HEÁHWOLCEN

FAIREVELLA
ENDORSA
ECKENBOURNE
Filifujol
Firgenholt
Portal
Orycheia
ELTA FOSSE
Maremohr
Mirabanie
New Salem
Felden Valley
THE BEORGDUN
Casa de Pietra
BONDRIE
PARAUMOR SWAMP
Ekstream
Silvurvaten
Ceoilhe
FLOATS
ODALI BIGA
Taberna Koste
THE HALTSE
CRYSTAL
Ummessgab
Halcyon Dales
The Bloodwood
Tehlalin
Claro de Baile
Tasveid Dunes
Samming Wall
Potevgod Granslavich Deutochta
Eneka
Duoria
Gahldir
Museo Botanico
Berzelsama
Tulip Fields
Museo Skoue
PALNA
Forêt Fossile
Xcthonya
Beaffunda Sceanara
AWHLAICA
Compotee
Terrabruixes
Ballanar
LA AZULIA
YLE DE L'EAU
Lothaire
TERRA NOIR
The Butchery
Maushus
Tusmorke Slot
Blacklodge Peninsula
Pretoria Fields
DEILT WATERS
Idalefime
Eastern Alluvia
DRAGON DE MAR
LOCH DU FLORS
SAGONGELWEVE
Evenshade
The Dunes
Vuurspuwer
Alluvia
Degalogesa
Saraced
Glethna
Calgant Nerthol
Felizita
Stadium Eduza
Stielhe
LOCH ARTUR
Aelchanon
Estmereamel
Feornham
Caislean
LAMHA DEALOCHA
Fusweald
Hláfjordstiepel
THUADH
LOCH LIATH
Faustdunleshire
TREAH

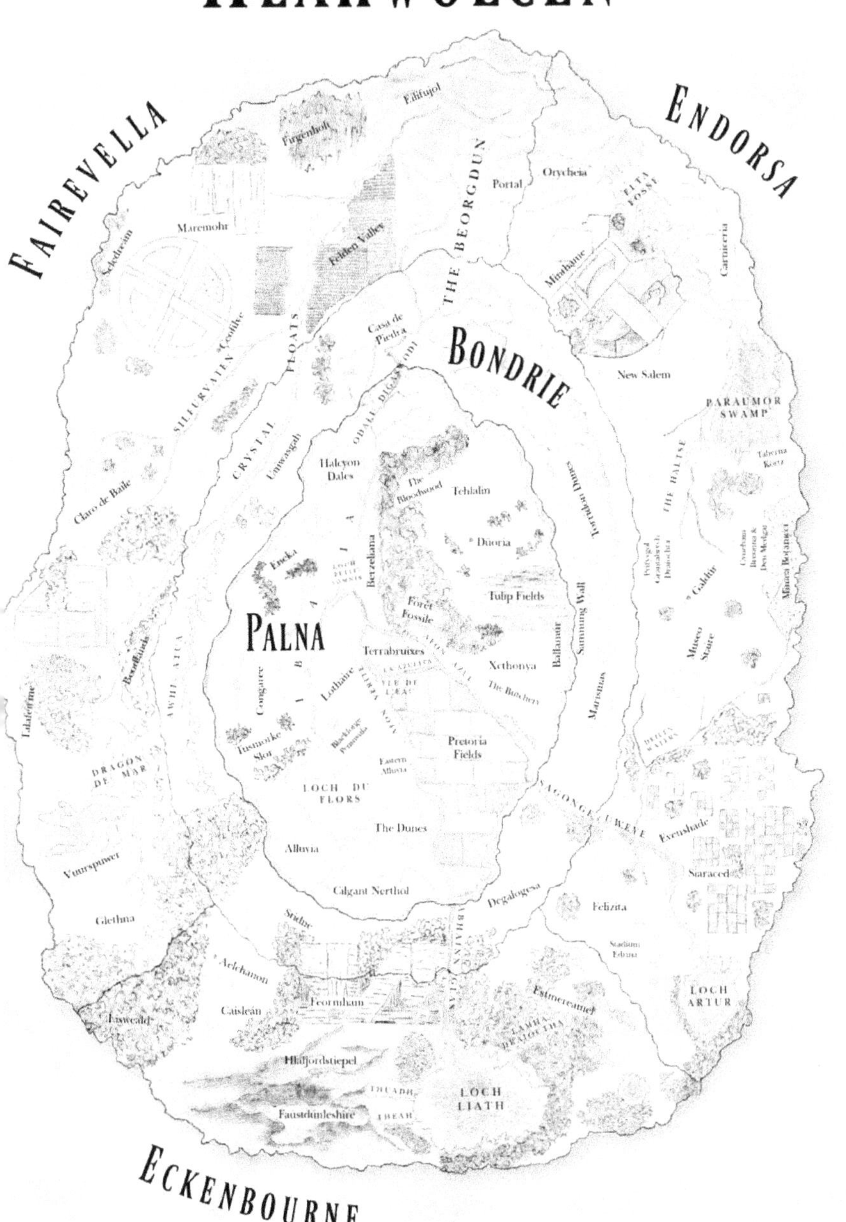

Triumvirate Rising

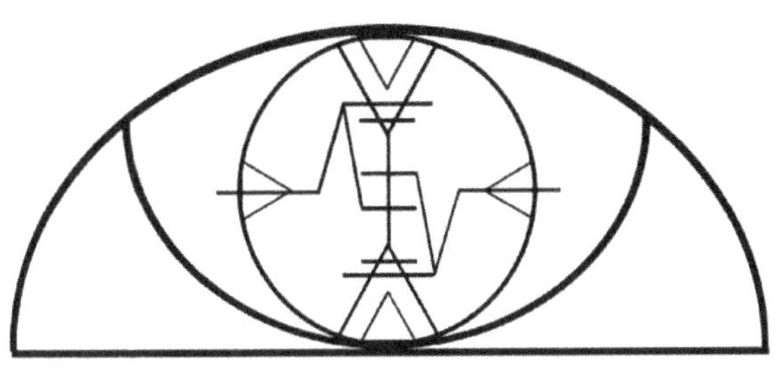

TRIUMVIRATE RISING

THE MERIDIAN TRILOGY • BOOK TWO

DALLAS ANNE DUNCAN

Dallas Anne Duncan, LLC
>> A Creative Publishing Co. <<
Athens, Georgia

TRIUMVIRATE RISING. Copyright © 2023 by Dallas Anne Duncan.
All rights reserved. Printed in the United States of America.
For information, contact Dallas Anne Duncan, LLC.

www.DallasAnneDuncan.com

Cover art, photography, layout, and design by Dallas Anne Duncan

Library of Congress Cataloging-in-Publication Data

Names: Duncan, Dallas Anne, author.
Title: Triumvirate Rising / Dallas Anne Duncan. — 1st ed.
Description: Revised edition. | Athens, Georgia : Dallas Anne Duncan, LLC, 2024.
Identifiers: Library of Congress Control Number: 2023918081
ISBN 9798985012132 (hardcover) | ISBN 9798985012149 (ebook)
ISBN 9798985012156 (paperback)
Subjects: High fantasy, fiction, fantasy fiction

The text of this book is set in 11-point Baskerville.

First edition: 2023 | First paperback edition: 2024

For those of you who reminded me
How to dream —
How to find joy in the little things —
But mostly,
How to rediscover the magic in me.
<3

And for my younger, much taller brother,
Dr. Barret Caldwell Duncan, Pharm.D —
I'm so glad you finished "Bright Star" by the time you got to read this dedication! Here's your forewarning that you have 'til November 28, 2025, to get through "Triumvirate Rising" before book three hits the shelves. Love you.

P.S.

There's an appendix and pronunciation guide in the back of each book in this series!

I remember the last night
The last time sleep took me
Under its gentle feathered wing.
The night called out – I heard my name
And where it beckoned, there I came
Then one night it didn't call
Not a whisper, not at all
But still, yet still, a girl must sleep –
And thus began the waking dream
The weeks and months and endless Time
Whirls around me, no end in sight.
I remember the last time
And after that it's all a haze
Weeks and months and endless Daze
Now it is I who calls out a name
Where are you? Will you come
To me, and we'll sleep again?
For sleep, she hath forsaken me
No longer does she proffer wings.
They say it gets easier
But whoever they are, they lie;
Nights don't get any easier
With the unending passage of Time
The nights instead grow opposite
In accordance with the aching of a Heart
Making every moment
Longer – H e a v i e r – Harder to endure.
I remember the last night
The last time sleep took me
Under its gentle feathered wing.
And oh, what I wouldn't give
To hear You call my name
Just once more
And wake me again
Into the Night we so adore.

— *Dallas Anne Duncan © 2021*

~ PROLOGUE ~

Ink-black midnight swirled through the air surrounding Heáhwolcen. It was a temperate night, not quite the balmy warmth of Southern summer eves, but the sort of weather where windows were left cracked open to let fresh breezes waft in, bringing with them gentle scents of emergent springtime and promises of warmer weather ahead. The sort of night pregnant with promise, when witches of old would have stirred from their beds and wrapped themselves in lightweight cloaks before converging on Whipple Hill to praise the spirits for this sign of good tiding.

Indeed, Nehemi wore a lacy wool shawl around her shoulders. The knitted stitches sparkled in the hints of starlight, for the yarn held the barest amount of milkfiber in its blend, which offered a pearlescent sheen to the peacock feather pattern it adorned.

Peacocks, the witch queen thought to herself, huffing aloud. *Artur Cromwell and his deity-damned peacocks.*

They were all over Endorsa, and by default, Heáhwolcen. They had been, for centuries longer than she'd been alive. The beautiful birds held such symbolism for the ancient, long-dead founder of her world. Every ruler of Endorsa since the 1700s had worn their own one-of-a-kind peacock crown and livery at official events. These late hours of the night were the only times Nehemi would be caught without hers on. It didn't make sense to wear her crown at midnight.

And, supposing they *did* go into this war with Palna … she smiled to herself. A rueful smile; Nehemi rarely ever truly smiled.

Only a fool wears a crown into battle, she remembered someone once telling her.

No, she would store her beloved peacock crown at Deu Medgar, the royal residence of Endorsa, should combat ensue. There were other ways for the wígend to know who in their midst was the mighty witch queen.

She shivered. *Mighty witch queen.* Nehemi knew what others called her, replacing the middle word with a more sinister rhyme. She did not balk from the insult. It was an honor to wear this crown, to represent and lead these beings, and she would not take that honor lightly. All her life she'd been raised to be "mighty". Her mother made it so: "princess lessons," they'd called her childhood. Every day, every night, she was tutored in the ancient arts of being a courtier. Endless years of manners, history — both of Earthen and magical realms; religion and spirituality, spellcasting and ritual, mathematics and business. The latter two, King Hermann told her once, were essential if one was to run a kingdom, not just a castle.

But it was the side lessons she learned from Queen Lalora's handmaiden, Naomi, that Nehemi used most often. Not just how to handle a state dinner for visiting dignitaries, which Heáhwolcen got quite a lot of ever since the Fairies began their ambassador duties again, but how to hone in and listen to what the dignitaries said. How to tell lies from truth. How to question *everything* without seeming to question anything. The art of being a servant was an artform indeed.

Before she was named queen, Nehemi would use this knowledge of Naomi's to sneak out of the palatial residence, and the other temporary residences that Endorsa held in neighboring nations. She'd not been to Earth, though — until *the accident* happened, Nehemi had been deemed too young to accompany King Hermann on international visits. Queen Lalora and Naomi never went.

Going to Earth was something Nehemi still wanted to do. Yet somehow, in the nearly seventeen years since she'd been thrust into the role of queen, the time to do so eluded her. She was always doing something. There was always some group that wanted her to preside over a ritual, always a Samnung meeting, always responsibilities; not to mention practicing her magic, the constant honing of skills and learning. And … Cloa.

Blasted, *blasted* bloody Princess Cloa of Endorsa. Sometimes Nehemi hated the girl. She scowled, annoyed that thoughts of the princess invaded her peaceful midnight walkabout. Even the air seemed to have stilled at the expression on the queen's face. She heaved a deep breath, forcing herself to calm down. To think about something other than the daft girl she wound up raising. The girl who would one day succeed her, take over everything she'd —

NO, a staunch voice inside Nehemi's head said. *You know what Lacnestre Pompié told you.*

Normally the queen would have been attended to by a lacnian, one of the head healers. But Pompié was different. She wasn't much older than Nehemi, perhaps her senior by fifteen years or so, and was one of the first of the lacnestres to choose to study mind-health. Pompié spent months at a time on Earth for her training. She would be the first lacnian of mind-health, Nehemi knew. The healer was one of the few blessings Nehemi came across in her years of life thus far. Without Pompié's expertise and constant obsession with learning, the queen wouldn't have a clue how to run her own life, much less oversee the lives of fellow government leaders and, deity forbid, all of magickind in their world above the world.

The burden of this was overwhelming. It was why the witch queen stole from her bedroom in the middle of the night on a regular basis, wrapped in this shawl that Queen Lalora commissioned for her. The shawl, of that shimmering yarn dyed a glimmering burnished bronze, had been presented to Nehemi the day of *the accident.* Queen Lalora was rushing about, chiding Nehemi over her "dealings" with Dominus and telling her for the umpteenth time that no, she couldn't accompany them that day. It would be a long journey with several stops, and the first official day back for Lalora after decades of being out of the public eye. Lalora needed to be seen out and about, but she wasn't ready to reveal her motherhood yet. Something they had all chosen to keep very, very secret.

For good measure, as it turned out. Nehemi knew the whole of Heáhwolcen shuddered to think what would have befallen Endorsa had she and Cloa been in the carriage that day, too. No one knew what would happen to the warded wall around Palna if one of those who wielded the magic *died*. Especially without an heir whom the ritual would then fall to.

And despite all the wary envy she had of the princess, the animosity she felt toward the next heir … at least she had this. This one, pivotal role she could play for Heáhwolcen, which all must be grateful for: keeping threats at bay, her powers combining with those of Eckenbourne, Fairevella, and Bondrie.

Now that the Ballamúr was powered though …

The queen wondered how long their defense would continue to last.

Though Galdúr was hundreds of miles from the Palnan border, Nehemi paused by the bay window in the upper landing and gazed out, imagining she could see it. See that mythical barrier surging up from the magical soil on which their world was grounded; rising higher than the eyes could see, higher than Hlafjordstiepel even, a constant throbbing power source that walled Craft Wizardry in and protected the rest of the worlds from the evil that could be wrought from its raw energy.

She squinted. Something caught her eye in the distance. Something coming her way, at a rather quick pace. Whoever was venturing toward her was being pushed forward via magic. Fairies would fly. Elves and Sanguisuges would run too fast for her eyes to make out the — Nehemi squinted again — bobbing light as they came toward her. The longer she watched, the more corporeal a form the figure took. She tilted her head and watched as it came closer: a figure on horseback, perhaps Unicorn-back, carrying a witchlight lantern. She knew it was witchlight because the gleam inside burned a pale acid green.

As the figure drew nearer, the witchlight illuminated its form. It was definitely a horse; she'd have seen the Unicorn horn glow by now. The figure was clad in gray leather, with chrome armor atop its shoulders and a matching helmet on its head. The helmet's face mask was lifted, but the face beneath cast in shadow.

A Bondrie guardsman, Nehemi realized. Her eyes widened. *Why in Hecate's name is a Bondrie guardsman galloping toward Endorsa at midnight?*

The queen pulled her wand from her houserobe pocket and flicked it slightly to the left, whispering "Cíegan Kharis" as she did so. A moment later, the wizened old man evanesced to appear by her side, in sleeping clothes as well.

"Majesty," he said, bleary-eyed but awake. Nehemi rarely used a summoning spell for her borhond. Their covenant bracelet sufficed unless she didn't feel like waiting on him to answer … or unless it was an emergency.

"Come," the witch queen told him. "We have a guest."

Kharis' brows raised. "At this time of night? Who?"

"A Bondrie guardsman, from the look of him."

The wizard's brows raised somehow higher. "With Corria?"

She shook her head. "He comes alone. And quickly."

Nehemi led Kharis down the staircase she'd just walked up, past the sitting room and formal tearoom to the front entrance. As they walked, she activated a thin cuff of Endorsan bronze on her left wrist, alerting her own guards to join them. By the time the queen and Kharis reached the doors to the residential entrance of the palace, they were flanked by guards of their own.

"Majesty," the Endorsan night commander addressed her.

"There is a Bondrie guardsman approaching," Nehemi said, all dreamy airiness gone and replaced with a tight air of authority. "There is no scheduled meeting. We do not know for what reason he is visiting."

Her face was set, and she hoped her eyes did not look too

worried. She hadn't seen an uninvited member of the Bondrie Guard in Endorsa in almost seventeen years.

It seemed like an eternity, but perhaps it was only a few minutes between the time Nehemi arrived at the front door and the guardsman reached the gate. She heard the horse's hooves on the cobbled drive, nearly a half-mile away, galloping as if lives depended on it. Perhaps they did.

There was the thud and clank of armor as he dismounted, followed by synchronized steps of the Endorsan guards as they stepped between the unannounced visitor and the front doors.

"I am here to see the queen," they heard him say, his voice thickly accented — the "th" sounded more like "zuh".

The Endorsan night commander looked to Nehemi for permission. She nodded to let the man in, hardening her expression in anticipation. The commander rapped on their side of the door, which opened heavily as the Bondrie guardsman darted in and nearly tackled the queen in the midst of his panicked entrance.

"I do not mean to affront, Your Excellency," he stammered, realizing who he'd run into. The man's eyes, visible now in the dim flicker of candlelight, were wild. He was coated in a thin film of sweat from the inhumanly fast ride.

Royal "princess lessons" would have had her offer him a glass of water, perhaps a seat somewhere more comfortable, before accosting him. But those were roles of queens who had the privilege of being married to kings. The mighty witch queen, whose might was questioned by none as often as herself, did not have such a privilege.

This was her kingdom. She wanted to know this man's business, right this moment.

"Quite alright," Nehemi said in polite forgiveness, though her tone was curt. "Who are you, and what is your business at Deu Medgar at this time of night?"

The Bondrie guardsman met her eyes, and she saw terror

there. He opened his mouth to reply, swallowed deeply, then spoke:

"They know."

~ And So It Begins. ~

There was an angry, audible *thud* as infuriated fists met solid hardwood, followed by a fragile splintering. Shallow dents remained in the table in front of Collum Andoralain, echoes of the helplessness and ire that had been flowing through his veins for weeks now.

"We cannot just leave her to rot in that hellhole!" he shouted.

The rest of the Samnung members exchanged glances. None met the fyrdwisa's eyes, and the magic in the room prevented him from hearing their thoughts, or even reading their emotions. Yet he still gazed at each, his jaw set, tone unyielding. He was the fyrdwisa. He brought them the Liluthuaé, the last hope for Heáhwolcen. For Earth. For fuck's sake, perhaps even for magic at large. And they were going to just … sit there?

Only Aristoces, Fairy of All Fairies, met his glare. Her eyes were pupil-less swirls of ink and slate, the nearly hypnotic whorls speeding up their rotation as they took in Collum, his fists now balled at his sides.

"What do you suggest, Fyrdwisa?" she asked. Aristoces sat back on her stool, her butterfly-like wings halted completely. He had her full attention.

"I … don't know," Collum admitted. "But is it not the responsibility of the Samnung to protect our world above the world? Should we not prioritize her rescue, above all else?"

Nehemi, the haughty Endorsan witch queen who hadn't liked Bridgette Conner to begin with, chortled. "Above all else?" she asked in disbelief. "Fyrdwisa, you think quite highly of your little Elfling, don't you? She was not what was promised. The true Liluthuaé would have avoided being trapped in the first place."

"We sent her in there completely unprepared!" Collum was

nearly ready to explode with anger. "Bridgette barely knows what she is capable of. The *wítega*, that blasted birth healer, spoke of a fully formed being, not an Earth-raised female who until seven months ago thought magic was a myth! Your forces, *Your Majesty*, were supposed to train her. To help her encompass and suppress her abilities."

"They did," Nehemi retorted, brows raised at Collum's insolence. "Watch your tone, Collum. The fyrdwisa is not irreplaceable."

He looked as though he might rip out her throat.

Before Collum could remind Nehemi whose idea it was to only allow Bridgette four weeks to cram what should have been four months' worth of training into her psyche and physical abilities, Aristoces raised a hand to silence them. But Trystane Eiríkr, the ard rialóir and Elven leader of Eckenbourne, spoke first.

"We cannot go in blind, Fyrdwisa," he said. "But I assure you, we will not let Bridgette *rot* in that deity-forsaken place."

Trystane's words did little to soothe Collum, who continued glaring at the rest of the Samnung. Kharis, the twisted little old wizard who served as Nehemi's hand and advisor, stared straight at the floor, avoiding the fyrdwisa's angry gaze. Nehemi's daughter, Princess Cloa, sat on her stool dressed in a gold and bronze gown, a coordinating bronze diadem atop her dark brown waves. The simpering fool was petting her damn one-eyed cat, Arctura, which for some reason was at *every* Samnung meeting. Next to her were Bryten, the beautiful, shirtless horned Baetalüan who did not lead a government, but represented the interests of sentient wood and water beings, and Verivol, the pale-skinned Sanguisuge who sipped from a flask of goat's blood. Wisps at the back of the room were nameless spirits; there was no leader of the in-between realm of Ifrinnevatt. Lastly, seated directly across from Collum, was Corria Deathhunter, the master swordswoman of Bondrie.

An empty stool was next to him: Bridgette's seat.

Or it would have been Bridgette's seat, anyway, if the magical government hadn't let its so-called spreca, the official leader of the Samnung descended from Heáhwolcen's founder, convince them to send the underprepared Elfling into harm's way for two weeks.

Her two weeks in Palna were supposed to have been up four weeks ago.

The fyrdwisa hadn't heard hide nor hair from his Elfling companion since he watched her cross into Palna. Bridgette had looked so determined, yet simultaneously terrified, that day. With one arm in Collum's and the other around her Fairy comrade, Ambassadora Emi-Joye Vetur, Bridgette walked from the sandy soil of Bondrie into the no-man's land that separated greater Heáhwolcen from the Ballamúr, the magically powered barrier wall erected by Palna's leaders. There were just a couple of miles between those two walls, but that day, they seemed to stretch on for eternity.

Once, years before Bridgette's birth, Collum stepped through that first wall, the only one that was supposed to be there. He was fyrdestre at the time, the right-hand assistant to the position he now held. Collum was charged with communicating with some of Heáhwolcen's spies, who'd been sent into Palna to keep an eye on what its leaders were doing. In those days, the covenant bands he and his contact wore acted as a communication channel. They were able to send bits of information to one another, which Collum could then report to the full Samnung or any others who might benefit from such details.

Before she made the crossing, Collum presented Bridgette with a covenant bracelet of her own, a constant channel between the two of them. But this time, he hadn't heard a word. It was as if the Ballamúr's magic, seeped in the ill-intent of the Craft Wizardry rituals that Collum and Bridgette suspected formed it, kept any other magic out.

Not hearing from Bridgette was aggravating at best, and sheer torment at worst. During their time together, Collum and the Liluthuaé grew incredibly close, incredibly fast. Being apart felt like a piece of him had been ripped off and hidden just out of reach. He hated it, and knew that if anything happened to his Starshine while she was in Palna, the being who'd pay the steepest price would be Queen Nehemi of Endorsa.

Nehemi was talking again, he realized, coming out of his thoughts and back into the Samnung chamber. The witch queen was going on about their plans for the Fórsaí Armada and renovations at Minthame, its training base in Endorsa. One of the Samnung's tasks while Bridgette was gone was to begin preparations for war. Though they would have no firm proof until Bridgette reported back, they all agreed that in the time since the Ballamúr was activated, Palna's leaders had been up to *something*. It was strongly suspected the *something* was an invasion of Craft magic backed up by a formidable militia. As such, Heáhwolcen needed to prepare its own forces. Preferably in secret.

Because they were still acting on suspicion and not an outright move of aggression, the Samnung members desired to keep any military proceedings hidden from Heáhwolcen's citizens.

Collum was torn on this idea of war against fellow magical beings. He didn't believe that every being and creature of Palna harbored any sort of ill will toward greater Heáhwolcen or the humans of Earth. Instead, both fyrdwisa and Liluthuaé agreed that it was the Tinuviels, Ydessa and her partner Eryth, whom they should rally against. Those two had ruled Palna for nearly Collum's entire lifetime. He had been but a youngling when the founder of Palna and first known wielder of Craft magic, Baize Sammael, attempted to lay waste to the world above the world. Had the wizard succeeded, his conquests would have taken him down the magical portal and onto Earth, where he planned to wreak ruin and havoc amongst humanity.

It had been the ruler's greatest wish that any humans who tormented magickind be destroyed.

The Samnung was caught unawares in the 1860s, when all of this came about. They intended, today in 2018, to be more prepared.

A kick under the table from Trystane jerked Collum back to reality again.

Collum tried to meet Trystane's eyes. But the ard rialóir was twirling a quill pen between his long fingers, pretending to be interested in whatever Nehemi was droning on about Minthame. Collum forced himself back to attention and tried to keep his thoughts from wandering.

"The herewosas assure me that they are quietly increasing the intensity and, as Herewosa Donnachaidh says, *lifelikeness*, of their training exercises," Nehemi said. "Until we are properly informed of the size of our enemy, I do not know how our forces will compare. When we have the intelligence in our hands, I believe we must prepare all of Heáhwolcen's citizens to fight for their homeland and against the Palnan threat."

"No."

Usually when Bryten spoke up against Nehemi, it was to be a bothersome contrarian, to add spice to dull meetings and break up the endless sharing of the queen's thoughts and opinions. It was exceedingly rare that he outright disagreed with Nehemi, and even rarer that he did so with such fire in his eyes.

"Your Majesty, it defies all logic —" Bryten began, but she held up a hand to silence him.

"I am not suggesting that we begin entering the home gardens of our citizens and hand them arrows and bows and swords," Nehemi said. "Not yet. What I do believe would be helpful in our preparations is to ensure that, should they want to be, every being of Heáhwolcen be able to be trained in select weaponry, combat, and magic. Very few individuals will want to hide in their homes or go underground if Palna attacks. They will want to fight. It is up to us to provide them with the tools to do so."

Collum scoffed inwardly. How hypocritical of Nehemi to argue in favor of proper training for magical beings when the very magical being who could fix this situation had been tossed to the pit vipers. He said nothing, though.

The Elf didn't disagree with Nehemi's idea. It was quite sound, actually, to make sure that those who wanted to fight would be properly equipped to do so, even though a few weeks or even a year wouldn't make a dent in what skills and practice they'd need to be able to battle alongside the Fórsaí Armada. He simply wished that Nehemi had given Bridgette the chance that the queen suddenly wanted to offer everyone else. For the life of him, he believed he would never understand what she had against the Bright Star.

"How would we even begin to do such a thing?" Bryten asked. His tone had softened, but he continued to look concerned. "It is impossible to turn our citizenry into fighting units if Palna is expected to attack us in the near future."

My sentiments exactly, Collum thought. Out loud, he offered, "We continue to circle back to the point I have been raising for several weeks. We continue to know nothing concrete until the Liluthuaé returns from her quest in Palna. Your Majesty" — he ground out the words — "I will not rest until she is back, and we know what she knows."

None of them knew he'd given her a covenant bracelet. None of them knew the Ballamúr magic barred the only method of communication they possibly had to Bridgette. All they knew is that she was in this other country, cut off from the world she'd grown up in and the second world she'd come to love. All they could hope was that the information she was supposed to glean was being gathered — and that his Starshine hadn't been caught gathering it.

There was a knock at the chamber door, an infrequent occurrence during a Samnung meeting. Most of the time if a meeting required an extra presence, the being or creature would wait in the formal lobby at the first floor of Cyneham Breonna until fetched.

The Samnung members exchanged glances at the unexpected sound. There were no guests or outside speakers on the agenda for the day.

There wasn't even an agenda to begin with.

Kharis, seated nearest the door, toddled over to answer the knock. He opened it to reveal, of all beings, the royal receptionist. Lucilla Von Detton stood in the doorway, wringing her hands as if she was nervous to interrupt the proceedings. Collum turned on his stool to face the witch, then blinked.

She looked … different. He saw Lucilla multiple times a week in passing, but supposed he hadn't really taken the time to observe her for a long while. Her usually platinum blonde hair was noticeably darker, more of a blush-blonde, and its tight ringleted texture was softened into gentler curls. She glanced at him, as if feeling his eyes roving her over, and he nearly fell out of his chair.

Lucilla's eyes had become a hazy shade of —

"Good afternoon, Your Majesty and Ceannairí. I apologize for the intrusion, but there is an urgent matter —" Lucilla was unable to finish her sentence as Geongre Akiko Chidori shoved her way into the room.

"Thank you, Lucilla," Akiko said, dismissing the witch, who gave a tight sniff of reproach in answer. The door had barely shut behind her when Akiko faced the Samnung and announced, foregoing all formalities, "We have a problem."

Collum was still reeling from the sight of Lucilla's glamoured violet eyes; of her attempt at titian, strawberry blonde hair. He clenched his jaw, feeling ill.

"Go on, Geongre, please," Aristoces said.

Akiko stilled her wings and plastered on a fake smile, the sort one does when they want the world to think that everything is hunky dory, when in fact, it is far from it. The kind of smile that doesn't meet the eyes. It looked out of place on her, a Fairy who was delightfully cheerful most of the time.

"We received a report this morning from one of our ambassadors to the United States. He happens to be in the American South, monitoring a heated political situation, and overheard a news bulletin about a missing woman named Bridgette Eileen Conner," she said. "He thought to report this information as the images showed of the woman clearly displayed Elven physical characteristics. He recognized the Elven eyes and pointed ears, and believed it was of utmost importance the Samnung be aware that there was an Elfling on Earth that had been reported missing."

Not even Arctura seemed to be breathing. No other ambassador or ambassadora, or ambestre, knew of Bridgette's nature except for Emi-Joye and Apostine, her second.

Akiko's smile widened even more painfully.

"A witness who knew Bridgette shared that there is one potential suspect, whom the law enforcement now searches for. A customer who came to her restaurant several months ago and who Bridgette told the witness made her feel uncomfortable." Akiko swallowed and said, "This witness described the suspect as being a tall male with wavy, dark brown hair, a brooding demeanor, and stunningly blue eyes."

Every face in the Samnung chamber turned to the fyrdwisa.

Oh fuck, Collum thought.

~ 2 ~

"One would think," Geongre Akiko said, her dark brown eyes trained on Collum, "that before one sent an Earth-raised Elfling into enemy lands, it would be prudent to ensure her extended absence from Earth would go unnoticed, so as to avoid a situation like this. One would *think* that she would have informed her foster parents that she would be gone for a long while, and not be able to check in regularly. One would *think* that perhaps it would be a good idea to withdraw her from her university classes for a semester, give notice at her job, pay advance rent on her *apartment*."

Fuck, fuck, FUCK.

What a fyrdwisa he was. Collum hadn't thought of *any* of that. Bridgette had told her foster parents, the Simmonses, that she was taking a year off — or some time at least, he couldn't quite remember — to study abroad and teach violin. She was, in fact, supposed to teach violin, but her students weren't in Europe, they were in Heáhwolcen. Children of local shopkeepers, as payment in-kind for their mothers making her clothing. But he hadn't imagined anything else would need to be done. He also thought that she'd be gone for a mere two weeks, with plenty of opportunities afterward to communicate more regularly with her foster parents, or anyone else from her life on Earth.

The blame wasn't entirely on him, he knew. It wasn't Collum who convinced Bridgette to drop everything and return to Heáhwolcen over the summer, without warning or any thought about loose ends that needed tying up. Come to think of it, with the way Bridgette had, as she once put it, "straight disappeared" after feeling sick in class, it was a wonder she hadn't been reported missing sooner. Or maybe she had, and this was just the first they heard of it.

"What does law enforcement think it knows?" Collum asked

Akiko.

Bridgette had bought a plane ticket in Nashville the day she disappeared. She'd taken a plane to Boston, then a taxi from the airport to the Witchcraft Victim's Memorial. She'd left a string of witnesses who could trace her to the city.

But praise whatever deities had her back, because the little devil had *flown* to his cottage, and there would be no way for her to be traced there or to the portal.

Collum's breathing caught in his throat. This was bad. Very, very bad, but it could have been so much worse.

"The local law enforcement know that she left class in June after fainting and never returned. She was reported missing months ago, when she did not come in for work that weekend, Fyrdwisa. A few weeks later, her foster parents called off the search, saying that Bridgette called them and apologized for being out of touch, and explained that she was taking time to study out of the country," Akiko said. "But the investigation reopened because her foster parents tried to call her. They assumed she didn't have adequate telephone signal overseas, but when they called the study abroad office to find updated contact information for her program, they were informed that no such program existed, and that Bridgette had not been enrolled in classes since June. She had lied, and they were worried."

That meant no one knew she'd gone to Boston. Bridgette must've paid cash for her ticket, tips saved from her weekends working at the diner. Collum's chest stopped heaving.

"How do we fix this?" he asked.

"We?" Nehemi choked out. She was livid. "*We* are not digging you out of the grave in which you've buried yourself, Fyrdwisa. *You* will fix this, and you will fix it very quickly."

Collum resisted the urge to reply with, "Or what?"

"Cheer up, Chief," Aurelias Parvhin, the fyrdestre, said a few days later, kicking Collum's shin with one of her thick-soled turquoise combat boots. "We'll get this sorted."

Collum groaned and batted her foot away. He was sprawled across one of the plush green velvet armchairs in Trystane's office, his fyrdestre in the other. Trystane was seated at his desk, staring into space, while his second, Njahla, tapped her long nails on the bookshelf she leaned against, eyes up at the ceiling.

"Will we?" the fyrdwisa asked. He'd draped the crook of one elbow over his eyes, feeling awfully sorry for himself. How had he been so careless to not even think about covering their tracks when it came to the studying abroad story? Had the Simmonses told Bridgette on that phone call about her being reported missing? Or had they been so relieved to hear from her, they didn't bother to mention it?

"Yes, of course we will," Aurelias replied. "Bridgette's not missing. We just can't tell anyone on Earth where she is. Not that they'd believe us if we did."

"I offer two potential options," Njahla said, still staring at the ceiling. "The first, we ask the help of the human leaders in her country who know of our existence. Perhaps they can smooth this over. The second, we —"

Collum laughed, catching her thoughts before they became words. "I appreciate the suggestion, Njahla, but somehow I think sending an army of magickind to alter the memory of every human who knew Bridgette is a bigger task than we have the forces to handle at this moment."

She gave him a long look, but didn't say anything else.

"What if," Trystane began, "instead of sending an entire witchcraft battalion down to Earth, we sent a ruse? We come up with a plausible cover for Bridgette's whereabouts these past few months and explain it will be a longer time before she returns. She was ill when she left her class that day. What if we claim Bridgette checked herself into a medical facility of some sort to take care of a mind-health problem that she kept secret? She could have lied to her foster parents about studying abroad to hide the medical diagnosis."

Collum groaned again, partly because this could be a story easily made believable. He listened to Bridgette's inner monologue enough when they first met to know that she truly did struggle with her mind-health. If they went that route, though, he knew there would be hell to pay. Bridgette would strangle him when she returned from Palna and found out all of her human friends and family thought she spent time in a hospital. He could picture the scene, and it wasn't pretty. Having twice seen the Elfling activate a bizarre internal power and go after someone's throat during one of those times, Collum had no desire to be on the receiving end of her strangling hand.

"She won't like that," he said.

"Yes, well, I don't like having to cover up the fact that this is all Mohreen Conner's fault to begin with, but we all must do things that we do not like from time to time, don't we," Trystane snapped.

"Ugh."

Aurelias kicked Collum's legs again. "She'll get a good laugh out of it since she jokes that you're a serial killer, anyway."

Collum lifted his arm from his eyes and glared at her. "Pipe down, Parvhin."

The eye that wasn't covered by an eyepatch winked at him, and he kicked back at her.

"Deity bless, will you two children behave?" Njahla said, her tone disapproving. The fyrdwisa and fyrdestre sneered at each other, but stopped kicking.

"There is another possible solution," Aurelias said, and the feigned innocence in her tone made Collum's ears perk up.

She was giving him an evil little smile, and he let his head drop over the armrest again. "Absolutely not, Aurelias. Don't even say it."

"Say what?" Trystane said, catching onto the nuances of glee in her voice and annoyance in Collum's.

Collum wrapped his head in his hands as Aurelias said, "We could always send in a body double. Has anyone else noticed how much sweet Lucilla resembles the Liluthuaé these days?"

Trystane choked back a laugh. "You know, Fyrdestre, that's not a half-bad thought."

"I hope both of your spirits wind up in the deepest pits of the darkest ditches of the bottom level of all seven hells," Collum grumbled. "This is a terrible idea."

"It's only terrible because you don't do want to do it," Aurelias challenged. She swung herself out of her armchair, turquoise combat boots hitting the wooden floor with a loud *thunk*. "We'll still have to glamour her, but I think it's completely plausible. Bridgette Conner checks herself into, what do they call those things? Asylums? And her doctors think it's best for her to stay there until she's in a better headspace. We let her be seen safely in the hands of a caretaker, maybe toss Lucilla-Bridgette in a straitjacket —"

Collum interrupted her. "As much as I would like to see Lucilla in a straitjacket" — Trystane coughed out something that sounded an awful lot like *"Bondage, much?"* — "I am afraid that I draw the line at putting our faux Bridgette in a mind-health facility. It would draw too many questions from her comrades on Earth. We could … suggest that she and this stranger she met at the diner …"

He swallowed hard at the words he was about to voluntarily let leave his mouth: "That she and this stranger she met ran off to Europe together, and she chose to upend her life to follow him, without considering the potential consequences of doing so."

Aurelias dissolved into laughter. "I don't know which thought brings me the most utter joy, Lucilla's face when she finds out she gets to masquerade as your romantic companion, or the fact that we wouldn't be lying at all with that story. Simply omitting the key fact that the two of you ran off to Heáhwolcen, not Europe, of course."

"And that we have any sort of romantic inclinations toward one another," Collum added, his strained voice barely audible.

Trystane was fighting a bemused smile, trying desperately to keep his leadership demeanor intact. But it wasn't working well at all. "Who wants to tell the lucky girl?"

"I will," Collum volunteered before Aurelias could speak up. He gritted his teeth. He could only imagine what torture his so-called *brother* and *second* would say or do to Lucilla if they broke the news to her that she was to be a stand-in for Bridgette Conner in the next few weeks. They'd have to glamour her still, as Aurelias pointed out. The blush-blonde wasn't quite Bridgette's reddish hue, and there was no way a witch could glamour her own eyes to be Elven. They'd have to do that themselves, for only the Elves could pull from the right energies and Nature to do that. It's why Nehemi was able to glamour Bridgette's eyes to the duller version of a witch or human when she went to Palna, but had it needed to be the other way around, only an Elf would be able to perform such a spell.

The grin was still plastered to Aurelias' face as Collum pulled himself to his feet and stalked out of the Caisleán, leaving her, Trystane, and Njahla to their own devices.

He walked into the dimming twilight, breathing in the freshness of fall night air. It was the day before Samhain, a Tuesday this year, and he had never cared less about the planned festivities. There was a strange irony to the fact that the night before a holiday celebrated by dressing in costumes, he was about to tell Lucilla she'd get to, as Aurelias said, masquerade as his female romantic companion. He wondered how she'd take it.

Lucilla had been the Endorsan royal secretary for nearly ten years now, and she spent a significant portion of that time chasing after Collum Andoralain. Her attempts at charm were at best annoying and at worst, entirely off-putting. Altering her appearance to look more like Bridgette, who for deity's sake was his *responsibility*, first and foremost, fell into the latter category. He'd never encouraged Lucilla, not really, but on occasion when he allowed himself to feel any sort of emotion, perhaps he'd given in just enough to let the witch believe whatever she did was working.

It wasn't. But the distraction, even for a few minutes, was welcome.

Until, in due time, Lucilla would say or do something that would cause Collum to throw all of his walls right back where they'd been for the last near-century. She wasn't mean, but deity bless, Lucilla could be vindictive. Once, after a holiday night where Trystane convinced him to let his guard down, Collum imbibed more than his usual share of Fae wine and came back to his senses to find Lucilla's lips pressed against his and her hands dragging through his hair. It was a small miracle he hadn't shoved her off, instead gently stepping back and bowing before retreating. Lucilla followed him and demanded, quite loudly, that he explain himself.

"Too much wine" was not an adequate reason, and she spent the next month only using pink paper for any reports she had to transcribe and share with the Samnung.

"So you'll always be reminded of the color of my shattered heart," Lucilla told him. She'd finally stopped because Nehemi told her the paper artisans were out of the floral dye they used to make that shade, and it was poor form for the Samnung to hoard every sheet of pink paper on the continent until more of the flowers could be procured the next season.

Then there was the most recent incident, almost three years ago now, the day Mohreen Conner visited the Samnung out of the blue and revealed to them that one, she was alive and well, and two, her offspring had been birthed and abandoned on Earth. Oh, and three, in case anyone had forgotten, the offspring was the legendary Liluthuaé, the Bright Star, the Elven legend foretold to be born only at a time when magic needed it most.

Collum had left that meeting lightheaded from shock and proceeded to spend the next several hours with his head over the toilet in sickness from shame at having failed the Samnung so miserably — though in retrospect, it wasn't really his fault that Mohreen was an absolute raging bitch who cared only for herself and her own reputation. Once he'd calmed down, Aurelias and several other leaders in the Fyrdlytta convinced him to venture into Endorsa for a rare night out and about. They'd run into Lucilla with a gaggle of her giggling girlfriends, and somehow between repeated dark ales and an empty stomach, the witch and fyrdwisa both wound up at the top of an alley staircase, hands gripping hair and skin in a wholly compromising situation. They had both been desperate. So desperate. Her, for his attention. Him, to forget he was worth existing.

Aurelias found them before things went further. After unsuccessfully trying to drag a thoroughly intoxicated Collum away, she kicked the Elf so hard in the side he saw stars — though that may have *also* been the dark ales' doing, in part. He'd stumbled back, reeling from the joined physical and mental pain, then nearly fell down the stairs, but he hit a railing and gripped it for dear life. Aurelias laid into Lucilla — he hadn't paid attention to that part, so caught up was he in his still-spinning head — and assisted him down the staircase. She'd forced him to drink some vile Old Magick potion before evanescing them to his apartment, where he ended the night exactly where he'd begun it: head hanging over the toilet.

Perhaps he should ask Aurelias what that was all about. He never had, just knew that he'd royally fucked up that time. Collum had never been so grateful to be sent out of Heáhwolcen a few weeks later, if only to escape the witch and the memory of what they'd almost done. What he never would have done, had he been of sound mind and soul.

Yet now, here he was, entirely sound in both regards … traversing to Endorsa to track down the very witch he wanted to avoid at all costs, and ask her to pretend to be his female partner. Collum wanted to shrivel into nothingness and die at the thought.

The things I fucking do for this deity-damned Samnung.

Collum stopped. He didn't know why he was walking. He could just evanesce, as it would take hours at this pace to get anywhere near Endorsa. The Elf felt torn: was it better to get it over with, to just appear at her doorstep? Or should he clear his head first? Figure out what to say to her? And who was to tell the rest of the Samnung this haphazard plan?

Nothing felt right. He sighed and slipped two fingers under a black and gold twisted cord around his forearm.

Bryten, I need a favor, the fyrdwisa thought into the void.

~ 3 ~

"You're joshing," Bryten said. He took a long sip of märzenbier, the crisp fall notes tickling the back of his tongue. "Whose brilliant idea was this?"

"Mine," Collum admitted. He stared at the toasted squash crisps in front of him, unable to eat. His märzenbier, despite being ice-cold and fresh from the tap, appeared equally unappetizing.

The two males sat across from each other at an outdoor table, situated well away from prying eyes and ears. A practically invisible ward-wall shimmered lightly in the moonlight, adding to the audio protection.

"Bridgette is going to go ballistic when she finds out," Bryten commented.

"You should have heard the first option. This was plan Z," Collum said.

"What in Hecate's name was plan A?!"

"First, Njahla suggested we send an army of witches to alter the memory of every being that ever met Bridgette, and then my darling of an ard rialóir piped in with the idea of claiming Bridgette checked herself into a mind-health facility, and we would use Lucilla to show that she was still alive."

"Fucking Chrysus," Bryten cursed, invoking the name of the golden god of the Baetalü. "Yes, this manages to sound more palatable. But Bridgette is still going to throttle the lot of you."

"You're being incredibly helpful and supportive in this time of need, you know."

Bryten grinned. "I do my best, Fyrdwisa."

Collum finally ate a squash crisp. It tasted bland, though that was due more to his stress-induced lack of any sensory experience than any fault of the kitchen's. He ate another.

"I need you to help me decide what to say to Lucilla," he said after a long moment. "I'm shit at this sort of thing."

"At what sort of thing?"

"You know," Collum gestured absently. "At … any sort of relationship."

"Collum," Bryten said, finally pinpointing the reason for the Elf's duress, "think for a moment. You're not asking Lucilla to truly be in a relationship with you. You are hiring her for a job. To work alongside you; to play a part. To be an aide to the Samnung. You do this sort of thing regularly. Just because it's a witch with whom you have a sordid past doesn't change that."

Collum chewed on that perspective. "Will she see it that way, though?"

"In truth? She'll probably be pissed off that what finally caught your attention was that she altered her appearance to look like Bridgette, and she will never let you forget it."

I'll add that to the laundry list of reasons to evanesce directly to the Samnung chamber lobby for the rest of my immortal existence, Collum thought.

Out loud he replied, "She shouldn't have made herself such a willing decoy. But what did she expect? That we *weren't* going to notice her attempt to portray Bridgette?"

Bryten leaned forward and swiped a few of Collum's squash crisps. "Females are an unusual breed, Collum. Lucilla's got it out for you though, and I think it's too far gone for it to be a win or lose situation. One of you is going to get your feelings hurt, and I daresay you don't really care about that."

The corner of Collum's mouth cocked upward. "It's not that I don't care, Bryten. But if it's a matter of Heáhwolcen's safety over Lucilla's incessant pestering, Heáhwolcen will be the victor. There is no question about that. I hope that Lucilla can overcome whatever her feelings or intentions may be and understand that, too."

"Then that, Fyrdwisa, is what you should say to our young comrade."

Collum chugged his märzenbier and stood, tossing a

crumpled piece of paper money onto the table. "Tell the proprietor those crisps need more salt."

He stepped away from Bryten, the ward-wall disappearing in his wake, and summoned Mithrilken. Collum knew Lucilla's late-night habits, particularly before a major holiday, would involve a substantial amount of wildness. It was still relatively early, but he nonetheless anticipated finding her at his least favorite place in the entirety of the world: Evenshade.

The Unicorn, his annwyl, arrived moments later — the two were never truly far from one another, their ceremonial bond cementing a deeper kinship than even that of blood. Mithrilken wasn't saddled and didn't ask any questions of Collum except that of their destination. But when the Elf replied, the Unicorn didn't move.

"What?" Collum asked. "Could we please go?"

"You dinnay like Evenshade," Mithrilken replied blandly.

"I am aware of this, but I suspect the being with whom I must speak will be there, pre-emptively celebrating Samhain. Trust me, I do not go to this space with a willing and open heart."

The Unicorn shook his head as if to say, "Whatever you wish," and galloped off into the blackness. The wind whipped around them and Collum tried his hardest to not get lost in his head, memories, or what-ifs. What Bryten said made sense: he was approaching Lucilla as he first had Bridgette. Except this time, he wasn't giving her a choice. Heáhwolcen and Bridgette Conner were both in danger, and whatever means it took to keep them safe, he'd take them.

Evenshade was, if there could be such a thing, the closest Heáhwolcen had to a magical nightclub. The witchlight within it was spelled to glow in shifting colors, and there was always loud, throbbing music leaking out from its windows and doors. There was a lengthy menu of drinks and spirit-enhancing potions available, which contrasted sharply with a food menu so small, it was hardly worth mentioning. Everything about Evenshade was loud and obtrusive, and though it attracted magickind of all species and ages, Collum would rather stay far away. He hated the writhing, twirling bodies dancing inside, many relishing in their psychedelic rituals of choice. Though he did genuinely like the psilocybin artisan who worked there, and the blind witch who ran the lights — she was a chakra energy master skilled at adjusting witchlight speed and color combinations based on the feel she had for the rooms within — the fyrdwisa had no desire to chit-chat this night. It didn't help that the psilocybin artisan reminded him of Heledd, the innocent-looking leader of the True Druids whom Collum, Bridgette, and Emi-Joye recently had the displeasure of cavorting with. Heledd turned out to be not nearly as innocent as his ancient, elderly demeanor put off, and Collum could do without any reminders of that debacle for a *long* time.

After a lengthy ride across Heáhwolcen, which Collum used to clear his mind, Mithrilken arrived at the venue in front of a large crowd of Dryads. The tree sprites danced around a massive witchlight "bonfire" on the lawn. Collum turned his head back to his annwyl.

"Would you like me to stay, Fyrdwisa?" Mithrilken asked.

Collum dismounted, feeling a bit of a burn in his thighs from holding the unsaddled position for so long. "No thank you, annwyl mine. I will evanesce home when my duty here is done. I do not know how long this might take, and I daresay you do not desire to wait for me any longer than I desire to be here to begin with."

The Unicorn snorted, tossing his head in agreement. "Should you change your mind, I am but a summons away."

Collum watched as Mithrilken trotted off, his annwyl's blue-black mane and coat rippling into nothingness as the October night swallowed him. The Elf turned to face Evenshade, already feeling the ground vibrate under his leather boot-clad feet as the music seeped into the earth. He couldn't deny there was an energy here, one that fueled certain aspects of youth and the vitality that his name suggested he possessed. The drums drew him in almost involuntarily, and he rolled his eyes as he followed the pull.

Opening the door was like entering an alternate universe. Evenshade, and its ancient cousin of a bar, Taberna Körtz, were polar opposites in many ways, yet both were places to let one's hair down. Both offered opportunities to experiment with others, with drink; with life itself, in certain ways. Collum didn't like either of the places very much, but he felt more comfortable in the tavern-like din and wooden walls of Taberna Körtz than he ever did in Evenshade. He allowed his eyes to adjust to the flickering, pulsating witchlight, and pushed into the crowd.

Collum knew the Fairy barkeep, and after thanking the deities and spirits above for this small blessing, he inquired if a blonde witch named Lucilla happened to be among the crowd. The Fairy laughed. She pointed to the dance floor, surrounded on three levels by tables on three sides, and shrugged.

"Do you see all the blonde witches out there?"

Collum smiled. "I'll take a black lager and go have a look." He paid for the beer in coin, despite the Fairy's protests of that not being necessary, and walked into the crowd.

An odor of cinnamon and Nag Champa filled the air, energizing the crowd and soothing any negativity. The band onstage was an opening act — it was too early for the intensive lightshow that usually filled the air for headlining musicians. The openers weren't very good, Collum noted, even for someone who detested this type of sound. And the vocalist wailed in such a nasaled tone that the fyrdwisa could hardly make out what language the words were in. They sounded Gaelic, but he could be very wrong.

The Elf sipped his mug of beer and scanned the crowd,

looking for Lucilla. He checked himself — he should be looking for Bridgette. For a dash of reddish blonde, for the light to glint off purple eyes.

This is going to get very old, very quickly.

No one in sight looked anything like Bridgette or Lucilla. He walked deeper into the dancing bodies that stretched from one corner of the glittering floor to the stage at the other end of the structure. The fyrdwisa opened his mind and scanned the crowd, listening for his least favorite inner monologue. He walked as he searched for Lucilla, dodging flailing arms and wayward wings. Collum glanced up to the one part of Evenshade he did like, the domed skylight, to watch Fairies and their partners dancing through the air. There were places like this in Fairevella, designed to ensure winged beings never felt confined to the ground. He would never take Bridgette here, not voluntarily, but those venues where she could fly herself? His heart thudded a little harder, and a familiar ache tightened his chest.

Collum closed his eyes and dredged up his own comforting scents, birch and tobacco. This was not the time. He was on a mission and right now, beings were starting to stare at him, finally taking notice that the fyrdwisa had crept into their midst. He groaned inwardly, but a little voice in his head told him this was probably for the best — if Lucilla was here, it wouldn't take long for word to spread that he was milling about on the dance floor. She'd find him.

But when fifteen minutes passed and Lucilla was nowhere to be found, Collum killed the rest of his ale, left the glass mug at the bar, and stormed back into the dark. Before he could second-guess himself, he evanesced to the royal flats where Endorsan government staff resided and opened his mind to listen for Lucilla's inner voice. He picked up on hers almost instantaneously, not because her flat was particularly close, but because she was thinking about *him.*

Wonderful.

He walked the long, well-manicured streets of these residences, a mixture of townhome-style cottages and four-to-a-building flats. Collum rarely ventured to this area of Galdúr; he'd never had much reason to. Most of the officials he dealt with lived in Deu Medgar, the residential palace that attached to Cyneham Breonna via a long glass walkway bridge. This area of the city made him think distinctly of human neighborhoods, and he was reminded of why he much preferred the less architectural, less structured flow of everything in Fairevella and Eckenbourne. There was a rigidity in the way witches did things that did not resonate appropriately with either himself or the nature of Elven magic.

Lucilla's inner monologue grew shriller the closer Collum drew to her door. Her whitewashed brick flat was on the top floor, and he trudged up the wooden stairs to find himself faced with a pink door. He rapped loudly on the bronze doorknocker and smiled grimly as the witch opened it. She stared at him, eyes wide.

"May I come in?" Collum asked. "We need to talk."

~ 4 ~

Alone in her bed, far away from the commotion of pre-Samhain festivities and magickind enjoying a night out, Ambassadora Emi-Joye Vetur tossed and turned, unable to fall asleep. She hadn't been able to sleep properly for ages now, not since returning from Earth. She was felled by nightmares of the True Druids, which she now regarded as vile miscreants who did not deserve access to any sort of magic, new or old. Sometimes, Bridgette's lilac eyes flashed into her dreams, turning a violent shade of dark violet before Emi-Joye woke, clawing at her throat. She'd spoken to no one about any of this.

Apostine, her second and ambestre, suspected something was amiss. He was very intuitive: his half-Tiefling heritage lent itself to him being able to feel one's despair or loneliness. He hadn't asked her to tell him, not yet, but Emi-Joye frequently caught him looking at her, a softness and concern to his eyes that made her want to cry. Whatever had been intervening in her energies these past several weeks caused her more torment than she wanted to admit.

The Fairy rolled out of bed. She rose quietly so as not to wake her parents as they slumbered in a neighboring room, then dressed in the darkness. At this hour, it was probably already Samhain, and she wasn't planning to participate in any of the rituals or celebrations. She needed to forget who she was, not just masquerade as a different being. The sort of costume she craved was one that covered her soul and mind, not just her body.

Clad in a charcoal gray shift dress that draped low in the back beneath her shimmering wings, Emi-Joye pinned up her braided hair, fingers finding the spots in the dark from years of practice and muscle memory. She cloaked the room in a silent ward-wall, which glistened faintly in the thin shafts of moonlight that winked in from her bedroom window. Checking a final time to ensure her parents hadn't woken despite her careful silence, she cracked open the window and flew out into the night. She was greeted with a chill that heralded both the autumnal season and the thinning veil between worlds that would permeate the air for the next few days. The veil was at its thinnest now, and Emi-Joye wondered faintly what this sort of magic meant for physical energy barriers like the Samnung's wall against Palna, and Palna's own Ballamúr.

The Fairy flew, wings catching the breeze like a soaring bird, letting Nature itself carry her away. She closed her eyes, floating on the gentle wind as goosebumps prickled her bare arms and calves. She hadn't been named ambassadora to the Antarctic for nothing. Even her surname meant "ice" in the language of her ancestral Fae. Emi-Joye embraced the cold. Thrived in it. Welcomed it. Feeling the pinpricks of frost meant she was alive. She paused in midair, fluttering her wings to keep herself aloft, and cupped both her hands in front of her face. Summoning the water molecules that brought this chill into being, her magic formed a minute snowflake that held court between her palms. It glistened in Fairevellan silver, a sterling gleam purer than any human jeweler could attempt to polish.

Emi-Joye flattened her hands out and blew the snowflake gently, watching it tilt in the breeze. She murmured his name, and with a whispered word of summons, the snowflake disappeared before her eyes. She fell back into the air, eyes closed, letting Nature again guide her journey. It may have been impossible to sleep in her own bed, but this motion put her into a near-meditative state.

After a time, the snowflake returned to her, landing gently in the hollow at the base of her throat. It carried his message with it, melting into her skin. She righted herself from the trance and flew to the darkened meadow he indicated to her. Emi-Joye had never been to Maluridae Wood. It was an open secret of sorts, used only by the Elven leaders and those to whom they extended an invitation, and could only be accessed by those who had seen it before. The things that happened there would be sealed inside, creating theoretical microcosms of Heáhwolcen. If walls could talk and homes held secrets, Maluridae Wood was a warded treasure trove of world-changing knowledge.

He promised to take her there when he could. Apparently, that was tonight.

They'd been doing this for ages now, these secret liaisons that no one knew about except the two of them. They had to be utterly careful to not cause any sort of suspicion, as it could harm more than just their reputations otherwise. Right now, he was the only one Emi-Joye trusted completely. There were things even Apostine didn't know — couldn't know — about her … though she knew he'd figure it out eventually. He was her second and deserved to not have any secrets between them. Except for *maybe* this one.

Her duties as ambassadora had been faltering recently. Everyone was bound to notice, and Emi-Joye was somewhat surprised that Aristoces hadn't yet. Or if she had, she'd kept quiet. The Fairy of All Fairies was a power unto her own, and it was not for an ambassadora to question her modus operandi. Emi-Joye had been avoiding her, too. The less she saw of Aristoces or other Samnung members, the less likely she was to get pulled back into this mess with Palna and Bridgette Conner and so-called Druids. She was afraid of all of it. That wasn't supposed to be her destiny, her legacy. She was Ambassadora Emi-Joye Vetur, representing Heáhwolcen and magical interests on what was ostensibly the *most* magical continent on Earth. Its power was hardly tapped yet — and she thrilled at being the one to help hone and research it.

But she hadn't even been to Antarctica since she returned from the trip to Wales. A significant stack of research proposals and data had been sent to her from the various human scientists and national representatives who worked on stations there, but she couldn't bring herself to read them. It was as if all of her joy, all of her passion for science and magic and ice, had been ripped away from her during those few days she spent with the Druids and the Bright Star. As if, when she glamoured her wings away for a few hours, she banished her own Fae talents and brought back a mere husk of herself.

It bothered her more than she let on that she could plaster the soft smile on her face for show, but there was a roiling black hole of *empty* that sucked her soul into it more and more with every day. Were it not for these midnight escapes and escapades, Emi-Joye would have let herself fade into oblivion. She didn't know what was wrong with her, much less how to fix it.

She looked down now at the treetops below her wings. *The meadow at the base of the mountains,* his message said. It was a wildflower field that the herbalists used, the only one on this side of Fairevella. The climate here remained cool and shaded for most of the year, thanks to the shadows put off by the giant monoliths of pyramidal stone that hovered above them. Things were challenging to grow, but somehow, these hardy plants managed to take care of themselves.

She beat him here, probably, and would spend the next bit of time wandering the wildflowers, though some weren't wild at all, more like experimental plantings by curious healers or horticulture enthusiasts. Emi-Joye's feet touched the ground in a field of late-season goldenrod, a heady scent of anise enveloping her, spicy and sweet. She smiled, reaching a hand down to pluck a few stems. They were usually long-dead by now, but the warmer days this September had kept them going.

Emi-Joye walked the meadow in the dark, wondering how lovely it must be in the day. She'd never been here before, but as her father was a poultice maker, he was likely well-aware of both its existence and how to properly utilize every part of every plant therein. She would ask him, but then she'd have to explain how she visited it in the middle of the night. And though she was a fully capable adult Fairy, there was still a twinge of fear at her parents finding out she'd snuck out of their house — ever, much less regularly for the better part of the last year.

She settled herself down at the base of a tree trunk, the vast mountain range of the Beorgdún to her back. The Fairy glanced up at the moon, centered now directly in the barely visible ring of red glow at the apex of the Meridian. He was always so late.

Her fingers wove stems and leaves of the plants she gathered, twining Celtic knots with blades of dying grass, the last vestiges of summertime, to secure a floral crown together. A stereotypical Fairy pastime, yes, but an enjoyable one. There was a twinge on her heart: what plant life could she find in her new country? What sort of Fae art could she create in partnership with its wonders?

The image of a frost-coated crown of moss and violets flashed in her mind's eye. It was the first time in months Emi-Joye had felt drawn again to her life, and she wondered if that meant this strange period of nothingness and sadness was finally ebbing away. She hoped so. She truly did not want to enlist the aid of a lacnestre. Such things might raise questions that Emi-Joye did not know the answers to.

She didn't know how long she waited for him. Emi-Joye had never been adept at telling time via the moon positioning. The sun, yes. But the moon? It had only been recently that she'd begun spending so much time out underneath it. She fitted the flower crown around her braids, then summoned a pool of reflective water from the dew forming on the chilling flowers still in the meadow.

"You are so very lovely," he whispered from behind her.

Emi-Joye smiled radiantly and rose to greet him, the moonlight slivers and reflection pool catching glimpses of his ice blonde hair and the gold of his gauges.

"Hello Trystane," she whispered, reaching for the ard rialóir's outstretched arms.

~ 5 ~

Collum wished he had a film camera to capture the portrait of shock on Lucilla's face when she opened the door and glimpsed him standing there. He supposed it might have been similar to what his face looked like this summer when Bridgette reappeared on his doorstep, looking deliciously disheveled, having come straight from a breakneck-speed Unicorn ride across Heáhwolcen to be at his side.

He, on the other hand, hoped he looked as uncomfortable as he felt, standing in the doorway of a witch whom he detested, but did not want to be cruel to.

"May I come in?" Collum asked again.

Lucilla blinked, those hazy purple eyes still throwing him for a loop, and collected herself. "Of course," she replied, opening the door wider for him.

She wore silken sleepclothes, which Collum was slightly annoyed to see were in shades of lavender. The woman may have absolutely lost her mind, and here he was, about to push her over the edge by asking her to live up to this self-created hype.

Lucilla sat on a floral-embroidered loveseat and patted the cushion next to her. Collum sat stiffly, and the witch procured two bottles of something pale pink and bubbly for them to drink. "It's a pleasure to see you twice in one day," she said, her voice less nasal-y and whiny than usual.

Hecate save me. She's even deepening her voice like Bridgette's.

"I came on Samnung business," Collum said, and her brows furrowed in response. Clearly, she thought him showing up this late at night was for a different reason. He didn't look at her as he continued, "It hasn't escaped our notice that you've altered your hair and eyes in recent weeks."

"What business is it of the Samnung's what I do with my appearance?" Lucilla bristled.

"Normally it wouldn't be, but when you're doing so to impersonate the Bright Star, it very much becomes Samnung business." There was no niceness in his reply.

She scowled. "I'm not impersonating anyone. I'm just trying something different."

Yes, trying something you know I like, he thought.

"Regardless," Collum went on, "I have been sent this night to ask for your help with a situation regarding the Bright Star."

"Oh?"

"Bridgette Conner has been reported missing on Earth."

There was a look of evil glee in Lucilla's eyes, and Collum fought the urge to get up and leave. But he calmed himself down, waiting until her eyes weren't so mean.

"Well, that sounds awful," Lucilla muttered finally, though her tone didn't seem to harbor a care that Bridgette's family and human friends thought she might be kidnapped or murdered.

"If by 'awful' you mean 'possibly putting the safety of Heáhwolcen at risk', then yes, it is awful. And that is why the Samnung is coming to you for this job," Collum said, putting emphasis on that last word. "We need for Bridgette to be seen on Earth by those who knew her. We need to address the situation by providing physical and visual evidence that shows she is alive and well. As her actual circumstances make this impossible to coordinate, the Samnung requires a stand-in. Thanks to your recent 'trying something different with your hair and eyes', as you say, you've been selected as the decoy."

"And what does that mean?"

"It means that the two of us will travel to Earth and weave the tale that Bridgette and I ran off to Europe together as … romantic partners."

The words sounded choked as he said them aloud. Lucilla really did smile.

"You mean that you and I would have to —"

"Whatever you are thinking, the answer is likely going to be 'no', Lucilla," he said firmly. "We just need to be a believable pairing and alter your appearance a bit more to turn you into a better likeness of Bridgette."

The witch fingered her hair. "You know that sitting stiffly next to me on a loveseat is not believable at all, Collum. Why should I say yes to this?"

"The Samnung is not asking you. This is a job duty being claimed of you as a matter of our security."

Lucilla's lip curled up at one corner. "I suppose it's also being required of you, then?"

"Yes."

"You know, after that night at Evenshade —"

"We're not doing this, Lucilla."

A rueful smile. "I suppose we'll have plenty of time to talk about it as we *pretend* to be romantically involved, won't we?"

He scowled. "This isn't about you and me, Lucilla. Think of it as a job in theater that the two of us were selected to take on. No audition necessary."

"Fine."

Collum tilted his head in a stiff nod. "Thank you."

"What else about my appearance do you need to alter?" Lucilla asked, and her inner monologue revealed incredibly inappropriate thoughts.

He held a hand up, though she hadn't spoken aloud. "Nothing of that sort, trust me. Whatever you think is going on between the Bright Star and I is incorrect. Our relationship has been purely professional, and at the most, friendly," he clarified. Collum took a moment to glance over Lucilla's pouting face. "The hair I think we can work with, but hers isn't as pink in hue. Trystane will have to glamour your eyes properly so that they appear Elven, and the right shade of lilac. And we'll have to get you higher-soled shoes and long pants to hide them. Bridgette's almost as tall as I am."

Tall enough to kiss you, her whiny mind-voice accosted him.

"Lucilla, you have *got* to keep your thoughts to yourself, or this is not going to work at all," Collum groaned, leaning his head back into the loveseat.

This is honestly the worst idea anyone in the Samnung has had in decades, he chastised himself inwardly.

She shut her mouth, and her mind, thankfully. A tense silence lay between them.

"Right. I'm going to leave now, and you are to report to the Samnung meeting next Wednesday for further instruction. That will give us time to get our story fully under control, so that we can … learn our lines, so to speak," Collum said, not looking at her. The pink bubbly concoction remained untouched in front of him. "Blessed Samhain."

He rose from the couch and let himself out, the few squash chips he'd eaten earlier feeling suddenly weighty in his gut. The fyrdwisa evanesced home, leaving the vengeful witch staring angrily at him from her front window.

Safe in his apartment, Collum kicked off his leather boots and threw himself on the couch. It had been weeks, but he was not used to being here alone again. The place still smelled faintly of vanilla and honeysuckle, reminders that somewhere, his Starshine existed. He was worried about her. The lack of communication bothered him immensely, and, as he did every now and then, he slipped two fingers under their covenant bracelet, concentrating on a mental image of her smirking face, on a memory of her flying in his home office, on the feeling of the night she fell asleep in his lap, wine-drunk from Ostara festivities.

Nothing. No energy. It was as if their line had been cut dead when she took those few steps between safety and uncertainty. He couldn't handle dwelling on it, not tonight.

So, he closed his eyes and willed himself to sleep, the tactile memory of Bridgette being next to him the only comfort to his fraying soul.

When Collum awoke, it was to a groggy burning sensation on his wrist.

Deity damn you, he silently cursed Trystane. He responded to the summons, sending a message of receipt and acknowledgement down their channel, and changed into fresh leggings and a different tunic. The Elf appeared at Trystane's treehouse, annoyed.

"What?" Trystane asked innocently as he answered the door. "You look an absolute fright, Collum. What happened last night?"

Though it was barely midmorning, Collum reached out a hand for one of his metaphorical brother's crystal goblets of signature burgundy spirits. "Give me some of that and I'll tell you."

He filled the Elven leader in on the night's events. Trystane listened without interrupting. When Collum finished, both took long draughts from their respective glasses. Collum's stomach growled, reminding him the only thing he'd eaten in the last twenty-four hours was a handful of vegetable slices.

"Now that I've done the dirty work to recruit our star actress, how the hell are we going to pull this off?" he asked, rising from Trystane's table to root around in the pantry for food. "The humans may not have Fae or Elven senses, but even they'll be able to tell she's not Bridgette if they see her too close."

"I do have a breakfast quiche we could warm up," Trystane offered in reference to the food hunt. "And if Geongre Akiko could procure us a photograph of Bridgette, and we get Lucilla close enough to the right height, we could do a full glamour on her facial features."

Collum suddenly wasn't hungry anymore. He closed the pantry door and returned empty-handed to the dining room. "That gives me no comfort, though I know it's the only thing that'll even remotely work."

Trystane gave him an apologetic look and got up to make the quiche. "I am sorry we're putting you through this. I know Lucilla can be a bit of a bother."

"You have no idea," Collum replied.

The Elven leader gave him a strange look. "What do you mean?"

So Collum explained. Told him everything, about the times he gave into her initial flirtation because it distracted him, about the night of the holiday kiss, and about the night Aurelias rescued him from doing deity-knows-what on the staircase outside Evenshade. About how, as a result, the thought of having to be in the same room with her was hard enough, let alone pretending that she was someone he cared about.

"It's not that I want her to die or be harmed," Collum clarified. "I simply do not want to be around her. Everything about Lucilla makes my innards squirm and put up emotional guards. It was easier when Bridgette *was* here because she didn't like Lucilla one bit."

"The Bright Star could pick up on truths like how strongly Lucilla felt for you."

"No shit."

Trystane chuckled from the kitchen. "This won't last, Collum. It'll be one trip to Earth to clear things up, and once we get Bridgette back, then the two of you really can visit her family and resume as normal a human life as she'd like to pretend she has. Nehemi blamed this all on you, but the truth is, we collectively didn't think about her having that aspect to work around. We were so focused on Palna that none of us — Her Majesty included! — bothered to consider the very human consequences of what Bridgette was about to do."

"We also thought we would have her back in two weeks, and this wouldn't have been nearly the issue it has become," Collum reminded him. He stood and leaned against the heavy wooden doorframe, watching as the ard rialóir pulled the warmed, rich dish from his oven.

"You're right," Trystane said, waving a hand over the heating coils in the appliance to remove the spell that allowed them to change temperature. "Here. Have a slice of this."

Collum picked at the perfectly cooked egg pie, which was dotted with chopped bacon, rings of bright green onion, and a decorative topping of paper-thin spicy radish slices. The buttery crust flaked at the touch of his fork. Had he not been questioning the next few weeks of his life, he probably would've gobbled half the pan-full, not just a slice. An earthenware mug of coffee appeared next to him.

"You need this more than you need spirits, brother mine."

The fyrdwisa smiled half-heartedly at Trystane, and said, "I hope Bridgette is eating half as good as this right now. Even though Ulerion seemed to love it in his reports, I've always thought of modern-day Palna as destitute and arid, a place where nothing grows but hate and deceit. I have nightmares sometimes where she walks past the Ballamúr, navigates Palnan guards, and enters into a desert of nothingness."

He chewed a bite of the quiche. "I hope I'm very wrong."

~ 6 ~

The first thing Bridgette Conner saw when she crossed from the no-man's land into Palna that day in September was a young boy. He stared up at her with eyes of a curious dull brown, flecked with golden sparkles that gave away some length of Elven heritage. The boy, with chocolate-brown curls and beige-gold skin, couldn't have been more than eight or nine years old, and he looked at her with such intensity that she thought perhaps she'd startled him.

"What are you?" he asked, his voice tentative and nasal-y.

"I'm — I'm an Elfling," Bridgette answered honestly, immediately put off by the ask of "what" instead of "who". "My name is Bridgette. What's yours?"

"My mumma said to never give my name to strangers," the boy replied. "Where did you come from?"

"From Earth, and then to Heáhwolcen."

"You come from the Outside? How did you get here?"

So many questions, Bridgette thought, her brain fumbling for a believable answer. She was still reeling from crossing through the Ballamúr. *I mean, this kid clearly saw me walk through the damn wall.* She ignored him for a moment, turning around to take in the scene.

And stopped abruptly, realizing why the little boy was so wary.

There was no wall behind her. Just miles and miles of bustling streets, full to the brim with a booming local economy, and far beyond that, fields of tulips. In the distance there was a stately building that could only be the home of the Tinuviels.

She turned in a full circle. No wall anywhere. She'd, for all intents and purposes, simply appeared out of midair in front of this child. A dark realization crept over her: two weeks from now, she was not going to simply be able to walk out of Palna the way she came in.

Oh fuck. Ohhh fuck. I'm in trouble now.

Bridgette breathed. She'd have to chance it. "The beings of Heáhwolcen have ways that let them walk through walls. There's a wall that separates where you are from where they are. They gave me permission to go through it, so I did."

"I don't see a wall," the boy said. He had an odd way of scrutinizing things.

"Yeah, funny you should say that, because I don't see it anymore either," Bridgette muttered. "There was a wall though, on the other side. But when I crossed over, it … well, I have no idea where the hell it went."

"My mumma says you shouldn't say swears like that."

The Elfling was not about to get lectured by an eight-year-old. "Your mumma isn't here though, is she?"

He scuffed his toes in the dirt, a muddy brown clay. "No, I suppose she isn't."

"Well, kid who has no name, I am Bridgette who has no filter. Pleased to meet you."

The boy looked up at her. Still scrutinizing. Beneath their glamour, Bridgette felt her eyes yearn to shift. Something was different about this boy. She wondered what that was and, just like the other times her eyes did this nonsense, wondered when the Universe would deem it appropriate to share the knowledge with her.

"Why are you staring at me?" the boy asked.

She hadn't realized she was. "Oh, um, sometimes I just stare when I'm thinking. I'm sorry; I know it's kind of weird."

"There isn't anything wrong with being weird," the boy replied. His voice was young, but he seemed wiser, perhaps, than a boy of eight or nine probably should.

"Why do you say that?"

"There isn't any adventure in being ordinary."

Bridgette grinned. She didn't know what it was about this

kid, why he'd been the one she appeared in front of, but deity damn it if she wasn't already attached to him after knowing him all of ten minutes.

"No, there absolutely isn't," she said to him.

They stood there awkwardly for a few moments longer. Bridgette hadn't expected to just show up in the middle of Palna: she thought she'd cross the Samnung's wall, then the Ballamúr, then perhaps have to speak with some guards and prove she was who she said she was. Appearing in front of a bewildered little boy, possibly an Elfling — fuck, possibly an Ealdaelfen! — had not been on her list of encounters to mentally plan for. But just as she was unable to figure out how to break from his presence, he seemed quite keen to stay near hers.

"Is this Düoria, the capital?" she finally asked, navigating the silence.

The boy giggled. His laughter had a musical quality to it. When Bridgette was growing up, one of her foster families attended a Christmas church service that included a handbell choir. As each song ended, the handbells that were still held aloft kept ringing, a melodious echo that then rang in the opening notes of the next tune. This boy's laughter was like that. But the magical noise of his giggles seemed lost on himself as he shook his head and answered her question: "No, that's Düoria, over there where the great castle is. The king and queen live there!"

Well, that's probably something the Samnung wants to know, Bridgette thought. *Nehemi will blow a gasket when she finds out Ydessa Tinuviel is calling herself queen of Palna.*

Bridgette looked to where the boy pointed. Barely visible on the horizon was a towering black shape. She initially thought it belonged to the Tinuviels and now assumed it was the "great castle".

"Well," she tried again, "if this isn't the capital, then where in the seven hells am I?"

"This is Xcthonya," the boy replied. He grinned at her use

of the language, since his mother wasn't around to scold them. "This is where I live."

"Ick-thone-ia?" Bridgette hesitated. She tried to remember the illicit map of Palna Collum once showed her. The name Xcthonya rang zero bells.

"Do you guys have like, a visitor's center? Somewhere I can find a map of Palna?" she asked. "I'm looking for a library, and probably a hotel. I came to your country to study your culture and history, but when I crossed the wall, nobody told me that I'd just kind of appear in the middle of your city."

How fucking unprepared we were, Bridgette thought to herself. She ran a finger under the lilac and cerulean covenant bracelet that now adorned her left wrist, its sterling silver beads cool against her touch. For all Queen Nehemi's talk of moving quickly and *not* being unprepared, the Elfling realized just how idiotic they had all been.

Well. Maybe not all of them. But the vocal minority was hard to oppose, even by those who had smarter heads on their shoulders.

The boy cocked his head, and those strange eyes went vacant. Deep in thought, Bridgette knew.

"I do not know. My mumma may can help," he offered. There was an unmistakable note of caution in his tone, and she felt her eyes fully shift beneath their glamour. The boy and his mother were important, Palnans who could and would help, but they would not trust outsiders like her right off the bat.

"Can I meet your mumma?"

She wished she could do Collum's scent spell to calm the boy and convince him that she wasn't dangerous. Not to him — and not yet, anyway.

"If she wants to meet you." He turned abruptly and began walking down an endless road of shops and bustling restaurants.

For a country that was supposedly ruled by the Wicked Witch of the West and her lover warlock from Hell, Palna mostly seemed like a brighter and less pompous Endorsa. "New money," the hoity-toity Southern humans Bridgette grew up with would call it, sticking up their noses at the altogether scoffing of tradition.

The Elfling followed her new tour guide. She noticed that although there were countless witches, Elves, and halflings milling about, and even a few Fairies and non-hominid beings, few of them made eye contact or even appeared to notice the two of them. When they did, they raised a fist to cover their hearts, a gesture the boy returned and Bridgette, desiring to blend in, echoed. Everyone kept to themselves or in small groups, and it gave Bridgette a nervous intuition. Though the residents of greater Heáhwolcen were clueless as to what the Samnung was up to, Palnans were acutely aware something was amiss. The air seemed to shift and become tenser.

The hustle of the market district ended after a mile or so of walking, and the boy turned down a little lane that led into a scrubby forest of bushes and low-growing, gray-leafed trees. Their branches sprawled rather than reached for the sky. Further down this lane, a small, wooden-planked building came into view. It was painted gray and had a thatched roof, making it blend into the surrounding wood. A woman was out front tending to a set of raised-bed gardens. She didn't register their approach until the boy was nearly upon her, Bridgette not far behind.

"Mumma, I brought you a friend," he said. The woman looked up and gripped her pruning knife.

"Who is this, Toby?" she asked, glancing from Bridgette back to her son. The woman kept her voice calm, but the tautness of the air increased sharply at her words.

"She said her name is Bridgette. She's from the Outside," he said. To the Elfling he added, "I suppose you know my name now."

"Leave us, Toby. I would like to speak to Bridgette alone,"

the woman said. He obliged without a word.

The woman knelt back down and continued silently trimming herbs into a basket. The only sound was the subtle *snick, snick* as she sliced through stems of mint, offering a lively aroma that cut the tightness of the air.

Without looking up from her work she asked, "What does my son mean when he says you are from the Outside?"

"Um," Bridgette began, gulping. It was the first time she'd uttered her full cover story out loud. "I'm an Elfling, and my human mother only recently told me about being half-magical being. She took me to this portal thing so I could come here to learn about my Elf dad. He died, apparently, and uh, I decided that I wanted to start studying at the University —"

"You are a student in Heáhwolcen?" the woman interrupted. She still hadn't looked up from the herbs.

"Yeah, I am."

"There is much learning to do there. How did you come to be in Palna?"

Bridgette breathed a sigh of relief. This part at least wasn't a lie. "I wanted to know about this country and the international relationships between your government and the Samnung. So I got special permission to come study here."

"I see."

Silence resumed. Bridgette wasn't sure for how long she stood, watching the woman at her feet. It grew hotter the higher the sun rose, and she felt beads of sweat trickle down her neck and tunic.

"Why did you come to my home?" the woman asked.

"Well, when I came through the wall, Toby was the first person I saw. I asked if there was a tour guide or a visitor's center where I could see a map, and he brought me to you," Bridgette answered. "And I asked him about a place I could stay."

The woman sighed deeply. "It is no coincidence you appeared to my son. I have no map, but I have much knowledge, an extra bed, and because he seems keen on you, I will help you, Bridgette of the Outside."

Phew, the Elfling thought. *Step one is done.*

"In return for your lodgings, I ask that you do not bring any other uninvited beings onto this land or into this home. I ask that you share with us what you learn, and answer Toby's many questions of the world outside these walls," the woman continued. "He is a curious little one, but he Sees something in you that I yet do not. I have learned to trust this ability of his. It shares much with the both of us, and I have come to know that he deserves much better than this life I wrought for him. Perhaps you will be able to teach our family as our country teaches you."

They want to escape. The knowing came to Bridgette like a brick to the skull.

"That's totally cool by me," she replied quickly. "I'm an open book."

... Mostly, she thought.

The woman stood and took her full basket on one arm. "I am Serrabinx Maudlin, and my son is Tobias. You may call me by my full name and him by Toby. Follow me; I will show you your room."

~ 7 ~

The inside of Serrabinx and Toby's house was inviting, but primitive. Candles and oil lamps provided warm-hued light, aided by large windows to let the sun in. Bridgette followed her hostess into the kitchen, where dried herbs and flowers hung in fragrant bunches on the walls. They covered every square inch, draping over a stone sink and surrounding wooden shelves full of jars holding spices and liquids in a rainbow of colors. It was incredibly rustic, and Bridgette remembered then that no magic was supposed to take place here.

At least it seemed this family abided by that decree.

"Are you a witch?" Bridgette asked, before she could stop her mouth from having a mind of its own.

A slap of air whipped across her cheek as hard as a hand — but Serrabinx was on the other side of the room, not even looking. Bridgette yelped in pain, rubbing the sting after recovering from the unexpected shock of it. She glared at the woman's back.

"I take that as a yes," Bridgette glowered.

"There are no such things in Palna," Serrabinx said sharply. "There were once, long ago. But as I am sure you are aware, they have been long forbidden."

"Well, ma'am, the air didn't just slap me of its own accord," Bridgette replied, her Southern accent coming out in her testy tone. "So clearly, not being *allowed* to perform spells doesn't mean you *can't*."

"You are shrewd, Bridgette of the Outside."

What the hell does this woman have against looking at me? Bridgette wondered, watching as Serrabinx carefully arranged her freshly clipped herbs into new bundles. Pre-arranged cuts of twine were laid out on the wooden countertop by the sink, and the not-witch busied herself tying precisely counted groups of sprigs together. These she proceeded to hang on nails sticking out of the doorframe that led to what appeared to be a small, intimate sitting room.

It wasn't an awkward silence in which the two of them now stood, one working while the other observed. There was a certain peacefulness, but a tense feeling remained around Serrabinx.

She clearly trusts her son's judgement, otherwise she wouldn't have let me come inside this door, but she doesn't trust me …

"What did you mean when you said Toby Sees stuff?" Bridgette broke the silence, but Serrabinx didn't answer immediately.

Bridgette waited for an answer about Toby. She watched out of the corner of her eye as Serrabinx tied and hung bunches of fresh herbs on the wall.

"My son is gifted, as I once was," Serrabinx said, keeping her voice low. "The deities and spirits of old and new work through him to aid those who need their guidance, but lack a direct line to them. He Sees in this same way, and forbodes what will come to pass, as I once could."

"Why is that such a secret?" Bridgette asked.

"You have much to learn about this country, Bridgette. While spell powers can be banned, as you already inferred, the gifts from deity and spirit are law unto their own," Serrabinx replied. "Should the Tinuviels learn of Toby's true self, I do not know what will happen. At the very least, I fear he will become part of the Collective."

"The Collective?" Bridgette questioned. She felt almost like she was back with Collum, having these illicit conversations behind the world's back, what with her new host's hushed voice and the noticeable avoidance of saying the word "magic".

"The Collective, on paper, does not exist. It is mere rumor if you ask most Palnans. But there have been too many instances in the past years of beings with such abilities disappearing. It is not a coincidence," Serrabinx declared.

Fucking fuck. Bridgette had barely been in Palna for a few hours, and her sierwan gifts were overflowing. Whatever the Collective was, it would be an formidable force of beings that the Fórsaí Armada would come to both spell and physical blows with.

"The guest quarters are down this hall and to the left," Serrabinx said, changing the subject completely. She pointed in the mentioned direction. "You may place your belongings there and make yourself comfortable. When you feel settled, please join Toby and I for lunch."

Bridgette thanked her and walked down the hall, where a bathroom and four closed doors lay. The "guest quarters" were small but sufficient, housing an iron bedframe with a white comforter and pillows on its mattress, a dark wooden dresser, and a square nightstand with an oil lamp. There was a beautiful rust-orange and golden yellow rug made from braided fabric scraps on the floor. A coordinating quilted pillow adorned the bed. On the wall hung a wood-framed mirror, its silvered surface tarnished like an antique, and round slices of tree trunks decorated with burned designs. One had phases of the moon, one a grouping of mushrooms, the third with a floral motif.

She unpacked the little bag of belongings she brought with her, just a week's worth of leggings and tops, socks, and underthings, two sets of Elven sleepclothes, hoping that she would be able to do laundry in-between wears. *Especially since it doesn't look like I'm getting out of here any time soon,* Bridgette thought.

There was a window facing east, hung with sheer white curtains. Bridgette stared out at the early afternoon sun. Her fingers brushed the covenant bracelet, and she hooked two fingers underneath.

Can you hear me? she thought to the bracelet, realizing that Collum hadn't told her how the thing was supposed to work. She'd seen him use his, and it always seemed so simple. But Collum could do magic. She could not.

There was no reply to her question. No twinge of power. No

staticky band of communication. Just peaceful silence, stuttered by the chirping of a few birds Bridgette could hear in the scrubby trees outside her window. She bit her lip, tamping down frustration, and leaned her forehead against the glass to stare out into the yard.

The flora here was something she noticed almost immediately. She inferred from reading Ulerion's reports that Palna's environment was different from greater Heáhwolcen's, having a generally drier climate with a set rainy season. But she hadn't thought how this would affect the plants. Where Eckenbourne especially was coated in tall trees and lush green grass, Palna was practically a desert.

Another sigh, as Bridgette resigned herself to spending a lot more time than she initially intended with these small trees as scenery. Bridgette gave up trying the covenant and walked back to the kitchen. Toby had come inside and stood on a stepstool at the base of the kitchen's firehearth, stirring a large cast-iron pot of something that smelled rich and meaty. The coals burned low underneath. Serrabinx remained at the counter, finely chopping a bundle of herbs — thyme, from the smell of it — and a crusty loaf of bread had been sliced into a napkin-lined basket next to her hands.

Bridgette felt like she'd stepped back in time a century or two. She knew Palna had been trapped inside itself since the 1860s, but being here felt like she was a reenactor in a traveling show of some kind. She was reminded distinctly of an overnight field trip one of her middle school classes took to a place in south Georgia called the Living History Village. She and her fellow students were asked to dress in period costume and take part in a few hours experiencing life as it would have been for thirteen-year-olds in the nineteenth century. The boys worked the fields and helped museum workers with livestock. The girls jumped rope, carded wool to stuff inside a pincushion they sewed, and helped make lunch.

Bridgette Conner might have many talents, but that day, she learned baking biscuits over a non-electric — or non-magic-powered — stove was not one of them.

A smile flickered over her face at the memory. She went to stand by Toby, as neither he nor his mother acknowledged her presence, and asked, "Whatcha making?"

"You speak strange," the child said. "This is beef stew."

"It smells delicious."

"My uncle brings us the meat, I grow the vegetables in my garden, and my mumma does the flavorings," Toby replied. There was great pride in his voice.

"How can I help?" Bridgette asked.

Toby hopped down from the stool. "You can be the stirrer now. I will get us drinks. Would you like milk and sugar with your tea?"

"Yes, please," Bridgette replied, taking the long-handled spoon he presented her with. She stood over the bubbling pot of stew, her mouth watering. A combination of anxiety and existential dread had made eating difficult the past few days, and this cauldron was the only thing that had smelled good for at least forty-eight hours.

"Where does your uncle get the meat?" the Elfling asked, not used to the silence that filled the kitchen.

"You will meet him. He is joining us for lunch, and his room is next to yours," Serrabinx said. She appeared next to Bridgette and dusted her cutting board of fresh herbs over the pot to add more seasoning. "Stir this consistently for three minutes, add one more pinch of blacksalt from the bowl on the mantle, and taste. If you detect the hint of smoked meat, it is ready. Here is a towel so you do not burn your hands as you move the cauldron from the coals. Set it on the counter trivet to settle."

"Yes ma'am."

Bridgette did as her hostess tersely instructed, astounded with how delicious the stew tasted fresh from the pot. *This is definitely one recipe I might need to take back into Eckenbourne and share with Collum —for cultural research and experience, of course,* the Elfling thought.

Toby set the table for four and handed Bridgette a proper little cup of tea with pressed cubes of sugar. "There is a milk pitcher in the icebox," he told her, pointing to what looked like an old wooden crate in the corner of the dining room.

"We keep it in here so the firehearth doesn't interfere with the ice blocks," the boy added, noting Bridgette's confusion.

She nodded as if that made complete sense. The Elfling opened the ice- and metal-lined box to find a chipped ceramic pitcher full of chilled milk. There were various other fruits and meats in the icebox as well, all separated in categories to prevent cross-contamination between thawed chicken or fish and refrigerated produce that would be eaten raw.

How funny, she thought, her eyes glittering. Martha Simmons, her human foster mother, was fastidious about keeping their home refrigerator set up similarly.

Bridgette added milk to her precious teacup, and as she straightened from the icebox, she became aware of a new presence in the room. The man entered on near-silent feet, and he seemed just as surprised to see the Elfling as she was to see him.

"Serrasweet," the man called over his shoulder, staring at Bridgette with a furrowed brow and stiffened posture. "Who is our guest?"

~ 8 ~

"Zedolph Maudlin, I introduce to you Bridgette, an Elfling from the Outside," Serrabinx said. "Bridgette, this is my brother, Zedolph."

"Nice to meet you," she said, sticking out a hand to shake it.

Zedolph looked at her palm, then back at his sister. "Why is she here?"

"To study our culture and customs as part of her research at the University in Heáhwolcen," Serrabinx replied. "Bridgette was raised on Earth by her human mother and recently learned that her late father was Elven. Her mother showed her how to reach these lands, and while studying, she became interested in our country."

The man didn't miss a beat. "And why is she in our *house*?"

"Bridgette appeared to Toby."

As if that's some hella clear answer, Bridgette thought, saying nothing. She wondered if she should put her hand back down, because Zedolph hadn't yet moved to grasp it.

"Tobias," the man called, and his nephew appeared. "Tell us what it is about Bridgette that made you bring her here."

Toby puffed out his chest, as much as his little body could. "Bridgette appeared to me in the square of Xcthonya. I hadn't meant to be in the square this day, but the wind said to me that something new was coming. Something that would need guidance. So, I followed the wind's path and it stopped in the square. I looked and looked, and suddenly, there she was. She came out of the air with a bag and looked lost, so I said hello. When Bridgette said she needed a map, I knew she was the one the wind sent me to."

"I see," Zedolph mused. "And Tobias, what is that you See about Bridgette?"

Bridgette stiffened. She had no desire to get her fortune told, or her story found out, after being in Palna for less than a day.

Mere hours.

"I have not asked to See her yet. It was rude," the boy said.

"What do you mean, See me?" Bridgette asked, trying to sound mildly interested and not as if her very destiny depended on him not Seeing anything.

"If you let me See you, I can catch glimmers of what the Universe wants from you," Toby said, confirming what Serrabinx indicated earlier. He regarded her curiously for a second, chewing his bottom lip. "But you have a strong wall around you. Someone protects you from being Seen without giving permission."

Bridgette's mind instinctively went to her eye glamour and her covenant bracelet, to the faces of her Samnung comrades. To the tidal pool eyes she wished were in the room with her. *Oh yeah, buddy. There are a lot of someones protecting me from being Seen*, she thought.

Zedolph watched her warily. Again, both he and Serrabinx seemed to trust Toby's judgement explicitly, but would need some move from Bridgette to prove whether she was worthy of their belief as well. She had no clue what that might be. Bridgette dropped her hand from where it hung awkwardly in the air, still waiting for Zedolph to shake it, and propped it on a hip.

"So, uh, now that I know I have some weird guardian Elf on the Outside ..."

Serrabinx tried to hide a smile at her guest's joke, and Zedolph seemed to relax. He asked if she would allow Toby to See her.

"I mean, sure?" Bridgette stumbled. "Although I don't exactly know how to break down this wall that he says exists."

She was grateful a split second later when Serrabinx stepped in. "After lunch, brother mine. You must be starving."

They served themselves ladlefuls of stew and thick slices of bread in porcelain bowls that matched the pitcher in the icebox. Bridgette got a vague sense that the dishes, and this house, might be priceless family heirlooms of the Maudlins'. As they seated themselves at the table, Serrabinx brought along a small wooden board and flat knife to add fresh butter and soft, creamy cheese to their bowls if they wished. The Elfling, starving from both her neglected appetite and the taste-test she'd given the meal, had to try very hard to keep her manners in check and not gobble down every morsel.

Bridgette distracted herself from eating too quickly by asking Zedolph and Serrabinx what they did as a living.

"My sister is an herbalist and téitheoir," Zedolph said, putting his spoon down to answer her. "And I am Xcthonya's butcher."

That explains the biceps the size of my face, Bridgette thought, glancing quickly at his bulkily muscled form.

"That's cool," she said out loud. "Do y'all like, have a farm?"

Toby looked at her. "What is a 'y'all'?" he asked.

Does NO ONE use that word outside of the South?!

Bridgette smiled at him, keeping the annoyance in her mind and out of her speaking voice. "It's a word from where I grew up, on Earth. It means 'you all', kinda like a shortcut way of saying it. I guess it never caught on up in Heáhwolcen."

"Well, *I'm* going to use it. Something new," Toby said, sounding satisfied. "We don't often have new things in Xcthonya. And today we have two! You, and this new word."

"To answer your question, Bridgette, we do not farm," Zedolph said. "Not livestock, anyway — my sister and most homes keep a well-stocked garden of flowers, herbs, fruits, and vegetables. The farmers in this city raise cattle, sheep, birds, and a few raise red pigs. In my butchery, we do not harvest or serve poultry. That is a different sort of operation and requires skills that I do not wish to learn. But the farmers bring their animals to the two butchers when they are at mature size, and we procure the meat and other items for use and sale."

Serrabinx smiled thoughtfully at her brother. "If you are to stay here, Bridgette, you do not have a way to pay room and board. Perchance my brother's butchery is hiring an assistant and you can work in exchange for your lodgings in our home."

Both Zedolph and Bridgette stared at her. He considered the suggestion and asked Bridgette, "Have you any experience with working in such a facility?"

"Uh, no," she said.

"Would this be an amenable arrangement for you during your time here?" Zedolph inquired.

None of them, Bridgette realized, had asked how long a time that would be. She wondered what it was about her, or about Toby's senses, that gave them such a high level of trust to not only bring her inside but offer her a job so quickly after showing up unannounced. But she nodded in agreement. She would think about those things later. The Universe graced her with both a bed and an excuse to stick around indeterminably, and Bridgette wasn't about to turn them down.

"I think so. I mean, you'll have to teach me everything. But I eat a lot of meat and stuff, so it'll be this like, connection to my food," she said.

Zedolph bobbed his head. "You will fit in well with our small team, I believe. We are different sorts of being than perhaps those you are used to meeting."

The fuck does that mean, Bridgette wondered. She took another spoonful of stew to avoid having to comment out loud.

Toby seemed horribly impatient as the mealtime went on. Bridgette chose to focus on her food and attempted to eavesdrop on the adult siblings, who were talking quietly to one another at the other end of the rectangular table. The boy finally resorted to tapping his toes against the table leg until his mother gave him a sharp look of reproach.

"Yes, Toby?" she said.

"I am finished with my meal and would like to See Bridgette now, please."

"Is Bridgette done with her meal?" Serrabinx asked.

Both Toby and Bridgette looked at the Elfling's bowl, empty save for one corner of a bread slice and the dregs of deep red liquid. She sopped the last bit of stew up with the remaining bread and swallowed shakily before saying, "Yep."

Toby hopped out of his seat and ran to her side of the table, nearly bouncing in excitement. The adults all stood, pushing their chairs in, and the boy came to face her. He was so *little* standing directly next to the Liluthuaé. Bridgette knew she was tall, but she was so rarely around children that she forgot sometimes that not everyone's head hovered six feet above the floor.

"Put your hands out flat, like this," Toby instructed. He held his hands with the palms facing upward, and Bridgette mirrored him. "Now close your eyes and think of a peaceful place. See it, sense it, smell it. Do not tell us where you have taken yourself, but stay there. You will know when it is time to come back to this house."

Bridgette closed her eyes and tried to relax, feeling warm energy from Toby's tiny hands gently pulsate over her open palms. A peaceful place? Her mind went first to Collum's office, but she couldn't risk the boy Seeing anything personal like that. Then she thought of Hlafjordstiepel, the misty mountaintop and highest peak in Eckenbourne's mountain range. That was peaceful.

She let her mind settle and visualized herself there, with Collum a nearby presence, surrounding her with calming scents of honeysuckle and vanilla. She imagined the air was getting cold, that it left tracks of goosebumps on her arms. She listened to wind whisper as it blew from mountaintop to mountaintop, heard the barely audible tweets of birds from the forests far below. She heard Collum's focused breathing and slowed her own to match it. She heard his voice, and though it had been mere hours since she'd heard him speak in real life, hearing it now in this forced meditation soothed a terrified scrap of soul. She smelled the cleanness of the air, saw the faint red circle of the Meridian at the top of the domed ward that provided invisibility and protection to the world above the world. In her vision, it was a sort of cloudy day, and she felt the air become wetter, rainier —

"Stop!" a woman's voice shrieked.

Bridgette's eyes flew open, and reality hit with such a jolt that it took her a moment to realize that what she was seeing was happening. The four of them were soaked to the bone and *rain* dripped off the ceiling and dining room table, as if an indoor shower had just happened.

"What the f — heck — was that?" Bridgette asked, eyes wide, catching herself before she let the curse slip in front of Serrabinx.

No one answered. Serrabinx and Zedolph stared first at Toby, then her. Toby looked confused; his head cocked to one side. He had a half-smile though, as if he may not have Seen anything useful, but he'd certainly shown them all something very big. From the looks of horror on the adults' faces, it was something very, very bad.

A memory tickled Bridgette's consciousness, of the day that she first met Mithrilken and Eloise, the day that was cold, misty, and icky when she and Collum walked out to the Unicorns' post. She hadn't liked that weather, and the two of them stayed dry. In her meditation just now, she'd *felt* rain, not just imagined it.

Something Collum said, months and months ago, reflected in her mind from one of the first times he told her about Baize Sammael and Craft Wizardry: *"It was power they had never known, an innate ability not to harness the elements and energies, but to control them. To become them."*

Bridgette's eyes shifted beneath their glamour, and something in Toby's own gaze lit up. She controlled the mist that day to keep herself and Collum dry. She just brought rain into a place where rain did not exist. She made it start and stop. Bent it to her will, without even trying.

She had done *MAGIC.*

She had done *CRAFT* magic.

No wonder Serrabinx and Zedolph were looking at her like she was something undead and rotting and horrible that needed to be thrown out of their house, preferably as a beheaded corpse that couldn't rise back up of its own accord.

Fucking seven hells, Bridgette thought, letting the sick realization sink in. *I'm a deity-damned Craft Elfling.*

Toby let out another musical giggle, breaking the stunned silence of the room. He smiled at her. "I See that you learned something new about yourself, Raisarch."

Bridgette crumpled limply to the wet rug-covered floor.

~ 9 ~

Having successfully skirted any and all Samhain ceremonies, except for being force-fed four of Aurelias' miniature molten chocolate cakes — "It's a *holiday*, Chief!" she'd whined at him, shoving the plate in his face — Collum spent the rest of the week ignoring all of magickind, holed up either in his bedroom sleeping or in his home office, dreading having to leave the safety of his apartment. He'd even sent in a written report, feigning ill, instead of attending that week's Samnung meeting.

It was only when Trystane evanesced into his living room Saturday morning with a paper bag of ham and egg sandwiches and two piping hot mugs of spiced caife mokka that Collum made half an attempt to rouse himself from his reclusive state.

"You. Up." Trystane shouted, banging on his bedroom door.

Collum grumbled from within. "Fuck off, please, I'm trying to avoid existing in the land of the living for the foreseeable future."

"First spiced caife mokka of the season. I'll be rather pissed if I woke up so early to be first in line for it, only for you to stay in bed moping and allow it to get cold and settle out," the ard rialóir called back cheerfully. He helped himself to some plates in the kitchen and opened the front door to pull in the morning's paper.

When Collum emerged a few minutes later in a long-sleeved tunic and loose sleeping pants, hair mussed and unwashed, Trystane stared at him.

"Have you slept?" he asked.

The fyrdwisa's answering grumble was unintelligible.

"You look like a Unicorn trampled you, Collum."

"Again, fuck off."

But Collum took his mug of spiced mokka and dragged a chair from the table, slumping into it before taking a sip. It was nigh on impossible to get the drink from the Coffee Cauldron.

He'd forgotten how much he enjoyed the blend of cayenne, cinnamon, and housemade vanilla syrup added to the witch sisters' regular brews of chocolate and coffee. Trystane had to have been up before dawn to secure two mugs. The gesture, despite Collum's sleep-deprived, work-stressed attitude, was genuinely appreciated.

Trystane chanced speaking again, now that the fyrdwisa had a few moments to acclimate himself to being in the company of another. "I'm not here to talk about Samnung things," he said, glad to see a look of relief pass over Collum's eyes at those words. "I feel we've let too much time go on without discussing the Aelys Frost documents."

"Ah," was Collum's only reply.

The week Bridgette crossed into Palna, he and Trystane began the task of combing through the antique trunk of papers and notebooks that had come into the ard rialóir's possession. But it was overwhelming, so they hadn't made much progress. The trunk spent the last month shoved into a back corner of Collum's bedroom.

Similarly, he realized then that he'd shoved a related topic to the back of his mind. He hadn't told Trystane about what happened between Bridgette and Emi-Joye when they were on Earth. Perhaps with all Trystane's talk of Maylemaegus, and with their impending deep-dive back into Elven lore, now seemed as good a time as any to bring up the incident.

"Trystane, there's something else you need to know about Bridgette's visit to Wales in August," Collum said. "When they first met, as you know, there had been that strange energy between her and Emi-Joye, which she called an aura. The two had a tense at best relationship for most of the time since, and the first night on Earth, in my cottage, things came to a head. After we'd gone to bed, Bridgette confronted Emi-Joye about some … inconsistencies, shall we say, in her story to us, when the ambassadora claimed to not feel the same aura. When Emi-Joye continued to hedge against being completely honest, Bridgette lost it and went after her."

A dark emotion filled Trystane's eyes. "Bridgette attacked the ambassadora?" he asked.

"Yes, and no," Collum replied. "It was more as if Bridgette was taken over by a power she couldn't control. Her eyes went purple, dark purple, like they had that time with Nehemi, but for whatever reason she became quite violent with Emi-Joye. She pulled that dagger of hers on the Fairy. Had her pinned to the wall by the throat, accosting her to tell the truth."

Trystane's already light skin had gone a paler shade of white. "What made Bridgette stop?"

This part, given that the only two beings in the world who knew about the ísenwaer were the fyrdwisa and the Bright Star, Collum couldn't exactly be truthful about. But he attempted: "I tried to pull her off at first. She elbowed me so hard it knocked the breath from my chest, so I used my calming spells on both of them. She snapped out of it and looked at what she was doing, as if she'd been possessed by a spirit or wraith. I've never seen anyone act like that. It was terrifying."

The ard rialóir was biting his tongue. "Was the ambassadora harmed?"

"Scared, I think. There were no visible marks left, and no blood drawn. They, strangely enough, were relatively friendly once the full truth was out in the open and after the ordeal with the True Druids occurred."

"Collum, why did you not think to tell me this until now?"

"I'd put it aside, I suppose, in light of what Bridgette was soon to do. I apologize if that was a decision of poor judgement."

Trystane gave him a long look. "It was atrocious judgement. Had we known, had *I* known, I could have ensured some sort of training be done with the Liluthuaé. Palna is a land of lying beings. What in the seven hells will happen if Bridgette snaps while she's within those walls? What if it's already happened and that's why she's not back yet?"

The thought of his Starshine in a Palnan prison, or at some whim of the Tinuviels', made Collum's stomach curdle.

"That's *not* why she's not back," Collum argued, refusing to admit the possibility.

"Well, something happened, Collum. Bridgette wouldn't have just stuck around for adventuring. That's not like her. Something, or someone, is keeping her there."

This conversation was not going in a positive direction. Instead of answering, Collum stood from the table to retrieve the trunk. Trystane shook his head sadly, muttering something about being in denial. Collum gritted his teeth and walked to his bedroom. One levitating spell later, the heavy trunk slowly floated in the air behind him, shadowing the Elf back to the kitchen. Levitating spells weren't his forte, and the poor thing swayed dangerously from one side to the other as he gripped with every ounce of mental strength to keep it aloft.

Trystane came to his rescue, and with each of them grabbing one of the rusting metal handles on the ends, they heaved the trunk onto the kitchen table. The wood creaked in warning under the weight, and both males reacted instantaneously, yelping in unison and moving the trunk safely back to the ground.

"*How* can paper be so heavy?" Collum sagged, his mind and magic needing a moment to recuperate. "Deity *bless*."

"History tends to carry much weight," the ard rialóir replied wisely, and Collum rolled his eyes at the quip.

Collum briefly felt guilty that he hadn't so much as looked at a Palnan ambassador report since September. He was so tired of going through paperwork by the time Bridgette deployed on her mission that he allowed himself to take a bit of a breather, and as no one stopped him, he kept on with his sabbatical from government paperwork. Then he became caught up in worrying about the Bright Star, and it was less and less of a priority to glance through one of Ambassador Fitzhugh's carefully scribed pages.

The documents in the trunk, however, were far more captivating than yet another droll account of a day minding Palnan border guards. Even protected with spells against aging, the papers, parchment scrolls, and texts were visibly ancient. Aelys Frost and her dúnaelfen had joined Artur Cromwell in Heáhwolcen in the early 1700s, breaking from the established Elven lands in England, Scotland, and Ireland. The ruling human monarchs established a religious agreement as part of their Union Act, which — in the eyes of Aelys Frost — put into permanence a dangerous form of religious intolerance. Though magical beings had long been tormented by humankind, the codifying of the religious persecution of "witches" as a government-protected right was an atrocity Aelys and her followers could not accept.

At a time when most magical beings on Earth became increasingly isolated, hiding deeper in woods and mountains than ever before, Aelys dreamed of a time when humans and magickind could coexist. Perhaps not in exact harmony, but at the very least, with mutual respect and tolerance. Yet the way European humans pitted religious doctrine against one another, she could see no way in the present moment for her dream to come to fruition. At least not in the British Isles.

The ancient Elf's dissent against her fellow leaders was a bitter period in Elven history. For the life of him, Collum couldn't understand *why* such a significant faction of Earth Elves wanted to remain in a place where they could be murdered simply for existing. A place where the state-sanctioned religion affirmed that such actions could be performed and even praised, seen as holy tasks that could help humans obtain their spiritual ascent to the heavens. If he ever had the opportunity to visit these legendary Elven lands from which his kind hailed, this would be the first question he would ask of its modern-day dúnaelfen leaders.

As Trystane lifted the trunk's lid, a musty, chalky, and somewhat sour scent filled Collum's kitchen. Coated with signs of age and ancient origin, a miniature museum of the Elven kind was inside. What Aelys Frost managed to smuggle out of the native Elven lands on Earth was a veritable treasure trove of history. They doubted anything would date back as far as Ceannairí Álfar itself, but — judging by the delicate yellowed pages made of both plant-based material and stretched animal hides — there were millennia-old records and stories in this trunk. Collum and Trystane placed shielding spells over their hands, and the former mentioned something about borrowing white silk gloves from one of the University magisters to protect their history as much as possible.

"Just don't ask Magister Ephynius," Collum added quickly. "Normal beings don't walk up to the library and ask to obtain two large pairs of archival gloves. He'll know we're up to something."

Trystane smirked. "This sounds like an ideal task for our fyrdestre, yes?"

"Aurelias will be just as bad about asking what in the seven hells we need them for, and if she can get herself a pair to help. Perhaps we should send Njahla," Collum replied.

He could see it now, the horned Elfling marching into his kitchen, whatever pair of obnoxious combat boots she wore that day stomping visible footprints into his spotless hardwood floors. She'd probably throw the pairs of gloves on the table and demand to know what they were doing.

To be honest, Collum didn't know why he hedged so much when it came to letting Aurelias in on his fyrdwisa duties, and on these side quests he had a tendency to get involved in. Perhaps it was a brotherly sense of wanting to protect someone he saw as his younger sister, but it was wholly unwarranted. She was the fyrdestre and proved herself worthy of that position the same way he had. Furthermore, she'd proven herself capable of succeeding him as fyrdwisa, should he be unable to fulfill his own responsibilities.

Collum sighed deeply. "Mayhaps I should go against my better judgement, and request that we send them both."

~ 10 ~

Herewosa Donnachaidh, the powerfully muscled witch who oversaw daily operations and combat training at Minthame, observed Emi-Joye from just outside her chosen fighting ring. He watched as she flipped her two favorite daggers in their respective hands. She usually came to Minthame once or twice a week unless her ambassadora duties required her presence on Earth, but he'd seen far more of her lately.

She always practiced in a dress, a simple shift of some sort that had high slits up each leg, allowing for maximum movement when the lightweight panels were left down. On occasion, she tied them off to one side by a knee. Donnachaidh admired this about her. There was absolutely everything feminine about Emi-Joye, and he was pleased to see that she and so many other females in this world did not let that stop them from pursuing whatever pastimes interested them — and in whatever attire they wished to wear while doing so.

Emi-Joye felt his eyes on her and the Fairy turned, her swirling irises stormy despite their light color. "What?" she called out to him, breathless. She'd been here for two hours already, slashing at and ducking from the swinging obstacles of hanging leather bags and wooden dowels that danced in the air around her.

He bowed his head. "You seem to be training more lately, Ambassadora. I believe I have seen more of you these past few months than I did the previous year in its entirety."

"Things change when you acquire a position such as mine," she said, sheathing her blades. "Training keeps my muscles fresh and my head cleared, as you well know, Herewosa."

An outright lie; a complete falsehood! she thought.

He considered this and reached a rosy-hued tattooed hand out to her. "That I do, Ambassadora. Join me on a walk of the grounds, if you would?"

The last thing Emi-Joye wanted to do was stroll the sprawling, acres-long campus of Minthame with the leading commander of the Cailleach. She didn't know why he was asking her when there was a veritable plethora of wígend and trainees around. But it would be rude to say no. She took a long drink from her white leather waterskin and slipped it over her shoulder for the walk. The Fairy gave a stiff smile to Donnachaidh and put her delicate hand in his, large and brawny and calloused, and off they went.

November dawned somewhat brisk in Heáhwolcen, but as most of the grounds of Minthame were spelled, she hardly noticed it. Or wouldn't, until they reached the areas that were designed to be harsh climates of snow and ice. None as cold and unforgiving as her own territory, of course — the chances of battle ever reaching such a clime were slim to none — but still permeated with the constant chill of winter. She did appreciate all the work her ancestors did here to perfect Minthame as training grounds. Even for beings who did not wish to ever join the ranks of the Fórsaí Armada, there were classes to teach basic swordsmanship and knife wielding, combat and shielding, even advanced spell magic. And for families who had little desire to vacation to Earth, Minthame's many habitats provided ample opportunity for beings to get away and have a new experience.

Her own parents did that several times while she was a youngling. Her father's guild of poultice makers and herbalists would gather the first week of June with their families and camp in tents and hammocks, cooking over open fires, spending the days foraging whatever habitat they'd selected for the trip. The evenings revolved around academic and scientific lectures on botany and horticulture. Her father had been to Earth many times, and Emi-Joye recalled him bringing humans up to Heáhwolcen to share their knowledge at these events — with explicit permissions from the Samnung, of course. Her father was born in Heáhwolcen and wasn't that much older than Trystane, though Fairies tended to show age more than Elves usually did. Emi-Joye's mother, however, was much older. She was born on Earth and fled to Heáhwolcen not long after it was founded. Her mother wanted nothing to do with Earth, and so the habitats at Minthame became her parents' compromise for fun overnight outings. So did visits to Loch Liath, the largest lake in the world above the world.

It had been years since Emi-Joye came here with her family, though. The moment she was able to focus on her chosen role as ambassadora, her studies and proficiencies took precedence over such things. Perhaps she should join them this coming summer. Perhaps, a strained voice in the back of her mind whispered, she should bring her friends. Apostine's father and hers had never met outside of professional or ceremonial settings. She felt as though they would get along as if they'd known each other their whole lives. She couldn't imagine Collum enjoying something as trivial as a family camping trip, though. Truth be told, she couldn't imagine Collum Andoralain enjoying much of anything.

But if Collum came, Bridgette would come. Emi-Joye wouldn't mind that. She liked the Elfling well enough, aside from Bridgette's insistence that they were meant to be connected to one another for roles greater than friendship.

"You seem to be lost in thought, Ambassadora."

The herewosa's voice startled Emi-Joye back to the present and she admitted, "I was thinking about the times my family came to Minthame when I was much younger. My father and his guild visit every summer still, but I have not joined them in some time."

She heard the wistfulness in her own voice, an ache for times much simpler than these. The long lives of Fae and other magical beings — even witches, whose lives were longer than those of humans, though not truly immortal — should mean an unending amount of time to pursue the things that interested them, to work in concert with Nature and Universe to design a better world.

"What is it that plagues you?" Herewosa Donnachaidh's question was curious, not pressing, and he squeezed her hand gently in comfort.

Emi-Joye sighed. She lifted her free hand and put an invisible barrier of sound around them before answering him, the sky magic breezing around the two figures.

"I am lost," she said, not sure why she was telling the herewosa this vulnerable *thing* that dwelled inside her these days. "The Bright Star was brought to us, which should be a time of great warning of threats and war and things we've not thought about for almost two hundred years. It should also be a time of great rejoicing for our Elven siblings, to be able to exist at the same time and in the same space as a legend such as she, wrought of Ylda herself."

"But?" Donnachaidh said, looking at her sidelong. The Fairy's gaze tracked straight ahead, staring ceaselessly at the wooded path before them.

"But there is a strange *feeling* between us," Emi-Joye continued. "Bridgette calls it an aura, and for her it is this tangible feeling that exists when she, myself, and Princess Cloa are in the same vicinity. We do not feel it when it is only two of us, but once, when all three were together, the air itself felt wrong to me. As I explained to Bridgette and the fyrdwisa, it felt more of a premonition, as if I experienced a fleeting presence of a deep energy that bonded us. But this was not a positive energy. Nor would I classify it as negative, but perhaps …"

Her voice trailed off. This was months and months ago that she'd felt the strangeness, and she still struggled to articulate it.

"I would very much like to be friends with the Bright Star," Emi-Joye said. "But I do not wish to be part of some grand ordained plan with her at the helm. I wish for my future to be my own, separate from whatever the Universe has in store for her."

Donnachaidh led her toward a sprawling springlike meadow,

full of lush green grasses that blossomed into tiny flowers of periwinkle and neon violet. "Ambassadora, I do apologize for my impertinence, and I mean no offense," he replied. "Your future is yours, as is the Bright Star's, as is your second's, as is mine own. But existence is an intricate web. To have one's individual future does not isolate it from being forever intertwined with that of another."

She frowned, although the discomfort was short-lived. The springtime habitat they'd walked into was for the moment free of practicing wígend, although the tree trunks surrounding it bore recent axe and sword scars of witness to hosting them not long ago.

"You speak wise words for me to think on," Emi-Joye said, looking at him with a half-smile on her lips. "Thank you for that guidance."

"You're most welcome, Ambassadora," Herewosa Donnachaidh replied. "I want to ask you something, because you *have* been training more than your normal regimen."

"I'm training to clear my head. You know better than I do, Herewosa, if war is on the horizon," she murmured, anticipating the question. Her guess was correct, and he chuckled.

"You always have been wise beyond your years," he said. "There are no true preparations that have been made, as much of what we may or may not prepare for depends on what knowledge the Bright Star brings back with her. Has she not returned yet?"

Emi-Joye shrugged. "No, unless the fyrdwisa has her squirreled away somewhere."

She didn't think he did, though. Collum had been too tightly wound the couple of times she'd seen him recently. Bridgette soothed and freed the rarely unshakeable fyrdwisa; reminded him that he was a being with a life to enjoy and not just someone with a job to do. The Fairy wondered if the Elf himself had bothered to see that yet, or if he had and just refused to admit it.

"Bridgette was supposed to be back earlier than this, yes?" Donnachaidh pressed, pausing their walk to run a hand over one of the tree's scars. Sap leached from its wound, the sticky substance issuing an amber scent. "Deity damn them, they nearly took this sapling in half. I'll have to get one of the Elves to come have a look and see if it's savable."

Such was the risk of training in a place like this. Ambitious trainees or hopeful future wígend tended to become overzealous, sending weaponry flying with too much force into the trees as they feinted after one another during group exercises. Though their weapons were spelled from doing harm against flesh, there was nothing to keep them from damaging the plant life that filled each of Minthame's habitats.

The Fairy left Donnachaidh to his examination and wandered further into the springlike environment. She wondered what it would be like to truly train as wígend and not just a skilled knife fighter. She wondered if she would need to, depending on what information Bridgette shared with them.

It hit her then just how dangerous, how precarious, things had become. If Bridgette let anything slip, if she couldn't stick to whatever story the Samnung concocted for her, they would be in trouble. If Bridgette wasn't able to find out anything or was somehow prevented from acquiring the knowledge they sought, they'd be equally doomed; poised for another potential surprise attack like the one that started the Ingefeoht. Heáhwolcen would be constantly on guard for the what-ifs.

What part was she supposed to play in all this? Was she to learn to fight in group formation? To wield her daggers aloft in the sky on command as part of the Caomhnóir Feeric? Were she and Apostine, along with the rest of the Fairy ambassadors, ambassadoras, and their respective ambestres, supposed to disappear to Earth and protect their territories? Surely if Palna attacked greater Heáhwolcen, Earth would soon follow. It was the humans Baize Sammael spent his entire lifetime aiming to destroy, humans who had no patience or understanding for spell magic and Old Magick, and the magical beings and creatures who did not want their mortal counterparts dead.

She did not like the answer that began to take shape, though a deep-seated part of her seemed to rejoice that *something* was changing in her. Emi-Joye's stomach twisted, an entire flock of butterflies and fear unleashed within her as this *something* clarified and took deadly form. It sickened her. Terrified her, and she did not want any part in what the Universe suddenly seemed to hint at. But if someone as unskilled in magic as Bridgette Conner was able to bear the fate of the world on her back, then Emi-Joye could certainly, albeit unwillingly, carry this new weight with her wings.

"Herewosa?" Emi-Joye called back to the witch. She turned from where she stood, lifting herself off the ground a few inches. The panels of her dark blue shift dress flowed behind her.

He glanced up from the tree, a notebook in hand — he'd been sketching the deep cut, measuring its angle and depth. "Yes?"

Emi-Joye wasn't sure she was breathing as she glided toward him, wings fluttering in the sky behind her. "I would like you to call a private meeting in the new year with the leaders of the Armada. Do not tell them who summons them. Do not tell the Samnung."

The Fairy's eyes were nothing but cold determination when they met those of the herewosa. He nodded warily.

"What should I tell them, then?"

The icy blue of her usually whorling eyes had gone deathly still. "Tell them destiny left her calling card. Some of us decided to answer it."

~ 11 ~

When Bridgette next awoke, she found herself nestled between the comforter and sheets on the guest room bed — her bed, she supposed, for the time being. It was bright out, brighter than it should have been, given that it had been early afternoon when she fainted on the dining room floor. She stared at the painted wooden ceiling, wondering what in the hell happened in those few hours she'd been there. The thought of moving from this bed was not a welcome one. How had it been only yesterday that she'd awoken in Collum's apartment?

It felt like a lifetime ago.

A gentle knock at the door, and Serrabinx entered. She smiled, noticing Bridgette was awake, but the smile didn't quite reach her eyes.

"A fair morning, Bridgette of the Outside," the not-witch greeted her. "How do you feel?"

"Morning?!" Bridgette was horrified. *How long have I been out?*

Her expression must have betrayed the question, because Serrabinx came to sit at the foot of the bed. The smile she bore now was soft, almost sad, but definitely more genuine than the one she first walked in with.

"Zedolph carried you in here when you collapsed two days ago. We've been unable to wake you since," she said. "The doorknob became painfully heated whenever we tried to enter once you had been tucked in. My son told us that this was a sign you were not to be bothered. He insisted on sleeping outside this door the first night, to make sure you were safe."

The Elfling balked. Two days? She'd been out for *two days*? And the doorknob had nearly burned them? Bridgette didn't know what to say. She just stared, mouth slightly agape, at the wall opposite her bed.

"Will you share with me what happened when Toby Saw you?" Serrabinx asked, after letting a momentary silence settle between them.

"I have no clue," Bridgette said, blinking hard, as if sleep still nestled in her eyes, as if the glamour was a dried-out contact lens she could feel like a physical presence. "I imagined myself in a peaceful place, like he told me to, and I was feeling and smelling and all the heavy visualization stuff. And in my visualization, it started raining. Then all of a sudden you yelled out to stop, and then there was rain inside the dining room …"

"I would like to know how that is possible," her host said. The tone was gentle, but it was a command, not a request.

Bridgette wished she knew how to answer. "Your guess is as good as mine. I can't do spells, no matter if I'm in Palna or Heáhwolcen or on Earth. I just kind of look like I can."

"Hmm," Serrabinx murmured. It was a noncommittal response, a sound to fill the void of silence between them.

It was so strangely silent in this room. Serrabinx was content with it, but her guest was not. When Bridgette woke in Eckenbourne, there were always birds chirping outside and that mysterious, faint sound of windchimes permeated the breezes. On the rare off-chance that it actually stormed, the wind whipped through the chimes, creating a delicious dance of tinny beats and soft melodies that contrasted against the whistle and the loud pitter-patter of too-large raindrops hitting rooftops. In Palna, the air seemed stagnant of sound.

"Can I talk to Toby?" Bridgette asked. That stagnation gnawed at her. "What he said at the end, I have some questions about that."

Maybe this was why she'd been out for so long. The shock of his words, coupled with her exhaustion from the days before crossing the barrier walls, combined to suck her into a period of cognitive non-existence, until she was ready to discuss what he revealed. The Bright Star wasn't quite sure that it was a revelation because it made absolutely no sense. There already *was* a Raisarch in Palna … and it was most assuredly not named

Bridgette Eileen Conner.

Serrabinx had stiffened noticeably. She still sat at the edge of the bed, but her expression hardened. Toby's words hadn't set well with her either, no more than the sudden rain shower inside her house did.

"My son will sometimes say words to get a reaction out of those in his presence. It is unfortunately and undoubtedly a childish prank that he played on you," the woman said, her words unnatural. A feigned tone of reassurance. "Allow me to apologize on his behalf."

She was lying through her teeth, and something deep inside Bridgette rumbled in anger and agony. The Elfling shook the feeling. She didn't have the mental capacity to deal with whatever bullshit her hosts were pulling on her. Not today. Not after apparently more than twenty-four hours without food in her system. She'd corner Toby later and get the boy to tell her what he knew about her that she, apparently, did not.

What a delightful theme of events when it came to nearly everyone she met in Heáhwolcen thus far.

"Oh," was all Bridgette said aloud, and her stomach growled.

Serrabinx let out a genuine smile at the noise and said brightly, "Shall we have a morning meal in the garden?"

Bridgette joined her an hour later, freshly washed up and in a clean pair of brown leggings and a lightweight silvery gray tunic. Palna had running water, thankfully, though by what means the Elfling wasn't sure. She wished she'd brought an entirely different wardrobe because it was swelteringly hot already in Xcthonya. This was a Deep South fall, Florida temperatures, not the New England fall she'd stepped out of earlier that week.

She still wished she had a damn map.

But she couldn't think about that now. Not here, not in this bright and vivacious expanse of garden that Serrabinx led her to.

Bridgette hadn't realized just how extensive the Maudlins' lands were. She'd only seen the front beds of herbs by the walk, not this backyard of blooms and fragrances that would have made even Nehemi croon with praise.

Serrabinx arranged their breakfast on a woven mat amidst a patch of sage green turfgrass, shorn short and apparently thriving in the drier weather of Palna. Though the air in the garden was still quiet, only dotted with the occasional tweet of bird or wisp of breeze, it felt less stifling as they sat surrounded by bright florals and heady perfumes. The birds might be silent, but the bugs and insects? They swarmed, emitting barely perceptible buzzes and hums as they flew from flower to flower, tiny legs and antennae and faces becoming coated in pollen of so many neon hues that they looked like tiny celebrants of Holi, or perhaps humans who'd done one of those color run races and been pelted with powdered chalk as they dashed from checkpoint to checkpoint.

It was so lovely, so vibrant. Bridgette was strongly reminded of Collum's home office.

"What is it that draws your attention?" Serrabinx asked, lifting a piece of toast. She'd smeared the crusty slice with a thick layer of fresh mashed avocado, spritzed with lime and dusted with a blend of Maldon flakes, pink salt crystals, and ground white pepper.

"Just … I didn't really know what to expect when I came here," Bridgette answered, reaching for her own plate. "Most of what we know about modern-day Palna after the Ingefeoht comes from Fairy ambassador reports. And that's only one guy's perspective, you know? There's only so much he sees and can tell us."

"How is what you have seen so far different from what is in the rest of our continent?"

Bridgette chewed a bite of toast. "This is insanely good, by the way. That's definitely one thing y'all share. The food up here? A lot of it isn't that different from things we have on Earth, but damn. Damn! It tastes so much better. Thanks to that grain festival last month, and from your meals, I've officially eaten food from every country of Heáhwolcen now, and ten out of ten all around. Like, whatever spices y'all use or cooking techniques, I don't know — something about it makes everything I've eaten wildly different. This avocado toast, for example. I eat avo toast all the time and it's usually nothing to write home about. But this?! With the citrus and the salt mix, I could die today and be happy this was my last meal."

Her host blushed at the rambling praise, but Bridgette was dead serious. She loved food and loved experiencing food. As much as she loved music, it was food that she couldn't get enough of exploring when it came to her rare instances of traveling.

"What is different in Palna?" Serrabinx asked again, still flushed.

"Okay, this may sound bizarre, but the air is totally different," Bridgette gushed. "Well, I haven't spent much time in Bondrie, but the three bigger countries, the air is clean and sweet. And it always has sound. You walk outside and the air sounds like there are these faint windchimes playing, even when there isn't a breeze. Birds do not shut up elsewhere in Heáhwolcen. They are literally always chirping, like it's constantly spring. Granted, I haven't done winter in Heáhwolcen, so that might be a seasonal thing like it is on Earth. Here though, in Palna, the air is way quieter. These little bugs are the most sound I've heard since I woke up. And the air feels different, too. Like it's tense or something. Kind of hard to explain, I guess."

Serrabinx watched her, and there was something in her eyes that made Bridgette's own eyes yearn to shift beneath their glamour. Her hostess hid much from her. This sierwan knowledge was something that would plague her until the woman decided to open up, whenever that may be.

"The way you describe greater Heáhwolcen makes me want to visit there," Serrabinx said. Her words were measured, and she stared into Bridgette's lilac eyes, dulled underneath their unseeable spell.

"Who knows, maybe one day you'll be able to," Bridgette said, put off by the stare. The first day she spent here, she learned through her sierwan gift that Serrabinx strongly desired to escape, and the knowledge roared back at her now. She ate more toast, wondering how in the hell any of them were going to get out of this place. "When I go back, you can come with me, if you want. And Toby, too."

She spoke those words offhandedly, but her eyes burned — actually burned — and Bridgette worried for a moment that the glamour was about to break as her eyes shifted rapidly and her vision blurred. This was a promise she'd just made. Something wholly adamant, a vow that the Liluthuaé would keep without fail.

The Maudlins wanted out of Palna, and Bridgette would be the one to help them escape.

~ 12 ~

Apparently, Bridgette's inner realization that she just made some sort of unbreakable vow went unnoticed by Serrabinx, who continued to eat her avocado toast as if the entire world hadn't changed. The two sat quietly again as they finished breakfast in the fall sunshine. It was Serrabinx who spoke first when they gathered their dishes to return inside.

"Zedolph would like to take you to the butchery tomorrow to introduce you to his slátraestres, and to begin your training to become one yourself," she said.

"A what? A slaw-tres-tray?" Bridgette's aberration of whatever word Serrabinx just said sounded like a Hollywood redneck mispronouncing "quesadilla".

"A slah-treh-stray," Serrabinx said, slower this time, trilling each "r" with a refined tongue. "It is the word for butcher's apprentice, as the butcher is the slátrari."

"Oh, duh," Bridgette blinked. "Yeah, of course."

"Today, however, my son has requested permission to show you more of Xcthonya, if you would be so willing to accompany him."

Bridgette didn't think she had much choice in the matter, so she nodded in agreement. It would probably be smart to begin roaming Palna with a guide who grew up there, so she could take notes as a way to support her ruse of being a University student. Plus, time alone with Toby would give Bridgette plenty of opportunity to peg him about the whole Raisarch nonsense. It *had* to be nonsense.

Her tour guide appeared by her side in short order, simmering with excitement. "Mumma says I am to give you a walk of our city!"

The Elfling couldn't help but grin at his enthusiasm. "Yes sir, so I hear. Can we look for souvenirs? I have a few friends I would like to get things for if I see anything that reminds me of them while I'm here. And I need a new notebook and pen."

"I will take you to the *best* shops," Toby promised solemnly, nodding his head in acceptance of this mission. "And I shall take you to the river market first, as it is a jewel of our city."

"Awesome," Bridgette said, her smile broadening. "Notebook first though? I can't believe I forgot to pack one, but I can't exactly study right if I don't have a way to write down everything I see and learn."

Before she and Toby made it out the front door, Serrabinx was at their side, walking up as soundlessly as a prowling cat. There was a flicker of worry in her expression as she warned them, "Do not speak to many others on the streets, if you can help it."

"Don't talk to strangers. Got it, Mom!" Bridgette quipped, intending to lighten the mood. Her hostess' response was another one of those smiles that didn't quite meet her eyes.

Like I am willingly going to go out of my way to draw attention to myself, Bridgette thought, though she knew the warning was as much out of concern for Toby as it was for her. This Collective, she had to find out more about it — confirm it existed, who was a member, how they were recruited … although from the sound of that warning, Collective members were as likely to be swiped up off the streets as they were to be actively courted to join.

Toby put his tiny hand in hers and nearly dragged her out the door. "We shall return by twilight, Mumma!"

Serrabinx watched them from the doorway. Bridgette could feel the not-witch's eyes boring into the back of her neck as she and Toby speed-walked to the main road. The sensation of being watched didn't dissipate until they rounded a corner and the house was out of sight. She shivered, not enjoying being mistrusted by Serrabinx.

I can't really blame her, though. I mean, her kid shows up with me like some stray puppy, I accidentally perform illegal magic in her dining room, her kid claims I'm the fucking Raisarch, and then I pass out for almost forty-

eight hours. Shining example of upstanding houseguest, she thought, rolling her eyes at herself.

The route they took back to the business district of Xcthonya was the reverse of how they walked to the house her first day. When they arrived, the streets again bustled with residents and shopkeepers, artists and customers. Though there were plenty of beings walking and flying around, both individually and in small groups, no one mingled or greeted one another. There were repeated instances of the fist-over-heart gesture that Bridgette caught out of the corner of her eye. The air still had that tightness to it. Bridgette wanted to study this, wanted desperately to understand what caused this tense feeling.

She looked down at Toby and whispered, "Does the air feel different to you here?"

"The air?" he asked, meeting the volume of her voice.

"Yes. It's like, *tight.* Like something is about to happen and everyone is waiting for it," Bridgette replied, hoping this served as a good explanation.

Toby tilted his head to one side as he led them toward a bookshop. "You wish to know what the wind tells me?"

The Elfling squeezed his hand in confirmation, and he obliged her request. Sort of.

"I can ask it this question, but it is not safe to share the answer with so many ears that would also like to know," Toby said. His confidence in being hesitant was almost answer enough. He definitely felt this same energy around them, but he had more of an ability to fish for answers in Palna than she did.

"Ask it, please. And then after I get this notebook, let's go where it *is* safe to talk," she said. "I have a lot I want to ask you about, actually."

"I know."

Bridgette gave him a wry look and he beamed up at her, the sunshine catching in those tiny golden flecks of his brown eyes. She hadn't realized how deep and wise those eyes were. Looking into them now, the Liluthuaé knew she would fight as fiercely to protect this magnificent, mysterious child as she would for the world that he deserved to grow up in. It was the same kind of innate conviction that convinced her to trust and follow Collum when he appeared in her life, wholly unwelcome, and changed the course of what she thought her future was meant to be.

They reached the entrance to the bookshop, which Toby proclaimed to be his most favorite store in the whole of the world. Or at least, the whole of the world he was able to see, he clarified for her. Bridgette neglected to mention the vow she made to his mother just a few hours earlier and couldn't help but visualize what his expression might look like when he walked into the University library for the first time.

Kid's gonna freak, she thought, the corners of her mouth twitching upward.

She followed Toby inside and the moment the doors opened, she understood why he loved the bookshop so much. Comforting smells of leather and crisp pages wafted toward them, complemented by the fragrant aroma of tobacco-scented candles. The store was overflowing with books and notebooks and — Bridgette stopped short.

The actual fuck are these doing here? she thought, reaching a hand out for a set of gray-spined titles she knew. She'd read these books. She'd *bought* these books. In high school.

On Earth.

Alarm bells started ringing inside her head and she was reeling, mentally reaching for answers that eluded her. Books from Earth should not be in Palna. Should they?

Maybe there's a completely logical explanation for this, Bridgette thought, trying to reason with herself. *Fairy ambassadors could easily have brought them in. There's probably some semi-secret exchange program happening, and that's why the Samnung leaders didn't think to mention it. Hell, maybe it started back before Mohreen's time as a spy, and beings were sneaking in books to try to educate Palnans to not be anti-human assholes.*

The logic calmed her, though something remained unsettled about the situation. Toby noted her discomfort and asked, "Do you know these books?"

"I do. I didn't expect to see them here," she said, tuning her voice to a near-silent whisper. "They're from *Earth*."

A sly little grin grew on his face. "Yes."

She stared at him, mouth slightly agape, as he pulled her deeper into the shop toward a display of writing tools and stationery. Leather in every color — every naturally dyed color, anyway — covered a wide assortment of hand-stitched and bound notebooks and sketchbooks. Bridgette found herself instinctively reaching for a notebook with a cover dyed a stunning shade of blue that reminded her so very much of Collum's eyes. It was in her grasp before her own eyes could even bother to take in any other color options.

"This one," she told Toby decidedly.

Bridgette clutched it to her chest as they turned toward the wall of writing utensils. The shelves overflowed with glass jars full of pencils and pens, quills and dipping jars of powdered ink, and small vials of liquid ink that could be inserted into pens to change or refill colors. Several pencils and a miniature Damascus steel penknife for sharpening their tips wound up in Bridgette's grasp to take back with her.

Toby pulled at her hand again, and they went around a set of shelves to find a display case of teas, chocolates, and coffees. Bridgette's eyes widened. The two ordered a half-dozen delicate macarons in a rainbow of pastel colors, as well as iced coffee with sugar and milk for her and bergamot cream tea for the boy. Her hands were getting full, but Toby guided her — his hand now gripped at the hem of her sweater — to one more section of books.

They looked far too advanced for a child his age, but what did she know? Hell, she'd been reading books above her suggested reading level since she learned the alphabet, and Toby certainly seemed precocious. He cocked his head to one side as he scoured the section, walking slowly and purposefully. She wasn't sure if he was on the hunt for a specific novel, or if he was simply letting his eyes wander and allowing whatever powers he pretended not to have show him what book he was supposed to add to their pile.

Bridgette let her own gaze flow over the spines. Again, more book titles she recognized and authors' names she'd heard before, all mixed in with books that had runes or different languages inscribed into their covers with metallic inks. Some had English titles, but clearly writers of magical origin. None had book jackets, so there was an odd sort of uniformity amongst the leather-bound covers, though the books themselves were different colors and heights with a variety of papers bound within. She glanced at Toby, who'd stopped walking and intently eyed a set of ochre books. They had runes etched down the spine in deep crimson ink. His little brow furrowed. Bridgette hung back, waiting patiently for him to make his next move.

They stood there for several moments until he made a decision and grabbed all three. They were each a good couple inches thick and probably weighed about two-and-a-half pounds each, a combined weight that his child's arms gripped with some difficulty, especially with his one hand clutching his pasteboard cup of tea.

"Wanna switch?" Bridgette asked, motioning to her armload, which weighed significantly less.

"No, but you may hold my tea."

She took the cup and followed him to the register, wondering what in the seven hells those three books were that he procured. The counter was a few inches taller than his head, but there was a stepstool that he pulled over with a foot and climbed on so that he could put the books down himself. The woman behind the counter gave him a long, appraising look.

"That is an interesting choice for you today, Tobias," she

said, raising a brow as she brought her fist up over her heart. "And you've brought a new friend?"

He nodded proudly, and both boy and Elfling responded to her gesture. "Yes. This is Bridgette. She is a guest in my mumma's home and will soon be working with my uncle at his butchery."

To Bridgette, he said, "This is my dearest friend, Glafida. This is her shop."

"Hello," Bridgette said, trying to sound more Palnan. "You've got quite a store here. I hope to visit it many more times."

Glafida inclined her head, then turned to Toby. "I heard news that there will be a new artist at the river market from Düoria this day. She is a skilled metalsmith. I believe your mumma might be intrigued by her pieces."

Toby's eyes lit up. "I will absolutely take Bridgette to the market as our next destination, then!"

As Glafida reached for their goods to place inside a cloth tote bag, she added, "Be sure to ask to see her garnets. Those are her most sought-after pieces."

Bridgette handed her a wad of paper money, which the woman frowned at slightly.

"Only the ambassadors use this sort of currency here," she said quietly, brows knitting together as she handed change back to the Elfling. "You'll like the garnets, too, I think."

~ 13 ~

Bridgette and Toby entered the bright sunshine again, eager to visit the river market and this artist. Bridgette had no idea why Glafida thought she'd like garnets. She wasn't even sure she liked the color red to begin with, much less that she wanted to purchase and wear jewelry or décor accented with the gems.

The river, which Toby said was called Afon Azúl, named for the blue sheen its currents took underneath the near-constant sun, was a lazily flowing wide body of water that swept south of Xcthonya, in the opposite direction of the castle that marked Düoria on the horizon. Afon Azúl's market was a decent walk from the business district of the city. Bridgette welcomed the cool breeze that hailed them as they neared.

She heard the market before they saw it as they crested a small hilltop that looked down over the edge of the river. Vendors were set up with multicolored tents of everything — food and drink, clothing, art, home goods. It was a much freer, more lively state of affairs than the bustle of what Bridgette decided to call "downtown Xcthonya", as children and younglings ran about screeching and shouting, animals barked and brayed, and merchants in wild colors and fabrics called out to invite passersby to their spaces.

It was, she decided, a farmers market on steroids.

Toby led her to a tent with an open fire next to it, and Bridgette balked momentarily at the added heat. She'd been sweating practically since she woke up. But the spicy, savory smell that crackled into the air along with the flames gave her pause. There was a wooden canoe moored to a post at the river's edge right behind this tent. A group of men was assembly line-style gutting, filleting, scaling, and cooking fresh fish right before their eyes. Another man headed up a long line of hungry patrons, furiously scribbling down and calling back orders to two girls and an older woman who were eyeing the meat, pulling it off the fire, and plating it as it finished cooking.

Bridgette's mouth watered in anticipation. They stood in line, fanning themselves idly to stave off the unending warmth, until the order-taker finally made it to them. He rattled off the available preparations of the shoal bass and channel cat his colleagues caught that morning: fillets with skewers of late-season peppers and caramelized onions; blackened and served sandwich style on fresh bread with spicy housemade pickles and avocado cream; or as bite-size fried poppers with cast-iron griddled potatoes. Toby ordered the third option, while Bridgette craved the sandwich.

They greedily ate their fish and a macaron each while seated under the shade of a miraculously tall fringetree, its drape of green leaves still clutching onto summer's fragrance. The lawn of the river market held many taller trees than Bridgette had seen thus far in Palna, perhaps nourished to greater heights by the proximity of this waterway.

Her stomach ached from so much walking, from the last week of beleaguered eating habits, and she lied down in the dappled shade with her arms underneath her head. "This has been a very intense day," she told Toby.

"We still have much day left," he pointed out. "And I would like to meet the garnet artist now, please."

She groaned, heaved herself onto her feet, and gathered their tote bag from the bookstore. Toby deposited their paper food wrappings in a metal compost bin nearby. When he walked back to her, she begrudgingly followed him down the packed lines of crowds, grinning at the small groups of children playing in the shallower areas of the river, which had been walled off with stacks of smooth stones to create swimming pools.

It wasn't long before Toby found the artist in question, though Bridgette did not know how he knew she was the one Glafida spoke of. But he approached the woman with confidence, and Bridgette was startled to see that it wasn't a woman at all, but rather a female Sanguisuge. She was rail-thin and petite, her skin almost black, but still maintaining the porcelain smoothness and near icy pallor that Bridgette had seen before with Verivol and the shopkeeper she met once in Endorsa, Lymerian. The artist's head was shaved, and she wore a stunning braided circlet of hammered brass across her forehead. It dripped with strings of garnets hanging over her ears and brow. Her eyes were as black as Verivol and Lymerian's.

The boy raised his fist and spoke first, his voice measured and quiet: "Tráthnóna mistéireach, friend. I welcome you to Xcthonya."

The artist acknowledged them with the same gesture. Her eyes narrowed. Cautious. "Tráthnóna mistéireach," she said, but did not flash the pearly, too-sharp canines that Bridgette knew lurked beneath her purple-painted lips.

Toby glanced around them, the movement of his eyes hardly perceptible, before whispering, "Viltu carleast?"

Good grief, he's talking in tongues, Bridgette thought, concerned. She knew the first traditional greeting from elsewhere in Heáhwolcen, but had no idea what he'd just asked.

The Sanguisuge wore a dress with fitted sleeves that went over her hands, thumbholes sewn in the cuffs. She performed a brisk movement with her right hand, pulling it out of the cuff and flashing her wrist, just long enough for Toby and Bridgette to note a curious tattoo that looked like an eye. Her sleeve was back in place in barely a second.

Bridgette pretended to look at some of the jewelry that the Sanguisuge displayed. Her style was minimalistic, characterized by geometric lines with direct angles that encased raw-cut stones and crystals. Druzy and glittery, they sparkled in the sun, the metal finishings either made of hammered brass, hammered yellow gold, or a dark charcoal metal that could have been rhodium. But there were no garnets at the jeweler's tent. The only garnets she had were the ones she was wearing, and

Bridgette stepped back in surprise.

The sierwan knowledge came to her at the same time Toby murmured, "Sóc Láttaew al Hringur."

Holy fucking fuckballs, Bridgette almost said out loud. *Glafida only told us about the garnets so we would know what tent to find this chick at, and her recommendation probably has nothing to do with jewelry.*

The Elfling was not sure she could handle yet another life-altering or destiny-confirming sierwan knowing until at *least* the following week. Maybe month. Maybe never.

If these past couple days were in a book, I don't know if I'd be excited to see what bullshit revelation comes next, or if I'd have thrown it across the room by now, yelling because what the actual *fuck,* she thought, leaning against the tent post to steady herself.

Toby and the Sanguisuge carried on quiet conversation, and Bridgette supposed she should either eavesdrop or entirely tune in. She chose the latter, and it was a semi-fortuitous decision. The two were indulging in a coded conversation, with many phrases of either metaphor or the traditional magical language that combined bits and pieces of modern and extinct Earthen tongues. It was hard for Bridgette, who'd only ever done moderately well in high school Spanish classes, to follow.

A couple walked up to the tent, and Bridgette coughed pointedly to alert the two to shut up before anything important was overheard. She pulled at Toby's hand, promising that they would return in a bit. One of the Sanguisuge's hammered gold necklaces with a stunning tiger's eye would indeed make a souvenir fit for Njahla.

When they were far enough away from the tent and alone except for more playing children, Bridgette plopped down onto the grass and pulled out the rest of the macarons. She turned to Toby, eyes narrowed.

"You. Talk," she directed him, handing over one of the treats. He may not know her true nature, but he discerned enough about her — through whatever overarching powers spoke to him — that she'd been deemed trustworthy of being part of something much, *much* bigger than she ever anticipated walking into when she stepped through the Ballamúr.

Toby gnawed thoughtfully on the macaron, kicking his shoes off to dangle his toes in the chilled river water. "Her name is Queylan, of no surname. She is an artist of Düoria who now wishes to expand her customers elsewhere in Palna. She is a Sanguisuge, which is a sort of being that has very sharp teeth and eats mostly raw meats and blood."

"What did you say to her in the language I didn't understand?"

"I was making sure she was who I was supposed to find."

Deity bless, this kid is cryptic, Bridgette groaned inwardly. She stared at him pointedly, and he looked right back at her. An impasse.

"And who where you supposed to find?" she pressed, getting frustrated.

Toby stood up and put his shoes back on. "Those people are gone."

Bridgette tossed her hands in the air and followed him back to the tent, itching to know the answers to all the questions that now peppered her brain. She couldn't let Toby know she was a sierwan, obviously, but if she was able to overhear a secret conversation, he would at least have the decency to fill her in on the significance of what she witnessed, right?

Good luck with that, the wind seemed to whisper to her.

She scowled, only half-listening to Toby and Queylan talk this time. She heard her name come up, followed by Toby explaining she was a friend who could be trusted. The Sanguisuge made a move of scratching her wrist where that tattoo was hidden under her sleeve. Toby shook his head in some sort of answer.

Queylan eventually looked to Bridgette, noting the Elfling's gaze on her jewelry, and asked if there was anything she'd like wrapped.

"Actually, yeah," Bridgette replied, flashing a hesitant smile the Sanguisuge's way. "This one is perfect."

The price marked on the tiger's eye necklace seemed wildly below what it should be for such a piece of art and craftsmanship, and Bridgette got a whiff of what sort of economics were practiced in Palna compared to the other countries in the world above the world. Coin and paper were jointly king here. There was no such thing as in-kind payment and friendly exchanges. No such thing, for most, of giving and creating for the joy of it. It was sheer capitalism, sheer Western human capitalism, and Bridgette saw that — with so many other artists in the river market, not to mention likely downtown Xcthonya too — Queylan likely priced her jewelry cheaply and competitively to entice new customers.

First the books from Earth, now *this*. The longer she was in Palna, even for as short a time as it had been, the stranger and more worrisome her situation became. Bridgette accepted her wrapped necklace from Queylan with only a brief word of thanks and turned to walk with Toby, the rich golden hours before sunset following them to her temporary home.

~ 14 ~

Serrabinx was in the kitchen. Fragrant smells of roasted vegetables and searing meat swelled from the firehearth. The flames burned low underneath a wrought-iron grate, and on top of it sat two cast-iron skillets. Serrabinx flipped pork chops in the larger of the two cooking vessels and gave the vegetables a stir before turning to greet Toby and Bridgette.

"How was your day?" she asked.

Bridgette gave Toby a skeptical glance. He'd refused to talk during their lengthy trip back from the river market, and she supposed she couldn't blame him. It would be just her luck to have asked a question with the wrong set of eyes watching or wrong ears tuned in, and get both of them in trouble. But she did have questions, and she absolutely would not let them drop. She also was not about to take the heat for whatever may or may not have occurred on their adventure into Xcthonya.

The Elfling smiled innocently at Serrabinx and began to walk toward her room, then remembered Toby's heavy trio of books that weighed down the tote bag slung over her shoulder. She reached inside to pull them out, but the boy stopped her.

"Those are for you," he said, and she cocked an eyebrow.

"Oh?"

"What are for whom?" Serrabinx jumped in, distracted from her cooking. She suddenly looked suspicious.

"I found for Bridgette the books that would be most helpful to her studies," Toby said. He sounded quite proud of himself, and Bridgette didn't have the heart to tell him that she couldn't read ancient runes, so she wasn't sure they'd be any help at all.

"What books?"

The suspicion remained in Serrabinx's tone, so Bridgette lofted them out of the bag. They really were lovely, and the Elfling made a mental note to plead with Collum to let her put a bookshelf in her room at the apartment. The deep golden color of these covers would contrast in the best way against the grays and blues of the bedroom's decorations. She handed the books to Serrabinx.

Serrabinx took one look at them and her nostrils flared. She practically ripped them from Bridgette's hands and gave Toby a look that would have had anyone else cowering in a corner. But the boy stood, arms crossed defiantly in front of his chest, as his mother seethed.

"Tobias Maudlin, you will explain yourself," the not-witch hissed through her teeth.

Bridgette interrupted by stepping between them. "Dude, before he gets thrown in time-out for buying some books — with my money, might I add — can someone please explain to me what these are and why you're so mad about them? I can't even read runes, so why do they matter all that much?"

"Why do they *matter*?!" Her hostess gaped at her. "Why do they *matter*? They *matter*, Bridgette of the Outside, because if they are found in this house, we are *all* going to be taken in by the Palnan Guard and questioned, at the very least, and eradicated, at the worst."

"Yeah, kinda figured it was something fun like that," Bridgette snapped, unable to stop the salt from entering her voice. "But again, I can't read runes, so your answer doesn't really do much to explain —"

Zedolph cut into the mix, having heard the beginnings of the argument before making his presence known. "Serrasweet, keep your voice down, for all our sakes," he said tightly, looking between the three of them. His sister still clutched the books, Toby had his little chest puffed out, and Bridgette was positioned in the middle, looking daggers at Serrabinx.

He reached out a hand to take the books from the woman, who only clutched them tighter. The look in her gaze was caught somewhere between rage and fear. Her brother sighed deeply before answering the Elfling.

"Those books, Bridgette, contain the history of Palna as it was written by this country's founder, Baize Sammael. I believe you know who he was," Zedolph said. "They are somewhat his autobiography, as well as his manifesto and vision for the future. All copies were supposed to have been destroyed more than one hundred years ago."

Not the Elusive Grimoire, Bridgette's sierwan gift assured her, but something … better. Something that no one in greater Heáhwolcen likely suspected still existed.

"Well, obviously somebody missed a set when they went all 'Fahrenheit 451'," Bridgette said. "Toby's right, though. This is exactly what I would have been looking for in a library. Unfortunately, for the *third time*, I am not going to be able to read them if they're written in ancient runes. Shakespearean English, sure. Spanish? Could probably work my way through it. Ancient runes? By the time I finish translating that, Toby will be old enough to drink.

"Plus," she continued, tossing her hands in the air with exasperation, "if these books are so bad and illegal, what the fu — heck — were they doing in a publicly accessible bookstore to begin with, where apparently little kids can get their hands on them?"

"That is an *excellent* question," Serrabinx said, eyeing the tomes in her hand.

"We didn't go to the bookstore," Toby said impatiently.

Bridgette threw him a *look*. There was no way his mother nor his uncle would believe that lie, not when his mother held the evidence of their shopping.

"We did not go to the bookstore," he repeated. "I took Bridgette to meet Glafida."

"Who *very definitely owns a bookstore*," the Elfling said, bemused at his continued fib.

Zedolph sighed again and went to pull their dinner from the firehearth before the vegetables burned. "No, she does not.

Glafida is a very skilled book binder and leatherwiph. Technically speaking, she does not sell books, but rather sells her services in leatherworking and binding."

The Elfling frowned, not seeing how this was supposed to play out. "But she had *these* books, and she had books that were from Earth, that anyone could have come in and bought."

"Yes and no," Zedolph said, and Bridgette couldn't hide the frustration from her face at this non-answer. He chewed the inside of his cheek as if pensively choosing his next words. "Glafida makes and sells writing supplies, such as leather-bound and canvas-covered notebooks and sketchbooks. She also provides these services for a fee to re-cover books that are owned by Palnan citizens. You will recall my nephew telling you it is rare to have *new* things in our country. Books do tend to fall apart as they age, particularly if they are poorly cared for, or are much beloved and read over and over. We are unable to prevent our books from this damage the way that they may be preserved in other parts of Heáhwolcen. Thus, Glafida's talent is in large demand.

"As for the books that you saw on the shelves, some of those are personal projects of hers and others are commissioned bindings that were not picked up by those who requested her services," the man went on.

Unspoken words were masked in his carefully selected verbiage, and a sharp pang went through Bridgette as she learned what he wasn't saying aloud: those who hired Glafida and neglected to pick up their commissions were likely dead — or *eradicated*, to use Serrabinx's word. Bridgette swallowed hard and Zedolph knew she understood his silent implication. She asked, "How did books like these ones wind up in people's possession though? How has Glafida not been caught with them?"

No one answered, but Zedolph gently took the books from Serrabinx's arms. She finally let them go with a soft hiss of displeasure, but didn't fight him on it.

"Bridgette will join me for dinner in my room this evening," he said, and inclined his head to the firehearth.

The Elfling didn't have much of an appetite as she loaded her plate in silence, wondering what on Earth her host wanted her in his room for and why they couldn't discuss whatever he wanted to tell her in front of Toby and Serrabinx. Maybe he was about to eradicate her, Bridgette thought, huffing a laugh at the irony.

But she needn't have worried, for when Zedolph closed the door behind them, he bade her sit on the edge of his bed and handed her a sharpened knife to cut her pork chop off its bone. He didn't seem tense or scared, or any of the same emotions Serrabinx emanated when she spied these mysterious books in her guest's hands. In fact, Zedolph seemed almost resolute as he placed the books out in apparent order on the bedspread between them.

"They are known as the *Sefnuskrá a Dyfodolden Draiochta Ceáird* — which translates in your English, loosely, as the *Manifesto on the Vision of Craft Magic*," he said. "There are three volumes. Technically speaking, the first is not part of the manifesto. It is Baize Sammael's autobiography, a history of the development of Craft, as told through his perspective. Although I suppose the history is largely supplemented with the research and experiences of others who practiced those arts, long before any of us were born.

"It is the second two books that are considered, *dangerous*, shall we say, if they found themselves in the wrong set of hands," Zedolph continued, running a finger down the red metallic runes. "I have not read them, as they were all supposedly gone, but I know enough about my country and its ... inhabitants of questionable character, to know what they are about. They tell of all the things Baize Sammael found wrong with humanity and Earth, all the things he wanted to change. And though from what

I understand, many of these views are well-founded and gained quite a bit of sympathy from fellow witches, and even Elves and Fae, the methods he outlines and later attempted to implement in order to achieve his vision were repulsive and brutal."

"Oh," Bridgette said, understanding. The *Sefnuskrá* had been destroyed to keep Craft and its creator's questionable philosophy from ever rising to power again. Which made her want to dig into these books even more. What was it that so many beings found compelling about Baize Sammael and his viewpoints, that they would go to such lengths to protect it? Witches and Elves and Fairies and more murdered their brethren in cold blood for these ideals. Bridgette wasn't naïve enough to think that Ydessa and Eryth Tinuviel — magic ban be damned! — were any different in the present day.

"How is it possible that this set got missed?" she asked.

Zedolph shrugged. "I do not know how that happened. I do not know how Glafida came to possess them. I do not know why she saw fit to sell them to you and my nephew. Perhaps you should ask our esteemed leatherwiph herself."

"Yeah, no shit," Bridgette muttered.

She felt she could trust Zedolph. Oddly, she felt she could trust him far more than she could his sister, even though Serrabinx was the one who unwillingly welcomed her into their home. The man might be big and burly, well-muscled from decades of hoisting cattle carcasses around his butchery, but for all his skill with knives and bone saws, it was his intuition and his quiet demeanor that truly defined his character. It was Zedolph, not Serrabinx, whom she could question and learn from.

Which was why she looked up from the books and asked him, "How did the three of you know what these books were, if they're written in ancient runes?"

~ 15 ~

Bridgette knew she'd caught Zedolph off-guard with her question, though it was an obvious thing to ask. Toby, she supposed, could have surmised — *Seen* — what the books were. But his mother and uncle, despite whatever powers Serrabinx hinted she once possessed, did not share that same gift.

"They're not ancient runes," Zedolph said, making Bridgette pause with her fork halfway to her open mouth.

She gave him a look of utter confusion. She'd watched enough Viking televisions shows to know what runes looked like, and the markings on this book most certainly fit the bill.

He glanced to one side. "What you know of as ancient runes are the runes of the Elder Futhark. They're Germanic, and while some powerful beings of old used them, other ancestors would have used the Ogham alphabet as their written language. It is similar, but not of the same lands. There was also the alphabet still used today by the ancient Greeks. And those are just a few samples of European glyphic language. There were and are more in every country. But the runes of the *Sefnuskrá* are very distinct because they're Baize Sammael's home language."

"Look at this one, for example," he said, pointing to a rune that looked to Bridgette like a Greek letter sigma, sort of an angular "E", with two horizontal lines extending out the backside. "It's a rune, yes, but not any sort you're familiar with. The Elder Futhark letter for 'S' is entirely different, as is the Ogham, as is every other written human language. None quite compare with the language spoken by Ceannairí Álfar."

Ohshit, ohfuck. Bridgette's eyes shifted as she understood. Her mind was reeling.

"You're telling me," she began, blinking swiftly, "that these runes are the language of the Fyrst? That Baize *fucking* Sammael knew the language of the *Fyrst?*"

"Keep your voice *down*," Zedolph said softly, placing a hand on her shoulder. "There is much indeed for you to learn about our country's founder, it seems."

Bridgette stared at her plate, appetite suddenly gone. She felt queasy. "Who else in Heáhwolcen knows the language of the Fyrst?"

"I do not know," Zedolph said, and the Elfling could tell he wasn't lying. "At least, I do not know that anyone in Heáhwolcen can or does, but there are magical communities on Earth that still speak and write Gemaere."

The Earth Elves. A magical group that Bridgette hadn't thought much about in quite some time, not since the Druids quashed most of her hopes of gallivanting with other magical beings on her home world.

She frowned, hoping Zedolph didn't notice any gleam in her eyes behind their glamour. "There's got to be someone in Heáhwolcen who studies this. Ancient languages at the University, maybe? I mean, a whole-ass language doesn't just disappear —"

But she stopped herself mid-sentence. Of course languages disappeared, at least from common tongues. As their speakers died out, assimilated to other cultures, or were enslaved or captured and forced to speak elsewise, countless languages became extinct. Perhaps the same was true of the language of the Fyrst, this Gemaere. Perhaps.

Bridgette didn't believe that for an instant. Whether or not Baize Sammael had used Gemaere to evangelize Craft Wizardry or not didn't make the language itself *bad*. Though she understood why magical beings would perhaps want to distance themselves from speaking it, especially outside of Palna, that didn't make it obsolete, particularly given the extra-long lives of those who could speak it. Gemaere was probably not spoken in Heáhwolcen because the world above the world contained beings descended from so many cultures and other languages, that —

She jumped up from the bed, staring at Zedolph.

"Gemaere isn't a dead language, is it?" she asked, her eyes again shifting so quickly beneath her glamour that Bridgette felt they'd look like flickering holiday lights elsewise. "It's been twisted around and assimilated, and written out in modern letters instead of runes, but Gemaere is the basis of what everyone up here calls the *magical language*."

Zedolph only shrugged. "I do not know."

Again, he wasn't lying. This was simply a truth he did not know. But Bridgette did: Zedolph only saw Gemaere as its original form, as the runes that would likely be difficult to translate. He didn't understand that the very traditional greetings that witches and Elves and Fae said to one another were the phonetic pronunciations of those runes.

It made sense for the modern "magical language" to be descended from the Fyrst. Ceannairí Álfar was the original magical being, and the language it imparted millennia ago would have been used and morphed on Earth with the existing languages of humankind. The Earth Elves would still speak fluent Gemaere. The True Druids probably knew it too, or at least knew of it. Heledd, in fact, surprised them all in Wales with a magical greeting. Gemaere predated Heáhwolcen by tens of thousands of years. Plus, Bridgette knew, much of the modern interpretation of Gemaere was heavily influenced by Welsh and Icelandic, Gaelic and Scottish, Olde English and a smattering of other largely European vernacular.

"Your mind has left us," Zedolph observed, calling Bridgette back to his bedroom.

"I guess," she muttered, moving the vegetables around uselessly on her plate. "Hey, how long do different magical species live for? Like, what's the lifespan of a witch or a Fairy?"

That question was easier for the butcher to answer. "Witches live longer than humans, usually to at least one hundred and twenty, and they are much slower to show age after turning thirty or so. But they do age, and they are much more susceptible to human diseases than Fae, Elves, Sanguisuges, and Baetalü," Zedolph answered. "Those species are, for all intents and purposes, immortal, though most choose to enter the spirit realms eventually. The creatures depend. Unicorns are extremely long-lived, though I do not know if they are immortal. The same for nymphs, wraiths, elemental sprites, and dryads. Other magical species, the smaller creatures, live decades rather than centuries."

Which means that if the Ingefeoht happened in the 1860s, there are definitely Elves and Fairies alive who heard of the Sefnuskrá, even if they didn't speak Gemaere, Bridgette thought. *But why would they pretend that neither ever existed?*

It was a thought that plagued her all night, long after Zedolph had taken their plates back to the kitchen and left his guest to her own devices. She walked the hall to her bedroom, knowing they both would be waking early in the morning to go to the butchery for Bridgette's first day on the job as a slátraestre-in-training, but she almost didn't care. As exciting as it would be to have something to *do* in Palna, she wanted to go back to Glafida's not-a-bookstore and question the woman. She still wanted to question Toby, since he'd been so evasive while they were out exploring, and she wondered how frowned-upon it might be to wake him in the middle of the night.

But she wouldn't. Not after she just scared the daylights out of Serrabinx, bringing contraband literature into the little house. There wasn't any need to overstay her welcome. Judging from the situation with the Ballamúr being miles away, she'd have plenty of excess time to learn about Toby's abilities, and about her temporary home.

Home.

The word clanged in Bridgette's head. It was a word she was cautious of, having been shifted from one foster "home" to another for the first thirteen years of her nearly twenty-three.

Even when it became clear that Doc and Martha Simmons weren't going to stick her back into foster care when she turned sixteen, Bridgette was wary of considering their house *home*. Houses were places to eat and sleep. Roofs over heads. Walls for protection from the elements. But the only place Bridgette ever felt at home, the only place she truly, with every fiber of her being, craved to return to — even when her stubborn, rancid brain tried to convince her otherwise — was Heáhwolcen.

Not even Heáhwolcen itself, with its magic and mystery, its unending beauty and insurmountable spirit, fit the word "home", the more she thought about it. *Home* was blue eyes and bath magic, Fae wine and gingewinde, an Elven apartment on one world and a Massachusetts cottage on another. It was vanilla and honeysuckle, illicit magic tutorials and an extra voice inside her head. It was Fyrdwisa and Liluthuaé, Bundy and Starshine, two twisted braids strung with silver beads around her slim wrist.

For the first time in a long time, the Bright Star cried herself to sleep.

<h1 style="text-align:center">~ 16 ~</h1>

It was a good thing the Samnung chamber was warded. Even Kharis, who usually kept quiet and let Nehemi do the speaking for Endorsa, raised his voice as each individual sought to be heard over one another. The chamber was unusually crowded, with the full Samnung plus Lucilla, Njahla, Aurelias, Geongre Akiko and her second, Geongrestre Etreyn, in attendance.

Only Cloa and Arctura sat in silence, though flickers of unusual intensity were evident in the princess' eyes. Her cat had his front claws slightly out, gripping firmly into the fabric of Cloa's toile gown. Arctura's eyes were shrewd; hers remained largely unfocused. Collum could only imagine what she thought of this absolute mess.

A week after conceiving the idea of taking Lucilla to Nashville, the Elves and Elfling fyrdestre had just presented their admittedly haphazard plan to the rest of the Samnung and the two lead Fairy travel deputies. To say they were met with mixed responses was to put it mildly. Nehemi and Kharis seemed most aggrieved that Collum approached Lucilla without the approval of her queen and all but ordered her to participate.

"Your ability to undermine the spreca of the Samnung is second-to-none, Fyrdwisa," Nehemi growled, before launching into what was possibly years' worth of angry commentary.

That was met with Aurelias nearly jumping across the table at the queen, always the feisty one to have Collum's back. She was stopped by Trystane grasping the Elfling's tunic to hold her down, but the damage was done. In situations like this, where Nehemi and at least one other Samnung leader spent far too much time shouting and arguing than doing anything productive, regaining decorum was impossible. Nehemi's only allies in this room were her hand, her daughter, and her daughter's cat, and the latter two weren't technically even part of the governing body. Even Corria, who usually tried to play the neutral role her country represented, gave up today and was snarling at the witch queen.

No one except Corria Deathhunter and Collum Andoralain knew that the master swordswoman had sworn fealty to the Bright Star before she crossed into Palna. Corria's intense representation of loyalty this day warmed the fyrdwisa's iced-over heart. He wondered just how much of that loyalty might push this governing body into a fractured grouping: Nehemi, and Endorsan rulers in general, expected the rest of the Samnung members to follow their lead. The current queen's ability to cause such palpable friction with the quirk of her head was almost a sickening superpower.

It was a dangerous thing, Collum realized. Whether this day or some other, if Nehemi made a decision that Trystane and Aristoces would not agree with, Corria would side with the two of them. And that could split Heáhwolcen into a very precarious position. The word of the spreca was final. To not follow it was an act of defiance.

The Samnung already had enough defiance to deal with on its continent. The members didn't need to dally with it amongst themselves.

"I, personally, am looking forward to this assignment," Collum heard Lucilla say.

"I bet you are," Trystane muttered, a queer sort of grimace on his face.

Nehemi was still shouting, now at her royal receptionist: "To have accepted such an assignment of espionage and deceit without the approval of your queen was a foolish choice, Lucilla! I do *not* appreciate my subjects taking such actions."

"It's not my fault the fyrdwisa presented this to me without disclosing that information!" Lucilla retorted.

With one look, Collum gleaned exactly what was going through the young witch's mind, though he couldn't hear her thoughts in the spelled chamber. She was terrified that Nehemi would stop her assignment before it began, quashing whatever hope she had of alone-time with the Elf. He was again momentarily thankful the chamber was warded, if for naught else but to keep the blush-haired witch's thoughts out of his head.

"Is it not the responsibility of the fyrdwisa to design such missions?" Corria asked. She stood menacingly close to where her sword, helm, and shield lay propped against the back corner of the room. "Has he ever had to have your explicit approval for doing the job the deities and Universe — and we ourselves — asked of him?"

Trystane caught Collum's eye. He could tell something was different about the way that Corria argued on their behalf. But it wasn't Collum's secret to tell. That was between the master swordswoman and the Liluthuaé.

The fyrdwisa didn't bother to listen to any more of the exchange between the two ceannairí, and he looked away from his own ard rialóir. The Samnung door swung shut with a castle-shuddering thud as Collum walked into Deu Medgar and evanesced away.

He'd be in trouble for walking out on the meeting like that, Collum knew, though one could scarcely call the shouting match a meeting. It was obnoxious, really, to have someone like Nehemi be spreca. There were many days when, as hard-headed as King Hermann had been, the Elf couldn't believe he fathered someone who'd grown up to become like the current queen. And his granddaughter!

Collum hadn't felt so perturbed by a situation since Bridgette ran from the very same chamber he just abruptly exited. The fyrdwisa, once safely in his own home, reached into his refrigerator and pulled out a bottle of cucumber-pomegranate elixir, a calming beverage he hoped would ease his over-consumed mind. He removed the cap and took a long swallow before bringing the bottle with him into his office. Collum needed to *think*.

The faux outdoor weather inside his secret paradise was on the vestiges of fall. It was cool, but not cold enough to warrant a second layer of long sleeves or a coat. He preferred it mild, almost always sunny, and gently breezy. Even in the deep of winter, his spells would only permit the softest dusting of powdered snow to fall sometime around winter solstice. The Elf walked to the creek he once found Bridgette by and settled himself amongst a crystal-lined circle. He'd been meaning to build a true meditation platform — several, actually — for convening with the higher powers that guided the roll of tide and shift of sand.

I should ask Aurelias to help with that, he thought. A sly smile came over his lips. *Perhaps I should invite Apostine to join us as well.*

That could be … fun. It was the first time in a while Collum intentionally thought of something *fun* to do, much less with other beings involved. How odd that it seemed so foreign an idea to want to do something besides what constituted his work. He supposed the sudden desire for contact and socialization had to do with the fact that his only upcoming interaction was with the being he would least like to interact with.

Collum lied down in the crystal circle, the elixir bottle half-empty and abandoned next to him on the earth. He stared up at the white clouds migrating slowly overhead and watched the gold, red, and caramel leaves wriggle in the wind until they shook loose and drifted to the ground beneath them. The Elf loved every season, but fall with its flaming vibrancy of colors was probably his favorite.

He let the entrancing movement of falling leaves lull him into a deep meditation, a somewhat neglected practice of late. Collum inhaled the cool air through his nose, feeling the breath flow into his chest and abdomen, then exhaling ever so slowly out of his mouth. His blue eyes began to glaze over as they lost their conscious focus, and his soul and mind shifted without prompting, opening themselves to receive whatever the Universe desired him to know.

Blurred edges of imagery flitted across his vision, none taking corporeal form. They were more like clashes of soft pastels dancing among circling orbs of black and burnt orange. It meant nothing to him, this lightplay, but it was dark and lovely all the same. Unsettling — usually a meditation calmed Collum, allowing him to either lose or find himself, depending on his mood. Not today, though.

He remained in his crystal circle for a while longer until the air around him stilled, quieting even the soft sound of windchimes. The Elf brought himself back to full consciousness, still feeling put off by the contrasting colors of light imagery. To be fair, just about everything for the past few weeks had him feeling agitated.

Perhaps I should go to a lacnian, he thought. *Nehemi brought that one witch to the Samnung once to share her research into mind-health … what was her name?*

But on second thought, the idea of going right back to Endorsa just after departing from it so spectacularly was extremely unappealing. Collum continued staring up at the sky, now annoyed instead of relaxed, and hoisted himself to his feet to walk back inside and do something work-related instead of moping unendingly.

He'd just stepped inside his bedroom when he realized his apartment wasn't empty. Both the voices and inner monologues of Trystane, Njahla, and Aurelias drifted toward him.

Fucking seven hells, he groaned inwardly, and pushed open the door to the living room.

"Fáilte, all," Collum said grandly to his guests. "To what do I owe this displeasure?"

"*There* you are!" Aurelias practically shouted. "I was about to waltz into Bondrie and demand to cross into Palna. We've been looking for you for an hour!"

Collum cocked his head to the side. "Why didn't you just summon me?" He motioned to the stack of covenant bracelets along his forearm.

"We did. You didn't answer," Trystane said from the couch.

The fyrdwisa whirled on him. "I have been in my home office this entire time, and no one attempted to summon me."

The three Elves and Elfling looked at one another, confused.

"What were you doing in your office?" Aurelias demanded.

"Meditating."

Njahla piped up, "Have you been able to be summoned in your home office before? Or summoned while meditating before?"

"Yes, both, and ironically at least once *while* meditating in my home office. There was no sign this afternoon that anyone was trying to contact me whatsoever," Collum reiterated.

"Perhaps you should check the strength of your wards," Trystane offered. It was an unhelpful suggestion; all four of them knew Collum's apartment and office were perfectly warded, and this was something *new* causing the disruption. However, all of them had enough *new* of late to not think about it too deeply.

"Perhaps it was just a particularly deep meditation, and I became so entranced I lost touch with my tangible form," Collum said, though he knew that was a lie. He'd experimented enough with astral projection while attending the University to know that even when one was outside his own body, he could still feel himself. It was only when a being chose to cross into the spirit realm that it actually lost touch with the body that encased its soul.

Collum didn't have any time to dwell on the situation further, though, as Trystane chose that moment to shift gears. The ard rialóir smiled at his companions and said jovially, "Friends, as we are all accidentally gathered here today, please allow the fyrdwisa and I to let you in on a little secret we've been harboring."

~ 17 ~

Toby was more excited than Bridgette was for her first day as a slátraestre. He bounded down the hall before the sun rose, knocking persistently at her bedroom door until she groaned out a promise of joining him in the kitchen. Bridgette was not a morning person — or morning Elfling, rather — and the thought of *existing*, especially after a night with little sleep, was not pleasant.

When she eventually joined the Maudlins in the kitchen, dressed in dark gray leggings, a lightweight, long-sleeved black tunic, and her black Elven boots, Bridgette was met with the scents of melted butter and sage. Serrabinx handed her a plate of toast topped with a fried egg and a thick smear of herbed goat cheese, then motioned for her guest to join them and eat. Hot breakfast tea was already waiting in a rotund ivory teapot in the center of the table, a cream and sugar set full of add-ins next to it.

They ate and drank in silence, which Bridgette was grateful for. Toby, to no one's surprise, finished his toast first and broke the peacefulness of their breakfast.

"Are you most excited about learning my uncle's art?" he asked. "He is very good!"

Bridgette grinned at him, appreciating how the boy described the work. "I think so. I don't know that I'll be any good at it, but I like learning new things, especially about food."

"No one expects you to be a savant on your first day," Zedolph assured her. "But I see in you a caring and generous heart, an empathy that is lost on many beings, and an ability to notice details. I have no doubt you will come to enjoy this work, and that you will develop a skill for it."

"Thanks, Zedolph," Bridgette replied to the unexpected compliments. She wasn't sure how the butcher picked up on anything about her in the little time they'd spent together, and she hoped she lived up to the hype.

Their walk to the butchery was unhurried. Palna, it seemed, favored slow and easy mornings. There was hardly anyone else out and about, and most of those who were appeared to be shopkeepers like themselves. The only sound was that of stones and dry clay crunching on the path under their boots. Zedolph's shop wasn't on the main square in downtown Xcthonya. It was a good distance down a side road, surrounded by grassy paddocks.

"We have to have a comfortable space for the animals to remain until they are harvested," Zedolph explained, noticing her gaze. "Today is not a harvest day, though, so there are no animals to care for."

The butchery itself was built of light gray wooden siding with a metal roof. There were massive windows along the front and halfway down either side wall, allowing natural light during the day to illuminate the meat cases within. The cases were empty at the moment, but Bridgette could visualize the veritable feast customers would see as they made their way up the gravel path. A pair of crossed blades — a cleaver and a boning knife — was painted on the building's black door, surrounded by swirls of oxblood and rich blue. There was no mistaking what was inside.

"I believe we have arrived first," Zedolph observed, unlocking the door with a metallic purple key. It eerily reminded Bridgette of the purple color she'd once seen in a recreation of Baize Sammael's armor.

She followed her host inside, wishing that she had an iced caife calabaza to sip on. Zedolph opened the sheer curtains to let in all the light, then began a grand tour of her new place of employment. To the left of the cases was a partitioned-off preparation room. Inside, shelves lined with spices, salts, mixing bowls, and sundry supplies surrounded a massive wooden worktable. A smaller wooden tower served as the base for a hefty meat grinder against the far wall, and a rack next to it housed several leather-wrapped bundles of knives and tools. There was also a massive icebox where unsold meats from the day before were stored overnight, alongside fresh meat waiting to be prepared for display.

The door behind the meat cases opened into a hallway down which Bridgette found a bathroom and sitting area. At the very end were the harvesting facility and walk-in icebox, where fresh carcasses hung to set before being broken down into case-ready cuts. It was clean and efficient, and though somewhat primitive — what with electricity and magic both being unattainable — Bridgette still felt firmly in the year 2018. It wasn't so much being in a time warp as it was being in a place where citizens modernized systems out of what they had … even if what they had was largely technology of the 1860s.

When she and Zedolph re-entered the front area, they were met with voices of the individuals she supposed were her fellow slátraestres.

"You must be Bridgette!" a melodious voice exclaimed. It came from a tiny male who stood barely taller than Toby, with rosy-hued skin, lavender-blonde hair, and cobalt blue eyes. The slightly pointed nails on his slim hands were a dark shade of blue as well, and Bridgette realized it wasn't polish. His fingernails, or claws, perhaps, were truly that shade.

"This is indeed Bridgette of the Outside," Zedolph confirmed. "Bridgette, this is Fincher" — he pointed to the blue-nailed male — "Muov, and Paxson."

Muov, who stood a head taller than Bridgette, was an Elf with dewy, dark brown skin and eyes of almost cherrywood color, flecked with opalescent amber. His black hair was loc'd, pulled back in a half-pony style, and a few locs were intricately decorated with metallic beads and colored fiber. They reminded Bridgette of the wire-wrapped tendrils Aristoces wore to Emi-Joye's ambassadora installation.

The Elf was muscular and well-built in a lean, trim sort of way, but Paxson stood next to him as an absolute tank. He was a

Baetalüan, his horns taller than Bryten's were, and they were a deep, gleaming forest green that sparkled in the morning sunlight. Bridgette thought Zedolph had biceps the size of her face, but Paxson could have crushed her between two fingers. His golden-hued skin gleamed like that of the Samnung leader's, although Paxson wore more clothing than Bryten. His caramel curls were tamed into a bun at the back of his head, and a few strands escaped to frame his square-jawed face.

I will not *get on that one's bad side*, Bridgette thought to herself. She stuck a hand out to say hello, but like Zedolph had that first night they met, no one reciprocated the gesture. She awkwardly crossed her arms in front of her instead.

"It has been a long while since we have had a full team of four," Zedolph said. "It's supposed to be my job as the owner to run the business side of things, and I perform the harvesting rituals as well as butchering. Paxson cares for the live animals when we have them and does much of the primal breakdown. Muov runs our curing shed — that's out back, I've not shown it to you yet — and our aging program. Fincher is the one who deals directly with customers."

Zedolph was interrupted by Muov snickering good-naturedly and muttering, "More of our resident know-it-all."

Fincher grinned. Obviously, this was a familiar jab, and one he was quite proud of.

"However," the slátrari went on, reining their attention back in, "we are supposed to have a fourth, one who does most of the day-to-day readying of cuts in the back and restocking them throughout the day. It was several years ago now that Ovidion entered the spirit realm, and though we have had a few attempt to fill that spot, none chose to stay."

Bridgette didn't have the heart to tell him that she probably wouldn't be remaining very long, either.

"Our new slátraestre will train under my guidance and in time, I hope she will be able to help Muov with some responsibilities they could share," Zedolph told his team, not noticing the Elf frown as he spoke. "As Bridgette is here studying, she will have many questions for us about our country, its history, and its culture, along with likely the customs and background of our individual species. Fincher, I believe you will have much to tell her about, as Kobolds are not so common. Please answer her to the best of your ability, and she will work here to the best of hers. It will be a time of great change for us, with new patterns and such to become accustomed to, but I daresay this will be an excellent shift for all involved."

Muov looked Zedolph straight in the eye and asked, "And what of those who inquire of her origins?"

That question struck a nerve. Zedolph narrowed his eyes. "Should anyone ask, she is of vuoristokylä."

"Should I know what that is?" Bridgette asked.

"Vuoristokylä isn't even a place. It's just a word for mountain villages, high and remote in the Beorgdún," Muov spat back. He didn't look at her, but at Zedolph. "Do you realize the risk you are putting all of us at by bringing her here? With no true explanation except that she is a guest in your house and a student in Endorsa?"

"That is explanation enough, Muov," Zedolph countered. "Bridgette will not spend time at the counter or with customers. We will minimize every chance of risk."

Why is it risky? Bridgette wanted to ask. She wished the ísenwaer could work with anyone she wanted, not just Collum.

But deep down, she knew why Muov was concerned. Though she told the Maudlins she was here on Samnung business, Xcthonya was a small enough town where indeed, *new* was cause for question. With the unending tenseness in the air, perhaps cause for suspicion, too. Bridgette could not rouse suspicion. It was one thing to wander around the business district and the river market with Toby, which hundreds of beings from all over Palna did every day, but it was a different story to permanently implant herself in daily life here with no one to confirm her story or vouch for her. She didn't blame Muov for his distrust.

Muov didn't say anything else to Zedolph, just shook his head and walked outside, presumably to the shed where most of his work lay. Paxson inclined his head to Bridgette before following, leaving her with Zedolph and Fincher. The latter scurried off to one end of the icebox, which was apparently a freezer, and began chipping away at ice to put inside the meat cases.

"First things first, you're getting an anatomy lesson," Zedolph said, and led his new slátraestre to the far end of the preparation room, where posters of livestock hung on the wall above the meat grinder.

An hour or so later, by the time the butchery was ready to open, Bridgette was sure she'd never crammed so much new knowledge in her brain so fast. Her notebook and writing utensils from Glafida's store were going to get well-used, Bridgette had no doubt. Not only would she have to remember the basic anatomy of cattle, hogs, and lamb, but she also had to know the names of primal cuts — the large sections a carcass could be broken into — *and* the individual retail cuts of steaks, roasts, and such that came from each. Plus, it didn't help that apparently humans had different names for certain cuts than magickind did.

By the time they emerged from the crash-course in meats, Fincher had expertly set up the two six-foot-long cases. The one on the left housed beef and lamb, and on the right, customers could find pork, sausages, and cured meats. In addition to the natural light now beaming in from the front windows, each case had a row of squat, lit candles atop it and in terraced shelves on either side, illuminating the meats.

Fincher stood in front of the sausages, chin held pensively in one hand. "Bridgette, may I get your opinion?"

Bewildered, she stood next to him. "What's up?"

"Tell me, if you will, does the drisheen, the dark red, look too starkly contrasted against the stippgrütze? That's the cream-colored one."

The Elfling stared blankly at the stacks of sausages, trying frantically to come up with some sort of feedback for her new teammate. She had no idea what those two words were that he just uttered. "Uh, not if you put both of those kind of in the middle, and had the reddish and pink ones like, evenly surround them?"

Fincher considered this suggestion. "A sound thought, that is!"

"Sure thing," she said, turning to look at Zedolph, who was smiling broadly at her, as if this was some sort of test she managed to pass.

What in the hell have I gotten myself into? she asked the Universe.

~ 18 ~

The more Bridgette learned about Zedolph's work, the more fulfilling and interesting she found it.

She couldn't care less about what he referred to as the "business side of things", which was largely working with farmers and customers, as well as keeping track of sales and wages. But the actual hands-on work he did required skills the Elfling could only dream of possessing. Zedolph used his knives as if they were extensions of his own limbs and spent an entire day teaching Bridgette the purpose of each one, as well as how to sharpen and care for the tools of the trade.

He taught her how to portion loins into individual chops and steaks, how to face hams and trim excess fat from roasts. She learned to correctly measure ratios for ground beef and pork, how to keep the meat from oxidizing and turning brown too quickly while on display, and the ways Palnans utilized everything they possibly could from a harvested carcass. Muscle and desirable organ meat were food. Undesirable organ meat, called offal, and the inedible muscle trim were bought and hauled off by a woman after harvest days to become compost. Hides were sold to tanneries and leatherwiphs like Glafida. Certain bits and pieces were purchased by a different woman who allegedly used them for "ceremonial" purposes. Bridgette hadn't met her yet, but she had a sneaking suspicion that "ceremonial" meant "illegal Craft Wizardry".

The work was mentally taxing, largely due to the sheer amount of information Bridgette attempted to record, process, and retain each day. Workdays were long, with she and Zedolph up before the sun and returning to the house by suppertime.

It was quite physical, too, what with moving and manipulating heavy carcasses and large portions of meat, not to mention the two-mile walk each way. Bridgette could easily pull an entire lamb from the carcass closet — which is what she jokingly began to call the walk-in icebox, much to Muov's eye-rolling dismay — but anything heavier was a struggle. Only Paxson, whom Bridgette soon learned was nonverbal and communicated by writing or with a form of sign language she was slowly picking up, could lift the cattle carcasses by himself without difficulty.

Most of Bridgette's days became a cycle of wake, eat, work, eat, sleep, repeat, and in truth she didn't mind it. But it bothered the seven hells out of Toby, who was already put out by her constant state of never being at home except to sleep. Zedolph promised his nephew that when Bridgette's training was complete, they both would have days off again, but it was important for her to learn everything first. The butchery was open five days a week, closed Monday and Tuesday, but those were the best opportunities for what the slátrari liked to call side quests: Bridgette's more individualized training.

One day, he took Bridgette on farm visits in Xcthonya and the surrounding smaller communities, introducing her to those who raised the livestock they harvested. She met the beings who harvested poultry and learned the difference between preparing birds and mammals for butcher cases. When she met new Palnans, Zedolph always used his made-up cover story, that she was an Elfling of the vuoristokylä apprenticing at his shop, having tired of the mountains and desiring a change of pace. It was always a brief aside, nothing they ever dwelled on, but every time someone asked her who she was, Bridgette clammed up and let Zedolph answer.

During her third week in Palna, the first full week of October, having long ago given up the concept that she would be returning to greater Heáhwolcen within the foreseeable future, the Bright Star finally got to observe a harvest day. The shop was closed down to customers so all of the team could work. Five steers — younger castrated male cattle — arrived two days prior, having been herded down the streets to the grassy paddocks around the butchery. Bridgette had hardly seen Paxson those two days. He secluded himself with the animals, calming and acclimating them to their temporary home, feeding and watering them.

"It's important the animals feel calm before the ritual," he wrote to Bridgette on a scrap of paper when she asked about it. "Animals that are stressed release natural compounds into their meat when they are harvested, and it can soil it, making it unsuitable for consumption. Too tough or off-flavored. In addition, these animals are giving their lives to provide nourishment. It is important this gift be respected and repaid as much as we can."

There had been several allusions to the harvesting ritual during her time at the butchery, and Bridgette was eager to observe it. Before she entered the harvesting room that day, Zedolph pulled her aside and asked her to be very calm and quiet throughout the process.

She stood at the front of the room with Fincher, who appointed himself her instructor for the day, and watched intently. Despite her preconceived notions of what such a room or warehouse might look like, the abattoir was less primeval slaughterhouse and more, well, *clean* and bright. Natural light poured in from the large open windows, and all the wood and metal were spotless inside. The first of the five steers was brought in, Paxson coaxing him with a thick length of rope, and he was situated in a wooden chute that held him gently but firmly in place. The animal had been bathed and fluffed dry.

Zedolph stepped in front of the chute holding an earthenware bowl that smelled strongly of licorice. There was a dark purple — almost black — paste inside. While Paxson laid a large hand gently against one of the steer's cheeks, the butcher stepped to the other side of him and began to rub fingerfuls of paste on the animal's poll, between its horns.

"Paxson and Zedolph stand off to the side because cattle are prey animals," Fincher whispered to Bridgette, his voice so quiet she had to strain to hear him. "Their eyes are on the sides of their head. In order to not startle them, we are calm, and we stand respectfully so that they may see us."

Interesting, Bridgette thought.

The slátrari began to speak as he applied more of the paste. His voice was soothing and even, and as the Elfling listened, she felt herself begin to go into a sort of trance. It wasn't spell magic, and it certainly wasn't what she assumed to be the evils of Craft magic, but a ritual much older than anyone in this room.

Old Magick, she learned, was ritual magic. It was conscious communion with the Universe and deities, with Nature and the elements. It took time and intention. Rituals were technically spells, at least with the chanted phrases involved. They offered more widespread power, both in terms of physical and spiritual space, and time periods. Modern spell magic on the other hand was almost a shortcut. It got the job done but was very specific and usually only covered one entity.

Bridgette gave up her vow of silence and whispered, "How can he perform a ritual when that's supposed to be illegal here?"

Fincher gave her a conspiratorial smirk. "It isn't illegal. It's ritual."

"Uh-huh," Bridgette smiled back, though she had to lean against a wall to calm herself as new knowledge hit her. Spells were forbidden. Craft Wizardry was absolutely banned. But Old Magick, ritual magic, some of which could *easily* be transferred surreptitiously into Craft magic?

Oh boy.

She'd fallen out of whatever peaceful trance Zedolph placed upon the steer, which now looked all but asleep in the chute. Muov, who had been standing in the back corner of the room, came forward with a lit candle held between his palms. Zedolph put his bowl on the floor and pulled two vials of herbal oil from his knife belt. Still chanting, he dribbled three droplets from each vial onto the candle, which sputtered and gave off a heady scent of lavender and chamomile.

Muov leaned the candle forward and carefully guided several drops of the hot wax to land on the steer's poll, where the thick paste created a barrier to numb the animal. Zedolph launched his hand forward suddenly and struck the heel of his palm against the cooling wax. The steer slumped to the floor, his head supported by Paxson.

Bridgette's eyebrows flicked up. She looked to Fincher, who explained in a more normal speaking voice now, "Zedolph has put the steer into a state of nonbeing. He is alive still, but we must now release the spirit of this animal back into the Universe."

He motioned for the Elfling to follow him, and the two drew close to where Paxson now loaded the steer into a rope and leather harness, using a pulley to hoist the animal over a clean metal bucket.

"Aside from the work in the butchery day to day, *this* is the reason why we need four beings with us," Fincher said pointedly. He smiled, a signal of both pride and invitation, then took one of Bridgette's hands and one of Paxson's. The four slátraestres encircled the steer — succumbed now into a deep, forever sleep — and Zedolph, who stood next to it in the center of their formation.

"We are North, South, East, and West," Zedolph began. "We invite the goddesses Artemis and Eirene into our midst; the god Shu. We form this circle for peace and respect, to open the portal and lift the veil that shrouds the spirit realm from ours."

The air around them shimmered: a warding ritual. Fincher squeezed Bridgette's hand reassuringly as her heartbeat quickened.

Zedolph approached the suspended steer and pulled a knife from his belt. Its blade shone in the sunlight that beamed in from the oversized windows, causing the swirling, blue-tinged

Damascus steel to glint like ocean waves. The handle was dark brown desert ironwood, nearly black, set with gold-rimmed garnets so deep red they too were the color of night. It was obviously a ceremonial knife, and the presence of it heightened the feeling of illicit magic in the air as Zedolph spoke:

> *"We give thanks to this animal for its life,*
> *For in its death it shall nourish many.*
> *We ask for peace as its flesh is pierced by knife,*
> *For the blood which flows shall nourish many.*
> *We express gratitude for those who raised him,*
> *For the meat that we harvest shall nourish many.*
> *We give thanks to Nature for green grass and sweet hay,*
> *For the meat it wrought shall nourish many.*
> *We ask for sacred passage for this animal,*
> *For the giving of its life begets our own."*

He chanted this four more times, each time joined by first Muov, then Fincher, then Paxson — who tapped his feet along to the rhythm of Zedolph's words — and finally Bridgette, who'd gone last both to observe and to learn the words she was supposed to say. But it was almost no matter; the words rolled off her tongue as if she'd spoken them her entire life. At her final line, all sound stopped. Zedolph placed the tip of the blade at an angle against the steer's neck and recited,

> *"By this, the Indryhtu Sciccel that marks mine art,*
> *By the power and blessing of all here gathered,*
> *By the power of three times three,*
> *As it is, so mote it be."*

The ward magic shivered as he slipped the Damascus steel into the animal's numbed flesh, and warm blood flowed in its wake.

~ 19 ~

Growing up, all Bridgette knew of butchering was what she read in books and saw in movies, or the occasional internet documentary. Like most Americans in the twenty-first century, she had little to no knowledge of actual agricultural practices. She expected butchering to be … different. Loud and fast-paced with a lot of gore. And though she was certain there were places on Earth that harvested animals in such a manner, that perhaps barely eked by the legal standings that had animal wellbeing in mind, seeing her own butchery harvest in the opposite way was a pleasant surprise.

She watched as the animal's blood ran from the knife wound in a torrent, then a trickle, then a dribble, before finally stopping. The ritual ward around them shivered one last time. As Zedolph lifted his blade to the ceiling — for the first time, Bridgette noticed a skylight window directly above them — the sensation of magic dissipated. Her body involuntarily whooshed forward, as if she'd been dozing off and was shaken awake. She blinked.

Fincher pulled her backward and they watched as Muov and Zedolph made work of the steer. The bucket of blood was covered with a beeswax wrap and moved immediately to the walk-in icebox. It would be used in sausages and could be purchased by Sanguisuges and other beings whose existence depended on it as a staple part of their diet. Bridgette watched the slátrari and Elf turn the body into a carcass, separating the organs into edible and offal, removing the hide so it could be taken to a tannery. The animal's head would even be used, though the brain would not. Fincher told her this was out of safe consumption concerns. Apparently, the brains of sheep and full-grown cattle could contain damaged proteins that, if ingested, might lead to severe mental deterioration in the predator.

"Yeah, we have that on Earth," Bridgette recalled, momentarily stunned by the similarity of her two worlds. "They call it Mad Cow Disease. I think I'll stay sane, thanks."

The Kobold grinned up at her.

They repeated the ritual process and harvesting for each of the remaining steers, and though Muov and Zedolph were extraordinarily speedy at their jobs, it was a *long* day. Even Bridgette, who expended the least energy out of all of them, was drained. She attributed this to the mental requirements of participating in multiple rituals, something that she noticed before had an effect on her. She wondered if the drain was compounded by performing Old Magick in a country that was so warded against it, as if there was a constant battle of energies between this ancient practice and the relatively new-fangled Samnung spells along the border wall.

After the floors, knives, rope, harness, and chute were spotlessly cleaned first with water and lye soap, then with grain spirits, all the Elfling wanted to do was collapse on her bed at Serrabinx's house. The Bright Star wished she could evanesce. It would have been nice to just grab onto Zedolph's shirtsleeve as a means of transportation instead of walking to the house.

Zedolph and Bridgette were thankful the butchery would be shuttered the following day to give their team some rest. For once, the two of them wouldn't be working on a closed day either, which Bridgette knew meant a day of adventuring with Toby was in the works. She missed her young friend, and she hadn't forgotten her slew of questions. In fact, the list had only continued to grow, but she started cataloging the knowledge she sought in two categories: questions for Toby and questions for his uncle.

"How was your first day of harvesting?" Serrabinx asked when they arrived at the cottage. A buttery smell of potatoes and cream arose from the cast-iron cauldron she stirred. "I've made potato soup with shredded chicken, leeks, and sweet corn for us. It'll be ready soon."

"Thank you, Serrasweet," her brother replied. He wrapped

an arm around her shoulders and took a whiff of their supper. "It was a most fruitful day. There are five beef carcasses hanging for preparation, and one of them had a stunning brown and white hide. I almost want to take its cost from my own wages so that we may keep it."

"It's your shop," Bridgette said, raising an eyebrow. "Can't you just like, pay the farmer and the tanner for their work and then keep it? Or trade them or something?"

Zedolph looked at the Elfling as though she'd sprouted horns. "… No," he said. "That would be considered thievery. All goods have a cost and must be reported. A portion of all sales we make at the butchery must be distributed to the crown for the good and conservation of our country. To keep such a hide without paying the tariff would have the Palnan Royal Guard at our door within days to collect what our leaders are owed."

"*Nowhere* else in Heáhwolcen collects mandatory taxes like that," Bridgette pointed out. "Everyone does what they're good at and pitches in to care for everything together. And if someone isn't able to do that, like some members of the Samnung because they're always busy, they get paper money. Most of the time though, shop owners and restaurants refuse to let the Samnung pay for anything. They say the work as a leader is payment enough."

Serrabinx scoffed. "That seems more like a fever dream than how to run a country."

"Yeah, funnily enough, the government on Earth where I'm from seems to have the same argument amongst itself like, *a lot*," Bridgette went on. "Sure, it seems weird and unattainable when you're used to something different, but I mean, societies existed before this kind of economics did. Like, *way* longer. It's possible if you're willing to work for the change."

Her hostess' eyes flashed, and Bridgette knew she touched a nerve. She shut her mouth tightly and turned to help Toby set the table.

As supper wound down, Serrabinx asked again how harvesting went. Bridgette answered honestly, explaining that seeing the harvest and participating in it was so contrary to what she thought it would be.

"The ritual was what surprised me the most though," the Elfling said in a quieter voice. "I was under the impression that rituals would fall under illegal practices, so it was really neat to be able to see and be part of that."

"It was helpful to have the right number present," Zedolph murmured. He looked to his sister, whose eyes dulled with pain. "We had gone far too long without someone to fill that role. It was a point of stress the day before harvests these past few years, when we only had three slátraestres, to find someone suitable to be our fourth and complete the circle."

Bridgette remembered the name "Ovidion" being spoken earlier in her training, and the sierwan knowledge came to her. Ovidion had been more than a slátraestre. He was Serrabinx's partner and Toby's father, and whatever happened to him wasn't something they liked to discuss. She felt a strong desire to know the circumstances there, though, and made a mental note to ask Zedolph about the deceased Elfling.

Later that night, after the dishes were put away and she was sequestered in her bedroom, Bridgette pulled out the volumes of the *Sefnuskrá*. The books were tucked into the bag she brought with her to Palna, buried underneath two sweaters that were far too warm for the weather here. Illuminated by the light of the oil lamp, she flipped through the runes of Gemaere, touching the stiff paper pages. They were heavy — so heavy! — both metaphorically and physically, and she yearned to know what secrets were written inside. She doubted the runic language could be translated directly to English. There would likely have to be a backdoor way to get there. Convert Gemaeric runes to their modern interpretation first, and then to English?

I wish I could ask you, she thought to the covenant bracelet on her wrist. *I wish I could tell you so many things.*

A sly idea entered her mind. No, she couldn't talk in real time to Collum like a true spy, like her mother, had been able to. But there were other ways. Bridgette grinned to herself and tossed the books back in her bag, then rolled off the bed to find her already worn blue notebook. She threw herself back against the pillows, flipped to a random page, and began to write. In-between her notes on butchering, she hid bits and pieces of the knowledge she gained — the barrier wall being invisible from within Palna, observations about Xcthonya, the tidbit about Ydessa Tinuviel having named herself queen of Palna. Bridgette wondered how that seemed to have missed being previously reported by one of the Fairy ambassadors, but it wouldn't surprise her if the Tinuviels were able to keep that knowledge very guarded.

She scribbled details about Palnan daily life in the margins of a page regarding butchering knives, and on a mostly clean leaf, recorded what she could remember of the harvesting ritual. Bridgette stared at the notebook, at the unpenned words she wanted to write but felt she couldn't — not yet, anyway — and heaved a sigh.

Journaling, even if it was for the Samnung, made the Elfling feel just a bit better. She promised herself that she would do better about recording her days in this new land. Bridgette wanted to portray Palna as she saw it, as it truly was, not as the preconceived notions she knew tainted greater Heáhwolcen's perception. There were good beings and creatures here who wanted out, who wanted the same change the Samnung members did, and she *had* to get the ceannairí to understand that.

~ 20 ~

"Why didn't you tell me about Bridgette attacking you?" Trystane asked. He traced a finger down Emi-Joye's cheek and angled jawline as she nestled against his shoulder.

Her body went taut, partly from his caress, but mostly from his question. "I didn't want anyone to know about that."

The accusatory undertone hinted wrath at whomever told the ard rialóir about it. Wrath because she couldn't openly accuse Collum Andoralain, as he'd want to know when Trystane had asked her, and the prying, mind-hearing fyrdwisa would eke the secret of their relationship out of her. She couldn't risk that. A dangerous, heated fire flashed on her creamy white cheeks at the thought of Collum's reaction.

"Obviously," Trystane crooned to her, tipping her chin up to meet his eyes. "But why not?"

Emi-Joye shrugged out of his grasp, annoyed. Angry. "Because it's embarrassing."

Trystane chuckled and shook his head. "She *attacked* you, Em," he murmured, the shortened term of endearment still feeling new to his tongue. "You have nothing to be embarrassed about. Do you think our ancestors were embarrassed when Baize Sammael attacked them?"

The Fairy scoffed. "That's different."

He looked away, and silence fell between them for a time. He knew her well enough to know that if he didn't press her, didn't goad her, she'd tell him when she was ready to. The moonlight cloaked them in soft silver, gleaming off their shared ice blonde hair. Emi-Joye eventually gave up on being stubborn and rested a hand on his thigh. Trystane turned to her, those lively moss green eyes flecked with both gold and mild curiosity.

"It's embarrassing because I knew better. Because I trained on sword and dagger work with the Caomhnóir Feeric. Because I know hand-to-hand combat. Because I know these things and have these skills, and a fully unskilled Elfling with no magic and a negligible amount of feoht experience was able to get the better of me. Because if Collum hadn't walked in when he did, she could have slit my throat," the Fairy said. Her voice was dull, though the memory drew up a feeling of deep anger. She chewed the inside of her cheek. "Bridgette launched herself at me before I could do any deity-damned thing to stop her, and I almost *died* because I didn't have my guard up. How could I claim to be a leader in our world, a magical representative on Earth, when I couldn't even hold my own against someone with what, a sixteenth of the skills that I have?"

Trystane slipped his fingers through hers and brought her hand to his lips. "You are magnificent and powerful, and skilled at many things."

She smirked as those last words took on a teasing note. "Am I, now?"

"You are," he said, and kissed each of her fingertips in turn. "So is Bridgette Conner. Her skills and knowledge lack in many ways compared to ours, but her magical abilities tower over what almost any being alive has ever known. We do not know how to teach her to use them. We do not even know what they *are*. I have never in my life encountered a sierwan. I have only heard legends about this strange brutality that she possesses. Bridgette doesn't know either, and somehow that makes this not knowing all the worse."

"What are you saying?" Emi-Joye asked.

"I'm saying that you were attacked by the Liluthuaé, a deity-ordained Elven being that has more power and abilities than any of us can fathom until we see them in play," Trystane elaborated. "I'm saying that Bridgette is more than an Elfling, and that you look at her as though she is half-human, or fully human, when she is not human at all. There are things about her past that you do not know, that I cannot reveal to you. But while she may not know how to handle her skills, that doesn't mean she doesn't have any to display."

"I think you're talking in circles, Trys."

He smiled. There was something about hearing this nickname that set him on fire. "I'm trying to nicely tell you that you have a horrible tendency to disrespect the most powerful being the modern worlds will ever meet. Stop being embarrassed about coming face-to-face with a magical legend and *surviving*."

Emi-Joye glowered at him. "I generally respect those who offer me the same. She doesn't."

"You know, you are incredibly lucky that it's the two of us having this conversation and not you and the fyrdwisa," Trystane said, his eyes glittering. "Bridgette has a load of respect for you. What she does not respect, and what I believe her to be genetically hardwired against accepting, are blatant lies. Had you been honest with her from the start about this aura that apparently surrounds her, you, and Princess Cloa, she likely wouldn't have had cause to be triggered to attack."

"So, you're telling me that this is *my* fault?" Emi-Joye was pissed.

He sighed. "It's not your fault she attacked you. Collum saw her do something similar with Nehemi once, very briefly, during a Samnung meeting before the trip to Wales," Trystane said. "Whatever this power is that possesses her, Bridgette doesn't know how to control it. *Yet.* That is primarily on her, and partly on us as the Samnung leaders for not helping her more. But hiding this truth from us? That, my sweet, is on you."

Emi-Joye tried to pull her hand away, but Trystane held tight.

"Like I told them in Wales, I don't want any part of *this*," she said, remembering too her recent conversation with Herewosa Donnachaidh. "I don't want some deep connection except with Apostine, Aristoces, and the delegates I work alongside in Antarctica. I want to further ease the bridge between human and magickind. I want to foster scientific research in the wildest of wildernesses! I want to help grow the fellowship between representatives of the different countries that work and live together, in harmony, on my continent. Is it simply too much for me to want what I was put on this world to do?"

Something she said made Trystane smile so wide his expression was almost feral. "Em, what if you were put on this world to do *more?*"

She blinked, and the question hung between them, nearly a tangible presence in the midnight air. Emi-Joye didn't know what to make of it.

"I don't know what *more* you imply," she said quietly, trying again to tug her fingers out of his grasp.

"Yes, you do," the Elf insisted, not letting her hand go. "Otherwise, why in seven hells would you have secretly summoned the commanders of the Fórsaí Armada to meet in January?"

The Fairy glowered at Trystane. "I don't know what you're talking about."

"Liar," he challenged. "I have it on good authority that the branch leaders have been requested to gather at a time and location yet to be announced, and that they are not to speak of it to anyone."

"Whose authority would that be, and what does that have to do with me?"

Trystane flashed a wicked smile and pulled Emi-Joye on his lap before she could wriggle away. "Oh, silly, sweet Fae of mine," he crooned. "Who is it that commands the Fyrdlytta?"

Deity damn me! she thought, cringing outwardly before she could stop herself.

The Elf laughed and kissed her across her frown. "The first thing the fyrdwisa did upon receiving that note from Herewosa Donnachaidh was evanesce into my office — where I was holding a very important meeting, mind you — and demand to know if *I* was the one who'd summoned them, to keep Nehemi from finding out whatever secret plan I was formulating.

"We deduced that it wasn't any of the Samnung members and then set to thinking about who else would know enough about the Samnung's plans with Palna to get directly involved," Trystane continued. "That leaves our seconds, Geongre Akiko, perhaps Geongrestre Etreyn, and exactly *one* Fairy ambassadora who might be the culprit we sought."

He couldn't help but smirk at the distressed expression that remained on Emi-Joye's face. She looked so defeated, and yet so utterly headstrong at the same time. It was irresistible.

"Let's say we discuss this in a more intimate setting, shall we?" the Elf whispered.

Her eyes flicked to his. "Oh?"

He evanesced them to his home with no further explanation.

After being gently deposited on the luxuriously large bed, covered with cotton sheets and an enviable forest green comforter, Emi-Joye crawled to the footboard and dangled her bare feet off the edge, waiting somewhat impatiently for the Elf to return with something delicious from his spirits collection. She couldn't *believe* she'd be so careless as to forget that Collum was the leader of the Fyrdlytta!

Emi-Joye was still sour when Trystane reappeared, two crystal goblets in hand. He sipped toffee-noted corn whiskey from one and handed the second to the Fairy, who accepted it with a muttered thanks. He leaned against one of the carved bedposts, watching her. She was the most beautiful being the Universe could have created, and he didn't think he would ever tire of looking at her.

"You're doing that thing again where you stare at me," she pointed out.

"I'm aware."

"Are you mad at me?"

He blinked. "Why would I be mad at you?"

"Because I did something rather stupid and foolhardy,

without talking to you or the Samnung about it, and you've caught me on it. You have every right to be mad."

Trystane sat next to her and tilted her chin up. "I'm not mad, Em. I do want to know what you're planning, though, and why you didn't want me to know about it. I feel like I have the right to ask those things, but I hold no command over you. When it is you and I, we are equals. When it is you as an ambassadora, I am not your ceannairí."

"I'm glad you're not mad at me, but I'd rather keep this to myself, thank you."

"My darling, I'm afraid that's not how this is going to work," Trystane replied.

"You just said you had no command over me."

"I don't." The Elf chuckled. "But I *do* know how to persuade you."

"You wouldn't dare —"

She was cut off as Trystane whipped them both around so that he crouched over top of her, sending their drinks floating harmlessly off to a corner table. Trystane traced a finger down her cheek, her neck, her collarbone, to the neckline of her backless crimson dress. He casually strolled his hand around the boatneck shape, watching as her chest rose and fell with each of her expectant breaths.

"Tell me, Ambassadora Vetur, what it is you want with the leaders of the Fórsaí Armada?" the ard rialóir instructed. "Please?"

Emi-Joye squirmed underneath him, legs and torso pinned firmly to the bed, wings splayed out behind her. She tried to reach an arm out to meet him but found an unyielding force of air pushing against her muscles, preventing her limbs from rising. Trystane smirked again.

Elven elemental magic, she thought with a hiss. She wouldn't be able to combat the binding spell, as her hands were just as immobile as the rest of her.

Trystane pulled his tunic over his head, revealing his taut and pristine warrior's chest. Unmarred by scars, because although Trystane was too young to have fought in the Ingefeoht, he was one of the most skilled weapon wielders in Heáhwolcen. Such an honorific made sense, given that his mother was known for her own combat and sword talents. But he was also vain enough not to lose, if for no other reason than to avoid the marks of battle claiming him.

"Do you want your arms free?" the Elf asked, leaning backward.

"No," Emi-Joye retorted, but her voice was a whine. *Yes*, she thought. *Absolutely yes.*

As if he could hear the wild thoughts coursing through her mind, her veins, Trystane's gaze intensified. She squirmed, pinned by his gentle magic.

"Liar," he said again. "I'll free your arms if you tell me …"

"I have nothing to tell!" she protested, writhing under her invisible bonds as the Elf reached behind her neck to unhook the collar of her dress. He slid it over her shoulders, letting the ties drape gracefully across her bodice. "Trys!"

"Nothing to tell?" he teased. "Nothing at all?"

The Elf stood and freed his calves and feet from leather boots, then ever so slowly — *tantalizingly* slowly — unlaced the front of his chocolate brown leggings. Emi-Joye let out a noise that was part hungry growl and part agonized protest. She was torn between sticking out the temptation, holding true to all the things she didn't want Trystane to know about her, and wanting to share every living, breathing aspect of herself with him.

"*Nothing*," she insisted, but the growl of wanton longing told him enough.

Void of even his undergarments now, Trystane knelt before the Fairy and began to kiss and caress and lick his way up her legs. Her calves and thighs flexed underneath his touch. Emi-Joye let out an involuntary moan of desire.

"Are you *sure?*" the Elf asked, in-between kisses.

This was too much — his touch, his sheer presence, what she'd come to know; what she, for deity's sake, didn't *want* to know. It had been a war within her for longer than Trystane would perhaps ever realize. Emi-Joye was positive about one thing, and had known it since she was a youngling, since before they were formally introduced two years ago. More than anything in any world, she wanted this Elf. As Trystane's hand pulled her silken undergarment to one side, as his tongue snaked temptingly between her legs, she caved.

He felt the change in her body language and looked up from betwixt her thighs as she stared at him and whispered, "Maylemaegus."

~ 21 ~

Trystane stopped moving for a moment. He was stunned. Of all the things he expected Emi-Joye to tell him, of all the options he tried to imagine, that word hadn't even been in the realm of possibility. He pulled back from her, simultaneously freeing her from the binding spell, and she sat straight up to reach out to him.

He held a hand up. "This —" he said, gesturing between his body and her own, now naked from the waist up as the dress had fallen to her hips, "— is not over. We will finish this. But first, sweet Fae of mine, you are going to explain, and then neither of us is going to say a deity-damned word about *that* word to anyone else. How do you even know of it?"

Neither he nor Collum had breathed the word "Maylemaegus" out loud to anyone except — Trystane rolled his eyes. "Did Aristoces tell you?"

"No!" Emi-Joye exclaimed. "What does Aristoces know about Maylemaegus?"

They stared at each other, both utterly dumbfounded.

"I told the Fairy of All Fairies that I suspect Bridgette is Maylemaegus brought to life," Trystane said. "Your turn."

Emi-Joye's stomach twisted. "My mother has an illustrated book of legends from when she was a youngling. It's ancient, really, you know how old she is. Sometimes when I get bored, I'll go into her study and read it," she said. "Once, several years ago, I flipped through it and happened upon a story I hadn't read before. The legends are written for younglings, of course, so I'm sure there's more to it, but it was the tale of how Ylda gave the first Fairies their wings.

"I know the story of the first wings, as it's one my parents told me growing up," Emi-Joye went on. "But the storybook version extended beyond that act. It tells that the deities were so pleased with the winged beings that they gave Ylda seeds of their own power as a gesture of thanks and blessing. Each seed represented a different aspect of divine power, Maylemaegus, that when combined with a being's own magic makes them akin to walking gods and goddesses themselves. The deities expected for Ylda to plant these seeds within herself, but she was a selfless being. She felt she had been gifted more than enough power, magic, and responsibility, and thus chose to sow the seeds in her most special creations so as to bless and protect the magical world as a whole."

"The Liluthuaé," Trystane said, sitting back on his heels.

The Fairy shrugged. "I suppose, given what we know and what you suspect, but the storybook doesn't specify. It's supposed to be a moral tale to teach younglings to share and care for one another as the Fyrst did, regardless of who has which powers and abilities."

"Em, what in seven hells does this have to do with you?"

With a heavy sigh, Emi-Joye told the Elf about that day at Minthame, about what Herewosa Donnachaidh told her and how his words about intertwined destinies struck her to her core. She told him that it awakened something within her, a magic she didn't yet understand, but knew dwelled deep in her soul. It was as if this magic had been waiting for her to notice and acknowledge it, patiently biding its time in the shadows of her very Self, before making its way fully into her.

"I felt this happen, like a spring coiling and uncoiling, like deadly butterflies in one's stomach," the Fairy said. "I remembered the legend and in those few moments, it made absolute, perfect sense. This power is Maylemaegus. And I think it has something to do with that aura Bridgette always talks about."

Trystane swallowed. "Hecate save us."

The aura, which made Bridgette violently ill and made Emi-Joye scatter like a mouse, only appeared when the two of them were in a shared space with Princess Cloa. The Elf felt sick. He looked up at the ceiling and said, "We have a very large problem, if the two of you are Maylemaegus in true form, and the princess' presence causes you both distress."

Emi-Joye fell back on the bed, covering her face with her hands. "I wish I knew what it meant, for her to be so contrary to us. Do we know anything of Cloa's father? Could he have been — something different?"

Trystane shook his head. He'd known Dominus. Not well, but in the sense that they were cordial to each other, and the witch was a trusted young aide to King Hermann. He was a couple of years Nehemi's senior, perhaps twenty or twenty-one to her age eighteen when she was revealed to the Samnung after his death. Young for a modern witch to be a mother, but not unheard of.

"Dominus was a good man," Trystane said. "He cared very deeply for the king and queen. In hindsight, we see that they were family to him by way of his partner and daughter. Whatever is wrong with Cloa is not his doing. But if the rumors were right, and Queen Lalora's womb *was* cursed …"

He trailed off, but Emi-Joye finished the sentence: "It is very possible that the ill-wrought magic passed to Nehemi, and Cloa is born of cursed blood."

Trystane's bedroom went silent as they sat there, horrified at what might be. If Cloa was indeed cursed by Craft Wizardry, there stood the chance that she — that *Endorsa!* — could be claimed and controlled by the very enemy which they sought to destroy in this possible fight.

"Deity damn me, I need a drink," Trystane said, summoning his whiskey to him again and sipping deeply.

He curled up against the pillows with her, and Emi-Joye shifted the rest of her dress over her hips and to the floor. She pulled her own glass over and laid her head against his chest, wings fluttering. There hadn't been much cause for strife in the young Fairy's twenty-five years. Some youngling spats with friends, of course, and stressing over schoolwork, but all in all, she'd been able to live a privileged existence. The mere idea that she'd become embroiled in a situation where something — something perhaps deadly and seen by outsiders as highly immoral — would have to be done to a descendant of Artur Cromwell made her skin crawl.

The ambassadora and ard rialóir remained thusly for the better part of an hour, both lost in thought amidst the shared quiet of the bedchamber.

"I can't stay," she finally whispered to Trystane.

"You're a fully grown Fairy, and can do whatever you'd like."

They regularly had this argument, although it wasn't really that. Trystane, whose father long ago crossed into the spirit realm and whose mother led the dúnaelfen of Lisweald, the stunningly wooded garden region of Eckenbourne, hadn't been under the rules of another's household since he was in his thirties. That was more than a century ago. Even then, his parents weren't the sort who kept close mind on their son, unless he was in the fighting ring.

Trystane therefore didn't understand Emi-Joye's insistence on continuing to appease her parents by something as simple as spending every night in their home. Unless she was in Antarctica, of course, but sleeping elsewhere on random nights throughout the week was an absolute no. She, on the other hand, had never known anything different and was petrified by the thought that her actions might cause her family any sort of displeasure.

She really needs to spend more time with Bridgette, he thought, but kept this feeling to himself. Instead, he looked up to the ceiling and not at the Fairy whose hands still rested upon him.

"You know we'd have to answer too many questions," she pleaded.

"*You* know one day we're going to have to answer them anyway," he countered.

"Yes, but not today," she said, a soft smile pulling at the corners of her lips. "Today I have to meet with Apostine to review research proposals for next year. Our liaisons narrowed it down from their scientists and academics, and we are allowed to select our top three projects to actively monitor and participate in."

"Have fun with that," Trystane chuckled, and kissed her on her forehead. He realized, as she rose from the bed and stepped back into her red dress, that they never discussed what she intended to speak to the Fórsaí Armada about. The Elf pocketed that conversation for another day.

The next morning, when Emi-Joye flitted through the Seolformúr — the magical gated entrance to the Seledreám, Fairevella's Noble House of Fae — she was so distracted that it took Apostine actually yelling at her before she realized someone was calling her name.

"What?" she snapped at her second, who responded with an appraising look.

"Sheesh, Vetur. What's wrong with you this day?" Apostine asked. He was genuinely concerned, of course. However, Emi-Joye was not in the mood to be hovered over. She was still upset about Collum and Trystane learning of her plans to speak with the Fórsaí Armada, and was upset with herself that those plans hadn't fully cemented, despite the fact that she still had more than a month to prepare.

In fact, she had outright lied to Trystane in the wee hours of the morning. She and Apostine decided weeks ago what research projects they would be working with in the new year. Today's agenda was of a personal nature. Emi-Joye had to — as the Bright Star put it — "get her shit together".

"I'm working on a project, and it's not … working," the Fairy said, answering Apostine in the vaguest fashion.

"Do you want some help?"

Did she?

It wasn't that she didn't trust her second. Emi-Joye trusted the Tief-Fae with her life, otherwise she wouldn't have selected him for the role of ambestre. But to accept Apostine's help in this would mean defying Aristoces and swearing the male to absolute secrecy. Apostine knew Bridgette was the Liluthuaé. They'd revealed that to him several months ago, when Emi-Joye accompanied her on the trip to Wales. But he had yet to be explicitly told *why* Bridgette was in Heáhwolcen, in terms of the potential for impending conflict. He'd been kept in the dark, to keep the number of beings who knew about that possibility at a minimum.

Out of anything in the world, disappointing those who believed in her and trusted her was Emi-Joye's greatest fear. She strived for nothing less than perfection in every aspect of her life. Her schoolwork as a youngling had been impeccable. Her knifework, pristine and efficient. Her stage presence and public persona, ethereal and professional. If there was a skill she attempted that left a gap in personal fulfillment, or if she was not immediately adept at it in some way, it was a skill she brushed aside and no longer pursued, as perfection in it would require more power than she cared to exude toward it.

The thought of disappointing Aristoces by breaking her ceannairí's trust, by telling Apostine about the true reason for the Liluthuaé to be in the world above the world, made her heart flutter in the exact opposite way Trystane did. It was a quandary, really, because having her second in on this plan would mean she had someone to count on, to guide and brainstorm with her, who wasn't intimately involved with the Samnung. She was half-surprised Collum hadn't already accosted her once he and Trystane deduced who desired to meet with the commanders, demanding to know what she was up to the same way the ard rialóir did just a few hours ago.

Perhaps only Trys figured that out, the ambassadora thought.

Making a split-second decision, Emi-Joye whirled in midair to face Apostine, moving so fast that he stopped flying and dropped a few inches before catching himself. She gripped the collar of his tunic and pulled him close, leaning in as if to kiss him, and whispered in his ear. When she pulled away, his eyes were wide with surprise and a sense of daring. He grinned at her. She hesitantly returned the expression, and the two soared hand-in-hand into the Seledreám.

<h1 style="text-align:center">~ 22 ~</h1>

Like Bridgette assumed he would, Toby knocked patiently at her bedroom door to wake her the next morning. She opened it to find him standing there with a warm cup of breakfast tea, seasoned with three sugar cubes and already whitened with fresh cream.

"Good morning, Bridgette!" he said grandly. "Mumma said we are to spend the day with each other, as the butchery is closed!"

Bridgette grinned. Toby tried so hard to be professional and a good little host, but she saw the light in those brown eyes of his. He was chomping at the bit to get out of the house with her.

"Oh, really?" she teased, accepting the proffered cup. "And what exactly are we going to do with ourselves all day?"

"We are going on a walkabout!"

"A who-da-what?"

Toby cocked his head. "Do you not know what a walkabout is?"

"That would be a negative, my little ghostrider. Please explain."

"What is a ghostrider?"

Bridgette snorted. "It's a stupid expression from Earth, 'negative, ghostrider'. It basically is a weird way of saying 'no' but adding a call sign on it, like how truck drivers use …"

And that was how Tobias Maudlin learned of the human cinematic classic "Smokey and the Bandit" and the associated phrase, "ten-four, good buddy".

"We should have call signs," Toby suggested as they wandered Forêt Fossile, the wild woods a lengthy journey northwest of his home.

"Alright then," Bridgette agreed. "Like secret nicknames for each other. I'll be Starshine. Only one other male calls me that. I don't think he'd mind if you shared it."

"Hmm," the boy mused, tapping a forefinger on his chin. "I've never given a nickname before. I don't know what else I would call myself."

Bridgette hopped over a thick root protruding from the ground, the soil here much richer and damper than anywhere else she'd seen in Palna. "Well, I guess a nickname is more something that someone else calls *you*, not something you come up with yourself. I'll think of one."

She reached a hand back to help Toby clamber over the roots, but he was perfectly at ease in these woods. It was a real forest, which surprised the Elfling, given the drier climate everywhere except along Afon Azúl. Forêt Fossile seemed like a veritable wonderland. The woods were lush, tree branches glittering with dew even though it was nearly noon, and the ground was spongy under their feet with layers of leaves, soil, and natural detritus. It was still and silent, almost eerily so, save for a hushed, constant white noise, the sort of sound that makes people wonder if their ears are working — if they actually hear anything, or if they're imagining things.

"Where is this place, anyway?" Bridgette asked. "What makes it so … wet?"

Toby laughed, the musical tone shattering the ghostly atmosphere, and Bridgette knew his nickname in that instant. She grinned at him and let the boy answer. "This is protected land, of course! The rain always falls here to keep the trees safe," he said.

The nickname was pushed to the back of her mind. "Protected land?"

"Yes," Toby nodded. "Queen Ydessa and King Eryth selected several sites and attractions in Palna to be protected, so even during the dry season right now they have a constant environment. This forest is one, our portion of the Beorgdún, the tulip fields of Düoria, and some others you haven't seen yet. I have not seen them all either, but I would so very much like to one day."

"Draw me a map, will you? Here in the dirt," the Elfling told him. She pointed with the toe of her boot to an area free of leaves.

Toby picked up a fallen twig and began to scratch into the ground. He sketched out a roughly oblong egg shape, added a few lines and circles and squares, then began telling Bridgette about the country he called home.

"These are the mountains, the Beorgdún, in the far north. It is not very cold here, but the further up they go, in the Outside, it is said that the winters last almost the whole year. I would not like to live there, I do not think. It would be much too cold for me," Toby said. "Below the mountains is the start of the forests. At the very base of the mountains is the most sacred of our protected lands, The Bloodwood. You must get special permission from the king and queen to go there, and the Palnan Guard must go with you. But the rest of the forests, from the bottom of The Bloodwood down to us, here," — he traced one of the shapes he'd drawn — "are open to all who wish to walk them."

Bridgette squatted next to the map, resting her weight on her calves. "This is Düoria, then? To the right of the forest ranges?"

"Yes, and the city of Tehlalin above that," Toby replied. "Tehlalin means 'moon soil', called so for the way the silver light of night and the mountains bathe it in shadow. It is said that Tehlalin was one of the old cities of Heáhwolcen, before Palna was Palna, named by the Fairy Galdúr."

"And the tulip fields?" Bridgette prodded.

The boy poked holes in a large swath of land under the star he drew to indicate Düoria. "The tulips are here, and other farmland. But we are known for our tulips."

"Where do they go?"

Toby glanced at her. "What do you mean, 'where do they go'?"

"Well … you said y'all were known for your tulips. So like, who buys them from Palna? Where do they go after they're grown and picked?"

The boy's brow furrowed, utterly confused.

"I mean, I've never seen tulips in Heáhwolcen," Bridgette explained. "I haven't been everywhere, so maybe I'm crazy, but it seems weird for Palna to be known for its flowers when there's nowhere to export them to."

"I do not know. They simply grow, and we are known for them," Toby said, still looking as confused as Bridgette felt.

"Huh," she said, turning her attention back to the map. An unease settled over her. Something wasn't right about the so-called protected tulip fields that no one outside of Palna knew existed, especially if everyone *in* Palna believed them to be prized elsewhere in Heáhwolcen. Bridgette tried to change the subject back to the map, and Toby was more than happy to oblige.

He pointed out the lines he'd drawn to represent the rivers that flowed through Palnan lands. The largest river was called the Ibaia, starting at the base of the Beorgdún and channeling down the western side of the country, ending near the southern border with a massive lake called Loch du Flors. A smaller lake — which was more the Ibaia widening significantly as it paralleled Düoria — called Loch Petit Somnis provided the branching point for the river named Afon Verité. It swung due south to the border with Bondrie, and off of it swept Afon Azúl and La Azúlita. The latter branched off Verité and reconnected with Azúl. The three rivers joined in such a way that they formed an island in the middle of the country.

"This is the *most* sacred land," Toby whispered reverently, pointing to that oddly shaped isle. "The most sacred land in all of our world. It is Terrabruixes, the Witchlands."

"Who lives there?" Bridgette asked, studying the place.

Though Düoria was the capital, it was bizarre to her that the most important land in a country *wasn't* the place where its leaders dwelled.

"I do not know," Toby said. His voice was solemn. "It is just sacred. It is like The Bloodwood, where only those who are given special permission may visit."

"But why is it so important? It's like an island. Or like a secret castle surrounded by a moat," Bridgette mused. "I kinda want to go check it out."

"We are not allowed."

"Well, why not?"

"Because we *aren't.*"

The Elfling gave Toby an annoyed stare. "That's literally not an answer. And no one said *I* wasn't allowed to go there, right?"

"That is because no one knows you are here."

"No shit, Sherlock — don't tell your mom I said that — so why not use that to our advantage and sneak over the river?" Bridgette pointed out. "It's stupid to have protected land that your people can't even visit. We have protected land on Earth, and where I'm from in America, they're called national parks. Anyone can go there. Sometimes they have to pay to visit, and the money helps cover the costs of the park rangers and landscaping and stuff."

Toby didn't answer. He stood from the map and announced, "I'm ready to return home now. It will be nearly suppertime when we arrive."

Bridgette bit her lip. "Whatever you say."

They made it about fifteen minutes back through Forêt Fossile before Bridgette couldn't stand her curiosity a moment longer. She stopped again and stared up at the canopy of trees above them — palms and oaks and pines and species she didn't recognize — and asked the question that had plagued her for weeks.

"Why in the seven hells did you call me the Raisarch that

day?"

Toby stopped walking and turned back around. He tilted his head to the side and gave Bridgette a long, appraising look before answering, as though wondering if she was worthy of hearing the explanation she sought.

"Because I Saw you," he said simply, finally, putting an emphasis on the verb.

"Okay, fine, but what do you *mean* you 'Saw' me?" she pushed. "I don't understand."

"When you allowed me to See you that day, there was much that I could not See around. You are protected. But there was a sight of you in leather, with a bow in your hand and quiver on your back, and your braid whipped in the wind as you flew toward a great sea of black and stars," Toby whispered to her. He was hard to hear, even over the eerie not-quite-silence of the forest around them. "It was a glimpse, but sometimes to See someone's self, that is all I need to understand."

The thought of Toby knowing she could fly was unsettling. She supposed the sea of back and stars was his power surreptitiously referencing her being the Bright Star. "So, you Saw me flying around at night with a bow and arrow, and that meant you thought I was the Raisarch?"

He scoffed. "*No*, you *are* the Raisarch."

"Toby!" Bridgette stomped toward him, breaking the quiet. "I am absolutely fucking *not*. There already is a Raisarch. He's somewhere in Palna. It's not me."

She glared at him and knelt to level their eyes. "You Saw a whole lotta shit, and you're keeping your mouth shut about it, which I appreciate, but I can assure you that whatever you Saw was not an indication that I am the Raisarch. I am here to *find* the Raisarch, and the Ealdaelfen he leads, and a bunch of other things you already figured out with your freaky-deaky little future-analyzing brainpower."

Bridgette hadn't meant to yell, but she was tired of being lied to. Although, she thought, maybe since she didn't pull a dagger on him meant that he wasn't lying … and she was not sure which of those thoughts was more disconcerting. Still, Toby stood in front of her, shoulders bared bravely as he took in her angry words.

"You do not know," he said.

"Yeah, well, sorry for yelling, but that's also not a helpful explanation. What else do I not know, because I'm assuming it's a helluva lot."

"You do not know that the Raisarch is both a title and a birthright," Toby said. "Now you do."

~ 23 ~

"A birthright?!" Bridgette trudged up a hill calling after Toby, who scurried ahead, knowing which roots to jump as he ran the path out of Forêt Fossile. "How is it a birthright when I'm not Ealdaelfen? And slow down, for Pete's sake!"

"You'll see!" Toby shouted back to her. He laughed mischievously.

She was annoyed. "My little dude, you're the one who Sees, not me, so I'd appreciate it if you did the polite thing and not skate around the bush here."

Her eyes flared, but it wasn't the shifting of sierwan knowledge. It was born of something deeper, something different, and the feeling came to her so unexpectedly that Bridgette's toes caught in a lifted root, and she went sprawling.

She yelped, feeling twigs snap under her weight as she fell. Something sharp ripped at her sleeve and stabbed into her arm, and her cheek scratched against the ground. "Ouch. *Ouch.*"

Toby jogged back toward her. "Oh no! Are you alright?"

The Elfling hauled herself to her knees. Her cheek smarted and she felt a trickle of blood and wet earth trail down the injured arm. "Probably."

"Probably?"

"Yeah, I'll be fine, but fuck, that *hurt.*" She glanced at her torn sleeve, where crimson now stained the cream-colored yarn of her sweater. "Dammit. That's unfortunate."

"I can help," Toby offered, reaching out a hand. "Tear off the sleeve and we can use it as a bandage to stop the bleeding. When we are home, Mumma can fix you a poultice that will reduce the scarring."

"Scarring? It's only a cut —"

"It is a most deep cut, to bleed so badly."

"Flesh wound," the Elfling sniffed. "I'll be fine, I've had

worse."

"Not from here, you have not."

Fucking hellfire, this kid is stubborn, Bridgette thought. "Why does it matter where the ground was that I fell on?"

"Forêt Fossile is *protected land*, Bridgette!" Toby said, but the significance of that fact was lost on her for the moment as she started to really feel the sting of her wounds.

"I don't know what that means about me bleeding, but fine, here's my sleeve." She cringed as the fabric ripped. Njahla helped her pick this sweater out after Lammas, and it was the softest fabric she'd ever worn. Tearing it apart bordered on disgraceful.

Toby took the proffered garment and tore it in half again, using one piece to dab the dripping blood from Bridgette's arm before folding and pressing it against the open slice. "Hold that down with as much pressure as you can," he told her, then proceeded to wrap her arm with the remaining half, tucking the ends in to secure the makeshift bandage.

"How did you fall?" he asked.

"I wasn't watching my feet," Bridgette admitted. "A root tripped me up."

"It should not have done that."

"No," she laughed. "It definitely should not have."

They reached the Maudlin home without further incident, though Bridgette was visibly limping by the time the house was in sight, and she felt ghostly pale and lightheaded. The blood dried on her cheek, but if wind hit it the right way, it stung something awful, and her arm throbbed. Her hand felt numb as blood struggled to circulate underneath Toby's tightly wrapped tourniquet.

"Mumma!" Toby shouted. "Mumma, come quickly!"

Serrabinx emerged from the garden, a basket hanging from her arm that overflowed with leaves and flowers of white geraniums. She gave one look to the Elfling's face and bandaged arm, and whipped her head to the boy. "What in the seven hells, Tobias Maudlin!"

"We were in the forest and Bridgette tripped over a root!"

"Which forest?" The woman's nostrils flared.

"Forêt Fossile, Mumma. Where we were on a walkabout. She fell and —"

"What root?"

Bridgette was close enough to hear the two talking, but after the gradual onset of pain, the long hike to the forest, and the walk back, she was too weary to say anything aloud. She wondered again why it mattered about falling in Forêt Fossile, and now why it mattered what tree tripped her up. She didn't listen to Toby's response, which from Serrabinx's tone was not the answer the woman wanted to hear.

"Tobias, fetch water and heat the fire under the cauldron. We'll use the heat to pull the venom out."

"Venom?!" Bridgette choked. "It was a *tree*, not a snake, Serrabinx."

Her host did not listen, but gripped the Elfling under her shoulder and walked her inside to the kitchen table. "How do you feel?"

"Currently very confused, thanks. I wasn't bitten —"

"Bridgette, listen to me," Serrabinx's eyes were fiercely sharp. She shoved Bridgette into a chair. "How do you feel?"

"I'm fine, Serrabinx, I swear; my cheek kinda stings when something touches it and my arm lost circulation a few miles ago. Toby's pretty grand at tying a tight tourniquet, actually. My right hip … well, maybe my whole right leg is pretty sore, but that's the side that I fell on. I just caught my boot under a root that was sticking up, and it took me down pretty hard. I was trying to catch up to Toby," Bridgette said.

Serrabinx held the back of her hand to Bridgette's forehead. "You're only a little warm. I believe we've caught it in time."

"Caught what, exactly?"

"Forêt Fossile is protected land, Bridgette."

The Elfling had to bite her tongue to keep from saying something she'd probably regret. "Toby said that, but I don't *understand* what that *means*. What the hell is protected land besides a forest that gets extra rain all year 'round?"

Bridgette looked up to see Zedolph standing in the doorway. "Ask and be answered, Bridgette," he murmured before turning to the firehearth.

Serrabinx nodded her permission and proceeded to examine Bridgette's cheek.

"What does it mean to be protected land? Why does it matter that I fell in it?" she asked the butcher. His answer sent Bridgette's head swimming.

"Protected lands are spelled to maintain their environment — to keep them as they should be, despite our country's otherwise rainy and dry seasons," Zedolph murmured. "Because they are spelled, power reigns within and can be utilized by those with the knowledge and power to do so. The land wards know who is welcome and who is not, and those who threaten their wellbeing shall be dealt with accordingly."

"Holy shit," Bridgette said. "All those lands, they're protected by the m-word I'm not allowed to say out loud? Specifically by the capital C-word type of m-word?"

Zedolph hesitated. "Yes," he said carefully. "The protection piece is a sort of power like those you reference. But the land wards can be accessed by any sort of power-wielder. Whether Craft or ritual, spell, Elven, or Fae, anyone with the ability to connect to the land wards may use and control the powers therein. Any Palnan citizens who have such abilities in their blood have the potential to do so, as does any outsider, whether or not demonstrating their skills is forbidden."

The Elfling's arm was shaking, and it was only partially from the injury. Toby emerged from the firehearth and handed a heated wet cloth and a glass jar to his mother. The jar reeked of heady herbs.

"This is a black sage poultice," Serrabinx explained. She used what looked like a mother-of-pearl cheese knife to spread the overly mint-sweet mush over Bridgette's arm. The Elfling chanced a look at her cleaned cut and was shocked to see that dark purple colored her veins, spidering them visibly against her fair skin.

The Bright Star's blood shivered and that strange sensation she perceived before, the one that caused her to trip, rumbled deep in her gut. She felt it stronger this time, maybe now because she was aware it existed. Any further consideration was gone a second later as Serrabinx's poultice started to take effect and both her arm and cheek gave almighty spasms that ached from her skin to her bones.

"What does black sage do?" Bridgette gasped out, gripping the table edge with both hands for dear life. Her blood felt so cold, yet her skin near the cuts burned feverishly. "This hurts way more than when I fell, holy cannoli."

Serrabinx pressed the heated cloth against the gash in Bridgette's arm and wrapped a strip of white fabric to secure it in place. "Black sage and the herbs in this medicine will pull out the venom, but because you two had been exercising, walking all that way back, your heart was well on its way to pumping it throughout your entire bloodstream," she said. "It's no small miracle that it did not spread more than this. It barely made it past the cuts."

Bridgette's eyes shifted, and the sierwan knowing sent a wave of nausea through her. She knew exactly why the venom was barred from fully taking over her blood. Craft blood of the Tinuviels, the ones who did the protecting and likely the interfering with the land wards, ran in her veins. The venom recognized that whomever this being was that tripped amongst the trees, she was not an enemy.

Bridgette swore the world trembled under her feet.

~ 24 ~

If anyone thought analyzing more than thirty years' worth of weekly Fairy ambassador reports to Palna was a daunting task, it was nothing compared to the centuries upon centuries of smuggled Elven history that Collum, Trystane, and their seconds now busied themselves with. It had been a long few weeks, yet again, of what seemed like endless research for the Elven leaders. For safety purposes, the fyrdwisa asked them to evanesce directly into his living room, lest anyone become suspicious of them constantly appearing in his hallway or at the back entrance that was — allegedly — a secret path for his personal use.

This time, they couldn't enlist the greater Samnung's help or even trust some of the other ranking officials and seconds to aid them. Though they could have used the assistance, given the sheer volume of documents, it would take too much explanation. It could lead to someone from the University becoming far too curious and involved. Things were questionable enough with the four of them having to obtain white silk archival gloves from the University librarians without arousing suspicions. Aurelias, too, was in the library or talking to magisters every other day, taking over Bridgette's old role of scouring shelves and brains to check facts and rumor.

The fyrdestre's former notebook of scribbles about Ulerion Mewt's ambassador reports had become lines upon lines of Elven history, scribed in the coded language of the Tieflings so that only she could read them. Her Elven companions were slowly but surely learning the secretive shorthand and complicated array of symbols. Aurelias and Collum had never before been so glad her ancestry included the horned, tailed beings and their mysteries.

Collum thought again about inviting Apostine to join this research team, if only to help translate Aurelias' notes into the common language for them, but he hadn't yet broached the subject of inviting the ambestre to be part of their gatherings.

Plus, Apostine had a tendency to get as excited as a young puppy when asked to be part of any type of mission and was likely to accidentally let something slip about a translation project. Collum wasn't sure who'd be more pissed off that Apostine was involved when they weren't, Aristoces or Emi-Joye.

Fucking seven hells, keeping secrets is too complicated, the fyrdwisa thought.

He forced his body out from underneath the down comforter, so warm and cozy on this late fall morning, and shuffled groggily into the living room. He barely recognized his apartment these days. It looked more like the underbelly of a museum than the dwelling quarters of a government official.

Collum's kitchen was covered with artifacts that chronicled portions of their kind's history. There was a rough categorization — loose-leaf documents here, handwritten texts and diaries stacked in that corner, papers with an air of government officiality were by the armchair where Trystane usually perched. There was hardly room to sit, and the trunk seemed endless. Collum thought they were barely making a dent in its contents. He began several days ago to suspect it was spelled; that the documents had been magically shrunken to all fit, and as layers were removed from the top, the open space allowed additional pages to show themselves.

The fyrdwisa surveyed the spread, grateful for a quiet morning. They stayed up long into the night two evenings ago, and Aurelias ended up sleeping on his couch. He hadn't had so many guests here at once — and not so often — for a very long time. It was nice to enjoy some small amount of peace at the moment, as his companions indicated they had prior commitments for the next several days. Trystane said this somewhat guiltily as he observed the mess they were making of the fyrdwisa's home. But Collum waved them out and brought Aurelias a knitted blanket from his linen closet, covering the snoring Elfling, who'd at least kicked off her combat boots before lounging on his furniture in her stockinged feet.

He sighed long and hard. He had no plans today, which meant his plans were to get back to this, alone, preferably in his office and not the living room. This area was beginning to take on a peculiar musty smell, like old chalk and stale cigar tobacco. He needed fresh air and solace.

And coffee. Definitely coffee.

Collum walked to his room and slipped into a long-sleeved black tunic and fitted black pants. He laced his rarely worn silver leather boots up his calves and covered his ears and head with a silvery gray knit beanie, the brim rolled slightly to let the length of the cap drape gracefully down toward his neck. It had been a winter solstice gift from Njahla, handknitted by her mother in fiber that complemented the flecks of color in his Elven eyes. The matching boots had been a gift that year from Trystane — who was terrible at presents, hardly ever gave them, and on the occasion he did, practically begged his second three days before the upcoming holiday to handle the shopping for him in exchange for, well, pretty much whatever bargaining chip Njahla desired. But these boots for once Trystane picked out himself, so Collum rarely wore them. They were too special to wear daily — albeit slightly flashy for his normal taste, though he loved them — and thus normally reserved for ceremonies or celebrations.

But today, Collum needed flashy. It reminded him of brighter things and better days, and the silver sheen was a complete contrast to the antique store that had overtaken his apartment. Collum splashed cold water on his face and did a cursory tooth-brushing, glancing to the side of his bathroom counter as he did so. A small pang went through his chest. There, a second toothbrush — one he swiped recently from his guest bathroom — shared the space. It was the only reminder that kept him remotely focused on this secret task of being an accidental Elven historian. Somehow, some way, it would play a part in bringing his Starshine back.

He slipped a thick black fur vest over his tunic to keep some of the chill at bay before evanescing to Endorsa. The smell of the Coffee Cauldron was the first thing to greet him, followed by the sight of a lengthy line out the door.

"Seven hells," he muttered to himself, trying to think about what day of the week it was. What day of the month, even. Unless it was a Wednesday with his presence required at a Samnung meeting, Collum barely kept track anymore. Judging from the past few times that happened, this was not a good sign for his mind-health. He sighed and tuned his mind into those around him, wondering what caused the crowd.

After scanning the inner monologues and outward conversations of the line ahead, his answer came in the form of a female witch whose thoughts concentrated on cranberry-orange honeycakes.

Collum groaned. He'd managed to arrive on the release day of the shop's winter menu, inspired by holiday flavors of the impending winter solstice the upcoming month. This was the only time of year the honeycake flavors didn't rotate as frequently as usual, as the witch sisters who ran the shop preferred to treat their customers to what were largely foreign human tastes. There would be orange and gingerbread, savory pine nut and hot honey, fragrant rum and vanilla, maple-cinnamon, and chocolate-pumpkin.

The only thing that could cause him further displeasure tapped him on the shoulder, and Collum whipped around to meet the bright gaze of Lucilla.

Fabulous.

"Hello, Fyrdwisa," she greeted him demurely. "It's a most welcome surprise to see you here. To see you at all, actually."

I fucking bet, his thoughts hissed, but he nodded in acknowledgement. "Well met, Lucilla. What brings you out this day?"

She indicated the long line of hungry patrons in front of them. "I heard there would be candied mint mokka this year, something we've not had before."

Collum decided in that instant that he no longer wanted solitude. He slipped two fingers under his covenant bracelet with Aurelias. She'd like candied mint mokka — caife mokka was her favorite beverage here, anyway — and even more, Aurelias would like to bug the seven hells out of Lucilla.

"I see," he said.

"And yourself?"

"I desired to get out of my apartment and find both caffeine and peace."

Lucilla snorted. "Well, then. You found one of the above."

"I suppose I have."

He didn't mean to be terse, but it was far easier to be short and not-exactly-sweet with Lucilla than it was to be intentionally kind and empathetic. Collum would not ignore her and wouldn't be outwardly rude, but he had no qualms about making it clear that he didn't intend to talk to her in public. Or ever.

The witch was deaf and dumb to his avoidance of her advances. Or maybe she thought that if she kept them up, she'd eventually win him over. He wasn't sure. Given that his preferred location was anywhere that was not inside her mind, he was okay with not thinking too hard about how she interpreted his behavior.

Aurelias arrived a few moments later, her impeccable positioning making her presence known: she had to dart backward into the fenced-in yard of a shop nearby to avoid evanescing on top of a very excited group of witches from the University, all of whom wore matching cream-colored tunics with a logo embroidered in glistening bronze thread. They shrieked at how close the fyrdestre appeared and looked moderately distressed as the eyepatched Elfling saluted them before joining her fyrdwisa.

"Well met, Chief," she said. "And Lucilla."

She glanced at Collum, who rolled his eyes just enough for her to see. Lucilla looked displeased but gave the fyrdestre a wan smile. "Well met, Aurelias. Although it is rather rude to be cut in front of in line."

Collum turned and smiled at her. "In which case the fyrdestre and I shall traverse to the back of the line, Lucilla, and relieve you of the inconvenience of waiting a moment longer."

"No —" the witch started, but her protest was a millisecond too late, as Collum grabbed his second and evanesced both of them several patrons to the rear. Lucilla pouted but didn't follow.

"Hecate save us," Aurelias muttered. "How are you going to put up with her next week?"

He'd forgotten. He let himself forget, actually, that in just a few days' time he and Lucilla-turned-Bridgette were supposed to visit Earth and show the Bright Star's foster parents, schoolmates, and colleagues that she wasn't missing, wasn't murdered, and remained very much alive.

In preparation for the trip, Geongre Akiko had taken it upon herself to enlist a team of Fairies from the Earthside portal in Danvers, Massachusetts, to hack into Bridgette's electronic mail accounts and send messages to select human parties. They arranged for her to see Joel "Doc" and Martha Simmons the week before the American Thanksgiving holiday. The Simmonses wanted to spend the day with Bridgette and this mysterious beau of hers — Martha's words, not Akiko's — but the Fairy, pretending to be Bridgette, was able to skillfully navigate the conversation. She gently reminded the Simmonses that in Europe, where Bridgette and Collum now supposedly lived, they did not celebrate this holiday, and the Bright Star's violin students required her presence. She could only take so much time away.

"I have no idea," Collum murmured finally, realizing he stared off into the trees instead of replying to his second.

Aurelias reached across his shoulders and squeezed him tightly. "You'll get through it. You always do."

He smirked. "Indeed, although I must admit, I do not always like it."

<h1 style="text-align: center">~ 25 ~</h1>

Despite spending weeks in Palna, Bridgette had yet to see the supposed king and queen who ruled here. She'd never seen her father, but deep in her soul, she knew the face that now stared at her was his. He looked nothing like she imagined such a vile character might. His features appeared pinched and elongated, with sloping brows, a weak chin, and narrow-set eyes. It was only the eyes that fit the bill of what she thought a villain such as Eryth Tinuviel would look like. They were dark, small, and unfeeling, with devilish wrinkles spanning around them. The kind of devilish that promised death and deception instead of mischief. The kind of devilish that froze her chest as she studied him. He saw her, but did he know her? Did he realize that who stood before him was born of his own flesh and blood?

Part of her yearned for a connection; some tie that bound them, that marked her as his daughter, even though she wanted nothing more than to throw him from the highest tower of the palace in Düoria, so that the red of his blood flowed as bright as the tulips that grew there. Eryth was the darkest, most despicable male to exist in modern magic — though she knew him to be far older, unusually old for a wizard or witch, as he and Ydessa had ruled since the Ingefeoht. Yet still she craved the connection of blood bond to him, this birth father of hers.

"What's a pretty little Elf like you doing here?" he asked. Eryth's voice had a nasally tone to it, a high falsetto which didn't fit the rest of his larger-set body, that of an athlete gone slightly to seed.

Truth be told, to answer his question, Bridgette had no idea what she was doing *here*, nor where *here* was. She'd been walking, exploring alone, and gotten lost. It was dark. The air stank of decay and burning tobacco, a smell like death and unbeing. A place where the Bright Star did not belong.

But *here*, she was not the Bright Star. She was an Elfling born of Earth who could do no magic and speak no words for fear of revealing what the king of Palna could not know. The Tinuviels were not supposed to see that the Bright Star shone among them. It was good she was nothing and a nobody, here in this strange place. She had never been more glad for that.

Eryth's mouth twisted to one side, his thin lips pursed as he appraised his charge. She realized he held a wand aloft, emitting an acid green light to illuminate her. Bridgette shut her mind off, tried to think of nothing except air and water, fire and soil, her breathing and the darkness. She wished she could do more than that. Wished she had Collum's power to hear what was going on inside her father's head. But Collum wasn't here, and she was, and she was defenseless. A frozen little bird, only her eyes moving to follow the movements of the man as he circled her.

How the fuck did I get here? she thought. It was dark, yet the black had as much color as a rainbow if she squinted her eyes just right. There was the thick, sticky orange of wet clay after a July rainstorm in Georgia; waves of navy; creeping rivulets of citron that turned into flashes of evergreen. Had she walked into Forêt Fossile? It was so dark she didn't recognize it. She wished it was Maluridae Wood. She felt safe there. She didn't feel safe here.

Bridgette felt a tug on her hair and she cringed. Eryth was behind her, whispering something she couldn't make out, but it sounded like a spell. She didn't like this one damn bit. The tightness in her chest increased, and the Elfling willed herself not to panic. She wondered for a moment if she'd been bound with magic to stand still.

A twig snapped underneath her bare feet. *Why the hell didn't I put shoes on? Was I sleepwalking?* she thought. *What the fuck is going on?*

Trapped. Bridgette was trapped, in this sick strange darkness that coiled around her and her father, who didn't know he was her father. She willed herself to breathe normally and keep her mouth shut as Eryth continued to circle her.

How did he even find me? It can't be normal for kings and queens to roam around at night, right?

There was a sound in the distance and Eryth turned. The dark changed colors, becoming more clearly blue and purple now, a shade of aubergine that matched the color of blood that ran along her injured arm. It was the color of the blood she and Eryth shared, and yet didn't, because how could this being have fathered the Liluthuaé? By what cruel, wicked god's snap of fingers had this happened, for the king of Palna, the only known living Craft wizard, to be determined as the father of his own antithesis?

Eryth was still turned away from her, listening to the faint sound. It was louder now. Something glinted in the acid green light of the king's wand: a dagger sheathed in his belt. Bridgette glanced at her own hips. She wore loose-fitting black pants and a matching top. Elven sleepclothes. No belt, no amethyst dagger. Had Eryth taken it? Did she even have it on her body when the two walked into each other? Not that she could use it now, bound with her arms to her sides, unable to move.

Whatever the noise was troubled Eryth. He started shouting orders at someone Bridgette couldn't see, the darkness caking them so thickly it seeped through her pores.

Of course he brought guards. He's an asshole, not an idiot.

Her father reached a hand for her, but it was as if she watched a movie in slow motion. Purple darkness swelled, hot and metallic, and a sense of peace overcame the Elfling as the dark shifted before them. The magic that bound her sparkled, a visible barrier for but a moment, then crumbled into nothingness. Bridgette took a deep, heaving breath. She was safe. Eryth and his guards wouldn't hurt her now, and indeed he moved his arm away as the new presence in their midst challenged him. How the presence found her, she didn't know, but she was glad it did.

Swords clanged too close for comfort. Everyone was shouting, and even though the magic bonds were broken, Bridgette couldn't move. She was frozen to the spot of her own accord, uncertain which direction to dart into. Eryth stood there too, turning angrily in place. He sensed the presence. Bridgette's eyes shifted. The presence was a sort of Old Magick. Eryth could not stand against it, not with sword nor with his own Craft spellwork. *Bastardized Craft spellwork, more like,* Bridgette realized.

Her realization seemed to please the presence. There was still no connection between Bridgette and her father. But perhaps the nothingness was not nothing, so much as it was the slightest tug toward the presence. The presence didn't have an exact form, but she felt it was male, and —

Bridgette blinked. "Collum?" she whispered, hoping beyond all possible hope.

But this wasn't Elven magic. The presence was older than the Elves. There was a faint brush of it against her skin and her body warmed. There was magic between them, deep and important, but the colors were wrong. The darkness was purple and there was a flash of coppery gold instead of dark brown —

Bridgette sat straight up, her throat on fire from the screams she hadn't heard herself make. It was a *dream.*

She twisted in bed, clawing at her sweat-soaked sheets, her right arm bleating in protest at the movement. There was blood on the pillow from her cheek, its scratches torn open again from thrashing in her sleep. Her chest heaved and the air was too thin. She struggled to calm her lungs long enough to take a breath. It felt raw and ragged going down.

Breathe, she told herself and squeezed her eyes shut, picturing Collum standing with her at the peak of Hlafjordstiepel, the mountains around them covered in powdery snow. Her fingers found the covenant bracelet and the Elfling gripped it for dear life. She knew there was no magic there, but it was still his touch in a way.

Breathe. There had been dark magic in that dream, something old that should have terrified her.

Breathe. But it hadn't been terrifying. What scared her was being trapped in place by Eryth Tinuviel, her dream-body unable to move, but her real body violently churning as she tried to break whatever held her subconscious hostage.

Breathe. It hadn't been Collum who saved her. But who the fuck was it? What was that presence? She swore she could still feel it in the room around her.

Bridgette lit the oil lamp on her nightstand. She ripped the bandage off her throbbing arm and promptly fell back against the bed. The aubergine blood hadn't moved any further into her veins, but it hadn't receded either. The wound was closed, and the veins shimmered in that same metallic sheen that coated the darkness in her dream.

Her stomach lurched and bile rose in her throat. She heaved forward and ran to the bathroom, where she spent the rest of the long night with her head pressed against the cold porcelain of the toilet.

It was Zedolph who found her, his hands heart-wrenchingly gentle and cool as he lifted Bridgette's head from the floor a while later. She was curled into a ball, hair splayed out in a thousand directions, arm throbbing, sleepclothes stuck to her from the sweat of the night before.

"I'm so sorry," she muttered, orienting herself to the calloused hands that moved her into a sitting position against the wall. "That stupid poultice —"

"Shhh," Zedolph reassured her. "My sister is very gifted in ways that perhaps we should not outwardly discuss. You do not need to apologize for being ill. An injury of that caliber is quite dangerous, and I am pleased to see that you made it through the night. How do you feel?"

He moved a hand to her forehead as if to check her

temperature.

"I've felt worse," Bridgette said. The light streaming in from the bathroom window made her eyes ache. "I don't think I'm going to be a very good slátraestre today, though."

"You are under no obligation to tend to the butchery this day. Or the next. Serrabinx will deem when you are fit to return to work," Zedolph assured her. Concern clouded his eyes. "What was it that made you so ill, if it is not impertinent to ask?"

The Elfling blinked slowly, forcing her eyes to adjust to the brightness. "I had a really, really strange dream where I met the king of Palna. Let's just say he was not a fan of me studying abroad here."

Her half-lie tumbled out smoothly, but her stomach churned. Bridgette heaved over the toilet. She felt Zedolph pull her hair back, then place a hand just below her neck. He stayed there with her until Toby stirred, the childlike patter of bare feet suddenly audible in the quiet morning hours. It was comforting, and so tempting as Bridgette leaned backward into Zedolph's caring embrace. She wished the sun would go back down so she could spend the day in cave-like darkness.

"Uncle, what is wrong with Bridgette?" There was panic in Toby's voice as he peered around the doorframe. "Is it her injury?"

"I'm fine, Little Lark," the Elfling said, her voice weaker than she wanted it to be. "That stuff your mom gave me made me pretty sick. I think I'm going to be useless today."

"Little Lark?" Toby whimpered, staring at his friend.

"Yeah. Your nickname. I guess I got distracted yesterday and kinda forgot to tell you."

Toby smiled as he silently crept back from the door and meandered down the hallway to the kitchen, where the sounds of brewing tea could soon be heard.

"You are kind to him, Bridgette of the Outside."

"He's a good kid. And he was kind to me first, anyways.

Who the hell knows where I'd have ended up if we hadn't walked into each other when I crossed over the Ballamúr," Bridgette replied. Her voice still sounded quaky. "Just being from Heáhwolcen doesn't make me a bad person any more than y'all being born Palnan makes you bad people."

Zedolph tensed. "An interesting observation."

"Yeah, well, it's true," Bridgette said. "There's so much discord between Palna and everywhere else. It's so stupid because nobody from Heáhwolcen really knows what happens in Palna and vice versa. Maybe it's naïve to think this, but what if everyone took the time to get to know each other and each other's customs without immediately shutting them down? I feel like the world would be at least a more compassionate and empathetic place. Not some utopia by any means, but more tolerable."

"Another interesting observation."

Yeah, no shit, and it'd be nice to know what you really *think about that, Zedolph,* the Bright Star thought.

~ 26 ~

Collum hadn't been to a séance since his time at the University, but sitting at this table in the Seledreám felt eerily similar. The atmosphere was different — much of Fairevellan architecture was stunningly glittery and bright white, with pristine floor-to-ceiling glass windows to let in natural light during the day. Solar panels on the roof, spelled to reflect the clouds in the sky, collected and channeled heat and energy to power flickering bulbs for nighttime meetings. He was glad for the moment that despite the company around him, they were gathered in the daylight hours. An evening meeting, even with the gentle powered light and blue candles, would have been disconcertingly too much like his University séances.

He could only imagine how crude Lucilla's thoughts would become if the group here met instead in the seductive dark of such an intimate spiritual setting.

They were seated in the gathering room in the Portal Authority's wing of the Noble House of Fae. There were several such meeting places, but this was by far the largest, at the moment accommodating the fyrdwisa, Geongre Akiko, Geongrestre Etreyn, Lucilla, Nehemi, Kharis, and Trystane. The lead travel deputy and her second sat across from him, Lucilla to his left, and the three other Samnung members were on a row of stools behind them. Collum faced one of the windows, looking out onto the grounds of the palace, and watched as a Fairy flew into a massive pecan tree. The harvester shook the branches to fill the buckets her comrades held out below.

He grinned. Those pecan trees made the best pie — his favorite seasonal indulgence. Collum made a mental note to tell Teale at the Coffee Cauldron that the harvest had begun, although she probably already knew. That witch stayed on top of crop planting and picking all over both the magical world and the human one. Teale was more knowledgeable about food pairings than anyone he'd ever met.

Sensation tickled his wrist, so faint it could have been a breath, and Collum glanced to his stack of covenant bracelets out of habit to see if someone was contacting him. His top bracelet was a simple band of leather with his initials stamped into it; a covenant with his parents, long since departed to the spirit realm. Below that, the bracelet that had been his when he was the fyrdestre, a constant bit of contact with his fyrdwisa, who'd been killed in the carriage accident that took the lives of King Hermann, Queen Lalora, and Dominus, who had been Nehemi's consort and Cloa's father. Then there was a delicate woven band of black and silver, which once served as his contact point with Mohreen Conner, Bridgette's mother and Elven spy to Palna. There were strands of navy blue threads intermixed with shades of green, marking his active covenant with Trystane. Another leather band, electric pink that clashed with everything he ever wore, was his channel with Aurelias. His most unique covenant bracelet was that with Mithrilken, a thin braid of the Unicorn's own hair. The one with the Samnung hung next, a complicated array of thin knitted cords and beads: moss green and gold for Eckenbourne, bronze and peacock blue for Endorsa, seafoam and silver for Fairevella, chrome and charcoal gray for Bondrie, glittering oxblood for Verivol, black and gold for Bryten.

But his last covenant bracelet, the one that sat closest to his hand, was the one he wished would go off a little more often than it had so far — which was never. The braided cords of lilac and cerulean, interspersed with silver beads, haunted him day and night. Whereas his covenants with the Samnung, Aurelias, and Trystane nearly vibrated with power if he concentrated hard enough, the covenant with Bridgette lay as quiet and ghostly as the ones of his late parents, the former fyrdwisa, and the expired covenant with Mohreen. Three of those beings were dead. One was somewhere, but that was a thought for another time. And

Bridgette?

Collum swallowed deeply, aware that Akiko had been talking while he'd been lost in his own thoughts. Again. The tickle on his wrist must've been imagined, because all the covenant bracelets lay dormant.

The fyrdwisa turned his attention to the table and finally began listening to the lead travel deputy. Geongre Akiko was spouting their itinerary for the visit to Earth in two days' time. She pointed to a hefty stack of pages that lay in front of him and Lucilla.

"Any questions that the humans may ask are answered here," she said, indicating a few pages held together with a folded metal pin.

It was a good thing that Collum started listening in when he did, because Akiko sent a thought directly to him.

You need to be the one to answer the questions, she told him mind-to-mind. *Our young friend is quite excited about her role, but she is untrained, overly eager, and more likely to screw this up and get us all in trouble if she talks too much.*

Collum gave Akiko the slightest nod of acknowledgement. He figured that part out already. Thanks to their planned glamour of her eyes and addressing the height difference with taller shoes and long pants, they could get away with her being not quite the Liluthuaé's identical twin. But the moment Lucilla opened her mouth she'd raise suspicions, especially with those who knew Bridgette best in her human façade.

"You'll portal down to Danvers the morning after tomorrow, and we have air transportation secured in Beverly to take the two of you to Nashville that afternoon," Akiko instructed, mentioning two cities in the quaint, picturesque state of Massachusetts. "You'll stay at a hotel in Nashville and be free to walk about the city that evening. I *never* say this to you, Fyrdwisa, but you need to make absolutely certain that you are seen. There is a map in these documents that shows the location of surveillance cameras utilized by the city's police, as well as a live camera that is used by one of the sports teams at its arena."

She turned to Lucilla. "These cameras show images of what's happening on the streets to the law enforcement officers. Think of them as moving paintings, instantly captured."

The witch nodded. Her eyes nearly glittered with anticipation.

"What about the diner?" Collum asked.

"*You* will not set foot in the diner, because the moment you do, someone is going to call law enforcement and report you," Akiko said. "Lucilla will have to go that one alone. In your folders are copies of the most recent menu for the diner, as well as a few notes you might find familiar, Fyrdwisa, as they pertain to who Bridgette's regulars are and her own personal preferences for what she ordered as her shift meals."

He grinned. He remembered precisely which notes she referred to, ones he'd jotted down and reported to the Samnung during his initial search for Bridgette. At the time he didn't know how useful they would be — perhaps he'd have to befriend some of these regulars in order to get close to her, the fyrdwisa once thought. But as luck would have it, and largely thanks to his abilities to calm those around him, Collum had been able to make the move on his own. He never mentioned any of this to Bridgette. Then again, she hadn't asked.

Collum resisted the urge to look down at his wrist again.

Akiko addressed his companion, sliding a handful of glass vials across the table. Each was stoppered with a piece of cork and filled with a precise amount of opaque, yellowed liquid.

Both the fyrdwisa and Lucilla blinked: *A glamour serum*, he heard the witch think.

"Is that what we think it is?" Collum asked. He leaned forward to get a closer look. Glamour serums weren't entirely unheard of, but he'd never seen one in his nearly two hundred years of life. They were fickle things to make, requiring exact amounts of ingredients and following recipes to the letter. Many a magical being had found itself either vomiting profusely or temporarily stuck with the wrong appearance after failed attempts went awry.

Akiko shot Collum a knowing glance. "If you drink it as instructed, Lucilla, you will be glamoured to temporarily appear as Bridgette would. The cameras and anyone you directly interact with will see Bridgette. Combined with the full glamour Trystane will perform on your eyes, along with how you'll dress, it will be a flawless illusion."

"Temporarily," Trystane piped up from the back.

"Yes, Ard Rialóir, only briefly," the Fairy assured him. "Lucilla, you will portal down as yourself, and you shall wear tinted glasses to cover your eyes. When the flight arrives in Nashville, our plane will land you at the international terminal at the same time a flight from London is scheduled to arrive. That flight, thanks to the work of our ambassador to England, has your names on the manifest as Collin Anderson and, of course, Bridgette Conner. You'll go through customs with those passengers as if you arrived the same way they did. There are luggage tags and passports in your folders. Lucilla, you will drink your first vial of this the moment you de-board the Samnung's plane, do you understand?"

Lucilla nodded, blush-blonde curls bouncing gracefully against her shoulders.

"The rest of the vials will be taken during the schedule in your folder," Akiko continued. "Our goal, as I said, is for Bridgette to be spotted in Nashville. As for the diner, it is *vital* that you stick to the script that we prepared for you. The coworkers Bridgette was closest to will not be scheduled to work on the day you go in. We have assured this to be the case."

Collum felt guilty for a moment. That sounded suspiciously like a job he should have been sent to do, but couldn't, for fear of being outed as a suspect and arrested before this asinine adventure even began.

"You are to walk inside, step to the bar, and ask for Jamie or Wade," the Fairy went on. "They will not be there. Whomever you speak with will tell you this information. You will say the scripted response, take one more wistful look around the restaurant, and leave. You will not dawdle. You will not go off-script, and you will not be inside for more than seven minutes."

The fyrdwisa caught half a disgruntled thought from Lucilla before she pouted out loud. "Do you *really* think Bridgette Conner would go into a restaurant and not eat? How is anyone to believe I am *her* if all I do is pop in and hop back out without so much as ordering an American sandwich?"

It took Collum a moment to process what happened next. One second, Lucilla was preening on her stool and the next, her head was backwards in Trystane's lap, the Elven leader glaring so close to her face that they shared breath.

"You are not going on vacation, Lucilla. You are going to perform a duty on behalf of the Samnung," he snarled. "You are not going to eat sandwiches and flaunt your false beau across the American South. You are going to stick to the script that Geongre Akiko wrote. You are going to take the glamour serum. You are *not* going to do anything to destroy this very delicate balance between the human and magical worlds, or so help me, I will personally ensure you are ousted from your position at Cyneham Breonna and spend the rest of your days as the Bright Star's personal assistant's back-up assistant." His voice was so sickly sweet in its threat that it could have spun a wad of cotton candy.

Collum couldn't bring himself to make eye contact with anything except the window. He couldn't believe Trystane *actually* said that out loud, that the ard rialóir gave such a warning to an Endorsan citizen in front of the queen of Endorsa. But even Nehemi, for once in her life, didn't so much as flinch. She, too, gave a disdainful stare at the young witch, whose heart beat so wildly that Collum was forced to ease the room. The chamber filled with enough soothing scents to run a candle shop, and Trystane shoved Lucilla gently back.

"Do not try me, witch," he warned. The Elf leaned back against the wall and took a long drink. "I am not in the mood."

Lucilla's cheeks were tinted pink with embarrassment. "My apologies, Ceannairí," she whispered, her voice cracking. "I am just trying to be believable as Bridgette, to save the fyrdwisa from being arrested and put in a human prison. I wouldn't be able to bear it if I was the reason he was shackled and shoved into a cage, because I hadn't made a good enough Bridgette."

You will never make a good enough Bridgette, Collum found himself thinking. He continued to stare at the window, willing his eyes to glaze over and his breathing to calm. The tension in the room tightened again.

"Stick to the script I've prepared for you, and you will do fine," Akiko assured her. "No one is getting arrested. Not this trip. So, you'll leave the diner, meet back with Collum, and then you will take a car from Nashville to the little town of Summerville, Georgia."

That certainly got Collum's attention. "That's on the wrong end of the state, Geongre."

Summerville was far northwest Georgia. The Simmonses lived in Madison, about one hundred fifty miles to the southeast.

"So it is, Fyrdwisa. It just so happens that Martha Simmons, and consequently her husband, will be in Summerville touring an eclectic art museum in the area. This is far more convenient to Nashville, and we couldn't have planned the timing better," Akiko replied, quite pleased with how it all shaped up.

Bridgette rarely talked about her foster parents, but Collum knew Joel, affectionately known as Doc, was a psychologist of some variety, and Martha did something with plants. From the way Bridgette spoke of her, driving hours across the state to see eclectic art was quite apropos for the woman.

Collum tuned out the rest of Akiko's instructions. They would all be in the folder for him to delve into later. This would be an easy mission, he hoped. His role wasn't that of spy this time. The hardest part was going to be meeting Bridgette's parents without their foster daughter by his side, where she should be.

He felt his stomach clench at the image that came to his mind.

This may be more difficult than I thought.

~ 27 ~

"What do all these signs mean about 'thickly settled'?"

Lucilla pressed her face against the tinted window of the hired sedan, gazing out as the backroads between Danvers and Beverly, Massachusetts, passed by. The characteristically New England homes, crafted with various colors of painted clapboard, were so close to the road that many years ago, Collum had once been tempted to see if he could reach out a car's window and pick a flower from one of the yards.

"It means there's a lot of humans who live in a small area," he answered her. "The signs are to keep people from driving too fast with so many others about."

"Are the people unable to just hop out of the way?"

The eye roll behind Collum's sunglasses was so exaggerated, he could have seen his skull. Lucilla's first visit to Earth lasted less than a half-hour thus far and they had already been some of the longest minutes of Collum's existence. He pulled his favorite navy blue beanie down further to hide Elven ears. "Lucilla, have you ever met a human?"

"I don't think so, except for our driver." She motioned to the mustachioed man behind the wheel of the car.

"Humans are *human*. They lack the same speed and reaction time of magical beings."

"Oh. So, they wouldn't be able to move?"

"Not if the car was traveling too fast, no."

"Are you telling me I need to move slower, then? To appear human like Bridgette?"

The Elf set his jaw and turned his gaze toward the sedan ceiling. "I do not know what poisoned wine they feed you in Endorsa, but between you, Her Majesty, and occasionally even Ambassadora Vetur all forgetting that Bridgette is not, has never been, and will never be *human*, it is a small miracle all three of you have not awoken to a throat slit by the Bright Star."

Lucilla stared at Collum, mouth agape. "Excuse me, *Fyrdwisa*, but did you just make a threat against the queen of Endorsa? In front of her royal secretary?"

"Why yes, Lucilla, I suppose I did," he smirked, turning his head from the ceiling, tidal pool eyes hidden behind dark lenses. "What are you going to do about it, go home? Tell Her Majesty I spoke aloud a truth she already knows?"

"You can be a really cruel piece of shit when you want to be, Collum."

He scoffed. "You have no idea."

By the time the Samnung's private plane deposited the two of them in Nashville, Collum was tempted to dump Lucilla over a bridge and see what her magic could do to stop him. He crossed a line with the remark against Nehemi; he knew that, but it did not make it any less true of a statement. Collum underestimated Bridgette enough himself, an internal struggle he was loathe to process. But it angered him that those who did not know or appreciate Bridgette like he did tended to forget that just because she was raised on Earth did not make her *human*. She was magic — a purer, deeper magic than most of them could ever dream of being.

Emi-Joye's feelings toward Bridgette he could handle, especially since the Fairy warmed up to her a tad after the traumatizing incident with the True Druids. Lucilla's thoughts, on the other hand, he was unable to be professional about.

Unfortunately, he had been professionally obliged to keep an occasional check on the witch's inner monologue throughout the rest of the drive to the Beverly airport, then again on the plane. He wasn't sure if Lucilla consciously thought horrid things, or if she simply forgot he could hear them if he wanted to.

"Lucilla," Collum murmured as they deboarded the plane and went to join the crowd flying in from London as planned, "I would like to take this moment to remind you that whatever happens between us on this trip is on behalf of the Samnung. I would also like to remind you that I can hear what you are thinking, and I am not above sharing some of your sentiments about the Liluthuaé with those who rule our continent."

She whipped her hair around a shoulder, and the glamour serum worked so well Collum was forced to concentrate to see through it. He slipped an arm over her shoulder. "Welcome to Nashville — again."

"I should have brought my guitar."

Collum blinked. "Bridgette plays the violin."

"Right. That one. I should have brought my violin."

You didn't read a deity-damned word in your script and backstory, did you? Collum thought to her, though he knew she couldn't hear him.

Out loud, he commented, "The documents in that folder from Akiko. You'll read those when we reach our lodging. That is not a request."

"I read them already."

"Not thoroughly enough. Otherwise you'd know what instrument you play, and what instrument you *teach*, for that matter."

Lucilla huffed a response, and the two didn't speak as they made their way through customs. A quick jaunt, as neither one of them packed anything larger than a carry-on, so they didn't have to wait nearly as long as those whose horse-sized suitcases were searched through for potential contraband. Their falsified passports were stamped, Lucilla's featuring Bridgette's driver's license photo, carefully edited by talented Fairies who specialized in human technology that made Collum's head spin. He could use a computer if it was a life-or-death situation, but he felt all of his one hundred ninety-nine years every time he was forced to find the power buttons on those silly machines.

A shining charcoal hatchback waited for him and Lucilla outside the airport. The driver deposited them at their hotel a

short while later, Collum and the witch barely speaking —
although for posterity's sake, at one point he did gingerly tuck a
strand of hair behind her ear and offer a smile that he hoped
looked tender and caring.

His stomach roiled. *I don't think I'll be eating much during this trip.*

Their hotel at least was nice. The one good thing about
Nashville being such a touristy city was that there was an
immense number of places to stay, so though Collum stayed here
multiple times, he'd never been to the same hotel twice. Given
that he was a wanted suspect in Bridgette's supposed
disappearance, this was probably a good thing.

Geongre Akiko picked out a location that was between
Bridgette's university and the bustling, unendingly crowded
downtown area. It was luxe, because the Samnung didn't skimp
on lodging, and thankfully had two beds in the room. Velvet
indigo curtains lined the large window, and plush pillows
coordinated in shades of deep blue, cream, and butter yellow.

Lucilla tossed herself on the bed nearest the bathroom. "This
is nicer than my flat."

*Yes, blue is far more soothing a color than the grimy shade of pink you
insist on decorating with,* Collum thought.

"Some humans do have an eye for design," he said. "I
suppose we should freshen up and go find somewhere to eat. You
may go first."

She sauntered into the bathroom, *oohing* and *ahhing* over the
vast mirror, and Collum promptly shut her mind out as she
turned on the water for the shower. *That* was something he never
wanted to think about, no matter what the Samnung members
asked of him.

While Lucilla showered, Collum took time to peruse the map
of security cameras on the street called Broadway, where most of
Nashville's bars, restaurants, and therefore visitors congregated.
This was an area of the city Collum generally tried to avoid. He
didn't understand the draw — country music fans aside — to an

area so slammed with bodies that it was nigh on impossible to move more than three inches from any given spot without elbowing a fellow patron, especially on the weekends. But given how populous it was, thousands of people would spot the two of them. They'd be seen on camera, effectively showcasing that Bridgette Conner wasn't missing.

Though Collum wanted Lucilla to be seen and mistaken as Bridgette on as many cameras as possible, he wanted to keep his own identity hidden. It was too much of a security risk for Heáhwolcen to have him parading around Nashville while suspected of a crime. Now, his usual haunt, which he discovered upon first venturing into the metropolitan part of Nashville? The bartenders there knew him by his false name, Collin Anderson, and by aesthetic. He was careful never to show his eyes or ears. In a city fraught with so many musical celebrities who didn't like being spotted, such behavior wasn't that abnormal.

The place was called Red Betty's, and it was just enough outside of town that most tourists rarely ventured to it. With warm yellow lighting, a burgundy carpeted stage and talented musicians that played something besides the required downtown "gig list" that could be heard echoing down Broadway, Red Betty's was as close to enjoying a bar as Collum could remember.

But he wouldn't take Lucilla there. He wouldn't take her to any of the little gems he discovered while he secretly followed Bridgette around, learning her ways and determining the best time to approach her and share with the Elfling that she was, in fact, not nearly as human as she'd been led to believe. When Collum found somewhere important to him, it wasn't a space he cared to share with just anyone.

"How do I look?" Lucilla emerged from the shower, wet hair braided over one shoulder despite it being chilly outside. She wore an outfit that was so unlike *anything* Bridgette would ever put on her body that Collum fought the cringe threatening to form on his lips.

"It's very … shiny," he commented.

She wore a fluffy sheepskin coat that hit mid-thigh, dyed a muted shade of purple, and a fitted white silk slip-dress that sparkled when the light hit it. It draped over her ample bosom — a physical characteristic that no amount of glamour serum alone could minimize and make more Bridgette-like — and curved seductively around Lucilla's hips. Had Collum not known precisely who Lucilla was, he supposed he would have found this an attractive-enough outfit, although the added accessories of white leather cowboy boots were too chintzy for him to appreciate.

"Well, *I* like it," she countered. "My dear friend Luthus, who is one of the travel deputies, showed me images of what humans wear and helped a sewist design it."

"I'm certainly glad you were able to spell your luggage to get that coat to fit inside it," Collum muttered. "You'll be hard to miss on the cameras."

Lucilla smiled dreamily. "What are you going to wear?"

He looked down at his dark blue chambray shirt, sleeves rolled up just past the elbows, and the black leather pants that clung to his legs. His only human shoes, a pair of navy blue high-top Chucks, were tucked underneath their hem.

"Um, this."

"You *always* wear things like that, Collum. You really should live a little, you know. How often do you get a night out in a city that's so exciting?"

"More often than you think, and it's usually not by choice," he said as he thrust the folder toward her. "Here. Read this, not just skim it, while I go remove the travel grime from my face. I do detest airports."

~ 28 ~

"This has to be the most beautiful place on Earth!" Lucilla squealed. She twirled on the sidewalk, almost slapping a passerby in the hip with the ridiculous see-through square handbag she just bought from the hotel gift shop.

"Sure," Collum said. He reached an arm out and pulled her close, looking to anyone who walked by like nothing more than a charming, aloof beau with a strawberry blonde beauty on one arm. The gesture was intentional: Lucilla was going to hit someone with that plasticene monstrosity if he didn't rein her in.

She leaned against his shoulder. "I could get used to this, you know."

"Your wet hair is very cold."

"You're so sweet to me, Collin," she crooned, using his human name. "Where are you taking me to dinner?"

"Is there a particular meal you are in the mood for?" He scanned the road in front of them, humming with the sounds of nightlife and sights of women in matching T-shirts, even though it was barely dusk. "There are, as you can see, quite a number of options."

They walked a few minutes until Lucilla pulled away and pointed at an industrial-looking building on the next corner, its dark brick the color of oxblood, purple stage lights dancing through the windows from every angle. "Is that a restaurant? That looks fun!"

"'The White Tank Top'," Collum read the sign. "I'm not sure, but let's find out."

It was a restaurant, with fairly expected Southern American dishes and bar food like barbeque and burgers on the menu, but even Collum had to admit the concept of a "beer can chicken" intrigued him enough to give the place a try. Not surprisingly, like most of the bars on Broadway, it was owned by a popular country music star who was known to visit and sometimes even take the small stage when he wasn't on tour.

That night's live music was a full band. As it was still early, the volume stayed low, making for pleasant background noise for those enjoying dinner inside.

"This music is catchy," Lucilla observed, tapping her foot to the wrong beat. She sipped her cocktail, some fruity concoction that included tequila, strawberries, and rose syrup. "And this drink is *delicious*."

Perhaps I will open an American-style restaurant in Endorsa when I leave Her Majesty's service, the witch thought. *We have nothing like this, and it would be so delightful!*

Collum didn't know if he was supposed to have heard her or not, but he offered a genuine grin across the table. "I believe you would have quite a draw. It would be a nice compromise between the atmosphere of our other well-known establishments."

"Precisely," Lucilla chattered. "Evenshade is one of my favorite places, but if I would like to go enjoy a drink and dinner, it is not the right spot. Neither is Taberna Körtz; it's so dingy inside and old. And so few restaurants in Endorsa have music!"

The Elf raised a brow, eyes revealed now since it was too dim in The White Tank Top for anyone to see the opalescent flecks in his irises. "They used to. Everything changed when — well, you know."

She fingered the end of her braid. "I was only a youngling when that happened, but I remember it. Seeing Queen Nehemi be crowned was one of the defining moments of my life, and I knew I wanted one day to serve someone as great as she. I don't think I truly understood then *why* she was being crowned. My parents didn't tell me what happened to King Hermann and Queen Lalora, but Nehemi was only ten years older than I when she took the throne. I saw in her such grace and power, and I wanted to be like her."

"What do you mean, 'like her'?" Collum asked. He sipped

his bourbon, curious as to what the witch saw in Nehemi that no one else did — or perhaps what everyone else saw that Lucilla refused to.

"The queen speaks, and everyone listens," Lucilla replied earnestly. "Her word is *law*."

He cocked his head to one side. "Yes, that is generally what happens when one is a queen."

She scowled. "Not all of us are blessed to be born with Artur Cromwell's blood in our veins, but we still shouldn't just be ignored or belittled."

"Lu — Bridgette, people don't ignore you. The Samnung would find it difficult to function were it not for you, or whichever being held your position. You're equally historian and librarian, recordkeeper and gatekeeper."

"Do you really think that?"

Exasperated, Collum shook his head. "Yes, of course. When I was fyrdestre, and in the years being fyrdwisa before you came to be the royal secretary, your predecessors were all heavily relied upon, just as you are now."

What annoys us is your insatiable, unsolicited solicitation of my affections, and your penchant for the color pink, he thought to himself.

"Well. That's an unexpected compliment."

Collum was spared the need for an immediate response as their food arrived, and Lucilla reached for her first taste of American food. It was a brisket sandwich, the slow-cooked, melt-in-her-mouth tendrils of beef accompanied by peppered cheese and spicy slaw, heat tampered thanks to a sweet whiskey-based barbeque sauce. The lightly toasted bun crunched as she bit into it.

"Holy gods," she gasped through the mouthful. "This is the most amazing food I've ever eaten."

It was hilarious, the more Collum thought about it, how Bridgette and Lucilla both thought the native foodstuffs from each other's home worlds were the best things they'd ever eaten.

"I'm glad you're enjoying yourself," he said. "I've picked out a few places for us to stop by — one this evening after dinner, and two tomorrow night when we return from meeting the Simmonses. I hope that will fill your desire to enjoy your visit."

"Only one tonight?"

Deity bless, how is pouting her primary expression?

"Yes," Collum replied. "We've got to be 'human' fairly early in the morning for you to pop in the diner, and I would prefer both of us have our wits about ourselves."

They spent time after dinner walking Broadway, Collum carefully navigating them toward as many security cameras as he could remember the locations of, before ending up at a bar with the exterior as purple as Lucilla's fluffy coat.

"Oh, my *stars!*" the witch exclaimed. She pulled Collum through the door by the cuff of his shirtsleeve. "Would you just look at this place!"

"This place" was so crowded that Collum put up a barely perceptible barrier of air around the two of them, just so they could have a few extra inches of breathing room. There was a live band here too, and a slim walkway between a wall covered with yellowed signed photographs and a bar with an extensive number of taps. He grabbed Lucilla's hand and led her to one of the open spaces at the bar, then shouted two beer orders at whichever bartender was able to hear him. A woman with a crop top, black jeans and neon orange ponytail leaned over and took the cash he proffered, then returned with a domestic lager and a bright pink sour in respective pint glasses.

"Here you go," the Elf said, handing the sour to Lucilla, whose eyes lit up with glee. "I assumed, based on what you enjoy drinking that is not beer, that this would fit your palate."

"This is beer?"

"Yes, a variety known as a sour ale. This one also has some sort of fruit component, hence that color."

Lucilla shook her head in wonder. "Humans are truly

amazing creatures."

"Maybe don't say that out loud?"

She laughed and guided him toward the band, where some of the crowd made enough room to dance near the stage. Between her glamour serum, his bourbon at dinner, and the beer he probably shouldn't have just bought, the witch looked too much like Bridgette — despite the height difference, which was more noticeable in her low-heeled boots than it would be tomorrow in long pants and tall shoes. Collum felt disoriented.

For the sake of the Samnung, he allowed himself to play nice, to twirl her around on the dance floor, though *diety fucking bless* Lucilla couldn't stay on beat if the drummer hit her over the head with a drumstick. He smiled and pretended, keeping a wary sort of mental awareness out. They hadn't discussed what should happen if anyone was to recognize her as Bridgette, though Collum knew he'd be able to hear the person's thoughts if someone approached.

As the night wore on and Lucilla neared the end of her third sour beer — she claimed she was on a mission to try all such flavors that this bar had available — Collum decided it was time to return to their hotel. He leaned into Lucilla's ear to share this with her, as it was now too loud to do anything but yell at one another, and she swallowed the last bit in her glass.

"I want to come back here tomorrow!" she cried to him above the din. "It's like Evenshade!"

It really wasn't. A honky-tonk bar with cowboy boots and denim-clad dancers was a far cry from the ground-shaking, electrifying bass and neon witchlight of the Endorsan venue. But he supposed he understood what she meant, in terms of it being a place she enjoyed going for a night out.

"We can come back," he promised. "And perhaps you should consider taking some time away from Endorsa to travel here on your own time and terms, without the itinerary of the Samnung guiding you."

"That's an idea," Lucilla slurred, and there was a flash of too-pink in her hair.

The glamour serum must be wearing down, Collum realized.

"It is an idea indeed," he said. "We should walk a few blocks, past the camera on this street, and then I'll evanesce us closer to the hotel. Your serum is wearing off."

"Mmmkay," she grinned, and looped an arm through his. "You can come with me when I come back. I need a tour guide, you know."

"Though I appreciate your invitation, and your confidence in my ability to guide you, I believe your friend Luthus or Geongre Akiko can set you up with a local resident who will be far more adept that I could ever be," Collum replied. "I am too used to coming to Earth, and Nashville in particular, for required purposes. I'd be more burden to your carefree trip than you would like."

She scowled. "You just don't want to come because I'm not Bridgette."

"I don't think Bridgette wants to come back either, frankly," he said. "The reaction you've had to this city is so similar to hers when she experiences new things in Heáhwolcen. She would come back for the Simmonses, I think, but not to live here. Not anymore."

He glanced down at their covenant bracelet, its silver beads glinting in the yellow of the streetlights, and hoped what he said was true.

~ 29 ~

Though Collum awoke the next morning anxious about Lucilla going off-script at the diner, he was pleasantly surprised the encounter went off without a hitch. The two were shortly on the highway from Tennessee into Georgia.

He made the witch try on three different pairs of platform shoes before they found ones that made her close enough to Bridgette's height, and then she spent twenty minutes pacing the hotel hallway, ensuring she could walk in them without tripping over the hem of her flared jeans.

"I want you to have every detail of this memorized by the time we get out of this car," Collum murmured to her. "The Simmonses know Bridgette better than anyone else on Earth, and they're going to be the ones to call us out if we muck it up in the slightest."

"You're really nervous I can't do this, aren't you?" Lucilla replied, halfheartedly flipping open the folder again. "I'm not dumb, Collum."

"No, you're not, but being smart and being able to disguise yourself effectively as the Bright Star, in front of the closest thing she has to parents, are two different scenarios," he said. "I spent months studying Bridgette, but no time at all with any of her foster parents. Tracing who she might be, before we knew she was Bridgette Conner, was difficult. All I had to go on was her last name. Mohreen hadn't told any of the Samnung what her first name was, nor any identifying characteristics. I only knew the year Bridgette was born because —" He stopped himself, cringing. "Because I was privy to that information, having been Mohreen's contact before she disappeared. In truth, Lucilla, most of that first year going back and forth to find her was tracking records in courthouses all over Georgia."

"I assumed you'd watched them."

Collum disliked how she and Bridgette made him sound like

a stalker every time they mentioned his tracking down the Liluthuaé. "No. I know their home address, but by the time I learned that information, Bridgette was already in her final year of college and no longer lived with them. It would not have made sense for me to visit them when I knew where she resided, so I recorded that information for my Samnung reports and moved on with my task."

"Collum." Lucilla turned to face him, glamoured eyes wide. "Neither one of us knows what these humans look like. But they are going to recognize *me*."

"And you are going to catch their eyes, and run up to hug them, while I smile and walk behind you," he said calmly. "We are going to be fine."

I hope.

"You're the young man who took my daughter away from us, then?"

Collum didn't know what he expected Joel Simmons to look like, but for someone who was nicknamed "Doc", it certainly hadn't been the imposing, burly man who looked as though he could deadlift a dragon.

I think his bicep is the size of my head, Lucilla thought to the fyrdwisa.

They stood with Bridgette's foster parents in front of a Summerville, Georgia, barbeque restaurant. Joel and Martha had wrapped Lucilla up in a giant bear hug upon seeing her, but the man now stepped away, facing Collum man-to-male.

Collum gulped. "I can certainly see why it's come across that way, and part of the reason I wanted to join Bridgette was to apologize in person for the misunderstanding."

He put a protective arm around Lucilla, reclaiming her from Martha's grasp, and the air filled with delicate scents as the Elf suffused the tension with his spellcasting abilities. "It would have been helpful, perhaps, if Bridgette had been more upfront with me about what she shared with you. For that, we are both sorry."

There was a brief moment where Collum thought everything was about to go awry, but then Martha elbowed her husband in the ribs and reached again for Lucilla.

"Oh, Bridgie! We're so glad you're okay. Y'all have no idea what this has been like, trying to find you. It was like you'd fallen off the face of the planet," she exclaimed, taking both of Lucilla's hands in hers. "We have been so worried."

The poor witch was frozen. "I'm — I'm really sorry, Martha."

Her voice in that moment was so close to Bridgette's, thanks to a higher dose of the glamour serum for the day, that Collum felt his chest cleave in agony. The voice wasn't quite perfect, but it was close enough that if he wasn't able to replay Bridgette's taunts and teasing over and over inside his head, he would have found himself doing a double take.

Something about the Elf's eyes changed, and his emotional gaze caught Joel's attention. Collum felt the man's energy toward him warm. Not much, but enough that it was a tangible shift in the tension.

"Y'all gave us quite the scare," Joel said. "But I reckon that's not any reason to bust your chops when we don't hardly know you. I'm Joel. You can call me Doc though, if you want. Most people do."

"Thank you, Doc," Collum said. He reached a hand toward the man. "I'm Collin Anderson. Bridgette talks about you all the time, and it's my pleasure to finally meet you. I am sorry we didn't do this sooner."

Martha, who hadn't let go of Lucilla, gave him a cautious smile. "Collin, I'm Martha, but you probably figured that out already. We appreciate y'all coming back all this way just to have lunch with us. How funny that the time worked perfectly for us to already be up this way the same time y'all were flying in!"

Lucilla laughed and squeezed Martha around the middle. "I

mean, I had to explain to everyone at school that I wasn't missing either," the witch said. "So, we kind of had to go to Nashville."

Good, Collum thought, wishing Lucilla could hear him. *She actually listened when I coached her about the way Bridgette talks compared to most of magickind.*

"Well, I can't wait to hear all about your recent adventures, babygirl. Let's go have a seat and y'all can tell us everything!" Martha smiled and led the other three through the door, where the smell of smoked pork hit Collum so hard his mouth watered instantaneously.

The four small-talked until their food arrived, and between bites of melted macaroni 'n' cheese, salted green beans, and massive barbeque sandwiches with various toppings, Collum did most of the talking about what he and "Bridgette" had been up to.

"I — and I know this sounds creepy, so I am sorry! — saw her at the diner once, through the window. I came in and just had to know her name," Collum said. "However, my nerves got the best of me, I must admit. I sat at the bar drinking coffee, watching her work, but I couldn't drum up the courage to say anything to her then. I did introduce myself a few days later, and I invited her to come with me on a trip over her spring break. Perhaps it was a crazy thing to do, but I couldn't help myself."

He is just *beautiful. No wonder Bridgie is head over heels for him,* Martha thought, sighing audibly. It was such an unexpected thing for Collum to overhear that the Elf actually blushed.

"It's like he put some sort of magic spell over me," Lucilla piped up, and Collum resisted the urge to kick her under the table. "It *was* a crazy thing to do, but we did it, and then we got into a fight about it —"

"And she returned to Nashville, and I went back to my home country," he interrupted. "Imagine my surprise when she reached out a few months later and asked if she could visit, and we could try again. This time it stuck, I suppose, although it would have been nice to know she had not been truthful to her school or to you about where she went and who she was with. I didn't realize she wasn't in touch with you regularly, either, though where I live is fairly rural and hard to get reliable communication service."

"Well — I didn't think I'd be allowed to go, so I thought maybe it was better to ask forgiveness than permission," Lucilla rushed out. "Then I got scared about saying anything, so I lied a little. It wasn't smart of me to do and I'm really sorry."

Collum sincerely wished they had rehearsed this part a bit better, but Martha and Doc didn't argue with Lucilla. Instead, they looked at each other, and Martha gave her husband a secret smile.

"Do you want to tell her or should I?" the woman asked.

"Tell me what?" Lucilla said, brows raising. Collum put a comforting hand on her shoulder, wondering what in the seven hells he would have to one day tell the real Bridgette, since this news that he could not detect was about to be revealed to her doppelganger.

Martha's eyes squinted as she gave the biggest, somewhat nervous, smile Collum had seen on anyone in quite some time. "Well, babygirl, Doc and I have been doing a lot of thinking while you've been gone. It's been real hard, you going off to college and only coming home for the holidays and maybe your birthday, and then these past few months we thought we'd *really* lost you. When you sent us that email, it was like a miracle. We'd had the police go and look for y'all, and your sweet friend at the diner, Jamie, was keeping the cops on their toes about the whole thing.

"I knew then that we had to do something," Martha continued, and the smile got bigger. "I looked right at Doc when that email came through and I told him we weren't dancing around this anymore. We know you didn't have the best things happen to you when you were little, and when we got you, you were *so* scared. We were scared too, you know — we'd never had a daughter before, but from the moment you first walked through our door, we never looked back. You were ours and we couldn't see it any other way."

Martha reached behind her in the booth for her purse and pulled out a manila envelope. "I know it's a few days late because we didn't see you on your birthday, babygirl, but we — and we understand if you want to keep your birth name but —"

She shoved the envelope into Lucilla's hands and Collum wanted to scream. He wanted to pull them out of that restaurant and evanesce far, far away. He knew now what was in that envelope. He could see it in Martha's eyes before Lucilla pulled the official-looking documents out. He read the title line, his heart pounding so loud the Simmonses could probably hear it.

Out of all the moments Bridgette should have had in her life, out of all the opportunities she missed because of her biological mother, this one would shatter her. It shattered Collum on her behalf, sitting there seeing Lucilla's eyes widen as she took in the enormity of what had been given to her.

They were adult adoption papers.

And a purple ink pen.

"Martha —" Lucilla gasped out. "I don't — I don't know what to say —"

For the love of every god of human and magickind, please do not sign that document, Collum mentally begged the witch, praying to whatever deity Lucilla believed in to intervene, to make this stop. *Please, please Lucilla. Please do not take this moment from Bridgette. I beg you not to do this. I will let you bed me if that is what you want. Whatever you want. Just please, please Lucilla. Do not break my Starshine.*

The restaurant had gone cold. Lucilla looked at Bridgette's foster parents. She stared, mouth agape, and Collum could not hear her inner monologue. It was as if Lucilla truly didn't know how to react. The Elf's heart was in his throat.

If he spoke, he might crack.

"Can I get y'all some more sweet tea? I'm so sorry to interrupt!" Their server came out of nowhere, brandishing an amber-colored pitcher. Collum could have kissed the man.

Glassware shuffled on the table. As the temperature of the room returned to normal, Doc spoke up.

"We know this is probably a surprise, because we should have done it years ago, Bridgie," he said, his deep voice a little choked. "You don't have to sign it now, but just know that we are gonna hold onto these at the house, and the pen, right here in this envelope. We're gonna keep it at the house, okay? And if you decide you want to sign them, if you want *us*, you got us, kiddo. We love you, you understand? Always have. Always will. This little paper just puts some icing on the cake."

"Thank you," Lucilla whispered. "I — that means a lot."

She gulped heavily and slipped the papers back inside the envelope. "This is just so unexpected. A good unexpected. I want some time to think about what it means? If that's acceptable? And I will let you know."

Martha nodded, her smile faltering a bit, and Doc chuckled. "Of course it's 'acceptable'. Look at you talking like you've never been to the South before. But we love you, even if you're starting to sound like some kinda British tea party attendee."

Collum did kick Lucilla under the table, and thankfully she picked up on the implication.

"I love you both too," she said, which caused the Elf to groan inwardly at the lack of the word "y'all" in that sentence.

"Happy birthday, babygirl," Martha said. She reached over the empty plates to squeeze Lucilla's hand. "We know y'all ought to be heading back so you aren't driving at night when all the deer are out, but it was so good to see you. And to meet you, Collin. Let us know when you make it back, and when you're able to visit again?"

"Yes ma'am," Collum answered for them both, and the

woman giggled at his manners.

She smiled at him. "You can come see us by yourself, even if Bridgie doesn't want to."

~ 30 ~

They said their goodbyes in the parking lot, tearful hugs on Martha's end as she hugged them both tightly, and then the four went their separate ways. The Elf and the witch watched as the Simmonses pulled out in their car, headed back toward the art museum. It turned out Martha was touring the grounds as a potential curator of its new seasonal landscape installations, an opportunity she was quite excited about. The artist was known for his religious-inspired works, and Martha planned to design gardens that utilized specific flora mentioned in human spiritual texts.

She seems quite the eccentric, yet loving woman, Collum thought, his heart still threatening to beat out of his chest. *As for her husband …*

He couldn't quite get a read on the man. Doc was a large presence, both in physical size and in energy. Doc was largely quiet, reserved, and observant — he tried very hard to accept "Bridgette's" story, but suspected the two were not entirely truthful — and it was evident how protective he was over the real Bridgette.

Collum was grateful neither husband nor wife had any idea, at least from what he gleaned from their inner monologues, that Lucilla wasn't the daughter they thought they were proposing adoption to. A part of him worried that Martha and her husband would turn their car around to bring the papers back and brandish the pen in Lucilla's face, begging her to sign them and make Bridgette officially their daughter. It killed him to see their faces, shining with excitement and hope, dim when Lucilla did not touch the pen except to put it back in the envelope.

The Elf knew, without a shadow of a doubt, that Bridgette would have signed those papers in an instant. He just wasn't sure if the signature would happen before or after Bridgette leapt across the table to hug her two parents. That's what the Simmonses were, after all, regardless of the legalities.

"When was Bridgette's birthday?" Lucilla asked, breaking Collum's reflective silence.

"October first."

She didn't reply. He turned to face her. "Thank you, for not signing those papers."

The witch scoffed. "I would have, you know. But I don't know what her signature looks like, and I thought Doc and Martha would be able to tell it was different. Consider it me not taking the risk you seem to believe I am destined to take."

It wasn't the response he expected, nor wanted. For her to have the gall to even think about signing them! Collum set his jaw and opened the car door for her. "Lucilla, whether or not you know what her signature looks like, that is not a decision you get to make for Bridgette."

"Aww," she crooned, and reached a hand for his face. "Does it make you mad when I get too into my role?"

He slapped her hand away. "Do not touch me."

The two rode back to Nashville without another word.

That night, for their second visit to the purple-colored bar, Collum paid no attention to what Lucilla wore. He didn't care. He knew she hadn't heard his promise to let her do whatever she wanted if it meant she wouldn't sign those papers, but the way she reached for his jaw made him wonder if the Universe and spirits were toying with him over a vow he hadn't meant to make.

He was stony-faced as the two meandered onto the sidewalk. Collum forced himself to keep his gaze down so the cameras would only pick up a male figure that vaguely matched the description of the "mysterious stranger" who allegedly kidnapped Bridgette. Collum knew the Simmonses would call off the missing person's search soon if they hadn't already. Now that the Fairies, through whatever means, had access to Bridgette's channels of electronic communication, he knew too that they would sort out the issues with her university, withdrawing her from classes and whatnot. He wondered if, when Bridgette returned, she would go back to Nashville to finish her last handful of classes and attend graduation.

He wondered too if she ever came to this bar. He doubted it. Bridgette liked to read and paint, and while she loved the Ostara celebration she attended in Heáhwolcen, he knew crowds sometimes made her edgy. With his suspicions regarding Bridgette and Maylemaegus, he assumed the edginess had something to do with her connection to Universal consciousness and reacting to so many energies.

Even when she thought she was human, a place like this bar would not have been her first choice. Where they *should* have gone, Collum groaned inwardly, was to her apartment complex to break her lease, in the event that had not already happened —

Dammit, he thought. *We still have so many loose ends. I will make a note of this one in my report and discuss if we can pay that fee and send someone to collect her things …*

The image made him grin. The last time a magical being portaled their entire existence from Earth to Heáhwolcen was approximately the time of the Ingefeoht. It would have been the last of those traveling to Palna to learn Craft Wizardry. Bridgette would appreciate the bit of irony.

Inside, the purple bar was even more crowded than the previous evening, and Collum again spelled a boundary of air around himself and Lucilla. He ordered a non-alcoholic drink from the orange-haired bartender, remembering at the last second to call it "soda" instead of "carbonated syrup water".

"Your friend's got pretty eyes!" the bartender said, scooting the soda and Lucilla's beer toward him. "So do you. I'd write a song about them if anybody in this damn town would let me play something that wasn't country music."

"What music do you play?" he asked.

The bartender glanced down at his navy Chucks. "Music

you'd probably like." She winked and turned away to help another customer.

He shook his head, grinning, and wished again that Bridgette was here with him. The Elfling would like this woman quite a lot.

"I'll get the next round!" Lucilla yelled at him a while later. Yelling to be heard over the band du jour, which played songs Collum remembered from the night before, though the band wasn't the same. This one had a lead singer who was off-key just enough to bother him, and the Elf managed to catch the bartender's eye a couple times as he twirled Lucilla. Judging by her eyeroll and inner thoughts, the bartender too was ready to pull the plug on the microphone.

Collum let Lucilla dart off to the bar while he did a cursory scan of the crowd, listening in again to hear if anyone thought they recognized the strawberry blonde with sparkling lilac eyes. Just as the previous evening, no one had. Collum sipped the soda Lucilla handed him as she danced back into the melee. He turned his lip up at the flavor.

"It's too sweet," he called out. "What did you get me?"

She shrugged. "The same one you got last time is what I asked for."

He took another sip. *Either the carbonation to syrup ratio is off-kilter, or they poured from the variety containing artificial sweetener. This is revolting, either way.*

The two danced a while longer, and despite his attempts to suck it up and drink the ill-flavored soda, Collum couldn't deal with either the drink or the off-key singer for another moment. His stomach was on the verge of rejecting the beverage, and he excused himself to forge a path to the bathroom. Lucilla waved him off, dancing alone with another brightly colored sour ale in one hand.

Collum leaned against the sticky door of the bathroom stall. It was covered with signatures in permanent ink, marks made by human males who used the metal as a writing board for appalling quotations, distasteful jokes, and canvases to draw their own genitalia.

Hecate fucking bless, humans can be such filth sometimes, he thought, though he knew magickind had its fair share of beings who acted in poor taste, too. *I want to shower the entirety of this bar off of me.*

His eyes opened, but he didn't recall closing them. The room wouldn't come into full focus, and Collum rubbed his eyes, confused. He didn't know how long he'd been in the bathroom, but supposed he should find Lucilla. His stomach was still in knots, and going back to the hotel seemed a smart plan.

Strange, flickering lights haunted Collum's dream. They were the same sort of springy pastels and muted earthtones he saw during his recent meditation after prematurely exiting that Samnung meeting. He couldn't see, but he was aware of the lights, so was he even dreaming? The lightplay blinded him, yet he felt her there. He could have sworn that flash of rosegold was a brush of her hair across his cheek, the blink of lilac her eyes closing behind velvet lids. He murmured her name, but no sound came out. She became more corporeal. Soft caresses and playful nips along his jaw, his neck; her hand resting on his chest. He was here in this dream-space with her and she felt so real. He didn't remember falling asleep, didn't remember walking back, but did any of that matter? Collum liked this dream and would rather remain in it, even if he was quite aware it was all in his head.

That hand on his chest lazily made its way lower. He wanted to sink deeper into this dream. He breathed her in, expecting honeysuckle and vanilla, but —

The fyrdwisa woke with a start and shoved Lucilla off of him.

Tried to, anyway: the problem with her being a witch was that she pinned him to the bed with magic.

"Fucking seven hells, you bitch!" he spat, but his mouth wasn't moving, and he still couldn't see. She'd bound him, gagged him with magic, and it suddenly made too much sense why his soda was sweet enough to make him want to throw it right back up.

Collum Andoralain could not move a muscle because she poisoned him into stillness, then amplified its effects with a binding spell he couldn't break without being able to move his hands. He struggled to breathe and the air that should have smelled like vanilla and honeysuckle reeked of lust and envy and his own anger. He was really and truly trapped.

"Do you know how long I've waited for this moment?" Lucilla murmured in an exact replica of Bridgette's voice — *deity fucking bless, she used the last of the glamour serum for this* — "Your fyrdestre ruined it for us that night at Evenshade, but I'm not dumb, Collum. I know what you want. You hide it, but you're still a male who has *needs*."

Her hand dipped lower until it was mere millimeters from touching him in a place where her hand very much did not belong.

"I wish it was *me* you wanted, of course, and not that humanoid Elfling you claim to care so little about," Lucilla went on, moving her hand and making Collum's insides squirm in exactly the opposite way of what she desired from him. "I wish you wanted *this* without me looking like her clone."

Her mouth hovered too close to his, and those damn lights in his eyes! He felt her breath trace his lips, smelled the sour honey of Lucilla's jealous words as if they too were coated in poison.

Make this stop! Collum begged inwardly. *End this. End this!*

His mind and spirit writhed furiously within the intangible bindings, heart beating wildly. He tried to become aware of his own limbs, but it was as if he was spirit alone, his body no longer part of him. For a fleeting moment, Collum lived an experience akin to Bridgette's when she first tapped into Universal consciousness and left her body on the ground below.

Bridgette.

He saw her face, saw her eyes and messy hair and oversized human T-shirts, her ratty cowboy boots and her mischievous grin, and hated with every sinew of his being the witch who now impersonated her, whose voice stole hers. For half a heartbeat, he thought his body twitched back into place.

The lights in his vision began flashing too violently to be part of the spell or an effect of the poison. Collum yelled inside his head, loud enough that he would have shattered Lucilla's eardrum had he not been gagged. He was no longer aware of what Lucilla said to him and where her hands were on his body.

You will pay for this! he shouted to her in his mind, willing *anyone* to listen to his voice in this darkness. He thought of Bridgette, of Aurelias and Trystane and for deity's sake, even Emi-Joye, and Apostine, Cloa and that stupid cat. How they would all make the witch pay for this!

The lights in his vision blinked emerald green.

You're dead, he thought, screaming at Lucilla without being able to scream. He had never before wished death upon anyone. Though he knew how, Collum never killed anyone, either. *You're the exception to the rule.*

His vision went black, then icy blue.

You abused your magic. You've committed an act of cruelty.

The lights became an angry shade of electric violet, and the voice inside his mind was no longer his.

We're going to fucking kill you, and we're going to fucking like it.

Collum's head throbbed, and there was a loud *thud* as his magic broke free and flung Lucilla against the wall. She shouted, her head slamming into the paneling, and Collum resisted the urge to roar as he saw Bridgette's form before him, crumpling prostate in pain. But this wasn't Bridgette, and he leapt over the bed before he even fully comprehended what was happening as his vision and senses soared back into his body.

He didn't care that he was naked and coated in a sheen of feverish sweat as he held the dagger to a whimpering Lucilla's heaving throat. He didn't care what she saw or had seen of him; a body was a body, and right now, his was a tool of life-altering action.

"Touch me again, Lucilla Von Detton, and it will be the last time you move," he hissed, the quiet threat a spell of promise. "Do you understand me?"

She nodded, eyes wide and terrified.

Collum jerked away, disgusted, and glanced at the knife in his hand.

The silver-bladed dagger with an amethyst-jeweled hilt. He stared at the weapon.

Holy shit. This is — how —

He felt his wrist burn as the silver beads on his covenant bracelet began to glow with heated fury.

~ 31 ~

"What the *fuck!*" Bridgette exclaimed, jumping out of bed. She fumbled to light the oil lamp, but there was already a source of light in the room.

The Elfling stared at her wrist, where gleaming silver beads cast an eerie glow, and her skin felt like it was on fire. She hissed and batted at the covenant bracelet.

"How the hell do you turn off?! Why did you go on? You don't work for almost two months, and suddenly at some unholy hour in the night *now* you decide to activate?"

Bridgette crept from her room, arm stinging, and tiptoed to the bathroom to splash cold water onto the fire. *For fuck's sake, stop burning!*

She was about to pull milk from the icebox and give that a try when, as quickly as the burning began, the beads went cold as ice and her arm throbbed in relief. Bridgette sagged against the bathroom counter, leaning her head into the sink. First the stupid protected lands injury, which she had to keep covered up to avoid unwanted questions, since the spidery veins of deep purple blood seemed a permanent accessory, and now *this?* She rubbed her hand over the bracelet, the skin around it raw, and wondered what sort of a mark it would leave in the morning.

There was no telling what time it was — somewhere between very late and far too early — and Bridgette knew going back to sleep was a fruitless exercise. She wasn't even sure what woke her, or rather, what caused her covenant bracelet to burn. Not that she was fully versed in communication magic, but she never heard of that happening before.

I wonder if Collum did something on his end to try to wake it up, something more than just touching it like he does with all his other ones, but the Ballamúr blocked the magic? Or the two magics kind of fought with each other and somehow my fucking arm got caught up in it?

She returned to her room, lit the oil lamp, and scowled at the raised marks the beads left. Tiny too-red welts pilled up on her fair skin.

Dammit.

Her mind raced in several directions, and she didn't know which path to chase. If she had her violin, she'd play it to have something to focus all of her senses on. But her violin was abandoned at her apartment in Nashville, an entire world away. Two worlds, really, given that she'd have to get out of Palna to get anywhere near Earth.

She did have her little notebook though, and maybe writing another secret report to the Samnung would help. It couldn't hurt, and it would be a better use of her time than lying against the fluffy pillows, unable to doze off and staring at the window until sunrise.

Bridgette flipped to a random page and, in cramped handwriting, recorded what she remembered about the bracelet activating. She was about halfway through a sentence about her being asleep, and it therefore being impossible for *her* to have activated the communication channel, when she stopped writing and nearly dropped her pencil.

Oh holy shit. What if my subconscious tapped into Universal consciousness?

The light from the oil lamp flickered against her bedroom wall.

How is that possible? I can barely tap into it when I'm awake, she thought. Bridgette stared at the unfinished sentence. She swapped her gaze to her throbbing new wrist injury, wondering if Collum now sported a matching set of wounds.

She closed the notebook and shook her head at herself. *You're such a hopeless romantic, Conner. So emo. Get a damn grip.*

But still. She wondered about it as she tried to drift back to sleep.

Hours later, Toby woke her like normal with a cup of tea and a soft knock at her door. He was surprised to step in and find the Elfling already sitting up, staring off into space, her oil lamp long-burning.

"Something's wrong," the boy said. He handed the cup and saucer to Bridgette. "You're supposed to still be asleep."

She reached one hand for the saucer and the other to scruff his hair. "I had a weird dream. Made it kinda hard to go back to sleep afterwards."

"Mumma can make you a tea for that, something to drink at night, if you would like," Toby said. He was stony faced, worried.

You know, Universe, it would be fantastic *if I could have one guy in my life who wasn't hyper-sensitive to my mental health*, Bridgette thought, exasperated, but she grinned despite her agitation.

"Maybe I'll take her up on that tonight. In the meantime, though, caffeine sounds like a great way to start the day."

"My uncle says to tell you to dress warmly," Toby told her. "The first of the frosts is on its way."

"Thanks, Little Lark."

He walked out of the room with one last glance over a shoulder. The boy was not convinced Bridgette only had a strange dream, and she wondered what the air whispered to him. Maybe it knew what haunted her subconscious that she couldn't remember now that she was awake.

It was indeed frigid outside as Bridgette and Zedolph walked to the butchery a short while later, warmed rocks stuck inside the pockets of their jackets. Bridgette borrowed an old woolen coat of Serrabinx's, having not brought a coat to Heáhwolcen, much less to Palna. She shoved her gloved hands deep to absorb as much of the heat as her dainty fingers could handle.

"You're quiet this morning," Zedolph said.

She was. Usually, they spent this time making small talk, Bridgette pestering her host with questions about farming, about his family, his favorite things to cook.

"Sorry," she muttered. "I didn't exactly sleep well."

Zedolph chewed the inside of his cheek. "I was wondering whom I heard."

"I woke you up?"

"It's quite alright, Bridgette. Occasionally people do wake up when they hear things they aren't expecting to in the middle of the night."

She grinned at the jest. "Yeah, I guess you're right."

Bridgette motioned to adjust the thick scarf around her neck and immediately wished she hadn't. Her sweater cuff had gotten caught in the coat sleeve and didn't cover her wrist, leaving the burn marks visible both to the biting November wind and to Zedolph's annoyingly observant gaze.

"What's that?" he barked, grabbing her arm. "Who did this to you?"

His eyes searched hers, and for the first time, Bridgette truly saw them. They were a similar dark, earthy brown to Toby's, not nearly as wise, and without the Elven flecks of opalescence. But Zedolph's eyes were warm and homey. Right now, they were also wide with concern, and Bridgette found herself shrinking involuntarily.

"I don't know," she muttered, hating the semi-lie. "Nobody did it to me, I guess maybe I just had an allergic reaction to the metal in my bracelet or something."

His eyes flashed. "We will cut it off at the butchery."

"NO." She snatched her wrist away. "No, Zedolph. This bracelet is really important to me, okay? I'm not taking it off. It'd be like losing a piece of myself."

"Bridgette, it *hurt* you."

"It's a fucking bracelet, Zedolph."

The butcher bit his tongue as she shoved her hand back in her pocket. "Some say the trees in Forêt Fossile are simply trees."

"Why do you care so much anyways? It's not like I can't work today or anything, I'm just a little tired and not particularly talkative," Bridgette snapped, disconcerted by his metaphor.

"I care, Bridgette, because you are my guest, you are my apprentice, and more than that, I would like to think by now you are my *friend*," Zedolph replied. He didn't look at her, just stared straight into the early morning light, watching his breath hitch in the frigid late November air. "I care because it's something good citizens do. Perhaps you are not used to that."

The Elfling walked a few steps before she could respond.

"No," she said softly. "No, I guess I'm really not."

~ 32 ~

The workload that day at the butchery was light. Soon though, Bridgette, Zedolph, and Muov would switch their focus from daily customers to making all of the specialty cuts available for Lunavidad, the name Palnans gave to the winter solstice, a sacred night for all of magickind.

And an especially sacred night for the Elves, Bridgette remembered, pausing as she cubed an unsold steak at the wooden worktable.

"The Elves celebrated the legend of this Bright Star at Yule during the winter solstice, the longest night of the year, believing Liluthuaé to be amongst the stars and most visible in that deepest of darks," Trystane once told her.

Bridgette wondered if the Ealdaelfen, or even Elves in Palna like Muov, knew the legend of the Liluthuaé. She supposed it was a legend the entire species knew, because of Ceannairí Álfar and Ylda.

"What are you so deep in thought about?"

The Elfling jumped. She didn't realize she'd been so mentally occupied until Zedolph appeared in the doorway, silent as a cat.

"Oh! Uh — actually, I was kind of wondering what all y'all do in Palna for Lunavidad," Bridgette said. "Samhain was so different than how we do Halloween, kind of the human equivalent on Earth, and Lunavidad falls around what a lot of people celebrate as Christmas and sometimes Hanukkah, so I was curious. You know, since we're supposed to be making all of the special meats and stuff."

"I do not know what Christmas and Hanukkah are," Zedolph said, walking into the back room. He ran his wide hands through his sandy brown hair, which was getting nearly long enough to pull back in the same way Paxson wore his.

"Religious holidays," Bridgette replied, hastily reaching for another steak. These were slightly brown from oxidation, but there was little to no waste in the butchery. They would be repurposed into grind, utilized by customers in soups and stews. Apparently, the concept of turning ground beef into cheeseburgers hadn't made it from America to Palna just yet.

"I assumed thusly," the butcher said. He smiled. "Lunavidad is the longest night of the year and holds different meanings. My family honors it with a private ceremony at our hearth at sunset, and then we join the larger village-wide celebration in Xcthonya. There will be entire roasted hogs, which we will be in charge of, and families may bring food to share. There are cauldrons of drinks, special ales, and the largest bonfire we can muster."

"Sounds fun," Bridgette commented.

"Do you celebrate the human holidays you mentioned?"

"Sorta," Bridgette admitted, conjuring up an addendum to her cover story. "My mother was raised celebrating Christmas, so that's what we did. We put up and decorate a tree, give gifts, have special food, that kind of thing. But we aren't really religious, so a lot of the symbolism and whatnot isn't something we ever got into."

Zedolph didn't respond. He continued to watch her turn the oxidized steaks into evenly sized chunks.

They stilled into near silence; the only sound was the delicate noise the knife made as it cut through meat and met wood. He typically watched her when he could, making sure that she was doing the right things, reaching around to correct her hand positioning or show her a new skill. But Bridgette couldn't handle it today, this quiet observance of her every move, and she felt Zedolph's gaze more intensely than usual. His concern bothered her.

Maybe what bothered her most was that *she* was wary of how much he cared.

Either way, Zedolph's presence felt heavier than it normally did, and the tangible essence of it was enough to drive her mad.

"How did the Tinuviels come to power?" Bridgette asked, out of the blue, determined to stifle the silence.

Zedolph paused. He fingered the edge of his boning knife and flicked it gently, almost absentmindedly, against the flat of his thumb. He knew she'd be asking him questions that pertained to her research, but this wasn't the inquiry he expected in the moment. He felt jolted back into cognizance.

"They came to lead Palna following the Ingefeoht," Zedolph answered.

"Well yeah, I know that. But how?" the Elfling pressed. "Like were they chosen by the Samnung?"

"No," the man said. "Ydessa Tinuviel was Baize Sammael's second-in-command. She is his spiritual daughter. She was always to lead Palna if Baize Sammael could not."

"Excuse me?" Bridgette said. She put her knife down and stared at the butcher. "The hell do you mean by 'his spiritual daughter'?"

Zedolph pushed the containers of beef and fat toward her and motioned to the meat grinder on a shelf. "Process this for ground beef, and I shall tell you the story."

Zedolph and Collum would get along really fucking well, they both love history so much, Bridgette thought. She eased the heavy grinder onto a table and procured a clean bowl for the beef to be ground into. Zedolph perched on top of the deep freezer — normally Fincher's preferred spot — and started talking.

"When Baize Sammael was gifted the land of Palna, beings of all sorts flocked here to learn from him," the butcher began. "His abilities were so different, so much more powerful, from what they had known thus far! Some beings came alone. Others brought their families. Ydessa's mother, Dahvñe, did so. She brought her lover and her two daughters. Ydessa was a mere youngling. She and her older half-sister practically grew up at the feet of Baize Sammael."

Ydessa has a sister? Bridgette thought to herself. She made a note to write that information in one of her surreptitious Samnung reports.

"One thing you must know of Craft Wizardry is that it is nearly the antithesis of the abilities we are — I mean to say, abilities that are common elsewhere," Zedolph continued, catching himself in such a way that stirred Bridgette's sierwan gift. "Where the power you experienced in greater Heáhwolcen was a synchronized dance between practitioner and practice, Craft is not. Craft is a skilled witch or wizard taking control of the world around them. It is a skill that takes far more willpower and practice to master — so I have heard — as the elements and Nature do not like to be controlled. The elements and Nature therefore rebel against Craft, which defies the natural order of how this power works. This rebellion, this lack of partnership, makes learning Craft very dangerous. It is easy for something to go fatally wrong, as is the case with Dahvñe and her lover."

"What, like a spell blew up in their faces?" Bridgette asked. She fed more meat into the grinder, ever conscious of Zedolph's use of synonyms to avoid saying "magic".

"Essentially," he answered. "It is my understanding that the two were working a ritual that they should not have been, one they were not ready for. You see — again, from what I have been told — Craft Wizardry requires the practitioner to be fully invested in order to dictate how a spell will behave. There is no room for empathy, for negotiation. This does not necessarily mean that a practitioner is a cruel being. Rather, it implies the practitioner is focused on their task, allowing nothing to distract them. The more advanced a spell or ritual, the more mind-strength is required. And, as with all forms of power, some beings are simply better suited to practice certain things than others."

The Elfling tucked these revelations about Craft in her memory.

"When Dahvñe's ritual failed, the daughters were left virtually alone," Zedolph said. "The half-sister disappeared —

not even her name is known. No one knows what became of her, but likely it wasn't pleasant. There were and are plenty of those in Palna with ill intentions.

"But Ydessa, who grew up without a father figure in her home, latched onto Baize Sammael right from the start," Zedolph went on. "Perhaps it was his charm? Perhaps she knew the two would be destined for something? Whatever the cause, they had a strange connection. Baize Sammael did not shy from letting it be known that he would protect this female from all the dangers the worlds might offer. Ydessa, likewise, would die for him. He took her in as a child, fresh from her mother's death, and raised her as his own."

"Didn't Dahvñe have a lover though? Wouldn't he have been a father figure before the spell killed him?" Bridgette asked. She refused to feel any level of sympathy or empathy for Ydessa Tinuviel, despite the minor similarities in their biographies.

"Dahvñe's lover was female," Zedolph replied. "Dahvñe was an Elf, and her first lover was too. This was the father of Ydessa's lost sister. Ydessa's own father is unknown. But he must have been a most unique creature, as Ydessa's supposed powers are not typical."

Bridgette dropped a handful of beef fat on the table in shock. "Wait. What do you mean, her powers *are*? Isn't the m-word not allowed in Palna?"

Zedolph smiled ruefully. "Do you really think that the most powerful witchling in the world, whose abilities were honed and taught by Baize Sammael himself, would be stopped by something as trivial as a border wall and an unenforceable decree? While everyone else is forced to abide by that law, the Tinuviels are simply good at playacting. Their powers are muted, of course, because of the Samnung wall's spell, but not gone."

"Who makes sure Palnans are abiding by the laws?" Bridgette asked.

"The Fairy ambassador for the most part these days,"

Zedolph said. "Before my time, when the Samnung's wall was erected and after Bondrie was established, there was a rotating number of guards who enforced the rules. Because the wall itself tampers powers, it was easy for the guards to put out the wisps of flickering flames that might remain."

Bridgette chewed the inside of her cheek. *Should I tell him about Ulerion?*

She shouldn't have thought about it.

"What's on your mind, Bridgette? I do not like this tension today."

Fucking seven hells.

"So — shit. I don't know how to tell you this. I don't know if I *should* tell you this, Zedolph, but what you just said about the Fairy ambassador? He's not doing or telling anyone in Heáhwolcen anything. In fact," Bridgette gulped, "I think he's probably dead."

~ 33 ~

"Dead?" Zedolph choked. "Ulerion Mewt is *dead*?"

Bridgette reached out a hand, narrowly avoiding nicking her palm along the edge of the knife he held. "No! I mean — I don't know for sure. I swear. I have no idea. He might be dead. He might not be dead. He might not even be in Palna."

She glanced around, making sure the other three slátraestres hadn't stuck their heads in the door at Zedolph's outburst. She lowered her voice, just in case, and gripped the butcher's wrist. The ground beef was entirely forgotten about.

"The Samnung hasn't heard from Ulerion since last August," Bridgette whispered. She fumbled for a few more plausible fibs about her faux backstory. "With Ulerion being gone, it made it super hard to finally convince anyone to let me come to Palna and study. The only reason I even got to go was because they thought maybe I'd run into him or someone who knew what happened to him."

Zedolph wasn't buying it, and Bridgette knew it.

"It just doesn't make sense for someone like him to up and disappear, you know?" she said quietly. "I think something happened to him and that's why no one's been able to reach him for more than a year. Maybe he isn't dead, but I get the feeling that he's like, no longer in range of being able to communicate. Maybe someone's kidnapped him or something. Got him locked in a coffin or a trunk made out of some crazy material that blocks his powers."

The man's eyes widened. "That is an interesting theory."

Bridgette let go of his wrist and resumed her meat grinding. "Well, I mean, where else would he be? He was in Palna, and then after the eclipse he suddenly wasn't."

"I recall that day."

"What was it like up here?"

The butchery's front door opened, and Zedolph glanced out into the building. "Finish making the grind, and I'll tell you on the way home this evening."

She nodded. Bridgette tried not to burst into questions the rest of the day, but the moment Zedolph locked the door after closing, she lost all hold on herself.

"You look like young Toby does when he is trying to be patient and is about to fail quite miserably," the butcher commented, a smile teasing one side of his mouth. "Go on."

"Okay. Tell me *everything* you remember about that day of the eclipse! That's it. Well, until I probably think of more questions while you talk. But start with that one, please."

He obliged, making the walk back to the Maudlin home much more energetic than that morning's had been. Zedolph's memory largely aligned with what Ulerion's report said. The Tinuviels, along with a host of advisors, started early in the morning the day of the eclipse traveling all over Palna, performing Old Magick rituals that, again, Bridgette strongly suspected were doctored a bit to be Craft.

"Each of us was given a ritual charm to wear during the ceremony," Zedolph recalled. "There were set areas we had to stand and move in. In fact, I'd forgotten this until now. A few weeks before, a member of the Palnan Guard came to Xcthonya to prepare us for the ritual. He demonstrated how we were to act so that we would be ready to join when the time came. The entire thing was rather fussy, so specific."

Oh yeah. Based on what Zedolph said about the particulars of Craft spells, those rituals were one hundred percent not normal magic, Bridgette thought.

"What's a ritual charm?" she asked.

"Nothing more than a memento of the occasion, but it was a small glass vial on a metal chain. The vial holds representative symbols of the four elements, as well as a commemorative blend of herbs. Everyone wore them while Ydessa and Eryth led us through the ritual. They moved onto the next town before the eclipse happened, and we had our instructions to stand in our spots until then," Zedolph said. "When that moment occurred and all of Palna was plunged into darkness, we were told to lift our faces to the sky and make one final ritual chant. As we did so, and the only light visible was the faint ring of red around the Meridian, the ritual charms glowed."

"They glowed?"

"Indeed. It was then we realized they were not all the same — there were several colors on display. It was quite lovely, to be in near-darkness and suddenly a rainbow is there with you."

"What was the point of all of the ritual?"

Zedolph chuckled. "Showmanship, of course. The king and queen made themselves known, they ordered citizens around, that sort of thing. It was the tiniest touch of power, a gift to us, if you will."

"Are you sure it was a gift and not a ruse?"

The words were out of Bridgette's mouth before she could stop herself, and she clamped a hand over her face. *Fucking fuck, Conner, you idiot.*

"A ruse?" Zedolph repeated.

Damn. It.

"Well, I mean, in theory," she said, trying to cover for her near slip. "The last thing Ulerion reported to the Samnung before he disappeared was about the eclipse and how they were, like, harnessing the energy of the Ballamúr."

Zedolph stopped dead and looked at her. "What is the Ballamúr?"

"I don't know," Bridgette lied, too fast. "It was just what he said in that last report. I read a bunch of them, and that sentence stuck out. Makes me think that maybe those charms weren't just mementos, you know? Maybe they had a real purpose in the ritual."

"You have many interesting theories and ideas, Bridgette of

the Outside," Zedolph said. He moved closer and put an arm around her comparatively narrow shoulders, then leaned in so that his warm breath tickled her ear. "If I was you, I would keep those thoughts to myself, or share them only in very secure company."

She shivered. "Right. Good idea."

He squeezed her in tighter and changed the subject to discussing the weather.

The next day's walk to the butchery was significantly less intense, and Bridgette managed to get through half the day barely speaking to the slátrari. It was only when he slipped into the back room and motioned for Fincher to scoot out — the Kobold and Elfling had been thoroughly engrossed in a conversation about chili, an American sort of meat stew with beans and tomatoes — that Bridgette felt she was about to get laid into about her theories. She wondered if he said anything to Serrabinx the night before. Her hostess had been strangely quiet after supper and barely bid them farewell that morning.

"Bridgette, something you said yesterday struck me in such a way that I had difficulty sleeping last night," Zedolph told her. "It is about your theories regarding Ambassador Mewt."

Yep, I figured that, she thought, nodding.

"It occurred to me that if the ambassador had not been seen in Heáhwolcen" — Zedolph paused mid-sentence and set his teeth heavily, as if he was fighting some unknown force in order to say his next words — "perhaps the ambassador *is not in* Heáhwolcen."

"What do you — hold the fuck up," Bridgette said as Zedolph's tone and word choice sunk in. Her eyes moved beneath their glamour with such ferocity that she pulled the knife out of the rib loin she'd been slicing and set it on the worktable. "Are you seriously telling me that this whole time, Palnans have been able to go to Earth?"

~ 34 ~

The last being Collum expected to see in Trystane's office was Emi-Joye. Njahla wasn't monitoring the door, so the fyrdwisa evanesced inside and saw the back of the Fairy's wings fluttering as she leaned gracefully over the desk, apparently engaged in heated conversation.

He cleared his throat gently, and both Fairy and Trystane jumped.

"Pardon me, Ambassadora," Collum said. "I do not mean to interrupt — I wasn't aware you had a visitor, Ard Rialóir. I can come back later."

Emi-Joye's initial thought was that Trystane let it slip that she was indeed the one planning the upcoming Fórsaí Armada commander meeting. But the fyrdwisa gave no indication that he knew, just a look of confusion at what she was doing in the ard rialóir's office. She darted back, her russet gown swooping at the movement. It was long-sleeved but dipped low in the back to allow her wings full range of motion.

"Fyrdwisa," she said, bowing her head. He inclined his in return. "It's been a moment since you've graced me with your presence."

Collum couldn't quite tell if that was professional observation or annoyed sarcasm. "Communication works both ways, Ambassadora," he replied, tone dry and open to her own interpretation. "It is good to see you though, truly. I was starting to think you'd been avoiding me."

I have, she cringed inwardly, and his blink let her know he heard — and was surprised.

"What brings you in so unexpectedly, Collum?" Trystane asked.

"I —" He started to reply and stopped, the icy blue of Emi-Joye's cautious stare reminding him far too much of some of the colors of lights that had been in his eyes three nights ago.

"There's something I need to tell you. You too, Ambassadora, actually."

"Something you need to tell me?" she repeated.

"Yes. First, may I have a glass of whatever you'd like to pour us all?" Collum requested. He sat in one of the office's green velvet armchairs. Emi-Joye perched next to him while Trystane conjured up two more glasses of amber liquid.

A shimmering ward-wall went up, separating Trystane's office from the small hallway in the suite, and the Elf looked to his fyrdwisa, concern clouding his eyes. Collum had not been himself for ages, and the way he presented himself now made it seem as though he was doing worse.

"It is something that occurred the final night of my trip to Nashville with Lucilla," Collum began. He had practiced this in his head the past two days, closed up in his home office, wondering whether he should tell Trystane, let alone the Samnung at large, what happened. He wasn't sure how he — allegedly a spy! — missed Lucilla poisoning him, a thought that irked him to no end. He pondered if the entire situation had somehow been his fault, even though the rational part of his brain told him that wasn't the case at all. Collum hadn't used magic with ill intent. *She* had.

The fyrdwisa took a gulp of spirits and a deep breath. He revealed everything, beginning with the moment they exited the portal into Endicott Park, the way Lucilla almost swiped Bridgette's choice of officially having parents, ending with the final night. He told them of the flashing lights, and of the unbounding burst of power that came from him — and yet not from him.

Sharing this event was in itself an unbounding of sorts. Collum did not shy from becoming emotional, from displaying the anger and pain he felt at being assaulted by Lucilla, a witch the Samnung members trusted, who betrayed them all in her actions toward him. When he finished speaking, his glass was empty, and he felt slightly heady from drinking so fast on a mostly empty stomach. Trystane's knuckles were white, gripped in tight fists, and Collum for once didn't use his magic to soothe the untenable rage that emanated from both the ard rialóir and the ambassadora. He was too exhausted from *everything.*

"Collum," Trystane whispered when he could finally speak, "Are you alright?"

The fyrdwisa spat out a laugh. "Absolutely not, Trystane."

"I want to assure you, my brother, my friend: what happened to you was completely, utterly unacceptable. It will be addressed and Lucilla will no longer hold her current nor any other post with the Samnung, so long as I breathe air in this body," Trystane said. His voice was low, aching, angry. "What do you need from me, from us, from the Samnung, in order to process and move forward from this?"

I need Bridgette back, Collum thought, but he didn't say that out loud. His eyes must've said it though, because of all things, Emi-Joye put a hand on his arm and stroked her thumb down toward his wrist.

He glanced up and offered an appreciative smile. She didn't move her hand, and he felt rather strengthened by it being there.

"I wish I knew, Trystane. Truly, I am glad you both believe me. We have so few beings in Heáhwolcen who use their magic with ill intent that I hesitated to say anything," Collum said.

"At the very least, I would like you to go see a lacnian. There is one, a witch called Pompié, who studies mind-health and healing," Trystane instructed.

Collum, who recently had that same thought — though for different reasons — couldn't help but let out a chuckle as he nodded in agreement. "I will. I promise."

"Good," his ceannairí replied. Trystane grimaced as he leaned forward, his next words measured: "That covenant bracelet that burned. It's with Bridgette, isn't it?"

Collum nodded. He resisted the urge to look down where it

lay innocently on his arm, harmless silver beads no warmer now than room temperature.

"When did you activate this covenant?"

"The morning she crossed into Palna."

"And it's never been active, until three nights ago?"

"Correct."

Trystane stared at the bracelets along his own arm. "In all my years, I have never heard of a covenant behaving like that, where neither one of you is able to contact the other, but the bracelet itself is able to tap into some form of power. Collum … this magic …"

"I know," Collum said, not letting Trystane finish thought nor sentence.

It was the only possibility that made remote sense, though the mechanics were still beyond him. If they were right about the Liluthuaé being Maylemaegus brought to life, and that was why Bridgette could tap into Universal consciousness, it stood to reason that she would be able to access some very deep power. But she couldn't have known what was happening to him that night, and he couldn't shake those colors and lights from his head. He felt they were on the right track with this train of thought, but something still was out of place.

Emi-Joye flinched. Collum spoke of Maylemaegus, though he never said that word to her. She and Trystane knew that *she* knew about Maylemaegus, that it was the "Old Magick" Collum once told her he believed Bridgette could connect to regarding her sierwan gift. The ambassadora and ard rialóir knew too that she suspected perhaps *she* was also connected to Maylemaegus, and that Cloa was cursed — Emi-Joye's head spun as she sat there, the three of them saying nothing to one another.

"Collum, there's something we should probably discuss," the Fairy said. She looked straight ahead at Trystane, who raised a brow, as if asking to be sure she wanted to go down this path.

The energy in the room muddied and Collum could no

longer read it. "Yes?"

"I've been doing some research of my own recently into Fairy lore, tracing my species to the Fyrst," Emi-Joye said. "I know about Maylemaegus, and I know it's what you think Bridgette has, or is. I think … I think I have it, too."

Collum stared, assuming this was knowledge Trystane already possessed, and wondered exactly when the Elf planned to share that information with him. "Go on."

"A few weeks ago, I became aware of a new magic that exists in my blood. I have yet to learn what it is, how it works, how to begin to access it, but it is there. I feel it sometimes. That reminded me too much of Bridgette to be coincidence, so I began to dig a bit deeper. I wanted to know if Ylda created anything else that she imparted the Maylemaegus gifts into, because she didn't keep them for herself. I wanted to know if there was any chance that the Fairies have a Liluthuaé, too," Emi-Joye said.

"And do they?" Collum prodded. Trystane perked up — this was a new tidbit for both Elves.

"Not exactly," she said, and Trystane scowled. "Let me explain. The Liluthuaé is, it appears, a very specific being with a very particular purpose. Ylda was originally given the seeds of Maylemaegus as a gift after she gave the first Fairies their wings. Though she then divided the Maylemaegus *somehow* — it's rumored there were three or four seeds of power; different texts I've found said different things — I was able to find evidence she created a distinctive Fairy lineage called the Duathanna. The Duathanna lived on Earth, dwelling in rolling hills and overseeing ancient lands of Fae and human alike, but they were set aside from other Fairies by their, and I quote, 'god-like power'."

Collum understood immediately. "The Duathanna were gifted Maylemaegus?"

"I believe so, at least some of them."

"What does that have to do with the power you believe you hold, Em — Ambassadora?" Trystane said, catching himself before slipping out her nickname.

Emi-Joye shot him a hard look before she answered. "My mother was born on Earth, and she is *very* old, is what that has to do with me."

"You think your mother is one of the Duathanna?" the ard rialóir asked. "Would she not then have this same magic in her, to then pass to you?"

"Perhaps." Emi-Joye's tone turned curt, and Collum gathered she did not enjoy her theory being questioned. He followed her line of thought and didn't disbelieve her, but …

"Ambassadora, I agree that it is possible your mother is Duathanna," Collum said. He turned and put her hand in between his. "But that does not explain why *you* have some deeper power —"

She balled up her fists and it took every ounce of self-restraint to not shout. "The Duathanna were rumored to have died out hundreds of years ago, defeated in a massive battle against humans, who drove them out of their native lands in Europe. The humans were aided by, and again I quote, 'men and femme whose abilities far exceeded those of common Man'."

"The fucking Druids," Collum murmured, already seeing where this was going, and still lost as to what this had to do with Emi-Joye and her potential Maylemaegus.

"That's one way to put it," the Fairy said, voice taut. "If my mother was descended from the Duathanna, who had god-like magic that could *only* be Maylemaegus, we should go pay a visit to our *dear* friend Heledd and ask him what his people know about mine."

~ 35 ~

Collum refrained from what he wanted to say, which was to whine out "Do we *have* to?" and said instead, in a most professional tone, "I would rather propose marriage to Nehemi."

Emi-Joye flashed him a wide grin, though it didn't quite reach her eyes. "Going back to that wretched place in Wales was not on my list of things to do in this lifetime, and yet I believe it to be the best option we have. This is a mystery, a legendary one, and we don't have to pretend this time to be anything we're not. Heledd and Gary, and their ridiculous guards, know who we are and know probably more about Maylemaegus than anyone in Heáhwolcen. Plus, this time it's personal."

"You two are becoming regular adventurers," Trystane commented. "This is shaping up to be quite the Samnung meeting agenda this week, Fyrdwisa."

Collum glanced at Emi-Joye. "You and Apostine should be there."

"Why Apostine?" she asked.

"Didn't he have to play ambassador while you were gone last time?" Collum reminded her. "And I suppose if you're willing to share with us what you've been researching, Trystane and I should play fair. Summon your second, and we'll summon ours. We're going on a little side quest to my apartment."

"Seven hells, Fyrdwisa, these are some impressive digs," Apostine whistled, his golden beetle wings carrying him in a circle around Collum's living room. "What's a Tief-Fae got to do to get a home like this?"

"Not live at your father's residence, for starters," Emi-Joye replied. She grinned at her second, who had the worst habit of picking up human expressions, but who was so earnest in everything he did that it was hard to really be annoyed with him. "Come down; your wings are going to send this paper scattering.

And watch your tail, please."

He flipped her the bird as his bare feet hit the ground, wings stilled and the end of his forked tail arcing to avoid swishing through the Aelys Frost documents. "As you command, Ambassadora. What are all these, exactly? It looks rather historic."

Apostine knelt amongst the semi-organized stacks, careful not to touch any of the papers. Emi-Joye was looking too, while the Elves and Elfling in their party stood, arms crossed, letting them take it all in.

"They are historic," Njahla said. "They're ancient documents of Elven history that Aelys Frost smuggled to Heáhwolcen. They wound up in a wooden trunk that Trystane managed to get his hands on. We've been going through them for weeks now."

"Found anything good?" Apostine asked.

Aurelias shoved a pair of white archival gloves toward the ambestre. "We're not sure yet. Most of this is figuring out what sorts of documents they even are. The damn trunk is endless. It's as if every piece of paper we pull out is replaced by two more."

"What is the point of going through them?" Emi-Joye asked. "Why not let the University scholars do this?"

"Morbid curiosity," Trystane joked. "We've been looking for anything we can find, anything at all, about Maylemaegus, about the Liluthuaé, and I suppose now, anything about the Duathanna."

Aurelias, Apostine, and Njahla exchanged confused glances, and the ard rialóir briefly filled them in on what Emi-Joye learned — carefully leaving out the parts where she believed she was somehow both descended from the Duathanna and connected to Maylemaegus. Collum caught Apostine's thoughts halfway through the lecture, though. The ambestre knew his ambassadora better than to accept the notion that she casually stumbled upon those topics. The male at least had the decency not to question her in front of the group, though his inner grumblings made Collum hide a chuckle.

"If I may suggest something," Emi-Joye began in a tone that suggested she was going to say whatever it was no matter what objections the others had, "Perhaps, instead of us all shuffling papers, it would behoove us to have one being categorize the documents, and the rest of us split up and read through what's been brought out of the trunk thus far?"

"That's a novel idea!" Aurelias said. She turned to Trystane. "Why in seven hells didn't we think of that?"

The Elf smiled, a glint of mischief in the gold flecks of his mossy green eyes. "I'm not sure, Fyrdestre, but you are most certainly up to the task of sorting them moving forward!"

She glowered at him.

Trystane continued smiling as he turned to the rest of the beings. "As for the remainder, I'll take the stack that looks as if it could be of governmental origin. The rest of you, pick a pile and get comfortable. I believe we're going to be here for a while."

They did take breaks — Njahla disappeared for a solid hour at one point before returning with earthenware mugs of hot tea and mokka from The Coffee Cauldron — but despite the time the six of them spent in Collum's apartment that day and long into the night, they seemed just as lost as they had when they began. No one came across anything that was remotely related to the Liluthuaé, Maylemaegus, or even Old Magick, much less Fairy lore.

Trystane and Njahla both left at some late hour, but Aurelias, Emi-Joye, and Apostine chose to remain.

"This is impossible," Aurelias griped, staring down into the trunk. It was just below half-full. "Why did Aelys bother to bring all of this to Heáhwolcen? *Why?* It's, aside from those bits that look official, just random. This entire thing is a chaotic collection of Elven 'history'."

"At least some of it's interesting," Apostine said. "Well. I say that as someone not of Elven blood. This stack I've got is diaries of some sort from different beings. It's not quite in order, and I notice distinct variation in handwriting, albeit all written in mostly the same language. But the language is gibberish."

"Gibberish?" Emi-Joye peered over at him from where she sat cross-legged on the rug. "What do you mean by that?"

He held out a piece of tissue-thin vellum. "They're all like this, all of these diary things. They could be poetry, perhaps? Lines of ritual? But the words are interspersed with strange symbols I don't recognize."

The Fairy furrowed her brow as she examined the page Apostine handed her. Collum and Aurelias joined her, looking at it as well. Some of the words were recognizable as either an old form of English or long-lost spellings of the common magical tongue of Heáhwolcen, but the symbols — series of lines and diagonals — were unfamiliar to all in the room.

"They could be runes," Collum mused, running a thumb over one of the lines. "But I don't know from what country, or what species. I've never seen anything that looks like this style of writing. It doesn't make any sense."

"As I said: gibberish," Apostine confirmed. "Anyone else having any luck?"

Aurelias gestured helplessly at the trunk, and the other two shook their heads.

Collum wandered into the kitchen and sent bottles of stout ale floating to his comrades, who accepted them in lieu of document defeat. He popped the cap on his own bottle before leaning into the trunk, where four columns of neatly stacked papers loomed. They looked so harmless, properly organized in their aging wooden box. An idea came to him, something he hadn't thought of in decades — something he and his friends would do at the University when they were studying and trying to avoid straining their minds too hard.

"Syndumir Maylemaegus," he whispered, flipping his hands

upward to lift the first stack of paper into the air.

Nothing happened. He tried the spell again with the second stack, then the third. On the fourth stack, however, a single sheet of paper floated out and landed at his feet. Collum peered into the trunk, where yet another layer of documents appeared, and swept his hand over the top of them, whispering the spell a final time. To his utter shock, the pages vanished, dissipating before his very eyes. Where they once were now lay a trio of slim, stitch-bound books, so ancient the leather of their covers cracked.

The Elf didn't trust his hands to touch these unprotected, not even with the archival gloves on. He lifted them gingerly with air alone: one a faded lavender gray, the second what could have once been green, and the third some murky shade of ashy blue.

"Hecate fucking bless," Collum breathed. He turned to the three beings in his living room, letting the three books drift before him. "I believe, as our dear Bridgette would say, y'all are going to want to see this."

~ 36 ~

Bridgette thought this must be what it feels like right before someone passes out from shock.

Zedolph looked at her, amused at her reaction. "No, not Palnans," he clarified ruefully. "But the Tinuviels? It has been alleged they have ways to do so. I am one who believes such rumors are more truth than fiction."

A slow, sinking heaviness caressed its way down to Bridgette's gut. Ulerion mentioned something akin to this in his reports. He wrote about the Tinuviels having some special mode of travel, and a word came to the Elfling's mind that she hadn't given thought to in quite some time.

"Holy fuck. Larivuria," she whispered.

The butcher's eyes snapped to hers. "What did you just say?"

"Larivuria," Bridgette repeated, barely audible.

His eyes became malicious. Zedolph grabbed her by the shoulders and pressed her against the wall before the Elfling could employ any sort of defensive maneuver.

Damn Nehemi and her four weeks of minimal combat training! she thought, thrown by her host's sudden shift in behavior. Those arms, which gently calmed her when she felt ill and just yesterday had pulled her in protectively, were *strong*.

"How do you know of that place?" the slátrari hissed, breath tickling her ear.

Zedolph and Bridgette were so close to one another that if Muov, Paxson, or Fincher walked in, it would be easy for the slátraestres to assume they'd found their owner and new apprentice locked in a lovers' quarrel. Bridgette came to her senses and kicked a leg toward Zedolph's kneecap, bracing herself to push him away.

"Take your fucking hands off my body, back up three feet, and maybe I will tell you," she whispered back. Slowly. Angrily. "Maybe."

As if he realized the position he put them in — as if he'd done so unconsciously! — Zedolph wrenched himself away. He put his open palms in the air, stepping further back. "Bridgette, I am so sorry. I didn't — I'm not sure what came over me. I should not have attacked you like that."

"No fucking shit, asshole," she said, glaring at him from lowered brows. He had grabbed her hard enough to bruise, as if she didn't already have enough arm injuries to contend with. Handprint-shaped red marks weren't on her list of things to have to explain to Serrabinx and Toby. She wondered briefly if her half-Elven blood allowed her to heal faster, if her half-Craft blood prevented true injuries like it had with the spidery design from the protected lands.

"That was untoward of me. I should not have reacted in such a manner," Zedolph said, not convinced Bridgette believed his apology. She wasn't sure she did, either.

He lowered his arms, glancing to the door. The tension was uncomfortable, but Bridgette wasn't going to be the one to soften it. Zedolph made this charge, this affront. He could fix it.

"The place you speak of. This is a conversation we should continue elsewhere," the butcher pleaded after a moment. "I do not know how you know of it. You should not know of it, and neither should I. It is information that could get you harmed. Possibly killed."

Fantastic! More fatal secrets, she thought.

"I would very much like to have that conversation," the Elfling said, voice stiff. "And hey, next time someone says something that freaks you out? Maybe try like, not gripping their shoulders so hard you leave marks."

Zedolph bowed his head, a defeated air lingering before him. "I don't know what came over me. I will learn from this error, and it will be one that shall not be repeated."

"Better fucking not," Bridgette muttered, wishing she had her dagger stuffed in her boot like she normally did. She usually slept with it under her pillow, but the damn thing disappeared at some point in the past few days. She hadn't been able to find it and assumed Serrabinx scuttled it away somewhere, fearful at the thought of a weapon in her home.

The butcher walked out of the back room, unsettled. Bridgette was momentarily reminded of the time she attacked Emi-Joye, but that had been different than Zedolph's actions just now. In the cottage, it was as if some unknown power possessed her and took over her body until Collum intervened. Zedolph's reaction was a knee-jerk response of sheer terror, and she wanted to know why.

Why was Larivuria such a deadly secret if the Fairy ambassador was allowed to be taken there? Why was he allowed to report on it? Did that mean no one from Palna read his reports before he sent them along to the Samnung? What other sorts of things had Ulerion unknowingly revealed in his decades of service, aside from the Ballamúr and Larivuria, that Palna had no idea the Samnung leaders knew about? Did the Samnung members even know what sort of treasure they had in their clutches, hidden in the ramblings of an eccentric Fairy who liked to send in notes on colorful sheets of paper?

Bridgette glanced over her shoulder to make sure no one was about to walk in. She chanced the opportunity to scribble her list of internal questions in her notebook.

Poor Collum when he reads this, she giggled. *He's going to have to pick apart what's meat knowledge and what's notable for the Samnung.*

That night, after a strained, mostly silent walk back to the house, Toby swung open the front door and practically dragged Bridgette inside. She hadn't seen him this exuberant in days and was grateful for the laughter it brought.

"Mumma let me make supper tonight, all on mine own!" he crowed. "It has some of the sage sausage from the butchery, and roasted tomatoes, kale, autumn squash, and cream!"

"And bacon," Serrabinx reminded him, smiling at her son.

She reached a hand to take Bridgette and Zedolph's coats. "He also made the sourdough rolls for dipping. Tobias is quite proud of himself, and rightly so. He's done a marvelous job."

The earlier tension, along with the promise to further discuss where the Tinuviels may or may not travel, dissipated in the festive air. Bridgette thought about her foster parents, and how this would be her first Thanksgiving soon without them, as it wasn't looking like she would leave Palna beforehand. She hoped the Simmonses hadn't been too worried, thinking she was in Europe teaching violin, and wished there was a way to contact them. But being unable to contact anyone in Heáhwolcen was hard enough. Maybe the Samnung had taken care of speaking with the Simmonses on her behalf.

"What are you thinking about?" Toby asked as they settled at the table.

"My mother," Bridgette said, not quite lying. "In America, where I grew up, there's a holiday called Thanksgiving. It's supposed to celebrate the settlers' first harvest after they sailed to America. When I was younger, I learned that it was a great feast held between what we called the Pilgrims and the Indians. As I grew up and learned more about human history, I found out we had been fed a false narrative — the settlers, or the Pilgrims, and those who came later weren't as nice to the indigenous people as we were taught to believe. Thanksgiving is a hard holiday now, because I don't like celebrating something that didn't really happen, but I always enjoyed having traditional fall food and gathering with my family."

Her real Thanksgivings ran the gamut, as many of her foster parents were not the type to put on large gatherings. There were years when it was just the parents, her foster siblings — some biological, some also in the system — and herself at the table. Other times, it was more of a grand affair, with a picture-perfect turkey surrounded by plated dishes that looked as though they'd been cut and pasted from expensive cookbooks.

Bridgette's years with the Simmonses fell somewhere in-between in terms of lavishness of Thanksgiving fare and décor. The food was impeccable in flavor, with the air of rustic homeyness that characterized Southern dishes — just the right amount of caramelized char on the sweet potato casserole; succulent giblet gravy with meaty bits if you were first to spoon it out of the saucepan; cranberry sauce straight from the can; and inevitably some uncle or aunt's retelling of how the turkey came to be that year. There were buttered rolls kept warm in the oven until just before serving and green bean casserole, a coveted side dish. The Simmonses always served the quintessential trio of Thanksgiving pies: apple with a picnic basket weave of crust on top, pumpkin, and sweet potato.

Bridgette didn't realize how far her mind drifted until Toby tapped her hand. She'd devoured her entire bowl of soup and several sourdough rolls without uttering a word. The Elfling offered him an apologetic grin and a compliment, assuring him his supper was so good, it transported her back to her human upbringing.

"I am most glad you enjoyed it," he said, beaming. "May I get you seconds?"

"Sure, Little Lark." She let him take her bowl back to the firehearth.

Serrabinx caught her eye across the table. "My brother tells me you've become quite adept at your job, Bridgette."

She flushed at the unexpected praise. "Um, thanks. I still really like it, so that's good."

"He thinks you should have a day or so reprieve tomorrow and the next," Serrabinx continued, nonchalant. "I daresay my son would be delighted should you choose to take his uncle up on this offer."

Bridgette hadn't had a chance to question Toby in ages, not since that day in Forêt Fossile. She looked at Zedolph. "Really?"

He nodded, and she realized this was his way of apologizing

for the attack earlier that day. "Yes, really."

The Elfling didn't have a chance to say anything before Toby was back, tossing Bridgette her bowl so hard that soup sloshed over its edges in his rush to hug Zedolph. "Thank you, uncle! I will have the *most* exciting days planned for us! This is a wonderful gift!"

After supper, when Zedolph rose from the table to assist his nephew and sister in cleaning up, Bridgette stilled him with a hand on his arm. She wanted to thank him for letting her have the next two days to enjoy Palna, but she *also* didn't want to let the man off scot-free. He did say he'd talk to her about Larivuria, and Bridgette had no intention of letting him forget.

Zedolph picked up on her intention. He met her gaze, something dark hiding in his brown irises. "Let us help wash the supper dishes. After my sister takes her leave for rest, join me in my room."

The Elfling nodded. "Sure thing."

Bridgette was antsy for the next few hours. Serrabinx was not one to go to sleep early, though she did have to coerce Toby into his bedroom with more parental force than usual — "You must be well-rested if you intend to adventure for the next two days, my love" — but finally, she bid her brother and guest goodnight.

Bridgette and Zedolph gave her about twenty more minutes to get settled, and then the butcher put one finger to his lips in a hushing motion, turned off the oil lamp in the sitting room, and beckoned for her to follow. The two walked the hallway to Zedolph's bedroom, careful not to let it sound like two pairs of feet traversing side by side.

~ 37 ~

Zedolph closed the door behind them and turned the knob so that it locked. He wasn't too worried about them being overheard. They were at the far end of the hall, separated from Serrabinx by Toby's room and the bathroom.

Still, he began speaking in a whisper, motioning for Bridgette to join him on the edge of the bed.

"I want to know why it's so dangerous for me to know the name of that city," she hissed, interrupting the start of his sentence. "Ulerion wrote about it in one of the reports I read. He said he took some kind of special route to get there. I figured it was special because he's a Fairy and perfectly able to travel anywhere he pleases for the most part."

Zedolph's brow furrowed. "This only further strengthens my thought that Ulerion is perhaps not in Heáhwolcen," he murmured. "When I was a boy, I came upon a book I should not have. Glafida had recently inherited her shop, the one you and Toby visited, from her father. I visited with my uncle, who raised me after our parents were killed" — he grimaced at that — "and this book ... it was the first time something had so *called* to me."

Bridgette understood exactly what that felt like, to be drawn inexplicably to an object or person, knowing it was somehow intimately connected to her. It was the same sort of instinctual pull that she felt toward Collum in the campus coffee shop the day they met. She nodded, and Zedolph went on.

"The book was lurid green, I'll never forget, and I begged my uncle to let me take it home," he said. "He didn't understand why I wanted it so badly. I came to learn the book had a way of hiding itself from those who weren't meant to see it. To nearly everyone else, including my uncle, the book appeared as the philosophies of a mathematician. But to me, and eventually to Serrabinx, it showed its true nature. The book told old stories of Palna and Baize Sammael."

"Old stories? Like children's stories?" Bridgette asked.

"Not quite," Zedolph replied. "They were true stories, written and illustrated in a style of epic tales. There were parts that were exaggerated, but there were also things that were not. It was a bit of detective work to pick out what was tale and what was truth. One story told of a great city by the sea, the first place for Baize Sammael to claim as his own powerful kingdom. It was called Larivuria, and it was described as a beautiful place. The book used words like 'tropical' and said the waters tasted of salt and brine, that they were such a bright blue they would blend into the sky."

"Okay, so city by the sea, cool," Bridgette said. "Again. Why is it so dangerous for any of us to know about it? It's not like anyone else in Heáhwolcen is barred from going to Earth."

"Because Ydessa and Eryth would like to continue in her spiritual father's footsteps," Zedolph said. "If Baize Sammael indeed had this 'city by the sea', as you call it, the Tinuviels would desire access to it as Palnan land by default. Though I do not know the details, it would make sense that they have a way to reach this place, as you confirmed for me earlier today. I believe the two of them have been up to no good for some time now. The Tinuviels are not the type to enjoy being challenged or to have their plans questioned. Palnans disappear, and no questions are ever really asked, although everyone knows *something* is wrong."

"You're saying that the Tinuviels are doing some shit going back and forth to Earth, and if anyone finds out, they're dead?"

Zedolph nodded. Bridgette almost shuddered from the intensity of his gaze. "I would very much like my family to stay alive," he said.

She thought it was a veiled threat at first, but the man continued.

"My nephew has special abilities. My sister does too, or did. I believe you have been warned about Serrabinx's suspicions regarding a rumored group of such Palnans?"

Bridgette gulped. *The Collective*, she thought to herself, and was suddenly reminded of her sierwan knowing that the Maudlins wanted to be free from this country. This was why. They knew too much, and strangely enough it sounded as though they had been gifted this extraneous, dangerous information. To what end, why *this* family, none of them yet knew.

Zedolph was still talking, saying something else about the Collective. This final question she had about his family frustrated her, and Bridgette ignored him, not caring at the moment about the secret group of magical beings who were kidnapped and probably tortured by their proclaimed king and queen.

Bridgette held a hand up. "I know I'm interrupting you again, but this is going to bug the shit out of me. Do you have any idea why that book showed itself to you? Why y'all are, of all the Palnan citizens, the ones picked to have all this dangerous knowledge?"

"No," Zedolph chuckled. "We do not, and though I cannot say any more on this subject, trust me when I tell you that we do not take the privilege of this information lightly."

She had no idea what to make of that cryptic statement, and the butcher provided no additional clarity. Bridgette took the hint and rose to head back to her own bedroom, bidding Zedolph good night on her way out.

It's like I'm being given pieces of a puzzle here, but I don't have the stupid box to show me what the end picture will be like, she thought. *I have no idea what to make of these little revelations they keep giving me.*

Frustrated, she turned off the oil lamp and threw herself under the covers for a fitful night's sleep.

The dreams that haunted Bridgette that evening weren't as visceral and vivid as the dream about Eryth had been, nor were they as strange and senseless as whatever caused her covenant bracelet to glow. She watched herself dance in Maluridae Wood, then stumble and run deep into the trees, unsure if she was being chased or if she was a detective hot on a trail. She dreamed of flashes of faces. Most she knew. Some she didn't. She dreamed of a puzzle, pieces coming together and not quite fitting.

"Are you more well-rested this day?" Toby asked when Bridgette made her way into the kitchen the next morning, having gratefully slept in an extra couple of hours on her gifted day off. "I kept your milk warmed in a saucer for tea. Mumma had to visit patients and make deliveries, so you mustn't tell her I stole the golden sugar to sweeten it!"

"That's sweet of you," Bridgette joked, winking at the boy. "Your secret's safe with me, kid. What patients?"

Having been so involved in the butchery, Bridgette hadn't gotten much chance to spend time with Serrabinx. She knew that Serrabinx was a doctor or healer of some sort, at the very least an herbalist, what with her apothecary garden out back, but wasn't sure of the specifics.

"The ones she takes care of," Toby said simply, as if that was answer enough.

"Right, I got that part."

He missed the sarcasm in her tone, and instead prattled on about the grand plans he laid out for the two of them. Bridgette half-listened, sipping her tea — whatever was in that golden sugar was *divine* — and waited until Toby took a breath before she jumped into the one-sided conversation.

"I had an idea about where to go today," she said. "I want you to take me to the border of Palna."

"What do you mean, 'the border'?" Toby asked.

"Like, where one country ends and the other begins."

The boy looked so confused that Bridgette tried again: "Okay. Remember when we were in Fôret Fossile and you started to draw the map of Palna? You drew kind of an oval shape and then filled it in with rivers and cities. I want to go to where the edge of the oval is. Whatever spot is nearest."

"You want to go to the edge of Palna?"

"Exactly."

Toby fidgeted with the hem of his sweater. "I'm not supposed to go there."

"What? Why not?" she asked, and his answer was a shrug.

"Mumma said I should never venture toward there. When Mumma says to do or not do something, it is best to listen," Toby replied.

Though her eyes didn't shift, Bridgette suspected that Serrabinx's warning away from Palna's borders was an attempt to keep Toby safe from any prying eyes and ears looking to harvest new members of the Collective. If there was anywhere Palnan guards were regularly stationed, the nation's edge stood to be a pretty fair assumption.

"Will you take me as close as you feel comfortable?" Bridgette pressed him. "Your mom didn't tell me *I* couldn't go. I want to do some research in that area, ask some of the homeowners if they had to cede land when Bondrie was formed."

Though it was a lie she made up on the spot, it was actually a question she now wanted the answer to. She didn't know if Bondrie was formed from land that was once Palna, land only from the other three countries, or a combination.

"I can do that," Toby agreed warily.

"Excellent. We'll leave after I get dressed."

The Liluthuaé didn't know what she expected to find at the edge of Toby's world, but it would be nice to see a tangible wall, something to prove there was a way out, instead of just having —

Bridgette nearly dropped her teacup.

"Holy shit. Toby, I'm getting my notebook. I need you to draw that map again," she declared, already halfway down the hall. She practically threw the notebook and pencil at the bewildered boy mere seconds later.

She watched as he sketched the oval, filling it in with rivers and markers for cities in his neat but childish scrawl. When he got to Xcthonya, her heartbeat quickened. The city in which they resided was nowhere near enough to the border for her to have just walked through the Ballamúr directly into it.

How the fuck did I get here? she wondered, trying with all her might to remember what it felt like to walk through the two walls. The Samnung wall looked like a massive tower of shimmering sand falling straight from the sky. It tickled with static electricity, like pulling clothes off and feeling the hair of one's arms stand on end. But the Ballamúr was like walking through a pit of sensory deprivation. In three heartbeats she'd gone from there to nowhere to somewhere else. The brief moment of time she spent in the nowhere was almost like she caught herself falling asleep, a blink that lasted one second too long.

Bridgette didn't know how to evanesce, and even if she had, it would have been impossible to evanesce in a location she was unfamiliar with. Yet by some magic or miracle, Toby had known she was coming to that place, that day, that *time*!

Her eyes flashed repeatedly beneath their glamour as some of the puzzle pieces sunk into place. The Elfling sank into a chair, Toby oblivious to her movement as he worked on the map.

These protected lands, the Ballamúr … this entire country was *sentient*, and it sensed her presence. It knew her. It was cautious of her, but still it called to her; was wary, yet wanting.

Bridgette was Eryth Tinuviel's blood, and so was Palna.

~ 38 ~

"Bridgette? Are you alright?" Toby asked. He finally looked up from his map to realize she was staring straight past him, her eyes glazed and locked on something he could not see.

She blinked. "I'm … not sure," she replied slowly, turning to glance at her young friend. The Bright Star wasn't sure how much she could or should divulge to him, or how much he knew about any of this — his mother and uncle's accidental secret-keeping, Palna's true history, even what he deduced about her. It was all so confusing, and hitting her all at once! She struggled to get control of her breath.

Toby's small hands came up on either side of her face and Bridgette opened her eyes, unsure when she'd closed them, to find herself staring directly into Toby's deep brown irises. Those tiny, tell-tale flecks of metallic gold and molten chocolate seemed to search her very soul, and Bridgette chose in that instant to let him See.

Bridgette allowed her body to unclench, her breath to flow evenly, her mind to wander the way it had that first day Toby Saw her in their dining room. She didn't focus on anything this time, didn't let concrete thoughts solidify in her mind. She thought about that moment of nothingness as she stepped across the Ballamúr.

Neither was sure for how long they remained there, frozen. After a time, Bridgette felt her anxiety ease and a strange lightness begot her. It was as if something had been pushing down on her shoulders for weeks and weeks. She realized with a start that she was about to let herself float upwards — a sensation she'd all but forgotten after the time in Palna.

"Oh!" she gasped out. Toby stepped back. He was smiling, but it wasn't a real smile. More of a gesture of reassurance to her than an expression of pleasure.

"Are you alright now?" Toby asked again.

"I do feel better, actually, but what in the seven hells did you do? I feel like you showered me in a muscle relaxer."

He grinned for real this time, taking the sentence as a compliment. "Mayhaps we should both get dressed and go for our long walkabout. We will be gone many hours this day, and I think you would like to ask me more questions."

"No shit, Sherlock," she replied, ruffling his hair. "Meet you back here in fifteen."

Bridgette threw on clothes while the boy packed them a light picnic lunch, complete with glass bottles of apple juice. While Bridgette and Zedolph had been busy at the butchery, Toby had taken up the new hobbies of breadbaking and juice-pressing, which he proudly made use of at every opportunity.

"Should we leave a note for your mom?" Bridgette asked, glancing around the kitchen for a scrap of paper.

"A most excellent thought!" Toby exclaimed. He opened a drawer and scribbled something, then dashed back to the front door. "Shall we venture?"

"Venture we shall, Little Lark."

It was a sunny day out, the November air crisp but still humid, and Bridgette was reminded again of a Southern American fall. She was glad she thought to wear layers, for in the bright daylight it was warm, but the moment the trees shaded their path, she resisted the urge to shiver from the sudden dip in temperature. Toby held her hand, their picnic lunch and beverages safely tucked in a leather knapsack that Bridgette wore crossbody. Her notebook, ready for questioning Toby, peeked out from the bag's back pocket.

Toby led the way, as Bridgette had no idea which direction led to the edge of Palna. Occasionally he would stop to point out a particular species of tree, or a bird chirping overhead, but that was the extent of their conversation until they reached what Toby declared to be a good spot to stop and sit. They leaned against the thick trunk of an aging, gnarled tree and pulled out the apple juice and sandwiches.

"What was it that made your mind leave today?" Toby asked.

"What do you mean?"

Toby chewed a moment. "When I was drawing the map, your body remained, but your mind did not. Where did it go?"

"Oh," Bridgette murmured. "I was thinking about the day that you and I first met, when I kind of appeared at your feet. I've been trying to figure out exactly how that happened, and I think … well, actually I'm still really confused about the whole thing, but I was fitting some stuff together. What did you do when you touched me? Did you See me?"

"I still cannot See you the way I can others," Toby said sheepishly. He toed at the ground, drawing a shapeless swirl in the dirt. "You are still protected, but your protectors let me ease your energy."

"Fucking little Reiki healer, aren't you?" she chuckled.

"What is a Reiki?"

"Never mind," Bridgette smiled. "It's an Earth thing. Maybe a Heáhwolcen thing too. I actually don't know. But anyway, go on about how you can ease my energy. What is it exactly you do when you See people, and how can you tell me so much stuff, like the Raisarch thing?"

"It is a lot to tell," Toby hedged.

"Cool beans, kid. I got lots of time. Let's go." She snapped her fingers in the air.

The boy sighed, defeated. "Each being is three. There is our conscious self, the being we present to the world. There is our esoterikos, the being that lives within our minds, that processes who we truly are and who we pretend to be. There is lastly and most importantly our true self, our higher being, our subconscious. Anyone with eyes can see the conscious self of the beings around them. But I can See the others within."

"I have a friend in Heáhwolcen who can listen in to hear

what he calls your 'inner monologue'. Like, he can hear you talk to yourself inside your head. Is that kind of the same thing?" Bridgette asked, wincing as Collum's face flashed in her mind.

"Mayhaps, but he is Hearing, not Seeing," Toby pointed out. "It is much easier to protect your esoterikos and your subconscious than it is your thoughts to yourself. Those are things you might not yet know about yourself."

The kid sounds caught between being a psychology textbook and a fucking medium, Bridgette thought.

"Can I have an example?" she asked.

Toby looked uncomfortable. "When I first tried to See you, I could not tell what you were thinking. I could not hear your thoughts or know where your mind transported you. But I could See that you were in a place of peace with a presence that comforted you, and you felt well and safe. That was your esoterikos. When we are calm and safe — or sometimes when we are very angry — the esoterikos is set away and the subconscious self becomes open, as when we are asleep. You became calm and safe in your mind, and so I could See some of the true self. But because you are protected, I could only See some things."

"Toby." Bridgette turned to him, her face deadly serious. "I need you to tell me what you Saw. I need to know what you know."

"I Saw that you aren't telling us the whole truth, that your conscious self is pretend," he whispered. "I Saw that there are things about you that you are afraid of. Your true self waits to be fully discovered, but I See a cycle of burrowing within you."

"Excuse me? A cycle of burrowing?" Bridgette repeated blandly.

"Yes," Toby continued, meeting her eyes again. "You know there is more to you, but you are scared to explore this power, so you pretend that all you are is your conscious self. You burrow this power down until something draws it up, and you feel challenged about who you are. But when these moments pass, you are afraid again."

His use of the word "power" was heavy with intention, and Bridgette's stomach clenched at the memory of her hand around Emi-Joye's throat. "How in the seven hells did you get from that vague explanation to telling me I'm the fucking Raisarch?" she questioned. She wondered if Toby was trying to make her angry, trying to bring out this aspect of her that they were both so very curious about.

"This power is *you*," Toby said with such a hard note to his voice that Bridgette felt dumb for not being able to comprehend what he meant.

"That means nothing to me!" Bridgette whined. "I don't understand what you mean, Toby. You say that you See I've got all this power locked up inside me, but I have no idea what you're talking about."

He winked at her. "You are lying to me. You will know what I mean when you decide to see what I See in you."

"Fucking fuck, Tobias Maudlin, you're driving me nuts talking in straight circles. I give up," she groaned.

He gripped her hand, still smiling. "No, don't give up, Bridgette. Think! Think about what I See in you, and the knowledge you will not share."

Bridgette didn't think, but she did snap out, "I want to know why you're convinced I'm the Raisarch when both of us know there already *is* a Raisarch, and it's one of the fucking Tinuviels."

Toby's eyes widened, and Bridgette realized she erred by speaking so loudly. They sat in silence for a moment, hoping the wind would not carry her words too far beyond their picnic spot.

"I'm sorry, Toby," she whispered. "I didn't mean to get snippy with you."

"There isn't a real Raisarch in Palna," he whispered back. "The real Raisarch is a title given by blood."

She blinked. "Come again?"

Toby nodded enthusiastically. "Anyone can call themselves

the Raisarch. It is just a word. But the true Raisarch is more than a name. It is an Elf bound to its warriors in a way no other can be. Only the original Raisarch's descendants may carry on this bond."

Toby was practically vibrating with anticipation.

Oh, fucking fuck, the Elfling thought. Toby knew she was lying about her last name being Roberts, about her mother being human and her father being a dead Elf. Toby knew that she was more than what she played at, although the words "Liluthuaé" and "Bright Star" might be unfamiliar, since he'd been raised by once-witches and not Elves, despite his late father's own heritage. She didn't know if Toby understood who she was — what she was! — but he knew enough to know that she was indeed an Elfling, and a special one at that.

Bridgette gritted her teeth and looked straight ahead into the grove of trees in front of them. "We'll get up early and walk to the border tomorrow. Today, I need you to tell me everything you know about the Raisarch and what it has to do with the history of this country."

The boy was crestfallen. He sensed she'd been on the edge of a personal breakthrough, but she hadn't quite gotten there yet.

"When I was a wee boy" — the term made Bridgette laugh, for Toby was a boy still — "Mumma and mine uncle would tell me stories about the Dark Elves that split away from the Ealdgecynd. They were called Eelings, and they were very bad beings. Why, they would start fires simply to watch them burn, and then come put them out with strange powers of water brought forth from the air! It was thought they were a gift from Ceannairí Álfar, the great first being of power."

That didn't sound so different from the bedtime stories Collum had been told as a youngling, Bridgette remembered. She liked in Palna though that the Ealdaelfen had been nicknamed "Eelings", a much easier word for little ones to pronounce.

"The Eelings were not very organized, Mumma told me," Toby continued. "Then one day, there came to be an Elf in their group who showed greater power than even they had, and he came to be their leader. They called him the Raisarch, and they bowed to him and him alone. He wanted to be the greatest ruler of all the Elves! And so, the Eelings did as he told them, for they wanted to please him. The Raisarch promised that when he came to rule the whole world, they would get gifts of his favor."

Toby sounded like a tiny little prophet as he spoke. "But the Raisarch's plans became known, and the other Elves rose against the Eelings. They did not want this dishonest male as their leader, for they learned that the Eelings were doing such bad things and pretending it was others! Pretending they were the ones saving Elvenkind when really, they were doing ill acts! It was a most frightful war and many Elves on both sides were lost to the ages." He paused to take a breath. "After the end of it all, the Eelings that remained were given a choice."

Bridgette's ears perked up. This was news to her. "A choice?"

"Yes," Toby said solemnly. "They could choose to renounce the Raisarch and remain in their dúnaelfen, or they would be banished, their powers and souls forever trapped underneath the earth."

"What about the Raisarch?"

"The Raisarch was killed."

Bridgette vaguely remembered Collum telling her that. "Right, so then how do we have another one?"

"I already told you," Toby chided her. "Blood."

Understanding dawned. "The Raisarch had an offspring."

Toby nodded.

"And Elves live fucking forever."

He nodded again, smiling this time. "Now you start to understand."

"Let me get this straight," Bridgette said. "The original

Raisarch of the big bad Eelings — or Ealdaelfen is what they're really called — managed to get offed in this war with the Elves. But before he died, he had a kid. Or a youngling. Whatever y'all call baby Elves. And this youngling, because Elves are essentially immortal, is still around and wreaking havoc with a new band of followers?"

"Yes, and no."

She tossed her hands up in exasperation. "Toby! You've gotta help me out here, dude. I'm trying to put the pieces together, but I'm fucking lost. It probably doesn't help that I was raised on stories about Cinderella and the Little Mermaid, and not Elven wars of the thirteenth century. But I'm gonna need a little bit more detail here if you're so damned determined I'll figure this out."

"The Raisarch does not have to take its role," Toby said carefully. "Especially if it does not know the role is its to take. It is said the true Raisarch now is a long-descendent of this first one, as though the Elves may live immortal lives, most choose not to do so, and most are still able to die."

Bridgette got it then. "You're telling me that the true Raisarch is biding his time out there in the world, and may not even know he's the Raisarch? And meanwhile there's this fake Raisarch, probably Eryth Tinuviel, pretending to rile up the new Ealdaelfen, probably to do — oh. Shit."

Probably to start destroying Palna from within, making it easy for faux Raisarch Eryth to blame these acts on the Samnung and drum up support for a war.

"Fucking seven hells, Toby," Bridgette whispered. "You know about what's coming."

He smiled, but not at her — more at the gentle wind that breezed across their faces and rustled through their hair at that moment, bringing with it a soft floral scent. Tulips. The boy leaned forward and drew a symbol in the dirt. It looked like a very angular, graphic eye, made of complicated lines and arcs filling a semicircle. The eye looked familiar, but Bridgette couldn't place it.

Then Toby whispered, in a voice quieter than fawn's breath, "Sóc Láttaew al Hringur." He looked at the Elfling, eyes wiser than his young years should have allowed, and waited for her to comprehend.

That phrase! The eye! It looked exactly like Queylan's wrist tattoo, and those, she could have sworn, were the same words he said to the jeweler. The sierwan knowledge hit Bridgette like a bomb. There was a Palnan resistance to the Tinuviels and this war they were trying to stir up, and the Maudlins were founding members.

Bridgette leaned harder against the tree trunk, utterly aghast. "What does this *mean?*"

"Sóc Láttaew al Hringur," Toby said again. "I am Guide to the Hringur. We speak for those struck voiceless. We are the prisoners of no one's walls. We are the power that should not exist. We are the Hringur, and we fight so that the Triumvirate will rise."

~ 39 ~

Each of the three notebooks Collum found had a faded symbol on the cover that was hard to make out but *could* have been a runic symbol like those Apostine saw. The two males, Aurelias, and Emi-Joye gathered around the floating treasures.

"Whatever these are, they're important," Collum murmured. He moved his fingers through the air, his magic gingerly flipping pages through the greenish one.

"Stop!" Aurelias gasped. "Did anyone else see that?"

"See what?" Apostine and Emi-Joye asked in unison.

Aurelias' silvery skin paled. "Flip through another one. Slowly. Watch the pages."

Collum did as she bade, and before their eyes, the bizarre runes handwritten upon the pages of the lavender-gray notebook morphed into the same sort of writing the ambestre pointed out earlier: a few of the symbols remaining between lines of comprehendible language. He blinked, flipped another page, and watched it do the same thing.

A shiver of something akin to fear stalked down his spine. "What magic would do this?"

"What does this magic not wish us to see?" Emi-Joye whispered, a strange cock to her head. "Why does it disguise itself so?"

The Fairy started to reach a dainty hand for the third notebook, but Aurelias slapped it away. "Have you lost your mind, Ambassadora? Maybe let's not touch these things with our bare hands. They're probably fucking cursed."

Emi-Joye rubbed over her palm where Aurelias hit it. She didn't respond. Collum frowned, as suddenly the Fairy's inner monologue was not a monologue at all, but a curious sort of humming and buzzing. Mental white noise. The fyrdwisa bit his tongue. He watched the notebooks floating in midair, as if waiting for one of them to combust or do *something*. But they simply bobbed there, waiting.

Yes, Collum thought. *They are indeed waiting.*

He felt a sentience, as if the notebooks had minds. As if they knew they were being watched by individuals they did not trust with the knowledge they held. As if they had been spelled to, or *knew* to, shift to hide their runes. Collum concentrated on the lavender-gray one, opening his mind to it, listening. He didn't hear words, not the way he could hear Bridgette with the ísenwaer or hear anyone's inner voice speaking to themselves. But the notebooks, hidden so well and for so long, were groggy. They still spoke to him, but offered glimpses of energy rather than sentences. They knew it was his air magic that cradled them, that found them in their hiding place.

Collum swallowed deeply. The notebooks were weary now, but they would wake soon enough. He didn't think his kitchen was the best place for them to be when that happened.

"We need to hide them," he said finally. He had no idea for how long he'd been having a stare-down with the ancient books. "We're taking the trunk to Maluridae Wood."

Apostine shot him a confused glance, and Collum half-thought it odd that Emi-Joye didn't do the same, but perhaps as an ambassadora she was privy to Aristoces' knowledge of the sacred place. The fyrdwisa used his magic to lay the notebooks back in the trunk, and then he turned to his comrades.

"Maluridae Wood, Apostine, is a secret, sacred space. It is only accessible by Elves who know of its existence. You two" — he indicated to the Fairy and Tief-Fae — "can only get to it by being evanesced with one who knows. The notebooks will be safe there."

It was as if the weeks' worth of work sorting the documents was irrelevant. The knowledge they sought was most likely between those cracking leather covers, as of yet indecipherable and distrusting of the four beings who discovered them anew. Aside from the pages Apostine found, and the lone paper Collum summoned with his spell, nothing else would have direct relevance to Maylemaegus. The rest could be taken back to the Caisleán or to scholars at the University.

Once the other Maylemaegus-related papers were added back to the trunk, Collum shut its lid and heaved the piece into his arms, significantly lighter than when it was full of documents. Aurelias, Emi-Joye, and Apostine each put a hand on him. In a flash of navy whirls, they reappeared in a clearing of silver rowan trees, scarlet berries dangling in the brightening light.

Dawn was on its way. The four had been up all night.

Collum set the trunk down at the base of a tree. He ran a hand through his hair, unsure how best to hide it. Air was his, and most Elves', specialty when it came to magic, but a floating bit of furniture was sure to raise questions, even tucked deep into the wood. He glanced to Aurelias. "Would you …"

"Sure thing, Chief," she grinned. The Elfling walked to the tree nearest the trunk and lay her palms upon it, speaking a spell into place that coaxed the rowan roots to lift themselves from the ground and wrap around the trunk, protecting it in their embrace.

The fyrdwisa summoned a breeze that moved twigs and fallen leaves into the roots, further sheltering the trunk. "I think that should do it, for now."

He was uneasy. The notebooks didn't like being cooped up again. *He* didn't like knowing what they were thinking, or that they could "think" at all.

"Deity Dhaoibh, these shall not be disturbed," Collum said. "Let us return to my home. You are all welcome to sleep there, of course."

Safely back in Eckenbourne, Aurelias claimed the couch, Apostine the chair in which Trystane normally sat — promising the fyrdwisa that his wings would be fine dozing upright — and Emi-Joye crept to the guest room that still smelled just barely of honeysuckle and vanilla.

Collum gargled a mouthful of water before lying down, the sun threatening to creep in through his bedroom window. Maluridae Wood was far away, and yet he still could not shake the energies that those notebooks gave off. He was plagued by this same thought several hours later when he woke to the sound of a sleepy Apostine opening the apartment door for Trystane. The ard rialoír returned with honeycakes and morning beverages, demanding to know what went on after he and Njahla left.

The fyrdwisa joined them in the living room, clad in his sleepclothes. He stifled a yawn and reached a hand out for one of the honeycakes. "All of this can be taken to the Caisleán," he said, motioning to the papers. "We found what we needed."

"You did?" Trystane's brows rose nearly to his hairline.

"An assortment of papers marked with unusual runes and bits of language that were incoherent, and three notebooks full of similar runes that, upon further inspection, changed languages in front of us," Collum said mildly. He took a bite of pastry. "Those notebooks are something *else*, Trystane."

The Elf furrowed his brow at the fyrdwisa's intonation, but it seemed lost on Apostine and Aurelias, both of whom were bickering about which one got to have the sole cranberry-orange honeycake in the bag.

"What do you mean? And where is the ambassadora?" Trystane wanted to know.

Collum inclined his head down the hall. "In Bridge — in the guest room," he caught himself. "We took the notebooks to Maluridae Wood and encased them safely at the trunk of a rowan tree. I can't tell if they're spelled to be so, but they are sentient. They have thoughts and energies. I can sense these — these moods, perhaps, is the best way to describe it, but they do not share sentences or words. They offer an innate understanding without speaking."

Is it because of your empath powers? Trystane thought to him. *Did you tell the others about this?*

The fyrdwisa met his eyes and shook his head. "I don't know, and absolutely not. You needed to know first. I want to go back and examine them, but as I do not know what they are and why I can interact with them like this, I did not wish to go alone."

Trystane nodded his understanding. "Eat and put on something warmer. We'll go as soon as you're ready and bring the ambassadora along."

"What?" That addition caught Collum off-guard. "Why Emi-Joye?"

"Because if she's right about herself, Duathanna or not, she at the very least felt the aura with Bridgette. Perhaps she will feel something similar about these notebooks, if they have anything to do with Maylemaegus."

Collum stopped mid-chew. He swallowed and nearly choked. "She does," he remembered, and shared with Trystane how, when he floated the notebooks amongst the four of them, Emi-Joye reached out to touch one in the strangest manner. "Aurelias hit her hand away before she could, but I would bet my annwyl bond that there's a connection."

"And I would bet mine that you're correct," Trystane replied. He inclined his head to the fyrdestre and ambestre. "Send these two off to the University with this collection of history, and I'll go wake the ambassadora. You and I must return in time for the Samnung meeting, which we invited both Emi-Joye and Apostine to attend, if you remember."

The fyrdwisa cringed. "I had forgotten that. I really would rather never set foot in Wales again; much less be in the same moldy cave that Heledd dwells in. Maybe the Universe will shine in our favor and these notebooks will reveal enough so that we do not have to make another trip."

Trystane gave him a look that very clearly said, "Good luck

with that", and walked off. Collum turned to Apostine and Aurelias — who decided to cut two flavors of honeycakes in half, like the sensible grown beings they were — and gave them the news that they were to collect and deliver all of the pages.

"Why can't we go back to the wood?" Aurelias pouted. "How come we get stuck lugging all of this around Heáhwolcen? And how are we supposed to transport the documents when the trunk they arrived in is no longer available for use?"

Collum hadn't had enough sleep to deal with the combination of anxiety about the notebooks, plus having to report Lucilla to the Samnung in just a few hours, *and* now his second complaining about having to do a mundane task.

"Deity forbid that not just I, but the ard rialóir, give you a job to do that is incredibly delicate in nature," he snapped. "I do not know how you're going to do it, but for fuck's sake, Aurelias, you are the fyrdestre of Eckenbourne and *you* can figure that out for yourself."

"Just because I'm your second doesn't mean you have to give me shit work, *Fyrdwisa*," she glowered. "I have just as much right as you do to be heavily involved in protecting our world and tracking down magical history. As your *second*, should I not be privy to knowing what you do? Or have you forgotten the partnership we had for so long? Just because I'm not the fucking Bright Star doesn't mean I get to be further distanced from you. You're hiding things from me and so is Trystane. Shoving me off to the side like this while you two go off to the wood and keep secrets isn't a good look for leaders who supposedly have the utmost trust in me."

Collum glared at her. The comment about Bridgette stung with a hint of truth. "If you don't want to do it, then don't. You can explain yourself to Trystane later. That's on you, Fyrdestre. I have more important things to do than listen to you complain about being entrusted with Elven artifacts and keeping these notebooks a closely guarded secret, which, mind you, is a very strong sign of just how deeply the ard rialóir and I trust you *and* Apostine."

She wouldn't cow. "You can be so shitty when you want, Collum Andoralain."

"And most of the time, I don't want to be," the Elf scoffed. He softened, a spark of anger igniting in himself for going off on Aurelias. "I'm sorry, Fyrdestre. I need you to accept we do trust you implicitly, but there are some things that … that I need to further research and understand myself before I am comfortable sharing them with anyone. Even you, and even the Liluthuaé. Some things, even Trystane."

Apostine cleared his throat, and they suddenly remembered the Tief-Fae was seated on the floor at their feet. "So, we're all friends again, yeah?" he quipped. "Because these have been a few very awkward moments of my life, and watching the fyrdwisa and fyrdestre get into a brawl was not on my to-do list this day."

"I'd beat him, anyway," Aurelias remarked. She gave Collum a sly glance. "Apostine and I will handle this. But you owe me a *very* expensive dinner, with scotch and steak, and a *lengthy* explanation, Chief."

He bowed his head. "That I do, Fyrdestre. This will not happen again."

She laughed. "Don't make promises you don't know if you can keep, Fyrdwisa."

~ 40 ~

"Em?" Trystane knocked at Collum's guest bedroom door. He glanced over his shoulder to make sure none of the others had followed, then slipped inside. The Fairy stirred at his entrance. She gave him a lazy smile as the morning sun beamed over the headrest.

"Well, Ard Rialóir, isn't this quite a way to wake up," she cooed, reaching for him. "Whatever would the fyrdwisa say?"

Trystane sat next to her, and Emi-Joye reached around to hug him from behind, her chin resting at his hip. He toyed with her hair, wavy from letting it dry braided the day before. "The fyrdwisa wouldn't dare challenge my judgement."

"Are you and I speaking of the same fyrdwisa? Because the Collum Andoralain I am familiar with would have *much* to say if he was to walk in this door right now."

The Elf flipped around, crouching over top of her. His filthy grin was ravenous. "Then let's hope he doesn't."

Emi-Joye's eyes widened with delight at his boldness, and she pulled him down to kiss her. They only stopped at the sound of raised voices coming from elsewhere in the apartment, and Trystane lifted his head, his Elven hearing able to make out enough to know that Collum and Aurelias were arguing over something. He sighed.

"What is it?"

"I have a feeling the fyrdestre is displeased I didn't invite her to Maluridae Wood with us," Trystane admitted. "We'd like you to join, though. Collum told me what happened with the notebooks last night, and that you seemed to have a connection to them?"

She blinked up at him. "Excuse me?"

"He said you reached for one, and Aurelias made you stop?"

Emi-Joye glanced down at her hand. "Oh. I suppose I did, but I don't know why." She gave Trystane a strangled sort of look. "Ah. This is the reason you would like me to accompany the two of you."

"Precisely, my winged maiden." He bowed back down to kiss her once more. "We'll leave when the both of you are ready, and then we have a Samnung meeting to attend to."

The Fairy groaned. "I don't know that I can go to that today, Trys. This is the same dress I wore yesterday, then slept in last night, and I won't have time to go home and change — I can't represent my station looking such a mess."

Truth be told, Collum didn't seem too keen on attending either, but he had no choice. "We'll discuss that later, then," Trystane promised. "I didn't say a word about another visit to Wales yet, so no one is even expecting you to be at the meeting, nor for the topic to be brought up on the agenda. Let us see what secrets these notebooks hold, and perhaps the trip can be postponed or disregarded altogether."

She wrapped her arms around his neck and her legs around his waist. "I do so cherish you, Trystane Eiríkr."

"And I you, Emi-Joye Vetur." He evanesced from her grasp and grinned as he reappeared at the foot of the bed. Her gasp of surprise raked over his core, and Trystane took a moment to adjust himself in his leggings. "Go freshen up before I do something brash and dangerous in this bed with you, sweet Fae of mine."

"You do so like to command me, don't you?"

"I rather do." He winked as he crept out of the bedroom, closing the door silently behind him.

Collum gave the ard rialóir a pointed look when he emerged back into the living room. "Where did you go?"

"I was discussing the Samnung meeting with the ambassadora," Trystane replied easily. "She is concerned about bringing up another trip to Wales —"

"You're going back to Wales?" Aurelias interrupted. She stared at Collum. "When were you going to tell me this?"

"Yes, tell *us*," Apostine agreed. "Vetur hasn't said a word about such an event either."

"Because we don't know if we're even going," Collum said. He tried to keep the frustration out of his voice after just having cooled off with Aurelias. "We want to further investigate the notebooks and any potential connection they might have to the Liluthuaé legend and the Fairy myths Emi-Joye told us about. Before we found the notebooks last night, she and I discussed possibly having to return to question Heledd further about what he or the True Druids knew about our species. If the notebooks are able to reveal anything, I will hopefully never have to see that man again in my lifetime."

Aurelias scowled. "Stop keeping secrets, Fyrdwisa."

"I wasn't keeping a secret!" Collum shouted. He threw his hands in the air, giving up on decorum. "Hecate fucking bless, Aurelias, just because I haven't thought to tell you something doesn't mean I am hiding it from you!"

He stormed into his bedroom and slammed the door behind him, just as Emi-Joye emerged from the other end of the apartment.

"Did I miss something?" she asked tentatively. Aurelias' eyes shot daggers at the door, which still vibrated from the force with which Collum slammed it. Apostine's shoulders were set and taut, and Trystane's expression was caught somewhere between amusement and embarrassment.

It was Apostine who spoke, not meeting Emi-Joye's gaze as he concentrated on stacking the documents in neat piles. "Trystane is sending Aurelias and I to the University. He just informed us of the possibility you could return to Wales."

"Oh," she said. "I hope we won't have to, but if we do, you'll know soon enough. Is that all? Why did that make Collum slam his door shut?"

Trystane snorted. "I'll let you ask him when he deigns to return."

By the time he, Collum, and Emi-Joye stood in front of the rowan tree, they only had a couple of hours remaining before the Elves had to report to Cyneham Breonna. Collum regretted his argument with Aurelias, especially as he stared at her handiwork that protected the trunk and its secrets within.

Deity damn me, he thought, sighing heavily. "Trystane, I might need you to undo this. You're far better with earthwork than I am."

Trystane ran a hand in the air above the coiled roots. "I'll coax the tree. You open the trunk when it releases."

They moved quickly, aware how little time they had to investigate the notebooks, which Collum floated in the air again. None of them had the strange runes they had the night before, just the even stranger combination of symbols, words, and half-sentences that made as little sense to Trystane as they had to the other four beings.

"I've never seen anything like this," the ard rialóir said. He used his own magic to move the blue-ish notebook to him, murmuring spellwords as he attempted to persuade the artifact to share its true nature and purpose.

They were still sleepy, and they didn't like Trystane's attempts to pry into their depths. Collum gritted his teeth at the awareness. He felt the notebooks' energy more this morning, but knew it would be some time yet before they fully woke. Like a youngling who protested being woken for lessons, so the notebooks resisted the Elf's whispered magic.

"What do you make of them?" Collum asked quietly. To speak loudly would irk the damned things, and he felt it best to let them rest as long as possible.

"These are not ordinary notebooks," Trystane answered.

"No shit, Sherlock," Collum chuckled, using a well-loved Bridgette phrase. "I should say they are not."

Trystane gave him a wry smile. "I mean that beyond the

obvious. This magic is deep. There is a heaviness to them, a burden. It permeates the air.”

“They’re sleepy.”

“Sleepy?” Emi-Joye stood at Collum’s shoulder. He hadn’t heard her flitter up to join them. “What do you mean?”

The fyrdwisa gave her the same explanation he gave Trystane, sharing his ability to sense them. “It’s very strange,” he admitted. “I’ve never had that ability with any inanimate object. Do you feel the connection you felt last night?”

Emi-Joye gave a long, hard look at the notebook that Trystane idly continued to flip through, its wafer-thin pages crackling from centuries of disuse. She didn’t remember *why* she wanted to touch it, and didn’t really recall reaching for it, but the sting of Aurelias hitting her hand and her pride were hard to forget. “I don’t know. I don’t think so.”

She walked closer to Trystane, keeping a professional distance between them, though her breath caught at the feel of his magic. The Fairy turned her gaze from his strong, lean hands manipulating the air, and focused her eyes on the notebook itself. It was ashen blue, older than any book she’d ever seen before, the leather so aged that to touch it with just any hand would cause it to crumble, to cry out in pain.

But her hands — *I can touch it.*

The Fairy felt her head lull about from side to side, as if meditating, while she watched its pages turn. *It isn’t a notebook, not really. Handwritten, but you weren’t a diary, were you? You* aren’t *a diary, even still. Will you wake for me? Will you show me your magic?*

She felt that tumble of power deep within. The notebook seemed to pause in response, as if it had a heart that skipped a beat in surprise. It didn’t fear her. No, it —

The power inside her trilled now, threatening to rise from where it slumbered, hidden so deeply that even Emi-Joye didn’t know how to access it.

You recognize me, she thought. *You know me. But how?*

A pulse of energy emanated from somewhere in the clearing and suddenly Trystane was before her, shaking her by her shoulders. The power grumbled, so angry! The notebook was nowhere to be seen, and she was empty and couldn't breathe and he was calling to her, but where *was* it?

"Ambassadora!" Trystane finally shouted, and the tone of his voice, the fear she heard in that sole word, shook Emi-Joye back into the present. Her eyes, the Fairy eyes of constantly moving whorls of color, had stopped entirely as she focused on the notebook. The only movement she made for those few minutes was her head moving, trance-like, until she reached her hand out and nearly broke through the ward Collum had hastily thrown up when they realized the notebook was putting her under a spell.

"Where is it?" Emi-Joye whispered. She looked around and saw Collum a few feet away, on guard in front of the trunk. "What did you do with it?"

"They're all back in the trunk, Emi-Joye."

She stared at Trystane, her eyes suddenly a whorling frenzy. "Why would you do that?" The Fairy launched herself at Collum, and the ard rialóir caught her around the hips, crushing her wings flat against his torso as she fought to free herself, her voice rising in pitch as she shrieked in panicked protest. "Give it *back*! Bring it back, it's *mine*!"

Collum couldn't calm her. He tried, but his scent spell wouldn't work. Emi-Joye was absolutely hysterical, screaming for Trystane to let go of her and for Collum to open the trunk. Her mind was the same unintelligible white noise as it had been last night, and the energy in that clearing of trees became pandemonium. It was like she summoned a storm: the mid-morning breeze picked up speed the more the Fairy fought.

"Get her out of here!" Collum bellowed over her screams, over the whistling wind. "*Now!*"

Trystane shot him a panicked look of his own as he

evanesced them away, and the flying leaves and loose soil settled gently into the quiet of the empty wood, the sound of Emi-Joye's shrieking still echoing in Collum's head.

~ 41 ~

"Where did you take her?" Collum whispered as Trystane slid into the Samnung chamber moments before noon and took a seat next to him. "Is she alright?"

"She's at my home with Njahla and Sigewíf Ilori," the ard rialóir replied, his body still tense and shaken from that morning's events.

"You summoned Njahla's mother to help?"

"No, I summoned Njahla, and her mother was visiting so she came along. A good thing, as Ilori is a téitheoir, one of the herbalist healers, and brought all sorts of potions and poultices along with her. Emi-Joye collapsed in my arms in the middle of evanescing, and I have never in my life been so scared." Trystane glanced around the table to ensure no one listened to their side conversation. "Had I not had to be at this blasted meeting, I would still be there. She was whiter than snow and unconscious when I left."

"The moment you two evanesced, the clearing settled," Collum murmured as Nehemi strode into the room to call their meeting to order. His stomach curdled with anxiety. "The objects are once again secure."

"She's going to want to go back for it," Trystane remarked. "I'm too afraid to let her."

Collum glanced sideways at him. "I don't believe that's your call, brother mine."

"Do the two Elves have something they'd like to share with the rest of us?" Nehemi said, her scowl settling on them. "Or are you blatantly ignoring me as usual?"

"We would never blatantly ignore you," Trystane lied smoothly. "However, there is indeed something we wish to discuss, as Collum would like to make a formal complaint regarding his recent trip to Earth."

Nehemi fixed her gaze on the fyrdwisa. "Would Collum also

like to make a formal report to the Samnung regarding his recent trip to Earth, as he has yet to do so?"

Trystane gave a supportive squeeze to the fyrdwisa's forearm as he stood to address the chamber. "Do not be afraid," the ard rialóir whispered, his voice so low that only Collum could hear.

"Ceannairí, I do apologize for my belated turnaround in sending in my full report," Collum began. "I will be happy to do so soon. It is, at this moment, impossible for me to turn in a truthful account of my days in America, as it seems ill-advised to turn in a formal complaint to the individual which the complaint is about."

He wished he could calm down; his legs were shaking. Never before had he had to stand and make a charge of such magnitude, especially in front of a room of individuals who held the assailant in such esteem, individuals who employed her. He chewed his lip for a second so hard it drew blood. The sharp pain grounded him, and he placed his palms on the table, leaning forward to steady himself.

"I, Collum Andoralain, fyrdwisa of Eckenbourne and Heáhwolcen, do hereby charge the witch and Cyneham Breonna receptionist Lucilla Von Detton with malicious, ill-intentioned use of magic in the offenses of poisoning and assault of a voracious, inappropriate, and sexual nature," he bit out, each word acrid on his tongue. "These were actions taken against me on our final night in Nashville, Tennessee, and I am prepared to undergo an evidentiary examination ritual for proof of wrongdoing."

He allowed himself one breath before giving the full story, omitting only the details about the lights, the covenant bracelet, and that the dagger that appeared to him was Bridgette's. Collum would have given just about anything to be able to hear what the Samnung members thought in the stunned few moments after he spoke. He lifted his gaze in the silence to meet each set of eyes in turn. Corria was stony with fury. Bryten looked pained, but not with pity — there was understanding there, and Collum gave him a slow nod of acknowledgement. The Baetalüan returned the gesture and straightened his shoulders. Next to him, Verivol's fists were balled so tightly that their knuckles were a paler shade of, well, pale, and Aristoces' expression was that of someone about to vomit. Kharis didn't make eye contact with Collum, and the Elf didn't need his energy magic to feel the seething rage that wafted from the queen of Endorsa, though he wasn't sure if she was mad at Lucilla or at him.

But Cloa. The princess' eyes were fixated on him. They were bright and clear, a far cry from their usual appearance. Her nostrils flared in what Collum could have sworn was anger. Cloa's hands were gripped tightly around Arctura, and the cat's one good golden eye had narrowed. It was as if the two wanted to say something — or Cloa did, at least — but there was an insurmountable barrier between her and the fyrdwisa. He'd never so strongly desired to speak with her, had never seen her eyes flash with such violence or, seven hells, even been this expressive.

When Nehemi finally spoke, the princess blinked rapidly as if her mother broke a spell, and she succumbed again to her usual glazed stupor, gazing up at the queen expectantly. Collum furrowed his brow. He was getting tired of seeing females go into trances this day.

"Fyrdwisa, no such ritual will be necessary," the witch queen said. Her voice quivered as she tried to keep her composure, but her hands were shuddering at her sides, one reflexively wrapped around her wand. Its tip glowed ochre. "Kharis, you are to summon Lucilla to the chamber immediately. She may bring with her an individual of her choosing for support. Ceannairí, I request you each summon a trusted advisor of your own, so that we may have witnesses."

Witnesses for what? Collum didn't ask out loud.

"We will recess this meeting for an hour so that the witnesses and accused may gather, for an Indictus Magnus Iudicium," Nehemi continued. She waved a hand at the table, and the day's luncheon appeared on it. "Please eat at your leisure, though I have lost my appetite."

She strode out of the room and Collum sat back on his stool, dumbfounded. An Indictus Magnus Iudicium — it was rare for Latin to be heard in Heáhwolcen outside the field of healing, and rarer still to hear that particular phrase. It meant that Lucilla would be charged by her government and questioned by fellow citizens, who would then publicly support or denounce the Samnung members' choice of admonition. Collum looked to Trystane, who was somewhat apologetic as he piled a plate with roasted potatoes and carrots. "You'll summon Njahla?"

"No," the ard rialóir said, and the response surprised Collum. "Njahla knows you too well to be an impartial witness, and she's otherwise occupied right now, if you'll recall. I'm going to request Bennameena."

"The shopkeeper whose son Bridgette was to give violin lessons to?"

"The very one. She knows you in passing and refused coin payment for the last three tunics of mine she mended. I happen to know Bennameena is enamored with human mystery novels, so to be able to participate in this will be quite a thrill for her."

"Well, then," was all Collum could say. He reached for a plate.

The meeting was called back to order, the Samnung chamber uncomfortably full of so many additional beings. It did not help that Bryten's witness was a Centaur, whose burly, muscled hindquarters took up three times as much room as anyone else. Lucilla stood at the front of the room, trepidation evident in her eyes, which were still the wrong shade of purple. Collum realized with a start that Trystane never undid their glamour. He sincerely hoped that would be taken care of while they all stood there.

Lucilla knew why they had called her; knew that she was about to lose everything. Her only hope was that some or all of the witnesses, after hearing her story as well as Collum's, would find the Samnung leaders' decision too harsh, and would speak out on her behalf. She held the hand of a Fairy with straw-blond hair and stormy gray eyes, his translucent wings a complimentary shade of charcoal. He wore the outfit of a travel deputy.

Luthus. The name came to Collum, though he couldn't remember why he knew what the male was called. The Fairy caught his gaze, then those gray eyes traveled down to where Collum now wore Bridgette's dagger at his hip. Luthus sucked in his cheeks at the sight of the amethyst hilt but made no comment.

The borhond presided over the presentation of charges. It was easier this third time for Collum to tell what happened, again omitting any details that could endanger the Liluthuaé. The witnesses were informed that the fyrdwisa went to Earth to handle a situation related to a missing Elfling who Lucilla had been glamoured to resemble. Kharis reassured the witnesses that the Elfling was not missing, but was on a mission that kept her from being in contact with her human friends. Lymerian, Verivol's sister, shot Collum a strangely knowing look when Kharis mentioned the glamour.

Collum answered questions from the witnesses, then the Samnung. Maqtok Spring Bearer, the shieldhand of Bondrie and Corria's second, was the one who asked Collum the question he hated having to answer: How did he not know he was being poisoned?

"I was concentrating on listening for any thoughts about the 'missing' Elfling's name from those in the crowd. I was not intent on listening for Lucilla's inner voice in those moments, but rather kept my eyes on her to make sure she was unharmed as she approached the bar alone," he said. "I do not drink what humans call soda very often. Her added potion simply made it taste strange, but not alarming in any way, nor bad-flavored enough that I was unable to finish the drink."

When it was Lucilla's turn to speak, the witch's voice was fraught with panic.

Hearing her for the first time since Nashville, even though it had only been a few days, still sent an angry chill down the fyrdwisa's spine. She used her voice, not her faked Bridgette voice with the terrible attempt at a Southern American accent. Collum was ready to jump across the table and strangle the witch if she said a word that could harm Bridgette.

He had let Lucilla live once.

He wouldn't do so again.

"Ceannairí, it was never my intention to harm the fyrdwisa," Lucilla croaked. "I only intended to make him recall the feelings for me that he once had. It wasn't poison, simply a potion, and it was of his own choice that he removed his clothing and lied down before me."

I couldn't lift my own hand, much less undo a belt buckle, you vile bitch, Collum thought. He glared at her, the silver flecks in his eyes flashing maliciously.

When asked what was in the potion, Lucilla listed its ingredients. They were innocent enough. Collum wasn't skilled at potion making or chemistry. He had no idea if it was indeed a love potion gone awry as Lucilla claimed, or an intentional attempt to paralyze him. It was only when Lymerian questioned Lucilla — doing so before anyone else had a chance — that the young witch's guilt was sealed without question.

The Sanguisuge stepped forward, her flaming red hair a chaotic mess of bouncy curls, and gave Lucilla a wild sort of smile. Then Lymerian turned to address the Samnung and fellow witnesses in the chamber.

"For those who do not know, I am Lymerian Rosu, sister of Verivol, gimmshoppe keeper, and Old Magick scholar. I happen to own the store where, from mine own hands, Lucilla Von Detton purchased her ingredients. She used paper money to do so — Samnung wages, it appears — and visited twice," Lymerian said. "The first visit, she did indeed leave with the ingredients she mentioned. Her second visit, she purchased crushed rose quartz and Malouetia bark. Malouetia bark, Ceannairí mine, is a paralytic ingredient. It causes the being who ingests it to be unable to move."

Lucilla stared at her in horror. Lymerian's grin went feral.

Collum recalled, somewhere in the recesses of his mind, that Bridgette once mentioned going to a curious shop owned by a Sanguisuge. He gave the Sanguisuge in question a smile that matched hers, and the two watched as tears began streaming down Lucilla's cheeks.

~ 42 ~

"How is she?" was the first thing Trystane demanded of Njahla and her mother when he and Collum evanesced into his living room several hours later.

"Resting," Ilori assured him. "I gave her a draught that put her right to sleep, but Ceannairí …"

Her voice trailed off, and the elderly Elf glanced toward the bedroom. Silvery gray strands glistened in her elegant twists as she turned her head. "I've never heard any being's heart beat so fast. It still continues to pace rapidly."

Is it what we think it is? Njahla thought to Collum, who gave her a barely noticeable nod of acknowledgement. She sucked in her lips, nostrils flaring. *Is it going to hurt her?*

The question took Collum aback. He hadn't thought of such a thing, that the Maylemaegus could harm those in whom it moored, slumbering until rudely jerked awake. Rather, it seemed more likely to cause the bearer to become violent: Bridgette's angry outburst toward Nehemi, her attack on Emi-Joye, and now the Fairy nearly losing her mind when that notebook was, as she seemed to think, taken from her.

Njahla still stared at Collum, the two of them ignoring her mother and Trystane, who were engaged in separate conversation about what could possibly ail the poor female. Ilori wasn't dumb. She knew her daughter was the ardestre, the second to the ard rialóir, his right-hand Elf, and that Emi-Joye's sudden collapse and racing heart weren't the normal sort of injury she was used to treating. But Ilori wouldn't pry, thankfully, unlike some of the other téitheoir and lacnians in Heáhwolcen.

Collum shrugged. He didn't know how to articulate his thoughts in such a way that wouldn't share too much information with Ilori. She may not pry, but the fewer beings who knew what the Elven leaders were up to, the better.

"How was the Samnung meeting?" Njahla asked aloud,

interrupting the other two. "Was it a favorable outcome?"

This, however, Collum did not want Ilori to hear about. He winced at the realization that Njahla knew about what happened in Nashville — though Trystane could never have hidden something of this magnitude from her, and probably told her the gist of it to spare Collum from having to do so. The fyrdwisa was somewhat grateful for this. He was tired of telling the arduous tale, especially after having had to relive it multiple times that very day.

"I could use something to drink. Join me in the kitchen and I shall fill you in," Collum said.

Safely out of her mother's earshot, Njahla put a comforting arm around the fyrdwisa. "Trystane told me," she confided. "Collum, whatever sort of support you need, please know that you can come to me, and I will do what I can."

He hugged her, a rare interaction between the two of them. "Thank you, Njahla. That means much to me."

She stepped back and met his eyes, searching for some sort of answer. "How did it go?"

At that, Collum flashed her a smile so full of vindictive glee that Njahla wasn't sure if it truly was the fyrdwisa standing in front of her. So unusual was that show of emotion from the largely guarded Elf!

"Neither I nor Lucilla was required to undergo a truth ritual, as our honesty was ensured by being in the Samnung chamber and being unable to perform magic therein. Nothing from either of us indicated that perhaps we were skirting the full story, although Lucilla did try," he told her. "Was it not for Lymerian, things might have gone differently. Lymerian is Verivol's sister and a shopkeeper. It was she who ensured that the full Samnung and its slate of witnesses understood that Lucilla's intent was indeed that of ill will. The witch bought the ingredients, including a paralytic plant, from Lymerian's shop."

"Did Verivol know that, do you think, when they brought

her in as a witness?"

"I am not sure. It's very possible they brought her because of her knowledge of potion-making ingredients, to provide any sort of insight from her expertise, and instead Lymerian recognized the accused," Collum mused. "Either way, it was a fortuitous choice. It seemed difficult for some of those gathered to fully believe I was both unaware I was being poisoned until it happened, and that I was unable to stop the assault despite being significantly taller and more muscular than Lucilla."

Her name tasted wrong on his tongue. He opened the refrigerator and pulled out a bottle of what looked to be wine, opened it, and took a long sip. He choked.

Njahla chuckled. "Well, now I know where Trystane has been hiding his chilled mead."

The honey liquor had a dazing effect on Collum and his mostly empty stomach, and he shoved the bottle back. "Remind me never to drink that again, will you?"

He shook his head to clear it, unwell from the flavor and the lingering Bridgette-like scent of sweet honey in the air before him. "Nehemi declared that Lucilla is no longer the Samnung's recordkeeper and receptionist. Her glamoured features were finally removed — though that was necessity and not part of her Indictus."

That delirious gleam returned to Collum's eyes, silver flashing on blue, as he told Njahla the final part of Lucilla's admonition: "Then they tipped her wand."

"They *what?*"

Collum nodded. "I could scarcely believe it myself, had I not heard Nehemi pronounce the admonition and watched it happen with mine own eyes."

"That's … incredible," Njahla breathed. "I would not have thought Nehemi capable of something of that nature."

"Nor I," Trystane agreed, appearing in the doorframe. "I sent your mother back to your home, Njahla, and assured her you'd follow quickly behind after I had a word with you. But yes, I must say, it gave me quite a thrill to watch Queen Nehemi, for once, turn her cruel consign onto someone who actually deserves it."

Collum stopped speaking in whispers now that Ilori was gone. "When Kharis brought forward that cauldron, you could have heard Aristoces' wings shiver. I believe we were all somewhat shocked that the queen would take such a measure. Not to say that it was an unjust sentence, simply an unexpected one."

"Nehemi had to read from the Endorsan Grimoire to perform it," Trystane added. "I don't believe I've seen that text brought forth from the Museo Staire since I watched the Samnung wall go up around Palna."

"What was the ritual?" Njahla was awed and entranced by their tale.

"I don't remember the full incantation, but Nehemi cleansed an athame and each member of the Samnung, along with any witnesses who felt so inclined, gave a drop or so of blood to the cauldron, pricked from our index fingers. Lucilla's palm was swiped for hers. Nehemi heated the cauldron as more words were spoken, our blood mixing and warming with the molten bronze Kharis poured inside. The way it popped and crackled … it was as if a new creature was being created," Collum said. He absentmindedly rubbed the sore spot on his own finger where the ceremonial knife touched it. "I do distinctly recall Nehemi pronouncing that by the power vested in her as the queen of Endorsa, spreca of the Samnung, and the magics voluntarily given of ourselves, that Lucilla should be so bound against using neither tools nor self to bestow her ill intent on another being.

"And then" — again that wildness in the fyrdwisa's expression! — "Nehemi dipped Lucilla's wand into the cauldron. The entire thing cracked, as a tree would if struck by lightning."

Collum's memory flashed to Nehemi's own face going

predatory as she listened to the spell force itself into the wood. The vast majority of witches required wands to transmit their magic, being too genetically similar to humans to access their powers and commune with Nature without help. The bronze cap that now dully gleamed on Lucilla's wand would forever be a barrier to that connection, a constant hamper to her magic.

She would find it exceedingly difficult to ever harm another being without her magic backfiring on her in the process.

For the first time in months, Collum felt peace settle in his bones.

It was short-lived though, for after Njahla left, the fyrdwisa and ard rialóir found themselves left with an ill Fairy, still passed out cold in Trystane's bed. Though Emi-Joye was tall, she looked dwarfed and sickly curled up as she was under the covers, a warm cloth over her forehead. She felt clammy to the touch and her breathing came in soft, uneven gasps. The room smelled strongly of conflicting herbs. Ilori had spread a poultice of citrusy feverfew and mint-like hyssop across Emi-Joye's chest, and lavender incense burned on the nightstand.

Herbs for sleep, for respiratory symptoms, and for anxiety, Collum thought. *Ilori is a gods-send ... but why does the ambassadora still sleep so fitfully?*

"Should we wake her?" Trystane asked.

Collum assessed the energies in the room. The Fairy was fitful, but far better than she'd been that morning. "I suppose we should. I don't believe she's in any sort of danger."

The ard rialóir leaned over the side of the bed and placed a gentle hand on Emi-Joye's exposed shoulder. "Ambassadora," he murmured, and she shifted in response to his touch. "How do you feel, Emi-Joye?"

She blinked up at him, slowly, as though her eyelids were weighted with iron. Her pupil-less irises whorled again like they were supposed to. Seeing them frozen as they stared at the notebook had been one of the most frightening things Collum ever experienced. He wasn't sure he'd witnessed a Fairy's eyes stop moving, and he had no idea what it meant for that to happen.

Emi-Joye took in first Trystane, then Collum at the foot of the bed. She squeezed her eyes shut, then opened them again, and groaned as she moved to sit up. "I feel like I've been thrown against a boulder and pinned there with an immovable wall of air."

Her usually bright voice was raspy — how loud did she scream that morning?

"That is an incredibly specific description, Ambassadora," Trystane replied. "Do you recall what happened?"

The Fairy's expression switched to one of anxiety, and Collum felt the energy in the room morph alongside it. She chewed the inside of one cheek and looked at the fyrdwisa.

I don't think I can explain it, she thought to him. He nodded his understanding.

Collum joined Trystane, both kneeling next to her. "I would like to summon Apostine and Aurelias to join us," Collum said. "They have a right to know what occurred. With your permission, Emi-Joye, I would also like for you to undergo a meditative interview. I want to ask you a few questions so that we may fully understand, or at least better understand, your experience. Would that be acceptable?"

"I suppose so, Fyrdwisa."

"Then I shall summon my second, and you yours. We will figure this out, Emi-Joye," Collum promised.

~ 43 ~

The four of them settled Emi-Joye as comfortably as possible in Trystane's library, reclined in a voluptuous velvet chair and covered in layers of blankets. Apostine moved the lavender incense into the room, and Aurelias — momentarily forgiving Collum for their spat earlier — salted a circle around the chair for protection.

Collum bade her, Apostine, and Trystane stand on the far side of the room. He entered the circle, seating himself on a stool to be eye-to-eye with the Fairy. He transfixed his entire mind around hers, calling forth the scents that calmed her most, gardenia and rain-studded grass. It was heady, and Collum had to concentrate to not let himself get sucked into the soothing massage of energy within their protected space.

"Emi-Joye, what we are about to embark on is a meditative interview, where you will find yourself in a state of free thinking and recollection. You are safe. You may ask questions at any moment, and should you find yourself in need of silence, you do not have to explain yourself," Collum said. "Please tell me when you are ready."

She was still woozy from Ilori's care, but the power in the circle strengthened her. Collum was with her, and so were Trystane and Apostine. Emi-Joye met their eyes, both staring concernedly from the opposite side of the library, before nodding to the fyrdwisa. "I am ready."

The Elf guided her into a state of meditation. Emi-Joye's breathing became deep and controlled, no longer the uneven rasps she had while in the bed. She kept her hands on the armrests of the chair and felt Collum's hands on her wrists, grounding her into reality as her mind lofted itself into subconscious realms. It was a strange sensation, being both *here* and *elsewhere*, but Emi-Joye listened to Collum's gentle instructions and assurances that she was well; she was safe.

He walked her through the events of the day. She responded dreamily, recalling waking up in his apartment, speaking with Trystane, convincing the ard rialóir not to make her attend the Samnung meeting. Then the visualizations took them to the wood, and the energy in the circle changed.

"It is wrong to call them notebooks, Fyrdwisa. They are vademecums," Emi-Joye told Collum, and his brows furrowed at the unfamiliar word. "One of the three *knows* me, and I know it. We are one and the same, though I do not know how. It is mine and we are meant to be as one. It trusts me and distrusts others. I can touch it, but you cannot. It will be strong in my hands, yet crumble to bits in yours."

"What do you mean by calling them 'vademecums', Emi-Joye?"

"They are guides, as grimoires."

"But they are not grimoires?"

She shook her head slowly. "A grimoire is a personal object, a compendium of spellcraft, created by each witch on its own. A vademecum is a guide of power, to be used only by those which possess it."

"Is that power Maylemaegus?" Collum's heart skipped a beat.

"I do not know, but I would suppose so."

"How do you know this about the vademecums?"

"It told me, when we were in the wood," Emi-Joye said. "Not in those words, but I knew 'notebook' was not right. The word came to me later, when I felt it ripped from me."

Now we're getting somewhere, Collum thought. "Will you tell me what that was like?"

Her hands clawed into the armchair. Collum heard Trystane wince as the fabric ripped under Emi-Joye's fingertips. "It was as if my magic was snatched before my very eyes," she said. "It was as if I had been whole for but a moment, finding a piece of myself that had been missing for so very long, an old friend and a lover, a partner and additive to my power. I was waking, only to be shoved back into stark emptiness. A starving being who reached for bread dangled before her face, only to find it was but a trick. I needed it *back*."

"Back?"

"It had been waiting for me. We found one another and there was a wholeness to my being. Then it was gone, and everything was *wrong* again."

Collum understood then, and the reason why he empathized unsettled him greatly. "And you would willingly tear apart the world to retrieve that piece of you."

The deep-seated power inside her thrummed outward, and the salt circle shifted into a starry spread of white crystals. Emi-Joye opened her eyes and stared into Collum's own, the whorling a hypnotizing frenzy of pain and need.

"Nothing can separate that which is meant to be together as one," she whispered, so intensely that Collum barely registered her voice was clear again and melodic, not the whisper she'd been using since she woke on Trystane's bed.

He pulled back from her as the thrum of power blasted outward, spewing the circle into oblivion, causing books to fly off the shelves and the incense to burn out in an instant. It whipped through Aurelias' dark curls and sent Apostine into the air, yet gently caressed Trystane, dissipating only as the Elf reached out to touch the invisible force.

Emi-Joye crumpled into the chair, exhausted, and Collum turned to stare at the other three. "What in the seven fucking hells is going on?"

No one had an answer.

Apostine insisted on transporting Emi-Joye home once she regained enough strength to move, thanks to the Elves and Elfling forcing food, water, and an invigorating elixir into her. She protested weakly, not wanting to have to explain to her parents where she'd been for the better part of two full days —

"My mother will *not* take 'I was working' as an excuse" — but when Trystane threatened to tell Aristoces she was ill, Emi-Joye gave in.

The Tief-Fae flew her to the Veturs' dwelling, and she gratefully cradled into him. He was so good to her, her second, even when she didn't deserve for him to be. They made quite a pair, her rosy-pale skin against his, a deep golden tan so metallic it was as if he bathed in sand.

"Thank you, Apostine," Emi-Joye whispered against his collarbone. "You really didn't have to do this."

"I really did though, Vetur," he said, squeezing her arm. "You'd have dropped faint somewhere over Aelchanon had you tried to fly yourself back. That would have been hard to explain to both your parents and our ceannairí, don't you think?"

"Fine. You're right," she relented. "But I don't want you flying me right to the doorstep, please. We can fly up the path together."

Apostine watched the clouds drift past. "You do realize that it is a bit juvenile to worry so much about your parents' opinion as a fully grown Fairy, do you not?"

Emi-Joye groaned. "I am not having this conversation with you."

"Do as you wish, Vetur," he grinned down at her. "I'm just saying it's going to be far easier to own up to who you are than to keep burying yourself down under the desire to please everyone for the rest of your existence. You are *you*, and those who love you, love you for it."

Tula Vetur met them at the door, disapproval on her face. "Where have you been, daughter mine? It's most unlike you to disappear for days on end without so much as a word," she scolded. "Hello, Apostine. Won't you come in and join us for an evening meal? We have plenty to share."

Emi-Joye gave him a pleading look and he accepted the invitation, doing his best to alleviate any tension between the young Fairy and her parents. Tula was a force to be reckoned with, being one of the oldest Fae in Heáhwolcen — so old that her age showed in gentle creases by her eyes and at the corners of her mouth, and her hair was silvery white. Her husband, Johannes, was much younger, and seemingly ignorant of the tension his wife felt toward their daughter. Most of the supper table conversation revolved around Johannes telling stories about new innovations in healing, and this day he was particularly delighted to share the recent news that American human doctors received government approval to use a cannabis-based medication on certain patients.

It was a light, energetic evening, though at the end, Emi-Joye fought to keep her exhaustion at bay when she bid Apostine goodnight. She hugged him tightly, hoping he could understand all the emotions she tried to put into the gesture, and assured him she'd be back at their offices in the Seledreám the following morning.

She managed to avoid answering her mother's prying questions regarding her whereabouts, assuring Tula there were some things that she as ambassadora was not able to discuss outside of a close circle. Namely Apostine, Aristoces, and her contingent of human leaders in Antarctica, of course. Tula tutted her lips, the disproving look returning, but she went to bed without further comment.

When Apostine arrived at the Seledreám the next day, he was shocked to find the ambassadora asleep at her desk, head down in her arms and shimmering wings drooped to either side of her body.

The ambestre was at her side in an instant, shaking her awake, still scarred from seeing her newly discovered power in action. It worried him to observe how this magic affected the Fairy. "Emi-Joye, did you sleep here?"

She gave him a groggy grumble in response and shoved back

into the crook of her arm. "Leave me be, to die of humiliation in peace."

"Humiliation?" He gripped her shoulder, wondering what happened after he left her house. "What's going on, Vetur? You haven't been yourself for weeks now, between this new magic and prepping for the meeting with the Fórsaí Armada. I think you've absolutely lost it. I've never known you to work like this or be so down on yourself."

She flipped him off, head still burrowed.

"Really, that's cute," Apostine smiled. He leaned over the top of her head and nestled his nose into her platinum blonde braids. "Come now. Talk to me. I'm your second, and besides that, I'm supposed to help you plan and present this damned thing."

The Fairy made an unintelligible noise.

"Listen," the Tief-Fae continued, "I'm going to check the post — I'm expecting a temperature fluctuation read-out from Dag — and when I get back, you and I are going to get breakfast and have ourselves a little chat."

"No."

Apostine chuckled into her hair. "You're a spiteful one this morning."

"Go. Away. Apostine."

"I'm going away for seven minutes tops to check the post for that report from Dag. Then I will be back, and we are leaving to get you fed and watered."

"You're going to marry that human one day."

He grinned. "Is that supposed to be an insult? Because I rather fancy the idea myself."

"I hope your wings spasm mid-flight and you're rushed to a lacnian, unable to continue tormenting me, so that I may perish in peace."

"Such a wee poet, she is!" Apostine teased. He pulled back from her and squeezed her shoulder. "Mayhaps I should alert our dear ard rialóir that the ambassadora is plotting her demise and penning her own eulogy as we speak."

Emi-Joye twisted on her stool so fast that she scared them both, and suddenly they were nose-to-nose, her eyes whorling in fury. "Do not get Trystane involved," she hissed. "I don't want to talk to him about this."

"Oh? As though you talk to him about other things?" Apostine's knowing smile was deliciously lupine.

Her cheeks turned a remarkable shade of rosy pink as she struggled for a suitable response. When her second's grin grew wider, the Fairy shoved him with all her might, pushing him toward the door.

"Get *out* of my office, Apostine, of no surname!"

He laughed heartily, pleased to have finally brought some life back into the wilting Fairy. "It's my office too, Vetur!"

She slammed the heavy wooden door shut as he called out, "I'll be back. Seven minutes!"

~ **44** ~

Emi-Joye groaned and slumped against the wall. She hadn't meant to stay overnight, but after sleeping most of the previous day away in Trystane's bed, she found herself tossing and turning, unable to drift off in her own. She didn't know what made her suddenly again so terrified and unsure about the part she decided to play in the task of the Liluthuaé, and she assuredly didn't relish that Apostine saw her like this.

She was an ambassadora! And the ambassadora to Earth's so-called final frontier to boot. Her entire life was to be built on unknowns, forging new paths of — as she told Herewosa Donnachaidh that day — claiming the role that destiny charged her with. How could she so quickly revert back to this level of apprehension?

Her eyes moved toward the stack of books she and Apostine secured from both the University library in Endorsa and their own Fae archives, books that told of war leaders and battles long past, both human and magical. They were next to a messy pile of paper, notes Emi-Joye compiled at home when she snuck into her mother's study at odd hours to research more about the ancient wars of magickind. The books in their office were all but defaced, with bookmarks and scraps of parchment sticking out that noted important passages and turns of phrase that once were used to rally the troops.

It was all propaganda. Apostine found it particularly fascinating that both Americans and the German Nazi party used these tactics to draw humans to their causes, one for ill will toward certain groups of people, and one to end the tyranny and fascism of the other. Even when the cause was just, it seemed so many of these leaders treated war recruitment as if it was a sporting event.

There was nobility in fighting for a good cause! There was glory in victory, it all seemed to say.

The Fairy felt sure that the leaders of the Fórsaí Armada would agree with that, to an extent, and perhaps they were not wrong. But why was it that the cause itself was not enough to fight for? Why tack on such auspicious things like honor, glory, and victory? It seemed selfish to her, fighting for something not because of the *something*, but because of the personal validation that would come from it. Admiration from one's peers, perhaps a promotion to a new rank; to have one's face and name forever sung by the bards of history.

It seemed hypocritical to have such thoughts, especially for someone who so loved combat. Emi-Joye craved the adrenaline rush of it. She felt complete with her knives in her hands, twisting and turning as she pushed her body to its limits, dodging and striking to best an opponent. To kill, if she had to. But personal validation in the training and competition ring was a separate beast than that of going into battle.

There would be no individual glory on this battlefield, only spilt blood and frenzy.

Somehow, this Fairy and her Tief-Fae second-in-command were supposed to convince the entirety of the Fórsaí Armada that this war was coming, and it would have to be worth fighting for not due to personal vendetta of the Ingefeoht, but because their entire world was at stake. Not just Heáhwolcen, but Earth as well, where many magical beings still dwelled. Emi-Joye did not want to use propaganda. She did not want to persuade the commanders and their fighting forces to go into war with Palna by sugar-coating the brutality they would face. She wanted them to understand that this war was something they went into not because they wanted to, but because there was no other way to free Palna and destroy Craft Wizardry once and for all.

That was the kicker. That was what killed her, the concept of turning these commanders into Palnan sympathists. All of them, she and Apostine included, grew up hearing horror stories about the Tinuviels, Baize Sammael, Craft magic, and Palna. Emi-Joye believed Bridgette to be right that most Palnan citizens lived in a bubble that — though it had been formed by the Samnung — was now manipulated by their own rulers. It would be an uphill battle convincing the Fórsaí Armada leaders of this idea, that the majority of Palnans deserved freedom, and the only ones who were destined otherwise were Ydessa, Eryth, and their supporters.

Emi-Joye's gaze moved to her office ceiling as she contemplated this for the millionth time. Like all offices of the Seledreám, the one she and Apostine shared was bright and airy, walled in on one side by a window made of stained glass in shades of crystal clear, pale blue, and watery lavender. The sun shone through to make a marbled pattern on the light-colored wood flooring, creating an illusion of water dancing along her feet. She watched this for a minute, seeing the blues and purples glide across her bare toes, and nearly jumped out of her skin when Apostine stalked through the wooden door, a male on a mission.

"Where the — oh!" he said, seeing the Fairy on the floor. "At least you moved from sulking at the desk to sulking on the ground."

Emi-Joye glowered at him. "I don't want to go on your stupid breakfast outing."

"And what would you rather do, Vetur, stay here and hide?" Apostine knelt down beside her. "That's not the Fairy I know. Come on! Seize the day! I'm going to drag you out of here by your dress sleeves if you don't come voluntarily."

"You will not."

"Watch me." He wiggled his fingers devilishly in her face. "No report from Dag, by the way, in case you care. I'm starting to worry about some of this icemelt. You did read the same data I did about —"

The ambassadora stood up, glaring down at her second. "I do care, thanks. I'm just a tad bit preoccupied by the other pressing matter on my mind, because as important as Antarctic habitat loss is, we won't *have* an Antarctica to worry about if Ydessa Tinuviel wins this war."

Apostine blinked. "That is an interesting shift in tone."

"What?"

"You said, 'if Ydessa Tinuviel wins', not 'if Palna wins'."

The Fairy sighed. She glanced past him into the empty hallway. "Fine. *Fine.* I give up. I should probably eat something besides my feelings anyway."

"That's my girl, Vetur." Apostine tossed a handful of wax-sealed envelopes onto the table in the office's small seating area, then reached his hand to her. "Mushroom toast?"

A smile crept involuntarily onto Emi-Joye's full lips. "Deity damn you, Apostine."

They walked out together, the Fairy cringing slightly at the thought of how disheveled she must look after a night sleeping at her desk, and took flight the moment they reached the open air in the central courtyard of the Seledreám. The two landed a short while later in front of a birchwood log cabin, its roof covered in thick moss and natural growth. Smoke puffed out from a squat chimney. Arranged on the lawn out front were stools and tables carved from fallen trees. It was a homey little place, more cottage than restaurant — the proprietors lived on the second floor — and was a frequent spot Emi-Joye and Apostine scuttled off to when they wanted to be left alone.

They found a clearing by the stream to speak and plan in private, although they didn't say a word until after they emptied their plates of the aforementioned mushroom toasts.

"So, Ambassadora mine, are you going to share with me why I walked in to find you so bereft this morning?" Apostine asked.

She sipped her bittersweet brew. "I'm worried I'm not making the right decision in bringing the commanders together, and that I'm just going to stand in front of them and make a fool of myself, and of you as well."

"Vetur, you're the absolute least likely being I've ever met to go and make a fool out of herself," Apostine assured her. "What's going on in that icy little head of yours?"

The words spilled out of her as though they had been waiting for the right cue. Emi-Joye told him how apprehensive she was to remove the propaganda aspect from war and how much she wanted the Fórsaí Armada commanders to understand what was at stake, when to their knowledge there had been no signs of conflagration to begin with.

"Then there's the matter of Palna itself," she choked out. "Bridgette's right. There are so many beings there who are imprisoned just because of their ancestry, not because they've done or intend to do ill will! We as protectors of magickind are charged with their protection, too. There continues to be talk about this being another war against Palna, but is it? Or is it war against the Tinuviels and those who follow their extremist views?"

"I knew something was up when you said a comment to that effect earlier," Apostine said. He pulled Emi-Joye in, letting her head rest upon his shoulder. "You know what will make them listen, Vetur?"

She shook her head, feeling a tear slink down her cheek. "Hitting them over their heads with a sword?"

"Ha!" Apostine laughed. "No, you silly thing. *You being you.* Propaganda is misleading or outright *wrong*, but you? Ambassadora Emi-Joye Vetur, you are honest. You want the world to think the best of you, but you will not and do not lie and weasel your way to that."

He turned to face her, putting both hands on her shoulders. "Vetur, you are going to go into that auditorium and say your piece. Perhaps not all will be convinced in one direction or another, particularly as we've no sure indication Palna *will* declare war upon us. But what those commanders will leave knowing and believing in is *you* and your deity-ordained loyalty to magickind as a whole. That, Ambassadora, is a cause worth dying for."

Apostine paused to wipe the tears from Emi-Joye's eyes. "Come on, you. Let's return these dishes. We have a pep talk to write."

~ 45 ~

Triumvirate.

The word clanged around Bridgette's head like a marble in a pie pan. She'd never heard of it, had no idea what it meant or what its significance was, and for a brief few minutes, this strange term overshadowed what else Toby just revealed to her. She knew in part what the Tinuviels' plan was, and there were citizens organizing a rebellion.

This is what Zedolph meant last night, she thought.

This is how he and Serrabinx weren't taking their "privilege of this information" lightly. This is why he told her he did not want his family to die. She thought he meant the Collective — and in a way, he probably did — but if Toby became part of the Collective, it would put them all in very deep danger. He was their little messenger, a small mouse with innocent brown eyes and a singsong laugh that threw off suspicion. Without him, organizing would become incredibly difficult. With him, the Tinuviels could siphon information to quash the Hringer, the resistance group, one by one — and likely manage to blame it on the Samnung.

Her eyes ached and her head throbbed.

At this point, I think it'd just be easier to walk around with lilac opals for eyes instead of the constant shifting. Fucking hell, Bridgette groaned inwardly.

"What," she started, rubbing the heels of her hands into her eye sockets, "the *fuck* is the Triumvirate?"

Toby didn't answer.

Bridgette was too busy thinking to say much out loud during their walk back to Xcthonya. Some things still made little sense — the Raisarch, for example. If the position was her birthright, as Toby claimed, and at the moment the position was held by a relative she didn't know, what was she supposed to do? Slay her great-grandfather? An uncle? With her paltry four weeks of combat training and a lost dagger? And what of Mohreen? It had to be her bloodline, too. If the Raisarch died, would she not have the choice to take on the role before Bridgette did?

This connection to Palna, to the lands here, was more understandable. The other half of Bridgette's bloodline was that of Eryth Tinuviel. She assumed he shared this link too, and she desperately hoped he wasn't able to sense it the way she did. That dream about him still haunted her. The vividness of it, that sight of rainbow darkness … even thinking about it now in the waning afternoon sun made her skin crawl.

Bridgette went to bed after barely touching her supper, but neither Serrabinx nor Zedolph asked questions. She slept fitfully and was up early, purposely waiting until she heard the front door shut — a sign the butcher at least was out of the house — before rising for her second gifted day off. She lit the oil lamp and dressed in her favorite cream-colored sweater, sleeves now shortened after the fall in Forêt Fossile. The aubergine leggings got tucked into her cowboy boots, and into her bag she heaved the *Sefnuskrá*'s three volumes and her blue notebook.

If I'm going to the Ballamúr and can get across it, I'm not passing up that opportunity, the Elfling told herself.

Serrabinx looked a bit surprised to see her guest up and ready so early. "Good morning, Bridgette. May I offer you some breakfast tea?"

"Sure, thanks."

The woman fussed over a teacup for a few minutes, and it wasn't long before Bridgette heard Toby's footsteps skipping down the hall. His hair was a mess, his long sleepshirt a goldenrod color that clashed fiercely with the grayish brown of the too-big socks that sagged at his ankles.

"Are we ready for another adventure?" he asked.

"And where is it the two of you are off to today?" his mother asked.

Bridgette had an answer ready: "I asked Toby to take me shopping. I don't know how y'all do Lunavidad, but most humans celebrate their winter holidays with giving presents. I kind of thought maybe I could start that tradition here, or at least be part of it."

Serrabinx gave her a surprised smile. "That's quite thoughtful of you, Bridgette. We do indeed exchange gifts, among other aspects to our celebration."

By the time Toby was dressed and both companions had their coats, scarves, and gloves on, Serrabinx had a satchel of lunch ready for them. She sent them off without a word into the breaking dawn. Toby waited until they got to the main road, shivering a bit despite his multiple layers, before speaking.

"Mumma is going to be most angry if she learns where we really went."

"Well then. Guess we're not gonna tell her, are we?"

He smiled up at her. "I will keep this secret between us."

"Me too, Little Lark."

Normally when Bridgette walked through Xcthonya this early with Zedolph, she concentrated on staying warm and trying to engage the slátrari in conversation about Palnan history, the Tinuviels, anything to answer or add to her ever-growing list of questions. It was refreshing to be able to experience these hours in silence, taking note of shopkeepers and workers busying themselves to set up for the day, and listening to the occasional atmospheric noises of bird and insect in the air.

The path they took was largely the same as the previous day, but instead of stopping by the tree they ate lunch at before, they continued walking. Little groups of homes popped up, along with the occasional restaurant or shop.

It was a long, long way to the edge from the Maudlin home. They passed no other cities on the walk, indicating that Xcthonya was either quite vast or most of Palnan land wasn't attributed to a specific place. Toby only marked a few cities on the map he drew, and the lack of commerce combined with the abundance of individual gardens and farms supported both options.

Toby finally stopped, panting slightly, and pointed to a row of houses several dozen yards ahead. The two companions were hidden from view by a cluster of young pine trees.

"The edge is after those homes."

"Are you sure?"

The boy looked shocked. "Of course, I am sure!"

"Just checking, sheesh." She ruffled his hair, and the Liluthuaé walked away, leaving the boy barely visible between the evergreens.

As she had when she crossed into Palna, Bridgette felt the barrier as she approached. But the Ballamúr was invisible, at least from inside Palna. In fact, from her vantage point within it, so was anything *else*. Beyond the back gardens of this last vestige of civilization lay a view of land so pristine, so untouched, that all Bridgette wanted to do *was* touch it. It was like looking through a clear window into what the first indigenous humans, or even the colonizing European explorers, might have first seen when staring upon the land that was now America.

She couldn't even see the no-man's land, much less the shimmering barrier of the Samnung wall ... and she absolutely could not see the natural landscape of Bondrie, nor the shadows of the Bondrie guardsfolk she knew were stationed along it.

How do the Palnans who live here not wonder what is in their own backyard? Bridgette thought as she gazed out into the open expanse of nature. *How can they wake up every morning, look out into this literal fucking great beyond, and* not *wonder or dream about what's out there?*

Bridgette meandered along the invisible barrier, straying far to the right of the residential fence posts and hedges that demarcated the edges of property lines. Even the ground she traveled on was mirrored in the strange mirage before her: where there was grass under her feet, there was grass there. It was a seamless extension of Palna, and one of the most beautiful sights Bridgette had ever seen in her now twenty-three years of life. Out of habit more than anything, she slipped two fingers under her covenant bracelet. It was still dormant, despite being this close to something else so magical, but she imagined perhaps at this exact moment, Collum stood on the other side of this wall, trying to figure out how she got in so easily and what held her back from getting out.

If she had to tell him the truth, the only thing holding her back was herself.

The past few months were supposed to be spent playing detective. Sure, she learned plenty, but Bridgette had the same number of, if not more, questions now than she waltzed in with. She found answers, but along with those came uncovering more things she needed to know, more unknowns that eluded her sierwan gift, and more thoughts to write in her notebook, hidden between reminders about the spice blends for sausages and how to calculate meat yields for customers who purchased whole and half-carcasses from the butchery.

One thing did not elude her sierwan gift. The closer she stood to the Ballamúr, the more her answer seemed to glaze through her glamour. All she had to do to leave Palna, to leave this place where her birth father dwelt and magic supposedly didn't, this place of protected lands and so many secrets, was to walk through this wall that did not fear her power. All she had to do to return home, to caife calabaza and feoht lessons, to her friends and the Samnung, to fly into the waiting arms of Collum Andoralain, was to take one step to her right.

She was so close she could taste it.

Bridgette looked once in the direction where Toby waited. She couldn't see him, having walked so far down, transfixed by the scenery that she was fairly certain didn't exist. There was a pang of guilt as she thought what the boy would do when she was gone for so long. Perhaps the wind would tell him. She wondered if he Saw this coming.

Does it even matter anymore?

Her eyes caught a glimpse of a willow somewhere in the false distance. She put her hand up to the Ballamúr, closed her eyes, and *wished*.

~ 46 ~

She'd dreamed of this moment for months.

She craved the smell of him, the silky sweet tobacco and crisp woodsy birch that permeated Collum's very existence. Fresh as New England fall air after a rainstorm.

Bridgette fell into the shellshocked Elf, hardly daring to believe that it was the black buttons of his charcoal tunic that pressed into her cheek. She felt like crying and dancing, but couldn't decide which, so continued to stand against him instead.

His arms around her felt like *home*. Not that Bridgette was unable to take care of herself, but there was a sense of safety and wholeness here that she lacked alone in Palna, and alone on Earth.

He felt it too, despite his best attempts to avoid it. Collum closed his eyes and caught his fingers in the thick strands of her braid. Her hair had grown longer, more lustrous, while she was gone.

I missed you, Collum thought to her, but she didn't reply. Just nuzzled her face closer against him, her breath grazing against his chest. He pulled away and Bridgette tensed.

"Shh," he whispered. "You haven't done anything wrong. I just — I need to see that you're alright."

"I'm fine, Bundy," she assured him. Her voice was wispier than he remembered. "I've got *so* much to tell you, like you won't even believe half of this shit."

He cocked an eyebrow. "You're a sierwan, Starshine, among many other things. What you speak is truth, not just truth as you know it, but the truth of the Universe. I'll have no choice but to believe you, as that is how this must work."

"Well, that'll make my job a hell of a lot easier then."

"I suppose," the fyrdwisa mused. "But now … Bridgette, I don't want to talk now."

"What?"

He tightened his grip in her hair, tilting her chin back to meet her eyes with his. "I would rather do this instead."

It was so unexpected, the shock of Collum's lips against hers, that Bridgette swore her heart skipped a beat. She became hypersensitive to his touch, sliding her hands up his tunic and to the back of his neck as he kissed her. This felt *right* in a way she couldn't explain. She wished she knew what he was thinking, but his mind-voice was empty to her. At the touch of his tongue against her mouth, she jolted back into herself to fully experience what was happening.

The world dissolved around them.

Collum wasn't sure what made him move to her like this, right now, but whatever caused the compulsion felt absolute, a fundamental shift in his existence that couldn't be undone. He'd kissed plenty of females, and he'd kissed this one on the forehead and in her hair more times than he could count. But *this* kiss — this feel of her lips, slightly chapped from months in the dry climate of Palna; this taste of her that was akin to warm dew on wild raspberries; the heat of her tongue as it caressed his — was different. It was final and both of them knew it, here in this moment in the middle of the deity-damned Caisleán front lawn for all of Eckenbourne to see.

Breaking the kiss was painful, but necessary.

"What do you say we take this, as the humans say, back to my place?" he murmured.

She nipped the bottom of his ear. "Pretty please, with sugar on top. Also as the humans say."

Collum whisked them away, and the feel of being kissed while evanescing was otherworldly. He almost dropped them both in the middle of somewhere that was definitely not his intended arrival place, so lost did he become in Bridgette's presence. But he managed.

Barely.

The moment their feet were safely on the ground of his

home office, the overwhelming scent of night-blooming plants in the air around them, Collum's fingers found the leather cord that tied Bridgette's braid and deftly undid it.

She laughed and stepped back, tossing her hair out and letting it catch in the breeze and moonlight. "Fucking hell, I missed you."

Her eyes glittered. So did his, the silver light glinting off the flecks that dappled his blue irises.

"That makes for good hearing," Collum said.

"I can't handle you, punk. Who says stuff like that in the middle of making out?"

His answer was to kiss her again, feeling her smile and laugh against him as she gave in. Collum slowed, no longer frantic with panicked relief that she was alive, that she was safe, that she was *home*. His heartbeat calmed, matching pace with hers, and he moved his hands from her hair to caress her jaw, her neck, her shoulders. He traced her outline, knowing every inch already. As his hands moved down Bridgette, her hands mirrored the movement, going up his hips to his chest and neck to nestle one in his dark waves and one against his cheek. Her touch felt like bliss given life.

There was a delicious, wanton feeling deep in his being, harsher and more potent than he'd ever felt before. Collum moved a hand to her jaw and pulled away. Bridgette's lips were swollen from the kiss, her eyes glazed.

"What?" she asked, blinking slowly.

And then she smiled, her gaze going razor-sharp, nostrils flaring in anticipation. Sierwan or no, she knew what.

The fyrdwisa's returning grin was sanguine, a look Bridgette had never seen him make except in her dreams. If it was possible for an Elfling to melt, she would have, then and there.

"Shall I?" he asked.

"Shall you what?"

"Proceed with you as I wish."

It was flirting in a way, but a question of consent and simultaneously a promise. Bridgette felt a lustful burning in her core at that pledge. "Fuck yes, you may, sir."

"You didn't even ask how I wish to proceed," he pointed out, reaching for her. That stunning white dress she wore needed to come *off*.

"I have a general idea of what you're implying," she said. Bridgette lifted her arms over her head as Collum slid the creamy dress from her body onto the grass. "Big fan of that plan. Whatever it is, I have a feeling I'm going to really fucking like it."

He stared at her, unclothed but for the skin tone-colored cotton undergarments she wore, and Bridgette wettened at his gaze alone. She'd never felt desired by anyone as much as she felt wanted and needed by Collum Andoralain, and she never wanted to be desired by anyone else ever again. She wanted him arguably more.

"You look like you want to eat me alive," she challenged.

"I was wondering when the ísenwaer would begin working again."

Collum didn't stop watching her as he unbuttoned his tunic. She squirmed as his beautiful, strong hands went from button to button, then to the belt at his hips. He kicked off his boots and stared straight into her eyes as the shirt slid from his shoulders, and the leggings and fitted undershorts fell to the ground.

Holy fucking fuck, she thought, taking in the sight before her. Bridgette reached for him — laughed as a snap of his fingers sent her undergarments fluttering off into the breeze — and hands met skin and they were crashing, falling, ever so madly. Bridgette wasn't sure where time ended and infinity began. She held him, stroked him, cupped him underneath as his hands slipped down her body again to truly touch her.

"Collum," she breathed, and his name on her lips was flint to his fire.

The Elf let two fingers glide inside his Elfling, and she

tightened at the feel of them, a cruel and teasing grip of pulsating craving for more. He felt her hand shift upon him as he crooked his middle finger within her, and the sensation overwhelmed them both.

Bridgette closed her eyes, frozen for a moment before she regained control of herself. "You are absolutely magical."

"And you put a spell on me, my Starshine."

His Starshine. She shivered with pleasure and pulled his hand from between her legs, keeping one of hers between his, rolling his head softly between her thumb and forefinger. "I want —"

"I know."

Collum lifted her up, kissing her deeply, feeling the world flip and right itself at the twist of their tongues and scrape of teeth against one another. "May I?" he whispered, and his voice was so quiet that Bridgette thought she imagined it.

"Please, Collum. Please —"

It was all the permission he needed, and Collum settled her onto himself, filling her.

This was ecstasy. A gift from the gods and the Universe.

"I missed you so much, but *this* was definitely worth being gone," she said, and rolled her hips toward him.

Collum held her, felt all of her lean muscle and taut skin against his own. He lost himself within Bridgette, their motions a mime of one another's. One moved, the other shifted in tandem, a rhythmic dance of sensuality and desire, yet so much deeper and more than a yearning for intimacy. It was just the two of them, as it was supposed to be, and it was like nothing else they ever imagined.

"I want you."

Neither was sure who said it. Perhaps they both did. But Collum took the cue to move her, and then he flipped her face-first against a tree covered with soft moss. Bridgette gripped the flora in her hands as he grabbed her hair in a ponytail at the base of her neck, her back arching for him as Collum resumed his place within her.

"Oh fuck, Collum!"

He was *so* deep that she could feel him in the place where that dark power rested and roiled, and it was indescribable. Collum pulled almost all the way out, tantalizingly slow, savoring every millimeter of Bridgette's craving for him, for *them*, and slammed his way back in, completely enthralled. Nothing mattered now except this, that she was safe, that she was his and he was hers, that she was here and *home* and wrapped around him.

"Deity damn you, Bridgette, you are everything," he whispered to her, feeling release begin to coil at his base. "You have destroyed me."

And for whatever reason, that was her undoing. Collum thrust himself deep again, pressing her to the tree. The Liluthuaé called out his name, spasming around him. He absorbed her orgasm like a shock to his system, and their sweat and her sweet climax was palpable between their legs.

It was too much for him to take. Collum cried out as he plunged one final time before pulling himself from Bridgette, the evidence of his pleasure spilling onto the small of her back, illuminated in the silver glow of moonlight. She turned to him, eyes wide, and locked their gazes together once again. Bridgette opened her mouth to speak, but something changed and —

Hundreds of miles from one another, as the full moon crested over Heáhwolcen, the Elf and the Elfling woke, the silver beads of their covenant bracelets glowing bright as miniature stars in the velvet darkness.

~ 47 ~

Bridgette was screaming.

Her sheets tangled between her legs, her arms wrapped around a pillow that was supposed to be a moss-covered tree. The air weighed her down, pinning her tossing, twisting body to the bed.

He had been here. Or she had been there. It was *so* real — every sensation of Collum's touch still warped her senses. She felt the ghost of his hands trace her jaw, his fingers in her hair —

The bedroom door swung open and Zedolph darted in, confused and worried.

"Bridgette! Bridgette, shh — it's alright, it was just a bad dream!"

But it *hadn't* been, neither bad nor a dream. Dreams aren't supposed to feel like that, to be that vivid and sensory.

Zedolph scooped the shaking, terrified Elfling into his arms. "Shh, Bridgette. It's going to be okay. You're in our home and you are safe. Nothing is able to harm you here."

She detected the unspoken meaning behind that promise and stiffened at it. It was a promise she didn't want. Not from him, especially not after …

"It was *so real*," she whispered.

"Do you want to tell me about it?"

"No. I — no." Her heart felt like it might either beat out of her chest or explode in anguish. "I'm sorry. I didn't mean to wake anybody up."

Zedolph smoothed her tangled, sweaty hair. "I believe I've told you this before. You don't need to apologize for having a bad dream."

They didn't say anything for a few minutes until Bridgette calmed enough to scoot out from his embrace. She wrapped her arms around her legs and pulled her knees to her chest.

"Was it something that happened when you and Toby went

off yesterday?" Zedolph asked. "You were so quiet when the two of you returned. You've been quiet recently, and it's most uncharacteristic."

Yesterday … it must be early morning then, Bridgette thought. She forced a deep breath of air into her lungs and tried to think of a sufficient story that would satisfy her host's curiosity without giving anything away.

"We went on a long walk is all, and then some psycho lady came out and yelled at us to get off her property. Kind of scared the shit out of me," Bridgette muttered. "Then we came back. It's been a long time since an adult has come at me like that."

It was close enough to the truth. Bridgette had been millimeters away from touching the Ballamúr, millimeters away from going home, when a woman really did come out of one of the houses nearby to shout at her.

"Young lady!" the woman had screeched, her voice loud as a fire alarm. "Just *what* do you think you are doing?"

The Elfling jerked back from the Ballamúr, thoroughly startled. "Uh — um, I — that willow tree —"

She had been stuck in place, not sure if she should approach the woman or run back to Toby. The woman made the choice for her, marching toward Bridgette looking absolutely murderous.

"That willow tree is on protected land, which *you* are most certainly not allowed on. Your parents should have taught you better! How *dare* you try to defile our queen and king's sacred spaces! You're lucky you weren't zapped into nonexistence, or worse. Get out of here," she shouted, her face so close to the Elfling's that Bridgette could see spittle fly from her mouth. "Get *out*, before I call the Guard on you!"

Bridgette ran, her legs moving faster than they ever had before, to where Toby hid in the trees. She grabbed his hand and ignored the wide-eyed, frightened stare he gazed at her with.

"We've got to go, right the fuck now," she instructed.

Where did that woman come from? she thought as she practically dragged Toby back to Xcthonya. *There was* nobody *around me.*

Whatever caused the Palnan to stop her didn't change where she was now, which was in the arms of the wrong man. Hell, she didn't even want to be in the arms of a *man*; she wanted the arms of an *Elf.*

She wanted very specifically the arms of Collum Andoralain, arms that still felt all too real if she stilled her mind enough to put herself back in that dream-state. She dreamed she walked right through the Ballamúr and wound up — as she had spontaneously appeared in Xcthonya all those months before — in Aelchanon, the capital city of Eckenbourne, on the lawn of the Caisleán. Right in front of her stood Collum, and dream-Bridgette could scarcely believe her luck. Was it luck or was it fate that he happened to be there right when she arrived?

Bridgette's thoughts were interrupted by her host speaking to her, again using a soothing voice meant to ease the troubles he sensed in her.

Zedolph tilted her chin up to look at him, though in the dark, Bridgette's half-Elven eyes had better sight than his did. What she saw was intense worry. She didn't necessarily like the idea of Zedolph having that level of feeling toward her, even if it was well-intentioned.

He told her, "I'm going to go get you some calming tea from mine sister's cupboard. It will help you fall back to sleep."

She nodded numbly, not sure that sleep was what she wanted to go back to.

Collum practically barged into Trystane's home an hour after waking from the dream. The bleary-eyed ard rialóir stared at him, thoroughly confused as to why his fyrdwisa stood on his doorstep while the sun still slept.

"I need to talk to you," Collum said. "Now."

He pushed past Trystane into the dark foyer, mind reeling,

half-wishing he'd showered more thoroughly before throwing on clothes that likely didn't even match, so blinded had he been by that … *dream*. Collum snapped his fingers and whispered a command, causing Trystane's parlor candles to flicker to life. The fyrdwisa threw himself on the sofa and laid his head between his knees, as if to stop himself from fainting or vomiting.

"What in the seven hells is wrong with you, Collum?" Trystane asked. "Do I need to summon a lacnian?"

"No."

"Then why," Trystane mused, pausing for dramatic effect, "are you in my house at three in the morning?"

"I had a dream," Collum ground out from his bent-over position.

"As one typically does, when one sleeps."

"A very vivid dream."

Trystane cocked an eyebrow. "Could this not have waited until daylight?"

"I dreamed I was with Bridgette, that she'd come back."

"Brother mine …"

Collum sat up and glared intensely at Trystane. "No. Not a wistful, sweet dream. All of my senses were as alive in my mind as they are now in this room. I could see her, smell her, feel her, fucking *taste* her, Trystane."

He didn't mention the ísenwaer not working in the dream-that-wasn't-quite-a-dream, which perhaps should have been a sign that something wasn't right.

"It was akin to an astral experience. That's the closest I can describe it as, but yet this was far more intense," Collum went on, forcing Trystane to understand that this wasn't a dream in the least, but something beyond, taking over the subconscious in sleep. "Astral projection is a mere hologram of the body. We are able to move in the setting we've placed ourselves, able to talk, but cannot touch, as it is our spirit alone that travels."

"I'm well-aware of what astral projection is, Collum,"

Trystane said wryly, though his voice was gentle. "What happened in the dream?"

Collum answered with a pained look. "We … it was … intimate," he choked out.

That wasn't the answer Trystane expected. "Fucking seven hells."

"I dreamed first I was at the Caisleán, and I heard a noise behind me. I turned to see what caused it, and there she stood. After a time, the dream setting took us to my home office. I became conscious nearly an hour ago, in the exact position I'd been holding her in — in my office, where I most assuredly had not laid down to sleep — and there was … physical evidence of our intimacy," the fyrdwisa whispered. "It was as if she evanesced away in a blink, leaving me frozen a moment later."

He had roared. She was *there*. He had held her! Had touched her, kissed her, felt her hair in his fingers and her hands upon him. He could still smell her scent, not sure if he conjured it himself or if she truly had been there and slipped away through some cruel trick of Maylemaegus. He stood there, in naught but his own skin, arms wrapped around air, and roared at the ghost of her that haunted him. He collapsed, aching and disoriented, against the tree where she'd just been, and sobbed until his head cleared. There was a fist-sized hole in the tree now, which Collum only somewhat regretted. He promised himself he'd bring an arborist out to have a look and help repair the damage he inflicted in his sudden state of grief.

And now, here he sat in Trystane's parlor, more lost than he'd been in a very long time.

"This is your second strangely vivid dream in less than a month," Trystane said. "You, stay. I'm going to make coffee and summon a few friends. You need support, and we need to figure out why this is happening."

Collum nodded and leaned back deeper into the sofa cushions.

When he woke again, it was several hours later and the sun peeked into the windows. He found himself stretched out on the couch, covered in a thick wool blanket. His boots were off — he had no memory of doing that himself — and a pillow was tucked under his head. Collum heard murmurs from down the hall and opened his mind to hear the inner voices of Trystane, Emi-Joye, Njahla, Apostine, and Aurelias.

The latter two didn't know about the first dream, or about what almost happened with Lucilla. He had a sneaking suspicion that Trystane wanted him to be the one to tell that story, while the ard rialóir and ambestre held Aurelias back. She might completely lose her shit and evanesce to Endorsa, aiming to tear the witch limb from limb. As crazy as his fyrdestre drove him, Collum loved her dearly and greatly appreciated her loyalty. But he did tend to draw the line at outright murder.

Collum rose from the couch and wrapped the blanket around his shoulders. He followed the sound of hushed voices to the kitchen.

"Good morning," he said from behind everyone, and they all jumped about a foot. Collum chuckled. "I apologize for startling you. I didn't realize I would be able to fall asleep again."

"Any more dreams?" Trystane asked. His moss green eyes searched Collum's ocean blue ones, concerned and perhaps a bit scared.

"None memorable enough to cement themselves into my mind," Collum replied. He turned to the others. "What is it that our ceannairí has shared with you?"

"Trystane and the ambassadora told us you'd been having some pretty weird dreams, Chief," Aurelias said. Her tone made him wince. He should have told her already, and he owed her a private explanation as to why he hadn't.

"The first dream to which Trystane refers occurred during my time on Earth a few weeks ago, when I was assaulted by my travel companion," Collum explained, and Aurelias' horns started to glow with a threatening amount of raging light. "I was poisoned and paralyzed to resist fighting back. But through means we are not sure of, a force within my mind broke the spell and I was able to gain control over my mental and physical faculties."

Apostine, who knew nothing about any of this, looked perplexed, both at Collum's brief story and at Aurelias' horns. The air was tight, but Collum chose not to diffuse the tension. He also chose not to go into further detail about what transpired with Lucilla.

He took a sip of the coffee Emi-Joye handed him. "That was not so much a dream as it was being blinded by this poison, and all I could see were flashing shades of light when I came to. Flashes behind my eyes, and I'd seen them recently during a meditation. A moment of peace then, and yet here they were again in this strange moment of torment," Collum reflected. "A voice spoke in my head as I broke free, and it was not my voice."

Collum pulled Bridgette's dagger from his belt and laid it on Trystane's kitchen table. "This appeared in my hand as the spell shattered."

All eyes stared at the blade, then back at him. He hadn't mentioned this before, and Trystane's eyes searched his for an answer none of them had.

"Isn't that Bridgette's dagger?" Aurelias asked.

"Yes," Collum said simply. "This weapon is quite something. It appeared to Bridgette out of thin air when she returned to Heáhwolcen this summer. She jokes that she summoned it, but as far as any of us know, Bridgette doesn't have the knowledge or power to summon an object, much less something she'd never seen before. After last night, I am further committed to the belief that this blade is related to Bridgette's ability to connect with Universal consciousness."

It was quiet for a minute.

"What was last night's dream?" Njahla asked out loud. *It was about Bridgette, wasn't it?* she thought to Collum.

The fyrdwisa gave her a pained jerk of his head. "Last night I dreamed that Bridgette returned to Heáhwolcen from Palna, but it was so vivid that I do not believe it to be a dream in the sense we are used to dreaming. I woke in my home office, where I must have sleep-walked. In one blink, Bridgette was there with me, and the next, it was as if she was never there. I have never in my almost two hundred years dreamed with such sensory perception. But unlike in real life, where I can hear the mind voices of those around me, I could not hear hers in the dream-that-was-not."

That was a safe enough revelation, and something that bothered him greatly. Why *hadn't* he been able to hear her, regardless of the ísenwaer?

Apostine flipped the dagger from hand to hand, admiring the amethysts on the handle and its blade, which turned a queer shade of purple depending on how the light hit it. Collum hadn't noticed that before, but it would make sense for the lilac-eyed Elfling to magically summon a color-coordinating sharp object.

"I am very confused," the Tief-Fae said, his bland comment breaking the stupor. "I feel as though I'm missing several things about Bridgette."

Emi-Joye put an apologetic hand on his shoulder. "To be honest, I'm not sure I remember anymore who knows what about her, what I'm allowed to say, and what we're keeping hidden from the rest of the Samnung. It's rather overwhelming."

No shit, Collum thought.

Aurelias chugged the rest of her coffee, choking a bit on the scalding liquid, and slammed her mug on the table. "If the Liluthuaé can connect to Universal consciousness when she's *awake*, what in the seven hells stops her from connecting to Universal *subconsciousness* when she's asleep?"

Trystane's kitchen went so quiet, they heard the candle flames flickering two rooms away.

<h1 style="text-align: center;">~ 48 ~</h1>

"Don't drop that!" Muov yelled to Bridgette, who indeed was about to drop a stone tray piled high with a pyramid of meticulously placed lamb chops, their rib bones frenched for maximum artistic quality.

The Elfling had overestimated her strength and promised Fincher she'd be able to carry his creation to the butcher case without one single piece falling out of place. But the stone slab was a beast. As she struggled with it, she wondered how the tiny Kobold got it into the back room to start with.

Palna's lack of magic wasn't enough to stop Muov's Elven speed, and thankfully he was next to Bridgette in mere seconds to help her carry the tray the short distance.

"Thanks," she gasped out, grateful for the usually moody Elf's aid. "I definitely didn't realize this was as heavy as it was. How did Fincher even get it over there?"

"He didn't," Muov chuckled. "I did."

"Ah."

They moved to the front of the case to examine their handiwork. Lunavidad was a week away, and the butchery was decked out for the winter solstice festivities. Toby and Serrabinx spent the previous Tuesday with the slátrari and slátraestres, turning the shop into a magic-free magical winter wonderland. A massive evergreen tree was now parked in the back corner of the shop, dangling with bundles of dried rosemary and twirls of citrus peels, and strung with handtied berry garland. It smelled bright and festive, accented further by the drops of orange and cinnamon essential oils that Serrabinx added to the candles along the counter.

Dried arrangements of pinecones, flowers, and feathers — some gathered by Toby in the woods and others donated by the poultry butchery — covered the windowsills. In the middle of the counter was a massive Yule log, its rough pine bark draped with more of the berry garland. Six small holes were carved in the wood, into which the slátraestres poured new wax each morning and lit the wicks for their homemade candleholder. For Lunavidad itself, Zedolph and Bridgette would bring the log back to the Maudlins' home to burn overnight in the firehearth, as tradition dictated.

It was deliciously cheerful, and Bridgette appreciated that even Muov was more spirited than usual. He still regarded her with a healthy amount of distance and gave her a stern look if she poked her head out while customers were inside, but he wasn't as openly hostile anymore.

"This is my favorite time of the year," Bridgette declared, gazing at the cases, practically overflowing with the specialty sausages and fanciest cuts of meat. She wished she could capture the scene, and though the Elfling had plenty of talent in that arena when she set her mind to it, she hadn't touched a paintbrush or watercolor paper since June. Now seemed a strange time to suddenly decide to indulge her artistic yearnings, but she studied the butchery anyway. All of its details, every inch that she could commit to memory, so that one day she could perhaps share it with others in Heáhwolcen.

Or maybe I can convince these dudes to portal in some twenty-first century technology, and just show up one day with a digital camera, she thought, laughing to herself.

"What's so amusing?" Muov asked.

"On Earth, we have cameras to capture instant images of things you see," Bridgette started to explain, but Muov stopped her.

"I know what a camera is, Bridgette."

She stared. "You do?"

"Of course. The Palnan Artifex Forum includes several photographers and film developers. They attend holiday celebrations to document Palnan history for future generations of younglings and children to learn from."

Well, hot damn, Bridgette thought. She grinned at Muov. "On Earth though, the humans figured out how to take photos without having to develop film."

The Elf scowled. "Earthen humans pride themselves too much on efficiency at all costs. It is, ironically, a most expensive philosophy to have."

He walked off, leaving Bridgette staring at the cases, hit with the truth of his words. Zedolph found her there a few minutes later and chanced putting a hand on her shoulder.

"Are you alright?" he inquired.

"Yeah, I'm fine," she said. "Just a weird conversation with Muov that got me thinking about growing up human. It's so weird how similar in some ways, and totally different in others, life is here versus there."

"I can only imagine," Zedolph murmured. "Perhaps one day you'll be able to show us what it's like there, and we can experience it ourselves."

Bridgette hadn't forgotten her accidental promise. "One day, definitely."

The hand moved off her shoulder, and Zedolph inclined his head to the back of the shop. "Customers will begin coming today to gather their holiday ingredients. Paxson would like for you to help him break down our dry-aged rib loins to fill their orders. He'll meet you in the workroom shortly."

She took that as her cue to move out of the storefront, and spent the rest of the day working in companionable silence with the Baetalüan. The shop was a flurry of activity, both Fincher and Zedolph aiding customers in the holiday rush. Every now and then, one of them would zip back to the preparation room to ask Paxson or Bridgette to work on a special request, or to bring them mugs of hot cider or other gifts from guests.

The workday passed quickly, and before Bridgette knew it, Zedolph brought her coat and bade her clean her knives, ready to get home before the temperature dropped any further. For its largely temperate climate, Palna was so similar to the Southern states Bridgette was used to, where the winter weather changed from tolerably cool to frigid with little warning.

"Are you looking forward to Lunavidad?" Zedolph asked as they walked, his voice muffled by the wool scarf wrapped around his nose and mouth to keep them warm. "You have seemed in much brighter spirits the closer we get to it."

It had been three weeks since her dream, three weeks since she'd been so close to the Ballamúr. Three weeks since Zedolph came flying into her room to comfort her, bring her hot tea, and soothe her back to a restless sleep.

The impending holiday *had* increased her joy. It was hard not to feel the excitement, a welcome break from the usual tightness Bridgette felt in the Palnan air. She and Toby really had gone shopping, after swearing to Serrabinx they didn't find the right gift for Zedolph the first go-around. The two spent many nights from these last three weeks staying up later than usual, wrapping their secret presents and discussing Toby's plans to decorate the butchery. It was his personal favorite holiday tradition. After seeing his handiwork each day for the past week, Bridgette tended to agree.

"I am, actually," she finally replied to Zedolph. "Definitely feeling the holiday spirit. All we need are some silver bells and some snow."

"Silver bells?"

She grinned. "It's a song. On Earth, the humans who celebrate Christmas — some are really religious about it, and some just do it because it's like, family and food and presents — sing Christmas carols. One of them is called 'Silver Bells' and when I was little, it was my favorite. Well, that and the one about the drummer boy, but that's mostly because I liked the drum beats in the background."

"We'll sing *carols*, I suppose, in the city celebration for Xcthonya," Zedolph promised. "Though we might need to teach you the words and the tune, if you'd care to join along."

A part of Bridgette's heart ached. She nodded wordlessly, very much caring to be able to join along, very much wishing that she could take part in Lunavidad and see Toby's eyes light up. She wanted to hear him squeal when he opened her gift, a handknit drawstring bag full of stones, feathers, and small mementos Bridgette found on her daily walks to the butchery and on their adventures together. The yarn was variegated with muted periwinkle, mint green, splashes of lilac that mimicked her eyes, and deep charcoal gray. Being a sierwan gave her the added talent of knowing he would more than like it. The same with Serrabinx and the similar bag she purchased for her, to be used for gathered herbs, and the fresh set of sharpening leathers for Zedolph. She wanted to sing carols and drink cider, to dance around bonfires and wonder at how, despite more than a century and a half of there being none to be had, Palna managed to make its own sort of magic.

But she would not be here for Lunavidad.

Bridgette was going back to the Ballamúr. She was going home.

Tonight.

~ 49 ~

Unlike most nights, when Toby helped his mother set the table for supper and put the finishing touches on their plates, tonight he took one look at Bridgette walking inside, scowled, and followed the Elfling to her room.

"What's up, Little Lark?" she asked, knowing full well he knew exactly what was up.

The boy gave her a shrewd, displeased look. "The wind says that you are going on an adventure without me," he whispered. "Why is it that you are leaving? Why can I not come with you?"

He pouted. Bridgette's heart lurched. Leaving him, even for what awaited her on the other side of that wall, was *hard*. It was the part she dreaded most. She knelt down to be Toby's height and put both hands on his shoulders. "I'm going to be straight with you, kiddo, but what I say in this room? It stays between us. Got it?"

Toby nodded, still pouting.

"Good. I need you to know that I didn't lie when I said I came to Palna to learn its history and its culture. But what I *did* maybe lie *a little* about is the part where it's for a University project," she admitted. "I have some very powerful friends in Heáhwolcen, and they want to know about Palna. I volunteered to be the guinea pig."

"What is a guinea pig?"

She rolled her eyes at herself for even using the saying. "It's an Earth expression, but it means like, the one who tests something out first before anyone else. Who makes sure it's safe and stuff. I had to make sure Palna was safe."

"Safe for what?"

Bridgette put a finger to her lips. "I can't tell you that yet, but I have a feeling you might figure it out, if you look and listen hard enough. And plus, I think you already know, even though you might not really understand it all yet. Hell, I don't understand it all yet, but I will. And when I do, and when the rest of my friends in Heáhwolcen get it too, I'll be back. I fucking swear to you, Tobias Maudlin, I will be back, and you will get to see the rest of Heáhwolcen and Earth, and you will get to live wherever you want, and be whomever you want, without any deity-damned fake queen threatening you."

"You promise?" his lip trembled. "You promise you will not leave for forever, like my Dah did?"

He meant Ovidion. His father, the Elfling she replaced at the butchery. She wasn't sure her heart could handle this. The biggest loss Toby ever knew, and here he was comparing her absence to it.

"I promise. I am going to come back, and you'll probably know exactly when I do," she grinned. "Just like when I got here first and I showed up at your feet, right? It'll be like that. I swear to you I will be back for you, and your mom, and your uncle. And even fucking Muov; I'll come back for him too."

Bridgette looked him squarely in the eyes. "But first, Toby, I'm gonna need your help."

She waited until Zedolph and Serrabinx were sound asleep, aided by Toby's carefully crafted tea that evening. He laced it with powdered valerian root, the most powerful herb for sleep that his mother had in her stores. The unpleasant taste he camouflaged with a spoonful of crystallized honey and a topping of frothed cream. While her hosts dozed unawares, the Elfling packed everything important in her bag and the shoulder bag she long ago adopted as her own. She dressed in her warmest clothes, working as quickly and quietly as she could. Two sweaters were layered under Serrabinx's loaned coat, and the borrowed scarf and gloves were slipped on. Toby handed her stones warmed in the firehearth ashes for her pockets, and a beeswax-wrapped package of hard cheese and dried beef jerky.

"For snacks," he insisted. "It is a most long walk, and you

will get hungry. How will you know the way without me?"

Bridgette smiled, deciding to share this little secret with him. "I'm a sierwan," she whispered, and watched as his eyes grew wide. "Don't tell your mom."

"I will not," Toby vowed solemnly, struck by the revelation. "It will be our secret."

She tapped him on the nose. "Good. I think I have everything, but if I left something — and if you see my knife, actually; I think your mom might've hidden that — will you put it somewhere safe for me?"

The boy nodded. "I am going to miss you, Bridgette of the Outside."

"And I'm gonna miss you, Little Lark. Be safe, okay? Promise me you'll be safe."

He threw his arms around her. "Please don't go! Please stay. You are *supposed to be here*!"

Those words struck a strange chord, and Bridgette knew if she didn't walk out that door this instant, she might not have another chance. Rather, she might not let herself leave without being sure Toby could come with her. She pried herself from his grasp and kissed his tear-stained cheek, biting back her own emotion. No one, not even Collum or the Simmonses, ever wanted her to "not go" with this much conviction.

"I'm coming back for you, Toby," she swore, and stepped into the night.

The air was so cold, it turned her own tears into frost on her cheeks in mere seconds. Bridgette shivered mightily and wished she could summon heat. Instead, she summoned the will to start walking in an effort to warm up. It was dark and foggy, but her eyes were magic enough to see several feet ahead without requiring a light. Bridgette did not want to attract a lick of attention to herself, a lone Elfling creeping in the witching hour.

Her gloved hands brushed the spines of the *Sefnuskrá* in the shoulder bag. If these three volumes weren't supposed to be in

Palna, they sure as hellfire weren't supposed to be in greater Heáhwolcen. Bridgette had a loose plan for when she crossed the Ballamúr. She would go to Eckenbourne first, of course, once she convinced whatever Bondrie guardsfolk guarded the border that she was with the Samnung and not a Palnan spy. Palnan sympathist? Yes, absolutely. But spy? Bridgette would spy for the Tinuviels over her dead body, and probably not even then. She'd rather haunt the castle in Düoria for the rest of eternity.

Once safely in Eckenbourne, after Collum knew everything, the two would gather their circle. She would show them the *Sefnuskrá* and tell them about Gemaere, and they would find a University magister or a wizened old Elf or Fairy who could translate it for them — although on second thought, turning Baize Sammael's manifesto over to a stranger might not be the best decision.

I'll keep thinking about that part, Bridgette promised herself.

A cold wind blew through leafless trees, shaking skeletal branches in its wake. It was eerie being out alone at night in Palna. There were no insect noises, no birds, no musical air sounds. It was silent save for the barely audible noise of her footsteps and the shrill whistle of wind. Bridgette felt as though something watched her, and never before had she been so thankful that her eyes adjusted more easily to the dark than others'.

Two weeks ago, on a dreary morning when the fog seemed to stick to her and Zedolph as they walked to the butchery, Bridgette decided she was going to take this journey. Her host hadn't let up about her strange dreams and seemed to have become more protective than ever, though for what reason the Elfling couldn't fathom. Sometimes it bordered on an elder sibling kind of air, a big brother wanting to keep his sister from harm. Other times, like when Zedolph's eyes flashed if he saw the covenant bracelet poking out from under her shirtsleeve, Bridgette got the sense it was a far deeper emotion. She spent twenty-three years now fending mostly for herself, and she didn't need some man — even a kind, knowledgeable man; hell, even a kind, knowledgeable, *attractive* man like Zedolph — suddenly swooping in to take over the charge.

If she was going to have a partner, Bridgette wanted someone who cared for her, not someone who wanted to put her on a pedestal like a damn doll. Someone who treated her as the equal she was to him, and not an object to be kept from danger. Someone who respected her independence, her abilities, and desired to embrace and encourage them rather than shutter them.

Zedolph had begun a rather annoying habit of staying up at night until Bridgette went to her room. He wanted to ask her more questions, though her sierwan gift didn't suggest what about. It lasted about a week before Bridgette decided she and Toby would scurry off after supper each night to work on Lunavidad gifts and preparations. It gave her a reason to smile at her host's soured look, but he loved his nephew and wasn't about to step on Toby's joy.

Bridgette knew she couldn't put Zedolph off forever. The only way to get out of his well-intentioned — but insanely off-putting! — emotional and physical embraces was to *leave*. She knew where the Ballamúr was now and how to get back to it. And, for the past fourteen or so days, Bridgette had been following a hunch.

She could connect to Universal consciousness. This was a known fact about herself. Thus far, it was not something she regularly practiced, because in truth, hearing trees grow kind of freaked her out. She also wasn't entirely sure the connection would work in Palna. The idea that it would work, but then somehow alert the Tinuviels to her presence here, *also* freaked her out. But about four o'clock one morning after a rough, sleepless night, the Bright Star came to the realization it was something she was going to have to get *really fucking good at*. Her covenant bracelet only worked during strange connections made in her dreams, which stood to reason that Bridgette could not only connect to Universal consciousness, but its subconscious as well. And if the latter worked in Palna, the former likely would too. She could make that connection, contact someone in Heáhwolcen, and go home.

In the darkness of her room, Bridgette started to practice. She never did it for very long — her fear of the Tinuviels was very real — but every night, Bridgette calmed her mind and focused enough to set the connection. It didn't always work, and when it did, she stopped the moment she felt the mental click into place. It was hard to get started. Everywhere else in Heáhwolcen, and even that time in Wales, it was easier because of the air. She had something to latch onto, be it the peaceful windchime sounds or her imagined orchestra when she first did it, but between her fear and the silence, connecting in Palna required significant effort.

After haphazardly successful attempts, one night Bridgette quietly stormed out of her room to splash cold water on her face. As she pushed her sleeves up, the purpled veins of her protected lands wound caught her eye.

Oh!

Her eyes widened with the sudden knowledge that she had all the tools she needed this entire time. *She* was the tool.

Palnan blood, Craft blood, ran through her. Fucking Toby tried to tell her once. She didn't understand then, but she understood now. The power of her blood made the venom from the protected lands stop its attack, because she was *of* the land. Her father was Eryth Tinuviel, and of all the things he gave her, this one she could be grateful for. Collum kept saying the Liluthuaé was Maylemaegus, and in their joint dream-that-wasn't, she felt such a strange well of power. It was there as if it had always been there, but looking back on those moments of subconscious existence, she finally recognized it. Now that she acknowledged it, standing stock-still over the Maudlins' bathroom sink, a part of her deep, inner core seemed settled, pleased, as though she had a purring kitten curled up in her lap.

The power of Maylemaegus previously acted through her, as it had when she lashed out at Nehemi and attacked Emi-Joye. It made sense that she didn't know it was there before. She spent her entire life scuttling away anything "special", because how often had she heard she wasn't? How often had foster mothers brushed her strawberry-blonde hair to hide the gentle point of her ears? How often had she been forced to pose for photographs to show off her eyes, because foster parents hoped to make money off a child's modeling contract? How many times had human children made fun of her for being so tall at such a young age, or so *nerdy*, with her nose always in a book, or a thousand other things they found to pick on her about until she burrowed into who she thought she was: an abandoned kid who nobody wanted … not even herself?

In that instant, Bridgette knew exactly how to connect to Universal consciousness, and the Maylemaegus inside her flickered. If she concentrated on that power, stoking it into being, she could float herself into the bizarre omnipresent projection that Heledd and his Druids once showed her she could become. She could search the worlds for the connection she wanted, and for the next few nights, she practiced finding members of the Samnung.

It was almost like Collum's power of hearing inner monologues, but not quite. Rather, she pictured a being's face, searching the endless vault of souls and spirits of living creatures, flora, and fauna, until she felt the one she sought. It took forever. More than one night, Bridgette either stopped herself because of a headache, or because she was jolted back into her body because Zedolph knocked on her door to wake her up. One of the reasons she'd been so quiet lately was because she had barely been sleeping for the better part of three weeks. Combined with the amount of manual labor at the butchery for the holiday season — they had almost double the usual number of harvest days for cattle and lamb since mid-November — the Elfling was utterly exhausted.

She paused on her walk to the Ballamúr to catch her breath, watching her exhales form into translucent foggy puffs in the air before her. Her heart raced, and she had no idea what time it was or for how long she'd been traveling. Bridgette closed her eyes and ran through the map in her mind. She was still hours away from the edge of Palna, even at the fast pace she'd been going. And her bags were heavy. Her already overworked shoulder started to ache from carrying the *Sefnuskrá* around.

Bridgette grinned to herself. She knew a faster way to travel. *Sorry, Bundy,* she thought, and launched herself into the sky.

<h1 style="text-align:center">~ 50 ~</h1>

Fucking hell, I missed this, Bridgette thought. Palna was dozens of feet below her. She flew a bit off-center, since one arm clutched her satchel of belongings to her chest and the other kept reaching back to make sure nothing fell from her shoulder bag onto a roof or treetop below.

She couldn't make out anything when she looked down, just jumbles of shapes that she knew to be clusters of trees, swaths of emptiness that were open land, and the *very* occasional spark of flame from someone's still-burning firehearth, keeping a home warm overnight. Bridgette flew fast, determined to get to the Ballamúr long before dawn. She left early enough from the Maudlins' that she would have made it by walking, but she was antsy to get back. Flying afforded her the ability to evade any potential members of the Palnan Guard or snooping women who might be lurking around in the dark.

Bridgette wasn't naïve enough to think that the Palnan Guard wasn't equipped with the ability to see at night. She also had a sneaking suspicion they wouldn't believe any tall tale she told them as to why she was wandering the area in the dark. They were less likely to think to monitor the sky.

The nearer she came to the Ballamúr, the stronger she felt it, a more internal pull than she had previously, as if it and the Maylemaegus within her reached for one another. It was still hundreds of yards away, calling her into its tickling, shimmering embrace. She loathed it and wanted it. Loathed because it had been erected by Ydessa Tinuviel and activated under false pretenses, possibly even causing the death of a Fairy she felt like she knew. Wanted because of this innate connection it held to her, a sense of possession she had for it.

When she finally reached its beautiful mirage and lowered herself to the ground, Bridgette greeted the Ballamúr like an old friend, letting herself connect to it. She'd known so long ago that it would welcome her, even going so far as to tell Collum that it kept Craft magic and blood inside Palna. Bridgette might not be able to do shit with the Samnung wall, unable to mend the alleged holes or weak spots Bondrie Guards found in its circumference, but this wall? The Ballamúr was hers.

Hello, you, she thought to it, feeling a new awareness surround the conscious connection she drew between herself and the wall. *You're a damn little well of mystery, aren't you?*

The Ballamúr cooed in response. It was Palnan energy, and as such it was her energy. It didn't belong here, for it was made of magic stolen from its own citizens, and she knew it would one day come down. Perhaps gently, perhaps with great force, but the Ballamúr was a temporary, involuntary barrier.

I'm coming back, she promised it, letting a finger trace along its edge, letting her heartbeat return to normal after her walk and flight to get here. *I'm coming back for you, for all of you.*

In the dark, the usually invisible Ballamúr now appeared as a sheen of fog like one might see on a mirror after a hot bath. She drew a heart into it, and to her absolute shock, the Ballamúr drew something back. It was a symbol of Gemaere, followed by another and another, until six square feet of barrier wall were covered with the strange runic language. The symbols were hard to decipher and flickered in and out with the night breeze. Bridgette's eyes ached as she furiously sketched the message into her blue notebook before it disappeared back into the miasma.

When she was sure she captured as much of it as she could, eyes watering with the concentration, Bridgette stepped again to the edge of the only world Palnans knew.

A voice that belonged to no being, and yet sounded of all beings, entered Bridgette's mind as easily as Collum's did: *You will know when it is time.*

The Liluthuaé understood.

She shot the Universe a determined smile and walked through the Ballamúr. Three heartbeats later, she stood in a different kind of dark, feet squelching in damp clay, surrounded by six members of the Bondrie Guard, all with weapons aimed at her and eyes wide with disbelief.

"Hey y'all," she said weakly, and the point of a spear tipped her chin up.

"Look what we have here," its barer spat, jabbing the point too close to her jugular for comfort. "Palnan fucking scum."

Bridgette's arms dropped to her sides weightlessly as two other guards snatched her bags away with their magic. Her wrists clasped together, bound by the same binding spell that once introduced her to magic, one that shoved her against an airplane seat what felt like a lifetime ago.

"Packed like she's coming out to make a home," one of them sniffed. "As if we would let that happen. You're coming with us."

"Perfect!" Bridgette chirped, wondering where in the seven hells this sudden energy came from. Her heart threatened to beat out of her chest in rising panic. "I need to have a little chit-chat with Corria Deathhunter."

She immediately regretted the line.

The spearpoint nicked her skin, and she felt the tiniest droplet of blood trickle down her neck. "The only thing our master swordswoman wants with Palnan scum is to see them *dead*," the guard sneered.

Oh fuck.

Bridgette's eyes shifted. She had seconds before one of them was going to gag her and take her to Corria, definitely, but likely with a pit stop by an interrogation cell first. She was not about to let that happen.

She twisted her hands in their invisible shackles until two fingers could slip under the covenant bracelet, and her body froze as her mind sought Collum's, pinpointing his apartment, his bed, his face, hoping beyond hope that this would actually work. She breathed in his scent as though he stood next to her, simultaneously casting a web over all of Heáhwolcen, to whatever minds were awake enough to hear, picturing various members of the Samnung. In the most authoritative voice she could muster, the Elfling spoke from both her body in Bondrie and her magic, which she heaved out to the world.

"I am Bridgette Eileen Conner, y gwyr yn erbyn y byd, the truth against the world," she said, loud and clear, repeating Heledd's Welsh words, part of her brain wondering how on Earth she remembered them and why they came out of her mouth now. "I am the Liluthuaé, I am the Bright Star, and I am coming home."

It took several moments for Collum to realize what stirred him from sleep. His arm itched and he closed his eyes, trying to remember what he had been dreaming about. Bridgette was there, he was sure of it, and he wanted to go back to that. To be asleep in a place where she was rather than awake where she wasn't.

His arm itched again, almost intentionally. Collum pulled it from under the covers, concerned, and stopped dead.

The silver beads of his covenant with Bridgette sparkled, and he heard her voice in his head: *I am the Liluthuaé. I am the Bright Star, and I am coming home.*

He evanesced to Bondrie in his sleepclothes.

Seven hells, it is frigid, Collum thought, still shaking sleep from his limbs. He'd been awake all of perhaps three minutes and took a minute to get his bearings, not quite sure where he landed. That was the problem with evanescing to a general space: one could end up anywhere. The Samnung wall was barely visible in the distance, indicating he must've arrived just beyond the border with Eckenbourne. He chanced it.

Bridgette? The ísenwaer felt rusty, a clogged channel after so much disuse. Collum let it take its time, hoping it would work, even if she was on the other side of the country. They never figured out how far it could bridge between them.

Nothing. He ran a hand through his mussed hair, knowing he looked quite a fright, and slipped two fingers underneath a different covenant bracelet, this one with Corria Deathhunter. *I'm about to pay you a visit, and so is the Bright Star*, he thought down the channel to her, and then disappeared in another flash of navy whirls.

This time, he knew precisely where he'd end up, which was the entrance to the stone fortresses at the Bondrian edge of the Beorgdún. The loudly flowing waters of Odalu Digsawosdi — Mountain's Tears, its name adapted from Cherokee — cascaded in front of the structures that were built directly into the landscape. The majestic river wound into Palna from here. When the sun set, it reflected in the water and gave the illusion that Odalu Digaswodi was on fire, a mighty symbol for the beings who chose to live in this country.

At the moment though, the waters were black as liquid pitch, and the only fiery colors came from windows carved into stone. Well, those, and the acid green witchlight torch carried by a Bondrie Guard who approached Collum.

"Tráthnóna mistéireach!" the fyrdwisa called out. "I apologize for catching you unawares, Thighearna."

"Fáilte, Fyrdwisa," the guard replied. "What is it that brings you to Bondrie at such an hour? It is either early or late; I am not so sure."

"Nor am I," Collum agreed. "I have come at this hour to see Ceannairí Corria Deathhunter on Samnung business. May I inquire as to if you've had other visitors this night?"

The guard studied him, something flickering in his eyes. "To my knowledge, we have not, Fyrdwisa. Should we have?"

"I suspect you'll have someone coming soon. That is actually what I would like to speak with the master swordswoman about. She'll be expecting me inside."

"You may follow me, Fyrdwisa."

Collum walked after the guard, whose chrome armor

glittered a sickly, menacing shade of metallic green in the witchlight. The male led him across a wooden bridge, past other members of the Bondrie Guard, then up and around several stone staircases before depositing the Elf in front of an entrance. The fortresses of Bondrie were mazes on purpose, extending deep into the mountain range in every direction.

The guard then pulled a polished ram's horn from the belt across his chest. He gave it a combination of short and long blows, a sound code, and the two waited for the carved wooden door to open. When it finally did, the guard stepped aside and presented Collum to his comrade.

"Fyrdwisa Collum Andoralain, here to speak with the master swordswoman," the first guard introduced.

Collum gave him a bow of thanks before stepping inside. The hall was dim, lit by a smattering of candles along its walls, illuminating the shadows of the Elf and the new guard as they walked down it, then around a ninety-degree corner and into a plush room lit by a roaring fire. Corria stood in front of the firehearth, a woven shawl draped around her broad shoulders.

"Fáilte, friend," she said, and the guard left them without a word. "I did not expect to be contacted by anyone in the Samnung this time of night unless Palna attacked."

The fyrdwisa smiled. "No attack tonight, Ceannairí. Although I do think we should intercept your guards before Bridgette crosses the barrier and surprises them."

"She already has."

Collum didn't expect this. "What?"

Corria indicated a massive black obelisk in the corner of the room. "The Bright Star appeared before a company of the Bondrie Guard toward the southern end of our border. I wondered if her call would wake you, or if I would be required to deposit her on your doorstep mine own self."

A scrying mirror, Collum realized, wondering what Corria meant by Bridgette's call. "Do you normally scry on your guardsfolk in the dead of night?"

The master swordswoman gave him a wan smile. "I do not always keep watch, but a wind whispered to me that tonight I should not sleep. I offered to be the Eye instead."

"I see," he laughed. "I am most grateful to have not woken you up."

"They are many miles away still, Fyrdwisa, as most of the guards are not able to evanesce, and this company does not have other means of transportation besides their own feet. Would you like to go to her?"

"Very much so, if you do not mind."

Corria, matching Collum's attire in little more than sleepclothes herself, reached for her longsword and scabbard. "Then let us go."

Bridgette was too busy arguing with the guards to notice that two figures were emerging from the dark before them.

"Listen to me!" she shouted, jerking her bound wrists away, angry that her one show of magic only made them afraid to touch her, not believe she was who she said she was. "I'm not some Palnan spy. I was in Palna on behalf of the Samnung —"

"We'll see what the master swordswoman has to say about that," one of the guards hissed at her. "Corria Deathhunter does not take well to liars. She rarely has much chance these days to show why she was chosen as our leader. I look forward to her demonstration."

"I'm not fucking —"

She bit her tongue mid-sentence, tasting the blood in her mouth, as the guard in front of her stopped short. The Elfling nearly ran into the back of him, halted just in time by a sharp pull of magic that froze her in place.

Deity damn you all, she thought, and almost cried at the mind-voice reply that entered her head.

Even me, Starshine?

Bridgette whimpered, unable to move a muscle past the

binding spell. She forgot how to think, she just *wanted*.

"Ceannairí!" one of the guards remarked, surprised. "A dark time of evening to see the both of you. We were —"

"Well met, Guardsmen mine. Let the Liluthuaé go," Corria commanded, interrupting him in a voice that offered nothing short of authoritative power. The guards looked nervously at one another. Bridgette dropped to her knees with exhaustion as the spell dissipated and her captors stepped back in unison. She spat blood on the ground, wondering if her neck still bled.

And then Collum's arms were around her, for real this time, standing her to her feet, holding her upright. Bridgette fought the surge of emotion, the pressure of waterworks behind her eyes, and stared hard at the guards. Though her heart still rattled, her smirk was worthy of a crown.

"I told you jackwads to take me to Corria Deathhunter," she said sweetly, then turned to Collum and the aforementioned master swordswoman. The tears finally leaked out. "Hello, Ceannairí. It's really fucking good to see both of you."

"As it is to see you, Bright Star," Corria replied. She swept into a low bow, her sword up. "Welcome home."

~ 51 ~

The guards stared, shocked, as their leader gave her fealty to the female they just held bound as a captive, an escapee from Palna. With expressions akin to horror, or perhaps those of a toddler caught misbehaving and rapidly seeking to rectify its wrongdoing, the guards joined Corria on the ground, kneeling before Bridgette. The spear that wounded the Bright Star now presented itself in submission before her.

"Thanks, Corria," she said, and the female and guards rose together. "I'm really glad to be back."

How did *you get back?* Collum asked her, mind-to-mind.

I'll fill you in later, Nosy Nancy, Bridgette thought back, flashing him a grin.

He took her in for the first time on far too long. The Elfling looked tired, like she hadn't slept in ages. Her eyes were still plain under their glamour, and a dried trail of blood disappeared into the knitted scarf around her neck ... Collum gritted his teeth.

That one. Bridgette ticked her head toward the guard with the spear.

"It appears as though the Liluthuaé was injured on her journey," the Elf said, staring not at the guards, but still at Bridgette. If Collum let go, she would fall to the ground in exhaustion. "You lot wouldn't happen to know anything about that, would you?"

The offending guard dropped again to his knees and held his weapon out to the fyrdwisa. "It was I who did it, Ceannairí. We did not know who she was. She simply appeared before us as a ghost might, coming straight out of the inner wall of Palna —"

"What do you mean, coming out like a ghost?" Bridgette asked, interrupting both the guard and Collum's train of thought about her injury. Thanks to the mirage from the Palnan side of the Ballamúr, she hadn't seen if anyone stood on the other side. She wasn't sure if she even ended up directly outside of where she walked through, or if the magic of the barrier deposited her elsewhere in the no-man's land, where a company of guards stood. "Did you see any strange symbols in the Ballamúr before I crossed through?"

The company exchanged glances. "Strange symbols?" one asked.

"Yeah. Give me that," Bridgette commanded, reaching for her shoulder bag. She yanked it back from a guard and pulled her notebook out, furiously flipping to the page where she sketched the Gemaere message. "Did y'all see these anywhere on the Ballamúr?"

"No, Sigewíf," one of the guards said. "I cannot say we have ever seen such symbols. What is this Ballamúr you speak of?"

Corria sighed behind them. "What is revealed to you this night will not leave the confines of this company. Is that understood?"

The six guards stood and stamped their feet, some sort of militaristic formation. "Aikalé, Ceannairí!" they shouted in unison.

"As you are not Elves, you may not understand the significance of the Liluthuaé, the Bright Star," Corria said, satisfied with their agreeance. "She is a most precious being, a legend come to life, and was in Palna at the request of the Samnung for reasons we cannot yet divulge. The Ballamúr of which she speaks is the name of the inner wall. It serves as a true border from our guard posts within the Samnung wall."

They were obviously familiar with the inner wall and could feel its power, but didn't understand its significance. Nervous, confused glances were exchanged between the guards before one of them, face half-hidden under a tightly wrapped black headscarf, spoke. Bridgette was surprised to hear the responding voice sound more feminine than the others.

"We say you are like a ghost because one moment we saw only the barrier and the next moment, you stood in front of it, as though you had been there the entire time," the guard explained. "We have seen others try to leave. The barrier morphs around their hands or bodies as they try to push through, but it will not yield."

That certainly didn't make Bridgette feel any better. She looked to Collum. "Was it like that when I walked through before?"

"It happened so fast, Bridgette. I could not say I remember," he replied apologetically.

The guard with the spear rocked from side to side. "You understand, Ceannairí, why we reacted as we did. No one has come through the barrier before on our watch."

Collum regarded him, a long look from the toes of his boots to the top of his chrome helm. "Your honesty is appreciated," he said in a tone that was more threatening than reassuring. "Let it be known that we now move into uncharted territory, and it would be wise to not draw blood from every being who walks through that wall unless they have the surname 'Tinuviel'."

"Aikalé, Fyrdwisa," the spear-wielding guard said, stamping his feet. "You have mine apologies, Sigewíf."

The fyrdwisa looked to the other five, his tide-colored eyes suddenly cold and commanding. "Is that understood?"

All six repeated the same military movement as they did with Corria, this time directed to Collum. He walked past them one by one, and Bridgette's heart surged with pride. Even in his sleepclothes, the Elf carried himself with the authority of his post. This was the leader of the Fyrdlytta. This was the second-in-command of all Elves and citizens in Eckenbourne. Here was the fyrdwisa of Heáhwolcen, and how well did he wear this mantle!

"We will take our leave now, so that you may resume your post. Do not forget what you have been told this night," Collum said. "Do not harm our comrades of Palnan blood."

Bridgette glanced at him. *Comrades of Palnan blood?*

We have much to share with one another, Starshine, Collum replied, mind-to-mind.

The Elfling reached for her other bag, still held by a guard who handed it back as though it would catch fire. Corria extended a hand to both Bridgette and Collum. She evanesced them back to her stone castle in the mountains, the three disappearing in a flash of wicked silver-gray.

It took every ounce of self-control for Bridgette not to immediately collapse into an oversized leather armchair once they arrived inside Corria's — well, she wasn't sure what to call the room, but it was warm from the fire and very cozy. She could use a long winter's nap after everything, especially since flying had been involved. Bridgette forgot how much muscle and energy the exercise used, and she knew she'd pay for it later that day.

Run-in with the Bondrie Guard aside, she could scarcely believe she made it out without a hitch. No one stopped her, not even the Ballamúr. It did the opposite, let her walk through unscathed … and invited her back.

She must have worn a strange expression, because Collum put another reassuring hand on her shoulder. "Bridgette?"

"Yeah?"

"What's wrong?"

Everything, she tried not to think to him. Now was not the right time to have this conversation. Now, all she wanted was endless sleep, a back massage with his healing salve, and bottomless caife calabazas.

I don't think the Coffee Cauldron opens for a few more hours, Collum jokingly thought to her. He tucked a tendril of tangled hair behind her ear. *The kitchen here in Casa de Piedra, however, does not sleep.*

Bridgette leaned into the side of his neck. *Do they serve naps?*

"No, the kitchen does not serve naps, I'm afraid," the Elf laughed out loud. "But I am going to go get us something warm and caffeinated, as I'm also afraid none of us are going to get any sleep the rest of this night."

He stepped into the hall and beckoned to the guard who stood there, asking for a guide through the fortress. Their voices disappeared after a moment. Bridgette really did collapse into the chair then. She curled into a ball, realizing she still wore Serrabinx's coat, scarf, and gloves. She tried not to think about Toby.

"You have had quite an adventure, Liluthuaé," Corria murmured from the firehearth.

"Yeah, you could say that."

The master swordswoman turned and surveyed the Bright Star, who was crumpled into the leather, wearing a bone-weary expression that suggested tiredness deeper than that of her physical body. "When was the last time you slept the full way through a night, Bridgette?"

"A couple weeks ago," the Elfling admitted. "I was practicing on how to get out, and it was easier to do it when the people I stayed with were asleep. How did y'all know where to find me?"

Corria indicated the obelisk she'd shown Collum shortly before. "I was the Eye tonight, and I heard your call."

"Wait, it *worked*?"

"Yes," Corria chuckled at Bridgette's amazed expression. "The wind warned me that I should keep watch, though I did not understand why until I heard your voice enter my mind. It was very strange to hear a voice other than mine own."

"Holy shit."

"How did you do that?"

Bridgette did her best to explain. She told Corria that she had strange, vivid dreams that made her wonder if she could connect to both Universal consciousness and subconscious, and she practiced until she thought she had it figured out.

"When those guards surrounded me, I used my covenant bracelet to hopefully get to Collum — the punk never explained to me how these stupid things work — but I kind of shouted in my head at anyone else's mind who might be awake," she said. "I had no idea if it would actually go through or not, because when I practiced in Palna, I only tried to do it with Samnung members. I stopped the connection as soon as I felt it connect."

Corria tilted her head to one side, thoughtfully regarding the Elfling. "I cannot speak for others this night, but I can speak for myself. I was awake, and I heard you. I can only assume others did as well."

She glanced toward the opening door from which Collum emerged, floating three steaming mugs of coffee before him. Bridgette watched him from the chair, nails from one hand digging into the opposite arm, the sharp pain centering her that this was truly real and not a dream; not some joke of the Universal subconscious she just spoke of.

"Thanks, Bundy," the Elfling said, smiling as he frowned at her use of the nickname in front of Corria. "You're the best."

You do love to test me, don't you? he thought to her.

Only on days that end in "Y".

You know, Starshine, I was going to say that I missed this, but now I think I'm rather changing my mind.

Bridgette looked mock-affronted. *Rude.*

He stuck a hand under her coat hood to ruffle her hair. "Drink this, and then I think it's time we both returned to sleep. May I take you back to Eckenbourne?"

"You may, Fyrdwisa." She wanted nothing more than to bury her face in his neck as he evanesced them back to his apartment.

The Elf perched on an arm of the chair, letting Bridgette snuggle into his side, her gloved hands wrapped around the mug.

Collum turned his face to Corria, whose pointer finger idly swirled above her own coffee, stirring sweetener into it with an invisible spoon. "How *did* you know it was Bridgette you should be scrying for?"

A smile tugged at Corria's lips. "Do you not realize the

grand fashion with which the Liluthuaé announced her arrival?"

"What?" He turned to the Elfling, whose lilac eyes were guiltily staring into the depths of her mug.

"Yeah, about that," Bridgette started. "I uh, kind of figured out how to maybe use Universal consciousness and also subconsciousness to like, send messages out?"

"You didn't just summon me?" Collum blanched, realizing what Corria meant earlier about "her call". "You summoned everyone?"

"Not exactly?" She cringed. "I was trying to use the covenant bracelet, but you never showed me how to do it right, so I used the one communication skill I did know how to use …" Her voice trailed off and she flashed him puppy-dog eyes. "Maybe I overdid it?"

He bit his lip to keep from smiling. "You don't say."

Corria took a long swallow, her own eyes glittering from amusement and the light of the fire. "Go get some rest, the both of you, before we're all summoned by the queen to Endorsa at the first rays of dawn."

Bridgette groaned. "Maybe Nehemi slept through that."

The master swordswoman raised a skeptical brow in response. "Perhaps."

~ 52 ~

Collum wasn't the least bit surprised to arrive at his door to find he and Bridgette had been beaten there by Trystane, Emi-Joye, Verivol, Aristoces, and Bryten. The five were clustered in various stages of bleariness, Aristoces still wearing her silk hair bonnet, and even Emi-Joye looked like she'd been pulled straight from sleep, her platinum blonde braids mussed.

"This is quite the welcome party," the fyrdwisa said, unable to stop the grin from spreading across his face as Bridgette blinked up from under his arm.

"Hey, y'all," she said, and then let out a gasping laugh as Bryten swooped in to pick her up. He pressed her against his golden chest, half-hidden by a fluffy sherpa-lined robe. "I'm definitely not sleeping tonight, am I?"

"Definitely not," Collum agreed. He pressed a hand to his door and ushered them all inside, wondering if he had enough mugs to serve coffee or tea to this many beings all at once. "Fáilte, friends. My home is yours."

We're missing a few, Trystane thought to Collum. *I suppose Njahla, Aurelias, and Apostine may join us?*

"Yes. Bring them all," Collum said. "I'll wake the fyrdestre."

He shot her a quick message of invitation through their covenant, then turned to see Bridgette, now nestled in Verivol's embrace, chattering animatedly with the Sanguisuge and Baetalüan. Aristoces was in conversation with Trystane and Emi-Joye. Collum watched as the latter formed a snowflake in midair, then slowly drifted it toward him.

"May I open a window and send this to Apostine?" she asked. "I believe he'd like to join the fun."

"Of course, Ambassadora, but what *is* that?" he replied, gazing at the meticulously crafted little thing. "It's beautiful."

"Thank you." Emi-Joye smiled at him. "I find covenant bracelets cumbersome and unnecessary, particularly when I can

- 344 -

send messages like this."

The perfect symmetry of its exterior crystals surrounded a circular message, formed in all capital letters with tiny diamonds separating each word: "Join us at Collum's. The Bright Star has returned."

"This is fascinating," the Elf said. "You truly are the ambassadora to the Antarctic, aren't you?"

"So they say," she answered. "It's not nearly as instantaneous as a covenant bracelet, of course, but so much better fits my aesthetic."

The Fairy walked past him to the kitchen, where she cracked open the window and let her message dance into the breeze.

"How will Apostine receive it, should he not have a window open himself?"

"He'll wake when he gets tired of hearing it tap at the glass."

Collum snorted a laugh. "Shall I make us some coffee?"

"Yes, please," Trystane answered for them all. He glanced out the window where the night sky slowly lightened into indigo. "Njahla will be here soon with breakfast."

"Thank the goddesses," Emi-Joye remarked. "I'm famished."

The fyrdwisa gave her a look. "How long were you outside my door?"

Trystane shrugged. "A fair hour or so, from when we heard her call to when you finally deigned to join us. I suppose you were right about her Universal subconscious connection, brother mine. Until Bridgette's message woke me, I was sleeping like the dead after the evening's calisthenics."

Emi-Joye coughed what could have been a laugh, but the ard rialóir ignored her and continued. "I couldn't tell you what I was dreaming about, but one moment I was asleep and the next, Bridgette's voice was in my head, almost as clear as if she'd been leaning over my bed, whispering in my ear. I believe I sat up so quickly that my head spun."

"I've never known anyone to do that," Verivol piped in,

appearing at the kitchen doorway. "I wasn't sure at first if it was a dream or not, but it seemed too *real*. There was power behind it, not just her words."

"How did you know to come here?" Collum asked, making movements toward his stove. He snapped a finger and flame appeared under one of the burners, ready to heat a kettle of water for fresh coffee.

"We didn't," Verivol replied. They turned to smile at the Elfling, who was blabbering to Bryten about a Baetalüan she met in Palna, one named Paxson. "My covenant with the Samnung was not activated, and when I first woke, I questioned whether or not I dreamt it. It wasn't long after that when Trystane contacted us all and told us where to go. That was when I assumed Bridgette was back."

She is, indeed, Collum thought, hoping that perhaps Nehemi may not have received the message. It would certainly explain why the queen hadn't activated the Samnung covenant or shown up at his home along with everyone else. He reached into his cabinets, frowning as he pulled mismatched earthenware mugs and a pair of double-walled glass tumblers onto the counter. *I believe I may need to invest in more dishes.*

There was a quick knock at his door then, followed by a tumult of laughter and an actual squeal from Aurelias, who from the sound of it either tackled Bridgette into the sofa or bear-hugged the Elfling so hard they both fell against the wall. The kitchen emptied as Collum's companions sauntered out to greet the fyrdestre.

"We thought you were *never* going to come back!" Aurelias cried, her visible eye gleaming with delight. "Trystane and I had a bet going as to whether or not Collum —"

The fyrdwisa appeared then and gave his second a shrewd look. "Whether or not I would *what*, Parvhin?"

"Disappear on all of us and try to break into Palna, of course. Clearly, I lost."

"Clearly," Trystane said from behind her. "Pay up, Fyrdestre. You owe me a week of service as my representative to Estmereamel."

Collum stared at his second. "*That's* what you bet? You hate going on tour duty."

Aurelias gave him a wry look. "Clearly, I also thought I was going to *win.*"

The living room erupted in laughter. Bridgette moved from Aurelias' embrace back to Collum's, letting one of his arms encircle her protectively. She watched them all, half-listening as they chattered together, awake from the adrenaline rush of her sudden arrival. The Bright Star wondered if any of the other Samnung members heard her message. There had been no word from Nehemi or Kharis, and Corria it seemed was determined to monitor her scrying stone until daybreak.

How are you, Starshine? Collum thought to her, relieved that this channel of communication was again open between them. The void he felt during her absence was gone.

Fucking exhausted, but I am just so happy to be back. I have so much to tell you, but I want to tell you first, before anyone else. Maybe Trystane can know, but … her inner voice trailed off, and she wrapped her arms around his waist. *You're cozy.*

He grinned down at her, nuzzling into the unruly mess of half-unbraided hair atop her head. *I missed you, Bridgette.*

I bet I missed you more, she thought back. *I wish I figured out the whole subconscious thing way earlier. My dreams would have been a hell of a lot more fun.*

Collum didn't have to look at her to see the devilish gleam in her eyes. *We'll talk about that later, when there is less of an audience.*

Their silent conversation was interrupted by another arrival. Apostine waltzed in without knocking, first greeting Emi-Joye with a quick hug and then skipping toward Bridgette, who was surprised at his reaction. She'd barely known Apostine before she went to Palna.

"You've been missed, Bright Star," the Tief-Fae said, and the amber whorls of his eyes spun with pleasure. "I think by this Elf the very most, although we all have much to share with you."

"So I'm gathering," Bridgette said, accepting his reach for an embrace. "Y'all must've been busy. I didn't know everyone was so concerned about me."

It was a little overwhelming to return and find that so many beings were this elated to see her. The Elfling wasn't used to friends, having rarely stayed with one foster family long enough to form such relationships until she was in high school. By then, it was such a habit to confide in no one but herself that what she considered "friendship" was little deeper than frequent acquaintanceship. Collum, she realized, and now Toby and sweet Fincher, perhaps even Zedolph, had become what friends were supposed to be. Now here she was, in an apartment full of magickind that cared about her — even ones like Apostine, whom she hardly knew.

By the time Njahla knocked on the door, bearing with her a basket overflowing with fresh pastries, the initial hubbub had died down and Bridgette dozed on the sofa, her head in Collum's lap. Emi-Joye was curled up under a blanket at Apostine's feet, resting against her second's knees. Verivol, Bryten, Aristoces, and Trystane turned the kitchen table into a meeting place, and Aurelias sat on the other side of Bridgette, using the Bright Star's thigh as a headrest while she read a book, her legs kicked over the arm of the couch. Collum and Apostine talked quietly with one another, the fyrdestre occasionally joining in, about what and how they were going to tell Bridgette of all they learned while she was away.

Collum shook the Liluthuaé awake at Njahla's appearance. Bridgette wiped the back of one hand across heavy eyelids. "Snacks?" she muttered hopefully.

"Breakfast," he corrected her. "Cinnamon caramel-stuffed croissants, jam tarts, and something with pistachios, from the smell of that basket. Which would you like?"

"All of them."

The Elf rolled his eyes and squeezed her shoulder. "As you wish, Liluthuaé."

They all moved to the kitchen, where Trystane had made a second pot of coffee and was cracking a dozen eggs into Collum's largest cast-iron skillet. Njahla heaved her basket onto the counter and helped herself to a mug.

She turned to Bridgette. "I see Aurelias lost her bet."

Collum gaped at her. "Truly, do the three of you know no bounds!"

"I guess she did," Bridgette laughed. "It's good to see you. All of y'all. Even if my eyes were" — she yawned — "kind of closed for a little bit."

"Escaping Palna was no easy feat, I would imagine," Verivol said from the table. "We would like to know how you got out, Bridgette, if you are up to telling us."

Bridgette groaned inwardly. She knew this would come eventually but had expected to be able to recoup beforehand. "It's kind of a long story."

"We've got all day," Bryten assured her. "Take your time. Have a croissant."

Someone floated one across the kitchen to her hand, and she chewed for a moment, forcing herself to become fully conscious. Bridgette hoped Bryten wasn't joking about having all day, because her plan to tell Collum all of this first evaporated as fast as the pat of butter Trystane now slid onto the skillet to season more eggs.

"It was the best of times. It was the worst of times, and now I'm a butcher's apprentice," she began, only Collum seeming to understand her human literary reference. There was a moment of exchanged befuddled glances before she added, "I think we're going to need more of that coffee."

~ 53 ~

Her companions said nary a word as Bridgette spoke, telling them as much as she dared about the past three months. She left out a few key details, namely that she might be the Raisarch by birthright, suspicions regarding protected lands, and some of the information Zedolph shared with her about the Tinuviels' and Ydessa's histories. The three books of the *Sefnuskrá* remained secret, too. But she did recount Zedolph's tale of the eclipse from the previous summer, and let it be known that no one in Palna understood the power of the Ballamúr. She told them about the mysterious barrier, too; how it looked from within the country's walls versus what the Bondrie Guard saw on its exterior, and what it felt like to walk through it.

In between sips of coffee and bites of pastries, the Elfling told them stories of Toby and Serrabinx, of being a butcher's apprentice and meeting her first Kobold, and what it was like to live within those fabled borders. She tried her best to describe how the air was so different than in the rest of Heáhwolcen, what characterized Palnan culture, and strangely, how the country was "known for tulips", except she only saw the flowers on the horizon toward Düoria.

Bridgette had no idea for how long they gathered in Collum's kitchen. An occasional chuckle broke through her tale, but all listened, taking in every sentence the Liluthuaé said. The sun was long risen by the time she finally started recounting the previous night's events and told them about her return. Again, she kept a few elements to herself. Though the Bondrie Guard knew about the Gemaere written on the Ballamúr, not everyone else needed to hear about that yet, and she knew Collum would skin her alive if she chose now, of all times, to reveal that she could fly.

"Then Collum evanesced us here, where I now" — Bridgette yawned dramatically — "have some extreme jet lag."

The fyrdwisa, who'd been sitting in the chair next to her this entire time, knees nearly touching, slid an arm around her shoulder and rubbed his palm comfortingly down her bicep.

You'll get some sleep soon, I promise, he thought to her.

She didn't get a chance to respond before Aristoces broke the pensive silence that surrounded them. "You have indeed had quite the adventure, Bright Star," the Fairy of All Fairies said, her words echoing those of Corria just hours before. There was a mischievous glint to her charcoal whorls, but her expression was somewhat grave. "It's a wonder you made it back without much challenge."

Collum's eyes flicked to the flakes of dried blood that remained on Bridgette's neck. "Much," he agreed.

Bridgette hadn't told them about her dreams, but she did mention the Palnan woman who stopped her from crossing through the Ballamúr a few weeks before.

"Yeah," she grinned at Aristoces. "Kind of why I decided to ditch in the middle of the night. I figured there would be less of a neighborhood watch by then."

A beat of scoffing laughter, a minute of silence, and then Verivol asked, "I'm assuming not everyone in the Samnung heard your message, or realized it wasn't a dream. Which one of us is going to tell the spreca and her borhond that you're back?"

"I will," Trystane volunteered instantly. "But not yet."

He looked directly at Bridgette, the gold flecks in his eyes flashing as they connected with her. "Lie low here for a few days, both of you. We don't have a Samnung meeting until next week, and that will give us time to gently break the news to Nehemi, which will be shortly followed by celebrations of the winter solstice. It will be difficult for even the queen to be dispirited with all of that to prepare for."

It will also give us plenty of time to share what we've been up to while you were gone, Collum added, mind-to-mind.

Bridgette nodded to both of them. To Collum, she thought, *I may have left out a few interesting tidbits of information. And you're going to need to bring back that old map of Baize Sammael's you've been hiding. I've got some stuff to add to it.*

For some reason that jogged Collum's memory. His eyes lit up and he stood suddenly, evanescing out and back into the kitchen within seconds. When he returned, he held out a blade.

The Bright Star stared, first at her knife, then at the fyrdwisa who proffered it. "How the fuck did that get here?"

"It appeared to Collum in a dream last month," Apostine volunteered. "Apparently he's been having some very interesting bedtime adventures of late."

You told them? Bridgette shot the incredulous thought to Collum, fighting to keep her cheeks from blushing. But the knife … she lost it, or apparently transported it here, long before *that* particular dream.

He handed her the blade and again put his arm around her shoulders. *Not specifics, trust me, Starshine.*

To the rest of the group, Collum replied aloud, "As much as I've enjoyed this gathering, I do not hesitate to say that I would also enjoy getting a chance to indulge in dreaming once again. You are welcome to remain if you'd like, but I will excuse the Liluthuaé and myself to our respective rooms for the foreseeable future."

Aurelias tipped her head toward them both, then winked at Bridgette. "We'll take that as our cue to exit, Chief. Summon me if you need anything, like two iced caife calabazas."

"Give me a few hours and I will definitely take you up on that offer," Bridgette grinned at her fellow Elfling. "They have some good food in Palna, but they do not have anything that perfect to drink."

There were a few exchanged hugs — Verivol couldn't resist and once again swept Bridgette off her feet in embrace — then the door shut and Bridgette and Collum were left alone in his living room, staring at one another, utterly sapped.

"I'm not going to make it down that hallway," she said, and turned to crash onto the sofa instead of walking toward her bedroom. "If I ever wake up again, I'm going to need some of that salve stuff. My back is dead from flying after being so out of practice."

"I am at your service," Collum said, sweeping into a mocking bow. He pulled a blanket up over her. She was already drifting into oblivion as he swept tendrils of her undone braid behind one ear and whispered, "Sleep well, Starshine."

Bridgette slept for nearly two days straight, all through Saturday and the majority of Sunday, waking only to use the bathroom and at one point to meander to her bed, which she sprawled on top of, still wearing the clothes from her final day in Palna. Collum hadn't made a peep that she heard, though the Elf crept in to check on her, silently as he could, every few hours. He eased the air in the apartment, making it warm and soothing, urging her to rest and relax. Bryten came by once, knocking softly and disappearing by the time the Elf answered to find a scrawled note next to a paper box full of venison brimlad — Collum's favorite snack.

"Solstice Week greetings, my friends," Bryten had written on his card. "From my family's hearth to yours. Sorry if the granola is too sweet; Mum was experimenting with a new honey."

Collum snorted, then shut the door behind him, bringing the gift to the kitchen. He'd only been able to sleep several hours, his nocturnal schedule not nearly as roughed up as Bridgette's. Most of the two days she slumbered he spent reading for pleasure, something he rarely made time to do anymore. It was a refreshing escape for his mind, knowing Bridgette was here and that trunk of artifacts, those horrific notebooks — vademecums, or whatever Emi-Joye called them — were far away.

When he finally heard stirring from her room, the Elf roused himself from his book, sliding Bryten's solstice card inside to mark his page.

Are you finally awake? he thought to her.

No answer entered his mind, but a few minutes later, the Bright Star's head peered around the corner, resting her cheek against the wall. Her hair was undone and tousled, remnants of braid long-gone, blanket wrapped around her shoulders like a heavy cape.

"Yes," she said, grinning. She still looked sleepy — still felt sleepy — but she was awake enough for now. Awake enough to change clothes, at least. "Can we get something to eat?"

She looked so preciously *human*, despite those delicately pointed ears poking out from her tangles. Collum resisted the urge to rise to greet her.

"Of course. Would you prefer me to cook, or to have Aurelias or Trystane bring us something from elsewhere?"

"What are the chances you can rustle us up a couple hamburgers and super-sized fries, Fyrdwisa?" Bridgette gave him a childish, sad-eyed look. "I'm dying."

"So dramatic," he murmured. "There isn't any such food in Eckenbourne, but I suppose I could send the ard rialóir to Endorsa. That sounds rather like a Taberna Körtz order, does it not?"

"Abso-fucking-lutely," Bridgette skipped out of the hallway, blanket-cape and strawberry blonde hair trailing behind her. She leaned over and gave him a kiss amidst his dark brown waves. "You handle that, and I will … bathe Palna off of me."

"I was wondering what that strange odor was," Collum said dryly.

The Elfling scowled. In all honesty, her clothes probably were a little rank, mostly because she wore them to the butchery, handling raw meat in the hours before her departure. Though dry-aged steaks were by no means rancid, they did tend to have a notable pungency that likely seeped into her sweater and pants.

"Punk," she replied, before turning and skipping back from

whence she came. "You better not have run out of any of those bath oils while I was gone!"

He shook his head, laughing to himself, and slipped two fingers under his covenant with Trystane. *We're hungry*, he thought down the communication channel, and not five minutes later the Elf rapped on his door to take their orders.

By the time Bridgette emerged from her bath — long, but not so much luxurious, given she had to wash and comb her mangled, wind-swept, sleep-matted hair — Trystane returned with four boxes, three containing steaming hamburgers and the last holding shoestring fried potatoes sprinkled with paprika seasoning salt. The Elfling gave him a gleeful hug of thanks. Her wet hair left an imprint on his tunic, but Trystane didn't care. His fyrdwisa hadn't looked this alive in far, far too long.

"I took the liberty of inviting myself to dinner," Trystane explained, indicating the third box. "We have just as much to tell you as you did us, but I assumed it would be best done in a more intimate setting, especially since several of those who welcomed you the other night also do not know that which we do."

"Cryptic," Bridgette said. She snatched a potato from the box, waving it in the air to cool it before shoving it unceremoniously into her mouth. "I told Collum this already, but I left out a couple of things that I only wanted to share with you two."

"Oh?" the ard rialóir prompted her. "Do tell, Bright Star."

"Y'all first. I'm going to pass out if I don't eat some protein," she replied.

But most of her burger lay unfinished as Trystane and Collum tag-teamed their own adventures. Collum glossed over the Nashville trip, intentionally not mentioning Lucilla or their meeting with the Simmonses. The revelation about the magical notebooks, though, made Bridgette stop chewing mid-bite.

She swallowed thickly. "I think I know what those symbols might have been."

~ 54 ~

Bridgette disappeared into her bedroom and returned with a thick stack of books, which she dropped onto the kitchen table. She looked first at Trystane, then at Collum before gesturing and asking, "Did the symbols look anything like these?"

The fyrdwisa gave her a hard look, concern shrouding the blue in his eyes. "Are you positive you were not injured other than by the guard with the spear?"

"What?"

Collum gingerly picked up the top book from the stack and read, "'Encyclopedia of European Fungi, Third Edition'?"

"What!"

Bridgette snatched it from his hands and furiously flipped through the pages. All English and Latin. Inked images of mushrooms on nearly every one of them. Her heartbeat sped up. The other tomes appeared as encyclopedias too, one covering flowers and the second herbs. She stared at them, horrified.

"What. The. Fucking. Fuck."

"Bridgette," Trystane began slowly. "What *were* these?"

He knew, then, that the books weren't supposed to be encyclopedias. She lowered herself into a chair again and took a deep, steadying breath.

"They're the three volumes of the *Sefnuskrá*," Bridgette revealed. Neither Elf gave any hint of recognition at the name. "It's got a really long title that sounded maybe Welsh or Gaelic. Both, probably, knowing how much y'all muddle up languages and call it 'magic', but they're written in Gemaere."

The Elves exchanged a glance, befuddled. Bridgette resisted the urge to ball her fists in frustration. How could two members of the Samnung not know this?

"Gemaere," she repeated again, gesturing her hands in front of her, as if she was tossing dice on the table. "You know? The language of the Fyrst?"

"The Fyrst didn't speak a separate language. Perhaps Gaelic or an old form of Irish or English, as Ceannairí Álfar was of that part of the world," Collum said. "But it assuredly was not its own tongue."

Bridgette gave him a long, hard stare. "Welp, Baize Sammael spoke it, and wrote it, and apparently enchanted it to hide or something, because here it is!" She again gesticulated to the three faux encyclopedias.

"Baize Sammael?" Trystane's skin went a tad ashen. "What does Baize Sammael have to do with any of this?"

"Y'all have never heard of Gemaere, and you're telling me that the word *Sefnuskrá* means nothing to you?"

"I cannot say that it does," the ard rialóir replied uneasily.

The air in the kitchen was charged now, tension from the Bright Star melding with whatever magic disguised those books. Collum bit his tongue to keep himself from easing the atmosphere. Bridgette looked so supremely irked at the two males that it was almost comical. She took another deep breath and finally answered, her tone an edged calm.

"The *Sefnuskrá* is Baize Sammael's autobiography and manifesto."

Trystane really did go pale, his skin nearly as satiny white as Verivol's. "Baize Sammael had a manifesto? And there are copies of these works in Palna?"

"Technically no — Zedolph said they were supposed to have all been destroyed. He and Serrabinx lost their shit when Toby and I showed up with them. He recognized the symbols and even though he couldn't read them, he knew what they were."
Bridgette regarded the three books. "I guess this explains why the leatherwiph, the woman who bound them with these covers, only remarked it as *interesting* for Toby and me to be getting them. They probably were disguised except around beings who are supposed to understand their significance."

The Bright Star sat back in the chair, marveling at how

much sense this made now that she said it out loud. Zedolph told her of the book that once presented itself to him in a similar manner, the so-called mathematician's philosophies that camouflaged epic tales of Baize Sammael and the founding of Palna. A rapid series of blinks overtook her eyes, and for the first time in quite a few days, she felt a near-physical blow as the knowledge came to her: the stories that Zedolph discovered were based on ones that were in the *Sefnuskrá*, watered down and illustrated to be more palatable and engaging to a younger audience.

But why us? she thought. *Why the Maudlins, and why me? Why do these books only show up for us?*

"I want to see the notebooks," she declared out loud. "If they changed from symbols to nonsense words right in front of your eyes, then whatever spell is on them is probably the same one that's on the *Sefnuskrá*."

The Elves exchanged a furtive glance.

What if she reacts to them the same way that Emi-Joye did? Trystane thought to Collum. They hadn't gotten far enough into the tale of the notebooks to reveal the ambassadora's terrifying reaction, nor the harrowing scare and interview that followed. Seeing Emi-Joye like that had given the ard rialóir such a sense of terror and panic that he knew if Bridgette went into any semblance of that state, Collum would lose it.

Collum, however, shook his head in response. "We'll take you to see them," he acquiesced. "But you have to promise us that you will alert us to any energies, *auras*, or feelings you have toward them. And please, please Bridgette, do not try to touch them."

There was fear in his voice, and Bridgette didn't understand why. "I mean, okay?"

"Thank you," Collum replied. "Please finish eating. We will go in the morning."

Bridgette made it another three bites into her cheeseburger

before her eyes widened in surprise. She pushed the chair back from the table so fast that it rocked backward as she ran out of the kitchen again. She returned with a notebook of her own, scanning pages as she walked, until she laid a spread out on the table before the Elves.

"Look," she pointed. "Symbols like these. This is Gemaere. Was the language you saw on the Aelys Frost notebooks anything like this?"

Trystane frowned at the scribbles. He hadn't actually seen them, not to the same extent Collum and the others had. He looked to the fyrdwisa for confirmation, but Collum only stared.

"This is the page you showed to the Bondrie Guard," he remembered. "You said these symbols appeared to you on the Palnan side of the Ballamúr?"

"Yep. Written in the mist, like something out of a horror movie. I tried to copy them all down."

"I can't say for certain. There are certainly similarities between this and what I recall being in those three notebooks, but that was weeks ago. And the symbols began to transform not long after we found them, so I did not get a good enough look at them to say for sure that they were written in what you say is Gemaere," Collum said, running a finger across Bridgette's scribbles. "Bring this with you tomorrow and we can compare the two."

"Yeah, if any of the symbols haven't magicked themselves away," the Elfling scoffed.

"A true observation," Trystane murmured. "Perhaps we will find ourselves lucky."

It was overcast and cold when the three set out to Maluridae Wood the next morning. The frostbitten leaves crunched under their boots as they walked to the clearing where the notebooks lay buried. It was eerily quiet; not even the birds seemed to have woken yet — either that, or it was too cold to chirp. Bridgette was thankful she kept Serrabinx's coat, now layered with a different scarf, and one of Collum's beanies shoved down over her head. It was a little too large, and she kept having to pull the folded brim up over her brow.

Why do you seem so nervous? she thought to Collum.

I don't like those … things, he admitted, mind-to-mind. *We hadn't gotten to this part of the story yet last night, but I can* feel *them. The notebooks have a sentience that goes deeper than their ability to hide what may be Gemaere from prying eyes. I've never been able to sense an inanimate object before, much less be aware that it senses me, too.*

Do they tell you things?

Not yet. I suppose I'd rather they didn't.

Bridgette took a step closer to the Elf and squeezed his fingers between her own. *Whatever they are, they're no match for the Liluthuaé,* she thought back.

She was only half-joking.

They'd evanesced close to the rowan trees, but not directly into the clearing. Upon reaching it, little evidence remained of Emi-Joye's torrent of power. The dirt and leaves she'd caused to spiral into the air around them were settled now under additional layers of forest detritus that fell in the time since that last visit. Collum could feel the notebooks as Trystane undid the fyrdwisa's magic, releasing the trunk from its hiding place. He'd done a shit job compared to Aurelias' first go-around, when she coaxed the trees to wrap their roots around the artifact.

Collum halted Trystane before he let the notebooks out. "Remove the glamour from her eyes, please," he said. "Aside from it being nice seeing them again, we'll be able to notice if they alter in any way." Glancing to Bridgette, he added, "These things have a tendency to entrance those who are intrigued by them."

She furrowed her brows, confused, but turned to Trystane to have her Elven eyes unveiled. The Elf raised a hand, his closed palm in front of her face, and spread his fingers out as he spoke:

"Bring back the vision of she who Sees,
For we no longer fear those who peek.
Unveil the truth we didn't want shown,
For in her task, success was sown.
By the power of three times three,
As it is, so mote it be."

Several blinks later, Bridgette's eyes — though they felt no different to her — must have visibly cleared, for Collum beamed in her direction.

I didn't realize how much I missed those, Starshine, he thought to her, and her core melted in nonverbal response. *Remember: Talk us through what you experience with these.*

"I'm not going to touch them," she said, winking. "Promise."

Though he wasn't sure he fully believed her, and a nauseating sense of worry fisted in his gut, Collum looked to Trystane. He nodded to the ard rialóir, whose hands were poised over the latch, waiting for instructions.

"Release them," the fyrdwisa commanded.

~ 55 ~

Bridgette didn't know what to expect when the three ancient notebooks rose into the air. They looked innocent enough, but the way they *felt* …

"I can feel them, too," she whispered to Collum. Whispered because she was afraid to startle them, as he had been. "It's like they're waiting for something."

"You have the same awareness about them as I do," the Elf confirmed. He reached for her hand, needing to feel her grasp, wanting to ground her in reality so that even if the notebooks entranced her as they had Emi-Joye — whose reaction Bridgette still knew nothing about — she would not devolve in the same way.

Trystane floated the notebooks closer to the two of them, following close behind. He was prepared to throw the vademecums back in the trunk at a moment's notice should Bridgette start to sense any negative or threatening energy. The ard rialóir watched her, but her eyes did not shift with either sierwan knowledge or into the deep violet that hinted at her connection to Maylemaegus, and often predicated her attacking someone.

It was the lavender vademecum that intrigued Bridgette most. The closer they got to one another, the more that notebook seemed as aware of the Elfling as she was of it. Bridgette kept her hand in Collum's, pulling him a bit as she walked purposefully toward this object. Its two companions appeared to hang back, their energies still palpable but muted in comparison to the draw she felt to the lavender.

"The purple-y one," Bridgette murmured. "I feel it more than the other two."

What are you? she thought to it, fully aware that Collum could hear this conversation. She wondered if he'd be able or inclined to chime in. *What do you want from me?*

She was positive now that the other two notebooks were entirely uninterested in her. But the lavender one floated boldly, its energy significantly more awake than it had been when Trystane first let it out of the trunk.

What do you want from me? Bridgette thought to it again. *You know I came here for you. Tell me why.*

The notebook shimmered and the same strange symbol Collum first noticed on it appeared for a millisecond. Bridgette stopped breathing and her heart started pounding.

Show me that again. Show me why I'm here, she begged it. The fyrdwisa's hand gripped hers tighter as he felt her energy shift.

Nothing happened. Bridgette furrowed her brow, concentrating her mind on the lavender notebook. She forced herself to calm, forced her mind into the state of connection that she'd become so familiar with. If this thing had any sort of consciousness, she could reach it if she focused properly, though admittedly her previous successful practice with Universal consciousness had included exactly one spoken message meant for the Samnung and one unintentional dream sequence. Connecting with this notebook was like scanning a room full of wandering eyes until they locked onto a specific gaze. Though the notebook had neither eyes nor mouth, she felt the lock, and sensed something like glee, or perhaps relief, pulse in response.

Show me, the Liluthuaé thought again, moving her mental tone from begging to one of authority. *Show me that symbol one more time.*

Her hand had Collum's in a death grip as the notebook shimmered, and the power that roiled in Bridgette's core blossomed. There was no other word for it. She felt it unfurl as fresh and joyous as a tulip opening to the spring sunshine. It moved to every part of her body, tickling gently, an exploratory feather swishing down from a great wind, coming to rest as it found home within her very nerve endings, her lungs, her heart. She felt it thrum as it came into contact with the wound left by the protected lands, and she *knew* …

Bridgette's eyes were wide with disbelief as the symbol again shimmered into view, and the eye of the Triumvirate sigil flared with glittering light before disguising itself once again.

Her heart was going to beat out of her chest.

"Did you see that?" she whispered to Collum. Her voice shook.

"The symbol looks like an eye," he said, remembering. "That's what was on all three when we initially pulled them from the trunk."

The Elfling didn't respond. She looked again at the notebook, *her* notebook, as strange as that felt to her. *Do you answer to the Raisarch?* she thought to it. Nothing, no bleat of energy in response. *Do you answer to the Hringur?* There was a skip of power, an acknowledgement of the word, but no, that was not their purpose in existence.

The Hringur? Collum thought to her, but Bridgette ignored him.

What do you want with me? she tried again, reaching out with her mind, with this fresh power that filled her. So caught up was she in her mental exchange with the notebook that she didn't see the physical surroundings alter as both Bright Star and vademecum began to glow.

"Collum," Trystane warned. But the fyrdwisa continued to stand next to Bridgette, the two Elves watching in mute terror as the female changed before their eyes, the expanding power altering her very presence. The neon purple glow didn't help, either.

The Elfling looked down at her empty hand, the one that wasn't attached to Collum's. She saw the glow, her skin tingling, the sort of intangible awareness one has when they enter a house known for its hauntings. This notebook was hers, its shabby, faded cover disguising the true power within. This notebook *was* her, in a bizarre way. Bridgette's power surged toward it, gently beckoning it closer.

"Don't touch it," Collum snapped, though he knew she wouldn't listen. "We don't know what will happen if you touch it!"

"I have to touch it," Bridgette whispered. "It's *mine.*"

The two Elves locked eyes, remembering Emi-Joye's eerily similar statement when she was presented to the trio. Collum remained at Bridgette's side as she walked closer and closer to the glowing vademecum, the shared bubble of energy brightening with each step. It was *happy*, he realized. The damned thing had indeed been waiting for its complement, waiting for longer than some magical species had even existed. It was as old as the Elves themselves, and how in the seven hells it and its companion volumes ended up with Aelys Frost was a mystery they might not ever solve.

But Aelys Frost had obtained them, hidden them, and smuggled them to Heáhwolcen, from where she entered the spirit realm of Ifrinnevatt shortly thereafter, leaving her trunk somewhere Trystane would later find it. And now that it had been unlocked, what came from its depths was *happy* to see the Liluthuaé. Collum felt as though they managed to open a veritable Pandora's Box, and that was the sort of Greek legend he would rather not have come to life.

He watched helplessly as Bridgette reached for it, her hand outstretched, palm up, waiting as though the vademecum was a bird or butterfly coming over to land. The fyrdwisa braced himself for the connection, his chest tight with anticipation.

Nothing could have prepared him.

Trystane shouted and both Elves ducked down, elbows crooked over their eyes, trying to cover their ears, as the lavender vademecum came to rest in Bridgette's hand. The world around them all but exploded and knocked the two Elves senseless.

The neon purple glow was blinding, the wind roaring as it had with Emi-Joye. All three were trapped in a column of whipping air, leaves, twigs, and dirt cycling up from the floor and rotating around the rowan trees. Particles of earth pelted Collum in the face. He shielded his eyes against the light and the maelstrom, and with horror came to the realization that one hand was clearly no longer attached to Bridgette.

He forced his gaze first across the clearing to Trystane, who knelt in a similar position, speckles of dirt staining his tunic and cloak, which was barely still attached to the Elf as the wind threatened to jerk it from around his neck and plaster it against the tornado of power that surrounded them. Collum bit his lip as he turned toward Bridgette, every ounce of movement feeling as though gravity had been multiplied.

Once, many moons ago, the fyrdwisa attended a human carnival and rode something called the Rotor, a sort of attraction that spun so fast as to push daring riders against the wall behind them, unable to move a muscle until the spinning slowed. Collum felt rather like that now.

He wished he hadn't looked, but now that he had, Collum Andoralain could not look away.

Bridgette had both hands out before her, the vademecum resting in her open palms, emanating *joy* and *completion* and *finality*. Her eyes were that violent violet, echoing the still-brighter neon glow that advanced to become pure white, the intense brightness too powerful even for Elven eyes to easily observe in the daylight.

What are we? Bridgette asked it. What at first had been an intense gaze became a palpable connection. The vademecum pulsed into her, its warmth in her hands not that different from Collum's. *What are we meant to do, and why do you answer to the Hringur?*

The Triumvirate sigil glowed on the cover.

That doesn't mean anything to me.

Below the sigil, a series of Gemearic symbols began to appear on the cover. It was like a computer screen glitching in reverse, sprinkles of glitter pixelating into solid being.

I don't speak Gemaere.

There was a whole line now, perhaps a sentence.

I need a cypher. A code, something to translate whatever you're telling me.

She felt a tap in her thoughts. An ask for permission. Bridgette blinked.

Go ahead, I guess?

✦ *We've been waiting for you, Liluthuaé.*

It had a voice now inside her mind, a whisper of consciousness that was unfamiliar to Bridgette, but as clear as the ísenwaer. The vademecum sounded croaky, its voice sore from disuse. There was a round deepness to it, something wise and feminine, with "queenly" being the best adjective the Elfling could come up with in the moment to describe it.

You've been waiting for me? she thought back.

✦ *Yes. For you, for the Triumvirate, for this time.*

This time?

✦ *Yes. For this time.*

Bridgette furrowed her brow, cocking her head at it. *Why?*

✦ *You have many questions, it seems.*

No shit, Sherlock. A glimmer of windchimes sounded in her head and Bridgette realized the thing was laughing at her.

✦ *All will soon be known, Liluthuaé.*

"Why is everyone and every*thing* so damn cryptic in this place?" Bridgette muttered out loud, scowling at her new vademecum.

✦ *Where are the others?*

Her brow furrowed further. *What others?*

✦ *The Triumvirate. We feel them here, have at long last felt their presence these many years, a gift from the Matla descended from the Demiurge that bore Ceannairí Álfar itself. Liluthuaé, Boireannach, Astridsí. The time hath come for all to be united.*

Matla, Demiurge … those words were semi-familiar to

Bridgette, something to do with magical origins and power that she vaguely remembered from a long-ago history lesson with Collum. But Boireannach? Astridsí? Those were new, and *new* never seemed to go particularly well when it came to things happening in Heáhwolcen.

I don't know what you're talking about. There's just me.

It seemed frustrated.

✦ *The Boireannach. Her scent is upon you. Where is Her Eminence? She knows where to find us. Why does she not accompany you now?*

There was a flash of ice blue light that transferred into Bridgette's mind from her vademecum, blinding the Elfling's eyes for a moment.

From his place on the ground where he still knelt outside of their glowing vesicle, Collum listened to their conversation. The vademecum's mind-voice was muffled, but Bridgette's rang loud and clear. He saw the Liluthuaé stiffen. And that flash of light that filled their minds' eyes?

That, he saw.

That, he recognized. It was the same shock of color that filled his vision shortly before he broke the spell Lucilla placed on him in Nashville.

Violent violet, icy blue.

The word "Boireannach" meant naught to him — and neither did "Astridsí" — but he knew to whom the vademecum referred.

Neither being was sure whose mind-voice said it first, but the object gleamed with pride as both fyrdwisa and Liluthuaé thought Emi-Joye Vetur's name.

<h1 style="text-align:center">~ 56 ~</h1>

The Fairy in question, meanwhile, was nearly knee-deep in snow at one of the enchanted Minthame habitats. Apostine followed behind her, a duo of humans standing watch a short distance away. One was Dagmar Nilsen, the other Noah Irwin, both of the Antarctic delegation that the two Fae worked with as ambassadora and ambestre.

"Anything?" Noah called out, shivering despite his multiple layers of clothing. Typical winter in Heáhwolcen had nothing on this place, where Fairies worked with Cath Draíochta practitioners to mimic the significantly harsher temperature and air conditions of Antarctica.

"No," Emi-Joye replied, her voice raised to be heard over the perpetual wind that plagued this particular habitat. "The receptors haven't picked anything up at all, at least not from what I can see."

She knelt next to what the humans called a collection core, a jerry-rigged, minuscule version of a much larger laboratory on the South Pole known as the Hexaxis. Protected by warding spells, the collection core gathered information from an octagonal arrangement of tubes that were buried deep in the habitat's ice, down to the core of Heáhwolcen's foundation, and extended beyond even what Fae eyes could see into the continent's atmosphere.

"And you're sure nobody's been messing with it?" the Australian delegate shouted.

"Positive, Noah."

"Damn," the man cursed. "Worth a try though, right?"

The ambassadora frowned at the collection core screen. This research device was one of the few things in Heáhwolcen that used a form of solar electricity. Magic-wielders didn't need such power, but human technology such as this tool did. She didn't understand exactly how such a thing worked, had never needed to before, and yet here she was, staring at something called a *computer* that showcased an endless scroll of numbers and symbols. They meant something to the human delegates, or would, once the *memory chip* — a bizarre-looking square cartridge lined with metal — was transferred back to the scientists at the main lab in Antarctica.

Emi-Joye pressed a button that deployed the existing memory chip and carefully installed a new one in the empty slot, her fingers tingling as they entered and exited the protective ward-wall that kept the core from freezing over. A hand touched her shoulder, and she found Apostine there, a sympathetic look on his face.

"They really want this to work, don't they?" he commented.

She gave him a half-hearted smile. "I suppose. The hypothesis is commendable. If the Antarctic version is able to detect these neutrino things from one end of the Earth, it makes sense that it's possible to try from the opposite end, too."

"I understand that, but I'm still not sure why they chose Heáhwolcen and not, say, the North Pole." The Tief-Fae took a moment to glance at the detector rods, such spindly tall towers of hopeful scientific discovery. "Would that not have made more sense?"

"Apostine, the North Pole is in the middle of an ocean," Emi-Joye chuckled. "Greenland might have been a more logical choice, or even Russia. Canada, too! But what Frosset told me was that because of Heáhwolcen's location *above* Earthen lands, the scientists wondered what could be detected differently, if anything, from such an elevation. We don't have the space to build a full replica of the Hexaxis, of course, but a miniature version might do … something."

"It's done a whole lot of nothing so far."

The Fairy swatted at her second. "Come on. Let's get these two somewhere warm before Noah manages to lose a finger from hypothermia."

Apostine tossed back his head with laughter, and the two trudged back toward their human delegates.

"Here you go," Emi-Joye said to Noah, depositing the memory chip in his open palms. "I made sure that we had this habitat reserved until the spring solstice next year. It's spelled so that only Apostine and I can come into it, along with our guests. No one's been here except for us and Ambassador Malvarma."

The Fairy led her three companions back to the edge of the wintry habitat, where they gladly stepped back into the normal winter temperatures of northern Endorsa: cold, but not so cold that Apostine's tail might fall off if it touched the snow for too long. It wasn't often that their human delegates came to the world above the world, but the collection core's construction changed that — for the Antarctic ambassadors, anyway. At least one, and usually two, human liaisons came every four months to check on it and change out the memory chip. To be completely honest, Emi-Joye wasn't entirely sure what it was that they were supposed to be detecting with this rather large contraption. Though Emi-Joye could create a snowflake from thin air and not think a thing about it, when it came to theoretical physics, her brain turned into white noise.

"When do we get to see them for ourselves?" she asked Noah. "The neutrinos, I mean."

"Everyone except a core crew is gone 'til after the holidays," Noah said. "Think you could come down to the station in the spring?"

Escaping to Antarctica after talking to the Fórsaí Armada seems like a fantastic idea, she thought. The Fairy looked back at Apostine, who was too busy twisting his fingers around Dagmar's snow-damp curls to pay attention to anything remotely like work. "I can't speak for Dag's biggest fan back there, but I don't see why not."

Noah chuckled "Maybe we'll get a Christmas miracle, and the core will spot one of the buggers for us before you come.

What a find that would be!"

"That would be a nice gift from the gods, indeed." Emi-Joye smiled back at Noah. He was older than she, perhaps in his fifties, but unlike Trystane — who had her beat by far more than that — Noah looked the age of her father. His skin was hardened both by plenty of summers surfing under the sun and too much time in the cold, daring hypothermia to take him on. Sometimes it did and sometimes it won, which was why the human now lacked two of his toes.

They dined that night at the Seledreám, flanked by the Antarctic ambassador emeritus Frosset Malvarma and his family, as well as Aristoces, several ranking members of her staff, the Veturs, and Apostine's father.

A musical trio provided light entertainment for the evening, the sounds of strings offering ambiance for the vast dining room that Aristoces selected for the meal. The glossy white marble table was laden with holiday dishes during each course, including an elaborate dessert of individual panettones topped with candied citrus slices and snowflake-shaped dustings of confectioner's sugar. It had been a long time since the ambassadora had been part of such an affair. Emi-Joye felt sure she couldn't eat another bite, but then someone brought in mugs of mulled cider and Noah pulled out a glass bottle of bourbon he claimed to have smuggled up the portal.

The next thing Emi-Joye knew, it was nigh on ten o'clock and she was dancing with her father, twirling to the tune of violins. Apostine danced too, flying with Dagmar balanced on one hip, her curly red hair flowing in the breeze the Tief-Fae created. To Emi-Joye's surprise, her own mother even joined the merrymaking. Tula Vetur and Aristoces had one hand joined and the other holding skirts to the side, their bare feet tapping out what had to have been a Renaissance dance of some sort.

"I'm proud of you, daughter mine," Johannes Vetur said to Emi-Joye, raising his voice to be heard over the music. "You've done so much in so few years, and this research you're a part of will be so vital to understanding more of our Universe!"

She laughed. "Thank you, Father. I only understand the very basics of it, but it is an honor to play such a part. This is research that can only be done right now in Antarctica, but we hypothesized that because Heáhwolcen is located higher in the atmosphere, it would be possible to capture neutrinos here as well."

The song ended and Johannes led his daughter back to the table. "What are they exactly, these neutrinos?"

"They're a bit like ghosts, I suppose," Emi-Joye replied. "Some humans call them that, 'ghost particles', because they're invisible and yet they're everywhere. The only way we can even sense them is if they happen to interact with another particle and leave some sort of trace. Supposedly they come from great happenings in the cosmos, supernovas and such, which the humans wish to learn more about."

"It seems to me that those are mysteries of the gods and Universe, best left alone."

Emi-Joye laughed. "I'd tend to agree, but humans are a curious sort. To them, a cosmic mystery is less a vast wonder to appreciate and honor, and more a detective story to be solved."

She took a sip of cider, hissing as the added bourbon glazed the back of her throat. "Noah says it's believed neutrinos are as individual as fingerprints, and that scientists could track their origins back to individual star explosions. Could you even imagine, Father? To be able to visualize a star exploding?"

"I'd rather not," Johannes said. "The stars are the homes of the gods, the keepers of the Matla. I do not want to know what anger would cause a goddex to explode its home, to send such ancient power plummeting across the solar system."

Something trilled at the back of Emi-Joye's consciousness when her father said that, but she chose to set the thought aside. She turned the conversation to a much lighter topic — the winter solstice celebration in a few days — until the festivities died down. The Veturs flew home in the chill night air, and after Emi-Joye bade her parents good night, she slipped into her room and let out a deep sigh.

This was followed immediately by a shriek of surprise as she turned and saw none other than Trystane Eiríkr lounging casually on her bed.

"Deity bless, Trystane! You nearly made me jump out of my skin!"

"I'd prefer you just jump out of that lovely dress, my darling Fae, but I suppose beggars cannot be choosers." The smile he offered was sanguine, but didn't fully meet his eyes.

"How did you get in?"

The ard rialóir smirked. "With magic."

She glowered at him. "And why, exactly, are you sneaking into my bedroom in the middle of the night?"

Trystane sat up and beckoned her to come close. "Firstly, my winged maiden, it's hardly past the witching hour, much less the middle of the night. In the second …" his voice trailed off, and his expression became taut. "In the second place, certain things happened today that I cannot hide from you. I could not sleep with those events on my mind, so I came to find you, only to discover you weren't here."

The Fairy frowned. She lifted her feet just off the floor and floated to him, wings fluttering softly as they deposited her onto his lap. "Why was this so important that it could not wait until the sun rose?"

Emi-Joye shivered as Trystane traced her neckline, down the open back of her dress to the sensitive muscles of her wing joints. He sighed deeply.

"The news probably could have waited," the Elf admitted. "But I could not. I have experienced more fear and uncertainty the last few months than I have in my entire life beforehand. I needed peace. I needed grounding, some reminder that what is meant to be, shall be."

He leaned his head over the top of hers, one hand still stroking between her wings. "I needed you, Em."

She didn't know how to say what she wanted to say, so she simply wrapped her arms around his waist and waited for him to talk again. It was a long moment before he did.

"Will you please allow me to evanesce us back to my home, where we can speak freely without the looming threat of your parents' Fae hearing?" Trystane asked.

"I will," Emi-Joye said. "Let me just go tell them that I had a note waiting on me when I returned. I can pretend that it was something Noah wanted to tell me about the collection core but didn't notice until he was examining data after dinner. It takes us long enough to fly home from Çeofilye that such a thing is very plausible, and it makes sense that a homing pigeon carrying a message would have beaten us to the house."

"Go on, then," the Elf urged, pleased that he managed to win what was usually their normal argument about her staying overnight. Though it wasn't a win, per se, as they still kept each other a secret. His core burned with something akin to envy as he thought about the Veturs receiving this news and assuming that Emi-Joye was using it as an excuse to spend the night with the Australian man.

Trystane didn't like that at all, even though there wasn't a speck of truth to it.

He waited impatiently for Emi-Joye to return and watched as she stuffed various necessities into an overnight bag, which she then wrapped across a shoulder before stepping over to him. The Fairy reached an arm for his, the ice blue whorls cooling in her eyes as he looked up at her from the bed.

"Well, Ard Rialóir, what are you waiting for?"

He kissed the hand she extended to him, then clutched her close and evanesced them onto a different bed many miles away.

~ 57 ~

One of Trystane's arms was stretched out beneath Emi-Joye's neck; the other crooked just under her breasts, pulling her close. She felt his warm, easy breaths blow gently over her ears and through her hair; felt the rise and fall of his chest against her back in rhythm with each inhale and exhale. And yet she could not sleep. Her mind was riddled with thoughts, struggling mightily to process the information the Elf dropped on her mere hours before.

"In those books of your mother's, did you ever come across the word 'Boireannach'?" Trystane had asked.

They'd been lying there, in not too different a position than they were in now, his hands winding through her unbound platinum hair, wavy from the braided crown she liked to wear it in. The question was so out of the blue that Emi-Joye, had been trying to decipher what sort of forest-y scent Trystane's skin smelled like, ignored him asking until he repeated himself a couple of minutes later.

"No," she had murmured, nuzzling her nose into the hollow at his throat. "Should I have?"

"I'm not sure," the Elf admitted. He paused playing with her hair and rested a palm against her cheekbone. "It's not a term I've heard of until today, when the vademecums spoke it to Bridgette and Collum."

Emi-Joye shoved away from Trystane and sat up, eyes wide. "They *spoke*?"

"In their own way. Collum has been able to sense them ever since they appeared in the trunk, but they also have power that allows them to have some variety of thought process and inner monologue, so he can hear them, too. One of them communicated directly with Bridgette's mind, and Collum listened in," Trystane said, giving Emi-Joye the briefest of explanations as to what he witnessed in the clearing. "The one that communicated with Bridgette knew she was the Liluthuaé, and it spoke of two other beings, the Boireannach and the Astridsí. The vademecum said it scented 'the Boireannach' on Bridgette, that 'she' had been in the clearing before, which is how we determined about whom it spoke."

"Me?" The Fairy gave him an incredulous look.

"You," he confirmed. "Whatever in the seven hells the Boireannach is or is meant to do, it's *you*, Em."

She didn't know what to say.

And now, tucked against his body and trying to match the pattern of her breaths to his, Emi-Joye Vetur still had no words.

The ambassadora was at a loss to describe the knowledge that she *hadn't* been crazy to think the gray-blue vademecum was a part of her, that she really could feel it. She didn't know how to explain what rattled inside her brain, that for all her internal conflict about what level of involvement she desired with working alongside Bridgette, she was flattered to find herself so equally favored by the Universe. But what *was* the Boireannach? Was it specifically a Fairy myth? She'd never heard of it before and wasn't sure where to begin to look or whom to ask. Would it raise questions to fly into Endorsa and ask a magister at the University?

The ambassadora allowed herself about five more minutes of staring at Trystane's night-darkened ceiling before she gave up on sleep entirely. She gingerly peeled herself out of his grasp, her wings almost cooing with relief after being pressed between the two of them, and drifted down the hall into his library. She had a feeling the ard rialóir hadn't bothered to look through his own collection of history and fiction to see if there was mention of this new myth. She lit the trio of candles on his altar and began her own search as the moon crested over Heáhwolcen.

What neither Emi-Joye nor Trystane considered, though, was the chance that Bridgette and Collum hadn't been entirely truthful with the Elf. Bridgette's vademecum — because it was hers; there was no getting around the fact now that it was out in the open — had gone smugly silent after the two of them concluded that whatever the Boireannach was, the *who* was the Fairy ambassadora. The tornado in the clearing calmed, the energy softened, and though Bridgette and her vademecum still glowed and her eyes were glazed with that deeper shade of purple, she was herself again.

They couldn't keep the revelation of the Boireannach from Trystane, least of all because though Collum didn't know what the word meant, perhaps the ard rialóir might. He didn't. Trystane evanesced out of the clearing to the Caisleán shortly after the three vademecums were once again safely tucked into their hiding place, leaving Bridgette with eyes the wrong color and words pulsating on repeat in the back of her mind.

Liluthuaé. Boireannach. Astridsí. Triumvirate. Hringur. Maylemaegus. Raisarch. Matla. Demiurge. Liluthuaé. Boireannach. Astridsí. Triumvirate. Hringur. Maylemaegus. Raisarch. Matla. Demiurge.

So there, protected by the magic of Maluridae Wood, where trees kept conversations close, Bridgette dropped to the ground and finally told Collum everything. Some if it repeated what she hinted at the first night she came back. Most of it was new or expanded details, things she didn't want known by anyone except him and possibly Trystane.

Collum realized at some point that his jaw must have dropped in disbelief, for after Bridgette finished talking, she reached forward and lifted his chin back into place. He didn't know how to reply. He opened his mouth to say something but shut it almost immediately after, then did the same motion a few more times, looking like a dumbfounded fish stranded onshore.

"Yeah, I know," Bridgette muttered. "It's a fucking lot. And I don't even know what half of it *means*. It's just all this stuff and these words that I keep hearing or seeing come up. Like the Triumvirate and the Hringur? The vademecums know about those. That stupid eye symbol has something to do with both of them."

She stared up at the open sky. "Do you know how sick to death I am of having to be a sierwan, but never getting to choose what information shows up in my brain? There are a gazillion dots I want to connect with all of this and they're just out there floating, stars unattached to constellations."

"That's a very Elven thing for the Bright Star to say," Collum said. A smile teased his lips as she kicked at him.

"Punk."

"And *that* was a most Aurelias-like move to make toward me."

Bridgette grinned. "I knew I liked her from the start."

"She likes you too, Starshine." It was Collum's turn to stare at nothing, his multiple arguments and tenseness with his fyrdestre as yet unresolved. Bridgette's reappearance softened much of his own anxiety, but he still owed Aurelias both dinner and an explanation. An extra-thoughtful winter solstice gift might be helpful in his apology as well, he thought.

The Elf turned to the Elfling. "Where do we go from here?"

He was relieved to see her eyes back to normal — or at least the normal color they shifted to as sierwan knowledge came to her — when she turned to him a few minutes later. There was a distressed sort of expression on her face as she answered him.

"Well, Bundy, I reckon we should see if anyone on this continent knows how to read Gemaere, and why the language keeps disguising itself. We've got a few really thick books to go through, and I'd really like to know what the fucking Triumvirate is and what it has to do with me."

Collum grimaced. "I'm still not sure it's a language —"

Bridgette interrupted him with a swift kiss on his jaw. "Just shut up and listen to me for once, will you?"

Her eyes really were back to normal when she pulled away, and the fyrdwisa gave her a relieved smile as he tilted his forehead to meet hers. "I always listen to you, Starshine."

"I'm not so sure about that, actually, but how about we take a little side quest to the University this afternoon and do a little digging?"

He frowned. "I don't —"

"Nuh-uh," Bridgette cooed, taking his face in both hands. "Not the main library, and definitely not to see Magister Ephynius. Let's go hunt for treasure in that dusty little trove of yours, Mr. Secret Society frat boy."

<h1 style="text-align:center">~ 58 ~</h1>

Bridgette hoped that by the time she was dragged to the Samnung meeting that week to surprise Nehemi and Kharis, she and Collum would have something of note to share about her time in Palna. She made it clear that it didn't make sense to start talking about the *Sefnuskrá* or Gemaere, the Triumvirate or the Hringur, until they had more of an understanding about what any of it was.

Her hope was a tad futile. Despite hours spent at the Coven House of Wand and Sword in the days between meeting her vademecum and coming face-to-face with the queen of Endorsa, the two made little progress. The difficult thing about the Coven House — aside from having to drink rancid-tasting potion every time they wanted to drift unnoticed between the main bar and the Alcove — was that the Alcove itself was, as Bridgette so glowingly praised it, reminiscent of a television show she once watched about hoarders.

There was no order, rhyme, reason; nothing to how things were haphazardly disorganized. Collum tried to use the same spell that worked on Aelys Frost's trunk to reveal anything related to the terms or history they sought, but all that managed to result in was a cyclone of dust, paper, disused quills, and for inexplicable reasons, an entire twenty-pound crystal ball flying around the room. The Elf halted the windstorm after several horrifying seconds — during which Bridgette dive-bombed to the floor faster than a fouled soccer player — then he cursed the number of tornadoes he'd been caught in recently.

To say that neither Liluthuaé nor fyrdwisa was in a good mood when they appeared at Cyneham Breonna was an understatement.

Please don't do anything stupid, such as provoking Nehemi, Collum begged Bridgette mind-to-mind as they walked through the plant-covered foyer.

I'm not making promises that I can't keep, Bundy. Plus, half the time — Bridgette stopped her thought mid-sentence and gaped at the sight of Njahla standing behind the reception desk instead of Lucilla. The Elf looked about as murderous as Bridgette and Collum both felt.

"Hey!" the Elfling greeted her, jogging up from the other end of the room. "What are you doing here? Lucilla's probably going to try and eat us all for lunch when she finds you in her spot. Although I don't think any of us would let her, but it'd be fun to watch her give it a go." She smiled conspiratorially at the ardestre.

Njahla gave Collum a pointed look and sent a rueful thought his way — *I see you've not explained the events of your Nashville trip to the Bright Star!* — before answering.

"It's my pleasure to inform you that Lucilla is no longer employed by the Samnung and the Endorsan royal courts," she said. "It is my displeasure to inform you that our beloved ard rialóir volunteered me as the stand-in until after winter solstice, when Nehemi intends to interview potential applicants for the position."

"Lucilla isn't here anymore?!" Bridgette didn't bother to hide the glee from her voice.

"No, she is not," Njahla replied. "It's a wonder she was kept as long as she was. Her organization is … abysmal."

Indeed, now that Bridgette was closer to the desk, she could see what Njahla meant. The Elf stood amidst stacks of folders and envelopes, looseleaf and bound pages, not to mention assorted supplies and mementoes that Lucilla kept around the desk. It was only a few degrees less cluttered than the Alcove. Bridgette scowled as she surveyed a scribbled note in Collum's handwriting, his neat signature at the end. It appeared to be an apology letter for turning in some report later than expected, and was weighted to the desk by an absurd pink crystal, shaped like a — Bridgette tried not to growl out loud.

"What the fuck."

Njahla bit her lip to keep from laughing. "I haven't been able to get either of those things off of here. It appears they are quite permanently attached."

"It's a rose quartz *dick*, Njahla."

The poor Elf didn't know if she could bite her lips any harder. "I am aware of this."

"It's on top of a note from Collum."

"I do see that, yes."

"What about me?" Collum asked, sliding up next to Bridgette. He glanced at the offending decoration. "… Oh."

His cheeks heated, caught between embarrassment and anger. And amusement: he couldn't help but enjoy the train of repulsive thoughts rolling through Bridgette's mind as she stared at the rose quartz phallus on top of his scrap of paper.

"Why in the seven hells is this here?" Collum asked. He reached forward and tried to remove the paper and crystal from the wood. They didn't budge. "Wonderful."

"Why can't you move them?" Bridgette gritted out.

"I'm not sure, but it appears they're quite content to remain. I suppose we could request for her to have permission to come clear out her belongings, and she could return to retrieve this … thing," Njahla said.

Collum put his palm along the small of Bridgette's back and thought to her, *There's no need to be angry, Starshine. Now is not the time, but I have something to tell you. Lucilla is well and gone, and she will be of no consequence to either of us anymore.*

I don't know why I hate her so much, but I fucking do.

I know. He rubbed his thumb up and down her spine. *I know why both of us dislike her. I was not sorry to see her go, and I hope to never voluntarily lay eyes on her again. Let us make it through this meeting, and then I shall share the story.*

Bridgette glanced over her shoulder at Collum. "I really hope she gets eaten by a hungry vampire."

He and Njahla burst out laughing, and the fyrdwisa dragged Bridgette up the stairs. Njahla listened as they made their way to the Samnung chamber, chuckling as soundbites like "stabbed by a unicorn horn" and "maybe fed a poisoned apple" followed in their wake.

The mood atop the stairs was tense since the rest of the Samnung arrived before the Endorsan delegation did. Verivol greeted Bridgette with a hug, then stood by her other side, both they and Collum with an arm each protectively wrapped around her back. No one said a word, though a few of the magical leaders sent thoughts to Collum. He relayed most of it to Bridgette through the ísenwaer. Though Corria would keep the visor lifted on her helm, she had no plans to remove her sword belt or lower her shield until all were seated peacefully. Bryten and Verivol had a bet going as to whether or not Nehemi would open the meeting by cursing them all for keeping this secret. Aristoces would do her best to keep the peace, but if it came down to it, she was not afraid of becoming physical with the queen of Endorsa. Nehemi was an incredibly skilled archer, Collum knew, but her quiver didn't come with her to Cyneham Breonna. Aristoces' blades, however, did.

Verivol's grasp tightened around Bridgette's waist as a trio of footsteps sounded down the hallway. Collum straightened his shoulders into the sort of stance that reminded everyone in that room that he was the fyrdwisa and leader of the Fyrdlytta, and that even if the individual needing protection *wasn't* the one he called Starshine, he would defend her at all costs.

There was a swish of fabric from Nehemi's oxblood skirts that preceded her appearance and an audible hiss of surprise that followed. The queen stood frozen, Kharis wide-eyed next to her, and Cloa oblivious a few steps behind. Arctura gazed at the Elfling, his one good eye appraising as if in approval.

Collum wished his listening skills extended to animals. He would have liked to know what the cat thought, but it certainly seemed content.

"How long have you been back?" Nehemi asked Bridgette. Her tone was measured. For once, though, she didn't seem angry at Bridgette herself — just everyone else in the room who kept this information from her.

"A couple days," Bridgette admitted. "I kind of figured out how to use some of my Universal consciousness connections to send out messages, but it's a little hard to target who actually gets them. I didn't know who heard and who thought it was a dream, 'cause it was the middle of the night."

"If I received such a message, I do not recall it," the queen said simply. "I presume you have much to tell us of your experience, and I'm sure the fyrdwisa will be glad to educate you on the proper ways in which to format and turn in your official reports."

Collum nodded. He relaxed. It didn't seem that Nehemi was on the warpath this day.

"Fáilte, Bridgette," Nehemi said, and turned to lead the Samnung members into their warded chamber.

When Collum had been fyrdestre, particularly around the time Mohreen started showing up to tell the Samnung she was carrying a youngling fathered by Eryth Tinuviel, there were some memorable, lengthy hours that the government leaders spent together. But that December meeting, the second to last in the year 2018, was perhaps the longest Collum ever attended as fyrdwisa. Much of Bridgette's story only Nehemi and Kharis hadn't already heard, but there were lots of questions to pepper Bridgette with from around the table. Only he and Trystane were largely silent, even Corria coming up with a few things she wanted to clarify. Her inquiries, though, were limited to the Ballamúr.

"You say it was a mirage?" the master swordswoman asked.

"Yeah," Bridgette confirmed. "When that one crazy

neighborhood watch lady — sorry, that's an Earth thing; it's like citizens who keep an eye out for crime and stuff — stopped me from touching the Ballamúr the first time I tried to cross it, I could see and feel that the barrier was there, but beyond it was like, trees and all this pretty scenery. It just looked like Palna kept on going, like no border actually existed."

Corria sucked in her lips, considering. "Our magic would not do that."

Bridgette wasn't sure if that was meant to be a question or a statement of fact, but she commented regardless. "If that's the case, then whenever the Ballamúr originally went up, it had to have been like that. And that's been, what, at least as long as I've been alive?"

A murmur went through the chamber.

Nehemi sipped from a glass of sparkling water. They'd been in the Samnung chamber for so long that both a hefty luncheon and early afternoon beverages and snacks had been delivered.

"I suppose it is time to attempt an official state of affairs visit to Palna," the spreca finally said.

Bridgette started so quickly that a bite of tea sandwich fell straight from her open mouth. "What?"

"It has been years since such a thing happened," Nehemi said. "Our ambassadors were able to handle that role quite well."

"Until Ulerion," Bridgette couldn't help but point out.

"Until within the last year, when Ulerion became unable to properly communicate with us," Nehemi said.

There was an uncomfortable silence at the table.

"Y'all are seriously telling me you could have waltzed into Palna at any point in time as the Samnung, and you never bothered to?" Bridgette looked to be on the verge of snapping, and Collum put a comforting hand on her thigh under the table. "Why didn't anybody bother to try this earlier, when Ulerion first disappeared?"

She scanned the room, all the Samnung members' gazes

directed toward the table.

"What the hell have y'all been doing? Ulerion could be *dead*; he could be part of the Collective; he could be literally anything and y'all do not seem to give two fucks about it!" Bridgette shouted. "I hate to break it to you, but Fairy ambassadors don't just disappear. Something happened to him, and from the atmosphere in that country, I don't think it's anything good."

Nehemi stood stock-still, nostrils slightly flared, as Bridgette went on.

"What did you think?" the Elfling shouted. "That you'd find the Liluthuaé, send me in, and hope that whatever ancient power y'all think I have would lead me right to Ulerion so I could solve this little problem of yours? That somewhere along the way, I'd run into the Tinuviels, and they'd tell this complete stranger with a twangy Southern accent exactly what they've been planning for who knows how long?"

The silence stretched, apt to break.

"Yeah, well, how's that going for you?" Bridgette said. Her voice was acidic.

"Not particularly well," Bryten muttered. He glanced down the table to where Bridgette sat, still glaring at Nehemi, and tried to catch her gaze instead.

Bridgette softened. She chewed the inside of her cheeks.

"None of us are sure what happened to Ulerion," Aristoces said, comparatively unfettered in the heat of the moment. "He was one of my citizens. It was less of a Samnung issue that he wasn't sending his reports in than it was one specifically of Fairevella. We knew about the inner wall, as you're aware, Bridgette. We did not — and I'm not sure I do now — consider him to be in grave danger. Ydessa Tinuviel is many things, but idiotic is not one of them. She wouldn't provoke the Samnung into attacking by murdering her ambassador."

The Bright Star huffed in response.

"I am sorry, Bridgette, that we put you into this position of no return," the Fairy went on. "You performed your duties admirably with very little time to prepare. You were the only one we could send in, because we needed an in."

"Oh," was all Bridgette said, not fully understanding.

Collum squeezed her leg gently. She knew how much he hated what his role in all of this had been and would still have to be for the foreseeable future. Collum couldn't have realized that by becoming the "handler" for Mohreen Conner, that when she chose to take on her abandoned role of motherhood, it would forever alter the course of his existence. He hadn't known what he and the Bright Star would mean to each other for the two years he tried to find her, and not even when he slipped into the diner that day and followed her home did he comprehend their growing importance to one another. Bridgette nudged her knee into his own, a silent sign of gratitude for his presence and support, and an acknowledgement of his apology.

Nehemi, in a rare show of empathy, nodded toward Aristoces. "None of us has ever been in such a position before, Bridgette. I do not apologize for what we asked you to do, nor will I —"

"Surprise, surprise," Bridgette, Collum, Trystane, Bryten, and Verivol all grumbled simultaneously under their breaths.

"— But Aristoces is correct. We needed, as she said, an in. The last Samnung leaders to physically go to Palna were King Hermann and Queen Lalora, and Kharis along with them sometimes. The last time they got near the border, they were killed." The queen drew her lips into a tight line. "As a whole, we decided we would do our best to avoid such a demise if we could help it."

"Fantastic! So, you sent a human-raised, magically inept Elfling instead?" Bridgette replied, deadpan.

Verivol chuckled, but kept their mouth shut.

"No." Nehemi gritted her teeth, any guise of kindness gone. "We sent in the Liluthuaé, who is also the daughter of the country's male leader, whether he knows it or not."

"Would've been nice if you'd, I don't know, maybe given her a little bit more time to get ready to save the world," Bridgette said back, not registering that Nehemi begrudgingly addressed her power and position. The Elfling's eyes flashed for a moment, and Collum fought the urge to actually grip her thigh instead of just rest his hand upon it.

Be careful, Starshine, he thought to her. She ignored him.

"So now I'm back, and because I managed not to die, *now* is when y'all are suddenly going to do a state of the union visit and check to make sure I'm not *lying* about what Palna's like?" Bridgette's voice rose a dangerous octave as she glared at the witch queen. "I. Do. Not. Lie, Nehemi."

Collum really did dig his fingers into her leg then. He felt her flex underneath his warning grasp, and then her fingers wove their way between his. When she looked at him, her eyes were the wrong shade of purple.

The smile she gave him met her eyes in a deeply disturbing way, and for a moment, the fyrdwisa wasn't so sure he was the one who should've been nicknamed after a serial killer.

"Do you understand me, *Queen?*" Bridgette hissed at Nehemi, the Cheshire Cat expression on her face both feline and feral. Collum didn't like the emphasis she put on Nehemi's title. It sounded off, mocking; and though none of them had much respect for their spreca, it wasn't normal for even Bridgette to talk to her like that.

"I am the Liluthuaé. I am y gwyr yn erbyn y byd, the truth against the world, Nehemi of Endorsa. What are you?"

The queen flinched, but no one except Bridgette and Collum noticed.

~ 59 ~

Collum spent the next couple of days walking on eggshells. Nehemi adjourned the Samnung meeting soon after Bridgette's outburst, and the Bright Star still hadn't quite gone back to her usual self. She was quick to anger at the smallest things and struggled to express why. Her eyes kept flashing randomly to violent violet, there and back again so fast that Collum wasn't able to hear her mind-voice or inner monologue when it happened.

Winter solstice celebrations couldn't come soon enough, the Elf thought. There would be festivities, of course. He, Aurelias, Trystane, and Njahla had to lead ceremonies in each of the cities of Eckenbourne. They would begin in Aelchanon at the Caisleán before sunrise, then moved to Lisweald, Faustdúnleshire, Feormeham, and finally Estmereamel at sunset. Each city's dúnaelfens and non-Elven residents would gather with food and drink, dancing and chanting along with the ritual spells. It would be a busy, long — albeit short in terms of daylight — day for all of Heáhwolcen.

Not entirely surprisingly, the concept of getting to see Collum in what she jokingly called "Elven formalwear" was Bridgette's favorite part of the holiday.

Is it weird if I stare at you until it gets too dark to see? she thought to him on solstice morning, halfway through the ritual at Lisweald. Bridgette was situated in the front layer of a circle of citizens directly across from where the Elven leaders led a chant.

Collum almost smiled, his eyes closed as he tried to concentrate more on the words he spoke aloud and less so on the voice entering his head. *I would not say it is weird,* he thought to the Bright Star.

Cool. It makes me think of this dream I had a while back …

The fyrdwisa's eyes flew open and he stared at Bridgette across the circle. She had a look of pure devilish glee spread on her face, pleased with herself. Aurelias, noticing that Collum quit speaking, tapped his ankle gently with her gold-tone combat boots.

You alright, Chief? she thought to him, keeping her own eyes closed and trained up at the morning sky.

He squeezed the fyrdestre's hand and resumed chanting, but still stared at Bridgette. *You're going to get me in trouble, Starshine.*

What, you're afraid that Trystane is going to put coal in your stocking? What?

You know, like on Christmas. Little kids hang up stockings by the fireplace and then Santa Claus and his eight tiny reindeer land on their roofs, Santa goes down the chimney and leaves them toys and stuff. But if you're bad, you get coal.

Collum had to say a solo line in the ceremony before he could respond. *It would seem to me that as coal is a fuel, it is a most practical gift.*

Fucking hell, Bundy. Only you would say that.

He smiled. *I suppose I should gift you coal, then.*

Bridgette raised a brow. *Oh, really? What'd I do?*

You distracted me so thoroughly that I forgot my place in the ceremony script and Aurelias had to call me back to attention. It's a most embarrassing situation to find oneself in as a leader of this country.

How did I distract you, exactly? The gleam in Bridgette's eyes was visible to Collum even across the wreath of Elves.

By bringing up a certain recollection that I also seem to recall.

Yeah? What is it that you recall?

Collum narrowed his eyes, fighting to keep his mind in two places at once. *A certain Elfling of great power returned to Heáhwolcen, at the Caisleán, and proceeded to come with me to my office.*

Uh-huh, Bridgette thought to him. *What happened there?*

I recall there being a tree.

She felt deliciously warm all of a sudden, despite being out in frigid December morning air. *You have lots of trees in your office.*

I do.

Why do you remember this tree then?

The Elfling I mentioned earlier found herself pressed against it for a short time.

Bridgette wanted to run clean across the damn circle, leap across the ceremonial fire, and force him to evanesce them both somewhere very far away and very private.

Did she, now? she thought to Collum.

He didn't respond, but just stared at her, the smoldering Yuletide logs matching the temperature of the emotion ensnared between them. Collum barely remembered to say his closing portion of the ritual — something about the long night to soon commence so that the sun again may rise anew — and invite each dúnaelfen leader to light their torch from the fire. For the next hour or so, as the residents of Lisweald danced, ate, and drank, the torches would remain staked in the ground. Afterward, the flames would then be taken to home hearths for each member of their clan to light and carry back to their own firehearths, a symbolic gesture of goodwill and connection.

The moment the solstice ritual ended, Collum broke from the grasps of Aurelias and the Elf on his other side, and skirted the dúnaelfen leaders as he strode toward Bridgette. She wore a most un-Bridgette-like outfit, a long, heavy velvet gown in a shade of gray that turned almost silver-white when the light hit it. It was open across her shoulders and fit snugly down her arms and bodice, the sleeves ending in pointed hand-covers that attached with silver rings to her middle fingers. The dress flared at Bridgette's hips, gliding to the ground to hide the supple black leather boots she wore underneath. The fyrdwisa had presented her with the same golden circlet she wore to Emi-Joye's ambassadora installation, its glimmering opal aglow in the midmorning sun.

"So this tree," the Elfling whispered to him the moment he found her in the crowd. "I'd like to hear a little more about that."

He pressed a kiss to her hair. "Later, Starshine. I have someone you should meet."

Bridgette gave him a bewildered look. "Who?"

She let Collum lead her back to the front of the ceremony space where Trystane was deep in conversation with an Elf she didn't recognize. The female was taller than Bridgette, with hair so ice blonde it was almost white, and her muscles showed through the fitted sleeves of her own velvet gown. It was similar in style to the one Bridgette wore, but jade green in color with a leather sword belt about the waist. The hilt that poked out was wrapped in bands of embossed emerald green leather, and a massive die crafted of faceted gemstones served as the pommel. The female turned as Collum and Bridgette approached, and she gave the fyrdwisa a wide smile.

"Fáilte, my son," she said warmly, and opened her arms to embrace him.

Trystane's mom, Bridgette realized. Now that she got a good look, the female's coloring was very similar to her actual son's.

"Well met, Cennestre," Collum greeted the Elf in return. He wrapped an arm around Bridgette and pulled her forward. "This is mine companion, one who I'm sure you've heard much of. Bridgette Conner, this is Callithys Eiríkr, Trystane's mother."

"Hi," Bridgette said, sticking out a hand. Unlike everyone in Palna, Callithys understood the gesture. She reached both her hands out to Bridgette and cupped the Elfling's open palm.

"It is wonderful indeed to finally meet you, Bridgette," she said. "My son does not tell me much about the secrets of the Samnung, but I do know how important you are to him, to his brother, and to us."

Bridgette bowed her head. "Just, uh, doing my job, I guess?"

Callithys smiled. "I'm most pleased to know you, Bridgette. You are welcome at my hearth and at those of my dúnaelfen at any time."

"Will she be welcome at your stone circle?" Trystane asked.

He put an elbow casually on Bridgette's open shoulder. "I daresay Herewosa Donnachaidh would appreciate someone teach our little legend the finer arts of swordship."

"'Our little legend'?" Bridgette laughed. "Wait. Swords?"

"Yes, swords," Trystane said, smiling. "My mother, as I believe we once told you, is a renowned seordwiph and swordswoman."

Bridgette turned back to Callithys, who still held her hand. "And you'd teach me? Like how to swordfight?"

"I do not believe mine son would give me much other choice." There was amusement in her eyes, which were nearly the same shade of Trystane's, though the tell-tale Elven flecks of opalescence there were onyx in color. "If it is what you wish, of course, Bridgette."

"I absolutely wish!"

"Good," Trystane commented. "I am glad that is settled then, and now we may attend to the festivities. I hear someone from Eulalia's dúnaelfen brought a mulled citrus brandy that I cannot wait to try."

"It's barely nine in the morning," Bridgette said. "We haven't even had good coffee yet."

Trystane tapped her on the nose. "Ah, sweet Bright Star. One cannot call it day drinking unless one begins in the morning, no?"

She shoved him in the shoulder and laughed. "I can't argue with that kind of logic. Let's go eat. Standing in magic circles is hard work."

Her hard work of standing continued throughout the day, until finally the sun set as the ritual in Estmeremel ended and the wreath of Elves dispersed. Bridgette was mentally spent. She didn't think she could stand one more second of staring at Collum's eyes across a massive circle without touching him as they watched one another. Aurelias locked arms with a female Elf Bridgette didn't recognize, and headed off toward the food.

Njahla took her leave almost immediately to evanesce back to her and her mother's home in Aelchanon, and Trystane barely bid them a good holiday before he, too, disappeared in a burst of evergreen whirls.

Collum looked to Bridgette. "Would you like to experience the Wynterwist of Estmereamel?" He gestured behind them at the various tables.

"Sure," she replied.

Bridgette followed the fyrdwisa to a line and then from table to table. Most housed various seafood dishes or small bites, along with a table for ice-cold spring water and two with white wines. They finished each course while socializing in line for the next, beginning with a scoop of smoked redfish spread and flaxseed crackers, finally culminating with miniature fruit tarts topped with greenhouse-grown peach slices and sprigs of basil.

The Elfling licked sticky syrup from her fingers as she swallowed the last bite of her tart. "That's going to go down as one of the most incredible meals I've eaten in my entire life."

Collum grinned at her. "I'm very pleased you think so, Starshine. Estmereamel hosts my favorite Wynterwist. I do not know if you counted, but there are seventeen tables in all, including those with beverages, each representing an hour of dark on this longest night, meant to nourish the ever-sleeping Bright Star."

The not-so-sleeping-anymore Bright Star chuckled. "I think they managed that pretty successfully."

JANUARY

~ 60 ~

Herewosa Donnachaidh looked at the ambassadora and ambestre. The latter appeared hesitant, the tips of his golden beetle wings flaring open and closed with nervous anticipation. Donnachaidh couldn't read Emi-Joye. The female had a talent for muting her emotions, portraying more mental strength than she really had. Emi-Joye's wings were utterly still under her Indryhtu Sciccel, the cape that symbolized her position, and the hem of her dress pooled gracefully at her feet. Donnachaidh had to watch her chest to make sure she was actually breathing.

Both the Tief-Fae and the Fairy wore official regalia, matching velvet attire in deep navy embroidered with silver and bright blue swirls, featuring the intricate shield knot of Fairevella embellishing each of their shoulders. Apostine fiddled with the high neck of his fitted sweater, visible beneath the open jacket and its deep shawl collar. His tail swished gently behind him, brushing the back of his skin-tight pants as he waited. This was his ambassadora's show; he was there mostly for moral support at the moment.

The leader of the Cailleach surveyed them a moment longer, running his tongue over his teeth and clicking it once before speaking. "If you are ready, Ambassadora, I will ward the room."

Donnachaidh received a curt nod in response and pulled his wand from his belt. Whispered words and a swish were all it took to secure the leaders of the Fórsaí Armada and the two Fae from the rest of Heáhwolcen.

The witch walked out first from behind the curtain. His thick Scottish accent boomed out over the small group of leaders who gathered before him.

"Tráthnóna mistéireach! Wilgiest winedryhtenen!" he called out. "It is with much secrecy that we gather here this day for a long-awaited meeting. What you hear today should not leave this immediate circle of beings, for in transparency, we are together to discuss things the Samnung — specifically Her Majesty Queen Nehemi of Endorsa — does not wish for us to yet know.

"However!" Donnachaidh continued. "There exists one being who believes it of utmost importance that we, as leaders of our Fórsaí Armada, be aware of and able to prepare for. Please rise in recognition of Ambassadora Emi-Joye Vetur and Ambestre Apostine, of no surname."

The herewosa stepped aside and opened his arm out, beckoning the two Fae forward. Most of the faces in the little audience looked confused, but Collum Andoralain was stunned. The glare he gave Emi-Joye when their eyes met was so hot with fury, it all but roasted her alive.

She grimaced. *I couldn't risk anyone in the Armada finding out ahead of time. Not even you*, she thought to him. *I thought you would have tried to change my mind.*

Collum wasn't sure what he would have done, nor what he was going to do now, but he was greatly angered by the situation. He glowered at her, wishing that he could say something, but knew it was advisable to keep his mouth shut. Meanwhile, the rest of the Fórsaí Armada leaders glanced over to him, a member of the Samnung, wondering amongst themselves what their fyrdwisa knew and why *he* wasn't the one calling this meeting or telling them something.

The Elf glowered at Emi-Joye as the quiet conversation in the room simmered down. They would have a conversation about this later. For now, he sat back in his seat, wondering what in the seven hells made the Fairy ambassadora to the Antarctic — of all beings! — call this meeting together and effectively throw him in front of a charging armed Unicorn. When Collum first heard about this unusual summons, he had evanesced directly to Trystane's office, full of concern. The ard rialóir appeared to be just as baffled as he was, and he wondered if Trystane already found out it was indeed this Fairy who orchestrated the event.

"Fáilte, friends," Emi-Joye began. "As Herewosa Donnachaidh said, I am Emi-Joye Vetur, and this is my ambestre, Apostine. Together, we represent Heáhwolcen's liaison to the nation and continent of Antarctica and its associated polar region."

Murmurs again rose in the seats, but the Fairy swallowed hard. She clawed one hand into a fist behind her back, nails digging into her skin so hard they threatened to draw blood, as she attempted to steady herself. She gave the audience a moment to survey her. They were but few — Collum of the Fyrdlytta; Donnachaidh of the Cailleach; Mxmillian Surefire, general of the Bondrie Guard; Sakari Torn Hand, the magister militum who led the Bródenmael; Oleandra Pappas, the aeris of the Fairy Mîleta; Djoser Fayek of the Caomhnóir Feeric; and Thorhallsson, who stood in the aisle, as it was difficult for the Unicorn calvary commander to be seated.

Emi-Joye didn't expect to be recognized or acknowledged, at least not at first. Only three of them knew her: Collum, Herewosa Donnachaidh, and Djoser, though she recognized Oleandra in passing. Most would underestimate her. And now, in this moment, all would watch her, questioning her every move.

She felt blood finally draw as her fisted nails bit into her hand. She breathed, forced herself to remain still. Apostine stepped closer to her and slipped a hand under her cape to comfort her, support her, and to remind her that she was not, and would not ever, be alone.

Collum saw Emi-Joye's posture shift and felt her anxious energy ease as Apostine touched the Fairy's back. The movement was barely noticeable, but in a millisecond, the Fairy's shoulders were elegantly looser, her back straighter, and the chin of her heart-shaped face more lifted.

One moment, she was mere Fae. The next, she was a prima

ballerina: alluring and authoritative all at once, the stage a platform for her heart and soul.

The room warmed to her, a bizarre energy change that accosted Collum while he noted it with everyone else. As Emi-Joye began to speak, it wasn't nervousness or insecurity that he heard in her voice. She captivated him — all of them — in a way that could not be escaped, as if they'd each been entranced.

The Boireannach, he thought to himself, and smiled despite his anger. Whatever it meant, whatever power its legends foretold, the fyrdwisa was here in the thick of it and he was going to pay attention.

"I am sure you are curious as to why you've been asked to be here. I am sure you are also wondering why it is a Fairy ambassadora, not someone of the Samnung or a fellow armed force, who requested this gathering," Emi-Joye said. "In full honesty, I too asked myself why I planned to do this. It is a question I have wrestled with most mightily for many weeks now. I have lost sleep over knowing what I know, and knowing what is being kept from you by order of Queen Nehemi."

She smiled at them then. "I, however, am not a member of the Samnung, and conveniently learned of this information without the restriction of being told to keep it to myself."

There was a titter from the crowd, and Collum relaxed a little. In that sentence, whether she meant to or not, she freed him from the burden of having hidden whatever news she planned to reveal to the Armada leaders.

"I report to the Fairy of All Fairies, and Aristoces never forbade me share this with you. My loyalty is not to the spreca, but to all of magickind. Given your chosen professions, I believe you to be of the same mindset," Emi-Joye said. "This room in Minthame has been warded by Herewosa Donnachaidh and myself so that what is said within does not reach prying ears. Unless you speak directly to someone you see within these walls, should you feel compelled to share the things you hear, you'll find yourself in a coughing fit, perhaps sneezing uncontrollably, or however your body chooses to respond to the spell of this room."

Mxmillian, a hulking male with deep russet skin and close-cropped hair, chuckled. "You're sharp as my blade, Ceannairí."

Emi-Joye blushed good-naturedly. "I appreciate your confidence, my liege," she replied. "Friends, comrades, I will make this a brief meeting, but I daresay it will be the first of many we might have in the coming months. I have no intention to make today a history lesson and share — yet! — what is a most complex backstory. But this, I felt you deserved to know."

She took a deep breath and looked quickly to Collum. He knew, and should have already suspected, what knowledge she was about to indulge the Fórsaí Armada with. He bit his lips, bracing himself for the impact of all the coalescing energies in the room when Emi-Joye said the first line of plans she would reveal to them during this meeting.

"Over a year ago, Fairy Ambassador Ulerion Mewt disappeared in Palna."

There was a sharp intake of breath from the two other Fairies in the room, Oleandra and Djoser. The two exchanged glances down their row of seats before looking back to the ambassadora.

"Early last fall, the Samnung sent a covert operative into Palna in the hopes of finding him and learning more about what life in Palna has been like since his disappearance," Emi-Joye continued. "It is the belief of the Samnung that the Tinuviels spent the last several years preparing for conflict, and it is under that assumption that our government leaders now quietly whisper of war."

The entire group — excluding Collum, who breathed a sigh of relief that Emi-Joye hadn't used the word "Liluthuaé" — hitched a breath. It took about five seconds before the full slate of commanders was on its feet, shouting to be heard over one another, outraged. There was as much mass chaos as a group of fewer than ten could create, including several calls of "Liar!" aimed at the Fairy.

She took it in stride, standing before it all onstage, and raised a hand to silence them. The same energy that befell them prior, that commanded their attention to her, again overtook the Fórsaí Armada. It fascinated Collum. Through sheer luck and happenstance, he and Trystane managed to keep both Bridgette and Emi-Joye away and distracted from seeking their vademecums since before winter solstice. They wouldn't be able to maintain the distance much longer, not after he saw the mysterious Maylemaegus gift of the Boireannach at work.

"I assumed, comrades mine, that you would be aggrieved and angered by this news," Emi-Joye said. "Hear my warning that this is not the time to be angered at the Samnung, and especially not the fyrdwisa, who joins us here this day. He was unaware as to my involvement until he walked through those doors. I requested this meeting as it did not seem fair to allow the Tinuviels to build their forces, to concoct a plan to break through the Samnung's barrier wall, while our own Armada went about daily life, unprepared even for the mere possibility.

"I am of the belief that it is imperative we take measures to ready ourselves," the ambassadora went on. "There are many unknowns to this situation. It is multifaceted, and the mysteries will linger until our operative returns."

Collum's blood went cold. *She will not go back.*

Emi-Joye started to pace the stage again, Apostine standing stoically a few steps behind her. "My ambestre and I have learned much as we researched and prepared for what comes next. There exists a breadth of information to share with you as we go forth from here. It will be up to each of you to decide how you handle this revelation and those to come with your divisions of the Armada. There are three simple rules for what is now our war council."

She had made her way again to the center of the stage. Apostine stepped next to her, and without hardly thinking about it, Collum evanesced himself to her other side. He exchanged a glance with her, and an encouraging nod, before the Fairy spoke again.

"The first rule is that we do not speak to anyone about illicitly fortifying our own fighting forces. The second rule: We do not speak of this except amongst one another. Our final rule is that we gather here in our makeshift war room on the first night of each waxing moon. It is then that the energy of motivation, change, and putting plans into motion is highest, and we will make much productive use of that time and intention as we move forward."

Collum took her hand. "All of this which the ambassadora tells you is true," he confirmed. "We have much to share with you but are limited in what we *can* at this moment. I am a member of the Samnung, yes. But I am also the leader of the Fyrdlytta and one of the commanding officers of the Fórsaí Armada. I am thirdly an Elf and a citizen of Heáhwolcen, and my ultimate duty is to protect our continent in the clouds. I ask of each of you to stand alongside Ambassadora Vetur, Ambestre Apostine, and myself in breaking allegiance with the Samnung on behalf of the future of Heáhwolcen."

"Will you stand with us?" Apostine called out. He let go of Emi-Joye's hand and soared over her and into the audience at Minthame. "Will you join with us against the spreca's wishes, for the betterment of our world and of magickind?"

There was a murmur that rippled through the gathered few, which became a resounding roar. It was impressive, Collum thought, to hear such a small number make such a large cry.

Emi-Joye squeezed the Elf's hand, then let go and flew to stand in midair by Apostine. They both raised their palms to the roof of the room and began to speak:

"We vow to share with each of you
The knowledge we receive,
Provided that you share with us
Your developing plans and strategies.
Do you swear to Heáhwolcen your allegiance?"

The roar of fury rose again from the floor.

"Then as it is, so mote it be."

A glimmer of energy pulsed over the room as the simple charge and ritual set. The two Fae lowered themselves to the stage, and Apostine eagerly clasped his hands together.

"Alright then, friends. Where shall we begin?"

~ 61 ~

She probably should have expected it, but Emi-Joye still flittered back a few feet when Collum evanesced directly in front of her the moment they exited Minthame. Despite his demonstration of support onstage, he was livid. The Fairy had never seen his blue eyes glitter with anything other than amusement, and she couldn't say she enjoyed being on the receiving end of this emotion.

"What in the seven fucking hells do you think that was all about?" he said. Collum had to physically restrain himself from touching her — grabbing her by the shoulders, or maybe taking her under the chin and shoving her head against a wall. His training of how to handle potential foes threatened to take over, despite his instincts telling him to keep his hands to himself.

Collum had to give her credit for reading his energy. The ambassadora flashed him a sour look and both hands drifted dangerously close to her knife belt. Apostine caught the movement and flew between them, sticking a hand against each of their chests.

"Absolutely not, you two," he ordered them. "Are you younglings? What sort of behavior is this about to be? You look as though you're keen to murder one another in broad daylight on a *most* public avenue."

"I might be," Collum said. He didn't take his cold stare from Emi-Joye's ice-blue eyes, the whorls of which had stopped spinning entirely. It was an eerie look, one the fyrdwisa didn't like any more now than he did when he saw it in the clearing.

"Attack me, and see who comes to my aid," Emi-Joye challenged. She squared her feet and pressed her body forward, forcing Apostine to shift closer to Collum. The Tief-Fae gave her an incredulous look.

"Oh? And who would that be, Ambassadora?" Collum replied. "Because the way I heard it, you threatened the Bright

Star in that room, all but saying her name in the process." He cocked his head to one side, waiting.

That did cause her to stop pushing against Apostine's barrier. "What?"

"You said 'our operative' would return to Palna. She will do no such thing."

Emi-Joye huffed. "That's not a threat, Collum. That's a fact."

"The hell it is," he said, paraphrasing something very Bridgette-esque.

"The hell it isn't," the Fairy spat back. "Do you really think Bridgette is going to be content to stay here and wait until Nehemi decides it's the right time to attack Palna, or until the Tinuviels make the decision first? Bridgette created an entire life there for herself, and perhaps you haven't picked up on it, but the Bright Star is not about to let anyone — no matter from what country — harm those that she cares about. There's no love lost between her and Ydessa and Eryth, for sure, but those people, or not-witches, she stayed with? The Elf and the Kobold and Baetalüan who worked with her at the butchery? The little boy?"

She huffed again. "Bridgette's going to go back, Collum, and there won't be anything you can do to stop her. You won't like it, and she will hate it with every fiber of her soul to separate herself from the rest of Heáhwolcen again, but she's not going to stand back and wait for war to come knocking. Destiny already has, and as I told Herewosa Donnachaidh last fall, there are those of us who are keen to answer its summons."

"With all due respect, Ambassadora," Collum began in a tone that belied any sort of respect due to her, "I regret to inform you that you called this meeting under guise of secrecy to your own detriment. Though I do agree that it's not the best route for Nehemi to keep the Fórsaí Armada in the dark about what we suspect the Tinuviels are up to, it's my duty to report that you might have placed your dainty Fae foot betwixt your own teeth."

"What are you talking about?" Emi-Joye retorted. Apostine took another step in her direction, confident for the moment that Collum wouldn't attack, but he was now less sure about his ambassadora.

Collum shook his head and stared at the cloudy January sky. "I'm talking about the fact that half the Samnung is taking an official visit to Palna in approximately two weeks' time."

"WHAT?" both of the Fae gasped.

Apostine recovered first, his gaze wide. "How did they come to this conclusion? Are you going with them?"

"No, I am not," Collum said. "It will be Nehemi, Kharis, Trystane, Corria, and Aristoces. Njahla wants to go, as does Maqtok Spring Bearer, but I believe the three of us and Hafiz will be the de facto Samnung in charge, along with Verivol, Bryten, and gods help us, Princess Cloa. They believe if I went, the Tinuviels would see it as a threat to have the fyrdwisa accompanying them and possibly 'planting spies' somewhere, a direct quote from Kharis."

The ambassadora looked defeated. "When were they going to share this with anyone?"

"I'm not entirely sure they planned on making it public," Collum replied. He stepped back from Apostine, still fully aware of how close his own dagger was if he needed it. "There are some logistics that must be worked through first, such as alerting the Tinuviels they're inviting themselves across the border for Imbolc."

"I'll say," Apostine muttered. He felt supremely uncomfortable. "Are you going to tell Trystane about today?"

"He already knows," Collum said, and the Tief-Fae's eyebrows went up in surprise. "After I received the summons in November, I went to him first thing, because I thought *he* was the one going behind Nehemi's back and plotting this. I did not expect to see the two of you up on that stage."

"What was your opinion on how today's meeting went?" Emi-Joye asked.

Collum gave her a long look. "I believe you made some well-thought-out and well-researched points, Ambassadora. I believe your premise to be genuine and presented with Heáhwolcen's best interests at heart. But again, I think this meeting was premature, and it was dangerous to go behind Nehemi's back. Whether you report to her or not, Aristoces and I both do in some form, and the queen does not like to have control wrested from her."

The Fairy pursed her lips. "Do you think it will make a difference then? That the Fórsaí Armada knows now that war could be coming, and that we should consider fighting it for the cause and not for our own personal glory?"

He considered that, and Apostine again shot a worried glance between them in the silence before Collum spoke. "I think that there is more than a century's worth of prejudice against the citizens of Palna amidst the ranks of our armed forces," the Elf said. "To reach the lofty ideals you set before us, those must first be overcome. What you did today, Ambassadora, was attempt to change how we see our enemy, and challenge us to reconsider who our enemy is. I do not know that the words of one Fairy ambassadora and her ambestre will be able to alter that, not even if those words are transferred down from the commanders to their respective legions."

Emi-Joye crossed her arms — Apostine breathed a sigh of relief that her hands weren't resting on knife hilts anymore — and chewed on her lips. She looked distressed. Collum did give her the respect of not trying to ease the anxious energy that she exuded in that moment. He couldn't tell if she regretted the decision to call this meeting or if she simply was nervous that all her work would go to waste. Perhaps both.

"This was just the first of many meetings," the Fairy finally said. "Mayhaps things will continue to move in the intended direction as time goes on."

Collum nodded in acknowledgement. "Mayhaps, Ambassadora," he said, and turned to leave. "But keep the Bright Star out of it."

He evanesced home, not seeing the dramatic eye roll Emi-Joye gave to his back.

~ 62 ~

"Bridgette, you have to talk to me."

Collum stood at the entrance to her bedroom — he ceased calling it his guest room the moment she came back to Heáhwolcen — and leaned against the doorframe. "Except for when you went to send a holiday greeting letter off to the Simmonses by way of the travel authority, you've done little else but hide in this apartment since winter solstice. It worries me. Please tell me what's on your mind."

You could just listen in and find out, she thought to him from where she was on the bed, eyes firmly positioned toward the ceiling. Even she didn't know why she was so … off, for lack of a better word.

"Yes, but that would be rude," the Elf said. He sauntered into the room and sat next to her. "Talk to me. Please."

She didn't look at him. "I don't know what's wrong with me, Bundy. When I was in Palna, all I wanted was to be back here. Now that I am here? It's like a different part of me is missing. Like I wonder if I'll ever feel whole, you know?"

He did know. Collum picked up one of her hands and threaded his fingers through hers.

Bridgette sighed. She sat up and curled herself around him, wondering if he'd move away, and breathed another small sigh of relief when he let her touch him in such a way. "It's like every time I get one answer to something, seventeen other questions pop up to replace it."

She held up a hand and started to tick off examples: how to read Gemaere, why the *Sefnuskrá* and the vademecums didn't show their true natures, what it meant that Emi-Joye was the Boireannach, who was supposed to be the Astridsí, why both the Maudlins and the vademecums spoke of the Triumvirate, and now the Samnung's sudden ability to visit Palna.

"Not to mention I'm worried sick about Toby. Zedolph too,

kinda. Serrabinx can probably fend for herself, but me leaving in the middle of the night left the city's slátrari without a slátraestre. I mean, *talk* about a complete lack of professionalism, ugh!" she groaned.

Collum gave her a wry smile. "You've been isolating yourself in this room because you miss cutting meat?"

"Geez, Louise, when you say it like that …" Bridgette chuckled alongside the fyrdwisa. She rested her head against his and sighed. "I haven't been isolating myself. I've just been … figuring out who I am again, I guess. I spent what, three months basically pretending to be someone else? And that was not that long after I discovered I spent more than twenty years living as not just someone, but some*thing* else entirely. It's a little whiplash-y. A part of me is here, obviously. But part of me is still in Palna, and there's another part that's still on Earth. I bet Martha's probably worried sick."

Collum bit his lip. "Starshine, there's something —"

"That's the one thing I didn't think about before I went to Palna. I know we didn't talk that much after I went to college, but we heard from each other at least once a week even if we didn't have a real phone call for days on end. They're going to be so upset; do you think the Samnung would let me visit? I know I'm not imprisoned here or anything, but I can just see Nehemi losing her shit if I try to escape back to planet Earth while I'm supposed to be —"

"Bridgette." Collum squeezed her fingers and turned to look at her. "The Simmonses are not worried. They think you and I ran off to Europe together and that you're teaching violin."

She blanched. "They what, now?"

"While you were in Palna, I was sent to Nashville to tie up some loose ends that none of us realized were left hanging," Collum tried to explain. He felt her concern rise as he told her what he probably should have revealed ages ago. "You've been withdrawn from your university thanks to some slick work by

Geongre Akiko; your colleagues at the diner know you're alive and well; and Doc and Martha think we ran off abroad together, which is why you lied to them about being on a study abroad program."

"You met Doc and Martha."

"I did."

"And they just accepted the fact that this strange man walks up to them and tells them, 'Hey, yeah, your foster daughter is my secret girlfriend and we've been living together for months. She's totally fine though, thanks for checking in'?" Bridgette narrowed her eyes at Collum. "I know you've got your energy talent and inner monologue ears, but I've known those two for a helluva lot longer than you have, and neither one of my foster parents would fall for that."

"I had … help," Collum admitted. He scrunched his expression. "I arrived in Nashville and visited your foster parents in north Georgia alongside a companion chosen for this assignment. Together, we were to do our best to convince those who reported you missing that there was no need to worry."

"I was reported *missing*?!" Bridgette shouted in his ear, making him wince. "You didn't think it was important to tell me this, I don't know, last month?! Come on, Collum! That's a fucking dick move — I've been here freaking out about all of this and plenty more, and you're just casually dropping this information? What gives!"

She stood from the bed, pacing with her hands raised in frustration, and went off, half of her emotions revealing themselves through her mind-voice as she didn't quite have the right words to express in her moment of shock. The fyrdwisa straightened his shoulders, letting his Starshine rage. He deserved it, he thought, her anger at him not sharing this with her. He let her yell until her exasperation was exhausted, then he dropped the final, most difficult part of the story: "You should also know that the companion who accompanied me was

Lucilla."

He wished he'd kept his mouth shut.

"You're. Joking." Bridgette's eyes didn't change color as she glared at him, but the depth of emotion that smoldered in them was a force Collum didn't desire to reckon with.

"I am not. Lucilla had already begun to alter her appearance to look more like you, and with a few glamour spells and a very hard-to-procure serum, we were able to have a near duplicate of you. It was … off-putting," he said. The Elf chose his next words carefully. "You should also know that while we were in Nashville, Lucilla slipped a paralyzing draught into a drink she purchased for me. I woke in my hotel bed, unable to move, hearing your voice come from the wrong female's mouth."

"Fucking *cunt*," Bridgette swore. "She drugged you? She assaulted you? While pretending to be me?"

"She did," Collum replied, and the scents of honeysuckle and vanilla filled the room like an automatic reflex to soothe her. Bridgette looked murderous. "I was pulled out of whatever spell she had me under by way of unusual magic taking over my body. It was then that your dagger appeared at my side, and I was able to subdue her until we could return to Heáhwolcen."

The Elfling's eyes shifted. She blinked, confused at the knowledge that flickered into her brain, and jerked the sleeve of her shirt up, revealing both her covenant bracelet and the barely visible scars from the burn marks they left after the nightmare she couldn't remember.

"Magic you hadn't experienced before?" she asked, then shoved her wrist in front of his eyes. "Magic that could do something like this?"

Collum took her wrist in his hand and ran his thumb over the tiny circles of skin a shade paler than the rest of Bridgette's arm. "I saw lights. Flashing lights, the same as we saw when your vademecum told us who the Boireannach was. They were blue, green, and purple. I've seen similar lights before, when I meditated once, but those were more playful than the ones in my vision while in Nashville. The lights this night were powerful and angry. It would not surprise me that they had something to do with Maylemaegus, but I've never known a covenant bracelet to harm its bearer. I'm sorry I caused this to happen to you, Starshine."

"You've got nothing to be sorry for, Bundy. Lucilla, on the other hand? I'm going to axe her."

He laughed and pulled her close, forcing the Elfling into his lap. "Absolutely not. She has already been dealt with, by Nehemi, of all beings."

Bridgette gave him a dour look. "There's a difference between being dealt with and dead. I don't usually want people dead, but I think I could handle Heáhwolcen existing without her in it."

"No murdering on my account, even if you are the Bright Star."

"Fine," she relented, and smiled. "At the moment, anyway. If I see her though? Good luck. I don't exactly know how to control this Maylemaegus shit, you know. I'm not responsible for how it reacts to evil creatures showing up in front of the Coffee Cauldron."

"Mmm," Collum murmured. "The Coffee Cauldron. What say you that we freshen up and visit your favorite place for a belated breakfast?"

"On Earth, we call that brunch, Bundy. I'm in."

Bridgette hadn't thought to ask where he'd been all morning, which was good, Collum thought, since he hadn't come up with a reasonable excuse. He didn't relish the idea of going into a coughing or sneezing fit in front of the coffee shop if he was to chance the seriousness of Emi-Joye's secrecy spell.

The two walked the streets of Galdúr for a time after their brunch, Bridgette's leather-gloved hands gripping the frosty mug of iced caife calabaza she insisted on, even though it was hardly above freezing outside. They said little to one another as they enjoyed their quiet companionship.

As much as she missed her life in Palna, Bridgette missed this more, just being with Collum. They hadn't talked about their shared dream again, not since winter solstice, and she hesitated to cross any lines she didn't know were drawn.

Maybe this is just what some people call seasonal depression, she thought, and Collum glanced at her.

Seasonal depression?

Yeah. You know, the winter blues and stuff. Scientists say it's a real thing, that not enough sunlight or something can cause it. I don't really know, but it is winter and it's been weird, so I'm going to diagnose myself.

He gave her a bemused look. *Would you like to visit a lacnian or lacnestre? There are some who deal with mind-health.*

"Good grief, Bundy, I'm not fucking clinical," Bridgette laughed out loud. "But thanks for your concern, seriously."

Collum put an arm around her. "You're most welcome, Starshine. And I must say, it is nice to be out in what little winter sun we are getting, if only to see you enjoying your winter solstice gift."

She reached a hand up to touch the edge of the handknit beanie, one in tones of purple and bright blue, made in the same pattern as the navy one Collum wore all the time — including the day they first met. He'd given it to her upon returning to his apartment after the Wynterwist, and the flurry of emotions going through her mind at that moment had been overwhelmed by her leaping up from the floor and planting a Fae wine-soaked kiss to his cheek in thanks, before presenting him with her own set of presents. There was a beautifully handcrafted notebook she bought from Glafida, along with her bedraggled blue butcher's notebook. Collum had looked at the latter book for a long moment before she explained to him that her unofficial reports were hidden inside, and he laughed as he commended her for the spy work.

Bridgette grinned now as the memory of solstice night flowed through her, and she nuzzled into the Elf's grasp. "I do enjoy my fancy new hat. It's kind of perfect, just like the weirdo who gave it to me."

"Your sass is unparalleled," he replied, then glanced to his wrist, where a warm sensation spread from his covenant bracelet with Trystane. "I'm not sure what else you wanted to do today, but it looks as though I might need to visit the Caisleán. Care to join me?"

"Always," she said, and readied herself to be evanesced back to Eckenbourne.

~ 63 ~

"Excellent timing," the ard rialóir greeted Collum and Bridgette when they knocked on his office door. "We're going to Bondrie."

"Bondrie?" Collum asked as the two followed Trystane down the short hallway to his desk. "For what reason?"

"As it turns out, the activated Ballamúr has made it quite difficult to get any sort of message across to Palna, which would indeed explain why there have been no reports from Ulerion coming in for such a long time," Trystane called over his shoulder. "Kharis and some Cath Draíochta practitioners attempted to break through whatever spells keep it together, but it holds firm. Earlier this morning, someone tried simply to shove a sheet of paper through it. The paper crumpled immediately, as if it was being pushed against a physical barrier."

Bridgette resisted the urge to remind the Elves that the Ballamúr *was* a physical barrier, even though it only appeared to them on this side as a shimmering mist. "So, what, y'all are going to send me back again, with even less training than before?"

Trystane stopped short and turned to face her. "No, Bridgette. But I do think that we could use your abilities to help in this matter."

He held out a hand for each of them to grasp. Bridgette gave Collum a pleading look just before the three were whisked away, reappearing moments later on a muddy, snow-laden path alongside most of the Samnung members, a handful of Bondrie guardsfolk, and a blush-colored Unicorn with a rose gold horn and hooves.

"Fáilte, all," Corria greeted them. She smiled, but the expression appeared tense. Bridgette understood why. When Aristoces said the Samnung needed an *in*, the Fairy meant, in part, that they needed to know it was possible for someone to cross the Ballamúr. Apparently, the fact that it hadn't been as open a door as they hoped was disconcerting.

"Hi," the Elfling replied. "What's up?"

"We have not, as of yet, been able to have our message received by the Palnan Guard or the Tinuviels," Nehemi said curtly. She scowled at Bridgette, who took the displeasure in stride. "Trystane thought that perhaps you might be able to shed some light on the situation."

Bridgette stared at the Samnung wall before them. "I want to see what you're talking about, please."

Corria beckoned them all forward, and the Bondrie Guard split into two smaller groups, one remaining in Bondrie proper and the other following them into the no-man's land that separated the two countries. Bridgette's breath caught at the Ballamúr, which again recognized her. She stepped toward it and felt Collum grip her shoulder to keep her back.

Chill, Bundy, I'm not going to cross it. I'm just saying hello, she thought to him.

You're going to explain to me later how this wall talks to you, yes?

The Elfling glanced over her shoulder. *Sure, but your guess is as good as mine. I know it won't hurt me. The Ballamúr likes me.*

I think it's rather difficult not to like you, Starshine.

She bit her lip to keep from smiling as she took another step toward the shimmering barrier. *Try telling that to Her Majesty Queen Nehemi of Endorsa, will you?*

Bridgette cocked her head as she traced a finger along the edge of the Ballamúr, much to the horror of the assembled audience, who had no idea what she was doing. She thought to the wall, to the magic, in greeting. Its glimmering façade rippled out from her touch in acknowledgement.

Hello, friend, she said in her mind. A pulse of pleasure ran through her, the Ballamúr's way of saying hello back. *I heard you're giving my friends and the queen a hard time.*

She felt wariness in response.

"Bridgette, what in the seven hells are you doing?" Trystane asked dryly.

She turned around to see him standing with one hand on his hip, the other around a mug of something that smelled suspiciously like warmed bourbon and cherries, even from several feet away. "I'm talking to a wall, Trystane. What's it look like I'm doing?"

"Exactly that. But why?" the Elf replied.

"Because it talks back." She winked and resumed "speaking" to the wall in question.

They're not going to hurt you, you know, she thought to the Ballamúr, hoping to soothe it. *Why are you so worried about them?*

Bridgette had forgotten the voice, but it again entered her head and she had to fight her instinct to step away from the barrier as it murmured, *They cannot be trusted.*

That was not the answer she expected. *But you trust me?* she thought, and pressed her full palm against the barrier, threatening to push through. *You believe me?*

Her answer was another pulse of pleasure. *Then I will vouch for them. They only want to see what's going on in Palna. They won't hurt anyone. I won't let them.*

She felt warmth spread across her fingertips. *Well. Maybe I'll let them hurt the Tinuviels, and anyone who tries to attack us. Is that okay?*

The pulse of pleasure was not as vibrant, but it was there. Bridgette grinned. *How can they get through to see what I saw?*

It was again the voice that answered. *They cannot.*

But I can. And she understood.

Bridgette traced a small heart into the exterior of the barrier, and it glowed for a brief moment before absorbing back into the Ballamúr. She turned around to face the gathered Heáhwolcen leaders and citizens, all of whom except Collum looked as unsure as the Palnan barrier wall felt.

"The Ballamúr was activated two summers ago using very powerful and very specific magic. Not anyone can just walk through it anymore, because the activation powered a spell to keep it intact unless someone with Palnan blood goes in or out," she announced. "I think that limits the number of us who can cross the Ballamúr to, uh, me."

"Absolutely not," Collum breathed.

"Not this time, and not like that," Bridgette replied. "Aristoces, y'all sent me in the first place partly to prove that someone can cross the Ballamúr, right?"

The Fairy of All Fairies nodded.

"Cool. So, what did we learn from my little adventure?" Bridgette gazed around the assembled group. "We learned that my blood can get through because of who my father is."

She kept her words vague; these Bondrie guardsfolk hadn't been warned to keep their mouths shut yet, at least not to her knowledge. Collum gave her a look of complete understanding, and his posture visibly relaxed. Everyone else seemed confused.

"Right then," she went on. "So y'all tried a bunch of ways to get the message through, and no dice. What was next on your list?"

A new voice, airy as an ocean breeze, responded. It was the Unicorn that stepped forward and volunteered, "'Twas I, my liege."

"You were going to try to cross the barrier?"

"Yes," the Unicorn replied. "I am Lessiel, the second-in-command to Thorhallsson, comandante of the Unicorn calvary of the Fyrdlytta. We thought perhaps if objects and avian messengers were unable to cross into Palna, the power of a Unicorn horn could instead."

Bridgette lowered her head in a sign of respect. "I am Bridgette Eileen Conner, Elfling and companion of the Samnung, born of half-Palnan blood and raised as a human. I don't think you're going to be able to get through the Ballamúr without help."

"What sort of help?" Aristoces asked on the Unicorn's behalf.

The Liluthuaé ignored her and again addressed Lessiel. "Do you have your message ready to go?"

"I do."

"Then can I have your permission to touch you?" Bridgette asked. Collum shot her a look of dismay as the Unicorn nodded and the Elfling pulled her amethyst dagger out of its sheath. Bridgette yanked her sweater sleeve up, revealing the spidery aubergine veins of her protected lands scar, and slashed the wound open again.

She winced — the rest of the Samnung members made sounds of varying degrees of horror — and wiped her dagger off on her woolen leggings. Then, Bridgette smeared the welling blood on her opposite palm and proceeded to gently paint the fluid across Lessiel's horn and hooves.

"There," Bridgette said. "I think that should be good enough to get you in and back out. There is something in that message saying you have to get back out, right?"

"We included a statement requesting a response be sent back with our messenger, yes," Nehemi confirmed. She did not look happy about the blood-covered Unicorn that now stood between the two barriers. "The Tinuviels have two days to confirm that they received our message, or face a less formal sort of greeting."

"Gotcha," Bridgette acknowledged. "Lessiel, do you know how to get to Düoria from where we are?"

"I do, my liege."

"Then we'll see you in forty-eight hours," the Elfling said, hoping that the Ballamúr wouldn't deposit Lessiel in the middle of nowhere. She placed a hand on the Unicorn's neck. "May the Force be with you."

Collum choked back a laugh. Bridgette walked over to him, trailing her hand reassuringly across the Ballamúr one last time. Together, she, the Samnung members, and the Bondrie guardsfolk watched as Lessiel trotted forward to the glimmering wall. She lowered her horn and pushed it against and gently through, parting the Ballamúr as if the barrier was naught but a curtain. Bridgette let out a breath she forgot she was even holding in as the Unicorn's tail disappeared beyond their sight, and the wall closed once again.

"I suppose if the Tinuviels respond positively to our request that you'll be smearing blood across our foreheads, too?" Trystane asked.

"Maybe someplace less conspicuous," Nehemi countered. "Thank you, Bridgette."

"Uh, you're welcome," the Elfling said. "So, what now? We just hang out here for two days and wait until Lessiel comes back?"

Corria nodded. "Select members of the Bondrie Guard will be put on alert for her return, and I will be the Eye until she does."

Bridgette grinned. "Fucking hell, I wish I could see what Eryth and Ydessa do when a Heáhwolcen Unicorn just shows up at their front door. They're going to go berserk."

I'm going to go berserk if your arm continues to bleed, Starshine, Collum thought to her. He put an arm around her waist. *What in the seven hells is that injury, and why is the blood from it purple?*

She glanced down and realized that dark, fresh blood was indeed still trickling down her forearm. Bridgette looked back to the fyrdwisa, who was giving her a death stare, and smiled apologetically. "Maybe I should go get cleaned up?"

~ 64 ~

It took nearly fifteen minutes to staunch the bleeding once Bridgette was barricaded in Collum's bathroom, where the Elf furiously tried washing the peculiar-colored liquid down his sink, then applying a tourniquet with so much force that he only stopped when she whimpered in pain.

"What is this?" he demanded. "How did you get this wound, Bridgette?"

She'd never seen him this angry at her. No, she thought better of it, not angry *at* her, but angry that this happened to her.

"You're real cute when you're being protective of me, Bundy. I tripped and fell in some dumb forest that Serrabinx and Toby kept calling 'protected land'. Apparently, you have to be a real idiot to harm this protected land, because if it feels threatened, it's still magic enough that it'll harm you right back," she explained. "Don't ask me why or how these lands have magic, because I don't know or even care, to be honest, but it uh, started wounding me and then got in my blood enough to figure out that hey, guess what, we're both Palnan, so I'm good to go. Still hurt like hell though, and then we had to walk back. It scraped my cheek, and my leg was sore, too, but only the arm got punctured."

"You received this injury from a *tree*?" Collum asked, incredulous. "A tree caused this?"

"Yeah," Bridgette said. She gingerly touched the tightly wrapped bandage that now covered her arm. "Serrabinx kept saying it was venom."

He furrowed his brow. "Trees don't have venom."

"No shit."

"I want a téitheoir to take a look at this."

Bridgette looked him straight in the eye. "I'm fine, Bundy. I swear. I want to know what the so-called venom is, sure, but other than the fact that I just sliced my arm open again — and

I'm about to do the same thing in two days — it's really okay."

"I do not like seeing you hurt, Starshine."

The Elfling jumped off the counter she'd been perched on and put her arms around his neck. "I'm a big girl. Big Elfling. Whatever. I may not be very good at combat yet, but I can handle myself most of the time, I promise."

He shook her off, annoyed with the situation, and walked out of the bathroom. Bridgette waited a few minutes, confused as to why he was so upset, then gave up overthinking and darted after him.

"Collum, what's got your panties all in a bunch? First, you're pissed off that I was wallowing too much, and now you're upset that I got stabbed by a tree?"

"Yes, I am," he said from where he stood in the kitchen, rummaging through a shelf for ingredients of some sort. "I dislike that I am supposed to protect you, and that despite this charge of mine I cannot seem to keep you safe. You were barely trained before we sent you into Palna. You were burned by your covenant bracelet — which I gave you! — and were wounded by plant life, the magic of which we do not know. My job is to —"

"Oh, fuck off with the job stuff, will you? We're way past that now." Bridgette came up behind the Elf and forced him into an embrace. "You have nothing to be sorry about. It's not your fault anything happened or might happen to me unless you yourself do it. I'm a klutz and I'm not particularly athletic. That's all, the end. You can't constantly be there to watch over me while I fuck up, and I give myself enough grief to not need anybody's help reinforcing it. So please, stop."

"I can't stop caring about you, Starshine."

She blinked, a slow smile growing across her face despite the aggrieved expression on his. "Well, that's nice to hear. Kind of hard to not care about you either, now that you mention it."

Collum smiled back. "You're truly a wonder, and your power of persuasion is a gift, as annoying as it might be at times.

Now, please leave me be while I sit with my emotions and cook us dinner."

It took less than a day for Lessiel to return from Palna. The fyrdwisa was again summoned, this time by Corria, to Casa de Piedra to hear what the Unicorn had to say. She'd been cleaned of Bridgette's blood by the time the fyrdwisa and Liluthuaé arrived. Lessiel stood before the full Samnung — save for Princess Cloa — to make her report.

"I cannay say that I entered into Palna unnoticed," Lessiel began. "I dinnay believe that they have many Unicorns remaining since the Ingefeoht, and the younglings noticed me quite soon after I crossed the border. I paid them no heed, but was not rude, and made my way toward Düoria. I regret to say that I dinnay make it the full distance before the Palnan Guard caught up to me on horseback. They questioned my presence in their country and I shared the Samnung's message with them before bidding them take me to the Tinuviels so that I could deliver it myself."

"Did you meet the Tinuviels?" Bryten asked. He glanced to Bridgette.

"I dinnay meet them, but I was escorted to Düoria and the palace residence. The Palnan Guard took the message inside and I remained out, waiting for the response. They then took me to the border again, and I crossed without difficulty, though I cannay say I enjoy the sensations of going through the strange barrier," Lessiel replied.

Bridgette shuddered. As fine as she was with the Ballamúr's presence and power, crossing it was definitely an experience.

The Unicorn presented the Tinuviels' response to a waiting Nehemi, who broke the purple wax seal and began to read. Her face was stony, its only movement the flicking of her eyes back and forth across the lines of the page.

Nehemi looked up from the paper. "They've agreed to host

us for Imbolc. We are to arrive the final day of January and leave following breakfast on the second day of February. They request that we arrive at the Düorian edge of the border with Bondrie. There will be a host of Palnan Guard and horses to lead us to the city, where we are to help lead the holiday celebration as honored guests."

Bridgette waited until the brief meeting adjourned before peppering Collum and Trystane with questions about Imbolc. The festival marked the coming of spring and included bonfires, candle ceremonies, something called "the forging of the swords", and poetry readings. Considered a time of cleansing, there were communal spaces set up where individuals and families could bring clothes, supplies, tools — anything that wasn't food — and put it out for others to take in.

"My personal favorite aspect is the sharing of the soil," Collum said. "Farmers bring bins and wagons overflowing with freshly composted earth, and each individual is asked to take some back to their home. When the wagons are empty, or as empty as we can get them, citizens in turn add recent food waste from their own kitchens, which will be taken and turned into community soil for the next spring."

"And you're in charge of it this year?" Bridgette asked.

"Somewhat. There are no ceremonies that I had to lead, such as what you observed during Lammas and winter solstice," Collum replied. "This will be more like Ostara, where we all gather and enjoy the festivities. It is more important that Samnung members have a presence."

Trystane sipped from his drink of the day, again something with whiskey notes in the scent. "I do wonder if Palna will do anything different. Each country always has for holidays, as we have so many deities that are worshipped and celebrated on our continent."

"You'll have to tell us all about it," the Elfling said. "When I was there during Lunavidad preparations, which is what they called winter solstice, it was kind of an interesting mix of stuff that seemed pretty witchy and some more human traditions."

Collum put his hand in hers. *I know you miss them*, he thought to her. *I hear it in your voice sometimes when you speak of Palna, how much that young boy means to you.*

She squeezed his fingers in silent thanks. *I keep calling him a boy, but I think Toby's technically an Elfling.*

Well, whatever he may prefer to be called, I do realize how deeply you care for him.

She wanted to kiss the fyrdiwsa, but held back as she realized that Trystane, oblivious to the ísenwaer, was telling them both goodbye.

"I've got a few things to wrap up before we leave next Friday, least of all being that I suppose I must tell my mother why I won't be at her hearth for Imbolc," the ard rialóir said. "I'll see you, Fyrdwisa, at the Samnung meeting?"

Collum nodded, and Trystane was gone.

~ 65 ~

It had been a few days since he'd heard from her, so Trystane already thought he might be in trouble the moment a Fairy guard welcomed him through the enchanted Seolformúr gate and into the Seledreám that afternoon. He knew he was in deep shit when a second guard guided him into the vast wing of international affairs at the Noble House of Fae, and it was so cold on the far end that he might not have bothered to come inside from the January air at all.

"Em?" Trystane began tentatively. He poked his head inside the office that bore her and Apostine's names out front. That was about as far as he got before the outraged Fairy swooped over from her desk and grabbed him by his shirtfront.

"What in the seven *fucking* hells are you *thinking*, Trystane? Going into Palna on a sanctioned visit? Just casually volunteering yourself as sacrifice to the Tinuviels?" she shrieked.

He shoved himself in the office and slammed the door behind them. "How do you know about that?" he whispered, horrified.

"Why does it matter how I know? The point is that I do, and that *you* weren't the one to tell me!" Emi-Joye shouted. "How could you hide this from me?"

"I wasn't planning on hiding it from you, Em, but I just haven't seen you, and besides, we only just got the confirmation from the Tinuviels today —"

"Excuse me, you *spoke* to them?"

Trystane didn't know it was possible for anyone's speaking voice to hit such an octave. "No, we sent a Unicorn messenger on our behalf. She returned today with a reply confirming that we were welcome as honored guests for Imbolc."

"I cannot believe you. I truly cannot believe that you think this is a good idea!" Emi-Joye ground out. "What if they attack while you're there? Do you have *any* idea how hard it is to pretend I don't know this information, because no one except for the Samnung is apparently supposed to know that most of our leaders are going into a country with which we would like to declare *war*?"

"Em. Please." Trystane walked toward her, but she zipped into the air, curling her feet up under her body so no part of her was within his reach. "I know you're mad at me because I didn't tell you immediately after it came up. I don't have a good reason except to say that, as with most of the plans concocted by Queen Nehemi, I rather hope they do not come to fruition and there is no need to worry about them unless they do. I left Bondrie moments ago to come here and tell you, because the plans are now confirmed. I will ask you again, who told you about this?"

"The fyrdwisa let that information slip the other morning after he tried to attack me following our meeting with the Fórsaí Armada," Emi-Joye said. She refused to look down at the Elf. "I don't want you to go."

"I have to go, Em. Ydessa and Eryth wouldn't dare try anything with five members of the Samnung, all fully powered, in their capital city at the same time. The four of us and Kharis are going as a show of unity for the rest of Heáhwolcen," Trystane said. He climbed to the top of the small couch in the office's sitting area and reached up for one of her shoes. "Come down, will you? Sit and talk with me, Em; I don't like this."

She stared at the ceiling. "I'm content up here for now, thank you."

"What would you like me to do, Ambassadora? Beg for your forgiveness? I will, if that's what would get you to come down from there," the Elf promised. "I swear to Hecate I will get down on both knees and *beg* for you to forgive me, forgive me for not telling you something that could *possibly* happen and worry you unnecessarily until it was something definite. I will beg for you, Emi-Joye Vetur, if this is what you wish."

The Fairy kept her nose turned up. She couldn't stand this

situation, that she was so upset and couldn't even put a finger on why. Of course Trystane should go to Palna with the Samnung; he was the ard rialóir, for Hecate's sake! That was his job, his highest responsibility and where his loyalty should most lay, and she was just … someone, wasn't she? It was a kindness that he hadn't told her earlier and caused her to panic, because now she was panicking and —

Deity damn these tears, she thought, squeezing her eyes shut to keep them from falling.

"Em, please," Trystane murmured. "Are you this mad at Aristoces, too?"

"No!" she shrieked, and holding the tears back was no longer of any use. "Of course I'm not angry at Aristoces, because I'm not in love with Aristoces, Trystane!"

The ard rialóir blinked.

Then he reached for her, and this time, Emi-Joye let him. He gently pulled her from the air and took her in his arms, where she sobbed. She was angry and sad and scared, for him and for herself. Everything was changing so quickly for her, and what she thought she wanted for herself felt out of reach, a pipe dream. She wanted to know who she was supposed to be, what with this Boireannach nonsense, and she wanted security and a stable sense of adventure, not to be thrust even more into an Elven legend she'd hardly heard of until the previous spring.

But most of all, and much to her surprise, Emi-Joye Vetur wanted Trystane Eiríkr, and the thought of him leaving in any capacity was unbearable.

"Please don't go," she whispered. His collar was soaked with her tears, a dark stain from her eye cosmetics evident on the white fabric. "Please don't leave me here."

"Em," he whispered, and pulled her tighter against him. Trystane pressed a kiss into her hair. "I have no choice in going to Palna. It is required of us all as the Samnung. Collum would be going too if he could. I think he *wants* to go. I cannot say that I do. Trust me, my winged beauty, I would rather spend my time wrapped around you than traipsing through an unseasonably warm tulip field."

She giggled. "I would trade good coin to see you traipse through anything, Trys. I don't think it's a move I've yet to see you make."

"It is not one I make very often," he said. "Did you mean that, what you said just now?"

"About you traipsing through tulips?"

"No, silly thing. About … about how you feel."

Her lungs stopped moving and Trystane noticed her eyes did, too. The whorls went wholly still, turning her eyes into ice blue orbs that seemed to stare directly into his soul. "I love you, Trystane Eiríkr," she whispered once she remembered how to breathe. "I have loved you for a long time now, and the thought of not being by your side is one that I cannot stomach."

There was a small smile tugging at his lips. "And I have loved you, Emi-Joye Vetur, from the first moment I saw snowflakes dance from your fingertips. I dislike not being with you either, but there is no other being or creature I would want waiting on me when I return to Bondrie next Sunday than you, mo chridhe, my heart."

Trystane took one arm out from around the Fairy and twisted it back toward the door. There was a click as the deadbolt connected, and then he took Emi-Joye's face in his hands.

"Do you still want me to beg for you?" he whispered as he kissed her neck, her jawline, the pointed tips of her ears. "Or would you rather me make you beg for more?"

Emi-Joye had never undone a belt so quickly in her life.

~ 66 ~

"Are you ready?" Collum murmured to Trystane and Corria as they once again walked through the Samnung wall into the no-man's land.

"I do not know what we are to be ready for," Corria replied. She looked empty without her usual longsword and shield by her side, but fearing what the Tinuviels might think if they saw a fully armed master swordswoman, she agreed to leave them behind. A somewhat larger-than-normal curved karambit, which Bridgette thought looked like a dinosaur claw, stationed in Corria's belt would suffice for the visit.

"Make note of everything you notice," the Elfling encouraged them. "Everything. The air, the smells, the people. I didn't meet the Tinuviels, and I never went to Düoria, so I have no clue what y'all are in for, but just … keep all your senses open, okay? Everything matters there."

She turned to look at Kharis. "You've been to the capital before, right?"

He nodded. "It has been many years since, Liluthuaé, but yes. I have been before."

"Then you'll notice what seems different," Bridgette assured him. "Don't try to write anything down or act like you're making a report. Just be normal, be you, but be observant."

"We are aware of how to keep an eye on our surroundings, Bridgette," Nehemi said in a warning tone. "But your concern is appreciated."

The Elfling huffed. "Yeah, well, since you're basically going for the sole purpose of deciding if you even believe anything *I* saw and experienced, I'm a little concerned about what the Tinuviels are going to show you versus what everyday citizens would. Look for weird symbols that resemble eyes. They might be tattooed on people's — I mean, beings' — wrists. If you see anyone like that, tell them that Bridgette wants Toby to know she's okay."

Nehemi gave her an annoyed look, but Aristoces assured Bridgette that they would be on the lookout for such a tattoo. "If we are able to check on your friends, we will do our best to make sure they know you are well," the Fairy said.

Bridgette gave her a nod of thanks. "Alright. Let's do this."

She rolled her sleeve up again, and Collum grimaced as she sliced her not-yet healed wound open for a third time. She dipped her fingers in the pooling blood and swiped a half-circle behind each of their ears. "I know this will be hard for you, Trystane, but don't wash your hair while you're there. Collum will be pissed as hell if you scrub this off on accident and find yourself stuck in Palna."

Trystane laughed, but it was empty. "Collum's wrath will be the least of my worries, should that happen. Clearly, you've not spent enough time with my mother."

Bridgette shoved him in the shoulder. "Be careful. Seriously."

The five of them — Kharis, Nehemi, Aristoces, Trystane, and Corria — joined hands, and together crossed through the Ballamúr. Bridgette winced as one of them shouted in surprise as the unsettling feeling of transition passed over the group, and then they were gone. She put a hand to the barrier, which seemed anxious.

Two days, she thought to the wall. *Please bring them back to us. They won't hurt anyone, but we need them back. They have my full faith.*

For once, the Ballamúr didn't answer her, and Bridgette stepped away, a bit unsettled herself. She looked to Collum and thought to him, *I want to get out of here. It's not happy with us and I don't understand why.*

He nodded. "We'll go to the Caisleán. Trystane asked that I, of all deity-damned things, water his plants. I need a housekey."

The spare housekey was secured quickly, but as the two left Trystane's office, they turned around in the hall and came face-to-face with a very harried-looking Emi-Joye, who stopped short mid-flight at the sight of them.

"Oh!" she gasped out in surprise. "What are the two of you doing here? Is Trys — I mean, the ard rialóir —"

"We are here because I do, on occasion, work from here," Collum said. He raised a brow at her. "Trystane and the others left this morning. We came to get his spare housekey so that I may care for his plants in his brief absence."

Bridgette looked from one to the other. "Hold up. How do you know about all of this? And why are you in Eckenbourne on a random Friday?"

"Long story," both Emi-Joye and Collum said together. Bridgette eyed them suspiciously.

"I found out about the trip on accident," the Fairy said, thinking fast. "And I'm here because … well, the ard rialóir also accidently told me something that the two of you found out, and I desired to speak with him about it before he left, which is that I'm something called the Boireannach?"

"Huh," Bridgette said dryly. "Really now. Fantastic."

"What is the Boireannach?" Emi-Joye asked. It was an honest question, even if it was her spur-of-the-moment cover story. Trystane had promised he'd see her before he left, and thanks to a meeting that ran over time, she missed him when he came to the Seledreám. Running into the fyrdwisa and Liluthuaé in her attempt to see him shocked the emotion out of her, and now she was stuck.

"You know, that's a great question," the Bright Star answered slyly. "Too bad I don't know the answer. Why don't we go have a little conversation with our favorite magical objects and see what they feel like telling us? We have nothing else to do except light sixteen candles for Imbolc tomorrow, right?"

"Sixteen?" Emi-Joye questioned. "Why sixteen?"

"Bridgette's making a human culture joke that she knows we might not understand," Collum said. He stared at the Elfling, who knew full well what sort of a mess she was about to create. "Do the two of you actually want to go to the clearing? Now?"

"Let's do it," Bridgette said. She looked at the Fairy, who gave a noncommittal sort of shrug. "There. Settled. Let's go."

Collum held up a finger. "No. First we're getting reinforcements, and then we'll go. The last time that one" — he pointed to Emi-Joye — "got near those things, we had to summon a téitheoir. We're not going unless I've got someone else who can get you out of there if something like that happens again. You've not both been around them at the same time. Given the propensity of those damned things to create windstorms out of thin air, I can only imagine what it will be like to have the two of you touching them at the same time. Njahla's still acting as Lucilla's temporary replacement, so she cannot go, but I'll get Aurelias and Emi-Joye can bring Apostine. The fyrdestre should be in our office, and you can tell your second to meet us there."

Emi-Joye nodded. "I'll send him a summons when we reach your office, provided it has a window I may use."

"Of course." Collum led them around the building and barreled unceremoniously into his office, startling Aurelias from her desk.

"Chief! And — well, hello you two. What are you lot doing here?" she asked.

Collum groaned. "For the second time in fifteen minutes, *I do work here sometimes*. These two are here because now that we don't have the Samnung breathing down our necks and telling us 'no', we're going to Maluridae Wood, and you and Apostine are coming with us."

"Really?" Aurelias said. She couldn't hide the excitement from her voice.

"Yes, although I am already regretting this entire debacle," Collum muttered. He strode over to the window and cracked it open for Emi-Joye. "Summon away, Ambassadora."

He busied himself at his own desk for a while as they waited for Apostine, shuffling papers until he came upon Bridgette's blue notebook. Collum opened a drawer, pulled out the leather-bound notebook she'd gifted him for winter solstice, and bade her come over. Bridgette propped up on a corner of the desk and grinned when she saw what sat before him.

"I need you to go through this and tell me what is news and what is how to make sausages," Collum said. "Dictate to me and I'll write it down. The only reason Nehemi hasn't been hounding you for an official report is because that's far too much work on Njahla, who's already balancing her job and being receptionist. It's the queen's fault she hasn't bothered to find someone to fill that position yet. We'd rather have our ardestre back, but I think Nehemi's holding onto Njahla out of spite."

"That sounds about right," Bridgette commented. She reached for her notebook and started flipping pages, calling out lines for Collum to write down.

"Is there any order to any of this?" he asked after a few minutes. "I don't believe what you're giving me are even complete sentences."

"Well, that would be because they really aren't," Bridgette confessed. "I didn't want to get caught, so I tried to make it look like it was just random notes and thoughts. Muov, the Elf who was a slátraestre with me, always acted suspicious of why I was there. I mean, he was probably right to, because I *was* lying my face off the whole time, but if anyone was going to get me in actual trouble, it seemed like it'd be him."

They were spared any further notetaking by a rap at the door, followed by Apostine letting himself in. His giddiness was palpable.

"We're going to find out about the Boireannach story, finally?" he said excitedly, and Bridgette shot Emi-Joye a strong look.

"Did Trystane tell *everyone* about this?" she asked.

"No, I told my second, because not all of us keep secrets from our seconds," the Fairy replied pointedly, causing Aurelias to flash her a sharp smile and a thumb's up, and Collum to scoff, insulted. "Shall we go, then?"

Collum eyed her as he stood from the desk. "I suppose we shall. Aurelias, you take the Fae and I'll take Bridgette."

True to form, the fyrdestre evanesced to the wrong clearing. Apostine picked her up and the two Fairies flew around until they found the circle of rowan trees, Collum and Bridgette waiting in the middle. They didn't make any comments as the trio landed, although Aurelias apologized profusely for her bad aim.

"It's fine, Aurelias," Collum assured her. "Will you undo Trystane's handiwork and release the vademecums?"

He walked to the opposite end of the clearing and stood next to Bridgette again, leaving Aurelias and Apostine by the trunk. Emi-Joye stood on Bridgette's other side, her wings flitting nervously as they waited for the magical things to be floated toward them.

If Emi-Joye starts to go into the same state she did before, I'm evanescing her out of here, Collum thought to Bridgette. *I'll come back for you, but I know you can hold your own.*

Gee thanks, I think, she thought back, laughing to herself. *I think we'll be okay. Just let them talk and don't try to take them away. Nothing bad happened when I touched mine, so I don't think anything bad will happen when Emi-Joye has hers, either.*

I hope you're right, Collum thought. He squeezed her hand as the trio of notebooks, more awake and sentient than ever, found their way to them.

Bridgette felt the tap in her mind. Given the startled gasp Emi-Joye gave next to her, the vademecums had just done the same thing to the Fairy.

✦ *You've brought us a gift, Liluthuaé.*

Is this the Boireannach? Bridgette thought, intentionally sending her question to all three vademecums, though again the greenish one hung back. Apparently, the communication included Emi-Joye now too, because the Fairy gave her a horrified look.

"Why are you in my head?" she whimpered. "What are they doing?"

"They're talking," Bridgette told her. "The one that just spoke is mine. Yours hasn't talked yet. And I'm not in your head, not like Collum can be. I think whatever Maylemaegus we have creates its own way to interact with each other."

✦ *You are wise, Liluthuaé. The Triumvirate will always be able to reach one another.*

You know, you haven't told us what the Triumvirate is, Bridgette thought. *Care to enlighten us now that we brought you the Boireannach?*

☠ *Her Eminence's presence is a delight to behold once again.* Emi-Joye's vademecum had a brighter voice, like that of a soprano singer compared to the alto of Bridgette's, as it evaded the question. *Do we frighten you?*

"I don't know how to talk to them," Emi-Joye whispered. Her heartbeat quickened, and she reached for the ash-blue covered artifact. "Can't I just talk like normal?"

It's easy, Bridgette thought to her. *It's like when you think something just so Collum is able to hear your mind-voice. But instead of thinking to Collum, think to one of us.*

Emi-Joye gulped down her fear. She glanced to Collum, who gave her an encouraging nod, before thinking to them all, *Yes, I'm frightened. I don't know what any of this means. What is the Boireannach? What am I? Why am I a part of this?*

Her questions were not what the vademecums expected, and there was a frigidity in their energy, a pulse of confusion that spread through the clearing. Collum was also confused: he expected terror and a power exchange, not this calm chatter. No one was glowing, either.

☠ *The Boireannach is the comandante, the most loyal, descended from the Matla, the power of the Fyrst Fae, a sworn protector of the time that is to* come. *The Boireannach is sibling to the Masterwork, the Liluthuaé, as is the sibling Astridsí. Where is the Astridsí?*

Bridgette reached for Collum's hand as she listened to Emi-Joye's vademecum speak. *This is following the same dumb line of script as the last time we were here, when mine asked about Emi-Joye,* she thought to him. *I don't think we're going to get the answers we need until this Astridsí thing is with us.*

Tell them, he urged her, mind to mind.

The Elfling again focused her attention on the vademecums and Emi-Joye. *We don't know who or what the Astridsí is. Can you tell us?*

✦ *How do you not know who carries the blood of the Fyrst Witch?*

An alarm bell went off in Collum's head. He squeezed Bridgette's fingers to call her attention back to him. *What in the seven hells do they mean by Fyrst Fae and Fyrst Witch? The Fyrst were Elves, Bridgette!*

She shot him a horrified look as she recalled the story of magical origins Collum once told her. Bridgette reached for her vademecum. *We can't do what we're supposed to do if secrets are being kept from us, you hear? There's no such thing as the Fyrst Fae or Fyrst Witch, there's only the Fyrst. The Fyrst were Elves, and Ylda created every other species of magical being and creature.*

Bridgette and Collum could have sworn the two vademecums started laughing. Emi-Joye was frozen — her eyes again going still as if in death — as the objects began to spin a yarn that spun Collum's world upside down.

✦ *What you know of your origins is a half-truth, Liluthuaé. There is a reason Aelys Frost had to hide us, had to imprison us in such a way while we waited until our time had come. Ceannairí Álfar was born in the Demiurge, the time that great blackness became all colors and life and power on the planets we now float above. The great Ceannairí bore the true Fyrst: the Elf, the Fae, the Witches.*

☠ *It is true that Ylda, the Fyrst Elf, went on to create many beings, and that your spirit was ordained and gifted back to the gods and goddesses for safekeeping. Ylda gave a great gift to her fellow true Fyrst siblings. While the great Ceannairí chose to evermore take Elven form and the offspring became known as the Fyrst, those initial generations of your kind, it would be impossible for the Fae and the Witches to go on without partners. That is when Ylda became the artist she is known as, and gave her siblings their heartsworn.*

"I'm sorry, but I think I just hallucinated," Bridgette said out loud. "What the fuck. So, what everybody in Heáhwolcen thinks is the story of how they came to be isn't entirely true? Why?"

✦ *The Elves were the oldest, Ylda born first. Ceannairí Álfar experimented, taking other forms suggested by the gods and goddesses, then birthing the Fyrst Fae and finally the Fyrst Witches. But the great Ceannairí preferred the grace and powers of what the Elven form was and chose that to be its legacy. All the rest was, indeed, by the heart and talent of Ylda. The Elves consider themselves to be the original biological descendants of Ceannairí Álfar and professed this tale forevermore.*

Okay, rude and kind of selfish, Bridgette thought to them. *So how do you know this story and no one else does?*

☠ *We are the grimoire of the Triumvirate. We know all that can be known.*

"Honestly, I think the only fucking gift you things got from Ceannairí Álfar is a talent to talk in a stupid circle the size of Texas," Bridgette muttered. "We still very clearly don't know what the Triumvirate is."

"I think they're trying to tell us that's what we are," Emi-Joye said slowly, so quietly it was barely above a whisper. "The Fyrst were three, one each an Elf, a witch, a Fairy. You're an Elfling. I'm a Fairy. That leaves a witch."

☠ *You, too, are wise, Eminence,* her vademecum praised her. *The Liluthuaé spirit is the work of Ylda, the Fyrst Elf. The Boireannach carries with her the power of the Fyrst Fae, and the Astridsí, a Fyrst Witch.*

You named Ylda, Bridgette demanded of it in her mind-voice. *What are the names of the other true Fyrst you're talking about? And if you say Heledd, I swear I am going to stab you, even if you're supposed to help me uncover our destinies.*

There was another pulse of laughter from all three vademecums this time.

✦ *Do not fear, Liluthuaé. The Druidic path of witchcraft practice came later.*

Thank fuck, the Elfling thought.

✦ *The Fyrst Fae had the name Duatha, and from she and her heartsworn were later born the Duathanna. The Fyrst Witches were two, a male who bore the name Biavis Scyllos and his elder twin, whose old name is long lost, but whom you know now as Artur Cromwell.*

Collum dropped Bridgette's hand and nearly fell to his knees in shock.

"Oh, you've *got* to be fucking kidding me right now," Bridgette breathed as she stared at the purplish vademecum. "Nehemi is the deity-damned Astridsí?"

~ 67 ~

"Are you sure it's her?" Aurelias asked Bridgette, not looking up from where her head lay buried in her arms at Taberna Körtz a short while later. "Because if this Triumvirate is supposed to do anything as a threesome, good luck with that."

The Liluthuaé pushed a spoon around in her bowl of chicken chowder. Thinking about food made her ill after this latest interaction with her vademecum. She fought mightily to keep it with her, despite its cursed revelation, but Collum insisted they go back in the trunk. He was in a daze — they all were — after the magical objects turned magical history topsy-turvy, and the fyrdwisa wanted nothing to do with them at the moment.

"There's no one else it could be. Even if Artur Cromwell was a twin, he was the oldest, so any offspring he had would have a right to the Maylemaegus gifts before his brother's bloodline got a chance to," Bridgette said. She forced herself to eat a spoonful of chowder. "After Imbolc when the Samnung gets back, how do y'all suggest we break the news?"

"I suggest we don't," Collum said, to everyone's surprise.

Apostine dropped both his jaw and the pot roast filling from his sandwich, so shocked was he at the fyrdwisa's declaration. "You think we should keep this a secret? That we shouldn't tell the queen that she's part of all of this? What about that everything we've known about our history is *wrong*?"

"Yes, precisely all that!" Emi-Joye agreed. "Not to mention the part where Artur Cromwell knew his own history and conveniently let that either die out or be lost to time, and that this version is what he spread to all of us!"

Collum shot the Fairy a look. "Is the pot calling the kettle black? Did you not come to us months ago and suggest that perhaps your mother was of a Fae sect known as the Duathanna?"

"Wait, what?" Bridgette asked. "You knew about that?"

"No, not exactly!" Emi-Joye tried to plead her case. "I came across the word in an old book I found in my mother's study, and after I suspected there was some sort of strange power hiding within me, I started to wonder — but how could it make sense for Nehemi to be the Astridsí if we believe her womb to be cursed?"

"Who believes that?!" Aurelias asked. "Where is this coming from?"

The shouting at their table began to get out of hand enough that even though Collum had warded them with a sound barrier, his companions' animated hand waving, leaning across bowls of soup to get in one another's faces, and slamming of a fist down upon the wood started to catch the attention of other patrons.

"Oy!" A sharp voice interrupted the arguments, and the faces at the table turned to see Sheridan, one of the barkeeps, standing just beyond their ward-wall. "What in the seven hells are you lot up to? You're disturbing the peace, friends. Not sure that's a good look."

Collum waved his hand, and the ward-wall dissipated. "We're quite sorry for any disruption to the tavern, comrade. We were simply having a discussion and it got a bit heated."

"Yes, well, might I suggest cooling your heads a bit by taking whatever your discussion is outside?" Sheridan said pointedly. He cocked his head toward the door. "I'm not above kicking even you out, Fyrdwisa."

"We'll finish our meal and be out of your hair immediately, Thighearna," Collum promised. "My apologies."

Sheridan scowled but walked away without another reprimand. The fyrdwisa breathed a small sigh of relief. The idea of explaining to Trystane and Aristoces why the five of them got in trouble at a bar — fighting on top of chicken chowder and pot roast sandwiches, of all things! — mere hours after the Samnung left seemed quite unappealing to him.

As it happened, Imbolc and the remainder of the Samnung visit passed both quickly and uneventfully, and Collum spent half of Sunday glancing at his stack of covenant bracelets. He was anxious to know that the ceannairí were back safely and unscathed, especially since he discovered over the weekend that it really was impossible for him to contact anyone through the activated Ballamúr.

"You're positive about that?" Bridgette asked from her perch in the Alcove. She had a favorite shelf, one that was not nearly as dusty as the others, and so tall that she "had" to fly to get to the top. It was a good vantage point from which to watch Collum whispering finding spells as the two continued their fruitless search for evidence or stories about Maylemaegus, and what they knew now about the Fyrst.

Very positive, he thought to her. *I tried to contact Trystane while we were in line at Taberna Körtz the other day waiting to order. He did not answer, nor did Corria a few moments later when I tried her as well. The channel itself felt deadened, as if there was nothing there at the other end.*

A pang went through his chest. *It felt the same as my parents' and former fyrdwisa's do,* he thought to himself.

The first time he realized his parents were both truly gone to the spirit realm was when he, out of habit, went to ask his mother if she would like some fruit from a vibrantly colored market he stumbled upon in Endorsa. He couldn't recall what the fruit was now, but he remembered with vivid clarity the devastation he felt when he touched that bracelet, and no magic tickled his fingertips. He'd bought the fruit in her memory and turned it into pastries that very evening. A pair of them he wrapped in a beeswax package and brought to the edge of Aelchanon to a public altar, where he left them as an offering to those whose spirits dwelt in Ifrinnevatt.

Bundy? You okay down there? Bridgette's mind-voice pulled him out of his memories. *You went real quiet for a minute.*

I'm alright, Starshine, he thought back, and glanced up to give her a soft smile. *It is difficult to have covenants that once worked, that no longer do.*

She jumped down from the shelf, tossed aside the useless pamphlet she'd been looking through, and joined the Elf where he sat cross-legged on the floor. "You were thinking about your parents, weren't you?"

"I was, and my former fyrdwisa."

Bridgette slipped her arms around his body and leaned her head against his shoulder. "I think they'd be very proud of you, you know. Not everybody gets to raise a kid — err, youngling — who grows up to help save the world."

He squeezed her arm in gratitude. "That's kind of you to say, Starshine."

There was so much more he could tell her, so many stories about those three that he wanted to share. He hoped to have time to, one day. One day — when there were no distractions, no foretold destiny looming over their heads — he would make that time. It was a promise he made to himself in that moment, sitting on that dusty floor, absorbing every feeling and emotion of their quiet, comforting embrace and committing it to memory.

You're very important to me, Bridgette Conner, he thought to her.

Collum felt her smile against his neck as she thought back, *You know the only reason I'm humoring this whole world savior thing is because I want to spend an unfathomable amount of time with you, right?*

I suppose I'm glad I'm worth saving, then.

She chanced a tighter embrace. *Oh no, punk; we're in this shit together. You die, I'm out of here. There's no point in saving Heáhwolcen if*

———

But whatever it was, she didn't get a chance to think it. Collum's covenant bracelet twinged with power as Aristoces, Trystane, and Corria collectively alerted him that they were back, and the Elf breathed a deep sigh of relief.

"Would you care to go to Bondrie for a spur-of-the-moment Samnung meeting in Corria's chambers?" he asked.

Bridgette gave him an annoyed look. "I don't think you're going to give me an option on that, are you?"

Collum swiftly kissed her on the cheek. "I will, but I'd much rather you come of your own volition instead of forcing me to convince you otherwise."

She rolled her eyes as she stood and brushed the dust off her leggings and the hem of her sweater. The Elfling stuck out a hand to help Collum to his feet. They kept their fingers together as he evanesced them to the entrance of Casa de Piedra.

They were led somewhere deep in the heart of the stone castle into a room arranged as a makeshift Samnung chamber. Similar wards had been placed on it — Collum felt the magic as he and Bridgette stepped through the doorway — and a circle of stools and chairs were arranged therein. Verivol and Bryten were there too, as was Njahla, armed with a feather quill and the notebook she once used to take notes on Uleron Mewt's ambassador reports. Only Cloa was absent.

Nehemi waited until Collum and Bridgette were seated before calling the meeting to order. Without a table to hide where his hands went, the fyrdwisa felt it necessary to keep them to himself, though he would much rather have had one hand in Bridgette's. He felt her tension rise the moment Nehemi stood from her chair, and wondered if these makeshift spells would be as strong as those that prevented him from using his scent magic in the actual Samnung chamber.

"We return today with much to share about our own time in Palna," the witch queen began. "I do not think it necessary to speak much on the Imbolc ceremonies themselves, but rather, to share what we observed during our time with the Tinuviels and in the capital city. I found the palace at Düoria to be quite ostentatious. It's the size of Deu Medgar, Cyneham Breonna, and the training building at Minthame combined, and houses only a few individuals. Those who work for the Tinuviels — save for their version of butlers, bodyguards, and handmaidens —

reside elsewhere in the city. There is so much room for so few beings, and to think that it was built originally by Baize Sammael himself! I do not know how one single male could require such opulence."

"I would assume it has not always been as such," Aristoces said. "I do agree with Her Majesty that it was quite an experience to be in the palace. Each of us had our own suite of rooms with a bedchamber, bathroom, and either study or parlor, despite the short length of our stay. The fabrics and materials are of expensive make and quality. I am not sure what I expected, but great care was taken to ensure our comfort."

I'm sure it was, Bridgette thought dryly to Collum. Out loud, she asked, "What do you mean by it being 'ostentatious' and 'opulent'?"

"There was an entire room outfitted in all the metals of Heáhwolcen, for one," Trystane recounted. "Everything in there was silver, bronze, chrome, gold, and an alloy we were told was called hepatizon. One room, which I found bizarre, held taxidermized remains of both magical and nonmagical creatures, including a Unicorn. It is said to be the steed that Baize Sammael himself rode into battle during the Ingefeoht."

Collum made an unintelligible noise of disgust.

"Speaking of Palna's esteemed founder — we did not get a chance to tour the grounds," the ard rialóir went on. "However, I had a view of a stone monument from my stateroom window, and I'm willing to bet I know precisely who that is supposed to honor."

"The library, too, was glossed over, but I imagine it was vast," Aristoces mentioned, speaking over Collum's second wordless grumble. She gave Bridgette a knowing look. "Though it seems the city you lived in had no such resource, there is at least one library in Palna."

"Duly noted," the Elfling replied. "How guarded was the palace?"

"Very," Corria answered. "We each were assigned to two members of the Palnan Guard, and they walked with us everywhere we went, changing shifts at night to stand outside our doors. Inside our rooms were the only places they did not follow."

I'd really like to see that library, Bridgette thought to Collum as she nodded her acknowledgement to Corria. *Something tells me if Baize Sammael had secrets he wanted kept, like how to read Gemaere, it's going to be in there.*

"What are the chances the Tinuviels do like, guided tours for their citizens?" she asked. "We used to go on field trips to places like that in school, the White House where the president lives, and that kind of thing."

"Very high, actually." Trystane raised his ever-present glass in a toasting manner. "We were kept from seeing any, a move I assume was meant to avoid the youths asking questions about who we were, but such 'field trips', as you call them, do exist."

I believe I know what you're thinking, and I lack a sierwan gift, Collum thought to Bridgette. *You want to visit Düoria for yourself, don't you?*

She flashed him a quick smile. *Abso-fucking-lutely.*

Njahla, who'd been taking notes the entire time, finally asked a question of her own. "Did you find that your beliefs regarding potential conflict are well-founded?"

There was a too-long moment of silence in the circle as the Samnung leaders looked at one another, unsure who should answer. Bridgette shot Collum a horrified glance before Kharis spoke, his wheezing voice more nasal than usual.

"We saw nothing that indicated there was disharmony amongst the Palnan citizens, nor any sign that preparations were being made to arm and train the Palnan Guard for anything but their normal duties," the borhond said. "We observed the contrary. It would seem as though all the Tinuviels want is for Palna to again be part of Heáhwolcen as a whole; for its citizens to know peace and again be able to practice their natural magic that has long been stifled by our own wall. Ydessa and Eryth do not appear to want any sort of confrontation between their citizens and those in the rest of Heáhwolcen."

"Really," the Liluthuaé said. She stared the elderly man down, watching his every move. Beside her, Collum watched *her*, prepared for her eyes to change at the hint of any untruth. Warded this room might be, but it was not made to protect against the Maylemaegus-infused wrath of Bridgette Conner.

"I speak truly, Bright Star," Kharis promised. Bridgette's eyes narrowed, distrustful, as she listened to him explain. "Of course, we did not make known our own suspicions, but we took part in many discussions regarding the Tinuviels' quest for integration. The citizenry holds much respect for their rulers, even to the point of several Palnans falling to their knees as Ydessa and Eryth walked by during a ceremony procession on the night of Imbolc. Their comradeship is like nothing I have ever seen: the rulers speak, their denizens listen. Palnans greet each other with a shared gesture, their right hands fisted over their hearts, and it is overwhelming to see swaths of beings do this for their leaders."

"What happened during the ceremonies when the Tinuviels said who y'all were?" Bridgette asked.

"If I recall correctly, the exact quote Ydessa said was, 'And now mine partner and I introduce to you our most honored guests for this blessed Imbolc, the leaders of the Samnung of Heáhwolcen, a body we hope to soon join on our own'," Kharis said.

Trystane held up a finger. "And the rest of that; she said something about, 'may the presence of their magic awaken the kinship that has been long-lost within our borders'."

"What in the seven hells does that mean?" Collum muttered.

Bridgette had her hands balled into fists in her lap. The fyrdwisa sensed her anger, felt her struggling to control it. He couldn't blame her. Everything she experienced was being countered by the Tinuviels themselves, and neither they fyrdwisa nor Bright Star understood what made such a dichotomy possible. How could the air in Xcthonya be tight with uncertainty when in Düoria, it appeared that everyone adored the Tinuviels?

Nehemi cleared her throat and again stood before the rest of the gathered Samnung. "It appears as though we might be somewhat premature in our assumptions that, because the Liluthuaé is among us, it means Palna is readying for war. Perhaps we are wrong entirely and it is not Palna that we should be worried about, nor the Tinuviels whom we must concern ourselves with defending against."

A strangled sort of noise escaped Bridgette's throat.

Nehemi didn't notice.

"What I observed during our visit is that Ydessa and Eryth, though indeed not my choices as allies in the Samnung, seek to revive the Palna they and their citizens thought was originally promised to them, without, of course, the presence of Craft Wizardry," she continued. "It was made clear to me they understand the danger of this magic and what it represents. As Bridgette has tried to make us see, Palnan citizens are not those who blindly followed the lead of Baize Sammael, and the Tinuviels are not their predecessor. For this reason, I am cautiously optimistic that some level of diplomacy can be attained."

Collum decided he didn't care about there not being a table to hide where his hands went, and he reached over to put his open palm on Bridgette's thigh. That's when he noticed she was starting to glow, the same way she had the first time in the clearing with her vademecum.

Oh no —

"You've lost your fucking mind, Nehemi," the Bright Star said.

~ 68 ~

Nehemi raised a brow. "Excuse me?"

"You've lost. Your fucking. Mind," Bridgette repeated, adding emphasis to her words. Collum went from flattened palm of comfort to near death-grip on her upper leg.

Bridgette … he thought in rapid warning. *Please, for once during a Samnung meeting, think before you do something irreparable …*

His warning was too late. Not for Bridgette, but for Nehemi. The queen walked across the circle and stood in front of the Bright Star, a daring glare highlighting her hazel eyes. She crossed her arms and stared down at the Elfling. "I might say the same to you, Bridgette, for daring to speak to a member of the Samnung with such an attitude."

That was it. Bridgette stood so quickly that had Collum not been paying attention, she'd have knocked him out of his chair. As it happened, he realized she was about to mirror the queen's movement, and he rose smoothly by her side. Corria, he noticed, was at Bridgette's other shoulder a moment later, the master swordswoman's hand on the hilt of the karambit in her knife belt.

"The only questionable attitude in this room is yours," Bridgette said to Nehemi. The glowing field around her deepened, slowly fluctuating colors from light to dark purple. "Your inability to see what lies before you does not bode well for what your own fate will be."

Collum choked back a breath; her voice was *wrong*. It sounded as though her vademecum's inhuman intonations melded with her own, giving Bridgette's words a hollow character. He didn't like that one bit.

"My own fate?" Nehemi barked. "Are you threatening me yet again?"

She took a small step toward Bridgette, but Corria intercepted her, blade glinting.

"This meeting is adjourned," the master swordswoman

commanded them. "I speak for Bondrie, and there will be no threats made against the Bright Star within our borders."

"You dare to go above your spreca?" Nehemi's voice rose a few notes in disbelief. "You dare to —"

The curved blade of the karambit was around the Endorsan queen's throat before she could speak another word, with Corria herself behind Nehemi, one arm trapping the witch's upper body against her own.

"Bondrie has sworn its fealty to the Bright Star," Corria said, and her upper lip curled in a strange movement of both delight and danger. In front of them still stood Bridgette, surrounded by the purple glow. "A threat to her is a threat to us. I will not tolerate it, and I encourage you to exit these walls before my blade slips."

There was a fury in Nehemi's eyes that Collum had never seen before, and a palpable astonishment as Corria's words struck home with the rest of the Samnung. Trystane shot Collum a look that, despite the fyrdwisa's inability to hear his brother's thoughts, clearly said, "What the ever-loving fuck?", and Collum tried not to laugh, given the gravity of the situation.

Nehemi, whose back was to Corria, glared at Bridgette for a heartbeat longer, as if considering whether or not she wanted to attempt to get physical. "Remove your hands and knife immediately, Deathhunter, and I will take my leave."

The master swordswoman, half a head taller than the witch queen, squeezed her quarry one final time before releasing Nehemi. Collum moved closer to Bridgette and watched as Nehemi took Kharis by the shoulder and exited the room. She stalked toward the door, looking daggers at them all, and her nostrils flared with each breath. The fyrdwisa had never seen her look so threatening. It unsettled him, but not nearly as much as what happened when the door shut behind them and the warding spells snapped off in their wake.

"*Fealty?*" Trystane shouted at Corria. No one was in their

chairs anymore, and Aristoces' eyes darted from glowing Bridgette to knife-wielding leader of Bondrie, who'd sheathed her blade and now stood toe-to-toe with the ard rialóir.

"Yes," the master swordswoman replied.

Trystane whirled to look at the rest of them. "Was anyone going to make that little tidbit of information known? And what is the deity-damned point of swearing fealty to Bridgette, Corria? There are at least a thousand ways to piss Nehemi off; why this?"

"I choose to follow the one who will lead us down the right path," Corria said. She was calm, more collected than anyone else in the room. "The gods and goddesses ordained that destiny for the Bright Star, not for the sitting queen of Endorsa."

Bridgette's glowing energy faltered. *I'm not so sure about that,* she thought to Collum. *If Nehemi is part of this Triumvirate thing too …*

He didn't want to think about it. He also didn't want to think about the fact that what just happened was *exactly* what he had been worried about for months — that suddenly it seemed as if the rest of the Samnung stood in opposition to its spreca — and again, the last thing they needed was infighting. Something told him that would only feed into whatever the Tinuviels wanted to convince everyone else they were not planning.

"Why are you glowing?" Bryten asked. He sauntered over to Bridgette and ran one of his golden-hued fingers down the edge of the purple light. It bounced at his touch, and Bridgette jumped, exclaiming that it tickled.

"I don't know why I'm glowing. It happened the first time I touched my vademecum —"

Blank stares met her eyes, and Bridgette clamped her mouth shut. *Oops,* she thought to Collum. *I just … really fucked that up, didn't I?*

"What is a vademecum?" Aristoces asked, and both Trystane and Collum groaned in unison. "Why does it cause you to glow?"

Bridgette cringed and stared at the ceiling. "Hell's bells, I really need to think before I talk sometimes. Why don't y'all take a seat, and let's get everyone caught up on the same page. If we could maybe have some beer or snacks or something, that would be great. We're gonna be here for a little while."

When the two Elves and Elfling finished talking, they were met with absolute silence. They'd told everyone everything, Bridgette and Collum even filling Trystane in on what they learned while he was in Palna, and it was as if they all now sat in the eye of a hurricane. The calm was false, everyone waiting for the other half of the storm to drop. While they spoke, Bridgette's glow faded as her heartbeat slowed and stasis resumed, bringing her body and voice back to normal, to Collum's relief.

"What now?" Verivol finally asked. "Are you going to tell Nehemi that she is this mysterious Astridsí?"

"I don't know," Bridgette moaned. "When the vademecums flashed the blue light at us, it was my sierwan knowledge that helped connect the dots of Emi-Joye being the Boireannach. That didn't happen when I wondered if Nehemi was the Astridsí. I don't want to tell her and then have to take it back. I may not like her very much, but that's kind of a bitch move."

Bryten chuckled, but Verivol still looked strained. "Aristoces, you are the eldest amongst us. Were you aware of such a Fairy history, of the Duathanna and this so-called Duatha?" the Sanguisuge asked.

Aristoces shook her head. She looked as drained as the rest of them. "By the time I was born, there were Fairies, Elves, and other such beings and creatures all over the world. Our history as Aziza was largely oral, and I grew up learning our origins are the same as all Fairies, that we were created by Ylda and gifted the first wings. The Duathanna I heard of loosely as a sect of Celtic Fae. My entire life until this moment, I considered the Duathanna an ancient Fairy variety of what the Elves call dúnaelfen. I would remind you all that there *are* multiple varieties of winged beings like ourselves. It is entirely possible that, though what are now known as the Celtic Fae were birthed by Ceannairí Álfar, my own Fairies were created later by Ylda. The reverse could also be true. I am unsure that we will ever now know."

"Did you know Artur Cromwell?" Bridgette asked her.

"I did not, Liluthuaé," Aristoces replied. "I remained on Earth with my own flock of Fae until after the Ingefeoht, when I was invited to consider the role I now have after my predecessor's life was unexpectedly lost. He was the son of Iontach ad Chéad Chaeannaire, Galdúr, and my distant cousin."

Bridgette let it slide over her for the moment that Aristoces was related to the co-founder of Heáhwolcen. Something wasn't sitting quite right with her. She knew Elves and Fairies, and to her knowledge, Sanguisuges, Unicorns, Tieflings, Baetalü, and a wide variety of other magical beings were all but immortal. Collum once told her that most of them chose to enter the spirit realm versus having a set lifespan. She knew, too, that witches were long-lived, but significantly less so than the rest of bipedal magickind.

How is it that most witches die of natural causes after two centuries, but Artur Cromwell lived … how long did *he live for?* Bridgette thought to Collum. *Was he even alive for the Ingefeoht?*

The silence had started to become uncomfortable. Collum gave Bridgette's shoulder an acknowledging squeeze, then addressed the room.

"I believe there are two places where we may find the answers we now seek," he said. "The first is within the pages of Bridgette's, Emi-Joye's, and potentially Nehemi's vademecums. They continue to veil their nature and purpose from us, and I suspect that may be the case until the third one is claimed. But they were the objects that revealed this new history to us and likely know a great deal more that they have yet to share."

He reached a hand to Bridgette, who allowed him to pull her again to her feet. "The second place, and it is with every warning flag waving inside my own psyche that I say this, is in Palna. The vademecums are written in Gemaere, this language that we know nothing of except to have seen it — some of us — with our own eyes and wonder what it means. The Ballamúr gave the Bright Star a message in Gemaere before she crossed back into Bondrie in December, hence why I hypothesize we might find aid there. It is imperative that we find out more about this so-called language. Where and how did it originate, and how do we translate it into the modern languages we now speak?"

Bridgette didn't expect to find tears in her eyes. She put an arm around Collum's waist, needing to touch him, to feel him there, as he gave her his blessing to go back. Back to Toby, to the native land of her father, to the place where she shared and spilled blood. But to leave him again? There was a cleaving in her chest, a dry and empty void that suddenly yawned open, her soul mewling in pain at the violation. Collum pulled her closer and rested his hand across the small of her back.

I would rather give up my own magic than allow you to endanger yourself once again on our behalf, Bridgette Conner, he thought to her. *But in the end, my permission is neither needed nor requested. No matter where you are, I am with you now and always, until the very end.*

His words echoed the promise he made the first time she stood at the edge of the Ballamúr, and Bridgette's heart gave an almighty lurch. She wondered if the rest of the Samnung members felt it too, or if they only saw her tears begin to fall, for there was an exchanged glance of concern between Verivol and Bryten, and Trystane's mouth hardened into a worried line.

It was hard to talk without her throat closing in on her words. Bridgette squeezed her eyes shut, willing the tears to stop. When they refused to obey, she stared at the ceiling again and allowed herself to feel their salt flow down her cheeks, her neck, burying themselves in the neckline of her sweater. She didn't know what to say anyway; there were too many thoughts and emotions warring with one another inside her head. There was a sense of déjà vu and for a minute, Bridgette found herself in a different room, telling some of these same beings exactly the opposite of what they hoped to hear.

And she recalled the barely-there flash of disappointment in Collum's eyes, and knew now, so many moons later, that his reaction had not been on behalf of Heáhwolcen. It was the first time he dropped the filter of being fyrdwisa and let her see *him*.

Bridgette stopped watching the ceiling and brought her eyes to Collum's, searching for very different answers in those soulful tidal pools as she finally spoke.

"I can't promise that I'll find out everything we want to know, and I can't promise I won't trip over another tree root and get stabbed by a stick again," she said. "Hell, I can't even promise I know what I'm doing. But I do promise you this: I will do everything I can to stop the Tinuviels and to reunite a renewed Palna with the rest of Heáhwolcen. I will find us allies against Ydessa and Eryth, and I will not let you down."

The Bright Star took a ragged breath. "I want a trio of covenant bracelets. One will be for Serrabinx, who should be able to work them, if y'all tell me how to do it. Magic is illegal, but not stamped out of everyone's bloodlines. The second one I'll wear, and the third is for the fyrdwisa," she said. "Serrabinx and I will be able to use ours between one another within Palna. I can use mine as a guide to channel Universal consciousness, to direct my thoughts to her inside the borders. There will come a time when she can use it to reach the fyrdwisa, too."

She smirked. "As for the existing consciousness connection between Collum and I? That's a power the darling Ballamúr won't bother to try and stop."

~ 69 ~

Bridgette stayed up far too late that night clearing her head by partaking in her favorite non-musical pastime, which was to stretch her metaphorical wings under the moonlit sky of Collum's home office. Corria suggested earlier that if she planned to return to Palna, she should resume her training immediately. The Elfling had meant to do so already, but it had been a challenge for her to readjust to life in Heáhwolcen to begin with, much less add anything else to her plate. Collum had been right, she supposed, telling her that she'd been mopey.

There had been a fundamental shift in her when she stepped across the Ballamúr that first time. Bridgette entered Palna with an objective, to learn everything she could about the culture and history of the country and find out what caused the Ballamúr to come into its newfound power. She immersed herself in the daily life there, developed a routine, made friends and even somewhat of a family unit. She had a job and responsibilities, not to mention needed to fulfill her initial task, then go above and beyond it due to the length of her stay, unlocking more secrecy and unanswered questions.

But the subterfuge of the entire operation! Bridgette laughed at her spy drama-like choice of language as she worked her shoulder muscles, forcing herself to work on shifting speed and direction as naturally as she would move to walk or reach to hold someone's hand. It was the constant pressure of living a lie, of being afraid of getting caught; knowing that the citizens who became her closest companions in Palna were willingly putting themselves at risk of getting killed — that was what chafed at her so much during the months she resided in Xcthonya.

It was hard to live like that, pretending to be someone she wasn't. Letting little bits and pieces slip to Toby made it easier because at least someone knew more of the truth. Plus, his own abilities didn't leave much to his imagination. Bridgette assumed being back in Heáhwolcen meant getting back to normal. But there hadn't ever been much normalcy here. There wasn't the same level of routine or expectations. Thinking back on it, most of her time in greater Heáhwolcen had been spent researching something.

There was only one reason she came back, and he was several dozen feet away, meditating on the ground, his mere presence providing the comfort and companionship she craved. She, meanwhile, had flown over the treetops, floating cross-legged over the canopy while she collected her scrambled thoughts. But she felt him stirring, attuned more than ever to his energy.

Starshine? Will you come down and talk to me? Collum's mind-voice called to her.

I'll be down in a minute, she thought to him. Bridgette unfolded her legs and stretched midair before spiraling herself to the ground. She'd gotten much better at this, though sometimes controlling her speed was still a fun challenge. The Elfling landed in a strong crouch, then popped herself upright to stand with the fyrdwisa.

"That was impressive," he complimented her. Collum leaned forward to tousle her windblown hair, stray strands glinting in the moonlight. "Nearly as impressive as your inability to keep your braid intact for more than a few hours at a time."

Bridgette shoved at his shoulder. "Rude. What did you want to talk to me about?"

"Walk with me?" he asked, holding out his hand. He led them down a winding dirt path, their jaunt serenaded by crickets. "I'm going to assume you have a plan."

He'd assumed as much earlier, when Aristoces mentioned the library in Düoria.

"Yes, and no," Bridgette confessed. "I'm going to go back, but I don't know for how long. I think I know what I need to do, which is mostly to continue what I had been doing to begin with.

There's got to be a way to get one of those palace tours of Düoria. I'm sure I can convince Toby to take me. I can check out the library, hopefully also check out some books while I'm there that talk about Gemaere and the Triumvirate. The kicker is that I also — don't freak out — need to be active in the Hringur."

Collum stopped dead. "The resistance?"

"Yeah," she said. "I mean, think about it. They've probably got all kinds of spies and informants, like undercover agents in the Palnan Guard or even in the palace at Düoria. That's where they're going to get information from, and that's the kind of information I think they'd wanna share with allies, especially if those allies had magic and weapons. And Unicorns."

She was right, and Collum didn't like to admit it.

"How soon are you trying to leave?" he asked. His question came out brusquer than he intended.

Bridgette raised a brow. "I wouldn't say that I'm *trying* to leave, but I don't know. It might be better to go sooner than later, since Nehemi's going to be on the warpath. If she really is the Astridsí, I want to have all the answers before the two of us and Emi-Joye have to be buddy-buddy."

"Why do you keep second-guessing her involvement?" he asked. Bridgette had said something similar in front of the Samnung a few hours before, and it hadn't sat well with the fyrdwisa.

"Like I told you already, there's nothing that cemented to me that she is the Astridsí," the Elfling snapped. "It obviously makes sense, because there's nobody else wandering around Heáhwolcen with a direct bloodline back to Artur Cromwell, also apparently known as a Fyrst Witch. But there's something about her having that kind of power that just doesn't feel right. We've got this giant jigsaw puzzle of shit to piece together. The Nehemi piece and the Astridsí piece look like they're supposed to snap into one another, but if you do that, it throws the rest of the picture off."

"That's quite the metaphor," Collum said, and rubbed his thumb over the back of her hand. "I didn't mean to upset you. I apologize for doing so."

"You're fine, Bundy," she sighed. "I didn't mean to get snippy. It's just stressful. Everyone's looking at me for answers I can't fucking give them, and I barely know where to start looking to find them. Y'all want timelines and strategy, and all I can give you is pretty much as soon as I know something, you'll know it too. It feels like I'm failing."

"I promise you that you are doing no such thing."

The Elfling flashed him a soft smile. "Thanks."

"Whenever it is that you choose to return, will you just be careful, Starshine?" he implored her. "Watch your step in those magic forests, and don't be afraid to bust the noses of any Bondrie guardsfolk who try to harm you when you come back. And for Hecate's sake, use *your* magic as often as you can to tell me what's going on. Things are not right when you're gone."

Bridgette turned to face the Elf and put her arms around his neck. He stiffened slightly at the movement but did not back away when she leaned in to rest her cheek against him. She didn't understand why he was still like this sometimes, but she no longer questioned it. She simply followed his lead and tried not to be hurt when he didn't seem receptive to her.

The whole time I was in Palna, I thought I couldn't wait to get back here. Home to Heáhwolcen, she thought to Collum, unable to form the words aloud. *But home was never really just this place. Home is you, Collum. It's always been you, ever since that Sunday you showed up and refused to order a stupid Wafflewich and instead drank that strong-ass coffee on repeat for about five hours.*

He threw back his head and laughed, and in a most un-Collum-like move, twirled her around until she started laughing, too. Their eyes danced together, Elven flecks of opalescence reflecting the starlit sky above them.

"That coffee was absolute garbage, and I cannot believe humans voluntarily drank it as if their lives depended on it," he chuckled. "As the fyrdwisa, I am happy to report that the Liluthuaé was most worthy of me forcing several cups of it into my system while I waited for her shift to end."

The corners of her eyes crinkled with amusement. "You really were stalking me, you creep. You're lucky a little sierwan voice in my head told me to trust you, and convinced me that you really believed magic was real."

"It *is* real."

"Yeah, I know that now, but I didn't know back then. Give me a break."

Collum pulled her into him again and smiled against her hair. "Are you truly telling me that the only reason you chose to come to Heáhwolcen was that you went from thinking I was a criminal to thinking I was perhaps in need of some mental health assistance?"

"No!" she scoffed. "I went from thinking you were going to stuff my corpse in a trunk to realizing you were a harmless weirdo trying to hit on me. Very different."

"And to think I was doing neither of those things …" Collum sighed dramatically. "Simply an Elf fulfilling my professional duties. Yet here you are, telling me you thought me to be attempting to steal your virtue."

"My *virtue*?" Bridgette cackled. She looked up to see the fyrdwisa barely holding back a wide grin. "If you'd been stalking me for any amount of time, I think you'd know there wasn't much of that left to steal."

Collum's eyes flashed. "Then, my Starshine, will you allow me to have what little remains?"

She didn't know if she actually answered or if she just moved, but either way, within a heartbeat her hands wound their way around his jaw, one cupping his cheek and the other in his hair as she pressed her lips to his, as hungry as dream-Bridgette had been what felt like a lifetime ago.

Except this was not a dream, and every sense was alive and aware. This was real.

Bridgette was falling, had been falling, for so long she didn't know anything else. Only it wasn't falling, not really, so much as it was sidestepping and sliding into place. A click; a turn of key into lock. The energy of Collum's presence was electric to her. He glistened with it, sparked and sparkled with a vibrancy of fireworks at midnight. The mere thought of him at any point — but at this moment in particular — warmed her core. Collum filled her chest with a tangible sort of heated tightness that grounded her, comforted her from the inside out.

Her hands roamed over him, caressing the planes of his face, sliding over the soft fabric of his sweater. Her hair was a hopeless tangle to begin with, and his hands winding between sections of her braid wasn't helping. They smiled against each other's mouths; pulled in closer as if to have space between them was painful. It was, in a way. Bridgette's mouth parted and she let out the most delicate whimper of pleasure that it almost caused Collum to laugh, but instead, he smiled wider and flicked his tongue against her teeth. The Bright Star moaned against him as he gently teased her further. He tasted so crisp, like water flowing from a mountain spring, and she found she craved that sort of drink.

They were breathless. Bridgette gazed up at him, entranced. Those tidal pool eyes that bespelled her from the very first moment she realized they were like hers, shared Elven irises, watched her intently. The world felt far away, and the Elfling realized she'd accidentally floated them a few feet off the ground.

"Oh!" she exclaimed, but Collum stopped her from putting them back.

"Not yet," he whispered. "Just allow me to hold you and pretend, for a moment, that there is peace in this world, and we are but two beings together, not two players in a very dangerous game."

Bridgette kissed him again, slower this time and softer. She memorized every detail that she could, and smiled when she noticed that as she'd flown them in her delight, Collum had used his magic too. The air smelled of springtime, coated with fragrant blooms and the hint of fresh grass after a rainstorm.

She slowly drifted them back to the ground, and there Collum held her, his head resting atop hers, fingers weaving themselves in her hair and brushing lightly down her spine. It wasn't a matter of letting her go to Palna, because he knew Bridgette would do what she damn well pleased no matter his opinion on the subject. It was more the thought of existing where she wasn't that caused him such grief. He'd mourned her absence twice already in their short time together, and each period was harder than the last. The thought of doing it again, so soon, made his chest ache.

They'd have to go inside if they intended on getting any sleep before Bridgette was to report to Minthame in the morning. He murmured the reminder into the strawberry blonde rat's nest they'd worked her hair into, and she sighed. She didn't want to move. She didn't want to break this spell, nor did she want the night to draw to an end.

She may have been fully clothed, but in that moment, held against Collum as if both their existences depended on the shared contact, Bridgette had never felt so visible in her entire life.

~ 70 ~

The Elfling awoke to her mattress shifting as Collum sat on the foot of the bed. He watched as she slowly came to full consciousness, and she gave him an effortless grin.

"Good morning, Bundy," she said.

"How did you sleep?"

Her grin widened. "I would probably sleep better if I didn't have to be alone."

Collum gave her a dry look in response. "I do not know that to be true. Aurelias once informed me I snored."

"I'd like to find that out for myself one day."

"Return from Palna in one piece, and perhaps I shall let you," he murmured. "I've been thinking about what you said regarding your preferred timeline to go back. There is an opportunity at which you might be able to slip away without Nehemi realizing we've all gone behind her back again. It is a holiday coming up called Lupercalia."

"What's that?"

"It is a surprisingly controversial celebration of fertility, once commemorated with animal offerings and chasing members of the opposite genders around the city while brandishing whips made of goat skin," Collum replied. His eyes twinkled at the disturbed expression that crept over Bridgette's features. "In Heáhwolcen, it evolved into a minor holiday with fewer sacrifices and more intimate coupling, a much more direct way to honor fertility, if you will. There are also blessing rituals performed for those hoping to add a youngling to their family, a feat much more difficult for magickind than for humans. Only witches seem to have perfected the ability to regularly procreate."

"You're kicking me out of town to avoid going to the sex festival with me?" Bridgette said. "That's good timing after certain recent events."

"Hold on —"

She kicked at him from under the covers, annoyed at what she took to be Collum reverting back behind the thin boundary line of friendship. "Would you move? I guess I have to get up and tell Herewosa Donnachaidh I'm back and need a refresher course on how to break Eryth Tinuviel's nose."

Bridgette was still in an angsty mood when Collum deposited her at Minthame. He walked a few paces behind her, trying to figure out why she seemed upset with him, as she strode into the familiar training arena, looking for the feoht trainer. They found him instructing a group of young Baetalü in what appeared to be a series of balancing exercises.

"Fáilte, Herewosa," Bridgette called to him, and he turned to greet them with a laugh.

"Bridgette! What a surprise this is!" Donnachaidh replied. He gave the younglings permission for a water break, and the golden-skinned, horned beings nearly collapsed in a heap with relief. The trainer jogged over to where Bridgette and Collum waited, then wrapped the Bright Star in a bear hug.

"How long have you been back?" he asked.

"Since about winter solstice," she said. "I would have come earlier, but there was a lot of stuff to do first. Training kind of went to the wayside, but I'm hoping we can pick it up again. I got a little rusty during my trip."

Donnachaidh beamed at her. "It would be mine honor, as always, Bright Star. Are you planning to be part of a particular division in the coming conflict? Basic combat skills will always be foundational, but I can cater your training depending on if you'd like to learn a specific weapon or be with, say, the Unicorn calvary, for example."

She frowned. "What are you talking about?"

Collum had a split-second mental warning that something was about to go *very* poorly when the herewosa gave them both a bemused look and replied, "You do not need to pretend you are unaware of the situation. We know how dire it has gotten elsewhere in Heáhwolcen. The Fórsaí Armada has begun its preparations to ready our forces."

"You've what, now?" Bridgette blanched. Collum just stood there, rooted to the spot, for the first time in a long time not sure what to do to fix whatever trust had just been broken.

Herewosa Donnachaidh finally had the good sense to look concerned. "Fyrdwisa, I assumed that this plan was orchestrated with the Bright Star at its helm …"

Deity damn it all, Collum thought as he watched Bridgette's eyes go the wrong color purple again. This time, the violent violet was aimed at him.

"What secrets have you been keeping, Collum Andoralain?" she asked him, her voice shifting with her eyes.

It dawned on him at that moment that her physical contact with the vademecum must have fully awakened or activated the Maylemaegus within her. But now was not the time for that conversation. Nor was it the time to come clean about the assembled Fórsaí Armada, thanks to the spell Emi-Joye had placed on them all during the meeting. The threat of suddenly going into a coughing fit without Bridgette knowing its context held him back from telling her everything, but he couldn't just stand there either.

"We cannot tell you," the fyrdwisa whispered to the Liluthuaé, and reached for her hands. He forced himself to stare into her eyes, begging her in his mind to understand that he wasn't lying. "But I can take you to the one who can. We have been forbidden to speak of it in direct terms, both Herewosa Donnachaidh and I. Will you let me take you somewhere?"

Uncertainty flashed on her face, and Bridgette became as if a holograph: there was a nearly invisible back-and-forth alteration between two sides of her, evident in both her eyes and energy. The Elf gripped her hands harder, forcing her to ground herself, to stay *herself* and not this other fleeting likeness that came and went, a ghost in the night of her power.

"Will you let me show you the truth?" he asked.

Bridgette started blinking quickly. "Get me out of here. Get me *out*."

Collum decided he didn't care about the young Baetalü in training, nor if they saw what was about to happen. He grabbed onto Donnachaidh and whipped the trio out of Minthame in an instant, depositing them in front of the Seolformúr. The unexpected explosion of navy whirls nearly unseated the two guards at the gate, and Bridgette felt a too-familiar wave of nausea begin to creep up her gullet the minute she realized where they were.

Her breath started to come too fast, too shakily and impossible to catch. *Why did you bring me to the Seledreám?* she thought to Collum, the panic rising in her chest. *You know I can't cross that fucking gate. Why are we here? Why is this happening to me?!*

When Donnachaidh had started speaking, she realized something prevented him from being forthright; that though he did not lie, there was an inauthenticity to his words. Bridgette sensed a sort of aura glimmering, teasing her as it hid the fyrdwisa's and herewosa's true intent. She couldn't process that sensation, that knowledge. All of her powers activated at once and grappled with one another for authority, and she couldn't control any of them. The flare of being the truth against the world and being lied to; the sierwan knowledge that she wasn't *exactly* being lied to; the very normal desire to know what the hell either of the males was talking about; and now her Craft blood feeling challenged by the energy surrounding the gate — Bridgette thought she might explode. All of her senses were heightened, and she wanted nothing more than to curl into a ball and shut everything off.

She only realized Collum wasn't standing with them anymore when one of the guards yelped out something about her glowing and drew her attention outward. Bridgette realized with mute horror that she'd walled herself off into a cocoon of purple light. The glow was new and unpredictable, having shown up twice now without a discernible trigger. Normally Collum would sense whatever caused her panic and reach to touch her. Just the brush of his fingers against hers, or a whisper of thought from him, was enough to ground her. But she felt nothing, and after a rapid twist in place, couldn't see him anywhere.

Collum! her mind-voice screamed for him, searching for him. It was like being in Palna again, too aware of her magic and unable to do anything about it; all alone in the throes of its pull.

Trust me, Starshine! His own mind-voice came to her from somewhere inside the Seledreám, only slightly quieter than if he'd been next to her. There was an undertone of anxiety in his own voice. *Think of Hlafjordstiepel.*

She was shivering inside her light. Bridgette clamped her eyes shut and tried to mentally transport herself back to that highest peak. She did her best to soothe her too-rapid breathing, inhaling through her nose and forcing the air out of her mouth, but it was impossible to calm her mind when the rest of her raged. The abyss of power in her core flared, furious that it was being tamped down, craving to lash out at whatever stood in her way. But what stood in her way wasn't Collum or Herewosa Donnachaidh, the latter of whom stood close enough to touch, guarding Bridgette where she smoldered in this strange light.

Calming herself the way she had on Hlafjordstiepel would not happen. All she could hope for was to keep the Maylemaegus at bay until Collum returned with whatever truth he promised.

The fyrdwisa had never before entered the Noble House of Fae without so much as announcing himself. He gave Herewosa Donnachaidh a warning glare, hoping the witch understood it as an instruction to keep an eye on Bridgette, and ran full force through the Seolformúr. Collum thought he must have looked absolutely mad barreling about like that, but he had neither time nor mental capacity to care at the moment. He evanesced from the Seledreám grounds into the building itself on a rabid hunt for

Emi-Joye, for only she had the ability and permission to reveal the Fórsaí Armada's plans to the Bright Star.

It had been a long time since he utilized such speed. Elves were quicker than witches and far faster than humans, their natural speed eclipsed only by those of the Baetalü and Unicorns. The fyrdwisa was a mere blur to most of those he rushed past as he searched the halls of the complex for the ambassadora, or even Apostine. He resisted the urge to call her name, though he had a feeling he was wasting time with this blind run.

"Fyrdwisa!"

Collum skidded to a stop and whirled around, chest heaving, to face Hafiz. "Well met," he gasped out to the guard. "I'm in a bit of a hurry, Hafiz, but how may I assist you?"

"I observed that, Fyrdwisa, and it is for that reason I called your name. It is I who wish to assist you, as there appears to be a disturbance at the gate. I assume that your haste has something to do with this situation?"

"Yes, I am afraid it does."

Hafiz furrowed his brow. His wings flapped tightly where he hovered. "What is it that you are looking for?"

"It is not a what, but a whom. I need to speak with Ambassadora Vetur, immediately."

"Please remain here," Hafiz instructed him. "I will return momentarily with her location."

The fyrdwisa watched Hafiz fly off nearly as fast as he himself had run through the halls. Collum tapped his feet anxiously. Hafiz's words about there being a disturbance at the Seolformúr did not sit well. *I'll be back soon, Starshine. Please do not fret.*

Where are you? Her mind-voice still sounded frantic when she replied, and Collum balled his fists by his sides. He hated the idea of her panicking, and loathed more that he was the cause of it to an extent.

I am inside the Seledreám, he thought back, careful not to tell her for whom he searched. He had a feeling if she knew it was Emi-Joye, a whole host of bad blood would resurface, despite how friendly they'd become. He hoped Bridgette wouldn't press him further.

Collum was not sure for how long he leaned against the wall, waiting for Hafiz to return. Every second seemed to last an hour; the worst sort of time-blindness. When he finally saw the guard appear at the far end of the hall, Collum started jogging toward him. They exchanged no words as Hafiz turned around in the air and beckoned the fyrdwisa follow, leading him rapidly through the building until they reached a secluded conference room which was quite chill compared to the area around it.

"You'll find her here," Hafiz whispered. "But be aware, she is meeting with the Fairy of All Fairies."

"Thank you, Hafiz." Collum didn't wait to see if the Fairy acknowledged his gratitude. He simply pushed his way into the room, where he overheard a split-second of angry conversation before the two females realized they'd been interrupted.

"Fyrdwisa!" Aristoces said, surprised. She glanced at Emi-Joye, who looked both confused and relieved. "Your timing is impeccable, as I was just speaking to the ambassadora about her involvement with the vademecums."

Oh, shit, Collum thought. He'd have to apologize to Emi-Joye for that at some point, for coming clean about their mysterious doings in Maluridae Wood, without telling her that he and Bridgette had done so.

"Well met, Ceannairí," the Elf said. "I do apologize for impeding your meeting. However, in circumstances not entirely unrelated to the vademecums, I require the ambassadora to come with me immediately."

He said something of the sort that first day he met Bridgette face-to-face. Collum meant it more, for if Emi-Joye was unwilling to follow him of her own accord, he'd do something he never would with Bridgette. Though the Bright Star would always get to choose her path, the Boireannach was sworn by pre-sealed fate to follow. Collum was willing to drag her — kicking, screaming, and flitting in midair — down to the Seolformúr.

"What's wrong?" the ambassadora asked.

"You need to have a conversation with the Liluthuaé," he muttered, aware the door was still open behind them. Aware, too, that Aristoces had no idea what else her young prodigy and the ambestre had been up to.

"About what?"

Collum didn't have time for her demands, nor a full explanation. "Consider this your first official responsibility as the Boireannach and come with me. This is not a matter of choice."

Emi-Joye gave him a bewildered look just before he grabbed her around the waist and whisked them away, both unprepared to face the turmoil of magic that awaited them outside the gate.

~ 71 ~

"You?" Bridgette choked, bewildered enough at Emi-Joye's sudden appearance with Collum that her magic faltered, and she gained control of herself for a moment. "What does this have to do with *you*?"

The Fairy looked just as lost. "I would appreciate it if someone told me what was going on, and why I was so rudely evanesced out of a meeting with Aristoces."

She glanced at Bridgette, then noticed who stood a few feet behind the Elfling: Herewosa Donnachaidh. Emi-Joye's eyes widened as she put two and two together. There would be little cause for the leader of Minthame to appear in Fairevella, accompanied both by Bridgette and a hefty dose of secrecy, unless the Bright Star had found out about the Fórsaí Armada.

"Well. That's unfortunate," Emi-Joye said.

Two words were all it took for Bridgette's eyes to shift, for her to understand that Heáhwolcen's armed forces were surreptitiously plotting a war they weren't even supposed to know was a threat, and that Emi-fucking-Joye was in charge of it.

Bridgette leapt at her.

It was the closest she'd ever come to having an out-of-body experience, fully embracing her Maylemaegus. Had she wanted to, she could have controlled it. Bridgette knew that; she'd known it for a while. But it was far, far more satisfying to lose herself in this raw magic, to let the air lift her and the wind sing a haunting melody in her ears as she danced with her amethyst blade, as though she'd always known how to do so.

The Boireannach moved, the Liluthuaé mirrored. Emi-Joye's two daggers were in her hands the moment Bridgette jumped. She hadn't consciously grabbed them, but she crossed the blades in front of each other to dissuade Bridgette's hands from going for her throat. The Bright Star's own knife thrust forward as if to split them, but that was a smart distraction. As her blade-hand aimed for Emi-Joye's daggers, Bridgette's other arm reared backward and she rammed her elbow up between the Fairy's wrists, forcing Emi-Joye's crossed arms to aim the knives toward herself instead of at the Bright Star.

The unanticipated movement was so quick that Emi-Joye had to turn her head to one side to avoid her own knives slicing into her face. She turned to the left, arms still raised, and round-kicked Bridgette, who hoisted herself in the air to avoid being hit. Emi-Joye swung her right arm out as her leg landed. The Fairy quickly stepped backward to regain her balance. She twisted her knives so both blades were pointed straight at the Liluthuaé.

The challenge of facing a fully trained Fairy was delicious. Bridgette moved on instinct, stepping toward Emi-Joye, using her knees and elbows with as much ease as she did her amethyst blade. The knife was an extension of her body, an extra-sharp limb. Such was the culmination of these months of held grudges, of neither female wanting anything to do with one another, of a tentative friendship fastened together by the thinnest of strands. What smidgen of faith established after Wales demolished in this clash of Fae and Elfling, both overflowing with magic beyond their understanding.

Bridgette's advantage was the longer awareness of what power she harbored. Ever since she caused rain to fall inside the Maudlins' home, she suspected that her father's Craft blood was related to the Maylemaegus. She didn't understand it fully, hadn't made tracks to explore it yet — but she knew it to be true in some form. That blood coursed through her veins as she twisted her body to avoid one of Emi-Joye's blades. It pounded in her heart while she switched her footwork, tiger-stepping forward to throw off the Boireannach's attack. Bridgette was truth, she was sky, she was infinity.

She hadn't stopped glowing, though at some point the pulsating border of purple light drew itself closer to her body. When her dagger next collided with one of Emi-Joye's — with such force that it set both of their teeth shaking as the two whirled off one another and reset their stances — Bridgette noticed that her opponent glowed as well, the pulsation of power matching the Fairy's heartbeat. The Elfling gave herself a moment to catch her breath as she surveyed the blue light. Her eyes met those of Emi-Joye's. She knew hers were the dark shade of purple and saw the Fairy's were dead-still orbs of ice blue.

Bridgette cocked her head to one side, waiting. She twirled her knife lazily in her right hand, left fist held to guard her face, and watched. She could be patient: if nothing else, being in Palna taught her that.

Emi-Joye regarded her. A mere three feet stood between them, the purple-shrouded Bright Star and herself. She didn't know where this anger came from, but the Fairy was done being a scapegoat for everything that pissed the Liluthuaé off. She would not let Bridgette get the best of her this time. She twitched forward, an attempt to fake the Elfling into moving, which would give Emi-Joye the advantage to attack, but Bridgette simply raised a brow.

It was as if she said, "I fucking dare you."

The Fairy dared. She gave a split-second warning, a cold-eyed smile, before she threw one of her knives into the dirt at their feet. Bridgette's eyes flicked down, and it was enough for Emi-Joye to flip forward and stab the second blade into the back of the Elfling's fist. Bridgette screamed, more with rage than with pain, and surged. The scent of her blood made the Maylemaegus within her wail.

Whip, she thought, and the air obeyed.

She commanded the ropes of concentrated element to lash out, forcing the Fairy back, making Emi-Joye's attention fall to fighting an invisible foe. With her remaining knife, the ambassadora sliced at the gusts of air that blew for her. Her free hand flew up and out as she guarded her face, ducking to avoid the villainous tendrils that Bridgette sent to her. Emi-Joye shouted, annoyed and unsure of where the air weaponry originated from, and completely aware that she couldn't stop it.

Bridgette used the distraction to her advantage. The Elfling waited until Emi-Joye was angled to the side, uselessly striking air that dissipated at her impact and reformed into tighter cords that grabbed for her wrists and legs. The Fairy's eyes were turned away as Bridgette started stalking toward her, twirling her amethyst hilt with such composure that the movement looked native, not learned.

Hold, Bridgette thought.

Emi-Joye shrieked as a coiled rope of air latched onto one ankle. She tripped forward, off-balance, directly into the trap that waited. She was frozen, prone, caught at an ungainly angle halfway to the ground. One arm outstretched, fingers barely able to hold onto her knife; the other jerked to one side. Her wings flapped hard behind her, trying to free her from the air that Bridgette controlled.

The Fairy glared up at Bridgette, her face level with the Elfling's thighs.

Bridgette simply smiled down at her. She knelt to meet Emi-Joye's gaze, then put the tip of her blade under the Fairy's chin. As she stood, the air followed her movement, raising the Fairy back into a standing position. It, too, acted as an extension of the Liluthuaé's very soul, and she relished in this connection to it.

Her blade was so gentle underneath the Fairy's jaw that it could have been a cold caress. She leaned close to Emi-Joye's ear, her words a whisper that sent a shiver of pleasure and daring up the Fairy's spine.

"Verta verestä, Boireannach," Bridgette murmured in a voice that wasn't quite her own. She grabbed the struggling Fairy around the neck, her own blood flowing from the wound deep in her hand, and deftly swept the tip of her knife across the join of Emi-Joye's throat.

The Fairy screamed.

The pitch of her shrill shattered the vortex of wind that neither female realized their magic had spun up around them. It collapsed with an almighty gasp, rippling wind through the winter-dry grass and dirt on the road. The ropes of air snapped away and Emi-Joye fell to her knees. Her second knife dropped to the ground as she raised both hands to stymie the blood that graced the shallow cut left by the Liluthuaé, dripping down her neck like a macabre choker of garnet and malice.

Collum was on Bridgette in an instant, his own magic wrapping around her so tightly and fast that she could've been in a straitjacket. It was instinct, both to protect her and to stop her, because what she'd just done …

There was a flurry of activity as Aristoces, Apostine, and Trystane rushed to the side of the wounded Boireannach. Collum had never seen such fury in any of their expressions. He'd summoned Trystane the second that wind tunnel formed, a colossal structure of air and dust that barricaded Bridgette and Emi-Joye inside. He only knew what was happening because of the ísenwaer, so completely in tune was he to his Starshine. Her mind was his, and his was hers. Through this connection he caught flashes of movement and understanding; could hear her thoughts as she planned her moves and processed those of Emi-Joye against her. Collum had been able to hear inside Emi-Joye's head too, but his gift was muted by the almighty roar that was Bridgette's mind-voice.

Collum stepped in front of the heavily breathing Liluthuaé, who needed no bodyguard despite his deity-gifted nature to be one for her, and stared across at the injured Fairy, who refused to move her hands to let anyone look at the cut. As he watched, the quiet drip from Bridgette's stabbed hand was as loud to him as a crashing waterfall.

Trystane was livid. The ard rialóir, who stood taller than Collum to begin with, now seemed to tower over the fyrdwisa as he stepped before the pair.

"What in the seven deity-damned fucking hells just happened?" Trystane whispered, his voice sharp, unhurried. His question was directed at Bridgette, the Elfling still protected by Collum's magic. Her eyes flickered between shades of purple.

Collum trusted that she wouldn't break through his bonds. She could if she tried hard enough.

"Tell the Boireannach to lift her spell from Donnachaidh and I," he told his Elven brother.

"Fuck you, Collum," Trystane spat, and the fyrdwisa winced at the tone, at the insult. "She nearly beheaded the ambassadora, and you want to make demands on her behalf?"

"Tell Ambassadora Vetur to remove her spell," Collum replied. He refused to back down. "If she does not, there will be no explanations. As it stands now, we are unable to speak freely due to her magic."

There was a glitter of fury in Trystane's opalescent flecks. "We're going inside."

"Bridgette cannot cross the Seolformúr."

Trystane huffed a laugh. "She can choke on her own vomit this time. Take her into the Seledreám, Fyrdwisa. That's an order."

"No."

"Collum." Bridgette's voice was thin, so tight was his spell.

He turned to her automatically, and the pleading in her eyes gutted him. She would cross the gate if she needed to, but the pain it would cause her was too much for him to consider. The Elf glanced over his shoulder at Trystane. He gave the ard rialoír a long once-over, then sighed.

"I'll make this up to you," Collum said. Before Trystane could so much as step forward, the fyrdwisa and Liluthuaé were gone.

~ 72 ~

"Deity damn them both!" Trystane cursed at the now-empty spot where Collum and Bridgette evanesced from. "Nehemi may get herself a new fyrdwisa after all if he keeps this act up."

He ran a hand through his hair, mussing the undone platinum blonde that had been a braid until the wind whipped his leather tie off. Hearing Emi-Joye scream like that did more than tug on empathetic heartstrings. It jerked him alive, though he'd been unaware he was in any sort of stupor to begin with. Then the blood? The Fairy still crouched to the ground, hands up under her jaw, whimpering. She refused to move, afraid that should her grip shift, she'd bleed out.

"I'm apt to kill them both for this," the Elf muttered. He walked across the small circle and knelt next to Emi-Joye. "Let me see it, Ambassadora."

"No —"

The ard rialóir would not accept that answer. He took her wrists in each hand and gently tugged them apart, though the Fairy tried mightily to stop him. Trystane breathed a sigh of relief. The cut was shallow, hardly deeper than a scratch, but enough to draw blood.

"You're going to be alright," he assured her. "Let us take you inside where we can properly have this healed, yes?"

Trystane glanced over her head to where Aristoces and Apostine each perched by Emi-Joye's shoulders. Herewosa Donnachaidh looked as though he might be sick. He was the odd one out here, with no idea about the Boireannach or Maylemaegus, nor the propensity for Emi-Joye and Bridgette to spontaneously form walls of wind these days. Trystane was not sure why the male was here. The ard rialóir was summoned with such a sense of urgency that Trystane dropped everything and evanesced, only to arrive to find Donnachaidh and Collum on either side of the columnar vortex, which he surmised quickly enough encased both Ambassadora Vetur and the Bright Star.

He reached his arms out and scooped Emi-Joye up with such care that Apostine gave him a shrewd look, one Trystane chose not to acknowledge. Together, they walked through the Seolformúr. Aristoces led them to an outbuilding on the grounds.

"I shall find both a téitheoir and a lacnian to aid us," she told Trystane after they got the ambassadora settled on a soft bed of plush pillows. "A wound of that nature may require sealing, not just a healing poultice, to avoid scarring and pain."

The thought of Emi-Joye forever being physically scarred from this made the Elf's stomach flip over. He knew it was a small blessing that the long slice was both razor-thin and all-but superficial. A part of him marveled at the skill Bridgette must have displayed to injure her like that — it was an intentional show of dominance more than an attempt to mortally harm the Fairy. And Bridgette! He blinked, remembering. Bridgette had been bleeding, too.

"Emi-Joye, can you tell us what occurred, and how you got this injury?" Trystane asked. He turned to look at her, his brow furrowed with concern. "There was another wind wall. We could not see past it to observe what was happening."

"I was attacked," she muttered, embarrassed. "Bridgette attacked me, and we fought blade-to-blade and fist-against-fist."

"Why did she attack you?" Apostine wondered aloud.

Emi-Joye gave him an exhausted sigh. "I am not sure how, but she became aware of a recent event that made her angry. She took that anger out on me."

Apostine took one glance toward Herewosa Donnachaidh, whose subtle nod was enough confirmation of what the "recent event" must have been.

"Ah," the ambestre said. "And who drew first blood?"

"I did."

"How?" Trystane asked her. "Is that why she chose to hurt you?"

"I stabbed her in the back of her hand," Emi-Joye explained. She carefully patted the warm, wet cloth Aristoces had placed across her neck to quell the bleeding until healers arrived. "I suppose so. Bridgette did the strangest thing while we were in there. We were both experiencing intense power, speed, and agility, as well as this queer sense of being able to know roughly how one another moved within our created ring. But I was only hurt because she used *air* to hit me, distract me, then finally to bind me."

The ard rialóir blanched. "She used air? What do you mean?"

"I mean precisely what I say, Ceannairí," Emi-Joye said. "I watched with my own two eyes and felt with my own magic as Bridgette voicelessly commanded air to be used as a weapon against me."

"That is impossible." It was Aristoces who spoke, and her voice, for the first time in any of their lives, sounded worried. "Elements cannot be commanded. They are our allies, our partners. We work with their powers to fuel our own."

"I speak truthfully," Emi-Joye whispered. "I did not know how to fight it. I tried. And as witnessed here, I failed. Once I was pinned and she held her knife to my throat, Bridgette said something I've never heard before, the phrase 'verta verestä'. I don't know what it means."

Apostine was still stuck on the fact that Bridgette convinced the air to attack his ambassadora, but to then hear that she did it without speaking? He sat on the floor and put his face in his hands, shaken. "How could she do such things? She cannot do magic like any of us can, not even Elven magic. I cannot fathom that Bridgette now has abilities that surpass ours like that."

"That saying …" Donnachaidh's voice trailed off, hesitant. "It is an old Nordic phrase. It means 'blood for blood'."

He looked up at the ceiling, needing to pause for a moment before speaking again. "Blood for blood, verta verestä; such was the maxim of Baize Sammael."

Across Heáhwolcen, Bridgette too had been laid upon a bed with plush pillows, though this was her own, and she shook so violently that it was all Collum could do to hold her still enough to guide her under the covers. He released his binding spell the moment they arrived in his living room, then had to grab the Elfling before she collapsed in a heap.

"Let me see your hand," he said, then reached for it before she could stop him. As if she could try, really, she was in such a state. The blood had started to clot, but Emi-Joye had gotten her good. The wound went halfway through Bridgette's hand.

Collum winced as he turned her hand over, ensuring her palm was intact. "I'm going to find you a healer, Starshine. This is not going to be a quick fix, even with your Elven blood."

She said nothing, just kept shivering under the covers. Her gaze swayed side to side, as if she was trying to ground herself and gain recognition of her surroundings. He wondered if she'd gone into shock. Regardless, she needed help and he didn't have the skills to aid her. Collum leaned forward to kiss her on the forehead. He gave her non-injured hand a squeeze of comfort.

"I'll be back soon, I promise."

It hurts, she thought to him, finally fixating on his eyes. *It's throbbing. I don't feel right.*

"I am going to Cyneham Breonna to find Njahla," Collum murmured. "Her mother, Ilori, is going to help you. Just stay here and breathe, please. You are home. You are safe."

His words echoed in her head as the fyrdwisa leaned forward again, this time brushing his lips across hers. "You're going to be alright. You're safe now."

As he vanished in the familiar whirls of navy dark, Collum couldn't remember the last time he'd done so much wild evanescing. He'd been to three countries today already, operating solely on adrenaline and the steaming mug of black coffee he had for breakfast. Trystane was going to come after him soon, he knew. He probably deserved some sort of admonition, but for Hecate's sake, Emi-Joye hurt Bridgette too, and yet the male was more worried about an ambassadora than he was the Liluthuaé. Plus, it would have been extremely unproductive to force Bridgette into the Seledreám in the condition she was in after the confrontation. She could barely speak as it was, much less give everyone a full report while she was under the warring energies that happened whenever she got too close to the Seolformúr.

Collum would take Bridgette to the Caisleán later, when she was back to herself, and ask that Emi-Joye and Apostine be present as well. The Bright Star needed to hear the full explanation about the Fórsaí Armada's plans, and only the Fairies were able to share what motivated them to take this matter into their own hands. But now, he needed to focus on healing Bridgette. That required the Elf he evanesced in front of, who was rummaging through a disheveled pile of what looked to be schoolbooks.

"Njahla!" Collum called to her, foregoing formalities. He zoomed to stand next to the shelf she was reorganizing. "I need your mother, now."

She glanced up from the stack of texts. "My mother? For what purpose, Fyrdwisa?"

"Bridgette has been injured," he murmured. "She and Ambassadora Vetur got into a bit of an altercation."

Njahla tapped her long, painted nails on the bookshelf. "An 'altercation', really? Would you care to tell me more about this?"

"Not really, no, but the ambassadora is privy to some information the Bright Star wants. Instead of sharing it, Emi-Joye remained silent, and our favorite ancient magical powers came out to play," Collum told her. "They both wounded each other. I'm not sure how bad Emi-Joye's was, but Trystane took one look at Emi-Joye's injury and went on the warpath. I took

Bridgette back to our apartment before he got a chance to drag her kicking and screaming into the Seledreám for questioning."

The female gave him an appraising look. "How much trouble am I going to get into by helping you, and why my mother?"

"You know why, Njahla. Your mother is the only one who knows anything about Emi-Joye and Bridgette's extraneous magic, and I'd rather keep that knowledge within a tight circle of trusted beings," the fyrdwisa replied. "Put the blame on me for this. You won't be in any trouble. But though I cannot speak for the ambassadora's injury, Bridgette's is a deep stab wound in the back of her hand. It's likely going to scar no matter what, but I do not know enough about wound dressing to do much other than clean it. Which, now that I think about it, I neglected to do in my panic."

Njahla sighed. She had a soft spot for him, but a bigger soft spot for Bridgette. "Damn you, Collum Andoralain. Go wash her up and I'll summon my mother for you."

He heaved out a relieved breath. "Thank you —"

"Don't thank me yet," she snapped, and shooed him away. "I will call in this debt if I need to, trust me."

Collum smiled, grateful. "You're a gods-send, Njahla. Call in whatever debt you wish."

"Go, Collum."

He bowed his head and evanesced back to the apartment, where he found Bridgette in the same position he'd left her, thankfully. She seemed to have regained more control of her breath, at least. Her lungs expanded and contracted in soft, even waves.

I need to clean your hand, Starshine, he thought to her.
Mmhmm.

Collum smiled, thankful beyond words that the only injury she sustained was able to be healed. He fetched a bowl from the kitchen and filled it with warm water, then soaped up a cotton cloth. Bridgette winced as he dabbed at the cut, wetting and wiping away dried blood, the active flow diminished to a mere trickle. He should have told her to put pressure on it while he was gone.

There was a soft knock at his door a short time later, and Collum left the now-calm Bright Star's side to let Ilori in.

"Mine daughter tells me one of your comrades was wounded by a knife?" the female said as she followed Collum to Bridgette's bedroom.

"Yes," he replied. "The Fairy you healed last year, Ambassadora Vetur, stabbed her in the back of the hand. It's a decent-size wound, made with a double-edged blade, going about half an inch deep. I do not believe any major blood vessels were involved, but I do worry about nerve and musculature damage."

Ilori put a comforting hand on his shoulder. "Worry not, Fyrdwisa. I will take care of her."

~ 73 ~

The Elfling wasn't sure what woke her, but when she next opened her eyes, there were both a strong, musty odor of anise in the room and a loud, incessant rapping at the front door. She registered that she was in her bed, she was alone, and it was daylight outside, though for how long she'd been asleep, she had no clue. Her hand itched. When she reached to scratch it, she noticed it was wrapped in a cloth bandage.

She wrinkled her nose. That's where the smell came from.

Bundy? Her mind-voice reached for Collum. She heard his actual voice, presumably talking to whoever had knocked on the door, but couldn't make out anything being said. There were two or three other voices, one male and the others female. She vaguely remembered someone coming in to fix up her hand, but it was all a daze.

Bridgette gave herself a moment to stretch in bed, muscles aching, and then heaved herself up. Her hand gave a gentle throb of protest. Bridgette looked down and realized she was no longer in the fitted leggings and long-sleeved top she'd worn to Minthame, which was the last thing she remembered feeling real. Everything after was too surreal to put a finger on.

After another minute of clearing her head, Bridgette opened her bedroom door and walked into the hall. She stopped nearly as soon as she started. Trystane and Collum were looking daggers at one another and whispering so furiously back and forth that the Elfling grew concerned they would start to fight in the deity-damned kitchen. She cleared her throat, and both males' heads turned in her direction.

"Good … morning?" she said, entirely unsure of what time it was. "What's going on?"

"It's afternoon," Trystane said curtly. "You owe us all an explanation."

"How long have I been asleep?" Bridgette asked.

"You've been recuperating for the better part of a week," Collum told her, and she stared at him in surprise. "The téitheoir I brought to heal you said it was imperative that you rest. You've been spelled to stay put aside from her daily visits to change your bandages, feed you, and handle your … other needs."

Bridgette gave him a *look*. "You're seriously telling me that I've been fucking Sleeping Beauty'd for like, four days, and some stranger's been taking me to the bathroom to pee?"

Despite his anger at the fyrdwisa and Liluthuaé, Trystane cracked the beginning of a smile. "I'm pleased to know that your time of recuperating has come to an end, and that you seem back to your normal self, Bright Star."

There was a tentative cough, and all three turned to see one of the females whose voices Bridgette heard earlier. It was the female she least desired to see, and the Fairy had an all-too apparent coral line of healing skin barely hidden by the collar of her turtleneck dress.

Oh, fuck me, the Elfling groaned inwardly. *You've got to be joking. I'm going back to bed.*

She turned to do just that, but Trystane stuck his foot out. "You are going to join us in the living room, and we are going to have a *civil* deity-damned *conversation* about what happened this week. That is not a request, Liluthuaé."

Bridgette crossed her arms, letting the bandaged hand stay on top. "Alright then. Let's talk." She inclined her head toward Emi-Joye. "But that one goes first."

She expected the ambassadora to protest. Instead, Emi-Joye nodded in agreement. That alone was enough to convince Bridgette to stalk the rest of the way down the hall and toss herself in her usual spot on the sofa. Collum settled next to her, while Trystane took a seat in the chair. Aurelias, the source of the second female voice, was already leaned up against a wall. Collum gave her an annoyed look as she rested the sole of one of her matte black combat boots on the surface.

Chill, Chief, the ambestre assured him silently. *I wiped them off on the rug, it's not going to scuff.*

He rolled his eyes and moved his attention to Emi-Joye, who stood nervously in the center of the circle they formed. The Fairy gazed at him, her expression pained and apologetic.

"It was never my intention to cause any of this, you know," she said, and Collum wondered at whom she aimed her apology. "Fyrdwisa, you are free from the binds which I've placed on you, and I now open the circle of discourse to include both the Bright Star and the fyrdestre. Trystane already knows, since you told him at least the bare bones of it."

And so did I, Emi-Joye thought to herself.

"All I wanted to do was convince the Fórsaí Armada that a united Heáhwolcen is worth fighting for, that our enemy is not Palnan citizens, but the Tinuviels and their supporters," Emi-Joye began. "Apostine and I called upon all the commanders to meet and begin quietly discussing strategy, preparing for war, but I wanted to do so under the pretense that Bridgette always presented — which is that very possibly, everything we've ever been told about Palnans and the country itself is a lie. We aimed to get in front of the inevitable propaganda that we suspected Nehemi would begin espousing if war became more certain. It will be useless for wígend to fight tooth and nail against Palnans for some unrequited grudge of nearly two centuries ago. That is not the objective the Bright Star aims for. It is to the Liluthuaé's purpose and to Heáhwolcen that I am loyal, for they are one and the same."

Bridgette was stunned. Whatever she expected the Fairy to say, that wasn't it.

"This meeting needed to be kept secret because I did not want Nehemi to find out. Truly, I didn't want any of the Samnung to find out, but I forgot that a member of the Samnung was also the commander of the Fyrdlytta," Emi-Joye went on, bowing her head toward Collum. "When he received the summons from Herewosa Donnachaidh, I learned the first thing Collum did was accost Trystane, believing *him* to be the one behind it. That is how the ard rialóir learned of the meeting. As for why Collum was unable to tell you everything when you asked him, I added a layer of security, enchanting everyone present against speaking about what occurred in that auditorium."

"But Herewosa Donnachaidh —" Bridgette started, confused.

Emi-Joye interrupted her thought. "Herewosa Donnachaidh incorrectly assumed that because I made this plan based on what your task was, that you were aware of it, or even the key leader of it. He informed me that he asked you about it, and it was then you seemed to get … angry."

"Yeah, no shit I was angry," Bridgette huffed. "This entire time I was back in Heáhwolcen, everyone's been hiding stuff from me. That's a pretty big deal."

"I was wrong not to tell you," the Fairy said. "I find that I have been wrong about very many things of late, and not making the time to inform you of the meetings with the Fórsaí Armada was one of them. I hope that you'll be able to attend them alongside us, so that we may all finally begin to work together and unite our magics instead of throwing them at one another."

That was a dig, and Bridgette frowned.

"There's one problem with that though," the Elfling said. "I'm going back to Palna."

Emi-Joye and Aurelias looked at Collum, then at Trystane. Both males were unphased, and the fyrdestre made a sound that could have been a growl of derision.

"You're going back?" the Fairy asked. She wasn't sure she heard right.

"Yep. Skipping town on Lupercalia. Someone doesn't want to be my sex festie bestie, so I'm out." Bridgette's voice was unexpectedly cold. "I don't know how long I'm going to be gone, but hopefully this time I'll come back with something more concrete, like plans for the resistance and important things about where exactly the Tinuviels are prepping their little army for ambush."

She went on to explain what she already told Collum and the Samnung. This time, the fyrdwisa heard no apprehension in her voice. Going back to Palna would be the right thing for all of them, and he would begrudgingly have to both accept and respect that fact.

When Bridgette finished talking, Emi-Joye let a mere handful of seconds pass before blurting out, "You're not allowed to leave without telling us how you controlled the air, and how you suddenly became far more proficient at combat than you should be."

"Right. That," Bridgette muttered. She glanced to Collum, who admittedly was as curious as the rest of them, having had the flashes of experience to know what was going on while she and Emi-Joye were trapped in their wind wall. "Well, I don't exactly know, to tell y'all the truth."

Emi-Joye scoffed in disbelief.

"No, hold up, let me explain," Bridgette said. She raised her hands in an ask for patience. "That entire fucking thing was like something else was controlling my body. I guess I can tap into my Maylemaegus, and when I do, it kinda takes over. I'm really sore actually from using feoht techniques I hadn't learned yet. As for the air? Sheesh. It was really weird. I knew it would listen, I just had to talk to it the right way."

"Can you do it now?" Trystane asked. He leaned forward in the chair. "On command?"

Bridgette shrugged. "I don't think so. I've only ever done anything like that a couple times. Once the other day, once I accidentally made it start raining in Serrabinx's house, and once I kept Collum and myself dry in the rain. I don't think I can sit here and be all, 'Hey, wind, blow all the candles out,' you know?

It wouldn't work like that."

As if to prove a point, Collum waved his hand in the air and the candles on his altar flickered. "Are you positive about that?"

She gave him a sour look. "Pretty damn sure. We all know I can't just wave my hands around and do spellwork like normal Elves can. I have to be tapped into the Maylemaegus to do it, but the only times I've ever tapped into it were total accidents. I'm not talking about Universal consciousness and subconsciousness here; I think I figured those out. I mean the creepy well of power that decided to show up and get real snappy when someone's lying."

"I would like to state that I was not lying about anything when you attacked me," Emi-Joye pointed out. "It was entirely unprovoked."

"Not exactly. It was your spell that prevented Collum from saying anything. Plus, you definitely didn't bother to tell me to begin with, so …" Bridgette let her voice trail off, as if daring the Fairy to contradict her again.

The fyrdwisa chewed the inside of his cheek. "Ambassadora, if I may ask, what was it like for you in that situation? Did you feel at all what Bridgette felt, as though there was magic within you that you allowed to take control?"

Emi-Joye hadn't wanted to talk about her own new powers she couldn't begin to understand. She glanced around the room, meeting no one's gaze in particular, before answering.

"I reacted to Bridgette's attack with my learned skills in combat. But there was, as I mentioned, an unusual sort of energy between us where we were aware of each other's movements. I felt faster and more agile than I normally am, but I would not say that I lost control in any way," she said. "The only time I felt out of myself with regards to this situation was when I first encountered my vademecum, and it was ripped from me before the full connection could be made."

Collum glanced to Bridgette. *You felt your Maylemaegus awaken more fully after you touched your vademecum, yes?* he thought to her.

Oh yeah. Big time.

I suspect that there will be more of that once the Astridsí is finally reunited with hers, and only then will we begin to comprehend the powers that the three of you will together wield.

It was not, Bridgette considered, any level of comforting thought.

~ 74 ~

"Toby?" Bridgette's voice sounded tinny. She wished it wouldn't echo so much around the cave walls. It looked like a cave, anyway. Dark and dingy, the ground spongey under her booted feet. "Toby, where are you?"

He was supposed to be here. She followed his tracks here from the house and would be the first to scold him for leaving footprints behind. Even though it helped her find him, it was a mistake. Anyone could have followed him.

Bridgette paused her search. Anyone *could* have followed him — she had only kept an eye out for his tracks, for child-sized shoeprints in the wet earth of the newly arrived rainy season. She hadn't been looking out for tracks of another, perhaps more ill-intentioned being. She cursed under her breath. She, at least, had the foresight to cover her own path, scraping away Toby's little imprints as she did.

The trail stopped at the mouth of this cavern. No side paths to indicate he went around, which meant he traipsed inside. Bridgette wondered why. She felt as though she'd wandered for hours after hearing the front door click shut. When had Toby gotten so fast? He was a mile ahead of her, at least, by the time she put on her oilskin rain jacket and boots, and slipped out behind him.

She supposed this could be a Hringur gathering, but then why would Serrabinx and Zedolph not be here as well? For that matter, why hadn't she been informed? That was the entire purpose of her coming back.

Where are you? she thought, though she knew Toby couldn't hear her mind-voice. She considered that maybe she could use Universal consciousness to find him. *Why didn't I think about that earlier?*

Out of habit, Bridgette glanced in the dark all around her. She saw nothing, smelled nothing, heard only the gentle drop of rainwater as it dappled the top of the cave architecture and trickled down the inner walls. There appeared to be no one else in the immediate surrounding. She winced as the oilskin fabric squelched under her weight when she sat down, the noise obtrusive. Bridgette crossed her legs and let her mind yawn open. She couldn't help but laugh at herself. She'd been so confused the first time she found herself in this headspace, thrust there by the magic of the True Druids. Now look at her, voluntarily drifting into the infinite.

She reached for Toby, but for the first time, felt a *block*. That was the first word that came to mind as she pictured him, opening her mind to greet him, only to be met with this stoppage point.

Where are you? she thought, unsure if he would be able to recognize her contact. *Why can't I find you?*

Bridgette didn't like this, not one bit. She stopped the specific search for Toby and focused on the cave, connecting tendrils of awareness to the moss that softened her footfalls, to the quietly creeping insects that explored its stone walls. Her consciousness snagged on something out of place. It wasn't Toby, but it was something more sentient than a plant or invertebrate.

She frowned. Her mind probed this new awareness. There was a block to it too, but less of a dead halt than what kept her from finding Toby. The Bright Star did not understand. She stood, and while keeping her mind trained on this other *being* that was in the cave with her, began to walk toward where she sensed it hiding.

The cave was so massive, so dark; an unending labyrinth of hallways that Bridgette finally realized began to spiral in on itself. Whatever the other being was, it would be in that most central room. She crept toward it, feeling more of the being's awareness come to fruition the closer she got. It was a beacon, calling to her, wanting her there. She knew it sensed her. It wasn't afraid of her, but it didn't exactly open up to her, either.

What are you? she asked it, her mind peaceful, unthreatening. *I am looking for a boy.*

The being tensed. She still couldn't see it, just feel its energy and a loose association of thoughts as it processed that another entity reached inside its head.

Where is this place? Bridgette tried again. She felt dizzy.

Come any further, strangeling, and they'll Collect you, too.

She froze. The connection stifled. The other being's message danced in her head: *They'll Collect you, too.*

"No!" Bridgette gasped out. "No, no, no — you are not going down like this, Little Lark."

She had to find that other awareness again. She had to find Toby. Bridgette could not fathom what lured the boy out of the house and all this way, deep into the belly of such a cavern. Her mind lurched for the voice that spoke to her, and she began running blindly, dashing through the endless ripple of concentric paths. Nothing. She felt nothing from the being, as if it had never been there to start with. Or perhaps it learned to block her, too. The Elfling cried out in frustration as she ran, her mind reaching for any stronghold as her feet flew under her, slipping on the damp earth.

Then there was a door, a door that appeared so unexpectedly Bridgette ran smack into it and pivoted backward down the path, ricocheting like an arcade game pinball. *Was the door the block?* she considered. *Was it open earlier, or was the other being standing outside? Is the other being some kind of guard?*

Only one way to know. Bridgette positioned her palms flat against the surface and began to push.

She was still pushing, completely entranced, when Collum and Aurelias arrived back from their dinner and found the Bright Star shoving against his closed bedroom door.

"Starshine!" Collum shouted at her. He'd never seen her like this.

The fyrdestre grabbed her by the shoulders and yanked her away from the door, which, to their dismay, was peppered with imprints in the wood, as if she'd hit and kicked at it with every ounce of force she possessed.

"Holy goddex," Aurelias murmured. She wrapped herself around the struggling Liluthuaé. "Collum, you have to wake her up; I think she's sleepwalking."

Bridgette grunted. She shoved against Aurelias' grip, turning back to the door. Collum wafted their favorite scents into the room. Bridgette's eyes were wide and unseeing. He wasn't sure she'd blinked since they walked back in the apartment.

"Starshine, come on," he said. When she didn't wake up, he gave the worried Aurelias a stern look. "I think she's either too deep in a dream, or more likely, she's immersed in Universal subconscious. She was musing about taking a nap just before you and I left. I'm going to try something that I'd prefer stay within the confines of this room — if she is dreaming, it's possible I can use my own mind to break the spell on hers."

"You can do that?" Aurelias was incredulous.

"I'm going to find out," Collum lied. He knew this would work, though the mechanics would be tricky. Bridgette invaded his dreams before. To do the reverse, with him instigating and being awake, might take some convincing. He closed his eyes and opened his mind to hers, prepared to call to her with his mind-voice, then jumped back a moment later.

"What is it?" Aurelias asked. "What happened?"

Collum's eyes were wide with surprise. "She's dreaming, but her subconscious is dreaming that she's connected to Universal consciousness. I think she managed to trap herself in somewhat of a mind-warp."

"Will she wake up?"

"Give me a moment."

The fyrdwisa put both hands on Bridgette's shoulders before he reached for her mind again. *Bridgette,* he thought to her. *You need to wake up. This isn't real.*

He repeated himself over and over, assuring her that she was safe, that whatever she dreamed was just that. He pleaded mind-to-mind for her to come back to him. Ever so slowly, he began to feel that the dream — which was just pushing against an unmovable door, from what Collum gleaned — began to flicker in clarity. He increased the intensity of the scents, nearly flavoring the room with honeysuckle and vanilla, birch and tobacco. There was even a dash of cinnamon-sugar and tart apple, which the fyrdestre offered him an appreciative hum for as she held Bridgette still.

Starshine, come back to me, Collum's mind-voice soothed the tangled thoughts of her fading nightmare. *This is a dream. There is no door, there is no dark. You are home, and you are safe. You can wake up now.*

The Elf lost track of time as he carefully eased Bridgette's mind back into wakefulness, speaking to her mind-to-mind as well as whispering aloud. It was only when Aurelias let out a gasp of relief that Collum shifted his own awareness back to the apartment. Bridgette was wide-eyed, but her eyes were normal. He nearly went to the ground in benediction.

"Toby?" she whispered. Her lilac irises met Collum's, and he held her gaze with as much care as he held her wrists now that she'd been let loose by the fyrdestre.

"Toby isn't here," he said. "You're home. You're safe. You were dreaming."

She crumpled against him and started sobbing. Collum gave Aurelias a beleaguered look as he hoisted the Bright Star into his arms, then onto his lap as he held her on the couch. The other Elfling went to the kitchen and returned a few minutes later with a bottle of passionflower elixir to soothe Bridgette's nerves, and two glasses of brandy, freshly poured from Trystane's winter solstice gift.

"This should help," Aurelias said grandly. She sat next to

Bridgette and curled into the female. "Buck up, Bright Star. What happened?"

Bridgette looked a wreck when she finally sat up and took the proffered elixir. She sniffed heavily. "I guess I fell asleep, and I must've been dreaming, but then I felt awake again. It was — I've had dreams like this before, where it felt so real it was like I was really experiencing them. I was back in Palna and Toby snuck out in the middle of the night, so I followed him to this cave. I walked in, couldn't find Toby, so I started reaching out with Universal consciousness."

The Bright Star told them everything she could remember. "I couldn't get out, and I couldn't get the door open to get to him," she said. "But Collum … the Collective has Toby. That's the only logical explanation for what just happened."

"Bridgette, I believe what just happened to you defies all logical explanation," the fyrdwisa told her gently. "You had a nightmare based on very real fears you have of losing this boy."

"Maybe you're right, but what if you're not? What if Toby has been snatched up by the Collective and they're holding him hostage in a cave like the one I dreamed up? What if this was a clue to help me find him?"

"You had a similar strange vision before you returned to Heáhwolcen, did you not?" Collum asked.

"I guess? I mean, I passed out and dreamed that y'all were in pretty rough shape without me."

"You came back to Heáhwolcen to find us spic and span, though I won't deny some of us missed you far more than others, and we were most pleased to see you again. Is it possible these vision-dreams are not visions at all?" he said.

Bridgette grinned. "Fine. You got me there. It's possible."

He took her chin in his hand. "Perhaps these so-called visions are your subconscious' way of pushing you in the direction you're supposed to go."

She leaned into his cupped palm, and Aurelias snuggled

closer behind her. They were quiet for a time, sitting like that.

"You're not going to wait for Lupercalia, are you?" the fyrdwisa asked.

"No, Bundy," Bridgette whispered. She felt more tears threaten at the corners of her eyes. "No, I'm not."

~ 75 ~

The next few days were a whirlwind.

It was utterly ridiculous, yet Collum couldn't help but feel a growing sense of envy for the little boy, his mother, and his uncle. Thoughts of losing Bridgette to this other family she established kept him awake at night. He was haunted by the mental image of her trying to force her way through his bedroom door, her eyes fixed in that shade of violent violet. To know that she was willing to go to such lengths for Toby Maudlin was a difficult truth for Collum to accept. It was in large part because of the boy that Bridgette volunteered to go back into Palna under even more questionable circumstances than she had before, now with her disappearing act to answer for, too.

There wasn't much time until she left again. It wasn't that much sooner than her original plan to go back on Lupercalia, but even the loss of a couple days set Collum's teeth on edge. He should have been more at peace knowing that despite her lackluster feoht training, the Maylemaegus gave Bridgette enviable skills if she needed to take on an unexpected opponent. He should have been able to breathe easier now that, thanks to her connections to Universal consciousness and subconsciousness, they had a better way of being able to contact one another across the Ballamúr.

He was not. If anything, Collum was more aware than ever of the threats she might face, and of her own volition, she'd face them alone. Two nights ago, he was so plagued with insomnia that Collum woke Bridgette from a dead sleep in the middle of the night and forced her to practice using Universal consciousness to find him while he moved from room to room.

She was pleasantly shocked to learn that after he stepped out of her bedroom, he'd evanesced to Çeofilye. They were able to contact one another as easily as if he was in his home office. Collum suspected that the communication would become one-sided once Bridgette crossed over. Though he would be unable to use their covenant bracelets the normal way, she could find him via her mental gifts.

"I want you to have a regular checkpoint with me," he told her one morning. "You must pick the time and day, but once a week I need to hear your voice. The Samnung will want to know what is going on, and I, for one, want to make sure you are well."

"Are you worried about me, Bundy?" She tried to make her tone teasing, but it was a mask. Bridgette was worried sick that Toby either *had* been taken by the Collective, or that something bad was set to befall him or his family.

"Yes. I am," Collum replied. "I dislike not knowing where you are or when you're to return. I dislike even less that I will be unable to aid you should you need it."

"Thank goodness our little friend Maylemaegus decided to show up and do some work. Hey, listen, I was thinking —"

"Absolutely not," the Elf said sternly, guessing what she was about to ask. "You're leaving the vademecum here. What happens if you run into one of the Tinuviels while you have it on you?"

"Fine," Bridgette pouted. She felt her magic grumble, displeased as she was at being denied. "Just promise you won't take Nehemi to the wood until I get back, okay?"

"I will not. I know you want to understand what the Boireannach and Astridsí roles mean before we upend all of our history and throw the three of you into a pit together. I will respect this and ensure that Emi-Joye and Trystane do as well," Collum promised.

Tensions had cooled between the four of them, though Bridgette intentionally avoided doing anything that could put her in the same vicinity as the ambassadora or the ard rialóir. Other than a stunning Unicorn ride through a late winter rainstorm and regular visits from Ilori, who came to check on Bridgette's still-recovering hand, the Elfling continued to stick close to

Collum's apartment. Her mood was brighter these days despite her introverted activities. No longer did she seem as lost and sad. Now that she had a set of expectations, a timeline, and a bit of experience, there was a newfound determination in her. Bridgette's tendency to flounder and second-guess herself only prevailed when she didn't have those things.

Collum didn't want her to flounder. He wanted her to do everything she was destined for, and on top of that, anything and everything she desired for herself beyond what her responsibilities as Liluthuaé demanded. Collum wanted Bridgette to believe in herself as much as he did. He never doubted her — only worried about her.

It was for selfish reasons he chose to worry. As he sat on the foot of the bed, wrestling with déjà vu and watching her decide which pairs of socks to bring with her, Collum decided to give himself grace for that selfishness. He would not beat himself up for caring so deeply for another being. It was not the worst thing to let himself worry about losing someone, about wanting something for his own for a change. This did not make him weak or prone: it made him alive.

Collum relished in that revelation. He silently prayed to whatever deities might be listening to keep his Starshine safe, to guide her from the moment she crossed over the border later that night until she returned to Eckenbourne.

"What are you doing?" Bridgette's bemused question drew his gaze back to reality.

"Requesting that the gods and goddesses, and whatever otherworldly guardians might exist, do everything they can to keep you safe, of course." His smile was soft as he looked Bridgette over, from the top of her half-dried mess of titian hair to the calloused soles of her bare feet. "I suppose it's rare these days for such prayers to reach them."

"I think I worry enough about myself to cover that anxiety for both of us," Bridgette replied. "But you really are cute when you get all panicky about me."

"Have you met yourself? I'm always panicking about you, Starshine." Collum guarded his face as she tossed a balled-up sleepshirt at his head. "For one, your aim with projectiles is atrocious."

"Hey!"

"As you said the other day, thank goodness for your Maylemaegus," he grinned. "Though I do hope it will stay under wraps unless you have no other choice but to use it."

Bridgette rolled her eyes. "It's not really using it. More like becoming it. Kind of hard to explain since I keep only doing it by accident."

"Then I hope you have no need to become it."

She leaned over the pile of clothes yet to be folded into her bag and kissed the fyrdwisa's cheek. "Same, trust me. As excited as I am to tour Düoria and the palace, I'd really prefer not to give Ydessa and Eryth any reason to find out that I exist."

Bridgette had no intentions of alerting any Palnans to her arrival, and so chose this time to cross the pair of boundary walls after dark. Her farewell with Collum was more subdued than before, both inwardly agreeing to keep their emotions close to themselves. Parting would be sorrowful enough without the addition of tears or words that might make it harder for the Liluthuaé to leave. A frantic, less-patient part of her wanted him to beg for her to stay; to wrap her in his arms and thread his fingers through her hair and refuse to let go. But Collum Andoralain would never forsake Heáhwolcen for his own purposes. It was why he went to Nashville with Lucilla, why he threw himself into work to avoid processing his parents' deaths, why he kept Bridgette at arm's length so often. In a way, it was admirable to see how dedicated he was to his country, his job, his fellow Elves. In another way, it was exhausting to feel as though she was on the very bottom of Collum's priority list.

It was far, far easier to keep these thoughts to herself than try to have that particular conversation, especially right before she was to leave.

They took their time going to Bondrie that evening. Collum surprised Bridgette with a final Unicorn ride, much drier than the one they'd taken a few days earlier. Mithrilken and Eloise intentionally paced themselves to a fast walk, and though it was far quicker a journey than it would have been on foot or even horseback, they still rode for several hours. It was quiet, chilly, and none of them said very much, simply enjoyed each other's company.

Bridgette soaked up as much of the magic around her as she could during their travel. She might be willing to do a questionable number of things on behalf of Palna's innocent civilians, but there was little love lost between her and the world the Tinuviels ruled over. It was their doing that caused the atmosphere inside the Ballamúr to be so strained. Bridgette's paramount desire at the end of this conflict was for Palna to have the same peaceful, easy feeling as the rest of Heáhwolcen.

For it to have the same seasonality of weather would be nice, too. Aside from whatever magic aided the protected lands, the remainder of Palna was strictly controlled by the Samnung's barrier. The columnar wall was capped by the Meridian of the continent's atmospheric bubble, and from what Bridgette understood, unable to be penetrated by precipitation in the same way the rest of the magical world was. She surmised that was so no Palnans would be tempted to fly up and over to escape. Thanks to the weather phenomena, Bridgette knew her reappearance would coincide with the country's rainy season, which stretched from February or March through about July.

Though the weather on the Bondrie side of the Samnung wall was cool and dry for the moment, Trystane stepped forward from the gathered circle of supporters who came to wish Bridgette well. The ard rialóir handed her a folded parcel of leathery dark gold fabric.

"To keep the rain at bay," he murmured, and she realized it was a hooded oilskin jacket.

Collum considered it a peace offering and he was glad Bridgette accepted it with gratitude and without question. It made them both think of the dream inside the cave, for in her dark visualization, the Bright Star had worn a similar piece of clothing to keep the rain at bay.

She slipped the jacket on. Eloise gave her an approving nicker — Trystane chose a shade of gold that complemented the eyes he was about to glamour yet again.

"I feel like an assassin, or maybe like I'm trying to steal the US Constitution or something," Bridgette joked. "Thanks, Trystane. I have a feeling I'll get a lot of use out of this."

"You're most welcome, Liluthuaé."

Once her eyes were again protected from giving away her sierwan gift — and hopefully her Maylemaegus as well — the master swordswoman secured Bridgette and Collum's newest jewelry to their wrists. The third of the matching covenant bracelets was spelled and placed safely in the inner pocket of Bridgette's new rain jacket, after assurances that the band would size and seal itself perfectly to Serrabinx's wrist once Bridgette put it on her.

The bracelets, Bridgette noticed right away, were fashioned of three strands of deep red cord, a single wooden bead in the middle. The same design was burned into the wood on each one.

"It is a symbol of one of the Bondrians' ancestral people, the Hopi'sinom," Corria explained. "The broken arrow represents peace."

Bridgette would have hugged her, was it not for the master swordswoman's stoic stature that never seemed very open to such a show of affection or appreciation. The Elfling turned her wrist in the glow of witchlight lanterns, admiring her small but growing stack of covenants.

A mark of truly being a citizen of Heáhwolcen, she thought to Collum. *How the hell do I use the one with Serrabinx?*

"To use them, if you have the same sort of magic most of us do, and I suspect is in Serrabinx's blood as well, all you do is put two fingers around the bracelet and bring that being's face to mind. Serrabinx will feel a connection. It might be slight; I am unsure how strong any magic of this caliber will be within the confines of Palna," Collum replied aloud. "When that connection is made, she will be able to think a message directly to you, and one day to either of us, when no walls separate the magic in Heáhwolcen. On your end, when she makes that contact, you will feel your band tingle or burn. The sensation differs on whom the communication is between. To receive what is being sent, you must also use the gesture of wrapping your fingers around it."

"That is definitely what I tried to do with our covenant, by the way," Bridgette said dryly.

He nicked her nose with his thumb. "I have no doubt, Bright Star. But you will have to use your own powers to communicate back. Your abilities supersede this magic."

You always know how to make me feel less shitty about not being able to do magic the way everyone else can, she thought to him.

In a rare public show of affection, Collum held her bracelet-adorned wrist in his hand and interlocked their fingers. They felt the eyes of everyone in that circle watching them, curious, aware perhaps for the first time that there was far more between these two than being simply colleagues and friends.

Do not ever feel as though your magic is less than, Bridgette Conner, the Elf thought to her. He pulled her hand to his lips and kissed it, letting the silver beads of their shared covenant warm against his breath. *Your magic is more than any of us could ever dream. It does not look like ours, nor should we expect it to. You will never stop astonishing me with your ability to be who you are, to wield such magic, more ancient and powerful than anyone else's alive, and to do so with an honest, kind heart.*

"I'll talk to you tomorrow," she promised, feeling that honest, kind heart soar at his silent words.

"And every Tuesday?" Collum prodded her, a reminder of their chosen day for weekly reports and a check on her wellbeing.

"Every Tuesday. Probably a lot more frequently than that, too."

The expression on his face tightened. He gripped both her wrists so hard that had she not been half-Elf herself, he might have snapped them. "Be safe, Starshine."

"Collum, I —"

The fyrdwisa let go of her hands and reached for her face, the move so swift it made her stop talking. He ran his thumbs over the panes of her cheeks, her jaw, their gazes latched onto one another.

"I know, Bridgette," he whispered. "I know."

~ 76 ~

How was it possible to want someone with her nearly every second of every day, and simultaneously understand that where she went, he could not follow? Bridgette had to wrench herself away, pull her face from Collum's hands and walk across the Samnung wall. She was through it before half the gathered audience processed that she left, and the tears started moments later. She could do this. Of course she could!

But she didn't have to like it.

The Ballamúr greeted her with a ripple of joyous sensation as she touched it and whispered hello.

"I told you I'd be back," Bridgette murmured, and she tasted salt on her lips. "I still don't know what you said to me when I left, that message in Gemaere, but I think I'll be able to figure it out. Thank you for keeping the Samnung and Lessiel safe, for letting them cross and trusting that I do not come or send others in with any intention of hurting anyone."

The ripple paused. Bridgette heard voices and assumed she was about to be followed through the Samnung wall. If she didn't go through the Ballamúr this very second, she would throw herself at Collum and tell him no, that she didn't want to go back; that all she wanted was to live an ignorant, peaceful life in Heáhwolcen and pretend that the problems of Palna and the hypocrisy of its imprisonment didn't exist. He wouldn't judge her for it.

He would, however, figure out a way to go to Palna himself and do this job in her stead. She refused to let that happen, and so she stepped through the glimmering wall.

The crossing once again upended her. Bridgette had to kneel for a moment afterward to catch her breath and get a handle on her surroundings. She had absolutely no idea where she was, even after letting her eyes adjust to the dark. It looked as though the Ballamúr dropped her in Forêt Fossile, for she was surrounded by trees and the soft pattering of raindrops, but in reality, she could have been anywhere.

Bridgette was beginning to think that the Ballamúr wanted to be helpful, and thus sent her where it thought she needed or wanted to go. That was how she wound up with Toby, miles and miles from the border, and how she ended up in Bondrie just in time to be found by a group of guards on patrol.

She sighed. "Fucking hell."

Her knowledge of Palnan geography was limited to knowing where large features and towns were, and a couple of rivers Toby once showed her. If she wasn't in Forêt Fossile, maybe she was by a body of water. Trees needed a sustainable water source, so that would make sense. She could find and follow the creek or river, perhaps. But that might take hours. She'd never been one for camping or the human organization known as the Scouts, so her woodsy survival skills were limited.

No wonder I had such a hard time following Toby in the dream, she thought.

Bridgette perched on a low-hanging branch for a few minutes, considering her options. None of them were that great. Her Maylemaegus seemed to perk up when she thought about flying again.

Calm down, you little twit, she told it, feeling strange for think-speaking to a part of her body that wasn't wholly hers. *How am I supposed to fly when I have exactly zero sense of direction here? I don't know where I am, much less the way to Xcthonya.*

✦ *You will be shown the path, Liluthuaé.*

Bridgette shrieked as the voice of her vademecum slipped into her mind. *What the — how are you talking to me? I didn't even bring you!*

It seemed to laugh. ✦ *Such is the way of the Triumvirate, Liluthuaé. We are one.*

"Fan-fucking-tastic, this really is some Three Musketeers shit," the Elfling grumbled. "So Maylemaegus and Universal consciousness with an old notebook can get through the Ballamúr, but normal magic can't. Got it. Great. Wonderful. Kill me."

✦ *You are most dramatic.*

She wished the vademecum had a face so that she could stare at it in annoyance. *Look, Thing One, I didn't choose to be the Liluthuaé. It got handed to me. I extra did not choose to be part of a magical little co-op of legendary beasts, and I very much did not get the option to pick who else was part of that trio. The ones y'all decided on would have been at the bottom of my list — a Fairy who can make snowflakes in midair but can't stop keeping secrets, and the ruling descendant of Artur Cromwell, who is one of the most arrogant, self-serving beings I've ever met. And I once had a foster mother who tried to make royalties off me as a child model.*

✦ *It is not for us to decide whom our bearers are. It is for us to serve and to guide them, to teach them in the ways of those who came before.*

"Cool," the Elfling muttered.

✦ *Have you considered, Liluthuaé, that perchance the Ballamúr is of our same magic?*

She glanced up and stared into the night. "Uh, no, but now I am very much considering that, actually."

The vademecum gave a hum of approval.

"So, what now?" Bridgette asked both it and the Universe. "I start flying and you show me where to go?"

✦ *If that is what you would like to do, you will be guided. The wind shall aid you.*

More weird air magic, Bridgette thought. To the vademecum, she asked, *Am I going to get told what the air magic thing means, and how I do it on command?*

✦ *The Triumvirate is soil, sky, and sea.*

"You are *so* helpful," she replied aloud. "The Ballamúr dropped me in these woods, so I'll figure the meaning of that out later. In the meantime, I guess we're ready for liftoff, huh?"

She chuckled at her joke. The vademecum did not.

Though she was grateful for the cover of darkness to keep

her flying form hidden, Bridgette was far less thankful for the raindrops that pelted her face and hair. The wind blew the hood of the oilskin jacket off, so aside from the quiet, instinctual guidance of the vademecum and the direction of the wind, she flew blindly. It was different to fly with the wind guiding her. Bridgette, so used to directing her own limbs and speed, was at odds for the first few miles in the air.

✦ *Do you fear falling?* the vademecum asked.

"Not. Exactly," Bridgette gritted out as she tried to keep from flipping sideways in a gust.

✦ *You are truth, you are sky, you are infinity. You know not where to go, but the wind does. Be one with it, as you already are, and you will not drop unless you choose to.*

Now, that was the most actual helpful thing the vademecum said to her thus far in their bizarre relationship. Bridgette stopped trying to control her flight. After an initial heart-stopping dip before the wind caught her, the Elfling adapted to the feel of being carried. She only exerted control to speed up when she felt the air begin to slow as she passed between areas of precipitation, or to position herself more comfortably when the rain picked up, doing her best to keep her hood in place.

It was in the midst of a torrential downpour — and nearing dawn, judging from the lightening of the clouds — when Bridgette finally felt the air start to change patterns. The wind was ready to deposit her and the Elfling had about two seconds' warning before she started to go straight down in a bellyflop onto the mud. She scrambled, regaining authority over her flight, and landed with an almighty squelch.

Yet again, she had no idea where she was.

Care to enlighten me? she asked the Maylemaegus, the vademecum. She wasn't sure which, because at this point, they seemed one and the same.

✦ *There is a street just ahead that you will recognize.*

Bridgette stomped into the deluge, letting her instincts, her sierwan knowledge maybe, guide her in the vague "just ahead" direction the vademecum spoke of. But before she reached any sort of road, she saw the backside of a wooden fence, acres of pasture, the outline of a shed, and further in the distance, the rear of a gray building that was nearly invisible in the rainfall.

Oh, thank fuck, she thought, and began to slog toward the butchery.

~ 77 ~

Bridgette had rarely been so elated to see a building in her entire life. She trudged through the thick mud and nonstop rainfall, wondering if she'd beat Zedolph to work. Wondering, too, what she'd say to him when they came face-to-face. Her planned excuse was to claim that she needed to return to the University for final examinations, but that wouldn't explain away the thief-in-the-night fashion in which she left.

The mud clung to her boots and splashed up the back of her leggings. Though she put her hood back up again after landing, it did little to guard against the rain. She shivered, feeling tendrils of cold, wet hair drip down the back of her sweater. For a country that espoused Florida-like weather during the dry season, this incessant downpour made Bridgette feel as if she was nearer to Seattle.

It didn't let up. By the time she was close enough to the butchery to see that none of the candles were lit inside — a sign Zedolph wasn't in yet — Bridgette was physically exhausted. Even though the wind carried her most of the way, the tension from keeping her body taut and in the air caught up with her. She groaned in relief as she slid to a crouch in front of the entrance, ready for a pause in movement. Her soaked bag hung heavily on her shoulder. Nothing inside would be damaged; Collum made sure of that. But the fabric exterior would need a solid two days by Serrabinx's firehearth to return to its usable state.

"Excuse me!" Zedolph's voice cut through the gloom. "What are you doing?"

A grateful Bridgette looked up to see him running through the mud. No, not running; Zedolph looked more like he was gliding. There were wide-soled contraptions strapped to his feet that could have been snowshoes, except that it wasn't snowing.

She pushed her hood back, and Zedolph stopped moving.

"Bridgette?" he asked, not believing his eyes. "Is that really you?"

Bridgette nodded as she stood, wincing at the protesting ache of her muscles. "I was kind of wondering if I could have my old job back?"

The man shook his head in amazement and resumed his walk toward her, less concerned now that he knew who she was. "Where have you been? We've all been worried sick, Bridgette!"

She gulped, but was spared an immediate reply by Zedolph swooping her into a bear hug. Their oilskin jackets squished against one another, and Bridgette allowed him a little more of an embrace than she normally would. It was nice to be hugged, especially after — *Damn*, she thought. *I flew all night and got no sleep again, didn't I? Where did the Ballamúr put me?*

The butcher pulled back from her, scanning her rain-soaked hair and wet jacket, the bag that dripped a puddle on his business' entryway, those once-black boots now caked in earth and forest detritus. His dark brown eyes held a far-away look, something painful and deep. Bridgette realized with a start just how badly her untimely departure affected him.

"Zedolph," she said quietly. "Have you ever tried to leave Palna?"

She didn't know why she asked that, but the unexpected inquiry seemed to knock some sense back into him. His eyes narrowed.

"No, I cannot say that I have," he replied. Bridgette caught a hint of wariness in his tone, as if Zedolph evaded a more detailed answer. "What makes you ask me this?"

"Because I had to go back to the University for my final exams, and to present the first phase of my first cultural research project." The lie rolled off her tongue smoothly, as though she practiced it for months. As though it was the truth. "If you never tried to leave, you wouldn't know this, but you can't exactly just walk through the wall and into Bondrie. There has to be special permission and all sorts of government bullshit. But when you get that permission granted and are summoned to leave, you have to go right then, otherwise it starts the whole cycle of permissions over again. It's really dumb. The Samnung members had to go through the same thing a few weeks ago when they were here."

"The Samnung was here?" Zedolph's curiosity was effectively piqued. He glanced around them for privacy, not that anyone could hear through the noise the rain made as it danced along the butchery's metal roof. "Don't answer that yet. Come inside and dry off."

He unlocked the door and led her in, the familiar environment as welcoming to Bridgette as Collum's apartment. She really did miss working here, in particular spending the mornings with Fincher as he set the cases. Even the brooding presence of Muov wasn't a deterrent, though she did not look forward to explaining her absence to him. She couldn't say for certain that the Elf knew she lied about her backstory, but he treated her with more distance and distrust than the other slátraestres did.

It was cold inside the butchery, though Zedolph made quick work of lighting all the candles to brighten the dim room. Bridgette warmed her hands over one of the larger ones that burned three wooden wicks together into a wide flame. The butchery didn't have a firehearth, as it was better for the meat to remain as cold as possible to preserve its quality.

"Now," Zedolph said once the candles were all glowing, "I would like you to tell me more about this Samnung visit."

They sat in the back room, ignoring the fact that the cases needed to be stocked, and Bridgette strung together a story that had enough truth so it wouldn't easily be questioned, even by Muov or Serrabinx. The Elfling told Zedolph that after the leaders of Heáhwolcen heard her cultural research, the spreca desired to see Palna for herself.

"She never went while her parents, the late King Hermann and Queen Lalora, were alive and visiting more regularly, or at least communicating with the Tinuviels," Bridgette said. "They sent a messenger who was met by the Palnan Guard and escorted to Düoria. It was all four of the leaders, not the full Samnung, but Queen Nehemi, her borhond, Kharis, Ard Rialóir Trystane, Aristoces, the Fairy of All Fairies, and Master Swordswoman Corria. They were in Palna over Imbolc and toured the castle and grounds in the capital city."

Her host chewed on his lip, processing this news. "We were not told this occurred. Perhaps it was only shared with citizens in Düoria."

"Maybe," Bridgette allowed. "There wasn't a bunch of time between them making the request and Imbolc happening."

More like they intentionally didn't give the Tinuviels a choice in the matter, she thought to herself. The Elfling found it odd, though, that the news did not spread in the days following the visit. She knew Palna had its archivists, which she loosely assumed were a kind of photojournalist, if they weren't full-blown reporters. But, come to think of it, she could not recall ever seeing a newspaper in Palna. Collum always had some daily publication that she never bothered to read in Eckenbourne, yet here? Either newspaper reading wasn't a popular pastime, or not everyone had access to the press.

"Do y'all not get the news from other cities?" Bridgette asked.

"We do," Zedolph replied evasively. "*The Watchword* is published thrice weekly."

"Hmm. I guess I've just never seen anybody read it, so I wondered. I figured it would be a pretty big thing for the Samnung leaders to come to Palna for the first time in what, sixteen years? Seventeen?"

The butcher shrugged. "I could not say for certain. As for the newspaper, all Palnans are required to receive it."

But they're not required to read it, Bridgette's sierwan gift confirmed.

She slowly nodded her understanding. "Got it. How come I've never seen it at your house?"

"Editions are typically on the doorstep mid-morning in Xcthonya, after I leave for the butchery. Should anything of note be found, that information is shared when I arrive home, as newsprint makes for both wonderful kindling and compost. Both of those tasks take place while I am at work."

The Elfling gave Zedolph a shrewd smile. "I think I'm picking up what you're putting down. That would definitely explain why I didn't know it existed if it's already been cleaned up during the workday. What kind of information gets shared with you?"

"Calendar meetings I might find of interest, for example." Zedolph took in a sharp breath and stared at the icebox for a moment. "There is one such meeting today I plan to attend, early this afternoon. I'd like for you to join me."

There was a devilish twinge in her gut. "Can I get a little hint as to what it's about?"

"It is a tea gathering."

Her face fell.

What is it with these guys and tea? Bridgette wondered, harkening back to meeting Collum for the first time, although she doubted the tea Zedolph invited her to drink alongside him would be chai.

"I mean, yeah, sure. Of course, I'll go with you," she agreed.

Zedolph stood and stretched. "Excellent. In that case, I believe your fellow slátraestres can handle the shop today. You look as though you haven't eaten properly, and the darkness under your eyes suggests you might enjoy a nap before our meeting."

~ 78 ~

"Where are we going?" Bridgette had to raise her voice to be heard above the nonstop rain. "And is this shit ever gonna quit? How is Palna not flooding?"

Zedolph smirked at her from under the brim of his hat. "It will slow, eventually. Every day is not like this during the rainy season, I promise."

"I hope not. This sucks."

The Elfling felt a tap at her consciousness. *What?* she thought to the spirit of her vademecum.

✦ *You do not have to allow the rain to touch you. The witch will not speak of it.*

By "witch", she assumed the thing meant Zedolph.

I don't think that Mother Nature is going to stop the rainy season just because I showed up in Palna, but thanks for that advice, Bridgette thought to it.

If the vademecum could give an exasperated sigh, the feeling that swept across Bridgette's mind was probably that. Suddenly, an image flashed in her head, a memory of Collum walking her through a misty morning, but the two of them stayed entirely dry. Her eyes shifted under their glamour, and what didn't make sense to her then now hit Bridgette with such perfect clarity she gasped out loud. She'd known — the one secret she hid from the fyrdwisa — for months now that her blood gave her the ability to do Craft Wizardry. But was it the blood of Eryth Tinuviel, or was it perhaps that Maylemaegus and Craft magic were not different from one another, mirrors of power separated only by their intention?

Very cautiously, she looked at Zedolph and waited until their eyes met. His brow furrowed, and she extended her mind to his: *Say nothing of what you see,* her mind-voice instructed him. The poor man gripped his ears and stared at Bridgette, bewildered. She wished she knew what he thought, but there was no ísenwaer with which to hear him.

Bridgette looked at the incessant water that poured around her, and — hoping she was doing this properly — reached internally for her core of Maylemaegus. It felt like flexing a muscle deep within, and though she was less phased these days by feeling the power move of its own accord, she had yet to intentionally activate it. When it happened before, it was second nature and just … happened. There was no pulling of a trigger like she attempted now.

Shield, she commanded.

It wasn't the water that eased, but rather the air that moved around her and Zedolph, creating an invisible wall that let the raindrops roll harmlessly away, imperceptibly shifting with every step they took so that it created an optical illusion for passersby. No one but the two of them would know that they weren't getting rained on.

Zedolph hadn't stopped staring at her. "What in the seven hells just happened?"

She grinned and shrugged a shoulder. "I was tired of getting wet."

"How did you —" the man stepped backward. "My nephew was right."

"Right about what?" Bridgette asked. "You still haven't told me where we're going, by the way. I'm just kind of wandering until you tell me to go inside somewhere."

Zedolph stopped walking, needing a moment to collect his thoughts. What he'd just seen! An Elfling controlling the elements; her thoughts inside his mind! Toby warned him and Serrabinx about this, though the boy was staunchly defensive of Bridgette after she left. Serrabinx threatened to box his ears if he didn't tell the adults what he knew, what he Saw, regarding her disappearance. He simply stood in front of his mother, prepared for the punishment.

"Tobias told us that you had abilities related to your

birthright," Zedolph said slowly. "He was not forthcoming with much else but did not deny when we began asking him questions about what these abilities might be. I began to suspect that perhaps your so-called cultural research here was not just for your University."

Bridgette squirmed. "Yeah?"

"I watched you twice perform a certain type of *ability* in my presence," he mused. "You caused it to rain inside my home and you just stopped the rain out of doors. This ability has been barred from within our country for more than a century. I once told you such a skill was one that required great ritual, preparation, intent, and training, and this is why Ydessa's mother died. However, what I just observed was you presenting that talent as innately as you would take a breath."

The butcher crossed his arms and gave Bridgette another once-over, his vision better now that rain wasn't being blown into his eyes. "I think you're going to find this meeting very fruitful." He turned and started walking again. "We're going to an inn. The barkeep will not question why I'm renting a room for several hours on a weekday."

"Oh, gross, Zedolph; I didn't want to know that!" Bridgette groaned but followed him anyway, the man's laughter deep and trilling.

The barkeep indeed did not care or question why his local butcher threw him a few coins for a quiet room on the top floor. Zedolph bought Bridgette a hearty bowl of warmouth chowder — "The fish is known as such for having teeth on its tongue," he said — and then let her enjoy the solace of a warm bed for a few hours.

Bridgette managed to sleep a bit, but the combination of anxiety from being in a strange place, of making a somewhat unwelcome discovery about her magic, not to mention curiosity about the meeting Zedolph would soon take her to, made full respite difficult. Still, she basked on the mattress, wondering how it was possible for a combination of dried straw and feathers to feel so soft and comforting. Her muscles loosened as she tried to meditate herself back to sleep. She resisted the urge to contact Collum right away, in the first place because she didn't want to become too dependent on that slim channel of communication, but she knew he was probably busy, especially now that underhanded planning with the Fyrdlytta was likely underway.

Plus, I have a feeling that this meeting is going to be really eye-opening, she thought. *I wonder what it's about, if Zedolph knows about my magic.*

There wasn't much time left to wonder about it, for the butcher knocked and let himself into the room shortly thereafter. "Did you rest well, Bridgette?" he asked quietly.

She nodded. "I did, thanks. Not much sleep, but I definitely feel more relaxed than when I got here. It was a long walk from where I crossed through the Ballamúr."

Her voice wavered on the word "walk". Zedolph pretended not to notice.

"That is most excellent to hear," he replied. "We've got a bit more of a trip ahead of us, I'm afraid. This inn is on the outskirts of Xcthonya, but we'll be having tea at Glafida's shop."

"Glafida's shop?" Bridgette asked curiously. Zedolph didn't give a further explanation, just stood patiently in the doorway, so she stood, stretched, and slipped back into the oilskin jacket to follow him once again.

She wished she'd been able to sleep more by the time they got to the downtown shops. Bridgette once again kept them dry, but the heavy mud was a different story. Zedolph's marshwings, as she learned his strange footwear was called, protected his boots from sinking as deep as hers did. The wet earth had begun to seep into the seams of her leather soles and between the laces. She made a mental note to ask about getting a pair of the marshwings for herself — otherwise, it seemed as though she'd be buying a new pair of boots every week to replace the ones that kept getting ruined in the wet weather.

The leatherwiph's storefront was a welcome sight. Bridgette and Zedolph stepped inside and were met by what must have been an apprentice, for the young girl took one look at their sodden forms and thrust forward with cotton towels and wooden coat hangers. She didn't even bother with the customary fist-over-heart move, so upset was she at their appearance.

"What mindlessness is this, Sigewíf!" she scolded Bridgette in an accent so thickly Scottish the Elfling struggled to understand it. "Your boots are a mess. Have you no sense to don appropriate footwear for the season?"

The girl, who might have been Bridgette's age, stuck her hand out. "Give those things to me, Sigewíf. I shall take your marshwings as well, Thighearna; there's no need for you to be walking around the shop all mucked up like such."

Bridgette and Zedolph shucked off their jackets and the Elfling peeled off her footwear, grimacing at the wet *thwap* noise her boots made as they came off her calves. The girl took them, not bothering to hide the disgust in her expression. She sauntered off, muttering something about "disrespect" and "crudeness of those bloody Elves".

"Right, then," Zedolph said sheepishly. "Sorry about that. Rainy season etiquette must be different elsewhere."

"Yeah, we don't have any," Bridgette muttered. She shifted the weight of her thankfully no longer dripping-wet bag. Her feet felt cold in their wet socks, which she noticed left damp footprints on the hardwood floor as she followed Zedolph deeper into the shop.

Only a few patrons browsed the shelves. One looked up as Zedolph passed, but as soon as they made eye contact, the customer looked away in a hurry, pretending he saw nothing.

That's weird, Bridgette thought.

Glafida bustled out from the back workroom with an armload of newly bound books, each with a note sticking out of the top bearing a customer's name.

"Well met, my friends!" she said. "What brings you out in this weather?"

Zedolph inclined his head, and Bridgette quickly mirrored his fisted gesture of acknowledgement. "Is it not time for tea?"

The woman winked at him. "Tea will be served shortly, my darling. Will you wait for me in the rear?"

"Of course, Glafida." Zedolph took Bridgette's hand. He walked her to the curtained-off workroom, which Bridgette considered a strange place to invite people over for tea, but the moment they walked through the fabric veil, she understood why there was some concept of secrecy.

"Viltu carleast?" A tall, foreboding Tiefling with skin the color of fresh peaches stepped directly in front of them. He crossed his arms and regarded Bridgette with some level of scrutiny.

"Etiam pro mundi," Zedolph replied. Instead of the normal fist, he held up the wrist that was perpetually covered by a fitted leather cuff. The butcher unlaced what Bridgette always assumed to be some sort of knife guard and revealed a familiar-looking eye-shaped sigil tattooed on his skin.

The Bright Star's own eyes went wide.

The Tiefling pulled back his sleeve, where a matching tattoo was imprinted. "Tunc Triumviratus resurget!" he called out.

"Ut nos liberant!" Zedolph responded in unison with a sizable crowd that now stepped forward from the surrounding walls. They all held their wrists high, except for one, who saw the Elfling in the doorway and ran forward with an almighty squeal of elation.

Bridgette nearly doubled over as Toby collided with her legs.

"You've come back!" he cried. "Oh, how I missed you while you were on your adventure. You must tell me about it!"

There was a light hand on the Elfling's shoulder. "I'm sure she will tell us many things about her time away," Serrabinx murmured. She gave Bridgette a strong look that caused the

Bright Star's Maylemaegus to flutter. "We welcome you back into your home here."

"Thanks, Serrabinx," Bridgette replied. She knelt down to go eye-to-eye with Toby. "Hello, Little Lark. I missed you, too. I'm going to hazard a guess here and say that this little group of friends is what you like to call the Hringur?"

~ 79 ~

It was, indeed.

There were a few more moments of quiet chatter before Glafida joined them and snapped the curtains shut. Someone did actually start sending around trays of sweets, a mismatched array of teacups, and several steaming pots of tea, each labeled with a different flavor.

Bridgette went for a breakfast blend. Those had the most caffeine.

"Fáilte, friends," Glafida began. She walked into the middle of the gathered crowd, which scooted chairs and stools into a circle around her. "It is with most joy that we welcome a new guest today in our midst. She is the friend of young Toby, an Elfling raised on Earth who has been living among us for a cultural immersion experience. She wished to learn more of our history and to share that knowledge with others in greater Heáhwolcen. I encourage each of you to get to know Bridgette as Toby and his family have."

The Elfling waved awkwardly from her seat. "Uh, hi. Thanks for having me, I guess?"

Zedolph held back a chuckle.

Glafida began to speak again. Much of what the woman said was hard for Bridgette to follow, because her sierwan gift started snapping so quickly that she gave up and decided she'd process it all later. It was too much to take in at the moment. It was only when Glafida introduced a second speaker to the circle that Bridgette stopped semi-dissociating. The speaker was Queylan, the Sanguisuge artisan that she and Toby met at the river market.

"I come with this month's news from our capital," Queylan told the Hringur. "I was present at the Düorian celebration for Imbolc, where artists were welcomed to sell our wares, and where I was quite shocked to see members of the Heáhwolcen

Samnung be welcomed as honored guests."

A murmur of astonishment rose in the room. Queylan waited for everyone to quiet before speaking again. "They were watched at all times by members of the Palnan Guard, each flanked by at least one to two at their sides. Attending representatives were the queen of Endorsa and her hand, as well as an Elf, a Fairy, and a female called the master swordswoman of Bondrie."

"Why were they there?" someone asked.

When Queylan did not immediately reply, Bridgette stood. "I can answer that, if it's okay," the Elfling offered.

No one objected, so she nervously stepped next to the Sanguisuge in the center of the circle. "I came to Palna, like Glafida said, to learn more about your country and its history. To do this, I had to get express permission from the Samnung. When I went back to greater Heáhwolcen before Lunavidad, I made a full presentation to members of the Samnung about what I experienced.

"They were curious about what I said and wanted to come for themselves," Bridgette continued. "Queen Nehemi hadn't been to Palna before, and other than Ambassador Mewt, I don't think anyone's been willing to come for a long time. I can't speak to the specifics, unfortunately, but Nehemi decided this would be the perfect time for a state visit."

"What did they find?"

Bridgette wasn't sure who asked the question, but she turned in the direction of the voice to answer. "The Samnung — well, some members of the Samnung — suspect that the Tinuviels have not been playing as peaceful a role as they pretend to be."

Another murmur and some chuckles of acknowledgment peppered the crowd.

She grinned. "Yeah, I kind of figured y'all might have the same suspicions. What I experienced in Xcthonya sounds pretty different than what it's like in Düoria. To answer your question, the Samnung found that the Tinuviels were pretty dedicated to their desire for peace and a fully united Heáhwolcen, without the presence or use of a certain type of *ability* that this country's founder was a big fan of."

"They believe the Tinuviels want peace?" someone called out.

"Nehemi believes this more strongly than the rest," Bridgette clarified. "Probably Kharis, too — that's the name of her borhond, her hand. But I think they all went into Palna expecting to see military forces and illegal powers in use, signs that for sure pointed to Ydessa and Eryth cooking up something that smelled a lot like war."

The Tiefling who greeted her earlier stood. "What do you believe?"

His question wasn't accusatory, but it reminded her of the same mistrust that Muov usually expressed. Bridgette faced him directly. "I believe that we are entering an unprecedented time of conflict to come," she said, surprised at how strong and steady her voice was. "I believe that there are things happening in Palna and on Earth that could have a negative effect on the world at large. I believe that the Tinuviels are preparing for something, given that they've been pretty much left to their own devices for almost twenty years and weren't closely monitored for a while before that.

"I believe Ydessa and Eryth found ways to skirt any monitoring they had," the Elfling went on. "Y'all confirmed for me today that there are citizens who do not want to support the Tinuviels in any coming battle, and that despite how secretive the so-called king and queen have been, there's a chance we can get an edge here. I know for a fact that Heáhwolcen's Fórsaí Armada quietly readies its forces, though not every individual is aware of why their training will intensify."

Bridgette paused to take a sip of her now-lukewarm tea. "I know also that those who fight for Heáhwolcen fight for *Palna*, not for the Tinuviels and their supporters, and that the prejudices and history that were taught for way too long about this country are being challenged."

Queylan glanced to the Elfling. "Who is doing such challenging?"

The Bright Star's eyes flashed. "I am."

More chatter filled the room, and a few members of the Hringur gave Bridgette guarded looks. She couldn't blame them. None of them knew her and here she was, without their matching tattoo, trying to tell them that just as there was a resistance brewing here, one existed against the Tinuviels elsewhere in Heáhwolcen. But Bridgette couldn't tell the Palnans gathered around her the full truth, partly because she herself didn't know everything.

She raised her hands in an effort to silence their voices. "Some of the Samnung members who think the way I do are aware that the Hringur exists, and that it's got a mission related to something called the Triumvirate," Bridgette said. "One of the reasons I was able to come back to Palna was because these ally Samnung members need to learn more about what the Triumvirate is supposed to do, how the Hringur is organized, and how we can help."

The Bright Star took her seat without another word. There were a few prudent glances between Hringur members. Everyone appeared to be waiting for Glafida — who Bridgette assumed was in charge — to say something. The leatherwiph, however, remained seated. She seemed as taken by surprise as the rest of them. A tense silence continued, peppered with uncomfortable sounds of feet shuffling and chairs scratching the floor.

"I'll tell you the story of the Triumvirate," a voice to Bridgette's left said. The Elfling turned her head to see who spoke. A tiny Pixie, hardly the size of a handprint, flittered out from the shadows. "If I may speak, Glafida?"

The leatherwiph nodded her permission, and the small being zipped to the center circle. Her voice was light and tinny, so hard to hear that no one moved a muscle while she spoke.

"It is a tale that has been passed down through generations, though some of the story was lost to time, and other parts shunned in favor of a more appealing truth," the Pixie said. "There are some species that prefer to consider themselves the original beings, though it is known that Ceannairí Álfar bore three."

This first part of the story the Pixie shared echoed what the vademecums told Bridgette and Emi-Joye. The Bright Star knew the objects hadn't been lying, but it still didn't make it any less chilling to hear the tale again.

"The deities were amazed by Ylda's artistry as she began to create other beings and populate the Earth with them. Presenting her siblings with their heartsworn was a selfless gift of such magnitude that the deities were moved," the Pixie shared. "At the time, the initial generations of Elves that began calling themselves the Fyrst had already begun to ignore the history of their creator's other offspring. The deities desired to honor Ylda for what she did, despite the outcry of the Fyrst."

As if for dramatic effect, the Pixie snapped her fingers and a sprinkle of fine, shimmering dust puffed into the air before her. She molded it into a floating orb as she continued speaking. "Matla, the mighty power of the deities, the ancients, was the precursor to the *abilities* that some of our kind possess outside of Palna. It is not of this world, and so cannot be contained in it."

The orb began to spin.

"Matla surrounds this world and all worlds. It is infinite, defying space and time, existing everywhere and nowhere at once," the Pixie said. "It is the beginnings of all elements and all consciousness; the ephemera from which all living things were born. The deities could not gift pure Matla to Ylda, for it would destroy her. But what could be gifted was an altered form, and thus the Maylemaegus came to be."

She toyed with the orb until it sputtered out three smaller spheres that began to circle within it. "Great power is always in three, and so mote it be. The deities presented Ylda with the three aspects of Maylemaegus: truth, passion, and loyalty. The power of truth brings complete knowledge of all that is, that was, that will be. Passion is a hyperdrive, an intense focus, the culmination of all feeling and emotion. Loyalty encompasses fierce protection, an understanding of battle and leadership.

"But what the deities gave to Ylda, she gave away. She felt it unnecessary, too fearsome a collection of power for one being to have. She offered two gifts of Maylemaegus to her siblings, and gave one to her finest creation, an Elven spirit known as Liluthuaé, the Bright Star," the Pixie went on.

Bridgette tensed. She watched as the three spheres inside the orb faltered their spin, then broke free.

"The Fyrst Fae, Duatha, accepted loyalty, and the Fyrst Witch, Artur Cromwell who founded this land, was given passion."

Fyrst Witch? I thought the vademecums said there were two, that they were twins, Bridgette thought. Her Maylemaegus, that truth power the Pixie spoke of, stirred in recognition. *I don't think anyone knows the full history anymore …*

She turned her attention back to listen to the Pixie again, hyper-aware of potential inconsistencies in the story.

"The deities made a bargain with Ylda. They knew that the time would come when the future of those with *abilities* would be threatened, and that it would take an act of great power to unite against such a threat," the Pixie continued. "They said that if Ylda was to take the Maylemaegus of the Fae and the witches, the same way she had with the Elves, and create two other beings to harness their portion of the Matla gift, they would keep the spirits safe until such a time came. It is perhaps a selfish request of the deities, of course, for by having specially powered organisms prepared to do such work, it saves the goddex from needing to intervene. Their only role would be to ensure that the spirits of the three, the Triumvirate, came to exist in corporeal form at the same time."

The three spheres circling the Pixie's orb of dust glowed faintly as they connected into one, now putting the original orb in their own center.

"When all are one, there will be nothing to fear."

The Pixie's final statement must have been a code, for the entire room began to chant together. Bridgette remembered Toby saying almost the same thing months earlier: "We speak for those struck voiceless. We are the prisoners of no one's walls. We are the power that should not exist. We are the Hringur, and we fight so that the Triumvirate will rise."

"Thank you for that story," Bridgette said to the Pixie, who bowed her head and snapped her orb away into dust once again. "How is it that no one elsewhere in Heáhwolcen knows of the Triumvirate?"

"Because to acknowledge the Triumvirate would mean acknowledging parts of history that the Fyrst tried to stop from being told," someone said. "It would mean convincing millennia of generations that they, too, were possibly descended from a true Fyrst three, and not an Elven creation. Admitting this could destroy everything."

Bridgette itched to tell them they, too, were wrong here; that Artur Cromwell had a twin. But something tethered her voice, urging her to keep that detail to herself for now. Instead, she tried a follow-up inquiry: "So, say Artur Cromwell definitely knew his own origin story, but chose for whatever reason not to brag about it. That might explain why the rest of Heáhwolcen has no clue they've been lied to, or at least misled. But it doesn't explain how y'all know about it, and how y'all got charged with whatever it is you're doing for the Triumvirate."

It was Glafida who answered. "My family has included

leatherwiphs for generations. We have bound books for many years. I believe you are aware of the unusual set of books purchased last year from my shop?"

The three volumes of the *Sefnuskrá*. Bridgette nodded.

"Then, Bridgette of the Outside, I believe it should come as no surprise to you that many such books have come surreptitiously across my family's worktables over the years. The legend of the Liluthuaé is well known in Elven culture. To learn that two other such beings exist was valuable and beautiful knowledge, and it became our duty to conserve this history and the promise made by the deities," Glafida said. "But the Hringur itself is a much more recent development in our efforts to preserve the true origins of our kind. There was a rumor in the wind that one of the foretold would soon be among us, and we chose to do our part to support their mission."

Bridgette grimaced. She wondered which one of them the wind whispered about, since both Emi-Joye and Nehemi were older than her.

"Do you know the names of the other two?" she asked. "And what's the deal with the eye tattoos?"

An Aziza stepped forward to reply. "This is the sigil of the Triumvirate. Glafida's family found it in one of the books they bound."

"Right, but what's it mean?"

"The sigil is a spell, of sorts," the Aziza said. "This one is particularly complex, but it is formed of lines and curves representing letters in the Trúwa, the divine vow of the Triumvirate. We do not know what that is, for only the Triumvirate's own grimoire can reveal such a thing."

Bridgette heard her vademecum's spirit stifle a laugh.

You know, Thing One, it's really annoying to have the ghost of you with me at all times, she thought to it.

"Why did you ask if the other beings had names?" Zedolph said. He and Serrabinx had been largely silent for the entire meeting.

The Bright Star sighed. *They're going to find out at some point*, she thought.

"I'm not going to share my source of this information, but I have it on really good authority that you can start calling the other two folks the Boireannach and the Astridsí, representing the Fae and the witches, respectively," she said. "In related news, I regret to inform y'all that though the wind may have told you one of them is alive and well, it must've skipped over the part where all three are hanging around here somewhere … but I don't think they have any clue that they're supposed to band together and save the world."

~ 80 ~

Sleep hadn't come easy to Collum since Bridgette left. He wasn't sure he'd ever before suffered such insomnia and anxiety, and he could not say that he particularly enjoyed either ailment. Once again, he found himself struggling to rest, his mind too occupied with the Bright Star to fade into oblivion. Hearing about the Hringur meeting mere hours after Bridgette arrived back in Palna was the most unexpected news of the year thus far. The fyrdwisa was half-tempted to tell her to come back now, before she got herself so ingrained again into life with the Maudlins and work as a slátraestre. But her first report back to him elicited too many questions — he could not ask Bridgette to cut this phase of her mission short.

For example, it made absolute sense when Bridgette's report revealed that the ambassadora's Maylemaegus represented loyalty, what with her chosen career. But passion? Nehemi? Collum rarely saw Nehemi show any emotion other than disdain. Her satisfied glee at Lucilla's wand tipping had been one of few recent instances.

Perhaps passion could mean great demonstration of emotion, and it manifests within the queen as righteous anger, he mused as he stared at his dark bedroom ceiling. *Passion can have so many synonyms; be such a broad term. Framing Nehemi's potential as Astridsí in terms of my own experience and interpretation could be stuffing her into a box and limiting how I perceive her.*

He would share this thought with Trystane and Aristoces the next time he saw them. They had taken the news of the Hringur meeting in stride, though like Collum were surprised that Bridgette managed to stumble upon it first thing. It was growing difficult to keep Bridgette's travels a secret from the witch queen. Collum knew eventually Nehemi would start to question why the Bright Star stopped showing up to Samnung meetings. When she chose to broach the subject, the fyrdwisa wanted to be prepared with a good answer, but nothing else of note had been learned. Bridgette's next two weeks of reports were relatively lackluster, and the fyrdwisa loathed that she was unable to hear his response. He thought the ísenwaer would be able to work between them now that she could intentionally tap into Universal consciousness, but it appeared the Ballamúr wanted to keep their private channel silenced.

Bridgette hadn't made any progress in learning Gemaere, much less translating the *Sefnuskrá*, although at least back in the Maudlins' home the volumes stopped pretending to be obscure encyclopedias. They were once again decorated with runes she could not decipher, and even asking the vademecum's spirit for help was of no use. It annoyed Collum to no end that of all magic, *that* damned thing was able to speak with the Bright Star while she was in Palna.

Apparently, the vademecum got very quiet whenever she asked about either the language of the Fyrst or the stack of books. Collum wanted to know if the vademecum would open up once all three of the Triumvirate had made their connections.

Mmm! The sudden thought hit him. *I wonder if it is possible to speak to the vademecums and have them pass along communication.*

It was worth a try, he thought, though the idea of facing Emi-Joye and Trystane with his suspicion was unappealing. The ambassadora's neck wound finally healed, according to Aristoces, but both the Fairy of All Fairies and the fyrdwisa worried that Bridgette's show of dominance and knife skills beyond her training affected whatever sliver of camaraderie stood between the two females. Emi-Joye hadn't asked about the Liluthuaé since she left.

Collum was finally drifting off when, of all things, his wrist began to prickle. Without warning, he was jerked to full consciousness, feeling a near-physical tug as if he was a fish at the end of a line. It took him a moment to catch his breath and process what woke him. After a disappointed realization that it wasn't his covenant with Bridgette going off, he shot out of bed at the sight of his entire Samnung bracelet starting to glow.

Collum had never been summoned in such a way before. He wasn't sure from which member the urgent request originated. The message was repeated over and over as he absorbed it: "The Samnung is summoned to its chamber. This is not a request."

He was halfway through tucking the hem of his sleep-pants into a pair of boots when loud knocks sounded at his door.

"Collum!" Trystane shouted through the wood. He didn't bother to whisper. Something was wrong. Very wrong.

The fyrdwisa sprinted to the entryway, his mind full of Trystane's rambling thoughts that didn't make a lick of sense. Something about Bondrie, Nehemi, and Palna. A trio of tidings that did not bode well for whichever of their comrades required their presence.

"Trystane, what —"

"I don't know!" The ard rialóir didn't care that Collum had neighbors. He was frantic. "Someone's come to Deu Medgar; there was a breach of the border wall —"

"A breach?" Collum dragged Trystane into the apartment by his forearm. "What in the seven hells do you mean, a breach?"

Trystane, who barely remembered to throw on a jacket — much less a tunic — in his rush to get to Collum, paced the living room shirtless in his velvet leggings. "I don't know, Collum! There was an initial summons sent to myself, Corria, and Aristoces, then the full Samnung covenant went off —"

Collum didn't let Trystane finish his sentence. "There was a breach in *Bondrie*, and the summons us came from *Endorsa*?" Surely he hadn't heard right.

"Yes; I don't know anything else!"

"Is it Bridgette?" The fyrdwisa couldn't help but ask. "Could she have torn a rip in the wall somehow?"

"I don't *know*, Collum! Put on a fucking coat. We need to go *now.*"

The covenant bracelets on their wrists were nearly vibrating, the summons was so intense. Collum threw a jacket on over his sleepshirt and let his brother evanesce them to Cyneham Breonna.

It was a bizarre scene.

Collum was reminded of the bleary-eyed group of beings who showed up in his apartment the night Bridgette came back, as every single member of the Samnung was in their sleepclothes. Well — perhaps Verivol wasn't. The Sanguisuge wore a long, feathered robe and flowing pants made of very sheer patterned lace. It could have been bed-wear or an outfit for Evenshade. Aside from them, though, everyone looked disheveled, a far cry from their usual finery and crested attire.

Aristoces adjusted the tie of her bonnet. Her wings were deadly still. Nehemi, Kharis, and Cloa were noticeably absent, though the Samnung chamber door was shut. Collum presumed the Endorsan delegation waited inside, leaving the rest of them in the lobby to panic, with no idea what happened while they were asleep.

Is it Bridgette? Bryten sent the thought to Collum, who glanced across the lobby with a slight shake of his head.

Despite him having asked Trystane that exact question himself, Collum knew better. No, if it was Bridgette, he would have known. Hell, Collum would have been the one summoning them, but not until several hours later after he had some time alone with the Bright Star.

The chamber door finally opened. Aristoces whipped her head around, charcoal eyes afire with heightened awareness and suspicion. "What is the meaning of this?" she asked, staring straight at Nehemi.

Collum was visibly startled by the sight of the witch queen as she and Kharis emerged. She looked terrified; small and shrunken. Nehemi did not answer Aristoces and instead beckoned them inside. For the first time since he arrived, Collum realized there was a palace guard lurking down the hall, doing a damned good job of thinking mundane thoughts. The fyrdwisa realized this was why Nehemi and Kharis, and presumably Cloa, stayed in the Samnung chamber. Their minds were protected by its wards.

He grumbled inwardly with frustration.

Nehemi stood at her usual place, Kharis by her side. Cloa, who of course held Arctura in her lap, looked at the queen reverently. The princess' eyes were more glazed than normal, which Collum attributed to her having lost as much sleep as the rest of them. He swore, despite once assuring Bridgette otherwise, that the girl was somehow deficient; not fit to succeed and lead Endorsa when Nehemi either died or chose to step down from her role. The fyrdwisa was not one to think females *needed* a counterpart in marriage, but for Cloa? She needed a partner with sense and sound mind by her side to advise and lead, while she remained the face and carrier of Artur Cromwell's bloodline.

Collum only averted his gaze from the princess when Nehemi at last started talking.

"It is with great urgency that you were summoned this night, and I am in each of your debt for your answer," the witch queen said. Her voice was shaky. "I would like to introduce you to MxMillian Surefire, general of the Bondrie Guard."

The chamber door opened and the palace guard from outside led another male into the room, one who wore gray leather topped with chrome battle armor. Only Corria did not look shocked to see him standing there. Instead, she looked pissed.

MxMillian entered and stood next to Nehemi. He gave his master swordswoman an apologetic, embarrassed glance of acknowledgement. "It is mine honor, Ceannairí, to be in your presence," he said. His accent was perhaps of Romanian descent,

Collum thought. "As a Bondrie Guardsman, I have two responsibilities. It is my job to ensure the continued wall stability of Palna and to maintain the safety of Heáhwolcen from any potential threat broiling over that border. To the best of mine ability, I have done that.

"I have been general of the Bondrie Guard for three decades, and established relationships with the leadership of our great countries." The man shuffled uncomfortably. "It was also mine honor to work alongside King Hermann and Queen Lalora. Upon their untimely accident — which perhaps you do not know I was the first to respond to — I was given a secret. I was sworn, upon my life and magic, to protect this secret as part of my duties."

He took a deep, shuddering breath. "This evening, the Bondrie Guard intercepted a Palnan citizen who … escaped."

There was a sharp intake of breath. Trystane, who already knew that part of their summons, still gripped the table and left deep gouges in the wood. Verivol's eyes flared, and Bryten's horns deepened in color, an outward sign of anguish. Only Cloa seemed unbothered by this news, by the knowledge that someone from Palna broke through not only the Ballamúr, but through the Samnung's own wall as well.

"How could someone get through the Samnung wall without permission?" Aristoces asked. "Our magic prevents such a thing."

"It should, yes. But as you know, Ceannairí, we have found weak spots that required reinforcement from time to time. Some exist now," MxMillian answered. "I cannot speak as to why these weak spots have begun to occur, only to confirm they have. The Bondrie Guard is not a large enough force to have someone stationed at every square foot of the Samnung wall at all times. We presume that some Palnans knew of these spots. There is one in the Beorgdún, and this individual took advantage of a chance to escape."

"Why do you refer to this individual as an escapee, as if it is someone seeking refuge?" Collum asked. Trystane nudged his foot under the table, a thank-you for asking the question also on his mind.

MxMillian grimaced. "We questioned him immediately upon seizing him. He claimed to not be Palnan by birth, but by *accident*."

The fyrdwisa did not like that emphasis. "By accident?"

"He told a very strange story to the guards who found him, and they brought me to see the captive where they held him at the border," MxMillian replied. "The male told me the story of a deep secret, something only a handful of beings knew. It was the same information I had been sworn to protect the day King Hermann and Queen Lalora died. This secret was also learned by Ydessa and Eryth Tinuviel, though how they came by such knowledge remains unknown. They know too where the weak spots are and suspect why they exist. They have plans to exploit those spots and have simply been waiting for the time that felt right. That time, according to our new refugee, is near. He sought to warn Heáhwolcen."

Bryten, whose horns still gleamed dangerously with the depth of his emotion, frowned at the guard. "Thighearna, I understand that this concerned you greatly, and you may perhaps not be aware, but the Samnung has long held suspicions that Palna is again readying for war, though we do not know in what manner or to what end. While I personally appreciate how quickly you responded to alert us of a potential threat, I cannot say that I understand why this knowledge required the single-most urgent summons I've ever received in my life, at perhaps three in the morning."

The guard glanced at Nehemi, who stood so still Collum kept watching to make sure she was even breathing. The queen gave MxMillian a sharp, curt nod.

"You were summoned here to know the truth," MxMillian

said, and the fyrdwisa's stomach gave a sickening flutter. "The Tinuviels know that Endorsa is led by a false queen."

The chamber went silent as a tomb. Nehemi started shaking.

"What did you say?" Aristoces' voice was barely above a whisper. Collum didn't need his magic to feel the waves of anger that roiled over the Fairy's body. The whole table, actually.

"How can this be? Why would the descendent of Artur Cromwell not be Endorsa's true queen?" Bryten asked.

The aforementioned descendent looked as though she was about to break, her body and features unable to remain as stoic as usual. But there was a sense of relief on her expression too as she looked down at her borhond. It was Kharis who answered the Baetalüan's question. Unlike Nehemi, his voice rang stronger than Collum had heard it in years.

"Many of you will remember our beloved King Hermann and Queen Lalora were wont to have a child," Kharis said, rehashing a tale the Samnung members were all-too familiar with. "It was their greatest desire, hers especially. It was discovered that the developing child would be born male, and King Hermann was delighted to know he would have a son. But the pregnancy, as you know, did not go as planned. The fetus died in Queen Lalora's womb. Though it is far easier for witches to conceive than other magical beings, they are also more susceptible to things that can take human life. After a period of mourning, it was quietly shared in certain circles that Queen Lalora was again with child. This pregnancy, too, did not go to fruition — nor did the one after it."

Collum remembered that period of time. Though he was unsure how many miscarriages Lalora endured and Hermann supported her through, the queen stepped away from public life for years following the second loss. That was when the rumors began circulating that there was a Craft curse placed on the queen's womb. They were quiet rumors, a hint of curiosity, of conspiracy here and there. No one would dare openly confront

King Hermann or any of the Endorsan staff with such a claim, but it was an open secret that such thoughts persisted throughout Heáhwolcen.

"Did any of you ever meet Naomi?" Nehemi asked. No one answered. Collum wasn't sure he knew of whom she spoke.

"They would not have," Kharis spoke for them all. "After Lalora stopped attending public gatherings and secluded herself to a separate estate, Naomi was chosen as her new private handmaid. The king needed to tend to his duties, and he desired someone to be with his wife at all times, especially when he was unable to be at her side. Naomi herself was a new mother, and her child's father was a witch who worked for Hermann already. It was, quite arguably, Naomi's friendship with Lalora that saved the queen's life.

"Lalora felt comfort with their growing friendship and encouraged Naomi to bring her daughter to the estate," Kharis continued. "Together, the two women and King Hermann raised this child. Eventually, their friendship became so close that Lalora begged Hermann to let the child be raised as one of their own. He agreed. Naomi, though herself a queen's handmaid and confidante, found herself the mother of a princess in all but title."

Uneasiness grew in Collum's gut.

"These were the happiest years of Lalora's life," the borhond said. "Our queen had a child she loved, a child that adored her, a husband who completed her, and a best friend. Only a few within the royal circle were aware of how the child was treated, namely the king's closest advisors and the girl's tutors, who eventually were housed on the estate grounds in their own cottages so that she could be trained as often as she wanted in a number of subjects and interests, which were many. After many years of being barren, Lalora discovered she again was pregnant. By this time, rumors of a curse dissipated, but she feared for her pregnancy and the developing child even more so. She kept this pregnancy a complete secret except for with her family, Naomi, and Naomi's child."

Nehemi swallowed thickly. "After a daughter was safely born, Lalora remained secluded to care for her new child for a little more than a month. They quietly returned to Cyneham Breonna — the queen's most extended stay there in years — and no one breathed a word of the new princess outside of this tight circle. There was a plan for a great reveal, a crowning. Mere days before the event was to occur, King Hermann and Queen Lalora began to travel to finally spread the news. They wanted all of Heáhwolcen to hear of this miracle child! First, they would go to Bondrie, for if the rumors of a Palnan curse ever *were* true, the king wanted all of the Bondrie Guard on high alert."

Collum thought he might be sick.

"On the way to Fairevella, the accident happened," Nehemi whispered. "Almost everyone died."

Almost everyone? Collum thought. He began a quick count: the king and queen, his former fyrdwisa, the carriage driver, advisors — and then the Elf looked to the borhond.

"You were on that carriage," Collum said quietly.

Kharis did not meet his eyes. "It was only by sheer luck that I survived. I could not return to Endorsa to crown a two-month-old infant as queen. MxMillian Surefire was the closest guard who responded to the accident site. I told him what must be done, what must be said, and bound him to secrecy. Only a fatal threat to Heáhwolcen would allow him to break this vow."

MxMillian looked apologetically at Corria, then at the still-speaking borhond.

"I evanesced back to Deu Medgar to find the young princess, and throughout the coming days, what was to have been her crowning became a funeral," Kharis said. "Preparations had to be made, of course, for the new ruler, and it was then we shared with the world above the world the news of the only surviving offspring of their late king and queen. A daughter intentionally kept hidden until she was old enough to protect herself from any ill-intended magic. This daughter, we were proud to share, now held in her arms the granddaughter of Hermann and Lalora, its father having perished in the fiery accident with the king and queen."

The fyrdwisa's blood went ice cold.

"It was our firmest desire and only drive to ensure that the intent and bloodline of Artur Cromwell be preserved," Kharis said. "And thus, we crowned our new queen, who would raise the princess as her own."

Nehemi began sobbing.

~ 81 ~

The once haughty, always proud witch queen slumped onto the empty stool in front of her, head held in her hands, sleep-crushed auburn hair piling over her arms as she cried. It was Nehemi's breaking point, this secret she kept for almost thirty-seven years, that she was raised as an heir would be … except she was no heir at all. There was a sense of release, too. Now that her deception was out in the open, the leash she and Kharis kept on her background could be tossed aside. She could be herself, not the queen's role she knew long ago her shoes would never completely fill.

Cloa regarded Nehemi with mild curiosity, though the hair on Arctura's spine bristled. The princess' eyes had woken some since Collum first beheld them in the Samnung chamber that night, but held that same glazed look. The fyrdwisa almost didn't care that they'd been lied to by Nehemi and Kharis, because at least for the past nearly two decades, Endorsa had a capable, sane queen to lead the country. Just because Cloa was the blood heir did not make her fit to rule.

"Why in the deity-forsaken seven hells was the remainder of the Samnung never consulted?" Trystane hissed. He and Aristoces had both been in leadership roles then. "What difference would it have made to tell us then, sharing the original intent of Hermann and Lalora to have Nehemi be their heir since they were unable to conceive? Cloa would have had to have a regent anyway; we could have vouched for Nehemi to openly have that responsibility until the princess was old enough to —" he grimaced, his thoughts drifting to where Collum's had "— take her place as queen."

"I am sorry, Ceannairí," Kharis said. He bowed his head demurely. "It was my only intention to protect Endorsa and the lineage of Heáhwolcen's founder."

"You did so at the risk of every single other being in this

world," Verivol murmured dangerously. Their black eyes were fixated on the borhond. "The Samnung wall must be reinforced by magic freely given by the leader of each country. No wonder a Palnan was able to escape, and no wonder the spells weakened in recent years. The one who should have been performing the ritual, whose blood is innately connected to the land wards of Heáhwolcen, can barely speak her own deity-damned name."

The Sanguisuge's comments sparked Collum back to the original call for this unscheduled meeting. The fyrdwisa raised the question, again, of who the Bondrie Guard found escaping from Palna.

"His name is Dominus," MxMillian replied. It appeared he hadn't told that part to either Nehemi or Kharis, as the queen stopped her choking sobs long enough to look up, wide-eyed, to stare in shock. Kharis went bone white.

"Dominus?" Nehemi repeated. "Dominus Falto?"

Collum couldn't believe his ears, either. "Dominus died in the carriage accident, did he not?"

MxMillian furrowed his brow. "When I came upon the site of the explosion, I came upon carnage. It was exceedingly difficult to identify the dead, and only by the sigils and colors on the carriage did I know it was the king and queen of Endorsa. Was it not for the borhond, who I found scattered furthest away from the wreckage, barely coherent, I would not have known whose bodies were so burned and destroyed."

The chamber door opened and shut: Bryten could not think of those images and excused himself, retching. Collum considered following suit.

"How long after the accident did you arrive, MxMillian?" Aristoces asked. She, too, looked a little green at the graphic description of the wreckage. "Is it possible that Dominus survived and was pulled into Palna while you were distracted by waking Kharis?"

"I am not sure how long it was. The moment I heard the

explosion, I leapt onto my horse, and we rode in the direction of the noise. There were no open flames, just smoldering damaged wood and … parts," he replied delicately. "I suppose it is possible that whatever Palnan caused the attack could have taken Dominus. We have not questioned him specifically about how he got into the country. The Guard thought our fyrdwisa should have that duty."

"In theory, then, you're not even sure it *is* Dominus Falto?" Trystane asked, one eyebrow cocked. "It could be someone who was involved in making the accident occur."

"You could be correct, Ceannairí," MxMillian agreed. "However, I do not think anyone in Palna would have known about Nehemi or Cloa."

He raised a fair point.

"So now Endorsa … has no true queen," Collum said.

Nehemi made a great show of shoving a pointed finger toward where Cloa remained in the corner, and Corria huffed.

"The princess has a kind heart, I am sure, but can barely participate in daily life. Perhaps it will sound treasonous, but I do not know that I trust Cloa to lead a country and work with commanders of armed forces. Not now, and not when she is eighteen and the traditionally youngest age to be queen," the master swordswoman said.

Kharis crossed his arms. "That is the other thing."

"What else are you not telling us?" Aristoces asked. Collum at once picked up on the borhond's shifty eyes that rose to stare at the ceiling, as though the witch considered whether or not he would answer the Fairy.

It took a long moment for him to say anything else, during which time the fyrdwisa wondered if he'd be questioning both Dominus and Kharis in the coming days.

"Cloa is shielded," the borhond whispered. The room erupted into shouts.

Collum stepped back from the fray. His head throbbed and

he could scarcely believe the experience he found himself in was real, for it felt like a nightmare. Trystane was beating into the Samnung table. Corria had a knife halfway out of its sheath and paused, not sure which of the Endorsan leaders to aim its blade at. Bryten returned to the room and almost turned right back around, but the fyrdwisa grabbed his arm and slammed the door shut behind him.

"Enough!" the Elf shouted. He slammed his palms down on the table. "Enough! We will have order in this deity-damned room!"

Collum turned his furious blue irises to Kharis. "Unward this room. Now."

The man balked. "Fyrdwisa, I cannot —"

"*Now.*"

Kharis pulled his knotted wand from his robe pocket. He gave Collum a frightened look and began to undo the spells that kept each Samnung member's powers in check while they were within its walls. When the last such barrier was gone, Collum brought a sense of calm into the room. New scents filled the air and the fyrdwisa watched closely as each individual in the chamber, including MxMillian Surefire, had their heartbeats and breath rates forcibly slowed. It seemed to take an eternity.

"Does Cloa know?" Collum asked Kharis.

"I do not believe so, Fyrdwisa. She has been shielded since she was a youngling, far too young to remember anything else."

Collum glanced at Corria, Trystane, and Aristoces. Each gave him a quick nod of permission. He looked back to Kharis and with the most authority Collum had ever exerted in his position, told the borhond to take the girl's shield down.

"No!"

"Remove the shield, Kharis." Collum did not and would not back down from this. "Do it now, while we are calm and some form of barrier still exists to her magic."

As Kharis turned the wand onto the princess, Arctura hissed, spittle flying from between his bright white teeth. The cat's sudden reaction startled Cloa, who gazed lovingly at the feline and started purring herself, whispering sweet nothings down to where the animal sat on her lap. The cat chattered at Kharis, then turned his gaze onto Collum.

Bridgette was right! the fyrdwisa thought. *That beast is far more than just a cat.*

But no one else registered Arctura's response as Kharis ever so slowly lifted the invisible shield of magic from Cloa, revealing both the young queen and the full extent of her magic.

"Astridsí," Collum found himself whispering in awe.

A very clear pair of green-gold eyes blinked themselves awake before him.

~ 82 ~

It was as if she walked out of a cool, dark cave and into heated, blinding sunlight.

Her pupils dilated and contracted; her body sprinkled with goosebumps and shivers before recalibrating. Her brain stopped working completely for a moment, adjusting itself to a strange feeling of openness.

Cloa blinked. Once, twice, then over and over again, taking in the scene that faced her. She recognized these beings. There stood her mother and Kharis, and the rest of the Samnung around them, all looking at her as though they waited for something. A reaction of some sort.

"Princess?" Kharis said timidly.

She cocked her head toward him, thoughts whirling in an unnerving manner.

"Yes?" she said, and her voice sounded vibrant. What noise was this? She knew her voice. It was airy and breathless, a dance across the tongue. Her mother once called it sing-song. Dreamy. This voice was not that. It wasn't hers, though it had come from her lips.

"What is happening?" she asked no one and everyone. Testing this new quality to her vocal cords, this compelling tone that was of deeper note and more regal in command.

The Samnung members all looked at one another, no one sure who would be best to answer her.

They looked different, as if before Cloa had seen them through a sheer voile curtain, an observer watching discreetly from the outside, rarely interacting with those beyond it. At this moment, the curtain was suddenly ripped back along its rod, displaying the characters before her in all their pure glory. She wanted to *know* them, not just see them. She yearned to be part of their space, to dive into the in-between and join them.

There was a Fairy named Aristoces and two Elves — an ice

blonde and a brunette; she couldn't remember who was whom. A golden-skinned thing with horns and no shirt was seated next to a pale-skinned individual who smiled at her with visible fangs. An armored female stood at Cloa's other side.

No one answered her question, and she was unsure how much time had passed since she asked it. The Samnung chamber remained silent, everyone staring at one another. How odd. Cloa remembered them talking nonstop and on occasion even yelling at one another.

Actually, she recalled, the ice blonde Elf and her mother usually yelled at each other *a lot.*

"What is happening?" Cloa asked again.

The Fairy spoke, her butterfly-like wings fluttering in a state of caution, or perhaps anxiousness. Maybe a little of both.

"Cloa," she addressed. "We were informed tonight that for nearly your entire life, we had been duped into believing that you are a princess. Though you were born a princess, the daughter of our late King Hermann and Queen Lalora, you are a princess no longer. You have been a queen since you were two months old. This information was intentionally hidden from us all."

Cloa stared at Aristoces. "I am a queen?" she asked. Cloa meant for her voice to sound timid, yet the strange new tone worked itself into those words. "But my mother is here."

Cloa knew of Queen Lalora, her grandmother. The late queen, king, and Cloa's father were killed in an accident many years ago. Her mother became queen at a young age as a result. But what this Fairy said made no sense! The Fairy female said that *Queen Lalora* was her mother. Mayhap she misspoke and meant "grandmother".

Aristoces met Cloa's eyes, and the princess realized the Fairy did not have eyes like hers. They didn't have pupils, just whorls of charcoal and silver spinning around endlessly, almost hypnotic.

"You are not *a* queen, Cloa of Endorsa," the Fairy said. Her voice was commanding, but not unkind, as if she wanted Cloa to understand something important. "You are *the* queen."

"How can this be?" Cloa asked. Again, she meant for her voice to be meek and kind, but it came out sounding much harsher. *What is happening to me?*

Even her thoughts to herself were different. In her seventeen years, Cloa realized, she never once truly *thought*. She remembered facts and figures, recognized faces and feelings. But *thinking* as she did now was … uncomfortable.

It was not the Fairy who answered her this time, but Kharis.

"Your Majesty, you must understand I never meant for any of this to happen," the old witch began, his watery eyes pleading. "You were mere months old when the tragic accident stole your parents from us. Your mother, believing it was impossible for her to bring a pregnancy to full term due to her cursed womb, instead raised her young ward as the royal heir — and did not tell anyone outside of her most inner council. When she was killed, it was the appropriate move for us to crown this ward as queen. She was old enough to hold the throne, and she could continue to raise you as her own child until it was your turn to be crowned."

Something stirred in the crevices of Cloa's mind: anger. Anger that she could not place.

"I do not know how to be queen," she said aloud, though her mind was spinning with new emotions and things that had been long hidden inside her soul.

The Elf with stunning blue eyes and wavy brown hair was trying to catch her gaze. He wanted to tell her something. She didn't understand any of what was happening. The beings at the circular table were all gazing at her with various faces of wonderment, pity, and uncertainty.

"Mother," Cloa began, and Nehemi jumped at being addressed directly by this new voice. "Mother, may I please go to my room?"

Her mother did not answer, but the golden-skinned male did: "Cloa, you are queen of Endorsa. You may do as you please, and do not need to ask anyone's permission."

He stared then at Nehemi, who Cloa realized had been crying. There were tear stains clearing paths down her mother's face from eye-corners to jaw.

Cloa of Endorsa didn't like this. Didn't like this one bit.

Cradling Arctura in her arms, Cloa rose from her stool and curtsied clumsily to those in the room. Her legs felt unsteady, but she forced herself to remain upright as she backed out of the Samnung chamber and bolted into the hall.

She was several steps removed from the chamber before she realized someone was following her. The someone wasn't running as she was — or as best as she could run in the floor-length nightgown her mother chose for her to wear. Cloa's feet kept hitting fabric with each footfall. She slowed and turned around.

It was the blue-eyed Elf behind her, who strode forward with an impressive air of command. His stride, his posture, made her think of this new voice that emanated from her mouth. This fit the Elf. It did not fit her.

"Why are you following me?" she asked.

"I would like to speak with you and answer your questions," the Elf replied.

Cloa swallowed. She would very much like to go back to bed and start this too-early morning over again. But the Elf, she could tell, was relentless, and would not stop until his quest here was satisfied.

"Will you answer me truthfully and not lie?" she asked him.

Something sparked in those eyes of his, but the Elf said, "I will, Your Majesty."

"Alright then," she said, wishing her voice would go back to how it was *supposed* to be. This voice was so hard, not at all delicate and dainty as a princess' voice.

She let the Elf come level with her. He was *so tall*, he had to be an entire foot taller than her! Long and lean, compared to her feminine curves. Curves that her mother discouraged her from showing, of course. It was unseemly for a princess to display herself in such a way.

The walk to her room was long, even if she hadn't felt the constant shadow of the blue-eyed companion following. The two had to go from the Samnung chamber in Cyneham Breonna all the way across the connecting bridge to the residential palace of Deu Medgar. Each footstep seemed an eternity, one full of strange new sensations and visualizations. Things that were supposed to be dull and dim were bright and colorful, and Cloa kept having to be careful to make sure that she took the right turns. What should have been a familiar walk she made daily — sometimes multiple times a day — was now unrecognizable in parts.

In fact, Cloa passed by her own bedroom door and only stopped when she felt Arctura claw into her forearm.

"Oh!" she gasped, turning around. The Elf stood by her and followed her movement as she shifted in place.

"I am sorry. This is my room," Cloa apologized, motioning toward the door-that-was-hers-but-wasn't. She did not remember the door being so *bright*. Its bronze paint gleamed and shimmered in a metallic hue that she swore had not been that way when she departed it a few hours prior. "The door must have been repainted while I was away."

She pressed a hand to the metal knob panel and it swung open at her touch.

Cloa stopped moving. This was her room. But it was not her room. Nothing matched. Everything was haphazard and done up in shades of gray and beige and cream that coordinated in a way that made her want to vomit at the blatant neutrality of it. How had she *lived* in this place with no life within it?

"You didn't live," the Elf murmured to her. "Not really."

She stared at him.

"Please tell me how you know what is in my mind," Cloa asked, although it came out as a terse, polite command.

He blinked. He seemed as surprised as she was at the new sound to her voice.

"I am gifted in the ability to hear the thoughts one thinks to oneself," the Elf replied. "I apologize if that startled you — it is common knowledge amongst the Samnung. I thought you knew."

"I thought I knew many things that I no longer think I knew at all," she murmured, the familiar singsong cadence finding new life with its queenly tenor. "Please, come inside. There is much I would like to ask you."

~ 83 ~

The lifting of Cloa's shield was a sensory vision that Collum thought might be cemented in his mind for eternity. He spent seventeen years, all but two months of this princess' — no, queen's! — life hearing her thoughts to herself, seeing her not-quite-there glassy-eyed stare. She was trapped in a magic cage, but not the sort of magic that should have ever been allowed to prosper in his beloved Heáhwolcen. There was no well-intentioned shielding of this nature. To have created such a shield as this, that not even Aristoces, the most powerful magical being Collum ever knew, was able to sense? It was nigh on impossible.

But the past few months taught Collum much about what was and wasn't possible — flying Elflings, to start with — and he would think about this shield and its origin later. For now, he must face these gold-green eyes that now saw everything, and answer the questions festering in a newly awoken brain.

Her eyes were positively electric with color and wonder. They were sharp, knowing. When she spoke, even her voice was different. It was deeper and focused. The energy that writhed around her, finally free after so many years, was tangible.

Though perhaps Cloa didn't realize it. She noticed the difference in her senses, according to what she inadvertently told Collum in her mind. But this energy …

His heart stuttered. The aura. This entire time, since the first day Bridgette, Emi-Joye, and Cloa shared close space with one another, the Maylemaegus of the Triumvirate tried to make itself known. But Cloa's shield prevented that: the deep power that locked the young queen inside herself was what caused Bridgette and Emi-Joye to feel so strange, and what led to Bridgette and Cloa becoming ill.

Collum remembered Emi-Joye's more recent suspicion that Cloa was born of cursed blood, which was why Cloa behaved in such a way and their energies felt so wrong together. But the aura had nothing directly and everything tangentially to do with Queen Lalora's supposedly cursed womb.

This is going to be a ruthlessly lengthy day, isn't it? the Elf thought to himself.

He tucked away the thoughts of the shield and the aura deep in the recesses of his mind, turning himself both physically and mentally to his new queen.

"What is happening to me?" Cloa asked for the fourth or fifth time.

Collum helped himself to a seat on a taupe settee. "I will be as honest and forthright as I can be, Your Majesty. But I would begin this question and answer session with a note of caution. There are forces at play here which I do not fully understand, and I do not care to lead you astray or share potentially incorrect information. If there is a question I do not know or cannot answer to, I shall tell you."

She nodded. "Please tell me what is happening."

"I do not know the mechanics of this magic, but what I can tell you is that you spent most of your life under a shielding spell," Collum said. He sounded emotionless. "This shield hid your mind and your magic. To us, you appeared outwardly as someone who was not fully present in our reality. I had, thanks to my abilities, slightly more insight into how your mind worked. However, even the thoughts I could hear from within your mind were distant and dazed. We were quite concerned about the future of Endorsa, for the Samnung and your own citizens believed you to be incapable of being much of anything besides a decorative piece at the ruling party's side."

Cloa's brows furrowed. "That's nice," she said bitterly.

Collum cleared his throat and continued.

"The shield spell was lifted tonight, after your true origins and position were revealed to us. I do not know what is *happening*, per se. But you are in a sense waking up, Your Majesty. Your body, your mind, your senses are becoming attuned to true existence. You felt as though a veil was lifted, and I believe that to be an apt description. I imagine it is a jarring experience," Collum said gently. "It is jarring for us as well, in a different way."

They sat in silence then, Collum waiting patiently for Cloa to ask more of him. He was so used to Bridgette wanting to know *everything*, toying with him until he either gave in and told her, or accidentally let his guard slip out of sheer annoyance. Cloa's quiet absorption unnerved him.

She doesn't even know who she is, he reminded himself. *Cloa has not been a cognizant being for seventeen years. It will take time, perhaps years, for her to express herself fully.*

Collum resisted the urge to chuckle. His own inner monologue just then sounded as though it came straight from Trystane's mouth. He watched the queen as she took a seat on the floor. Her back was to him, her face and body aimed due east, where the sun began to rise. Its pale rose-gold light streamed into the window at them, illuminating Cloa in a devastatingly beautiful silhouette. The fabric of her nightgown draped gracefully around her, and her long, wavy brown hair was no longer a shade of dull earth. It shone with the force of a thousand sun-drenched trees, the dark black-browns of forests as old as time, that withstood storm and fire, hell and high water, and did not falter. The gown was modest, as Cloa's usually were, and looked something out of a human storybook that dressed its characters in corsets and too much fabric.

Collum knew this queen would never wear a dress like that again.

She turned to him, realizing he watched her. The sunlight caught in those eyes, and his breath caught in his throat. The gold glinted. The green glowed. Her irises flashed like stars.

Had the fyrdwisa been standing, he would have instantly fallen to his knees before her. It was a feral feeling, an instinct to give this act of reverence. These were the eyes of his queen and commander. He was helpless before them, and a deeper, wilder part of him roared inside at the feeling of such magic in the air. The blood of Artur Cromwell flowed in front of his eyes. He craved to bow before Cloa not just because she was the rightful queen of Endorsa, but because a missing puzzle piece was found when that veil lifted. A shifting of the very worlds occurred.

Cloa watched him from her seat on the carpet. Her head tilted to one side in a move that once Collum considered silly and daft, but now? Now that head tilt could have just as easily been the considering stare of a raptor, homing in on its prey with deadly consequences. He did not deserve to be seated above her, and he could not explain this feeling.

"Stand up," he rasped out. She did so, a confused look flitting across her cheeks. Collum slid to one knee before her.

"I am Fyrdwisa Collum Andoralain, commander of the Fyrdlytta, heir successor to the ard rialóir," he said, reciting words he had not spoken for seventeen years. Not since he'd said them out loud on a stage, swearing fealty to an imposter queen. "I am yours forsworn, Queen Cloa of Endorsa. My swords and arrows, my movements and destiny, are yours to command and to claim. I will protect your life and the lineage of Artur Cromwell with mine own, as I will so protect and fight with your sisters of the Triumvirate. I swear this by the power of three times three, by the magic of soil, sky, and sea. As it is, so mote it be."

There was another shift in the energy between them. Cloa reached out and touched his shoulder.

"Rise, Collum Andoralain," she said, feeling his name on her tongue.

A flicker of thought crossed the Elf's mind — she didn't know his name until now. He realized she got him confused with Trystane all the time.

Collum stood, again looking down at his queen. There was

such a fierceness in those eyes!

"I do not know what it is to be queen, nor do I know why you say I have sisters," the young queen said. "But I would very much like to learn, I think, and I trust that you will keep your promises you've made to me this day. I think I should like to go back to sleep now."

He blinked. The ancient magick was still palpable, but he hadn't exactly expected a dismissal. Cloa didn't seem to register it as a dismissal, however. She just seemed, well, exhausted.

"Of course, Your Majesty," Collum said. He bowed his head slightly and retreated from the room. Before he closed the door, he turned back to face her. "Your Majesty, I am at your service. You may call upon me at any time."

She nodded in acknowledgement, a slightly dazed look returning, and watched as his languid form exited her bedchamber. The door was about to click shut when her small hands yanked it back open, and the queen stuck her head out in the hallway.

"One thing, before you go?" she asked.

"Of course, Your Majesty." He stood at attention.

"Please don't call me that. It's just Cloa, to you." The queen grinned up at him and winked, then the door ticked shut behind her.

Collum groaned. He knew that grin all too well. It was usually on the face of Bridgette Eileen Conner, and was usually a precursor to something absolutely wicked.

Seven fucking hells, these females, he thought, and shook his head as he began the long walk back to find Trystane.

~ 84 ~

Cloa snapped her back against the door the moment it closed, and breathed a heavy sigh. She still felt as though this was a strange dream; that at any second, she would sit straight up in bed and her room would look normal, her voice would sound right, her mother had always been her mother, and she would have many years before anyone referred to her as a queen.

These overnight events, what Collum said to her! She sat on the floor and put her face in her hands. There was a coo from the ground next to her, and without looking, Cloa reached out for Arctura. He snuggled between her arms and curled into her lap. She remembered finding him. It was her earliest memory.

It might be the only real memory I have until tonight, the witch realized with a shudder.

She had been quite young, walking with her mother — it would take a long time for her to consider Nehemi as anything else — along the paths of Mimea Botanicci, the vast botanical gardens behind Cyneham Breonna and Deu Medgar. Cloa distinctly recalled hearing a sound in some bushes and beginning to toddle toward it. Nehemi saw the injured kitten first, mewing in anger as it fought off whatever animal attacked it. Cloa could not remember precisely, but felt strongly it had been a large bird. She recalled yelling something, a noise loud enough to startle the predator.

But more than the actions of the day, which wound up with Nehemi placating the toddler by scooping up the bleeding, terrified feline and carrying both kitten and child into Deu Medgar, what Cloa remembered about finding Arctura was the instinctual gravitation toward the creature. She would not be complete without him in her life. He was given the name Arctura by the kind lacnestre who did her best to heal the cat's injured eye, the moniker short for "Arcturus", one of the brightest stars in the galaxy.

"He's such a wee thing," Cloa remembered the lacnestre saying as she handed the bandaged kitten back to Nehemi. "It'd be proper luck to name such a little one after a big, bright star like that, I think."

Arctura was her constant companion ever since. Of course, he would disappear for a period of time every few days, but never strayed far, and knew in mere heartbeats if Cloa needed comfort.

It was so bizarre to think back to who she thought she was, who she'd been, only hours before. That Cloa always needed comfort, needed something to keep her hands busy. Especially at the meetings her mother took her to. She tuned most of them out, preferring to stay inside her own mind, rehashing lessons and having pretend conversations with the ones she did not feel comfortable talking to. Which, it turns out, was nearly everyone.

The witch picked Arctura up fully and rested him half-against her shoulder, as she would a baby. "I cannot say I enjoy this," she told him. "I feel conflicted. It's waking from a dream, in a way, you understand?"

Arctura nuzzled into her. Cloa felt his agreement. She always knew the cat's emotions, though it was a different ability than what Collum had. The cat did not think the same way that bipedal creatures did.

Cloa watched his fluffy tail flick against the bodice of her nightgown. "Hmm. I wonder, if I am truly the queen, does that make you a prince?"

Collum walked a few lengths of hallway in Deu Medgar before he got turned around. Though a different sort of architecture than Casa de Piedra, both were similarly maze-like. It also didn't help that he was wandering the residential palace on a significant lack of sleep, paying more attention to his mental recap of the night's events than in which direction he walked. The fyrdwisa paused in the middle of a decadently carpeted area and reached for his covenant with Trystane.

Where are you? he asked.

A one-word answer drifted to him shortly after: *Home.*

The fyrdwisa hoped he wouldn't shock Trystane too much by immediately evanescing to his front doorstep. The ard rialóir didn't even come to the door, just swung it open with a gust of air and invited his brother inside.

"I'm cooking breakfast. How many eggs would you like?" Trystane called from the kitchen.

Collum hadn't even thought about food. "Two, please," he responded as he walked through the treehouse, ears and mind picking up on the handful of voices that accompanied the Elves. "You made quick work of that debacle, I see."

He was glad that Aurelias was here, along with Njahla, Emi-Joye, Apostine, and most of the Samnung. Nehemi, Kharis, and obviously Cloa were not crowded around Trystane's kitchen table or perched on his countertops and windowsills. Collum graciously accepted a steaming mug of coffee from Bryten, whose seat was nearest the coffeepot.

The fyrdwisa took a long sip, relishing in the burn. A little too much burn. "Did one of you put whiskey in this?" he asked, sniffing over the rim.

"Don't ask questions you already know the answer to, brother mine," Trystane warned. "How did facing off with our new queen go?"

"I would not call it 'facing off' so much as explaining in more detail what occurred in the Samnung meeting," Collum answered. He took another sip. At least it was good whiskey. "I spoke the Hyldájj of the fyrdwisa to her. It rather tumbled out of me at one point."

There was a beat of pause in which Trystane's spatula stopped moving in the massive pan of scrambled eggs. "Did that go over well?"

"I believe I did little more than confuse her," Collum

admitted. "We need to know how much magic she knows, and I personally care to learn more about the shield itself. None of us detected it. That worries me."

"Who put the shield on her?" Aurelias asked.

"Kharis, I think we collectively assume," Bryten replied. "As he was the one who took it off, that makes sense enough to me."

Did you tell her about the Triumvirate? Emi-Joye thought to Collum. He glanced up to where she and Apostine floated quietly in midair, the ambestre cradling her in his lap. Collum shrugged, and she answered with a frown.

"What are you going to do about Nehemi and Kharis?" Njahla asked aloud. *And does this mean I can have my regular job back?* she thought to Collum. He chuckled.

Trystane began serving heaping platters of eggs and sliced honeyed ham. "I believe the correct mode of action would be for Nehemi to publicly be reported as stepping down from her role. I don't know that it should all come out that the entirety of Heáhwolcen was duped for seventeen years by a reckless decision of the legacy borhond of Endorsa."

"You think it better to continue lying now that we are aware of the truth?" Verivol asked. "I respectfully disagree, Ceannairí. Our citizens were lied to the same as we were. Mistakes are not the end of the world, and yes, this is a sizable mistake that is embarrassing to admit. But it is not our fault. We had no reason to suspect anything was amiss. Regardless of it being Nehemi or not, Cloa would have needed a regent until about now, anyway."

The Sanguisuge stood to serve themself a plate of the ham. "I also would like to remind everyone gathered here that *Kharis*, not eighteen-year-old Nehemi, was the perpetrator of this charade. She was little more than a child herself and thrust into both motherhood and queendom, one of which we don't know if she wanted. Her life was upended just like Cloa's was, albeit in a lighter fashion. We keep harping on her as if this is her fault, and it's not."

Verivol made a fair point.

Bryten jumped in to back them up. "She's made running an effective government body challenging, I'll say, but wouldn't anybody in her position? Think about it. I wasn't in the Samnung until after Nehemi was crowned, but *no one* knew about her before then. Seven hells, I doubt if either she or Cloa even know who they are as individuals. I think Verivol's right. Sure, have Nehemi step down, but don't keep up the lie. That's ridiculous."

"Why not allow Cloa to make this decision?" Corria wondered aloud. "Nehemi raised her. Should she not get a say in her foster mother's fate?"

The term "foster mother" set Collum's teeth on edge. He wondered which of the travel deputies had been put in charge of pretending to be Bridgette the past several weeks, sending electronic communication back and forth with the Simmonses. They weren't taking any chances this time about her being reported missing.

"Oh, fucking hell," Collum muttered. "I suppose it doesn't matter now that Nehemi doesn't know Bridgette's gone, but Cloa … the new queen is so integral to everything that's going on, everything that we've been trying to keep Nehemi and Kharis from knowing about. We should probably brief her at some point."

A pointed silence. Aurelias chuckled. "By 'we', you know you mean yourself, right, Chief?"

The fyrdwisa rolled his eyes. "I will add that to my lengthy list of individuals to question. Beginning with the alleged Dominus Falto," Collum said, looking over to Corria. "I'd rather get that over and done with soon, if you don't mind."

She nodded. "Of course, Fyrdwisa. Let us finish this meal and we can evanesce in fast fashion. I have a few questions for Dominus myself."

The fyrdestre joined Corria and Collum at Casa de Piedra.

They were all three still in sleepclothes, though Corria requested they stop by her personal rooms so that she could at least put on her pauldron and swordbelt. It was quite the getup when she emerged, and the rag-tag trio descended into the bowels of the Beorgdún.

There was not a prison, per se — though Bridgette might object, had she seen it — but the subbasement of Casa de Piedra was a cavernous maze of little-used rooms. Most were for spiritual practice, meditation, and even feoht training if wígend did not care to train at Minthame. It wasn't dark or damp as one might expect an underground to be, but rather cool and peaceful, with ever-burning torches and lanterns of acid green witchlight lining the tunnel walls. MxMillian, who joined them upon Corria's request, led his master swordswoman, fyrdwisa, and fyrdestre to a hallway offshoot. Two guardsfolk were casually stationed at the hallway entrance. They immediately stood to attention when they saw who approached. Corria nodded her thanks to acknowledge their gesture, but the foursome passed without a word. Collum could see an arched doorway at the end of the short hall.

"You'll find him in here, Ceannairí," MxMillian said.

"Password?" Corria asked. She didn't look at the guard. It was evident how furious she was that he'd gone to Endorsa instead of to her, no matter what secrets Kharis should never have forced him to keep.

"Hilina'i," MxMillian replied.

The master swordswoman gave him a bemused look. "Native Hawaiian?"

MxMillian shrugged somewhat bashfully. "My new apprentice recently began to learn the language of his cultural ancestry. I have picked up a few things from him. The word means 'trust'. I thought it prudent given the situation in which our uninvited guest stays with us."

"An interesting tale, MxMillian Surefire." Corria pressed

both open palms to the doorframe and whispered the word against the wood. It swung open to reveal a cozy suite of bedroom and small bath. The man's back was to them, situated by the firehearth.

He looked over his shoulder. "Fáilte, Ceannairí. It is a relief that you have come."

Collum wasn't sure it was a relief at all. Part of him wished Trystane joined them — the ard rialóir knew Dominus. Not well, but well enough to readily recognize if this was indeed the witch seated in front of them. The fyrdwisa moved forward and held a hand to stop the man from rising from the chair. Two whispered words had him seated and bound. He didn't seem to like that, but Collum was not dumb. He was not going to believe the man was Dominus without a thorough investigation.

Aurelias and Corria watched as the fyrdwisa ran his hands over and through the various energies that the man emitted. Collum searched for any glamour spells, any instance of a shield. The previous night's experience, Collum's embarrassment at not detecting Cloa's shield, weighed heavy on his mind. He would not let that happen again.

It was a lengthy process, this quiet examination of the man's aura and mind. The witch sat still through it all, uncomfortable as he was with the magic keeping him stuck to the chair, but all Collum heard in his mind were thoughts wondering what was going on, and who the females were. The man recognized MxMillian as the guard who found him, and he, oddly enough, recognized Collum, though he couldn't remember the fyrdwisa's name.

The Elf had only seen Dominus in passing, and that was years ago. Witches may not age as fast as humans, but the man was clearly in his late thirties or early forties, older and more haggard than the spry young aide to King Hermann that Dominus would have been before the accident. Collum gave him a final once-over, using a modified revealing spell like what he used on Aelys Frost's trunk, searching for any remaining tells that would give away ill intent or deception. He wished Bridgette was here. Her Maylemaegus would come in quite useful in rare situations such as this.

Satisfied, the fyrdwisa stepped away from Dominus and unbound him. Dominus pitched forward and stretched his shoulders and arms. "I have seen you before, a long time ago," he said to Collum.

"I am Collum Andoralain, fyrdwisa."

Recognition bloomed. "You were the fyrdestre when —" His voice cut off with a grimace, but Collum nodded.

"I was. Behind me is Corria Deathhunter, master swordswoman of Bondrie. You likely knew her predecessor, Druan Heart of Stones. The Elfling is my fyrdestre, Aurelias Parvhin," Collum said. "We need to hear everything you can tell us about what happened when King Hermann and Queen Lalora were killed, how you got into Palna, what happened whilst you were there, and nearly as important, how you got out."

Dominus sighed. "Is Nehemi …?"

"She is in good health," was all Corria volunteered. She was willing to use the false queen as a bargaining chip if she needed to. "Your story, Dominus Falto."

It was a lengthy tale. When Collum and Corria reported it back to the rest of the Samnung the following day, they had just as many questions as they had answers. From what Dominus remembered, the explosion that destroyed the carriage and murdered his king and queen, the fyrdwisa, Naomi, and supposedly himself did take place near the Samnung wall. But the explosion burst forth from behind him. Dominus had been driving the horses and was pitched forward when the blast came.

They were astonished to learn that Dominus had not been kidnapped.

"I flew off the seat and bashed my head against the ground," he said, and indicated a long-healed scar under his sandy hairline. "I couldn't tell you how long I was out for. But when I came to, I saw that the carriage was destroyed. It burned. I saw limbs and fragments of clothes on the ground. But the screams … I still hear them screaming. It was as if some passengers remained trapped in that damned box, but when I tried to stand the world tilted out from under me. I saw Kharis, though. He wasn't inside; I suppose he'd gotten out. He was saying strange words and I know the wizard is an old cod, Fyrdwisa, but I couldn't tell you what language he was going at. I've chalked it up to my head being concussed, and it still bothers me, because whatever he said made them stop screaming …"

It was about that point that Dominus had caught sight of dust blowing in the distance, which would turn out to be MxMillian on horseback. But Dominus didn't know that, and in his panic, he crawled through the Samnung wall to escape the carnage.

"The wall isn't soundproof, not like the Palnan inner one is," Dominus recalled. "I heard Kharis start saying that it was an attack, that the Tinuviels were obviously behind it. But I swear to you, on my life, that I looked around inside that barrier, and no one else was there in either direction. The borhond told the guard that he was the only survivor, and then he began pointing out whose body parts were whose —"

He'd had to stop speaking then, and Aurelias had gone a touch green with horror. It had been hard for Collum to function for a moment too, so wretched were these memories and this energy of remembered panic and fear that surrounded Dominus. The fyrdwisa gave him a moment to collect himself before asking him to continue.

"Bottom line being, I backed myself into the no-man's land and everyone in Heáhwolcen, my betrothed included, was about to hear I was very, very dead. Kharis told the guard about his plan, that the princess babe could not take the crown, but

Endorsa could not *not* have a ruler," Dominus said. "He swore the guard to secrecy, that nothing he saw at the accident site could be shared, that the truth of what happened needed to stay there unless the guard had no other choice or Heáhwolcen was threatened. My head was spinning, I was apt to be physically ill, and something inside me knew that if I was to go back through the Samnung wall, I would no longer be welcome in Endorsa, no matter if my beloved was queen or not. So, I went the other way."

Getting into Palna was far easier then, before the Ballamúr was fully activated. It was as flimsy a physical barrier as the Samnung wall could be, provided one had permission to go through it. Dominus had been close enough to the Beorgdún when he crossed into the country that it was easy to hide, to start a quiet life.

"They called where I lived the vuoristokylä, no real name for cities and towns, but remote villages. I found work with a shepherd and lied about where I was from, though I think eventually he caught on that I was not telling the full truth. When he passed into the spirit realm — I would assume Palnan souls still enter Ifrinnevatt — the farm became mine own. I kept to myself, raising sheep for meat and wool, only going into a real city when I had no choice," Dominus said. "Market days, mostly. But I happened to be in Düoria not that long ago when a group of unexpected visitors were announced as honored guests for Imbolc."

As Collum relayed this story to the Samnung, Trystane's jaw dropped at that part. "Dominus saw us in Düoria?" he asked, incredulous.

"He did," Collum confirmed. "I'm sure he recognized you, but he saw Nehemi and knew that Kharis' plan would soon come to fruition."

Dominus had seen Kharis as well, and the fury that welled in him at the sight of the borhond nearly made him reveal himself to the queen as she strolled the capital city streets. The man told Collum, Aurelias, and Corria that he did not expect to ever see anyone from greater Heáhwolcen for as long as he lived, but to see Nehemi with Kharis at her side? The man could hardly stand it.

"He nearly made himself crazy remembering all the things from the day of the accident," Aurelias piped in. "I can't even imagine. Just standing there, minding his own business, when suddenly the woman he loved and the wizard who betrayed them waltz into the life he created."

Aristoces frowned. "What do you mean by 'betrayed', Fyrdestre?"

The Elfling let out a harrumph. "Is it not obvious? Dominus is pretty convinced that Kharis blew the deity-damned carriage to bits."

~ 85 ~

No one mentioned a word to Nehemi, and especially not to Kharis, about Dominus' interrogation or whereabouts.

The man had spent days after the Samnung visit to Palna creeping along the border, trying to get back through the way that he came. It was nigh on impossible, as the activated Ballamúr had leniency for only one magical being. But Dominus was persistent, and either the sentient wall took pity on him — Collum thought that it may have understood the man's mission would be important to the Bright Star — or the Ballamúr had weak spots just like the Samnung wall did. By a stroke of luck, Dominus tumbled through. He found himself in the no-man's land for a brief few moments before the Bondrie Guard found him.

The Samnung decided, with Corria's blessing, that Dominus could remain at Casa de Piedra until they figured out what to do next. After being questioned, he had been moved to a different level of the residence, one that had a window and a balcony that the man quickly took to spending his days on, usually reading.

Cloa hadn't seemed to care one way or another what happened to the man she'd been led to believe was her father. It had been two weeks since she learned she was queen, and the poor girl kept waffling between being excited for her new role and wanting to crawl into her closet and never emerge into society. The only individual she wanted to talk to thus far, aside from the tutors who still visited her, was Collum.

He sat on the settee for the third time in four days and did little more than watch Cloa dart around her rooms, directing various artists and designers about colors and fabric choices. Her first order of business as rightful ruler of Endorsa appeared to be making her personal space, well, hers.

"Cloa, what say you about taking a trip?" Collum asked, interrupting her holding five swatches of too-similar gemstone greens against her final three curtain fabric options. "You're going to have to go out in public at some point, you know. It might be better to do this particular venture before everyone knows of your new role."

"Where do you want to go?" She didn't even turn around to look at him.

Collum's favorite thing about Cloa was her obscure ability to have an entire conversation with him and simultaneously carry on a different thought pattern inside her mind. She was the only being he ever encountered who constantly had a soundtrack playing in the background of her inner monologue. He observed this for years, and it was more prominent now that she was out from under her shield.

He tried not to think about the shield. It made him think about Kharis, about the idea that the borhond might be responsible for the murder of his former fyrdwisa. Kharis had been forced to seclude himself in his chambers. Though the Samnung members still argued over Nehemi's fate, they agreed that for now, Kharis should have as little influence over Cloa as possible. She would be told about Dominus soon, about his suspicions regarding Kharis, and it would be up to the new queen to decide what role, if any, the longtime advisor might play for her.

"Do you recall when I gave you my Hyldájj and I mentioned your sisters and the Triumvirate?" Collum asked.

"Yes." Cloa turned and gave him a shrewd look. "Are you going to explain that now?"

"I'd like to, yes. But not here."

"What's wrong with my room?"

He cringed. "Well, this information is … sensitive, only to be shared with the Samnung and a few other trusted advisors. Nehemi did not know the full extent of it, but you should, as it involves you. I hesitate to share these things in a room where so many guests are coming in and out."

"Right. That makes sense." She gingerly laid the paint swatches down upon a footstool. "Where are we going instead?"

"A place called Maluridae Wood," Collum replied. "It's sacred to the Elves, but others can go with our blessing." He glanced down at her outfit, a loose-fitting dress that hung to the floor. "I would suggest wearing something a bit more outdoorsy."

"Are you sure this is a good idea?" Trystane muttered as he and Collum led Cloa and Emi-Joye to the clearing of rowan trees, where the vademecums slumbered. Or their physical forms slumbered, anyway. Collum was keen to find out if Bridgette's vademecum cared to act as a conduit for his intended message.

"I am not," he admitted. "But I want to give the queen as many tools as I can to prepare her for both leadership and the unasked-for responsibility of being part of the Triumvirate. Her vademecum will be able to give her answers that we cannot, and to questions that we ourselves want to ask."

Trystane glanced over his shoulder to see the Fairy and witch interacting with one another. They seemed tentatively at ease, though the only time they met previously had been at Emi-Joye's installation. The ard rialóir was deeply worried about the ambassadora after her last run-in with Maylemaegus. Though the scar around her throat was barely visible anymore, the image of her wounded like that was seared into his brain.

"Collum, have you ever heard the phrase, 'verta verestä'?" Trystane asked.

The fyrdwisa gave him a sharp glance. "Once. It's what Bridgette said to Emi-Joye the day they fought."

"Do you know what it means?"

"I'm going to hazard a guess and say that you do."

Trystane chuckled. "Your hazard is well-placed. Donnachaidh told us that it was the battle cry of Baize Sammael. It means 'blood for blood'."

"How in the seven hells would Bridgette know that phrase to

begin with, much less the significance it would have had to the Ingefeoht?" Collum asked quietly. "She said it right before she wounded the ambassadora, as if it was a sort of challenge."

"It concerns me that she said such a thing."

"And me as well," the fyrdwisa admitted. "Bridgette told me that she *becomes* her Maylemaegus. I surmise that this ancient power has knowledge we do not, such as those words, and when she is fully Liluthuaé she has that same knowledge. It is possible too that Baize Sammael picked up that phrase and didn't come up with it, and Bridgette saying it to Emi-Joye has nothing to do with him."

The ard rialóir considered that. "I hope that to be the case."

Cloa and Emi-Joye caught up to them as they entered the clearing. During their walk, the ambassadora had given the queen a debrief about the Triumvirate, its history, and what they understood of its mission and their roles in it. Cloa's mind was brimming with questions, reminding Collum fondly of how Bridgette reacted when the magical world was first thrust into her life. But the witch chose to voice only a few inquiries.

"These vademecum things, they're keys to unlocking our destined power?" Cloa asked.

"That's a concise way of putting it," Collum replied.

"And my power is supposedly passion?"

"Yes, and as Emi-Joye is the Boireannach and Bridgette the Liluthuaé, you are known as the Astridsí," Trystane reminded her. They'd had a brief version of this conversation already.

"Astridsí," Cloa murmured, feeling the name on her tongue. "When is Bridgette coming back? Will it make a difference that there are only two of us?"

"I don't know, and I also do not know," Trystane quipped. "That being said, your crash course in being the Astridsí is the same as ours. We have hardly a clue what any of this means, and one of Bridgette's jobs while she's in Palna is to learn everything she possibly can about the legend of the Triumvirate. Our entire history has been thrown upside-down over the course of a few weeks, and while I do feel terrible for throwing it on you in even more of a harried fashion, we do so because completing the Triumvirate will change everything."

Collum gave him a look. "Everything?"

"Perhaps that was a bit dramatic," Trystane admitted. "But it will mean that whenever the Tinuviels decide to make their move, our arsenals will be fully powered. I realize this is a lot to throw at you. However, I am not willing to soften the blow just because you are seventeen — not if it means to do so would cost us time to train, work, and learn together."

The ard rialóir undid the magic that kept the trunk in place. "Stand back. I'm going to let them out now."

It was, Collum thought, akin to setting a chained animal loose. The three vademecums were barely in the air for an instant when they realized who else was in the circle.

Your Eminence, you've brought us our Reverence!

The third vademecum, the greenish-colored one, spoke for the first time. Collum watched as Cloa froze, stunned by the feel of this new sentience that reached for her.

Welcome, Your Reverence. We have been waiting for you.

Cloa gave a frantic glance to the fyrdwisa. "What do I do?"

But Emi-Joye answered her, and Collum saw that the Fairy's eyes had gone completely still. "The vademecum is yours. It is your grimoire, your paradigm. Think of it as a gift from the gods and goddesses who created our Maylemaegus, a way for us to understand our magics, as no one else living can teach us," the Fairy said encouragingly. "The vademecums can speak to all three of us — you, me, and Bridgette — and Collum will hear their consciousnesses as well. You may speak to them or to yours alone, and you may do so out loud, or by concentrating your thoughts on the object you wish to hear you."

"What if I mess up?" Cloa's voice went up a note. "What if they don't want me?"

✎ *Your Reverence, we assure you that we do.*

It was as if the queen's vademecum understood precisely how young she was, how inexperienced in any magic. Once, at Lammas the previous August, Cloa told Bridgette she couldn't study the raw arts, and neither the fyrdwisa nor Bright Star understood what that meant. But Collum got a blink of comprehension now as he watched the terrified witch finally extend a hand for the green notebook. Either Nehemi or Kharis must have long ago suspected that Cloa would have great magic, and that was why she had been so strongly shielded. At least one of those two, which Collum began to think was Kharis, did not want Cloa able to tap into or control such a thing, so her magical instruction became highly guarded and rudimentary.

"I don't really know how to do any magic," Cloa told the vademecum, as if she heard Collum's train of thought. "I mean, I have a wand! But it's — I only know some basic spells, nothing extraordinary or queenly."

✎ *Fear not, Your Reverence. You are not alone anymore. What news have you of the third?*

"Are you going to tell Bridgette about me?" Cloa asked.

✦ *The Liluthuaé will soon know that our circle is complete,* the Bright Star's vademecum promised.

"I'm going to take that as a 'no'," Collum muttered.

"Emi-Joye said I should touch you?" The queen phrased her request as a question, and her vademecum laughed.

✎ *You should, and you must, for it is our first taction that connects us. You will feel the difference, Cloa of Endorsa, and it will be strange to start.*

"Is there going to be another tornado?" Trystane called out when he noticed the queen start to reach for the vademecum. "Someone tell me so that I may mentally prepare myself this time."

But it wasn't a gust of wind that started when Cloa took hold of her vademecum for the first time. Instead, the earth trembled under their feet, causing both Collum and Trystane to jump further back from the two females.

Emi-Joye leapt into the air with surprise, but the witch only blinked as she processed the shudder.

"Why did that happen?" Cloa whispered. She traced her fingers over the eye-shaped sigil that was barely visible on her vademecum's green cover. "Why did the ground just pitch?"

It is the soil shifting to meet the future. The soil, sky, and sea are aligning.

"Sea?" Emi-Joye gave her vademecum a questioning look as she lowered herself back down. "When Bridgette and I both touched you, there were wind vortexes that formed around us. No sea to be seen."

There are no seas in Heáhwolcen, Boireannach. The water nearest you in this space is the dew drifting through the air.

Collum heard the wheels turn in Emi-Joye's mind as she worked through this revelation. Her snowflake messages, her draw to ice … sea there might not be on the world above the world, but water? There was plenty of that. The Fairy's eyes stilled as she concluded, accepted, that — as Herewosa Donnachaidh and Trystane both once suggested — she had always been meant for this future. There simply hadn't been a name for it until now.

"I'm taking this with me when we leave," Cloa announced. It seemed that she, too, on some level comprehended what the Boireannach just realized about herself. "Emi-Joye should take hers, and Collum should make sure Bridgette's stays safe until she comes back."

The idea of keeping that object in his apartment made his gut turn.

"Cloa, I'm not sure that's smart —" the fyrdwisa began.

She gave him a dour look. "It's inconvenient to have to come find you to take me here every time I want to practice my magic. Everyone's said this vademecum is *mine*, and I desire to keep it with me."

As smoothly as a hologram, Cloa's eyes shifted. The gold of her irises moved and gave her pupils the appearance of being star shaped. Even for someone who was used to females' eyes changing in his presence, this one was particularly unsettling. Collum knew better than to tell Cloa no.

"Then so you shall, Astridsí," he murmured.

<h1 style="text-align:center">~ 86 ~</h1>

✦ *The circle is complete.* Her vademecum's voice entered her mind out of nowhere.

Bridgette, who'd been in the middle of de-boning pork chops, put her knife down on the worktable and stared emptily at the wall. "I'm going to kill Collum. I *told* him, and he *promised* not to tell Nehemi anything!"

✦ *The fyrdwisa broke no promise to you.*

"Yeah, well, the fact of the matter is he lied, and I really don't fucking like it when that happens," she muttered. "What now, is Nehemi going to come barge through the border walls and drag me back?"

Her vademecum went silent.

The Bright Star was frustrated. Zedolph had indicated there would be a Hringur meeting approximately once a month. But after five weeks, she heard nothing else about it, and still never saw a newspaper with the alleged calendar that would tell them of another gathering. Nor did Bridgette have any news worth reporting back to Heáhwolcen, aside from how different Ostara was in Palna than in Fairevella. But still, she religiously spent the first few minutes of her Tuesdays sending blasé summaries to Collum. She hated not being able to hear him, even though she knew he was listening. Sometimes, *sometimes*, their shared covenant warmed against her wrist, and it made her smile to hope that he was thinking about her at least a fraction of how often she thought of him.

Bridgette looked guiltily at the other covenant bracelet on her wrist. She hadn't yet given Serrabinx the matching one with garnet cords. It was safely hidden in her bedroom. Her hostess was less enthused than Zedolph and Toby were that she returned, and it had been a tense few days after the Hringur meeting as they became used to living together again. The woman was cold toward the Elfling, not that Bridgette could blame her. The Bright Star had left in the middle of the night without so much as a farewell and told Toby secrets that the adults did not know. Then she proceeded to show up in as abrupt a manner as she left, revealed all sorts of information to the Hringur, and expected to acclimate pretty quickly back to the daily life she enjoyed before Lunavidad.

I'll talk to Serrabinx tomorrow, Bridgette promised herself. *I'll tell Collum I have no updates and that I am going to axe murder him for telling Nehemi about the Triumvirate. Then I'm going to talk to Serrabinx. Maybe she'll be less offended by my presence once I give her the covenant.*

"Bridgette?" Zedolph stuck his head in the workroom. "Would you mind keeping an eye on the front counter for a few minutes? Fincher needed to go to the herbalist for some new recipe he wanted to try. I told him yes, but forgot I promised Muov I'd help him back in the dry-aging shed."

"Uh, sure."

She stayed in the back and continued her work, listening for any sign of customers up front. There were custom orders that needed to be filled before the butchery closed for its day off, so the Elfling busied herself with filling requests and stocking them away in the iceboxes. After a while, she heard the unmistakable tingle of bells at the door, followed by a few hushed voices. Bridgette wiped her blade and hands on her apron, then walked out to greet the guests.

Her breath caught mid-hello.

The four Palnan guards who stood in the butcher shop looked ready to pick a fight, not pick out a steak. Their uniforms were almost identical to the one Baize Sammael wore in the immersive cinema room Herewosa Donnachaidh once showed her in Minthame: deep purple leathers with metallic armor over their shoulders, knees, and chests. They each cradled their helms under an arm, and across their hips and chests hung belts of knives. Two of the four had longswords strapped to their backs, easily within reach between their shoulder blades. One wore a quiver of arrows and a bow. The fourth lazily twirled a whip made of studded leather and delicate aubergine metal chains in her hand. The first three appeared to be not-witches, but the fourth, the only female, was either Elfling or full-blown Elf.

Ealdaelfen, Bridgette's mind corrected itself.

"Hello!" she gasped out and quickly threw her fist into the expected greeting. She forced a welcoming smile on her face and hoped that whatever gods and goddesses were out there, they would not let the guards see her shaky knees. "What may I get for you this day?"

Bridgette carefully altered her speech pattern, her diction, to appear more like someone Palnan born and bred.

"We have an order," one of the sword-wielding ones said. His voice was gruff and muffled, as though he had a jaw full of chewing tobacco. "For the queen and king."

The Bright Star's brows furrowed. "I'm so sorry, friends, but I do not recall offhand that an order was placed for Their Majesties," she replied. "May I ask what was in the order? Perhaps another slátraestre filled it, or it was mislabeled."

She felt the ghostly imprint of a hand at the small of her back and straightened as if on command. The feel of it triggered her memory. Bridgette had no idea from whence the presence — an unexpected echo from her long-ago dream about Eryth, now in very real time — came, but understood it was there to offer strength.

The archer gave her a disdainful sneer. "We did not request our order yet. We are here to place the order now."

"Oh!" Bridgette's smile became more genuine. She reached for the stack of papers Fincher used to take orders and dipped one of his feathered pens in ink, ready to write. "I would be happy to assist with this request. What is it Their Majesties would like?"

"We will have three blaccattle carcasses, skinned and whole, ready for the spits. The abomasums will be preserved, along with the livers and hearts. The hearts must be marinated in the usual truffle fire oil," the other swordsman recited. "We will need the carcasses and prepared offal delivered to Düoria three days before the Gathering of Games."

Bridgette furiously scribbled down the instructions. "Delivered?" she repeated. She'd never seen any of the slátraestres or even Zedolph take meat anywhere but their own homes. She supposed, however, that the Tinuviels considered themselves above trivial things such as business policies.

"Yes, delivered," the archer sneered. He seemed to think it an intimidating expression. It reminded Bridgette too much of the cocky fraternity brothers she used to run into while out in Nashville on the weekends. She gave the archer a cool glance, refusing to acknowledge his attitude.

"I will make note of that request," she promised. The four turned to leave, but Bridgette halted them before they took another step. "I need your names."

"You do not."

Fucking frat-hole, Bridgette screamed internally at the archer. She gave him a look that anybody else from the Southern United States would have been able to translate as "bless your heart" from three miles away.

"I do need your names," she said. "It's our slátrari's policy. Surely if he or one of our slátraestres has a question, it would be improper to trouble either of our rulers?"

The archer glared at her, but the female spoke up. "You may say that Chalamet of the Palnan Royal Guard made the request."

She spelled out her name, which Bridgette dutifully wrote down. "Thank you, Chalamet. We'll have that ready for you."

Bridgette watched the four guards walk out and Chalamet tossed her a sidelong glance, a curious look in her eyes. Then the guard shook her head, as if thinking better of whatever thought just entered her mind, and exited the butchery.

Holy fuck, Bridgette thought, once they were no longer visible through the front windows. She sank to her knees behind the counter. The ghostly handprint squeezed her shoulder, then disappeared. *What just happened?*

She'd never heard of "blaccattle", though she assumed it meant "cattle with black hides", and what was that stupid truffle oil they asked for? And an even bigger question — what was the Gathering of Games, and why would it require three entire beef carcasses? Her heart felt like it was going to beat out of her chest. Did the Palnan Royal Guard know if someone was or wasn't a citizen? Would her sierwan knowledge alert her if she encountered any other Ealdaelfen?

"Bridgette?" Fincher had entered the butchery so quietly that the bells on the door hadn't sounded. He peered around the cases to see her squatting against the wall. "What's wrong? You look ill! May I fetch you some water?"

She motioned toward the ink-blotted paper on the counter. "We just had a group of customers I didn't expect to see. It was a little uncomfortable."

"Who?" the Kobold asked. He pulled the page down and sat next to Bridgette on the floor. "Oh — *oh*. I didn't expect that order to be placed for a few more days. I am so, *so* sorry that none of us thought to warn you they might be coming! Where is Zedolph? Does he know?"

"He's with Muov." The Elfling's stomach churned, full of unexpected anxiety. "What is the Gathering of Games, and what the hell is a blaccattle?"

Fincher put a comforting arm around her waist. "The blaccattle are a very specific breed descended from the finest beef cattle known on Earth. There is much marbling in the meat, so tender that it melts on one's tongue like butter. They are raised only by one farm in all of Palna, and we are the closest butchery to it. As for the Gathering of Games, it is a multi-day gathering for all of Palna that occurs at the end of each April, leading into

Beltane. The country all but shuts down, so many citizens attend. There are feasts, bonfires, but most of all, the Games themselves. These are great feats of athleticism, showing strength and prowess, leadership and skill."

"What kinds of games?" Bridgette asked.

The Kobold smiled. "Many! There are competitions for archery and longsword, racing, even artistry. Each major city in Palna has one to two entrants in each sport or show of talent. It is quite a fun time, though three long days with little sleep and too much wine."

She grinned at Fincher. "Too much wine? As if."

"Believe me, Bridgette. Three Games ago I woke up on the final day wearing clothes that were not mine, lying next to an Elf I did not know and an Elf I knew quite well, with a pyramid of wine jars built between us," he admitted. "I have no memory of anything that occurred after watching the upriver distance swimming race in Afon Azúl."

The Elfling laughed at the mental image. "That sounds insane. What's the point of it? Like, what do the winners get?"

"Ahh!" Fincher said. "The winners of each event are invited to move to Düoria to train as professionals, for competitions elsewhere!"

That struck a chord. "Elsewhere?" Bridgette asked. "Where … else? No one regularly leaves Palna except the ambassador."

Fincher shrugged. "I could not tell you. That is simply what is known."

Bridgette tried to laugh it off as she stood back up to resume her duties in the workroom. She had a sinking suspicion that she now knew how the Tinuviels were recruiting for their budding fighting force.

~ 87 ~

Zedolph didn't seem nearly as fazed by the Palnan Royal Guards' order as Bridgette or even Fincher were. The slátrari took it in stride, commenting only that it was an honor that the Tinuviels continued to source the beef from his shop, when there were others the blaccattle could be sent to.

The next morning, despite it being her off-day, Bridgette struggled to sleep in past the rainy dawn that broke outside her window. She activated her covenant bracelet with Collum and sent him what felt like the most interesting report in weeks: *No word about another Hringur meeting. Yesterday, four members of the Palnan Royal Guard came into the butchery and put in a big order for this thing called the Gathering of Games. Fincher told me it's this giant competition-slash-festival, with music and food and all of these novice athletes. It sounds like a mix between the Olympics and like, Highland or Renaissance games or something, just from what he told me. I asked what the prizes were. Get this: the winners are invited to live in Düoria to train professionally. There's nowhere else for them to compete but think about it. Gifted athletes and strong individuals, being trained under the eye of the Tinuviels? Collum, I'm fairly certain — not sierwan gift certain! — this has something to do with how the Palnan army is recruiting wígend.*

She let the message hover between them for a moment, feeling the indescribable mental flow settle smoothly. It was silly, she knew, but like checking her phone to make sure a text message sent, there was a sort of in-her-head confirmation of the same. Bridgette allowed herself a few more minutes to wake up before stirring, then finally reached for the carefully wrapped package that held Serrabinx's covenant bracelet.

Bridgette found her hostess in the kitchen, making something that smelled like pickles. She wrinkled her nose at the amount of vinegar in the air. "Morning, Serrabinx. Where are Toby and Zedolph?"

"My brother took his nephew fishing."

The answer was so strikingly normal that Bridgette took a second to process it. "Gotcha," she replied, disappointed. She originally hoped she and Toby could go to Düoria, but clearly that would have to wait at least a week. "Hey, Serrabinx?"

"Yes?" The woman still didn't turn to face her. Bridgette was reminded of the day they first met, when Toby deposited the Elfling at his mother's feet in her garden.

"Can I talk to you about something? It's … kind of important."

That got Serrabinx's attention. She glanced over her shoulder. "What is it, Bridgette?"

"Here." Bridgette handed the package to Serrabinx. "It's a special kind of bracelet. It matches this one that I have, and a third worn by an Elf in Heáhwolcen."

Serrabinx opened the package and fingered the cords. She ran her thumb over the carved bead, contemplating. "Why do you give me such an object?"

"Because I'm not going to be here for forever; I have to go back again," Bridgette whispered. "Also, because at some point after I go back, there are going to be fewer walls separating us than we have now. I'd like to be able to stay in touch, whether we're both in Palna or not."

"Is this a *covenant*?" Serrabinx hissed. Bridgette couldn't tell if it was with shock or with gratitude. "Between myself, you, and some unknown-to-me being?"

"Yes," the Elfling replied. "I can't make you put it on, of course. But you'll be able to use it to send messages to me in Palna, and once the walls are gone, to my friend, too. My friend is powerful, and he and I both swore to do everything we can to get your family out and keep y'all safe. This bracelet is one way to make sure that happens."

Serrabinx gave the jewelry a furtive look, then wrapped it back up in its paper packet. "Thank you, Bridgette. I shall think about this, if you do not mind."

Bridgette did mind, very much actually, but wasn't about to say anything. She changed the subject instead. "What are you making?"

"Pickled greens," the woman replied. "I have a patient who is struggling in her pregnancy, and I believe incorporating such vegetables in her diet will help as her youngling develops."

The Bright Star chuckled. "Weird how even in a whole 'nother world, pregnant folks still crave pickles and ice cream."

"She does not eat enough salt and protein," Serrabinx said, not taking note of Bridgette's quip. "If that continues, the little one will enter the mortal plane quite ill. This offspring is strongly desired by its mother-to-be. I am going to do everything in my power to ensure the pregnancy does not fail, even if the aforementioned mother gets violently ill every time she thinks about meat during these months."

"Do you have a lot of patients who are pregnant?"

"A few," Serrabinx replied. "I have many patients, of many species and medical needs. Do you care to have younglings one day, Bridgette?"

The question caught her off-guard. "Uh, not really. Why?"

"I ask out of curiosity. You get along well with Tobias. To be a mother would come easily for you, I believe."

Bridgette felt suddenly defensive. "I think if a female wants to have offspring, she should," she said. "And if she doesn't want to, that's fine too — and *both* females should have adequate access to resources, support, and medical care. Or healing, whatever they call it up here."

Serrabinx stirred her pot of pickled greens. "That is an interesting perspective, coming from an Elfling who was almost terminated."

Bridgette stared. Stared long and hard at the not-witch. Surely she hadn't heard right. But with the way that the woman froze immediately after speaking, there was no doubt to the clarity of her words.

"How," Bridgette began slowly, "the fuck do you know that?"

Serrabinx didn't move. The vinegar mixture in the pot bubbled, its simmering a tangible sound for the tension between the two females that stood next to it.

"Serrabinx," Bridgette said. "Look at me and tell me how the *fuck* you know that."

Her host was frozen, wide eyes glancing wildly in all four directions. Bridgette wanted to shake the woman. Her Maylemaegus ached within, straining to break free the way it had when Emi-Joye dared to draw blood.

"I'm going to give you one more chance to answer me." Bridgette's voice was ice cold and razor sharp. All her careful plotting regarding her cover story went out the window. "How did you know what my birth mother did? How did you even know that I *have* a birth mother?"

"You are not the only one in this house with powers beyond what should be given, Bridgette," Serrabinx whispered.

The Bright Star was at Serrabinx's throat before the not-witch knew what was happening. Bridgette snarled, her lilac eyes shifting to the violent shade of purple, burning with rage. Burning so hot that there was no longer a glamour protecting them from being seen by unsavory gazes. *Lies* were the work of ill intent, of the very thing she and this voltage of Maylemaegus could not coexist with. Serrabinx lied to her and had been lying this entire damned time.

It felt as though Bridgette's heart was about to beat out of her chest, as if electricity was to spark from her fingertips. The Ballamúr couldn't stop her. Nothing could stop her, not even the scream that rose from Serrabinx as the Elfling leapt upon her. Screamed and screamed as Bridgette growled in response, a raw and feral question her very existence demanded answer to.

"You will tell me who you are, Serrabinx Maudlin. You will tell me who you are, and how you come by this knowledge!"

Bridgette demanded, her voice deep and angry, almost disembodied. It was the voice of her vademecum fusing with hers, and her magic writhed with pleasure at their union.

The still-Elfling part of Bridgette's mind hoped that whatever the winds whispered to Toby, they kept him and Zedolph far away. Yet this thought was buried so far beyond the demand for truth that it was nothing more than a gnat to be swatted away by the overarching command of Maylemaegus.

Bridgette repeated herself, over and over, one arm at the throat of her host and the other pressed them against the kitchen wall, bracing herself. Serrabinx's screams dulled to pained whimpers the longer they stood there. The Elfling reached to palm the hilt of her dagger.

"Do not *lie* to me, Serrabinx Maudlin," the disembodied voice said from Bridgette's mouth. "I am Truth. You will not lie to me."

As if it sensed that the woman was breaking, the Maylemaegus power ever so slowly began to recede, slinking back millimeter by millimeter into the Elfling's core. It was beautiful, this deliciously wicked magic nestled deep inside her very sense of Self. Bridgette's eyes cooled, the feeling of fire within her dipping back down to room temperature; the deep purple calming back to opalescent lilac. She blinked and stepped back.

"Who are you, Serrabinx?" Bridgette asked, her voice again her own. The amethyst dagger was halfway out of its sheath.

The not-witch heaved and gasped as the Elfling released her throat. She clawed at her neck, her whimpers raspy and horrified.

"I'm — sorry —" Serrabinx whispered, her voice a stammer as she regained her breath. "Bridgette — I know — who you are."

"I'm gonna need you to elaborate," the Elfling said. She massaged the hand that had been gripped around Serrabinx's esophagus. "Look. I don't generally enjoy when I accidentally torture people, so the faster you spit it out, the less likely it is I'm going to do that again."

"You've done this before?" Serrabinx whispered.

Bridgette rolled her eyes. "Yeah, a couple times. Like I said, not a fan of it happening. Ten out of ten would prefer to not unleash the beast, although I bet it'd be fun to see what happens when Ydessa Tinuviel lies through her teeth in front of me."

"Bridgette, I — I'm sorry," her host said, voice still near-silent. "I've suspected who you were since Toby brought you to my door. I do not know how you came to be here. At this moment I do not wish to know that story. One day I will ask, but the time is unripe for those questions."

Bridgette stared impatiently. *Get to the point*, she silently urged the woman.

"I am Palnan born and raised, but my whole life has not been spent within these borders," Serrabinx said. "It became known that I had … abilities. Abilities beyond the scope of what should have been possible for me to express, given the Samnung wall. My great-grandparents were from Endorsa. They were the ones who'd come to Palna to study under the tutelage of Baize Sammael himself. Little did they know how they doomed us with that choice. They told my grandmother, who then told my mother, about Endorsa and Fairevella, about Eckenbourne and Earth. Preserving our history, so to speak. My mother therefore knew what was possible, and she knew too that there was a Fairy ambassador sent to keep watch over the Tinuviels."

The woman breathed deeply, tears sparkling at the corners of her eyes, before continuing. "My parents sacrificed *everything* to get Ambassador Fitzhugh to smuggle me out. They believed that with proper training, I could become something more than what this deity-forsaken country and its *leaders* ever would allow me to be. My mother especially was worried about my abilities becoming known to the Tinuviels. She feared that I would be taken to Düoria, stolen to join the Collective, and they would never see me again.

"And so, one day I left. Simply went with the ambassador through the Samnung's border wall into Bondrie — which my parents never told me of, as it did not exist when my great-grandparents came here," Serrabinx went on. "I was fourteen. I spent the next fifteen years studying to be a birth healer, honing my gifts all the while."

Bridgette's sierwan eyes, now relieved of their glamour, shifted into opals. "You learned how to really be a witch in Endorsa and figured out sneaky ways to have power behind the Tinuviels' backs."

Serrabinx smiled, finally gazing up at the Elfling. The tension in the room eased.

"Yes," she said simply. "I am also what is known as a wítega. I have the gift of foreboding."

Suddenly a puzzle piece snapped into place. Bridgette huffed a laugh.

"You're the birth healer who convinced Mohreen *not* to have an abortion," she said.

"I am," Serrabinx confirmed. "I would like to clarify that I am not in the business of convincing females to use their wombs in any way other than the way *they* feel fit. It is my responsibility to ensure that any potential mother knows every avenue open to her. Should your mother have decided to terminate her pregnancy, either the deities would have found ways to change her mind, or they would use their own powers to find another vessel to serve as the tangible form for Liluthuaé.

"There are some wítega who can forebode at a moment's notice," the woman continued. "I am not of that ability. I do not sit in a dark tent or shop corner, waiting to discern the future of those who hand me coin or paper money. My gift is to know the outcome of an injury or health condition. When the fyrdestre brought Mohreen to me, I did what I always did: examined her in body and in spirit; examined the health of the fetus' spirit and developing future body. It was then that the deities shared with me *this* was no mere fetus, no mere future Elfling. The deities chose Mohreen to carry the Liluthuaé."

"Wait." Bridgette held up her hand. "Are you telling me that you saw my future? That you know how everything I'm supposed to do plays out?"

"I did not see such a thing," Serrabinx said, somewhat apologetically. "My gift allowed me to know that should I carry on with the requested procedure, I would be destroying the first-choice vessel that carried the most important being to all of magickind, not just the Elves."

She paused to again massage her throat. "But I could not know this fetus' future in the sense of who it would fall in love with, or if it would grow to be a warrior or healer, or even whether it would be deemed traditionally female or male. Most fetuses of sentient, two-legged beings like us do not develop any sort of cognition until the middle third of pregnancy. It is even later for the species of beings that have longer gestation periods. It was impossible to detect the fetus' *thoughts* at that visit, though it is conceivably possible the fyrdestre may have been able to do so as the pregnancy went on."

Bridgette shuddered at the thought of fully-grown Collum Andoralain listening in to future-her's formulative thoughts in utero. *Gross.*

"How did you get back to Palna?" she asked Serrabinx.

Serrabinx leaned back against the wall — *had they really been standing this whole time?* — and looked up at the ceiling.

"I told you my parents sacrificed everything to get me out," the woman said quietly. "I had not heard from them for so many years. There was a new Fairy ambassador, Ambassador Mewt, and I wanted to know what had become of them. I requested that he look into the Maudlin family."

Tears slipped as Serrabinx whispered, "My parents were

both killed in a fire two weeks after I'd gotten out."

She struggled to breathe, remembering how it felt to fall to her knees and scream as she read the letter that shared such soul-breaking news with her. The worst day of her life.

"That was the first time the deities saw fit to let me forebode something of myself," Serrabinx continued, tears still falling. "It was an unclear vision, but a calling to return. As it was your destiny to embody the spirit of Liluthuaé, it was mine to be here and make what difference I could. So Ulerion Mewt brought me back, on the last trip citizens of greater Heáhwolcen could choose to come here as spies. Ulerion told me my brother had been taken in by our uncle. He was so young when I left, still very much a boy, younger than Toby is now."

Her tone changed, subtly but abruptly. "We began to build our lives together, the two of us and my beloved Ovidion, and now Toby. We aim to create something better than what we'd been allotted after being born Palnan, because the Universe chose us for something more."

~ 88 ~

When Zedolph found Bridgette that afternoon, she was curled up in her oilskin jacket, burrowed against the thick trunk of a tree miles away from the Maudlin homestead. Her cheeks were tear-stained, despite hours of rain washing down her face. The damned salty trails kept starting again as soon as she thought they were under control.

"Oh, Bridgette," the man murmured. He climbed the wide, low-slung branches until he reached her about midway up the trunk. "My sister told me what happened. Are you alright?"

She shook her head. The Elfling feared that if she opened her mouth, she would either begin sobbing again or start screaming. She wasn't sure which outcome would be preferred, so she pulled her lips tight as more tears prickled the corners of her eyes. Bridgette let Zedolph cradle her. The warmth of his arms was a welcome contrast to the chilled rain that fell endlessly around them, and despite her efforts to the contrary, she found herself crying against his shoulder.

"Did you know?" she asked, her voice barely more than a whisper.

"I do now," Zedolph replied. "It explains rather a lot. I knew that Serrabinx spent many years of my life elsewhere in Heáhwolcen, but that was all. The rest she shared with me after Toby and I returned from fishing. He does not know. I believe my sister would prefer it stay that way, for now."

Bridgette nodded numbly. She didn't know how to feel. Swindled? Angry? Confused that everyone in Heáhwolcen knew more about her origins than she did? Serrabinx and Zedolph couldn't know that her biological father was Eryth Tinuviel. She had a feeling Mohreen wouldn't share any information that made her seem a villain in this tale. Having a few night stands' worth of time with the king of Palna might not go over well for Mohreen Conner's self-serving personality style.

"Since you know," Bridgette gulped, "I want you to know that I need to go to Düoria. When the Samnung was here in February, they told me that there was a library in the palace. I think it's the only place in all of Heáhwolcen I'll be able to find anything about Gemaere, because no one outside of Palna has even heard of it. I'm sure I could go question a few Earth Elves and probably the fucking True Druids, but honestly, I think everyone would rather avoid having to do that."

Zedolph tucked a tendril of escaped hair back behind her ear. "Is that something you would like to do tomorrow?"

She looked up, surprised. "Tomorrow? The butchery is open tomorrow."

"It is. But we survived while you were, as you say, taking your final examinations." He winked. "I believe we can handle a day more, if you and Toby want to visit our capital."

"Yes!" Bridgette sat straight up and had to float herself back onto the branch before she toppled out of the tree with surprise. "Yes. Please. Thank you so much, Zedolph."

He gave her a look so filled with emotion that it made her heart strain. "I would do anything for my world and my future, Bridgette, even if it is as simple a task as obtaining two horses for you to ride. Düoria is too far a walk, and even so, you'll need to leave before sun-up. How long do you expect to be gone?"

She had no idea. "Most of the day, I guess? I want to do the tour of the palace and definitely spend some time in the library."

Zedolph offered her a kind smile. "I look forward to hearing what you learn."

If Bridgette couldn't wait to explore Düoria, her excitement was nothing compared to Toby's when he learned he'd be going on such a grand adventure with her. He barely slept the night before, and the Elfling had to escort him back to his bedroom twice in the middle of the night, so convinced was he that it was time to wake up to leave. Zedolph's secured horses were sheltered from further threat of rain by being tied near the house, able to come under the porch roof if they desired. They each bore a simple leather saddle. Bridgette, used to riding Eloise bareback, helped Zedolph lift Toby onto his horse and get him situated before she went astride the gelding assigned to her.

"You'll let us know when you arrive and when you set upon your return trip?" the butcher asked. He motioned his head toward Bridgette's hands.

Serrabinx must have told him about the covenants, Bridgette realized.

"I will," the Elfling promised.

She nudged the heels of her boots into the horse's side and together, she and her young companion began their journey in the dark. Toby seemed to know the way, so Bridgette let him lead and adjust their pace. They began at a slow walk but sped up the moment it was light enough outside to see the path without the oil lanterns they each carried in one hand. When the overnight showers finally paused, Bridgette and Toby cantered for a few miles, then stopped to take a break for snacks and to water their steeds.

"Have you ever seen a Unicorn, Toby?" Bridgette fished around in her saddlebag and pulled out a pair of beef jerky sticks. "Not a picture, but one in real life?"

"No. Mumma has told me of them though! She says they are the most beautiful horses and that they sometimes sparkle, and each has a very important horn on its head. I would love to see one someday, but I do not know where they live in Palna. Mumma says they are secretive and hide."

The Elfling chewed on her jerky for a minute. "I don't know where they live in Palna either, but I saw them other places in Heáhwolcen. Do you remember what I told you before I left? About how I'm kind of like you a little bit, and I can know some things that others can't?"

Toby nodded.

"Well, that makes me kind of important to the Samnung in

Heáhwolcen," Bridgette explained. "Sometimes, important folks get to have their own Unicorns."

She laughed at how far Toby's jaw dropped. "Your own Unicorn?" he gasped.

"Yeah, not like a pet, but more like a partner," the Elfling said. "Unicorns can choose to be annwyl, to be bound to a rídend. There's a fancy ceremony, which I haven't done yet, but yeah, I have a Unicorn assigned to work with me if we both want. Her name is Eloise."

"When will I meet her?" Toby demanded.

"One day, maybe soon," Bridgette said. "We'll see."

She helped him to his feet and back on the horse, and they were off once again. The closer they got to Düoria, the heavier the air felt around them. At first, Bridgette attributed it to the humidity from the rainy season, but it went deeper than that. She recalled the tenseness that pervaded the downtown square of Xcthonya, and thought it multiplied significantly in the capital.

Rain-soaked fabric banners began to decorate the path, some branded with a symbol that looked like a longsword stabbing through an upside-down crescent. Eight stars were depicted on the sword blade. Other banners showed the silhouette of an unknown bird carrying the crescent in its claws, wings outstretched. There were more such symbols the longer they went on this stretch of path. Uneasiness crept over Bridgette. They hadn't seen any buildings or other beings for miles.

"Hey Toby?" she asked, scared to raise her voice. "Are you sure we're going the right way? This feels … weird."

"Of course!" he replied, so self-assured that for a moment, Bridgette thought she was imagining the difference in air and tension.

Hey Thing One, you there? she thought to her vademecum. It stirred in acknowledgement.

✦ *Follow the youngling. This is the path you must traverse.*

Oh, come on. Did I wake you up from your beauty sleep? Hundreds of years not enough for you? Bridgette was halfway trying to make the object converse with her so that she could distract her nerves from the growing sense that something was wrong about this road.

✦ *Are you listening, Liluthuaé?* There was a hint of irony there as the vademecum's consciousness shut itself off from her, and Bridgette's eyes shifted with recognition.

"Shit," she muttered. "Toby? I need you to hold my reins and guide both of us for a few minutes, okay? I've gotta … do something."

The boy gave her a curious look, but took the reins without question. He stared ahead, continuing to guide them, as Bridgette drifted herself into Universal consciousness. She kept her heels firmly down in her stirrups and her hands on the saddle horn, grounding her body in the here and now as her mind began to wander. She wasn't sure what the vademecum meant for her to listen for, but this is how she would find the answer.

It was *noisy* in the consciousness of this forested road, or as forested as Palna got outside of its protected lands. The trees were gangly little things, greedily soaking up every ounce of water they were afforded. There were more insects and small mammals than Bridgette expected, yet few birds. She was reminded of the dream in the cave. Her consciousness then had snagged upon whoever's mind it was that led her to where dream-Toby was being taken into the Collective.

Who am I looking for? she thought to whatever beings or creatures might be out there. *What is it I'm supposed to listen out for?*

Bridgette was about to give up when she heard a sound in the distance, but she couldn't tell if it was the physical distance from where her body sat on a horse, or a mental distance. She reached for it with her mind anyway, curious about why, out of all the noises in her head when she tapped into Universal consciousness, this one demanded her attention.

What are you? she asked. *What do you want from me?*

The sound had been a voice. A sharp laugh, deep and throaty; likely male. She reached out for it again, mentally scanning miles around where she and Toby rode, searching for who laughed. Her consciousness stopped of its own accord. The male laughed again. He was close.

He was too close.

Bridgette ripped her mind out of its reverie and flew back into herself. "Toby!" she hissed. "Stop walking. Stop *now.*"

"But why —"

"Shh!"

The Elfling grabbed his hands and pulled, doing her best to stop both their horses from moving forward. They stopped, but Toby's horse let out a dissatisfied whinny and stomped in place. A branch cracked under its hoof, and the woods went eerily still.

Please don't see us, please don't see us, please don't see us! Bridgette begged internally. She squeezed her eyes shut, hoping beyond hope that whoever laughed was still too far away to have heard the horse. *Just walk by, mind your own beeswax, we are not even here. This is a blank space, baby. Just an open spot on the road …*

For a few moments, during which the Elfling thought her heart might beat itself into a pulp, so intense was her anxiety, there was nothing but silence and the eerie stillness. She thought maybe, just maybe, they skated by. The too-quick cadence of her heart and breath thrummed in her ears. Bridgette was about to tap into her power again to see if she could get an idea about how close the male might be, when the ghostly hand again placed itself at the small of her back. She jumped, terrified it was what she wanted to run from, but no one was there.

Bridgette had the sensation of an invisible thumb caressing her spine. *Trust.*

It wasn't her vademecum's voice. It sounded more like the Ballamúr, but also wasn't so much a voice as it was the same kind of instinctual command she used when she spoke to the air.

She didn't have time to puzzle it out, because an indistinct humming started to sound in the trees next to them.

"We're going to be okay," she whispered to Toby. "Just let me talk."

The boy gave her a confused look at the same moment a duo of Palnan guards emerged from the trees. Bridgette groaned. One of them was the asshole archer from the butcher shop. The other she didn't recognize.

"Well, well, well!" the new guard said. "What do we have here?"

Bridgette swallowed hard.

"You're that slátraestre, aren't you?" the archer asked. The Elfling didn't respond. She glared at him, which caused the male to revert back to his characteristic sneer of distaste. "Who do you think you are, female? You dared question a member of the Royal Guard because of *shop policy* and now you cannot say two words to explain what you're doing on a road that citizens aren't allowed on?"

Bridgette shot a glance to Toby, who looked confused. "My young friend and I must have taken a wrong turn on our way to Düoria. It was dark when we left Xcthonya. We were not aware this was a forbidden route."

"Why is the boy not in school?"

Toby answered for himself. "My mumma teaches me all there is to know."

The archer's sneer grew darker. "You're not a registered student? No wonder you and your Elven friend struggle to remember the appropriate way to greet those of higher station than you."

The fist. Bridgette winced. She'd almost forgotten in the shop that day when the archer and his three fellow guards came inside, and now she and Toby were both caught with hands on reins instead of placing one over their hearts.

"I apologize for our lack of decorum in the moment. We

were simply surprised to see anyone else on this road, although now knowing that this is an exclusive road to Düoria, that explains why it's been so quiet," she said, trying hard to cover for them. *Let us fucking go.*

"Two wayward travelers on horseback, heading to the capital city. One is a boy who should be in classes. The other is Elven and has an attitude problem. What say you, Caracas? Shall we take them into Düoria as they wish?" the archer asked. He turned to his companion just as Bridgette felt the ghostly handprint on her spine again.

Trust! the otherworldly voice implored her.

Trust who?! she thought frantically. *These fuckers? Absolutely not!*

Trust! Safe!

It was as if whatever the ghost or spirit was, it couldn't communicate in complete sentences. Bridgette's heartbeat quickened.

"I say that it's a marvelous idea. I'm sure Her Majesty would love to know why an Xcthonyan matriarch refuses to enroll her child in school," the guard named Caracas said. "Get off your horses, citizens. You're coming with us."

~ 89 ~

Cloa's first official Samnung meeting as queen was a bland affair, compared to some of the more recent ones.

Bryten tried to be helpful and came in bearing an agenda of items to discuss. He began the list with choosing a new spreca, then deciding how to handle Nehemi and Kharis, respectively.

"I'm impressed," Collum told him. "I don't know that we've had an agenda like this since I became fyrdwisa."

The Baetalüan fluffed his blonde curls dramatically. "Thanks, Collum. New queen, new era, or something to that effect. Thought I might as well go all-out and start things off with a new sense of propriety."

His last sentence was directed at Trystane, who simply raised his glass in acknowledgement: "Long may Queen Cloa and our novel sense of propriety reign!"

The spreca discussion was easily resolved. Cloa, who continued to sit in the same spot as usual, Arctura in her lap, told them she had no desire to be spreca.

"Yes, I sat in on nearly every meeting that took place in this room for a lot of my life," she said. "Yes, I am the queen of Endorsa, and normally because of Artur Cromwell's bloodline, that ruler is automatically spreca. But I don't know how to be that type of leader. I don't know that I can represent that level of authority, in the first place because I am seventeen, and secondly because I don't have the physical presence that I think is necessary for it. If I have to look to you all for inspiration, it makes more sense for one of you to be spreca instead."

Collum stood, so pleased to be able to suggest what had long been at the back of his mind when it came to the Samnung. "Ceannairí, I would like to nominate Aristoces as our spreca."

The Fairy of All Fairies bowed her head graciously. "The decision is not mine to make, but should the full Samnung agree, I will accept this role."

Not surprisingly, the full Samnung agreed, and moved on to the next order of business with Aristoces presiding over the table. They had repeatedly pushed aside the decision on what to do with Nehemi. Both Trystane and Verivol voiced their previously shared thoughts. Collum thought the chatter went in circles, but after about thirty minutes of hearing the same options presented with slight variations, Aristoces silenced the discussion.

"I would prefer this be a unanimous decision," the new spreca said. "What we all expressed regarding the former queen and her departure are valid thoughts and concerns. I propose that we let it be Nehemi's decision, perhaps aided by Cloa, as to what to put in the public mind. We will do our duty and share the news of our new Endorsan queen, and simply tell those who ask that the decision for Cloa to succeed at her age was one made personally between family members and advisors. Nehemi, as several of you so thoughtfully said, is as much a victim in this situation as Cloa is. We can pay her this respect."

Though the discussion regarding Nehemi was diplomatic and succinct, deciding what to do with the former borhond was the exact opposite. Corria went so far as to suggest exile, to which Bryten stared at her, incredulous, and asked, "To *where*, Corria? The moon?"

Collum wanted to interrogate the man, who was one of the few beings that still referred to himself as a wizard. The term fell out of fashion decades ago, after Fairy ambassadors discovered some factions of Americans were using the term "great wizard" to refer to leaders of a hate-spreading, murderous cult disguised as a political interest group. Now that the Samnung suspected Kharis might have had something to do with the deaths of their former king and queen, fyrdwisa, and Nehemi's mother, the fact that Kharis still wanted to be called a wizard rubbed Collum the wrong way. He agreed with Bryten that exiling the former borhond would do more harm than good — where could they send a suspected murderer that other beings would be safe from death?

Trystane brought up the idea of tipping Kharis' wand, as Lucilla's had been, assuming, of course, it was determined he was the ill-intentioned individual Dominus hinted he was. They continued to keep Dominus secluded from both Nehemi and Kharis, and Collum planned to use the refugee as a blindside tactic if he needed to while questioning the borhond.

"What would you have us do with the man who essentially ruined your life, whether or not he was involved in the death of your parents?" Trystane finally asked Cloa, who had been largely silent during the animated chatter. He leaned forward to hear her answer, which she chose to think about for a few more moments.

"If Kharis is found to have caused or participated in the accident, then his admonishment should be wand tipping at the least, and a bar from magic at most," Cloa replied. "Do we plan to ever tell the citizens of Heáhwolcen the full truth of my birth and shielding? If we do not, then to have Kharis pay for the lives he took with that of his own would turn him into a martyr. Endorsans loyal to my moth — to Nehemi — will rage at his death. They will see such a move by the Samnung as a direct attack on Endorsa, perhaps on the bloodline of Artur Cromwell himself. It could go very poorly."

"Do you desire to have Kharis admonished for what he did to you?" Corria inquired.

"Losing his station and likely some, if not all, of his magic is punishment aplenty. Kharis had one young queen on the Endorsan throne that he could lead like a puppet," Cloa said. "It will be humiliating for him to be unable to do the same with me, and for me to have the knowledge of why he cannot and will not be trusted. I don't want the ilk of his life on my hands, but I will do what I can to ensure he knows little to no pleasure for what years he has left on this mortal plane."

The fyrdwisa wanted to leap across the table and hug her.

He smiled, but Cloa wasn't looking at him to see it. There were glimpses of her Maylemaegus in how she considered her emotions, her empathy in the way she spoke to others.

"You speak with forethought and honesty beyond your years, Your Majesty," Aristoces told Cloa. "I second your suggestion as how we should proceed with the former borhond."

There was a murmur of agreement around the chamber, and the Fairy declared it to be so. "Fyrdwisa, you will speak with him soon?"

Collum nodded. "Yes, Ceannairí."

"Have you word of Bridgette?"

"Yes, I do," Collum replied. "She gave her weekly report to me yesterday morning, which I already shared individually with some of you. Four Palnan Royal Guards visited the butchery and placed a large order for beef to have at a massive athletic competition. The specifics of such an event are largely irrelevant to us, but the prize awarded to the winners is not. Bridgette claims the winners are invited to Düoria to train professionally."

Cloa raised a questioning finger. "I know much less about Palna than the rest of you, but I do find it curious that a country with closed borders wants to train athletes that have already bested everyone else within those closed borders."

Nods and mutterings of "fair point" and "true, true" went up around the room.

Collum held his hands up to quiet the Samnung. "Bridgette also suspects that, for the precise reasons Queen Cloa does, the Tinuviels are not training athletes at all. She thinks that is how they find new wígend for the fighting force they claim not to be building."

"Shrewd!" Verivol exclaimed. "I would never have thought the Tinuviels capable of strategizing like that."

"We don't know for sure, but it makes sense. Bridgette said her sierwan gift did not alert her to confirm this suspicion," Collum clarified. "I assume she will learn more as this event nears."

The rest of the discussions on Bryten's agenda, plus a few others added as conversations spun off from one another, were all addressed in the most diplomatic and respectful manner that Collum had experienced in close to a decade. He said as much to Trystane as they walked out of the chamber. Whatever the ard rialóir might have thought was masked, though, as the first thing they saw back in the lobby was Emi-Joye, floating cross-legged in midair and waiting impatiently for the meeting to be over.

~ 90 ~

Trystane gave her a look of delighted surprise. "Fáilte, Ambassadora. What brings you to the Samnung today?"

"I have an appointment with the new queen of Endorsa," she replied brightly.

The two had become fast friends after their time in the clearing. Emi-Joye thrived having someone figuratively under her wing to teach and work with, though with the number of times she'd flown them around Heáhwolcen, literally under her wing as well. Most of their shared experiences thus far revolved around learning about their vademecums and Maylemaegus. Given that the former were written in Gemaere, and the latter was still unpredictable at best, the Boireannach and Astridsí typically ended up dissolving in giggles on the floor of one of their bedrooms.

Cloa consistently expressed how she felt an outsider in her own body because she'd been clothed, styled, and treated as little more than a doll for so long. She didn't know what she liked, what she wanted, and everything she *thought* she desired, Cloa was just as apt to second-guess: was it really her idea, or was it something ingrained in her from her shielded years? Both she and the Fairy assumed this was why it had been far more difficult for the witch to activate her Maylemaegus than it had been for the Boireannach and Liluthuaé. Emi-Joye would never admit it out loud, but part of her sorely wished Bridgette was around to show them the ropes. She envied how easy it was for the Bright Star to tap into her powers.

Today though would not be about Maylemaegus, or magic of any sort. Emi-Joye wanted to spend pressure-free time with the queen to hopefully help her overcome some of the hang-ups she had about creating a new sense of self.

The witch exited the Samnung chamber, talking quietly with Verivol. Arctura was at their heels. He meowed at the sight of

Emi-Joye, who dropped down to scoop him up. The cat rubbed his head under the Fairy's chin and began kneading softly into the base of her neck.

"Ouch, you rascal," she murmured. "You're going to have to stay here today; they're not fond of cats at the places I'm taking your queen."

Arctura gave her a disdainful look, then turned to Cloa as if to ask if she was going to enforce the Fairy's ultimatum.

"Well met, darling!" the witch cried, breaking out of her stride with Verivol. "I hope you weren't waiting long; we had a lot going on today."

Collum glanced at Trystane. "When did these two become so chummy?"

The ard rialóir shrugged, though he shot Emi-Joye a curious glance. "I haven't the slightest. Care for a round of chess?"

"Only if you swear you won't use that damn king's gambit opening. It's become quite predictable," Collum replied.

"So predictable, yet you haven't beat me in the last six games I used it in, have you?" Trystane gave him a sly grin. "If you win, I'll hand over my last bottle of cinnamon-pomegranate mead from winter solstice."

"You're on," Collum told him. He turned to Emi-Joye and Cloa. "Well met, Ambassadora. Enjoy your afternoon with the queen."

"Oh, I will!" she promised him. "If you find your chess match becomes too taxing, we'll be at Taberna Körtz should you two care to join us." She offered the fyrdwisa and ard rialóir a conspiratorial wink before putting Arctura on the floor and reaching for Cloa's hand. The two descended the staircase together and stepped into the sunny, spring-like weather of Galdúr.

"Where exactly are we going?" Cloa asked as they took to the skies. She was always impressed at how strong the Fairy was, to be able to just scoop her up and carry her with little effort.

"You keep telling me that you don't even know who you are anymore," Emi-Joye said. "When I feel at a loss about my own emotions, I usually go stab something at Minthame. Sometimes it helps to make a change in my appearance. I have a feeling your blade skills are even more minimal than Bridgette's, so instead of bringing you to the fighting ring, we are going to my favorite coiffeure."

"Your favorite *what?*"

"You know, an artist of the hair, a coiffeure! Her name is Sixsi and she was born in Bondrie, but now has a salon in Çeofilye; you're going to love her."

"What's wrong with my hair, Emi-Joye?" Cloa asked in horror. "Moth — Nehemi always said it was supposed to be worn long, that it's royal like that."

"There's nothing wrong with your hair, not objectively. It's a lovely color. But do you like it? Or do you keep it styled the way Nehemi taught you because you've never known anything else and are afraid to take a risk?"

Cloa didn't answer. She was unsure what to say.

Once the queen was seated in her chair, Sixsi Windwraith gave Cloa an appraising once-over.

"You look uncomfortable," the artist remarked.

"I've never been in a place like this," the queen responded.

"A place like what?"

"Like this. Where hair and fur are cared for."

Sixsi raised a brow. "Are you telling me that you've never had your hair styled before?"

"Of course I have!" Cloa shot back, insulted. "By a palace-selected artisan that Nehemi chose, every few months for as long as I recall. They always came to my chambers."

The coiffeure snorted. She fingered a lock of Cloa's dark brown hair, twining it around fingers of sienna skin marked with holographic swirls and symbols. Cloa supposed that's where the salon's name, Hologrimoire, came from.

"Your palace artisan was improperly trained," Sixsi said. "These split ends are horrendous."

"What's a split end?"

Sixsi threw back her head in laughter. "Deity bless, Your Majesty."

"That's unhelpful."

"It wasn't meant to be helpful," the artist replied. Her dark eyes glittered with mirth. "How can I be of service to you today?"

Ah. There it was. The inevitable reminder that for whatever reason, Cloa had been selected by the gods and spirits to be different. She *hated* this. She loathed the air of subservience that half of Heáhwolcen and all of Endorsa put forth to her. It was why she barely left her rooms since the shield was removed unless she was going to be with Collum or Emi-Joye. She also hated that she felt so ridiculously stupid, so out of touch with the world above the world. How could she be so completely unaware of herself as to not know something as vain as how she wanted her hair to be? Nehemi required that her hair be kept long, with soft curls, easily able to be styled in updos for rituals and official events. Otherwise, it was to be worn down — perhaps half-up, with side portions pulled back and wrapped around the ends of her tiara and pinned in place. Demure. Princess-ly. Sweet.

Cloa nearly choked on the thought of those words.

Sixsi glanced Cloa, who hadn't yet responded. The artist wasn't sure if it would be impolite to ask again.

It would have been, if Nehemi had been on the receiving end of the conversation, but Queen Cloa couldn't give two shits. She just wanted to have a normal talk with someone who was like Emi-Joye and Collum, someone who wasn't trying to impress her or care for her. Sixsi, with her chin-length glossy black bob and slightly slanted chocolate brown eyes, with her septum pierced by a ring of rose gold studded with tiny pale blue sapphires, with her effortless white shift top and black leggings, was someone who Cloa wanted very badly to think well of her. She looked back toward the entrance, where Emi-Joye chatted animatedly with another artist who now cared for the Fairy's hands and nails.

"I want …" Cloa began, then stopped. She closed her eyes and attempted to do Collum's scent therapy on her own. She pretended that he was there, his comforting presence surrounding her with the rich, smoky perfume of amber and fruity cassis.

Sixsi raised an eyebrow again, glancing down at the queen as she … meditated? The coiffeure wasn't sure what was happening. Cloa didn't know how long they stood there in silence, as her mind worked through layers of thoughts and ideas, peeling back pieces of identity. No one, no being in any world known to her, would have the capability to craft who they were in the sense that she now did. *Who am I?* she thought to the open expanse of the Universe, waiting to see if someone or something might provide clarity. She wished she had Bridgette's skill to connect to that level of consciousness, and wondered if the Bright Star would be able to use such a gift to give the queen any more idea of self.

A jarring vision sparked behind Cloa's closed eyes. Just a moment, a mere second of image, but her eyes opened, and she gasped. Apparently, she'd been holding her breath. She faced Sixsi, crossed her arms in front of her chest, and smiled a smile flickering with wild abandon.

Two hours later, Emi-Joye stood behind the chair with Sixsi, openly gaping at the witch that now sat in front of them. The Fairy scarcely recognized Cloa.

Gone were the gentle curls that draped midway down the queen's back. Gone, too, was the innocent air of *princess*, replaced instead with a roiling energy of *ruler*. Cloa's hair had been given side-swept bangs and cut almost to her shoulders, then treated with Sixsi's custom blend of oils and shampoos to remove seventeen years' worth of improper care and treatment. Her brunette waves, the texture brought back to life following two different haircare rituals and the application of a sea salt scrub infused with crushed abalone shells, gleamed in the sunlight that glowed in through the salon's open windows. Something else gleamed, too.

Emi-Joye leaned in closer to see. She blinked rapidly at the strands of gold and Endorsan bronze fibers that were now attached to the queen's hair.

"Is that actual gold and bronze?" she asked.

Sixsi grinned proudly. "I couldn't just let the deity-damned queen of Endorsa walk out of here without a crown on, now, could I?"

Cloa's reflection smirked at both of them from the mirror. She reached up to touch the dark brown hair that tumbled around her, loving how it felt soft and nearly alive with crackling energy. Day in and day out, she awakened more and more. Today, perhaps for the first time since having the shield removed, she thought that she looked awake, too.

"It's fucking amazing," she said, grinning. Cloa turned to thank Sixsi, but was instead met with two gawking females. Emi-Joye flushed.

"On behalf of the Samnung, please allow me to apologize —" the Fairy began, but Cloa hopped out of the chair and gave the ambassadora a look that said *shut the seven hells up.*

"Sorry for breaking the mold and shattering expectations. But this is fucking amazing, and I have never in my life felt so like myself," the queen said. "I'm not even sure who I am yet, not really; but this? This helps so much more than I could ever express."

Cloa reached into a satchel for money, but Sixsi put her hands out.

"No, Your Majesty," she protested. "The Samnung does not pay here."

"The rest of the Samnung members can do whatever they damn well please with their money, but you provided me a service — a really good one — and I don't have a way to compensate you for your time and skills other than coin. So please let me, Sixsi Windwraith. And I will need some bottles and hair potions for regular maintenance at home, so add in however much that will cost." Cloa's voice was firm, and for possibly the third time in as many weeks, she was glad the singsong quality of her vocal cords was gone.

She loved how the improvised crown caught in the sun as Emi-Joye flew them back around to Endorsa for their dinner at Taberna Körtz. Cloa had heard much about the tavern and couldn't wait to experience it for the first time. She dutifully followed the Fairy inside and almost immediately had to shrink into the wall to avoid being squashed in the fray of moving bodies. The place was always packed to the gills, but arriving just as the evening crowd showed up meant an extra level of close proximity. Emi-Joye flattened her wings against one another to keep them from impeding patrons' paths, then grabbed Cloa firmly by the hand and pulled her toward the counter.

"Sheridan!" the Fairy shouted.

"Back of the line, Ambassadora!" The barkeep didn't even look up.

Cloa smiled. She couldn't see whom Emi-Joye spoke with, since everyone nearby was at least a head taller than her, but she automatically appreciated that no one was going to give them different treatment simply because of their jobs. *It's a sense of equality, and I like that.*

They waited in line for what to Emi-Joye felt like an eternity, but the queen was enthralled. She took in the sights, the scents, the somewhat sticky texture of the floor, the raucous banter occurring over tables covered with mugs of ale and platters of meat and potatoes. By the time they got near enough to the barkeep's station to actually see the bar, a pair of paper menus floated to them. Cloa thought her stomach might melt directly into a puddle.

So many options — and that was only skimming the page that offered drinks. Cloa was occasionally allowed to indulge in a glass of Fae wine but had typically been prohibited from imbibing such fermented beverages.

"It's busy tonight," Emi-Joye told the barkeep once they were in front of him. "Is the pot roast sandwich still on?"

"Come on, Em! We do this every year. Do you see it on the menu? No. If it's not *on* the menu, it's off the menu," the barkeep's voice snapped.

"Deity bless, you're in a mood," the Fairy muttered. "Give me a minute to think. Cloa, do you know what you want yet?"

"Yes, I —" Cloa started to say, still scanning the menu, but the barkeep interrupted.

"Cloa? As in, *Princess* Cloa?" he hissed to Emi-Joye.

The Fairy, too, had resumed perusing the menu. "It's actually Queen Cloa now, but yes," she said idly.

The aforementioned queen finally glanced up from the menu to see the barkeep's profile as he gave Emi-Joye an exasperated open hand gesture. "What in the seven hells, you blasted Fae! You should have said that earlier!"

"I tried to get your attention, but back of the line it was," the ambassadora reminded him. "I'll have the crawfish po'boy with kettled chips and a glass of sparkling Riesling. Cloa?"

Cloa stepped forward as the barkeep turned to make eye contact, still visibly annoyed with Emi-Joye. The queen opened her mouth to start talking, but instead, she found herself staring intently into eyes that seemed to glare right inside her very soul. They were layers of brown, a reddish gingerbread near the center that deepened into chocolate, encircled by a border of rich umber. She saw herself reflected in those irises as if they were a mirror. Her chest warmed and there was an overwhelming sense of *rightness* that filled her with peace and joy, safety and *home*. Her Maylemaegus trilled; the warmth in her chest spread.

"Are you two alright?" Emi-Joye asked.

The world spun. Cloa wasn't sure how long they'd been staring at each other; it could have been an eternity, but in reality, it was only a second or two. She broke her stare and turned to the Fairy, who gave her a horrified look and motioned to her own eyes. Cloa winced; they must have shifted into the star shape. Her heart felt like it would thrum across the counter.

"I'm — I'm fine," she stuttered. "Tráthnóna mistéireach, friend. I don't believe we've met."

"Your Majesty," he murmured in reply. "Sheridan Ifans. How may I be of service to you?"

Cloa cleared her throat. "Um. I will have the vindaloo curry with rice. And a drink."

"By 'drink' she means she's going to want the lightest ale you have, Sheridan," Emi-Joye directed him. "One step above iced water."

"Yes, of course," Sheridan said absentmindedly. "Preferred method of payment, Em?"

"Service, please."

Sheridan turned around to look at a notebook. "I can put you down for a pit shift next week, or you could come in early this Saturday and run a prep line; we've got all of them open. Your choice."

"Friday night in the pit, thank you," she said brightly.

The barkeep scribbled something on the open page. "Be here by five o'clock. Your Majesty, you don't pay here, so please go take your seat. Your food will be out as soon as I can get it, and drinks before that. Refills will be on the house for both of you this night."

Emi-Joye started to thank him, but Cloa stepped back in front of her. "Thighearna Ifans, if I may. I ask of you no preferred treatment, as I am more than happy to pay for my meal in the same fashion as the ambassadora."

He faltered. "I … alright then, Your Majesty. I shall see you both in two nights."

Cloa hoped she would see him far sooner than that.

~ 91 ~

This, Bridgette decided, was not what she had in mind when she planned to visit the palace in Düoria. Not the run-in with the Palnan Royal Guard, for starters. Definitely not the Samnung-prohibited, invisible magical handcuffs and gags forced upon her and Toby during their guided escort into the capital city down the back road. And most assuredly not the part where the two of them were separated and locked into poorly lit rooms behind heavy black doors.

She tried several times to reach Serrabinx through the covenant bracelet.

The Elfling got a sick sense that perhaps, if he was still alive, this was where Ulerion Mewt was being kept. She thought they were on the lowest level of the palace: they were definitely in the massive building. But when they had approached it, led the rest of the way down the so-called prohibited road by their pair of guards, the path ended at either a back or side entrance, not opulent front gates. Bridgette wondered then if that was why the road was protected, and wished she could question Toby as to how he knew about this route in the first place.

It had been two days since they were deposited here.

Bridgette was given a change of clothes and presented with three square meals a day. Nothing special, but well-made and nutritious. The suite was bare, with a small bathroom that housed a shower, toilet, and sink. There was a mattress tucked into a carved alcove instead of stacked on a bedframe, a firehearth that never stopped burning, daylight from a small window high in the ceiling, and a solitary wooden chair. The chair befuddled Bridgette. It was positioned in the middle of the room and, though there were no bolts holding it to the floor, seemed rooted to the spot. She couldn't budge it, change the direction it faced; nothing.

Though the Bright Star generally did not mind being alone,

she was close to her tolerance level for being in this room with no answers and no Toby.

Serrabinx and Zedolph must be out of their minds with worry, Bridgette thought.

When one of the Royal Guard brought her dinner that night, she shoved her foot out to hold the door open. "How long are Toby and I going to be down here for?" she demanded. "His mother needs to know he's alright, and all we wanted to do was tour the palace and see the tulips!"

The guard, whose face was hidden behind one of those purple metal helms, didn't say anything. He didn't shut the door, either.

"Look, friend," Bridgette went on, taking the opening, "I hail from vuoristokylä and have only been in Xcthonya a few months. This was my first chance to finally see our capital city. We took a wrong turn, ended up on a road neither of us knew we weren't supposed to be on, and suddenly our exciting trip turned into us being locked in barely more than a dungeon. We came to enjoy ourselves and instead are being treated as enemies."

"Your dinner, Sigewíf," was all the guard said. He pushed the tray of food toward her.

Bridgette took it with an annoyed glare. At least it smelled good. She was halfway through eating it when there was a knock at the door, followed by the same guard poking his head in.

"You've been summoned to a receiving room, Sigewíf. Present your hands so that you may be protected on your way," he instructed.

Protected, Bridgette scoffed inwardly. *More like, 'Let me tie your hands so you don't try and escape before we do whatever we want with you.' Fucking assholes.*

The guard led her out of her suite and through a dim hallway, which reminded Bridgette too much of the cave dream to be a coincidence. They reached the bottom of a winding staircase, which was rickety near the base but eventually widened and became much more ravishing the higher they went. The first section was wrought iron; the second, wood; the third, marble. It was on this level that the guard opened a gate and pulled her through. Her mouth had been magically gagged again, otherwise Bridgette would have gasped.

This was the part of the palace the Samnung must have seen. Not for the first time in Heáhwolcen, Bridgette thought she'd stepped into a fairytale. The guard didn't let her see much of it as he guided her around a corner and into what must be the aforementioned receiving room, but what Bridgette did observe in those fleeting moments was an open atrium covered wall-to-wall in plush navy carpeting. Three other staircases, these going straight up and out, were on the remaining sides of the room. Marble columns marked the boundaries of each staircase, and an abundance of tropical plants lined the walls. The ceiling was stunning, a vast painting depicting the galaxy. Gold, silver, bronze, chrome, and that metallic purple were everywhere; constellations catching the sunlight streaming in so that their model stars were made to sparkle.

Bridgette turned to catch one last glimpse before the atrium disappeared behind her. *Blue carpet, plants on the walls, stars up top … soil, sky, and sea,* she realized. A shiver went down her spine. She recalled what Zedolph once said about his children's storybook and Baize Sammael's Larivuria, the mysterious "city by the sea", and wondered …

No. Absolutely not. I refuse to even acknowledge that train of thought.

Her Maylemaegus, active for the first time since the guards found them on the road, stirred at her inner musings.

"You'll wait here until you're received," the guard said suddenly. He stopped walking and removed Bridgette's magical binding. "Don't touch anything and don't speak until you're addressed. Do you understand?"

She nodded.

"I will return you to your stateroom shortly."

Bridgette nodded again, despite her eyeroll at the concept of her cave-like suite being considered a stateroom. She heard the guard's soft footsteps as he stepped down the navy blue carpet, and she was alone. She walked to the massive window and gazed out upon Palna. From this vantage point, she could see flat land dotted with villages, the rise of the Beorgdún far in the distance. Her back was still turned when the eeriest feeling came over her. The Elfling felt covered in oil, similar to what she experienced when she, Cloa, and Emi-Joye were first together.

It made her skin crawl, this unexplainable energy that coated her. It reminded her of the darkness from her dream about Eryth, but worse, because she knew she was very much awake.

"Hello."

The voice oozed curiosity. Soft and sweet, like the saltwater taffy Bridgette used to buy from beachfront candy shops as a child. But the tainted energy behind the remark soured whatever unassuming cool was meant to present itself.

The Bright Star turned around and braced herself, unsure if she was prepared to finally see the face of Ydessa Tinuviel.

"Uh, hi," Bridgette stammered. It wasn't anxiety that caused her to stutter, though it probably should have been. What stopped her cold was how unnervingly unlike her imagined Ydessa that the queen of Palna actually was.

In Bridgette's mind, Ydessa was dark and wicked — so many fantasy novels she read growing up depicted the female *villain* as someone with either flaming red or dark-colored hair, usually paired with either ice pale or deep golden skin. None of those characteristics stood before her, for Ydessa was several inches shorter than Bridgette, with voluminous honey-blonde curls, a rosy-hued heart-shaped face, full pink lips, and perfectly proportioned buxom hips and breasts sandwiching a trim waist. It was only the steely blue eyes that gave away the innocent woman's true nature, and the dainty aubergine tiara that snaked around her hair that displayed her as a self-proclaimed queen.

Ydessa watched as Bridgette eyed her up and down, then slowly cocked her head so far to one side, her ear was inches from her shoulder. "What are you?" she asked. Bridgette watched in fascination as the witch's pupils morphed into serpentine slits. An invisible energy brushed across her throat and the Elfling swallowed hard.

"I'm Bridgette, and I am an Elfling," Bridgette answered, thrown off by Ydessa asking *what*, not *who*, she was, just like Toby once did. Instead of what was supposed to be her cover story, she thought it safer to revert to what Muov told butchery customers about her if they asked; the same thing she told the guards upon her capture. "I was born and raised in vuoristokylä, and recently became a slátraestre to the butchery in Xcthonya."

"How did you get here?"

Bridgette wasn't sure Ydessa's head could tilt any further to the side without falling off her shoulders.

"Uh, I came with the slátrari's nephew," the Elfling replied. "We were coming to see the palace and hoped to take a tour, but then some guards found us on the road and brought us here. They said we were on a route where citizens weren't allowed."

Ydessa hissed a breath. "How interesting."

Oh boy.

"We must have taken a wrong turn in the rain," Bridgette chirped conversationally, fighting to hide the anxiety that gripped her lungs. As she'd done with the guards, she tried to change her diction to sound less human. "It was pouring when we left the other morning. I don't understand why we were housed in the palace though for what, two days? Three? I haven't kept perfect count. The food is quite good, but it has not been the reception Toby and I hoped for. He was put in a different room and I would like to see him. I feel terrible; I promised his mother I would have him home by nightfall the same day we left. Is this something you could help me with? What is your name, friend?"

Whatever Ydessa expected out of her newest guest, that response wasn't it. She looked at Bridgette, aghast, and blinked so hard her eyes became normal again. "I am Ydessa Tinuviel, queen of Palna."

"Oh, Your Majesty! I am so sorry; images of you are hard to come by in the Beorgdún. I did not recognize you!" Bridgette gave Ydessa a wide smile. She made a mental note to share this visual recollection with Collum and Trystane the moment she saw them again, because she couldn't wait to see them collapse in laughter at the memory of how she greeted this self-proclaimed monarch.

Ydessa responded with a sneer. "Evidently, I must speak to my archivists about this oversight. It is rare to have a citizen not know their own queen."

"I cannot believe I am standing here talking to the *queen* of *Palna*!" Bridgette rambled. "I am honored, truly, Your Majesty. I told the guards who found us about my and Toby's desire to see this palace and the tulips. I had no idea it would glean me an audience with the most powerful female in Heáhwolcen."

Her flattery wasn't lost on Ydessa, whose lips thinned into the flash of a smile. "You are very talkative, Bridgette."

"May I ask why we were brought here?" the Elfling asked. "And when we can expect to return to Xcthonya?"

The queen regarded her for several long minutes, head moving side to side in a trancelike motion. "Finding citizens on this road raised many questions. You were brought here because my guards wanted those questions answered."

"As I said, Your Majesty, we simply took a wrong turn —"

Ydessa held a finger up to silence Bridgette. "But did you? Or is that simply a convenient tale to tell?" She laughed softly. "Bring the lad in and close the room off, Taurus."

Taurus, one of the guards who must have been waiting outside, entered the room. Bridgette was horrified to see him nearly dragging Toby in by the collar of his shirt, the boy kicking and silently screaming behind his invisible bonds. He looked miserable. The Bright Star moved to run to him, but Ydessa stepped between the two. She snapped her fingers, and Bridgette found her arms and legs pinned together, turning her into a sentient statue. Toby started screaming out loud, but no one could hear him. Closing the room was code for Taurus to shield any sound inside, and the same sort of veil that made the Palnan side of the Ballamúr appear as though it looked out over a garden now coated the doorway. Bridgette tried to scream, too.

Another snap and Toby was bound, though the queen didn't censor his voice like she had the Bright Star's. He was terrified. Bridgette fought inside herself, aching to wake her Maylemaegus. *Why won't you fucking activate?*

Ydessa circled the boy, the obsidian pupils of her steely eyes narrowing again to venomous snake-like slits. The vile smile that slowly shaped her lips gave her the look of a starving carnivore, defied for years from being able to eat meat, now presented fresh food on a golden platter.

"A wrong turn, from someone like you?" she whispered. "Perhaps your Elfling friend would believe that, but I do not. It is not often someone who Sees finds their way into Düoria, not anymore."

Oh shit. Oh SHIT! Bridgette thought. *Wake up, you stupid magic!*

"It is rarer still that a young Seer joins me. I welcome you into this special place, Tobias Maudlin. You'll find that your life has much more purpose now, my sweet. A talent such as yours would be wasted in Xcthonya, but not here." Ydessa's voice fluctuated between feline purr and serpent hiss. The self-proclaimed queen of Palna reached a finger out to stroke Toby under the chin with one of her coal-black nails.

Her smile widened. The boy whimpered.

An acrid smell filled the air. Bridgette watched, furious and embarrassed, as Toby's fear overtook him. The dark spot formed at the crotch of his light brown leggings and slowly trickled its way to the floor, widening into a flooding puddle that deepened the blue of the carpet as he wet himself. Ydessa frowned in disgust, stepping aside as the humiliating torrent of piss-sodden floor threatened to touch the hem of her flowing lavender gown.

"How crude," the queen scolded. "A true Palnan would find honor in being invited to be a permanent guest in our palace."

Bridgette roared, her Maylemaegus with her.

✦ *It is not the time*, her vademecum's spirit whispered in warning. *Do not betray yourself, not here, Liluthuaé!*

The Elfling didn't care. What she wouldn't give to be able to magic herself free and shove her jeweled dagger into Ydessa's neck.

You fucking bitch. If it's the last thing I do, I am taking you down! the Elfling thought to herself as she screamed a voided song for Toby, for herself, for Palna. The invisible bonds tightened around her biceps, her wrists, her ankles. She was well and fully trapped.

To break her bonds with Maylemaegus would get her thrown into the Collective right alongside Toby, or worse. There was nothing she could do, not at this precise moment, as she watched Ydessa Tinuviel conquer her young friend by presence alone.

~ 92 ~

The Palnan guards had to sedate her. One of them held Bridgette in a modified headlock as they forced an intimidatingly large syringe under her skin and plunged an unknown liquid into her bloodstream. She let out one final scream of frustration and got a solid kick into a guard's kneecap before she passed out.

When Bridgette woke again in her so-called stateroom, with no Toby and more agitation, she had no idea how long she'd been down there for. It was dark aside from the firehearth, so she hoped she'd only been out for a few hours, maybe a day at most. No meals had been left for her. It reminded her of when she woke after healing from her hand wound. Then, she had flashes of memory of Ilori changing her bandages and aiding her in walking drowsily to the bathroom, but this time she woke with nothing. It was one minute of consciousness to the next.

Her lungs burned and her throat ached from screaming. She got Toby caught and swiped right into the Collective. He had to have known that route through someone in the Hringur. Angry tears threatened to fall.

✦ *Be at peace, Liluthuaé. This is of no fault of yours.*

"Easy for you to say," Bridgette muttered to her vademecum. "You didn't willingly take your friend and easy target into enemy territory. I should have just gone by myself and not asked Toby. Serrabinx is going to kill me, and I don't blame her a bit."

✦ *It was known the boy would take this path.*

Bridgette sat straight up in the bed, furious that she couldn't see or throttle the vademecum's spirit. "You told me that this is the path I had to take! Why the fuck would I take it if I knew it would lead to Toby getting swiped into the Collective? Did you see how scared he was? They're going to kill him, and it's all my fault, because I listened to you."

✦ *The intertwined fates are aligning. This is the path you must traverse.*

"Well, fuck you, because I don't *want* to traverse *this path*, you dumb notebook!" Bridgette's shout was scratchy and lacked the rage she wanted to get across. "You said to trust you and your stupid ghost handprint, and you broke that trust. Why would you tell me to believe you when now we're both in danger?"

✦ *'Twas not I, Liluthuaé. Another.*

"Another *what?*" she groaned. "One of the other vademecums?"

But no — as soon as she said that, it sounded incorrect. She would have known the voice of Emi-Joye's and would be able to determine immediately if the ghostly mind-voice was that of the third. Her vademecum didn't elaborate further, and Bridgette didn't have the mental capacity to process what it could mean, that yet *another* unseen force or magic was with her. The Elfling put her head back on the pillow and curled into a ball, body sore from exerting itself earlier against unshakeable bonds.

Why doesn't my Maylemaegus work in here? she thought. *What about this room is barring it from being activated?*

✦ *Did you not observe the closing of the room, Liluthuaé?*

How come I can talk to you, but not access my magic? Bridgette thought grumpily, though the vademecum's words began to sink in. Her eyes shifted in acknowledgement. There were spells in this castle that acted like modified versions of the Ballamúr, giving the Tinuviels the ability to censor what magic could occur inside.

"That doesn't make sense," Bridgette murmured. "Not if the Ballamúr and the protected lands recognize me, or at least my blood. The power everywhere else in this castle should abide by that same rule, right?"

✦ *Your power comes from within, Liluthuaé.*

"No shit, Sherlock," she told the vademecum. "Why do you think I keep trying to activate it?"

✦ *Your power is not something to be turned on and off. It simply is.*

"Are you *ever* going to be less cryptic?" She glowered at the darkness. The vademecum spoke true, however. When she *became* her Maylemaegus, as she once told Collum, it was a split-second switch with no warning. One moment she was herself, the next, she was … not. Standing outside the Seledreám the day she fought Emi-Joye was the closest she came to being able to consciously differentiate between these two sides of self. Stopping the rain from hitting her and Zedolph her first day back in Palna — and most mornings and evenings afterward on their walks to and from the butchery — was what she called triggering the power. But was it really so much triggering as it was accepting the gift of the deities?

Bridgette might not be physically able to leave this room yet, and it might bar her normal ways of communication, but she had a way out. She closed her eyes, wrapped her entire hand around her covenant with Collum, and coaxed herself to sleep, visualizing the Elf's face and chanting his name inside her mind as if it was a ritual.

Collum knew he was dreaming this time because the ísenwaer didn't work. He could only speak to this subconscious version of Bridgette out loud, or as out loud as the dream version of himself could.

"You meant to do this," he murmured, and took her in his arms. She felt so real. It killed him to know that whenever this dream ended, he would wake, and she would still be so far beyond his reach. "How did you teach yourself?"

"Magic."

He chuckled. "So snarky, my Starshine."

"Do you really want to know?" Bridgette asked him. "It's kind of a lot."

"Everything about you is somewhat of a lot, Bridgette Conner. I suppose it is a good thing that I rather enjoy such a quantity of things."

She kissed his cheek and stepped back. They were in his office again. But this would be a different sort of dream, though none less powerful. Bridgette gave him a mournful sort of smile.

"You told me a long time ago that magic isn't inherently good or evil, that it just *is*," she said. "What if Craft Wizardry is the same? What if the only reason you think it's evil is because you've only ever heard of or seen evil beings use it?"

Collum gave her a curious look. "What are you talking about?"

And so, she showed him.

Maybe it was easier because they were dreaming, but it felt like second nature to become the pure connection to all that was and is and would be. No longer did Bridgette whisk her mind from her body when she reached for any of her power. A simple moment of inward focus opened the unending chasm. It took a mere heartbeat to just *become*.

Collum choked out a shout. In the space of a breath, Bridgette appeared as herself, but altered. The fyrdwisa stared at the otherworldly presence that floated in midair before him.

Her eyes were her own, and the smile on her face was soft. She was cradled in the arms of a nonexistent breeze, save for the churning cyclones that appeared in her upturned palms. Wind whipped through her hair. It pulled tendrils loose from her braid, the motion of the air moving reminding Collum more of a rolling tide than that of an impending storm. Electricity sparked between them, both metaphorical and visible.

Bridgette lifted a hand, beckoning to the velvet navy of midnight. Every tree within a mile inside his secret paradise danced in her midst. Blades of grass bent toward her. The atmosphere itself thrummed as if the same heartbeat powered them both.

Because it did, for the Liluthuaé was Maylemaegus come to life, and hers was Maylemaegus gifted to a bloodborne child of Craft magic. Collum could not separate the two, for they were innately so Bridgette, the same way her fears, her hopes, her heart were. The truth of this brought him to his knees.

Collum fell as he had for Cloa, but it was something deeper. That had been a matter of duty, a response to the rise of a queen; a sworn promise to the mission and legacy she represented. But this? Deep in the recesses of his unconscious mind, the fyrdwisa acknowledged that when he awoke from this dream, he would be as wet in real life as he was getting now in the rain that began to fall. He struggled to see, to breathe properly.

The rain soaked him to the bone, torrents coating the soil as if it gifted the ground a promise of sustenance. And in the sky above him, floating like a goddess, hair blowing in a gentle breeze and drier than desert sands, was the Bright Star.

She tasted hot salt mixed with the rain that fell. Bridgette descended the few feet to the ground and cloaked the Elf and his tears in a breeze. He was dry in seconds, though the rain continued to fall around them. The ground beneath Collum's knees felt unstable. He understood now what she meant.

Perhaps it had been bastardized by Baize Sammael, but Craft Wizardry was as old a magic as the gifts of Maylemaegus were. Together, they were unstoppable and incredibly dangerous. It was no wonder Bridgette couldn't do magic the same way everyone else in Heáhwolcen could. She didn't need to. She existed as pure power, able to command the elements — air coming easiest — as if they were extensions of her own consciousness. Which, Collum considered as he stared up at her, they were.

Words failed him.

You never cease to astonish me, Starshine, he thought to her, and knew that even though the ísenwaer would not work in this dream, the meaning of his expression conveyed the thought perfectly.

Bridgette lifted them both into the air, not even touching him, so firm and sure was her grasp on her power. Collum felt the air strong and steady as it pulled him beside her. He wished again that this was real and not a sequence of events occurring in his subconscious mind. Collum traced her arms, up her shoulders and her neck, bringing his hands to rest at the base of her jaw. He tucked some of those flyaway strands of her hair behind an ear. There was another spark of electricity, but he didn't shy away. The unspoken question lingered between them.

Collum moved forward first, then just as quickly pulled back, unsure if this was the right moment to do such a thing. Bridgette let the air drop him, and he gave a shout of surprised protest as he shot down a few feet. It caught him a moment later and raised him back up to again face the Elfling, who glared at him wryly over her crossed arms.

"You're a real damn tease, Bundy," she scolded him.

"Bridgette, I'm sorry. This is … much to process," he started to say.

She barked out a laugh. "Oh, you think this is a lot to process?" Bridgette chortled. "Wait until you hear why I *actually* decided to come invade your dreams tonight."

~ 93 ~

Tula Vetur was not fond of having to answer loud knocks before sunrise. She tore open the front door, ready to shout at whichever being so rudely presented itself, and then realized she stood face-to-face with the fyrdwisa.

Her shout died on her lips. "Oh!"

"Sigewíf Vetur, I am so sorry to be here without prior warning and at such an hour, but it is with extreme urgency that I request an audience with the ambassadora," Collum said. He spoke so fast that he wasn't sure the Fairy caught everything he said. "May I come in?"

"Of course, Fyrdwisa, but I do not believe my daughter is home this morning. She was with the queen last night."

Shit, Collum thought. He bowed his head to the female. "Thank you for that information, Sigewíf Vetur. If she happens to arrive home and we miss each other in transit, please let her know that I am in need of her, and she'll be able to find me at the Caisleán in my office."

The Elf evanesced to Deu Medgar without giving Tula a chance to say anything else. The Fairy closed the door on the now-empty stoop, shaking her head in disbelief.

But Emi-Joye wasn't in Cloa's rooms either.

"Emi-Joye wasn't here last night," the queen told him. "Come inside, Collum, it's not even time for the cocks to crow. Why are you looking for us so early?"

He started pacing the new shaggy rug on her floor. Arctura leapt into his arms and clawed into the Elf's shoulder, causing Collum to snarl at it. But he calmed, answering the request of the feline, before turning to answer Cloa. "We told you before that Bridgette is able to do something I refer to as dream walking. She's done it before without realizing what was happening. Last night, she did it intentionally, and she is in trouble."

"In trouble?!"

"Yes," Collum replied. "She accidentally found herself and her young comrade, Toby — the boy I mentioned to you who has certain unusual powers — trapped in Düoria, in the palace. The boy was kidnapped by the Tinuviels to be part of a group known as the Collective, which we believe to be part of Palna's secret military forces."

"Are they going to take Bridgette, too?" Cloa had to sit down. She stared at Collum.

"I don't know. She doesn't know. We have to do something to get her out; I cannot just sit here *again* and wait for her to come back!" The Elf wanted to punch something.

"Can't you just … go in? Wear a cloak so you won't be recognized?" the queen asked.

Collum looked at her, distraught. "Unfortunately for us, the only one who can cross the Ballamúr is apparently Bridgette."

"How did the rest of the Samnung get in?" she demanded.

He sighed. "That barrier wall recognizes Bridgette's blood. For what purpose, I cannot say. But she hypothesized that by sharing her blood with whichever individual wishes to enter Palna, it is akin to giving it her blessing. The Ballamúr honors that," Collum replied.

"Is this the part where you tell me that you have a vial of her blood saved somewhere in your home?" Cloa asked with a gleam in her eye. Collum looked at her in revulsion.

"Do I appear as a Sanguisuge to you?!" he asked. "Why in the seven hells would I have a vial, or even a droplet, of Bridgette's blood?"

"I don't know," Cloa said coyly. She twirled some of the bronze strands in her hair. "I don't know what the two of you get up to when you're not amongst the rest of the living."

Collum unceremoniously dropped Arctura to the ground and almost grabbed the queen by the shoulders. "We get up to nothing like what you're insinuating, thank you, and I'll thank you too for keeping such notions and thoughts to yourself!"

She only smiled, her irises dancing into the star shape. "Say what you wish, Fyrdwisa, but it's useless trying to keep a secret like that from this member of the Triumvirate."

"These fool powers of yours, I do swear," Collum muttered. His cheeks flushed a warm pink. "I would still not have a vial of her blood, regardless. That is … not my style."

The queen made a noncommittal "hmm" noise and walked past him to an inlaid shelf filled with a series of labeled pulleys. Cloa tugged on the one for the kitchen and was about to join Collum on the settee — which had finally been reupholstered to get rid of the drab beige of its former life — when the Elf jumped up with a shout. He ran a hand through his hair and stared at the witch.

"Cloa!" he cried. He walked a circle in place, elation written across his features. "I believe there is a way we can enter Palna without having to *enter* Palna!"

A knock at the door announced the arrival of a kitchen witch. Cloa held up a hand to silence the fyrdwisa and answered the woman. "I'm sorry for calling upon you so early, Sigewíf, but this is a rather urgent and impromptu meeting. We need a carafe of breakfast roast coffee and some sugared croissants," she said. "Please bring them at your convenience. I realize this is not an ideal time to request fresh baked goods."

The kitchen witch promised someone would bring the ordered items as soon as they were prepared. After bidding her farewell, Cloa shut the door again. "Go on, please," she implored Collum.

"Are you familiar with the concept of astral projection?"

Cloa blinked. "Astral projection? As in, sending our spirits elsewhere while our bodies remain grounded behind?"

"Yes."

"You believe that you or I could project ourselves into Palna and find Bridgette?" Cloa was skeptical. "But what are we to do once we find her? Astral projections cannot physically touch, they can only observe."

"I'm aware of that. The point of this exercise will be to find Bridgette, assess her health, and see what needs to be done to bring her back," Collum said. "She can't sit in that room and wait to be let out. The Tinuviels were already known to take prisoners or to eradicate those who disagreed with them. If Bridgette steps a toe out of line, especially after the way she reacted when Toby was taken into the Collective, it could trigger something none of us is prepared for."

Cloa, who had yet to sit down again, began pacing along the rug. "Let's assume this works, and we're able to project our spirit-selves across the Samnung wall and the Ballamúr. None of us have been to Palna, much less inside the palace. How do we make sure we send ourselves to the right place?"

She raised a fair point.

"It's possible that once my consciousness is in Palna, Bridgette will be able to sense it," Collum said. "I am willing to take that risk."

His actual plan, of course, was to see if the ísenwaer worked via astral projection, but Cloa wasn't to know about that.

"You think she'll know we're coming?"

"She knows I'm going to get in that damned place. I told her as much tonight when she dream-walked me awake," Collum said. "Whatever connection she has to Universal consciousness will let her know that something is awry."

Cloa hummed nonchalantly. "And I'm sure her vademecum will help."

Collum glanced at her. "What are you on about?"

"She has her vademecum, of course. Not physically, since as far as I know hers is wherever you and Trystane hid it," the queen said. "But when we touched them that first time, it cemented some kind of spiritual connection. Bridgette's vademecum is able to communicate with her because of it."

That's certainly a convenient piece of information she left out in her reports, the fyrdwisa grumbled to himself.

"Do they all three speak with you?" he asked.

Cloa shook her head. She hiked the hem of her house-robe up to reveal a leather harness around her thigh. The green notebook glowed in hello as it recognized Collum.

✗   *Hello, Fyrdwisa, fanner of the flame.*

"Does the queen speak truly, that Bridgette's vademecum is able to guide her?" A plan began to form in the back of Collum's mind.

✗   *The Astridsí speaks the truth.*

"Is it possible for us to speak with the vademecum, and it share a message with the Liluthuaé?" The Elf felt off-put when he realized he spoke out loud while staring at the witch queen's bare legs. "Or if we were to project ourselves into Palna, could your spirits sense that of your sister and lead us to Bridgette?"

✗   *A message could be transmitted, yes. For such magic of which you speak, we cannot be certain. We have never undergone such an experiment.*

Further conversation was momentarily halted as a second kitchen witch arrived, bearing their requested treats. The steaming mug of coffee was a jolt to the fyrdwisa's system. He sipped quietly and watched Cloa continue to pace circles around her rug as she chewed a croissant. Sprinkles of powdered sugar snowed to the ground with each bite.

"How soon do you want to go ahead with this plan?" she asked.

Collum leaned against the wall in thought. "Soon, preferably. The less time Bridgette spends at the mercy of the Tinuviels, the better."

"Then we should probably find the ambassadora. Shall we visit her home?"

The Elf blinked. "She's not at her home. I went there first and her mother told me she was here, which she clearly is not. Perhaps she stayed at the Seledreám?"

"I don't know," Cloa commented. "Can you not summon

her?"

"Can *you*?"

They were at a standstill. The queen glowered. "Fine. I'll tell my vademecum to tell *her* vademecum that the fyrdwisa is in my rooms and would like to speak to her immediately."

"No," Collum stopped her. "It'll take her hours to fly here. Have it find out where she is and I'll evanesce us to her."

The Fairy's shriek of panic woke Trystane from a dead sleep.

"What?!" he gasped out, reaching for her as his eyes adjusted to the waning darkness. "Em, are you alright? What woke you?"

"I have to go." She was already out of bed, rummaging through the pile of clothes that decorated the floor from the previous night. "Cloa decided to use our vademecums as a way to transmit a message. She and Collum want to know where I am, so that they can evanesce to me and discuss something supposedly urgent."

"What?" Trystane was not a functional morning Elf. Not this hour of morning, anyway.

"As our vademecums speak to us in that strange way of theirs, apparently they can be used as a means of communication. Collum has important news and went first to my house, then to Deu Medgar. Now they both want to know where to find me for some clandestine meeting in the middle of the deity-damned witching hour," Emi-Joye said hurriedly. "Where are my undergarments, Trys?"

He motioned vaguely to a corner of the room. "I believe I threw them over there. Did your vademecum tell you anything else?"

"No, but they can't evanesce *here*, and they'll expect an answer soon. I have to be anywhere else, but not my house because that will raise too many questions!"

Emi-Joye's voice reached a high-pitched wail of desperation. Trystane had known for some time now that they wouldn't be able to keep this a secret too much longer, not since she began spending more nights away from her bed. He supposed her excuse of visiting Cloa was not the smartest choice, as evidenced by the events unfolding before them.

"Em," he said gently, "Why don't you breathe for a moment, collect yourself, and allow me to evanesce you to your office? It is perfectly reasonable that you would be there overnight, or at least early in the morning. We all know you're dedicated to your work, and it would not be the first time you fell asleep at your desk."

She paused, holding her rumpled dress in one hand and a pair of silken undergarments in the other. Her exposed chest heaved with panicked energy. "Right. Yes. Let's do that."

"Don't answer them just yet. Come here first."

"Trys —"

With a crook of his hands and a whispered spell, the Fairy was tossed unceremoniously back onto the bed. Trystane wrapped his arms around her and breathed on the shell of her ear. "Will you tell me why you're panicking, and how I might help?"

Emi-Joye felt herself mold around him, skin against skin. She reached for one of his hands and snaked her fingers around his. "I don't want to spoil this."

"Is that why you're panicking, or are you trying to tell me you don't want to answer?"

She giggled softly. "I don't want to answer, thank you, but it's so hard to keep this — the two of us — a secret. I feel as though I'm lying to everyone, but I don't want either of us to have our lives affected by the knowledge that the ard rialóir has a female distracting him from his duties. And an ambassadora at that!"

Trystane furrowed his brow. "Do you truly think that I consider you, and the depth of my feelings for you, as distractions?"

She nodded against his chest.

"Oh, Em," the Elf breathed. "I am sorry if I did or said something that caused you to have such a thought about yourself. I assure you, my darling Fae, that you couldn't be a distraction to me if you tried. I've had my share of such dalliances. But you? You, Emi-Joye Vetur, hold my soul within your grasp, my essence in your energy. That is a gift to be possessed in such a way, with such warmth, by someone so fierce. I want the entire world above the world to see you the way I do — though perhaps, if I may request, the rest of Heáhwolcen sees you with more fabric upon your body than I am honored to get to."

His thank-you was a kiss. "You daft cad," Emi-Joye teased. "How do you manage to lift my spirits when I least expect it?"

"Always expect such an action from me, my love." Trystane resisted the urges both to deepen their kiss and to tell Collum that he could fuck right off. "Put that dress back on and go tell my brother and your sister where they may find you, before I change my mind and keep you here indefinitely."

~ 94 ~

There was not enough coffee in the entirety of the Seledreám's kitchens to prepare Emi-Joye — nor Trystane, who to his displeasure was summoned by Collum not long after the ard rialóir had evanesced himself back under his bedsheets — for Bridgette's late-night dream walking report.

Are you alright? Trystane's first concern, once he heard the story, was for Collum's welfare.

The fyrdwisa barely looked at Trystane as he shook his head. No, "alright" was nowhere near what Collum felt this night. He knew Bridgette was perfectly able to hold her own. Watching her fight Emi-Joye and experiencing her magic at its gentlest mere hours ago assured him of that. But Ydessa had been able to get the upper hand and bind her once. So had the Palnan guards who brought her to Düoria. Collum wasn't sure if the Bright Star would be able to break through such magic despite what they knew of her powers. He did not want her to have to find out.

"Do you really think this will work?" Emi-Joye asked Cloa. She glanced at the two Elves. Collum was anxious, though the Fairy couldn't blame him.

The queen sighed. "I don't know. My moth — Nehemi — was so careful about any magic that I learned. I was tutored in magical theory, but actual spellwork? I think my wand is more for show." She pulled the stunning carved taper of basswood from its holster on her belt and slowly spun the object, allowing morning light to accentuate the shadows of its labyrinthine swirls.

"It is a lovely wand," Emi-Joye replied.

"Thank you. I wish I knew how to use it better." Cloa felt her vademecum's spirit tap her mind as she murmured that desire.

⚡ *The Triumvirate needs no wands, only one another.*

"Aren't grimoires supposed to be, I don't know, helpful?" the queen grumbled. "Aren't they also supposed to not eavesdrop on their bearers' conversations?"

⚡ *Simply because you do not accept the help we offer does not negate that we offer it.*

Cloa glanced down at the harness hidden under the nightdress she still wore. "Emi-Joye, does your vademecum insist on being as clear as mud, too?"

"It is as if we have been handed younglings to take care of, but they were born into this world with the wisdom of the ancients and the lack of manners of the deities," the ambassadora grinned. "It is a lost cause to control them. I mostly ignore mine."

☠ *And the Boireannach wonders why it is more challenging for the two of you to be your true selves than it is for the Liluthuaé.* Emi-Joye's vademecum seemed to let out a harrumph.

"Rude," the Fairy muttered. "You're quite useful, I will admit, when you are not acting as an insect, buzzing in my ear."

☠ *You will need such buzzing should you wish to achieve your goal of finding the Liluthuaé in the astral plane.*

"I'm glad your vademecum, at least, seems to think this idea has merit," Collum said. The Fairy shuddered. She forgot for a moment that the fyrdwisa was able to hear and sense them the same way the Triumvirate could.

"When do you anticipate us leaving our physical bodies, and where shall we ground ourselves?" Emi-Joye asked.

Collum hadn't thought that far. He wanted to do it *now*, not at some vague point in the near future. But that was an impulsive, self-driven motivation. If they wanted this to work, with or without the added boon of having the vademecums' spirits along as guides, they had to be intentional and take their time.

He gave them three days.

Cloa volunteered a meditation room in Cyneham Breonna for their journey, and after the Samnung heard the plan, Verivol volunteered their sister, Lymerian.

"My sister has guided others many a time," they said. "She'll know how to prepare the room, Your Majesty, if you'll allow her early access."

"Of course, Verivol. Thank you so much," the witch replied. "Please tell her to visit tomorrow so that I may show her the space and allow her to ready it as she needs. This is a generous offer from both of you, and one we greatly appreciate."

Collum chuckled at Cloa sometimes. It was hard to remember that she was so young, so green in all that life had to offer, when she acted like the queen she was born to be. It angered him to think about all the time she lost due to Kharis' actions. He couldn't wait, though he found himself required to, to question the former borhond. They had more pressing matters to attend to than the old wizard these days. The fyrdwisa did make regular checks on both he and Dominus, and occasionally even Nehemi. He spoke to Dominus, but for the other two, he chose to converse with the guards that stood outside their doors. Kharis was watched to ensure he wouldn't do anything stupid, but Nehemi secluded herself in such a state that Collum was starting to worry if he should implore Cloa to send the former queen's lacnestre of mind-health in to visit her.

As he listened to the Samnung members decide who would be in the meditation room and for what purpose, the fyrdwisa's mind drifted. He felt so much anger, so much anxiety of late. His feelings for Bridgette aside, a part of him hated the deities for placing such burdens on individuals so young. Their souls and magic may be older than anyone except the Fyrst, but their physical manifestations were hardly fully grown. The females of the Triumvirate should be spending their existence balancing feoht and power training with things they enjoyed, not pigeonholed into the time crunch of fulfilling their destinies.

It scared him to think what that fulfillment might entail; what sacrifices these three might be required to make.

Those thoughts haunted the fyrdwisa the closer they came to

being able to try this half-brained idea of astral travel. Bridgette hadn't contacted Collum again, though the vademecums assured Cloa and Emi-Joye their message was received. He didn't know what he expected — that Bridgette would start dreamwalking to him every night? — but the silence worried him incessantly.

Collum, you are too tense to undertake this journey right now, Trystane thought to him as the two walked down a hall in Cyneham Breonna. *I am of the mind to call this off. You know better than any of us that to overthink or not be relaxed during astral travel could prove disastrous.*

"I'm aware," the fyrdwisa snapped back. "Am I not allowed to be worried?"

The ard rialóir put a comforting hand on his shoulder. "You are, brother mine. But I sense in you a most *unlike* you energy these days. You have been ill-tempered and do not appear to be sleeping well again. You are worried for things that will not come to pass, Collum. I am hesitant to let you proceed under such mental strain."

"I'll be fine, Trystane. I just need to get in there."

Trystane sighed. "You will. I only ask that you be smart about this."

Collum didn't say anything else as they continued walking. The room Cloa offered was beautiful and quiet, secluded toward the end of this winding hallway, and spacious. He and Trystane entered to find Lymerian, her firetruck red hair pulled back, surrounded by a series of crystal bowls. A trio of soft pallets had been made and arranged on the floor, and the air was heady with herbaceous and floral scents of lavender, rose, and chamomile. A repeating pattern of crystals encircled the room, stones meant to guide, protect, and bring light.

The entire Samnung, plus Apostine, Njahla, and Aurelias, milled about, waiting for the time to come. Emi-Joye and Cloa looked nervous but determined. Collum gritted his teeth. He could do this. They all could.

"Are we ready?" he asked Lymerian.

She smiled, her fangs glinting in the candlelight she used to brighten the room. "We are, Fyrdwisa. You may each enter the circle and lie down. Please hold one another's hands so that you all three transport to the same space." Lymerian gestured forward. "I ask, Your Majesty, that as I guide your journey, you and the ambassadora focus on following Collum. As you begin to drift, visualize yourselves holding his hand, going where he takes you. It is important that you do not allow yourself to separate from him. He has the strongest connection to the Bright Star."

Collum stretched, loosening his muscles as he got comfortable on the pallet. He placed himself in the middle and held one hand out for each Cloa and Emi-Joye. The rest of the party stood just outside the crystal circle and held hands as well.

"I invite you to inhale deeply and follow your breath as it flows through your body. Allow it to pause. Feel it nourish you. Exhale," Lymerian instructed. Her voice was melodious as she spoke, a quality emphasized as she slowly began to play music on the bowls that sat before her. "You will remain grounded here, aware that your physical bodies are not with you. It is up to you where this journey takes you. Be at peace, for you are safe. No harm can befall you, for you are grounded here."

Lymerian began to speak of Düoria, describing it in such poetic, vivid descriptions that somewhere, deep in the recesses of his drifting mind, Collum knew she studied every word in each of the Samnung members' reports from their visit in February. He latched onto these visualizations, seeing flashes of rooms he'd never been to before. They became clearer and lengthier, until finally a room with taxidermized creatures came into full view. He knew that room. Trystane told him about this room.

Collum leapt, dragging Cloa and Emi-Joye along with him. Their ghostly presences tumbled onto the floor.

"What is this place?" the Fairy asked. She dusted herself off and reached a hand to touch the shaggy dark green fur of what had once been a cù-sìth, the long-extinct species of Fae hound.

Her fingers went right through the beastly remains. "Oh. Right. We can't touch anything."

The fyrdwisa scanned their surroundings. "We're in the palace. Trystane mentioned this room in his report." He began to walk the museum-like display of creatures. "How do the Tinuviels have some of these? The cù-sìth have been gone for a thousand years, and I believe *that* is — deity fucking bless, is that truly a chrysomallos?"

The golden-fleeced, golden-horned sheep stared back at him with deadened eyes. "This should not be here. None of these should be here."

Collum could spend hours cataloging the international collection of creatures. It was abhorrent for the Tinuviels to keep such a macabre set of decorations and parade tour groups before them, showing off what they, and presumably Baize Sammael before them, had in their home.

Bridgette? Collum sent a thought to her, but as in the dreams, the ísenwaer did not work. He cursed under his breath.

"One of you needs to use your vademecum and get us down to wherever Bridgette is being kept," the Elf instructed Cloa and Emi-Joye. "Fast. I'm not sure how long we're going to be able to stay projected."

Emi-Joye pulled hers from her knife belt. "Where is our … sister?" she asked, making the last word sound as though it hurt her to utter it. "Can you lead us to her?"

Like the ísenwaer, the vademecums' ability to speak to their bearers was lost in this form of magic, but their energies were not. The objects began to glow. Cloa smiled, relieved.

"They'll get brighter as we get closer, and dim if we go off-course," she said.

Better than nothing, Collum decided. "Let us go, then."

It felt like hours that they wandered the palatial residence. Even though the spectral trio could walk through walls and closed doors, they played a constant guessing game of which direction to go next. At some points, Emi-Joye and Cloa argued over whether or not their vademecums' glow was dimming, and they went several wrong directions — and once in a circle — before getting back on track. Having to avoid being seen or heard by Palnan guards and palace staff was an added layer of challenge, for being astral did not prevent being perceived. Collum tried to keep all three of them calm.

"If we lose our way and our focus, there's a strong chance we will be called back to our physical bodies," he warned them. "We've come too far this time to go back now, not until we've found her."

Collum realized after a while that the taxidermy room must be on an upper level, because the vademecums led them down various staircases as they searched. Finally, they reached a blue-carpeted atrium, surrounded by more staircases. There was no other way out of the room except to go up or down. Only one of the routes descended further, and Collum didn't need a guide this time to know which way they needed to go. He walked across the vast room and picked up speed as he led the Boireannach and Astridsí deeper and deeper. He would have thought they were underground, was it not for the occasional window through which moonlight peeked.

The vademecums' lights turned bright white and pulsating at the base of the stairs. There were rooms down here and the surroundings looked to be nearly cave-like. Collum paused. He did not see any guards, which meant the doors must be strongly warded. That explained why Bridgette might have trouble accessing her full power; not because she couldn't, but because she was apt to encounter a barrier and assume she wouldn't be able to. He huffed.

"Walk in front of each of these doors until we find hers," he murmured to his companions.

This part, at least, was simple. The vademecums went dark except for at the first door nearest the stairs. *Thank Hecate,*

Collum thought. He grabbed the females and they plunged through the door, no such spellwork able to stop the energies of three ghosts.

- 647 -

~ 95 ~

"Still shining, Bright Star?" a new, young voice asked.

Three figures were silhouetted in front of the small room's firehearth. Twin pulses of energy, one green and the other blue, shone from two of them. Bridgette shot out of her bed, shaking in relief.

"Holy shit, it worked!" She threw her arms around Collum, only to find that she could not embrace an astral projection. "Well. That sucks half the fun out of it."

He chuckled. "It did work, though the vademecums are disappointed to learn they cannot speak in their usual manner while in the astral realm."

Bridgette turned to flash a smile at Emi-Joye, and then to the third figure. "Hi, Your Maj — what the fuck. Cloa?"

She didn't recognize the witch. Gone was the dazed princess with long hair and longer gowns. In her place stood a petite young woman whose leather armor fit her so skin-tight, Bridgette could see the outline of every muscle in her body. Across Cloa's hips lay a sword belt with looped chains. The hilt of a dagger stuck out of one boot, and a harness around one thigh was presumably where the vademecum typically stayed. Her hair had metallic strands woven throughout. But the energy, specter or not, was remarkable.

"You're the Astridsí," Bridgette breathed. "But *how*? When my vademecum said the circle was complete, I thought Nehemi —"

Collum wished he could touch her. "Much has happened since you left, Starshine. We do not have time for all of the details, but what is important to understand is that Cloa is both the rightful Astridsí and queen of Endorsa."

Bridgette was horrified. "Is Nehemi dead?"

"No!" Cloa said, laughing. Bridgette was struck by the difference in tenor of her voice, so strong in that one word compared to the few other times she heard the now-queen speak. "Nehemi's not dead. She's essentially exiled herself at Deu Medgar. Everyone in Heáhwolcen was duped, myself included, to believe she was the child of my parents. She's the daughter of Queen Lalora's handmaiden and was raised to be the heir when Lalora thought that she could not have a child of her own womb."

"She's not actually your mother?!"

The Elfling was brimming with questions. Collum didn't need the ísenwaer to see that — there was a gleam of hunger that sparkled in her eyes — but he held up both hands to stop the chatter. "Again, we don't have time, friends. We need to get you out."

Bridgette poked a hand through Emi-Joye's spectral shoulder — "Ugh!" was the Fairy's response — and then made an open-handed gesture of annoyance. "Y'all are gonna be real helpful with that, being ghosts and all."

"You can break down that door, you know," Collum said. "It won't hold Maylemaegus."

Why haven't you done it already? he wanted to ask her. *Why have you remained here instead of using your magic to get out? Why do you stay in this deity-forsaken palace instead of returning to Eckenbourne?*

But the answer to his questions was painted plainly on Bridgette's face. She wasn't leaving until she knew Toby would be safe. Collum watched her for a moment as she took them all in, dressed as if they were prepared to fight. They would be, if they were here in corporeal form.

They were dressed not all that differently from how Corria Deathhunter looked on a daily basis, thick fighting leathers reinforced at the joints, topped with metal armor over their shoulders, shins, and the upper portions of their chests. Bridgette imagined that if battle truly was to break out, there would be matching helms. Cloa's leather was the deep peacock green of Endorsa, embossed on the cropped chestplate, forearms, and thighs with bronze-colored symbols. Emi-Joye's leathers shifted in hue like a holographic image, going from seafoam to mint to turquoise, glittering softly in the firelight. She had a short, flowing skirt draped under her ever-present knife belt, and the silver shield knot insignia of Fairevella was emblazoned across her torso. On each shoulder was an arrangement of silver stars that signified her ambassadora status.

It was hard to look at Collum and know she could not feel him. She'd never seen him dressed as fyrdwisa — only in formal attire for holidays and ceremonies — and the sight of him in that fitted navy blue leather nearly undid her. His armor was a gold so rich it looked molten, glistening so against the fire, and the familiar intricate "E" of Eckenbourne shone from his shoulders. The colors accented his tidal pool eyes, which were filled with a set of emotions Bridgette yearned to unpack.

Bridgette wanted to know everything. She didn't know why she hadn't put it together already, that something was amiss with Nehemi and Cloa other than the now-queen's former personality. Her eyes shifted and she was hit by a startling realization. The reason there was something wrong with their aura that first meeting was because there had been some magic that kept Cloa from being her true self. That magic should not have been able to contain the Astridsí, for no magic should be able to contain the Astridsí.

It unsettled her. Bridgette resisted asking about it.

"I'm not breaking down the door," she told them. "I'm not leaving here yet. I can't."

The Bright Star recognized the agonized glimmer in Collum's eyes. She'd seen it once before, the day she ran from Heáhwolcen the prior spring. "I'm in a prime spot to figure out what the hell these two are up to," she explained. "We know that Palnan citizens are being brought here for both the Collective and for the country's armed forces training. What we don't know is where they're doing all this bullshit and how they're keeping it hidden from the rest of the country."

"So, you're going to keep yourself locked in the basement of Baize Sammael's homeplace until you change your mind?" Emi-Joye snapped. "I wouldn't call that entirely helpful. There are ways to do that without putting yourself in danger of revealing our existence."

There was a flicker of that ghost hand again, this time on Bridgette's shoulder, and her vademecum chuckled. The Elfling's nostrils flared.

"You think I'm going to reveal the Triumvirate to the Tinuviels? You seriously think I'd be that stupid and put any of us at that kind of risk?" Bridgette aimed to take a step forward. The ghostly hand gripped her harder. "I'll leave this place when I'm ready to, Emi-Joye. Quit questioning where my loyalties lie. That's not what your power should be used for."

Collum stepped between them, putting one hand against the Fairy and the other uselessly toward Bridgette. "If the two of you don't stop arguing, there won't *be* a Triumvirate to be loyal to. Stop it. No one is questioning anyone's magic or loyalties. We all want you back, Bridgette, but we will *respect*" — he glared at Emi-Joye — "that your role requires you to remain here for some time longer. As for you, Starshine, I'm going to ask that you continue to report to me every night in the way you communicated with me the other day, since you're determined to stay in this room and not risk taking the door down with your magic. Is that an acceptable compromise?"

Invade your dreams every night? Bridgette though to him, though she knew he wouldn't hear. *I'm definitely not saying no to that invitation.*

She nodded and gave him a wink. "Heard, chef."

Collum raised a brow. "Your humanisms, particularly the food-related ones, are always so well-timed."

"Thanks, Bundy. It's a talent," the Elfling grinned. "Someone's gotta keep you old Elves up with the lingo of the humans."

"You're insufferable," he laughed. "I'm going to take these two back now. But I will hear from you every day, and when you are ready to leave, we will assist in your escape. Please be safe, Bridgette."

She wanted to hug him. Wanted for Cloa and Emi-Joye to not be here watching. But this was not a time for wanting, and Bridgette knew that. She nodded, and tried not to let her tears show as she watched the three spectral bodies seize in place before snapping into nothingness.

The firehearth crackled in their absence, and that ghostly hand finally slipped from her shoulder.

~ 96 ~

There was a dizzying jolt as Cloa's spirit zapped back into her body. Her eyes flew open and she promptly rolled to her side as a wave of nausea swirled in her gut.

"Oh, hell," she muttered. She closed her eyes, trying to get used to the feel of having a real form again. On the other side of Collum, Emi-Joye was in a similar state of discomfort. The Fairy looked as green as Cloa's leathers.

"I am *never* voluntarily doing that again," the ambassadora declared. She tried to move and immediately regretted that choice. "I don't think I can sit up."

"Don't try to sit up," Collum told both of the females. "I apologize for not preparing you for the callback. That is my mistake. Breathe and slowly flex your muscles until you feel harmonized with your bodies once again."

Lymerian had stopped playing the sound bowls. She looked to Collum, who, having projected himself plenty of times before in his younger years, knew how to reacclimate himself following astral travel. The Elf was prostrate, breathing slowly and deeply as he gingerly tensed and relaxed muscles in his body. Lymerian watched him flex his toes and calves, thighs and glutes, abdominals and chest, fingers and arms, until finally he slowly moved his neck in a circle before opening his eyes.

"One day, Fyrdwisa, it would be nice if you remembered there are other members of the Triumvirate to consider, not just the Liluthuaé," Emi-Joye grumbled. Trystane coughed from the audience, hiding a laugh.

Collum didn't respond. She had a point, of course. Aurelias had said something similar to him on multiple occasions. But their being correct didn't minimize that his responsibilities to Heáhwolcen were deeply intertwined with the fate and actions of the Bright Star, and that without her, there would be no Triumvirate. This trivial rivalry between her and Emi-Joye frustrated him endlessly. He didn't know how to end it, and truthfully didn't know that he held either that ability or that duty.

"How is the Bright Star?" Aristoces asked from the circle.

The fyrdwisa slowly sat up, doing his best to soften the inevitable lightheadedness and blurred vision that befell him after astral projecting. "She is determined not to leave until the boy is safe and she knows more about the Tinuviels' plans for their armed forces."

"So, she's fine, in other words," Bryten joked.

"Her magic could easily get her out of there," Collum went on. "She chooses not to use it, and to maintain whatever story she told Ydessa. She does not want to risk anyone discovering she has power."

There was an uncomfortable silence in the room.

"We didn't tell her everything that happened," Cloa volunteered. She still had her eyes closed, lying curled into a ball on her pallet. "Just the bare minimum, that I'm the Astridsí and the queen. She doesn't know about Dominus or Kharis."

She may not know there's a way to get out of Palna through the Beorgdún the way Dominus did, the queen thought to Collum. *Why didn't we think of that before we spirited ourselves across the country?*

Collum glanced to her. "The Hringur is without its Seer and likely suspects that he and Bridgette are held in the capital. I will ask Dominus where he was able to exit the Ballamúr. If Bridgette is able to get a message to the Hringur either while she's in Düoria or once she decides to leave, we may be able to use his exit route to our advantage. It is likely that it crosses through weak spots in both walls and can be a way to evacuate innocent citizens when the time comes."

Evacuating Palna, he thought. *Never would I have imagined I'd be part of such an undertaking. Never would I have pictured myself looking forward to the day it came to fruition.*

"What happens now?" Apostine asked. He crouched next to Emi-Joye and helped the Fairy up from her pallet. "Are we supposed to wait until Bridgette decides to show back up again in the middle of the night?"

"She will give me nightly reports," Collum said. "We must wait, yes, but I cannot say what the final straw will be that brings her back."

He didn't like not knowing. It was the only reason he was at Evenshade a few nights later, semi-voluntarily. Collum wanted to distract himself from this ever-present uncertainty that loomed over his days like a storm cloud. The fyrdestre suggested a night out to celebrate his two-hundredth birthday, although "suggested" was a weak synonym. Aurelias all but threatened to start sleeping on his couch overnight if he didn't stop being so gloomy.

Collum begrudgingly acquiesced. He knew she was serious about the couch. He knew she was just as worried about him as he was about Bridgette. The Bright Star stayed true to her word, entering his dreams for a handful of blissful moments every night. She hadn't run into the Tinuviels again yet, nor anyone else except the Palnan guards who brought her food and books. She had apparently complained to one of them that it was ever so boring in her warm new home — a word Collum wanted to choke on — and a guard presented her with a stack of books from the palace library the next morning at breakfast.

Her vademecum's spirit did its best to keep her company. Bridgette mentioned something about a ghostly presence that sometimes empowered her, and other times helped keep her Maylemaegus in check. The fyrdwisa didn't doubt that spirits inhabited the palace like they did elsewhere in Heáhwolcen. He sent up a silent prayer of thanks to whichever deity or long-dead soul stood at the Bright Star's side when he could not.

"Are you going to drink, Chief, or are you just going to brood about some more?" Aurelias asked. She slid onto the barstool next to him. "I invited you to come tonight so that you'd escape your mind for a change."

Collum smiled down at the stout beer that he'd barely touched. "I cannot escape my mind, Aurelias. It has an unfortunate habit of being attached to me at all times. Your efforts do not go unappreciated, however."

"Gee, thanks," she replied. "But you know Bridgette wouldn't like knowing you're sitting at a bar, too busy worrying about her instead of living your life. She's doing what she needs to do and so should you. And I happen to know, Chief, that what *you* need to do is stop thinking about all the worst-case scenarios that could potentially befall Bridgette Conner. That Elfling is as capable of wreaking havoc as I am, probably more so, and the worst thing that could ever happen to her is that someone finds out she's the Liluthuaé and then makes the mistake of trying to off her."

Collum chuckled. "You're right."

"I know." Aurelias ruffled his hair. "Come outside to the bonfire for a bit. The band in here is about to take its intermission."

How she knew that, Collum had no idea, but he lifted a finger and requested the barkeep hand him a fresh beer. The Elf followed his fyrdestre outside but didn't make it to the bright green bonfire of witchlight before he stopped in surprise.

"Well met, Ambassadora; Your Majesty," he said to Emi-Joye and Cloa.

Emi-Joye, in her attempts to take this Triumvirate sisterhood concept to heart, convinced Cloa that she should leave her rooms more often. The queen had been quietly ruling Endorsa for weeks now, and it wouldn't be too long before the Samnung would make shared announcements that Nehemi stepped down from both her throne and position as spreca, opening the positions to Cloa and Aristoces. The ambassadora thought it would be good for Cloa to be seen out and about before that news hit the papers. No one thought it would be beneficial for

Endorsa to have another jarring transition between its leaders.

Being queen filled Cloa with more trepidation than she liked to admit. Though she knew her anxieties weren't warranted — knew that she'd be a perfectly adequate leader, if not an exceptional one! — the thought of messing up or failing in some way made it challenging to fill her very public roles within Heáhwolcen. Truthfully, the only part she felt comfortable playing was that of Astridsí, which wasn't so much a role as it was leaning into a deeper, higher version of herself.

"Well met, Fyrdwisa," Cloa said to Collum. "And Fyrdestre; how are you, Aurelias?"

"Can't complain, Your Majesty," the Elfling replied. "You look … nice."

Cloa groaned. "It's not my fault most of the clothes I own are too formal for everyday wear, or places like this. All Emi-Joye said was to dress for a night out, and I didn't have time to ask for a dress to be altered to better fit this atmosphere!"

She felt woefully overdressed, and far too warm. Her hair was left down, but the formfitting black dress, like all of her dresses, dragged the floor at her feet. The fabric was heavy, more suited to a winter dinner than the beginnings of spring. The boatneck collar flattered her immensely, showing off her sharp collarbones and the growing muscles on her shoulders, thanks to her new hobby of joining Emi-Joye and Apostine at Minthame.

Flattering or not, Cloa thought she looked too much like what Nehemi thought a queen *should* look like. It was, until recently, what Cloa also thought a queen should resemble. But it didn't fit the type of queen she would be, and that juxtaposition irked her.

"What are the two of you doing out this evening?" she asked Aurelias and Collum. Her gaze skimmed over them as she took in the exterior of Evenshade. She'd never seen such a place: it looked absolutely alive.

"It's the fyrdwisa's birthday!" Aurelias chirped. Collum

inclined his head in acknowledgement.

"In that case, may this coming year be one of good memories and bright tidings," Cloa said, her mood instantly improved. "May we join in on the celebration?"

Collum's grumble that it wasn't exactly a celebration was overshadowed by Aurelias' gleeful shout of "Absolutely!", and it was in that guise that the four of them turned to walk back inside.

The music thrummed in Cloa's ears, reverberating and undulating with drums and the screaming whine of stringed instruments. Her heart felt as though it beat alongside the backdrop of the melody. Evenshade glowed from the inside out, the pulsating witchlight shifting from cerulean to citron in tune with the drums. Beams of violent white light — *Triumvirate* glow, she thought to herself — streamed from the building's open windows, criss-crossing one another in geometric formations that reached endlessly out toward the stars in the night sky above them. It was a beacon, and Cloa felt called to it.

"Well, hello Em."

The voice interrupted the foursome's walk, and the queen's heart soared. She knew that voice, though it wasn't directed at her. She wished it was.

"Sheridan!" Emi-Joye cried. "Fancy this, you're not at the tavern. What an occasion! Will you join us? We're celebrating the fyrdwisa's birthday."

The barkeep gave Collum a curious glance. Collum's dour look made him laugh. "The fyrdwisa seems quite pleased you're celebrating him."

"The fyrdwisa would rather eat a sock," Collum muttered, and Sheridan laughed harder.

"I see that," Sheridan said. He turned his attention elsewhere. "It's a pleasure to see you again, Your Majesty. I'm sorry I was unable to supervise you and the ambassadora during your tavern shift the other night."

Cloa felt certain her words squeaked out of her throat. "It is good to see you too, Sheridan."

He extended an arm toward her. "May I walk you inside, Your Majesty?"

To touch him? "Of course, but please — unless we are on Samnung business, don't refer to me by any honorifics. It's just Cloa."

"Well then, 'just Cloa'," Sheridan chuckled. "I have no problem meeting that condition."

She crooked her elbow around his, damning the long sleeves of her dress that prevented her from feeling his skin against hers. Cloa relished the warmth of him, wondering if he felt her heartbeat speed up.

The moment they stepped inside Evenshade, Cloa knew she walked into somewhere incredibly special. It was one thing to be mesmerized outside by the lightshow, but indoors? The entire atmosphere goaded her limbs into moving with graceful fluidity. She felt compelled to twirl, to grind her body against the rhythm that danced into the recesses of her mind. The air smelled of cinnamon; the drinking vessels adorning the bar were made of blue-dyed glass that captured the fluctuating colors of the witchlight spectrum.

"Welcome to Evenshade, Cloa," Sheridan said, speaking louder than usual to be heard over the din. Witches lacked the more sensitive hearing of other magical beings. "What do you think?"

"I think I'm going to have a drink," she said decidedly.

Sheridan didn't loosen his grip around her arm. He didn't know if one so young should partake in some of the enticements made available at Evenshade. He did know, however, that it wasn't his place to enforce whatever arbitrary rules may have been placed on Cloa of Endorsa, and so he walked with her to the bar.

The barkeep this night was a female Fairy with solid matte

black butterfly wings, her skin so dark brown it was almost as black. She'd painted her shoulders and collarbones with a fine dusting of dark purple glitter. Save for the purple X smeared directly across each nipple, she was unclothed from the waist up. Her black hair was braided and twisted into an updo.

Cloa had never seen someone so free. Having spent all but the last few weeks of her life confined to fashion norms established by Nehemi — the dress she now wore being a prime example — the queen relished the idea that such wild abandon of expression and style existed to all of Heáhwolcen's citizens, including herself. As she gazed upon the Fairy barkeep, Cloa praised the deities for that shield being removed from her body, soul, and magic.

"I'll have …" her voice trailed off. She didn't know what she'd have. "Pick something for me, Sheridan?"

The quiet smile he bestowed upon her sent her eyes starry and heart fluttering. She had no idea what drink the Fairy barkeep made, nor did she care. All that mattered in that moment was that he was with her, that he chose to be next to her.

Is this what it feels like to be alive? the queen thought.

Somewhere in the recesses of her mind, she thought she heard her vademecum chuckle.

~ 97 ~

It had been one week since she saw Collum. Though Bridgette now visited him every night, there was something different about him being *here*, in the space she found herself inhabiting. Dream-Collum was a figment of their shared imaginations, in a way. Where she found him in his subconscious was wherever he felt like being, usually in his home office, though two nights ago her report was given while sitting at the Coffee Cauldron.

She found herself struggling after the astral projection visit. The books that the guards brought helped. Part of her was tempted to ask if they could procure a violin — she was so out of practice. But despite the distractions, her desire to see Collum again was nearly enough to send Bridgette careening off the course she set for herself.

Her days in Düoria were patterned by waking up and worrying about Toby; trying unsuccessfully to contact Serrabinx via their covenant bracelet, the fruitlessness of which was something that concerned the Elfling to no end; eating breakfast and reading. Then there was more worrying, perhaps a quiet attempt to use her Maylemaegus on the doors — or maybe it was Craft Wizardry. At this point, Bridgette considered them one and the same. Lunch would be delivered, then more reading. A guard sometimes came in to stoke the fire and bring clean bedsheets or linens for the bathroom.

Bridgette waited impatiently for nights to come. Supper was by far the best meal of the day, and nighttime was usually when the guard who brought books would stop by. He didn't say anything to her usually, just held a hand for the ones she finished, then returned an hour or so later with something new. Her current read was on the history of Fae, which conveniently skipped over the existence of Duatha, the Fyrst Fae, and obviously the Duathanna.

She was halfway through a chapter when a knock sounded at the door. Bridgette glanced up at the window. It was getting dark out, but the evening meal had been delivered and she already turned away the offer for a new book or two. The knock sounded again, and Bridgette went to answer it.

Her blood ran cold at the face that stared back at her.

Eryth Tinuviel looked exactly the same as she dreamed him up months before.

"Hello," she said cautiously. "You're not the usual guard who comes for dinner."

"I'm not a guard," he replied. He pushed past her into the room. "Sit," he directed, and pointed to the immovable chair. "I've got questions for you."

Bridgette sat. "Who are you?"

"I said *I've* got questions. You don't ask them. You answer them."

His eyes were as beady as she recalled. But their color hadn't been a trick of the light in that dreamed-up cave from last fall. They were dark brown, nearly black, a realization that sent Bridgette's sierwan gift into overdrive. *Holy fuck, that's impossible —*

"Why were you on that road?" Eryth asked. He started circling the chair, the wand he shouldn't possess, much less be able to use, twirling deftly between his thick, stubby fingers.

"As I told the queen and the guards, we took a wrong turn on our way to Düoria," the Elfling said. "Who are you?"

He scoffed in mock horror. "First you do not recognize my wife, your rightful queen, and now you claim to not know me as king? Surely the elders of vuoristokylä teach their younglings better than this."

"I apologize, Your Majesty."

"As you should. Where did you take the wrong turn, Elf?"

She frowned and chose to not bother correcting him about her identity. "I'm not sure. I've never been here before. My young friend was my guide."

Eryth sneered at her. "Your young friend proves most challenging to speak to."

Good, Bridgette thought, glad for the indication that Toby had not given into the fear she knew he felt toward the Tinuviels. To her father, she replied, "He certainly has his ways."

"Do you know what is most interesting about the route you took?"

"I cannot say that I do, Your Majesty, but it was lovely despite the rains."

The compliment didn't faze him. "That route should not be known to citizens. It is for the Palnan Royal Guard, my partner, myself, and our closest circle of advisors and friends," Eryth said. "A common boy, Seer or not, would not have knowledge of this road. Not unless someone told him about it."

Shiiiiit. Bridgette hoped her face remained blank. "I would assume someone told him, as Toby is not the type to wander aimlessly when he has a destination. Perhaps he asked, and that was what he learned. I don't pretend to know who he talks to or gets information from."

"My queen and I find it most telling that our new friend was not in school."

"Should he be? I was under the impression he was schooled at home, with his mother teaching him lessons and skills," the Elfling answered. That comment confused her. Why would it matter where Toby went to school?

"It seems we have much to discuss with our citizens of the vuoristokylä," Eryth said scathingly. "They do not seem to read that which our archivists send. All Palnan younglings attend school, where they learn all that makes them productive citizens contributing to the betterment and progress of our great nation."

Oh, you've got to be joking. That's straight out of the Third Reich playbook, Bridgette realized. She knew now why Toby was expected to be in school. Her eye shift, evident since they'd broken from the glamour that day with Serrabinx, was a sure sign that Eryth Tinuviel would figure out something was different about her, too.

"Your eyes," he said immediately.

Her nostrils flared. "What about them?"

"They did …" he peered at her, so close that she scented the too-saccharine flavor of his breath. "They changed. I watched them. Do that again."

"Do *what* again?" She couldn't shift them on command if she wanted to.

Eryth leaned closer still. "Make them change again, Elf."

"It's *Elfling*, actually, and I don't know what you're talking about. I can't make my eyes change except to blink or close."

"Your attitude is abhorrent. No one behaves so in front of their king."

Good thing you're not my king, Bridgette thought. She glared at him, not saying a word.

"Change them," Eryth demanded again. "Alter your eyes, you damned bitch."

"How?"

He slammed his hands down so hard onto her shoulders that Bridgette gasped in shock. "Change your eyes!" Eryth shouted. "I observed this of my own accord! You will not lie to me!"

"I'm not lying, Your Majesty." She fought to stay calm, though her heart pounded and her Maylemaegus churned at the accusation. "I do not know how to change my eyes. The sun is setting; perhaps they look different in the light to you?"

He didn't take his eyes from her face, as if waiting to see her sierwan gift manifest. Bridgette hoped he wouldn't know it was a sierwan trait, even if they did shift again in front of him. He may not think it was anything other than a party trick; some curious magic unfamiliar to him. Collum hadn't even recognized it at first.

"Do you think you'll be in trouble for your magic?" Eryth sneered. Spittle flew from his angry mouth. "Do you think the

Samnung is in charge here; that they will have you throttled, tarred, and feathered for daring to let the dark wizardry inside you fly free?"

Bridgette willed her eyes not to shift, but she knew it was useless.

"HA!" the man shouted, victorious. "You lying bitch. To tell me that you cannot change your eyes and then to do so — do it again!"

Like Hell I will, she thought. Her eyes had shifted because suddenly something made a scary amount of sense: the activated Ballamúr negated the power of the Samnung wall. Without Ulerion, wherever he might be, dead or alive, there was no one left in Palna to enforce the rules against Craft Wizardry. It was only by citizens' own belief of the power the outer wall held that they kept their magic hidden.

The Tinuviels had no desire to hide Palnan magic. Now that there were no repercussions, not since the Nunta Alchimica, they wanted to use it. And if the Bright Star wasn't careful, they'd try to find a way to use hers, too.

"Do it again!" Eryth yelled. He began shaking her. "Show me your magic, Elf!"

"I don't have magic!" she screamed as her Maylemaegus writhed, itching to overtake her. "No one has had magic here since the Ingefeoht!"

Her head whipped back as Eryth hit her square across her left eye. Bridgette screamed again, this time with pain and shock. She tried to move a hand to her face, only to find her arms were bound to her sides.

No, no, no, NO! she thought. Her head felt like it might burst, so intense was the agony of this injury. She struggled against the invisible bonds, desperate to get out, to use the magic she just swore to Eryth she didn't have.

Bridgette gasped as his hands went around her neck. The pain by her eye all but disappeared as she felt the blood flow taper off. Keeping her eyes open became a revolting chore. She couldn't *breathe*. Eryth's grip tightened, and her hands splayed open, clawing in place by her sides. Her feet kicked uselessly as she fought to stay conscious.

"Show me your magic," he yelled. "How dare you try to deceive your king!"

Her vision swam as she choked. *Fuck you, asshole!* she longed to scream. She couldn't have done anything magical restrained like this anyway, even if she had normal Elven abilities. Her only thought was getting out from his too-tight clutch.

"SHOW ME!" he bellowed as he pushed himself onto her, his weight straddling her on the chair where she kicked and screamed in place, unable to see or move or hardly *think*. There were tears streaming down her cheeks, and they were angry tears, furious bolts of liquid lightning she wanted to electrify and burn him with. Eryth was screaming at her with such voracity that Bridgette gave up listening. This was worse, so horribly, sickeningly worse than her dream about him, because in that dream there had been *help* —

As if on cue, she felt a pair of ghostly hands scramble against her, eking their way under the grip Eryth held against her throat, seeking to lessen it; to make some kind of barrier to stop him from hurting her any further. Bridgette wanted to kiss the ghost. Her head throbbed again, forcing her back to consciousness where Eryth was still screaming.

"CITIZENS OBEY THEIR KING!" He started to shake her by the neck, his body and binding spell holding her to the chair. The ghost hands wrenched themselves between his fingers and her neck and she heaved a breath. He roared wordlessly, furious.

But this wasn't her magic. She didn't know to which spirit it belonged. All Bridgette knew was that it gave her a chance to get air into her lungs again. It was enough. She sunk into herself without a second thought and tore through Eryth's magic with her own.

"YOU ARE NO KING OF MINE!" she screamed, and jabbed her fist forward into Eryth Tinuviel's nose before he could process what happened. The appendage shattered with a satisfying crunch, and he went demonic.

Bridgette had about half a second to guard herself before Eryth went for her injured eye a second time. Her elbow went up and blocked his punch, and she slipped her head to the side on instinct, grateful for whatever combination of ancient power and Herewosa Donnachaidh's training that saved her in that moment.

Eryth didn't like being foiled, and he didn't like playing clean. He spat in Bridgette's face. She yelled in disgust, which gave him the edge he needed to lift himself off of her and thrust his other fist in her gut. Bridgette pitched forward on reflex and her head slammed into his waiting raised knee. A choked scream left her lips and she was no longer sure if it was her blood, her tears, or Eryth's saliva that slid down her face and neck.

His hands were back at her, one shoved under her jaw and the other at the base of her hair, forcing her head back as he leered over her. "Citizens obey their king, bitch," the witch rasped. He jerked her head to the side, eyes flaring with delight at her hiss of pain. "You'll show me your magic, or I'll make sure that boy —"

Whatever Eryth wanted to threaten Toby with didn't matter. She didn't let him finish the sentence.

OFF! she commanded, and the air obeyed.

The so-called king of Palna was hurled against the wall without warning. He hit it with a sickening crack, and as his body fell to the floor, Bridgette swayed with him, unable to stand the pain any longer.

~ 98 ~

Bridgette came to before Eryth did.

She didn't know why she was glad he was alive. She wished he wasn't. It was the ghost hands and a constant, terrified whispering of her vademecum in her mind that brought her back to full consciousness from the heap she'd become on the floor. Her skull throbbed. Her eye ached, though it thankfully did not appear to be swollen shut. Her stomach roiled from the gut punch. It hurt to try to hold her head straight.

Help, she begged the Universe. She didn't think she could talk. *Please!*

✦ *He cannot remain like that,* her vademecum said quickly. *He must be restrained.*

How? Bridgette thought to it. *I don't think I can move.*

✦ *The sheets, Liluthuaé!*

The Bright Star's legs and arms weren't sore like the rest of her, but *oh,* how the movement affected her! Bridgette crawled, agonizingly slowly, toward the bed. She could bind and gag the witch. The ghost hands, both of them again, touched her upper back. *We'll help,* they seemed to say.

Or maybe they did say. Her mind swam too much to process what was real and what she might be making up.

She yanked the pillowcase and loose top-sheet off, shouting at the sharp pain in her torso at the movement. A glance back assured her that Eryth remained unconscious.

I probably gave the fucker a concussion, she realized with a flash of glee. *Good.*

It took a significant amount of maneuvering and gasps of misery in order to work the sheet and pillowcase into a sufficient set of ties. Though Bridgette initially was glad she didn't bring her dagger into Düoria, given that it'd probably have been confiscated by the guards on the road, she wished she had it now to help rip the fabric into long strips. Instead, she twisted the flat sheet into a length of rope. The ghost hands helped by touching her shoulders and arms to guide where and how she should thread the makeshift rope between Eryth's heavy, dead-weight limbs so that he wouldn't be able to get out of them.

The binding took an age. Bridgette was exhausted but pleased at the sight of Eryth Tinuviel trussed up like an American Thanksgiving turkey.

✦ *You are sending the message?* Her vademecum's voice was laced with urgency.

Bridgette hadn't been given a choice — revealing her Maylemaegus to Eryth or getting beaten to a pulp because she didn't obey him were equally bad options — but she just put herself into a very dangerous situation. At some point, someone would expect Eryth elsewhere in the palace. She couldn't keep him tied up here forever, especially not if and when he woke up. Guards would come to bring her meals and books; servants to change her linens again.

One of them would see him in the corner.

She had to get out of this place before they did.

I'm going to Collum now, Bridgette thought to her vademecum. *I need you to pull me back here if Eryth wakes up or if someone comes to the door.*

✦ *Liluthuaé, your power will hold doors.*

Her vademecum was right. Bridgette looked at the door and slipped into her second skin of Maylemaegus as easily as if she would a sweater. *Hold!* she commanded the air. *Hold as if our lives depend on it.*

The air in the room became taut. It thinned, pushing as much pressure against the door as possible, making it difficult to breathe on the other end of the space. Bridgette glanced to where Eryth's chest began to rasp a little harder for breath in his passed-out state.

"You better not die, asshole," she choked out to him. "I'm not ready to kill you just yet."

Tonight, there wasn't time to quietly drift into Universal subconscious and Collum's dreams. She wrenched her mind into focus of the conscious sort and raced, faster than ever before, through all the minds and sentience of Heáhwolcen, searching for his. Only when she felt that unmistakable click of connection did she allow herself to sink slowly into his dream, heaving a sigh of relief to be in Collum's presence.

He must have been waiting for her report, for dream-Collum was seated at his kitchen table. It appeared to be morning in his subconscious, as he was doing his customary skim-through of the newspaper, drinking a mug of coffee.

"Hey, Houston, we've got a problem," Bridgette said in greeting. Her voice sounded as hoarse as it would in real life. "I just fucked up, and I'm gonna need to get out of here like a bat out of Hell."

"Hello to you too, Starshine," he said, not having glanced up yet from the newspaper. "What do you mean?"

"I mean I fought Eryth Tinuviel. And won."

Collum knocked the mug of coffee all over the paper. He didn't bother to clean it up. "You what?!"

The fyrdwisa took one look at her blackened eye, the bruised handprint around her throat, and swore. His blue eyes flashed with rage. "What in the seven fucking hells happened? How did he do this?"

"He showed up to question me and bound me to the chair. Collum … with everything that happened on the way to Düoria, there's kind of a big thing I forgot to mention that happened right before. It didn't seem to really matter as much as Toby and I getting kidnapped, until now," Bridgette said. The words physically hurt. "I had a run-in with Serrabinx after she let it slip that she was the wítega that told Mohreen her Elfling fetus would be the Liluthuaé —"

Collum thought he might pass out, even if it was a dream. "Serrabinx *what*?"

"Yes, listen, I know; just shut up for a second. My stupid Maylemaegus broke through the eye glamour when she told me that. Ever since, my eyes have been sierwan shifting in front of anyone who notices, and tonight, Eryth noticed," the Elfling went on. "He demanded I show him my magic, but like, I can't; I can't control when my eyes shift into opals! He went crazy, bound me to a chair and started attacking me and choking me. It was rough, Collum, but I'm fine, I swear. I got a good punch in and broke his nose, and then I Maylemaegus-ed him with air so hard against the wall I think he has a concussion. He's still knocked out. I got him tied up thanks to my new guardian ghost and my vademecum."

The fyrdwisa never before — including the day of King Hermann and Queen Lalora's carriage accident-and-possible-murder — had to process so much crucial information in such a little amount of time. "But he's alive?"

"Yes. I didn't kill him. I'm not *that* dumb."

"I don't mean to insult your intelligence, Starshine, but I think you underestimate your own power. By yourselves, the Liluthuaé, Boireannach, and Astridsí are dangerous. Together, the Triumvirate is lethal. I want you to remember that; to be glad for it, but to use those great and dangerous powers with as much tact and consideration as you can."

She wanted to cry. How could she ache so much while being in someone's dream?

"Why did you come here instead of blasting that door open and leaving Palna?" Collum asked. "Now would have been the time!"

"Because I don't know who's waiting on Eryth to come back! I don't know how to get out of there, especially not if I have to fight off a slew of guards, and maybe you haven't noticed, but I'm not exactly in prime condition to run off!" Bridgette motioned to her face and neck. "He punched me so hard in the stomach too that if I was human, he'd have ruptured something.

I can't run around or even sneak around like this."

Collum winced. "I'm sorry, Bridgette. What do you want us to do?"

"I want you to do the deity-damned craziest horseshit thing I will probably ever ask you to do, Bundy," she said. She squeezed her eyes shut, which hurt as much as it helped. "I think the Ballamúr will let Mohreen into Palna. She doesn't have the blood of Eryth Tinuviel, but we share blood. I think if you use her the way the Samnung did me as a means to get in, you can get through."

"To what end, Starshine? What will bringing Mohreen into Palna do?"

Bridgette took a long gulp of air. "In the first place, she's how you, Emi-Joye, and Cloa will be able to get across the Ballamúr. Secondly, there's something I'd like to chat with her about. And third, I think it's time the Triumvirate really gave this thing a go."

"You realize what you're saying, don't you?" Collum's blood chilled. "You realize that this could trigger everything we've been talking about?"

She nodded, somber. "It could. But not yet. My number's probably up for attacking the king of Palna, but they still don't know who and what I am."

"You're not making sense, Bridgette."

"Do you or do you not know where Mohreen Conner is?" she hissed at him. Her eyes went violet, the deep purple clashing against her bruises.

The Elf didn't really want to answer. "I have my suspicions."

"Good," Bridgette said. Her irises softened back into lilac. "I don't know how long I can keep Eryth tied up like a turkey. You have to hurry."

"What aren't you telling me?" Collum knew her well enough to see she was holding something back. "Why do you want to do this?"

"I don't want to," she whispered. "I have to."

The fyrdwisa was still reaching for her when he woke up. He stared around his darkened bedroom. It was the middle of the night, and the vision of Bridgette so battered made him want to break Eryth Tinuviel's neck. Collum could not wait to have that chance. His Starshine, one eye surrounded by a swelling socket discolored to terrifying shades of oxblood and fuchsia, and that *handprint* around her throat! It was a discolored, perfect stamp of the Palnan king's appendage. The Elf yelled into the void of the night, his voice so loud his cup of water vibrated right off the nightstand and shattered against the wooden floor.

Collum didn't care. They wouldn't get away with this, the Tinuviels. He would make sure of it.

Bridgette was right. He had been hunting for Mohreen Conner for the better part of a year now, ever since Bridgette ran from that final Samnung meeting of her first visit. He latched onto enough of the female Elf's scent and energy while they were in the chamber together that he thought — even though their covenant was supposedly shattered — there could be a way to track her through the once-active channel.

The fyrdwisa had been right. The only problem was that Mohreen wasn't an idiot, and at some point, found out she was being tracked. But in the middle of the night, Collum might have the upper hand. Especially if he had help.

He slipped fingers underneath first his covenant bracelet with Trystane, then the one with Cloa. *Eryth Tinuviel attacked Bridgette. We need to move quickly. My home. Bring Emi-Joye and your vademecums.*

And then, Collum waited.

~ 99 ~

I have to drag him to the corner, Bridgette realized. If Eryth's body remained where it was, any servant or guard who cracked open the door would see him first thing. But if she pulled him — a thought that made her pained body wail with exhaustion — off to the far corner, the one that could not be seen from the entrance unless the door was fully open, she could keep uninvited guests at bay. They'd see she was injured, perhaps, or she could lie on the bed and say she was ill; to please just leave her food and not enter in case it was contagious.

She wasn't even sure illnesses worked the same way with magickind. It was a chance she'd have to take.

The ghost hands were back, this time smoothing down the tangled mess of hair on either side of Bridgette's head. It was a gesture Collum did sometimes, and one that Joel Simmons used to do when she was upset.

"Don't let anybody tell you that you're not powerful, babygirl." Her foster father's words came to her clear as day. The tears, hot droplets of anger and sadness, for the life she thought she'd get to live and the future she was determined to create, streamed down her angry, aching cheeks.

"Listen, buddy," Bridgette said to the ghost hands, "I don't know who you are and frankly I don't give two shits. But I'm going to pull this fucker into the corner, and you're going to push. Got it?"

There was a tap on her shoulder. She took that as a yes.

Together, the Bright Star and her unknown guardian managed to get Eryth's body into its hiding spot. She eased the air's hold on the door, just a little bit, if only to make breathing less of a hassle. If anyone came asking for Eryth, she'd tell them he left ages ago, not long after dark. The supper tray was still where she left it, next to her face-down book. It was still the same night, though it felt like a lifetime had passed since the king of

Palna knocked at her door.

Bridgette knew her plan would work. She knew Collum, Cloa, and Emi-Joye would be able to enter Palna with Mohreen's help. "Help" might be a bit of a strong word; Bridgette didn't think her mother would voluntarily assist anybody who wasn't herself. But with Mohreen's coerced aid, they would make it here. They knew where to come once they reached the capital, having astrally projected themselves into her little room. And once they did …

Bridgette smiled up at the ceiling. *That's when the fun begins,* she thought.

Cloa — who first had to be caught up to speed with the shortened version of Bridgette's life story — wanted nothing more than to go back to bed. She'd been in the middle of a delicious dream about Sheridan, reliving the recent night at Evenshade when he invited her to dance and figuratively swept her off her feet. Instead, here she was in Collum's kitchen, awoken yet again at an hour so early that she wondered why she bothered to sleep at night at all.

"What do you want us to do?" she asked.

"We're going to find Mohreen Conner, and then we're going to Düoria," Collum replied. "We've got to get Bridgette out. She's too injured to leave on her own, but if they — when they! — find out she's got an unconscious, likely concussed king of Palna trussed up in her bedchamber, it will be far, far worse. We need to act quickly."

"How quickly is quickly?" Emi-Joye wanted to know. She glanced at Trystane, whose face was white with worry. The ard rialóir didn't want her going into Palna now any more than she wanted him to go when the Samnung visited.

"I don't want Bridgette to have to be in the same room as Eryth Tinuviel for any longer than a day," Collum said frankly. "Put your leathers on, your weapons, and the longest hooded cloak you own. I want you all back here before daybreak. This is not a request."

It felt odd to say such a thing to the queen of Endorsa, but she was not the typical sort of queen he'd dealt with before. In the Samnung, she had sway over him. But outside of that? Cloa and Collum were equals. They might be the Triumvirate, these three females of soil, sky, and sea, but there was always a fourth element, another direction to complete the quadrant. There had to be a spark. Collum Andoralain had been their fire, burning longer and with more devotion than any of them could have known.

His ultimatum was met with solemn nods. The time, finally, had come. It was the era of the Liluthuaé, the long-foretold culmination of her legend, but the Bright Star would never be asked to shine alone.

They carried helms this time, slung over their shoulders and hidden underneath their cloaks, along with a satchel that held first-aid supplies and Bridgette's feoht training clothes. She didn't have true wígend gear yet. But she would, soon enough.

Collum and Trystane evanesced the females to a dense wooded area in Lisweald, the last place the fyrdwisa found evidence of Mohreen. Bridgette, though she didn't know it, came close to discovering what he was up to the day she learned about the Ballamúr and barreled into the woods, riding Eloise. He'd been in that very forest, perched in a tree, listening to the minds of residents as they walked trails and paths. Mohreen kept a house here, tucked high in the canopy, and largely stayed under the radar. No one in this village knew her real name, but they knew her essence.

What he'd been quietly tracking for months wasn't even Mohreen at first. He'd been keeping an eye out for tulips.

There had been a bouquet of them on the credenza when Collum stepped into the foyer after Bridgette ran out of the Samnung chamber last March. He didn't think anything of it at first, but there were never flowers there. Weeks later, he offhandedly mentioned their appearance to Nehemi, who'd frowned and told him they were a gift from Mohreen.

But tulips, outside of a select few varieties at Mimea Botanicci, didn't grow in Heáhwolcen. Collum decided there was a way to find his former contact: learn where she got the flowers from and as a result, find out where she'd been hiding all these years. It took ages, sneakily inquiring about the tulips with various scientists and botanists, floral artisans, and University magisters. Eventually, Collum was able to trace a quiet Elf in Lisweald who kept to herself but was known to cultivate and sell the rare blooms.

He found the house that day Bridgette found him in the woods. But it had been abandoned — or at least shuttered temporarily — and he thought hope might be lost. Until, that is, the Bright Star told him Palna was "known for its tulips". Collum realized then with a sinking heart that Mohreen must be the center of that horticultural market. Collum didn't know how it was possible, but he felt certain it was. He was also fairly certain that when she wasn't hiding in Lisweald, Mohreen was going in and out of Maluridae Wood. It was the only place she would be able to truly hide, for it sealed so many secrets inside.

"Where are we going?" Emi-Joye whispered to him.

"Mohreen Conner's Elven home," he murmured back. "I found it months ago but it was boarded up, as though she temporarily resided elsewhere. I've been keeping an eye on it since and got word not long ago that its occupant might be back. I cannot say for certain that the occupant is Mohreen, but the probability is high."

His "gotten word" was that a florist in Lisweald promised to let him know when tulips were again available. Pinks and yellows were, allegedly, coming into season.

"What do we do if she says no?" Cloa asked.

"She won't say no." Collum didn't plan to give her the

option.

The sun was peeking through the treetops as they neared their destination. Collum held a finger to his lips, then pointed straight up and over. The treehouse was barely visible from the ground, camouflaged with moss for an added layer of protection. At first, it looked like there wasn't a way to reach it without climbing the trees themselves, but Collum motioned for them to shift their perspective. Shallow grooves were carved neatly into the tree base, a natural ladder that, if the light hit it right, was invisible to even Elven and Fae eyes.

He mouthed out a word: *evanesce.* A nod to Trystane, and the four disappeared and reappeared a moment later, the navy and green whirls not having vanished at the trunk before they were at the front door. Collum smelled peat. There was a fire burning inside. Someone was home.

He and Trystane whispered warding spells on the door, windows, and the entirety of the porch that surrounded the cylindrical house that erupted around the tree. Mohreen, or whoever might be there, would be unable to evanesce directly from the residence. The fyrdwisa put on his helm and the others followed suit. Collum's and Trystane's nearly matched, the only difference being the colors and formation of the plume of spikes that rose from the metal. Trystane's were gold and arranged as if he wore a crown. Collum's, alternating blue and gold, curved down his head like a dragon's spine. Emi-Joye's silver helmet gleamed nearly gold in the morning sun, and Cloa's resembled the ard rialóir's, bronze all over with a crown of spikes.

The queen put a hand on the hilt of her shortsword. Emi-Joye's knives were already out of their sheaths, ready. Their vademecums glowed from their thigh holsters, and the matching purplish one trilled from within the bag of clothing for Bridgette.

Collum took one more breath. He straightened his shoulders, and then he reared back and kicked the door in.

~ 100 ~

It was as if she'd been waiting for them.

Mohreen Conner sat calmly in front of the peat fire, hands in her lap, a smirk on her face. "Tráthnóna mistéireach, Ceannairí. You're going to pay to have that door replaced, I'm sure."

Collum wanted to smash in her teeth.

"You're being summoned for a task on the order of the Samnung," Trystane said. "But I'm going to suppose through your own means that you gleaned enough information to suspect something of the sort."

She shrugged, the movement exaggerated by oversized shoulder epaulets on the unnecessarily formal dress she wore. It was velvet, a stunning dark blue-gray. Collum wondered if she owned clothing in any other fabric. He'd only ever seen her in velvet and velveteen, even when she was supposedly spying for them in Palna.

"I assume you're here because of my daughter," Mohreen said lightly. "What has the Liluthuaé gotten herself into this time?"

"She got into a fight with her father," Collum said dryly. He was surprised to see a flare of actual emotion dart across Mohreen's face. "Bridgette has been in Palna for several weeks now. She's badly injured, and we need to get her out before anyone finds out what she's done."

"Did she kill him?" The female's words were a sharp slice.

"No," Emi-Joye answered. "And he doesn't know that she is either the Liluthuaé or his daughter. We'd like to keep it that way."

Mohreen looked conflicted. "How is it that I am supposed to be part of this?"

"You've been part of this from the start, Mohreen," Collum reminded her. "We need your blood to get across the wall, and your daughter wants to have a word with you. Therefore, you will be coming with us. Now."

"Now? Surely, Fyrdwisa, it would be foolish to —"

"*Now*, Mohreen." Collum's order was finite. "Put on your cloak. I am done wasting time."

He cocked his head in a motion to Emi-Joye, who twirled her knives threateningly as she edged toward the female. "You heard the fyrdwisa," the ambassadora said. "Get up and put on a cloak. You could at least pretend to care that your daughter's life might be in danger."

Mohreen stood, but she huffed at the Fairy. "My daughter is the Liluthuaé. Her life is the last one we need to be worried about. Haven't you heard? I carried and bore her to bring forth the one who will save us all!"

Is she always like this? Emi-Joye thought to Collum.

He couldn't answer quietly, not with his eyes and mouth hidden behind his helm. "I'm delighted to see that you have not changed, Mohreen. I do regret to inform you that there's more to the story than simply the Bright Star, but we do need her at her healthiest in order to proceed with fulfilling her destiny. Get a move on."

Mohreen glowered at him from under the hood of the cloak she pulled over her head. "What does my daughter want to speak to me about?"

"That is not for me to say," the fyrdwisa answered. "But as we have you with us now, I would be most interested to learn how you've managed to procure Palnan tulips all of these years without anyone noticing or questioning you about them."

Mohreen didn't say anything. She stood still as Trystane warded her from being able to evanesce of her own accord, though her face soured once she realized what he was doing.

"We're crossing through Bondrie as near to Düoria as we can," Collum said. "You'll get us across the wall, and you're in charge of getting us to the castle unseen. Is that understood?"

He took the angry flare of nostrils and sucked-in cheeks as a begrudging *yes*. "Good. Let us go."

Corria was waiting for them inside the Samnung wall. The master swordswoman, whom Trystane contacted before they left Collum's apartment in their armor, looked even more forboding than usual with her helm on. The chrome of Bondrie gleamed so pristinely that it became almost a mirror, a way to ensure those who met Bondrians on a battlefield would be able to watch their own grisly ends.

"Bring her back, Fyrdwisa," was all Corria said before she jerked Mohreen's left hand out in front of them and unceremoniously slashed across the palm with a knife.

The Elf cried out in surprise as blood welled.

Trystane removed one of his leather gloves. "Take off your helms so that I may put this on you," he told the remaining trio.

They did as instructed. Mohreen's blood tingled against their skin as the ard rialóir brushed a line of it behind each of their ears, despite the giver's protestations. He hesitated almost a moment too long giving Emi-Joye that swath of protection, and her eyes looked pleadingly into his. She wanted to tell him so very many things, but there was no time. The Fairy felt a small hand curl around hers. Cloa's eyes flashed starry for a heartbeat as she looked at the ambassadora. The queen squeezed her sister's fingers in understanding.

Passion, Emi-Joye laughed to herself. *I suppose that cat is out of the bag.*

Trystane put a spell on the gash in Mohreen's hand to protect and heal the skin. He stepped next to Corria, and they all exchanged a glance before sliding their helms back over their shoulders.

"Hoods up," Collum said. He crooked his arm through one of Mohreen's. "Try and run, Conner, and Hecate help me, I will break you."

⚡ ✦ ☠   *We'll help*, the three vademecums said in eerie

unison. The Elf, for the first time, looked scared as the voices drifted across her consciousness.

Collum gave one final look to Trystane and Corria. "Do not wait for us."

He linked arms with Emi-Joye, who pulled Cloa close to her side, and the four stepped through the Ballamúr.

The sensation of crossing, though both Emi-Joye and Collum were somewhat prepared for it thanks to Bridgette's detailed accounts, was disconcerting. The fyrdwisa felt as though he flipped upside down and spun in a dizzying circle before being able to reorient himself. Cloa retched to one side, and it made Emi-Joye shiver. Only Mohreen seemed unaffected.

"Do you know how to get to Düoria from here?" Collum asked.

Mohreen pointed in front of them. "You can see it. That massive building is the residential palace. It shouldn't be more than a couple of hours' walk."

"Are we walking, or are we evanescing?" Emi-Joye asked quietly. "The more we walk, the more likely it is someone's going to see us. These hoods keep us well-hidden, but they do make us look suspicious."

She had a point.

"We'll walk for a few miles, get a lay of the land. We're going to need to come back once we have Bridgette —" Collum grinned at the Fairy with sudden realization. "Boireannach, what say you about adding some rain to our cover?"

Her eyes widened. "I don't know how to command it like Bridgette does; she just thinks, and it happens!"

The fyrdwisa started laughing. "Emi-Joye Vetur, I have watched you summon snowflakes from midair with mine own eyes. You have *always* had this power with water, to make it bend to your will. If you stop fighting your destiny, I believe you'll see that it's quite easy to be at one with your Maylemaegus."

Emi-Joye's vademecum glowed and warmed against her leg

in encouragement. She gave a hesitant glance at the fyrdwisa, then extended a hand as if she was to mold one of her snowflakes. She felt the daintiness of mist as if she was a magnet for it.

Perhaps I am, she thought. *Pour.*

The bottom dropped out on command, dousing the entirety of the brushy woods they hid in all the way to the distant tulip fields in a downpour. Lightning crackled somewhere, followed shortly by a roll of thunder.

"You're a madwoman!" Cloa shrieked with childlike elation. "You just made it storm out of nowhere!"

"Yes, well, I suppose I overdid that *a bit*," Emi-Joye said. She bit her lip, then started laughing at the slack-jawed face of Mohreen. Water dripped from their hoods; they were already soaked in less than a minute. The female Elf looked horribly confused at both the storm and the Fairy who called it into existence.

Collum did his best to put up a bit of a shield against the rain as they continued walking, but it did little to help. Their boots squelched in the thick mud and the hems of their cloaks heavied as they dragged through the muck. Emi-Joye experimented briefly with this new understanding of her magic, and finally got the rain to lighten up in their immediate vicinity so that at least the fyrdwisa's shield wasn't being constantly pelted.

"How did you know we were coming?" Collum finally asked Mohreen. The question had been bothering him since they found her.

She stared straight ahead. "I didn't. I was waiting for someone else when my door was so rudely kicked in."

"Who were you waiting for?"

"A friend."

Collum chuckled. "I wasn't aware that you had friends, Mohreen. Tell me about the tulips." He knew she would continue to hedge, for whatever ill-gotten reasons she concocted, but he wanted to try.

"I've been growing them for years. I saved the seeds from the gardens in Düoria. I thought it a shame that such lovely flowers were so poorly received elsewhere in Heáhwolcen, simply for having Palnan origin," Mohreen replied.

There was truth in that answer. Somewhere.

A flicker of warmth flashed across his wrist, and Collum's attention flipped from one Conner female to the other. "Bridgette knows we're here," he said, smiling with relief. "Let us step off the path for a moment so that I may attempt to have a conversation."

It was the sweetest sense of peace when the ísenwaer worked for them this time.

Holy shit, Bundy, that was a fast turnaround!

He smiled, keeping fingers around his covenant bracelet to maintain the illusion that they could only communicate via that channel. *I could not stomach the idea of you being in the same room with the man who attacked you so viciously. How are you, Starshine?*

Someone tried to come in to give me breakfast. I told them to leave me alone and that I was sick, and to just put the food tray right inside.

Has anyone inquired about Eryth? Collum thought to her.

There was a beat of silence in their communication. *No. Not yet. But he's stirring. I may have to go bash him over the head. Maybe Maylemaegus can break the spell on this stupid chair, and I can WWE him with it or something.*

What? What do you mean, 'WWE'?

Human thing, Bridgette thought back. *People like to watch this sport called wrestling and there's usually someone getting hit over the head with a chair.*

Collum's face must have looked horrified, because Cloa interrupted the silent conversation. "Is she okay?" the queen asked.

"She's making it," he replied. "Keeping the guards at bay by pretending to be ill. But Eryth may be starting to wake."

We should evanesce now, Emi-Joye thought to him.

Collum didn't disagree. He glanced up to the sky. They hadn't been in Palna long at all, judging by the sun's position, though the anxiety of the sleepless night, morning, and now having to stay in the same square footage as Mohreen Conner made it feel as though they'd been walking for a week. The fyrdwisa sent one more message to Bridgette.

Unward that door, Starshine. We're going to evanesce in before anything else goes awry or someone spots us. There's no need for the Palnan Royal Guard to have all of us in locked rooms.

You got it, dude, Bridgette thought back.

<h1 style="text-align:center">~ 101 ~</h1>

Bridgette was on pins and needles until the blast of navy whirls erupted in front of her. She didn't realize she'd been holding her breath until she let it out in one shaky gasp that tore from her angry, swollen throat.

"Collum!" was all she managed to say as she stumbled from the bed, her stomach throbbing repulsively, and staggered toward him.

He caught her and neither cared that his rain-soaked cloak got her just as wet as he was. "Let me look at you."

She stepped back and almost toppled over. Cloa was at her side in an instant, leaving Emi-Joye to guard Mohreen, who glanced at the still-unconscious tied bundle in the corner that was Eryth Tinuviel. Bridgette looked a wreck. The dream version of her from a few hours before must have been filtered through Collum's mind's eye, or some deep subconscious desire for him not to see her like that, for the real-life Elfling that now faced him had been through the ringer. Her face was black and blue from Eryth's assault, and the handprint on her throat …

The fyrdwisa came embarrassingly close to losing it. "Show me the torso wound," he said gently, but there was no hiding the deep hatred in his voice.

Bridgette lifted her shirt to reveal a ghastly bruise, worse than the one around her eye, and colored nearly the same as the handprint. "It's … not great," she rasped out.

"You don't say," Cloa muttered.

Mohreen stood stoically next to the Fairy. She said nothing, just took in her daughter as the Elfling displayed her injuries for them all to see.

"Hi, Mom," Bridgette said. "Glad you could make it."

"Do you want to sit down?" Collum asked gently. "I brought what little healing supplies I had, some arnica salve for the bruising, elixirs for muscle relaxation and rejuvenation, and your feoht leathers to change into."

Bridgette cocked her head toward the bed and instantly regretted moving her neck. "There. Not the chair." The Liluthuaé didn't want to be anywhere near that piece of furniture unless she was using it to beat Eryth.

Cloa and Collum walked her to the bed, where the fyrdwisa knelt to begin seeing to her wounds. "Go to Eryth, please," he told the queen. "Make sure he's going to stay unconscious."

The Astridsí walked off wordlessly, leaving the fyrdwisa and Bright Star together. Bridgette reached for him. "I'm glad my theory was right," she said. The words came out as half-whispers.

"Don't try to talk, not until after you've taken these elixirs," Collum murmured. "Drink the one with the blue label first; that's the muscle relaxer. It should ease the pain in your throat and stomach."

Bridgette chugged it. *This tastes like ass, Bundy,* she thought to him as she forced herself to swallow it. *Y'all have got to come up with better recipes for this stuff, eugh. Can I get a palate cleanser?*

He grinned. "I'm glad to see that your father's attack didn't injure your sense of humor."

He's not my father, the Liluthuaé replied, mind-to-mind.

Collum paused for a moment. He still hadn't told her about the adoption papers that Lucilla nearly signed for her. Now was not the time, though he wasn't sure there would be a right time for that revelation. "No, I suppose he isn't," was all the fyrdwisa said in response. He pulled her vademecum from the satchel. "Here. We thought you ought to have this now."

How are we getting out? Bridgette thought to him. She caressed the pages of her vademecum, which began to glow softly in her grasp.

"I suppose we'll evanesce the same way as we did in, and then cross the Ballamúr again once we walk close enough."

She winced at the word "walk". *I need to talk to Mohreen here before we go. There are some things I need her to clear up for me. For us.*

What aren't you telling me, Starshine? Collum asked her again, reverting to his mind-voice. *You have never voluntarily asked to see or speak to her. Why now? What changed?*

She put her hand under his jaw and lifted his gaze to hers. *I changed.*

He furrowed his brow, the meaning not making sense. "Are you alright? You don't usually keep things from me, not like this."

Bridgette sighed. She gave Collum a soft, sad smile. *I think it's time Mohreen Conner met her daughter for who she truly is. I don't think she's going to like it.*

"Mohreen likes two things, and they are herself and velvet, so this does not surprise me," the fyrdwisa muttered. He rubbed a final dollop of salve ever so delicately along the handprint-shaped bruise. "I don't like seeing you hurt, Bridgette."

"It's not my favorite either, trust me," she said. Her voice sounded less raspy, but speaking still twinged her throat. Collum handed the feoht clothes to Bridgette, who nearly started crying again as she slowly changed out of the clothes from the Tinuviels and into the familiar fighting gear, a lighter and less regimented version of what her companions wore.

"You three should probably stand back," the Bright Star warned them as she put her boots on.

"What?" Cloa asked.

It hurt to raise herself off the bed. *Assist,* she commanded, and the air carried her, acting like a vertical sling for her entire body so that Bridgette Conner could stand to face the Elf who birthed her. The Elf who betrayed her, whose lies and deft mistruths were at the heart of this entire conflict.

Bring her, she told the air, and Mohreen was thrust forward, eyes wide at the magic that enveloped her. *And the blade?*

A moment later, something clattered to the floor. Bridgette jerked two fingers up and her amethyst blade was in her fingers. She had no idea from where the dagger came or how it got here so quickly. All she knew was that once, she subconsciously sent it a world away to Collum in the middle of the night. If she'd done it once, she could probably do it again. The evidence twirled in her hand. She smiled, strengthened by Collum's salve and elixirs, and by those who stood beside her.

Bridgette might be wounded, might ache from head to toe with exertion and pain, but the Liluthuaé would not be stopped by a few mere bruises. She closed her eyes and went into herself, and when she emerged, she was the same being Collum remembered from the dream in which she'd shared the truth of her magic.

Show them how, she implored the vademecums. Bridgette stared at Mohreen, violent violet eyes seeing everything in the Elf's essence, and waited.

⚡ *You are the Astridsí.*

☠ *You are the Boireannach.*

Bridgette listened as the two vademecums repeated themselves to Cloa and Emi-Joye, as they worked their magic to guide them into the same form of Self. The Self that was one with Maylemaegus, that could be slipped into by a mere breath and desire. The Self that was both impassioned leader and veritable weapon. The Self that defied existence on a binary scale, that rose above mere magical intent and instead existed as power that gave and destroyed in the same measured breath. Theirs was the power that created worlds.

Once, Bridgette felt the way they did. It seemed a different life ago. In a way, it was. That Bridgette didn't know her purpose. That Bridgette was scared, wanting to be loved for who she was and not what gifts she gave. That Bridgette couldn't do magic like everyone else, and it made her feel weak, a failure. That Bridgette played herself far too small.

The same way Cloa did, so worried was she that she would fail at being queen.

It was the way Emi-Joye did, focusing so much on her

chosen line of work, wanting to give her all to something that mattered, something that fit within the plan she had for herself.

Bridgette watched the Astridsí and Boireannach shift the same way she had. She felt it, in that strange, shared consciousness of the Triumvirate that the vademecums communicated through. She saw them become *themselves*, stepping into their power as easily as they would a pair of shoes. Cloa's eyes went deep emerald with starred pupils, the gold of her eyes flecking around them like constellations. Emi-Joye's ice blue whorls became stiller than death.

The air in the room pulsed.

Bridgette again turned to Mohreen. There was no pain now. She would allow herself to feel it again later, to ease the ache and soothe the anger. For now, she would relish this moment. It was not supposed to come to this, and yet there was no way it could *not* come to this. Bridgette Eileen Conner bore her mother's surname, her Elven ears and metallic-studded irises, but that was where the resemblance ended. There was only one thing Mohreen Conner could ever give her, and it was the one thing she would never give up.

The Bright Star twirled her dagger again. Her expression was feral as she looked the female Elf over one more time.

"How long have you known that you're the Raisarch, Mohreen?"

~ 102 ~

Mohreen Conner looked at her daughter and did not answer. Her purplish gray eyes, duller than the lilac of Bridgette's, were cold and unforgiving. She radiated disdain and annoyance.

"Tell me." It was a command now, from Bridgette.

The Elf glared in response.

Collum's heart soared, and the grin on his face was sanguine as the Liluthuaé approached her prey. Their shared covenant burned against his wrist, but it wasn't the sort of flame that would harm. No, this was the fire that heated air, that turned water to boil, that renewed the earth. He felt ravenous.

"You will tell us what you know, Mohreen Conner." The voice came simultaneously from the Triumvirate's mouths, but it was theirs and their vademecums speaking in unison, a glorious symphony of magic and wisdom, charm and demand, three all-but-goddesses claiming what was due to them.

"I know nothing, daughter mine," the female finally said, deflecting. It was her idea of a challenge, and thus began a battle of words, a fight for truth the Liluthuaé required. "Surely you know the Raisarch is no longer."

Bridgette smiled. Mohreen wasn't lying about that. The Raisarch that preceded her was long dead. But she was, at least right now, very much alive.

"The original Raisarch is long-gone, sure," Bridgette said, her voice flitting back to being her own for a moment. "A wise little kid once told me that being the Raisarch is a birthright. Why don't you tell me about my grandparents, *Mom*?"

"My foremother and father are long since gone into the spirit realm, Bridgette."

Bridgette started to pace an agonizingly slow, measured circle around the Elf. "Your father would have perished first, yes? Was that before or after Dahvñe found herself with another male instead of him?"

Collum saw Mohreen's nostrils flare. She said nothing. *What are you on about, Starshine?* he thought to Bridgette. *What do you know that I don't?*

"And how did you feel when you found out you were going to have a little sister? Was that a shock to you, Mohreen?" Bridgette tossed the knife up in the air and caught it. She flicked the blade toward the female. "Let me tell you, when I found out that being the Liluthuaé meant I had not one, but *two* sisters, it was a surprise. A nice one for the most part, so long as the Boireannach stops pissing me off, and especially since the sister I got as the Astridsí is a thousand times better than the one I thought I was gonna get."

"I have no sister," Mohreen said. She eyed her daughter warily.

"Well, I'm sure she wouldn't recognize you these days, because she didn't when you were here spying on her, did she?" Bridgette said sweetly.

The fyrdwisa's blood went cold. *You are joking. You ARE joking, yes?*

"It had been too long since she saw you, hadn't it? You ran away when she was so young, after Dahvñe died, but you never forgave her for being chosen, did you?" Bridgette mused. "*You* held the birthright to being the Raisarch. *You* were a full-blooded Elf. *You* were the eldest of the favored female's daughters. It should have been *you.*"

A muscle flexed in Mohreen's jaw. "Who told you such lies?"

"Mmm, Mom. The Liluthuaé doesn't do lies. I deal in truths," Bridgette chastised her. "Being a sierwan with access to quite a lot of Palnan history over the past few months has made a few things super clear. I think it's a good thing you and I don't look much alike, because I think dear Aunt Ydessa would have had a lot more interesting questions for me when I met her the other day."

You were not joking, Collum thought weakly. *Deity fucking bless, you were not joking.*

"That's the reason you decided, firstly, to have your little one night stand with ol' turkey jerk over there in the corner, wasn't it? To prove to your precious little sister that *you* should have been chosen, right?" Bridgette stopped pacing and smiled contentedly. "And that's the only reason you decided not to terminate your pregnancy. It had nothing to do with whether or not you felt fit to be a mother. It was because finally, *finally*, the Universe and deities saw fit to choose *you* for something. To bear the legendary Liluthuaé."

Mohreen did not respond, but her body language suggested fury and confusion, a volcano prepared to erupt. She couldn't deny any of it. Collum wondered how much more Bridgette figured out this past year; how much she kept inside, waiting for this very moment to reveal it all.

"Wanna know something else interesting, *Mom*?" Bridgette leaned heavy on the emphasis there. She seemed to be enjoying herself. "I think it's super neat that your little sister has been ferreting Palnans to and from this quaint little beach town on Earth called Larivuria, when no one's been able to go from Palna to Bondrie since the Ingefeoht! Isn't that *wild*?"

Collum glanced to Mohreen. She had started to sweat.

"It's almost as if no one except the two sisters, the daughters of Baize Sammael's favorite follower, knew how to get there," the Bright Star laughed. "How funny! I suppose it's a good thing Baize didn't tell everyone about his second portal, otherwise it would've been even harder for the Samnung to keep Ydessa in check over the years."

Emi-Joye and Cloa had begun to inch forward, keeping all eyes on Mohreen in the center of Bridgette's circle. The air in the room crackled with electricity.

"And how do you feel about Ydessa calling herself a witch, just because she's Baize Sammael's *chosen daughter*? She's an

Elfling, just like me, and wants to bury that part of herself. I bet that doesn't feel good, does it? It's like a slap in the face to your mother, I bet," Bridgette went on. "I was surprised when I found out, too. She hides her ears in that blonde hair. I'm not sure if they're pointed or not."

Mohreen couldn't hide the disgust from her expression. "Ydessa Tinuviel can die a deeply painful death, for all I care. She has run this country into the ground."

"I'll say," Bridgette chirped. "Speaking of ground, what do you know about protected lands? I've been to one once, Fôret Fossile, but there's another one I'm *really* curious about. It's something super sacred that a friend of mine said was called Terrabruixes, the Witchlands?"

She blinked innocently at Mohreen, whose breathing became evidently heavier. "Terrabruixes is a sacred place, yes."

"When was the last time you went there?"

The muscle feathered in Mohreen's jaw again as she evaded answering. Bridgette circled in closer now, a shark hungry for blood.

"Do you want to know what I think has been going on, *Mom*?"

"I cannot say that I do." Mohreen's words were almost a staccato, as if she thought the wrong words might get that knife too close for comfort.

"Well. I'll tell you anyway because I'm sick and fucking tired of your lies and deceit. It'd be nice to have this all out in the open, don't y'all think?" Bridgette mused.

Satisfied nods from Cloa and Emi-Joye. Collum joined in.

"Excellent," Bridgette said. "I think that you've been using your so-called theater background to disguise yourself and go to Earth, then zip right back into Palna via the portal that goes from Larivuria to Terrabruixes. Who got you a Palnan Royal Guard outfit so that you could fit the bill and not be questioned for so many trips?"

Mohreen was so stressed that she was chewing the insides of her cheeks.

"Do you have *anything* to say for yourself? No denials, no evasiveness, nothing?" Bridgette taunted.

"It's a mother's delight to know her daughter grew to be such a wickedly gifted, intelligent creature," Mohreen finally said. She looked anything but delighted.

Her daughter smiled. The expression was feral again, devilish with the grotesque injuries accessorizing it. "I'm so glad we could have this little chat, and so glad you chose not to lie anymore — although I will say, this whole not answering me thing is getting kind of old. We need to know what your sister and her husband are up to in Larivuria."

Mohreen clearly had no loyalty to Ydessa, but she wasn't about to go down easy. "What happens outside of Heáhwolcen is not my concern."

"Hmm. It should be," Bridgette murmured. "I'm going to tell you a secret. Would you like that? Something just shared between us, my sisters and my mother, and the fyrdwisa?"

"We'd like to hear your secret," Cloa and Emi-Joye said in creepy unison.

Bridgette feigned a whisper directly into her mother's ear. Mohreen flinched as the Elfling's breath blew by. "You'll never succeed Ydessa and Eryth as queen of Palna, Mohreen Conner. No matter what havoc you think the Ealdaelfen will wreak on your behalf, because half of them believe Eryth is their leader, and you will *never* have the full power and might of the Raisarch. You had your chance to earn your title. It's someone else's turn now."

Whatever hold she had on Mohreen broke, and faster than Collum could take note, it was Elf versus Elfling. He had no idea Mohreen was armed — a rookie mistake; he should have checked both her dress and her cloak before they dragged her out of the treehouse — and watched in mute terror as the two went after one another. Emi-Joye and Cloa stood back, patiently waiting. This was not their fight.

It wasn't Collum's, either, but he could barely handle it. The two of them moved incredibly quickly, and Bridgette played fair for the moment. They went knife to knife, and the fyrdwisa took in the Bright Star's movements. When the Maylemaegus receded, she would pay for this entire scene. He tried to process what was going on before him at the same time his mind worked to unravel the threads of history that stitched themselves anew. Mohreen Conner was Ydessa Tinuviel's older sister. Bridgette's *aunt* was the leader of Palna, the hand-picked spiritual child of Baize Sammael selected to succeed him should he die. Baize Sammael had, at some point, founded *another* magical realm, a place on Earth, the mysterious Larivuria that Fairy Ambassador Ulerion Mewt once visited. Larivuria was an active outpost, most likely the place that the Tinuviels sent their armed forces and athletes out to, where they could train and not be detected by the Samnung.

But the worst part of it all was that no matter what the Samnung had tried to do after the Ingefeoht, Baize Sammael succeeded all along. He had another portal. It had always been there, and no one besides him and a select few followers knew that it existed.

A shout of pain drew Collum's attention back to the fight that played out in this dark basement bedroom. Mohreen decided she didn't want to use knives anymore and resorted to magic without warning, sending a pulse of air directly into the Bright Star's injured eye. Tears streamed down Bridgette's cheek as she reared back. Collum watched Bridgette try to restrain herself.

"I don't want to. I have to," she had whispered to him not even a day ago. He didn't understand it then, but it made sense now. It wouldn't hurt her any less, to want versus be compelled to. It was almost as if Bridgette waited for a trigger, for Mohreen to

make a move she could not come back from. Bridgette didn't want to do this of her own accord. The punch of air had almost been enough, and he saw her reserve falter.

Mohreen, on the other hand, appeared to have no qualms about injuring yet another being who sought to take what was hers. She said some spell that sent Bridgette sprawling — another grunt of pain; the Bright Star landed on her stomach — but the Triumvirate stepped in. Mohreen went to her knees as the ground shook. Cloa wiggled her fingers devilishly at the Elf, and Collum had to stop himself from cackling out loud.

The distraction was enough for Bridgette to get back to her feet. She came again at Mohreen with her knife, and the Elf leaned backwards to avoid being cut. Another gust of air went at the Bright Star, this time for her other eye. Bridgette didn't dodge it in time. She screamed.

That was all it took for her to stop trying to keep her magic under wraps. Bridgette exploded.

There was no other word for it, as she came to one knee and with an almighty swipe of her arm, churned half the air in the room into a bolus of pressure. It hit Mohreen square in the chest, and she staggered back, gasping. Collum had never seen anything like it before. Bridgette was naturally gifted at what he knew now was Craft Wizardry, though there was a subtle difference in Maylemaegus versus what Mohreen had been taught growing up. One was innate, a gift. The other was a bastardized attempt to imbue the gift upon others who could never wield it to the same strength or success, nor with instinctual ease. The two fought tooth and nail. The fyrdwisa wasn't sure which female would best the other, and he glanced nervously toward Cloa and Emi-Joye. They seemed unperturbed, observing the fight as if it was no more serious than a sporting competition.

A loud boom echoed through the room, and the altercation faltered. Collum had forgotten they were in the basement of the fucking castle; that Eryth Tinuviel was in the room with them; that they were probably making a significant ruckus in a space that was supposed to be inhabited only by an Elfling.

If anyone else comes in, we are in very deep trouble, Collum thought to Bridgette.

"Hold the door!" he shouted to the Fairy and witch queen. Their magic responded immediately. Water droplets summoned from the air fixed themselves to the doorframe and froze solid. Tiny branches began to grow from the floor, trees sprouting out of long-dead wooden planks, and rooted into the door. It would hold. But not forever.

"Tell me what you know, Mohreen!" Bridgette bellowed.

What the fuck else is there to know?! Collum thought. He was torn between aiding her and watching. *What else are we missing?*

"I gave you life! I owe you nothing!" the Elf screamed back. She shoved another punch of air, and another right after. Bridgette dodged the first but didn't shift fast enough to miss the second. It slammed into her shoulder.

"I want the fucking *truth* about who I am!" the Liluthuaé bellowed.

An unforgiving wind slammed Mohreen so hard into the firehearth mantle that something cracked. The world slowed. The Elf fell to the floor, her body jerking as blood dripped down her hairline. Her breath came more raggedly than Eryth's.

"You want … Raisarch?" The words heaved from Mohreen's mouth, slurred and thick. "That … want?"

Bridgette towered over her. "I want the truth, Mohreen."

Someone outside started ramming at the door. Mohreen Conner let out a shaky laugh as Emi-Joye called out, "This is not going to stay up much longer!"

"Truth," Mohreen coughed, mocking the Bright Star. Blood pooled in her mouth. "Ask … him."

"I can't. I'm asking *you,*" Bridgette snarled. She dipped her face close to Mohreen's, both of their chests heaving from exertion. "Tell me who I am."

Mohreen reached a shaking hand for Bridgette, as if to cup her daughter's face, to finally show some sign of affection after twenty-three years. She grabbed Bridgette's ear and twisted it. The Elfling scrambled, shrieking in pain.

"Already … know!" Mohreen rasped and started cackling. "Already! Know!" She kicked Bridgette away from her. Blood pooled at Mohreen's back from the crack in her skull as the laughter grew, both in volume and level of maliciousness. Something glinted in the red by Mohreen's side. Collum had a millisecond to shout, to warn —

Bridgette screamed as her mother drove the blade into her own neck.

~ 103 ~

"NO!" the Elfling shouted. "No, NO!"

Collum wrapped himself around Bridgette as she strained forward, fighting his grip on her in a futile effort to get to Mohreen. She kept screaming, as if the world ended. It had, in a way.

The world she thought she knew was dissolving and reforming before their eyes. There was a nauseating sound as Mohreen gurgled a final exhale around the knife sticking out of her throat, and an awful odor as her body expelled itself. The fyrdwisa threw a ward-wall around Mohreen's fresh corpse to contain the stench. His other arm gripped Bridgette against him.

"Starshine, stop!" he cried. Collum looked to Emi-Joye and Cloa, who stood terrifyingly still, their Maylemaegus on full display independently of their bodies as they battled to keep the door shut, to stop what sounded like a hoard of Palnan guards from coming inside. The fyrdwisa was legitimately scared. He started barking orders, something he'd been trained in, but never once required to do. "Emi-Joye, untie Eryth. Put the sheets back on the bed. This needs to look like he killed Mohreen. Cloa, hold that deity-damned door. Bridgette, Starshine, STOP!"

He felt the ghost hands first on him, as if to let him know they were there, and then they moved to her. Collum was shaking with the effort to focus and keep the Bright Star in check. *What have we done? What did we just cause to happen?*

They had to get out. They had to get Eryth's body near enough to Mohreen to make the scene believable. And then, he'd evanesce them somewhere. Anywhere.

The door cracked in the center. "Collum!" Cloa screamed.

Collum gave her a terrified look and then twisted Bridgette around, making the Elfling's screams of anger blast in his face. *Anger!* He had a sudden realization that she wasn't losing her mind over her mother's death, but rather, the death of the truths that died with Mohreen.

Oh, thank Hecate. That he could deal with it. His breath came easier.

"Bridgette, listen to me!" Collum gripped her by the shoulders, the ghost hands reinforcing the touch. "We have to get out of here. We have to go soon. You can tell me where to go, yes? Where do we go from here?"

Her breath came in furious exhales. The room became fragrant as Collum forced both soothing scents and peaceful energy to form around them. It was a challenge; there was so much intensity and heat from the fight and the events preceding it. Another boom hit the door. They were running out of time and luck.

"Collum."

His name on her lips in that moment was an answered prayer. The fyrdwisa clutched the Elfling to him so hard that she winced, even though the pain of her injuries was still numbed by Maylemaegus.

"Bridgette, we have to leave. Where do we go?"

The Bright Star's eyes flittered between her own and the deep purple. "Baize Sammael's map," she said. "If I show you somewhere to go on that map, can you evanesce us there?"

He wasn't sure. But what choice did they have?

Collum summoned the stolen map of Palna from wherever it lived in the recesses of time and space. Emi-Joye had sufficiently posed Eryth and Mohreen together and rejoined Cloa to help hold the door. The Fairy flashed them a worried glance.

Let's get a move on, shall we? she thought to Collum. He gave her a quick nod of understanding as Bridgette scoured the map. It was larger than the one Toby once drew in the dirt for her, the one she copied into the blue butcher's notebook stored safely at the Maudlins' home.

"There," Bridgette pointed. It was a spot near the center of Palna. "Will you take us there?"

"Bridgette, I'm not sure I can evanesce us somewhere I've never been!"

"What if you have a guide?" she asked. "What if the vademecums show you?"

Collum didn't have enough headspace to focus on managing the panic that filled the room as another crack appeared in the door, answered by frustrated yells from the Boireannach and Astridsí. He looked to Bridgette. "I don't know! I'm the fyrdwisa, Starshine, not a deity; I can only do so much!"

His eyes were so wide that Bridgette, for once, softened first for him. "You can do plenty, Collum Andoralain. Especially with we three bitches on your side. Okay?"

"I take offense to that, actually," Emi-Joye called out. She gritted her teeth as ice chips flew from the door. "Are we leaving, or are we about to fight the Palnan Royal Guard?"

"We're leaving," Collum said.

Thing One! Bridgette thought to her vademecum. *Now would be a great time to do some of that guide shit you keep claiming y'all do. Get us to Terrabruixes. Now.*

The fyrdwisa felt the object's consciousness tap into his mind at her command. He saw where he needed to go. There was no warning as he scooped the three females into his arms and blasted them away in a flurry of navy.

"HEAVE!" someone shouted from outside.

Without any more magic holding it, the door came down. Chalamet, face hidden behind her helm, started barking orders. The scene was horrific — trees grew directly from the floorboards, puddles of what she hoped were water dotted the ground. There was so much blood, and pages ripped from books still fluttered down from the air.

"His Majesty!" one of the guards yelled. Eryth was curled in a pool of blood at the side of a very dead female Elf, a knife protruding from her throat. "He's alive!"

Chalamet took a careful spin around the room. There was

no way in or out of this place other than that door, or burning oneself to a crisp climbing up the chimney — and it was a long, long way to the top of the palace from here. Despite all of those obstacles, someone had managed to go missing. The commander cursed.

"Find that fucking Elfling!" she roared.

The fucking Elfling in question was busily fighting down waves of nausea on the island of Terrabruixes. Surrounded by three different bodies of water that acted as a moat for this area of protected lands, Terrabruixes was somewhere that none of them should be found. Bridgette had a sense that though travel to and from Earth might not be as heavily monitored here as it was in Fairevella, there would be guards watching the portal. The portal that shouldn't exist.

Yet there it was, a replica of the one Artur Cromwell originally constructed when Heáhwolcen was founded. Baize Sammael's biggest secret wasn't nearly as wide, judging from the outside. Unlike the true portal to the world above the world, this one was a glistening column of opaque light that had no surrounding buildings. It simply seemed to go all the way up, to what Collum once told Bridgette was the Meridian point, and down.

"Are you alright?" Cloa knelt by the Liluthuaé. The queen's skin was pale and her dark hair mussed. "Bridgette, I'm so sorry about your mother."

"Don't be," Bridgette rasped out. Her throat was starting to hurt again. She dreaded the upcoming moment when all of the pain that wracked her body would come back into full existence. "She mostly just fucked my life up when she abandoned me on Earth. But I turned out okay, I guess."

The queen apologized about Mohreen's death, but not about Eryth's attack. Apparently, judging from that omission, there were still a few secrets being kept amongst the Triumvirate.

Bridgette looked up to her two sisters. "Sorry I called you bitches."

Emi-Joye gave her a dry look. "You're forgiven, so long as you don't pull any more knives on me. Are you going to tell us why we're here, and where *here* is? And what the seven hells that portal is doing here? And how you knew it was here?"

Bridgette grinned. "This is Terrabruixes, the so-called sacred Witchlands. Half of what I said to Mohreen back there started out as hunches a few months ago. We don't have time for everything now, but I swear I'll explain this all soon. Really soon. The short version is that Baize Sammael had this concept of creating magical worlds on soil, sky, and sea. Soil, he had Palna. Sea is this place called Larivuria. Sky is … I guess he died before that part happened. Small silver lining to the Ingefeoht."

Collum had been walking the shoreline while Bridgette retched. "I see no guards. This worries me."

"Yeah, that's uh, not what I would have expected. I won't complain about it though. It's kind of nice to not be pursued for the first time in a few days, sheesh," the Elfling admitted. She flashed a grateful smile to Emi-Joye and Cloa. "Y'all did great, by the way. That was … that was really cool what you did to hold the door. Thank you."

"What now?" the queen asked.

Bridgette reached for Collum's hand. "I think we have ourselves a little beach vacation ahead of us."

"All of us?" Emi-Joye said skeptically.

"You two need to go back," Bridgette said. "Endorsa can't be without *another* queen, although I bet Nehemi would come out of hiding for a few days if she needed to. And Cloa needs help getting out of here."

The Elfling motioned to Emi-Joye's wings.

"There's something I need to do first though," Bridgette said. "Or, well, Collum, will you help?" She held out her wrist, and he understood immediately.

"Send your thoughts to me, and I will send them to Serrabinx," he said. Neither of them felt like surprising the woman with a message conveyed via Universal consciousness. The fyrdwisa slipped two fingers around the carved bead and let Bridgette's message flow into his mind.

I don't know if you'll get this, but if you do, I'm so sorry, Bridgette thought. She tried to keep her sentiments brief. *The route we took to Düoria was guarded. They have Toby. I got out. I'm coming back for him.* She wasn't sure what prompted the tears this time, but they stung like hell leaking from her blackened eye. *One more thing, Serrabinx. Mohreen is dead. Eryth Tinuviel attacked me. I guess that's two more things, so here's a third: the Triumvirate has risen. Ready the Hringur for our return.*

Collum squeezed her around the shoulders and pressed a kiss to her hair. "We will be alright, Starshine. All of us."

I thought I would feel different, the Elfling thought to him. *I thought taking my birthright would change me; change my magic. But I just feel numb.*

You've had a traumatic few days, Collum reassured her, mind-to-mind. *Give yourself grace and time to heal. Perhaps the numbness is a gift until the goddexes know you are ready for this next turn along your path.*

"I guess this makes the whole Triumvirate thing pretty official then," Bridgette said out loud. She leaned into the fyrdwisa's chest.

⚡ ✦ ☠ *You must first speak the Trúwa,* the vademecums sounded.

"The what?" Cloa asked.

Bridgette recalled the word from the Hringur meeting. "It's like an oath," she explained. She motioned to her sisters. "I guess we should do that, yeah?"

"What are the words to this Trúwa?" Emi-Joye asked. She stood with Bridgette and Cloa and joined hands. "Are we supposed to know it?"

In answer, the voices of the vademecums entered their

minds, and all three females' eyes snapped into their Maylemaegus forms. There was a gentle breeze and mist began to cloud around as the trio froze, almost in a trance. When they spoke in one voice, of one mind, Collum felt compelled to kneel in respect. It was as if they knew all the words, all along, all their lives. As if this moment was the perfect time, as close to perfect as any, here on this island in the middle of Heáhwolcen, for destiny to unfold.

The three began to glow, green and blue and lavender, and their shared Trúwa, the divine oath of the Triumvirate, slipped from their lips:

"We are truth, passion, and loyalty.
We are soil, sky, and sea.
We are time, space, and infinity.
We are the Triumvirate,
And as we will it,
So mote it be."

There was a whisper on the wind, an echo of promise, as the world above the world rippled in place. Trees bowed over. Waves formed in the rivers and lapped at the sandy shore. The ground trembled. Terrabruixes went still, the land holding a bated breath. The air went tight around them. And then they heard the crash. The three broke their handhold and without warning, the ghost hands were on Bridgette, one turning her toward the shimmering portal, the other on her lower back, ushering her along. "What the —"

There were more crashing noises in the brush behind them, followed by shouts. Bridgette's body went taut. She whipped around to grab Collum, her eyes opalescent. "We used magic! With the covenant bracelets, then whatever the fuck we just vowed is a spell. The Samnung made it illegal, but the Tinuviels monitor magic — don't ask me how, I haven't figured that out yet! — to find out who's still got power. That's their prime recruiting method for the Collective."

The shouts were getting louder. Bridgette pulled her dagger from where she'd stuck it in her boot and slashed her hand open. "What's one more scar from today?" she muttered, and then smeared the blood across Cloa and Emi-Joye's stunned foreheads.

"Put your hoods back up and fucking *fly*, Emi-Joye. Call the rain and use it to camouflage yourselves!" Bridgette implored her. "Get out of here and tell the Samnung what happened. Tell them Mohreen is dead, that Eryth attacked me, that there's this secret portal. And tell the Fairies to send someone to Earth, directly below the Meridian. Tell them to send someone we can trust."

They hesitated. It was long enough for an arrow to soar out of the woods, aimed directly at Emi-Joye's wings. Bridgette hurled forward and tackled her to the ground. She stared at the Boireannach, eyes wide.

"GO!" Bridgette shouted. "Get the fuck out of here!"

She didn't look to see if they listened. She turned to the bushes and commanded the air to shield, to hold, and she *ached*. Every bone in her body screeched in protest and Bridgette implored her Maylemaegus to hide the pain for just a little longer. Her shield of air blocked arrows, and it hid her and Collum from the guards, most of whom had eyes and aim on the fleeing Fairy and queen. A few of the guards skirted the blockade of air and ran for the two remaining fugitives. Collum, helm still slung over a shoulder, drew his sword and swung. Metal met metal and sparks flew as he took on three, then four at once. Bridgette held her shield, shooting fleeting glances to where Emi-Joye was in the sky — not high enough to escape the volley of arrows that would pelt her the moment the shield came down — and the Bright Star urged the air to *punish*. She didn't care how the element interpreted this command. She just had to keep the

Boireannach and Astridsí alive.

By the grace of the Fyrst, it started to pour. Bridgette had to look down to stop the rain from stinging her eyes. More shouts echoed from the bushes. Collum tapped her on the shoulder, echoed by the ghost hands. Four bodies, two without heads and two bleeding out from disemboweling gashes across the intestines, were at his feet.

"Starshine," he said. His eyes were so blue they could have been gemstones.

It was now or never. She grabbed the fyrdwisa's outstretched fingers and they bolted through the torrents of precipitation toward the shining beam of the portal, chased by the sounds of more guards. This was why there were no guards on Terrabruixes. Only those with permission or illicit magic dared to come here, and usage of the latter would be an instant call to arms to guards across the country. The Elf and Elfling crossed the breadth of light and stopped dead at the edge of the windtunnel inside. This portal went straight down and straight up into nothingness in both directions.

Bridgette gave Collum a sideways glance as the wind whipped around them. Shouts started to sound louder, closer, outside.

"Hey Bundy!" she managed to yell above the cacophony of swirling air. "Nice job back there. I always knew you were a serial killer!"

Collum smirked and cocked one eyebrow at her, amazed that she was even still standing. "I prefer … trained assassin," he said.

The fyrdwisa met her adventurous gaze and grasped her hands tightly. He pressed a kiss to her lips; the furious, heated sort of contact that said so much more than words ever would.

"Don't drop me," she whispered, and together, they jumped into the void.

Please note the below pronunciations are based on the English pronunciations, unless they are specifically words derived from other languages.

Bridgette Eileen Conner *(Brih-d-jet Eye-leen)* — your protagonist

Sorts of Beings

African Aziza *(Ah-zee-zah)* — A species of Fairy that originated in Africa, known for having wings of insects including beetles, moths, and butterflies

Baetalüan/Baetalü *(Bay-tah-loo-ahn / Bay-tah-loo)* — Magical species with human-esque builds and limbs, who have simple, small horns growing from their heads

Celtic Fae — A species of Fairy that originated in Europe, typically with gossamer-like wings, though rare Fae are born with bat-like wings

Centaur — Horse-bodied creature with the chest, arms, and head of a human

Chrysomallos *(Chris-oh-mal-ohs)* — Golden-fleeced, golden-horned sheep

Cù-sìth *(Coo shih-hee)* — Long-extinct species of Fae hound

Druid/True Druid *(Drew-ehd)* — The magical beings and human "masks" who practice a specific lifestyle that furthers the bond between sentient being, Nature, and the Universal consciousness; only the True Druids are able to perform magic utilizing this bond

Dryad *(Dry-add)* — Tree-dwelling spirits and guardians

Ealdaelfen *(Eel-dehl-fen)* or Eeelings *(Ee-lings)* — The legendary sect of "dark Elves" that haunt bedtime stories of magical younglings

Ealdgecynd *(Eel-d-geh-send)* — An old term for Elves, used before

the Ealdaelfen sect formed, describing them as beings who are
One with Nature

Elf/Elves — Humanoid beings with pointed ears, opalescent-
flecked eyes, and elemental magic

Kobold *(Koh-bold)* — Mischievous and joyful little sprites, noted
for having unusually colored skin, blue nails, and occasionally
horns or tails

Pixie *(Pick-see)* — Tiny winged humanoid being

Sanguisuge *(Sayn-gwih-sooj)* — Magical being that requires only
meat and blood to survive and perform magic, known for the
healing powers of their own blood. Accidentally created
vampires by biting humans who did not die, but instead were
infected with Sanguisuge blood and became a new type of
being entirely

Tiefling *(Teef-ling)* — Solitary beings with horns like those of a
ram, very adept at magics of subterfuge. Rumored to have
been related to "demon races" at one time due to a
characteristic pointed tail many Tieflings have

Witch / Wizard — Humans with magic in their veins, able to
harness powers and elements by way of tools such as wands,
staffs, and guiding words

TITLES

Ambassador/Ambassadora — Lead Fairy liaisons between
Fairevella and the various countries of Heáhwolcen and Earth

Ambestre *(Am-beh-stray)* — Second-in-command Fairy to each
ambassador or ambassadora

Ardestre *(Ard-eh-stray)* — Second-in-command to the ard rialóir

Ard Rialóir *(Arrd Ree-ah-lohr)* — Head of the Elves in
Heáhwolcen

Astridsí *(Uh-strih-d-see)* — A mythological witch

Boireannach *(Bore-ee-an-ach)* — A mythological Fae

Borhond *(Boar-hund)* — The witch king or queen's lead advisor

Ceannairí *(She-an-air-ee)* — Both a generic title for magical leader, and a specific title that can be used when addressing a magical leader, similar to "Your Majesty"

Cennestre *(Sin-eh-stray)* — Elven and Fae term for mother

Fairy of All Fairies — Leader of the Fairies in Heáhwolcen

Fyrdestre *(Fuh-yord-es-tray)* — The Elves' second-in-command to the fyrdwisa, and second in line to succeed the ard rialóir

Fyrdwisa *(Fuh-yord-wee-sa)* — The primary Elven spy and military leader, first in line to succeed the ard rialóir

Geongre *(Gay-awn-grey)* — Lead Fairy travel deputy

Geongrestre *(Gay-awn-greh-stray)* — The Fairies' second-in-command travel deputy

Iontach an Chéad Cheannaire *(Eon-tack ahn Chay-d She-an-air-ee)* — A title Fairies use when referring to the founding Fae of Fairevella

Lacnestre *(Lack-neh-stray)* — Apprentice healers to the lacnians

Lacnian *(Lack-nee-an)* — Specialized healers who use a mixture of practical tools and ritual magic to address ailments

Liluthuaé *(Lih-loo-thoo-aye)* — A mythological Elven being

Master Swordsman / Swordswoman — Warrior leader of Bondrie

Raisarch *(Rye-sark)* — Leader of the Ealdaelfen, the mysterious and legendary "dark Elves"

Sigewíf *(See-jweef)* — Title of respect for a female/feminine being

Slátraestre *(Slah-treh-stray)* — Butcher's apprentice

Slátrari *(Slah-trah-ree)* — Butcher

Spreca *(Spreh-ka)* — Lead voice of the Samnung

Thighearna *(Thee-gar-nah)* — Title of respect for a male/masculine being

THE SAMNUNG (SAHM-NUN-G)

Arctura *(Arc-tuhr-ah)* — Princess Cloa's mysterious and ever-present cat

Aristoces *(Ah-rihs-toh-sees)* — Fairy of All Fairies, leader of
Fairevella, and wisest being in the Samnung chamber

Bryten *(Brighten)* — Baetalüan elected to represent horned beings
and the minor populations of magical folk in Heáhwolcen;
frequently absconds shirts

Cloa *(Cl-oh-ah)* — Princess of Endorsa, addled by an unusual lack
of mental presence that causes frequent discomfort during
meetings

Collum Andoralain *(Call-uhm And-or-ah-layn)* — Elven fyrdwisa
and Bridgette's stalwart companion

Corria Deathhunter *(Cor-ee-uh)* — Master swordswoman of
Bondrie, quiet but quite adept at her gifts of leadership and
warrior arts

Kharis *(Care-ihs)* — Nehemi's right-hand wizard, the borhond

Nehemi *(Neh-heh-mee)* — Witch queen of Endorsa, haughty and
proud

Trystane Eiríkr *(Tryst-ayn Air-ih-kur)* — Ard rialóir, leader of
Eckenbourne; Collum's best friend and symbolic elder
brother

Verivol Rosu *(Veh-rih-vole Roe-soo)* — A gender nonbinary
Sanguisuge chosen to represent the coteries of their kind.
Loves fashion and immediately brings Bridgette into their fold
and heart

BEINGS ON EARTH

Dagmar Nilsen *(Dahg-mahr Nihl-son)* — Norway's leader of the
human Antarctic delegation

Gary — The Druids' human gatekeeper on Earth

Heledd *(Heh-led)* — The ovate adept, or Ilwyn Gyfrinach, of the
True Druids

Jamie and Wade — Bridgette's co-workers at the diner in
Nashville

Martha and "Doc" Joel Simmons — Bridgette's most-present
    foster parents
Noah Irwin — Australian leader of the human Antarctic
    delegation

Beings of Bondrie

Druan Heart of Stones *(Drew-an)* — Former master swordsman
Maqtok Spring Bearer *(Mack-tock)* — Shieldhand of Bondrie and
    Corria's second
Mxmillian Surefire *(Mix-million Sure-fire)* — General of the
    Bondrie Guard
Sakari Torn Hand *(Sah-kah-ree)* — Magister militum of the
    Bródenmael
Sixsi Windwraith *(Six-see Wind-wray-th)* — Hair artisan who
    works in Endorsa

Beings of Endorsa

Artur and Felicity Cromwell — Witch founders of Heáhwolcen
    in the 1690s. Escaped persecution in Europe to journey to the
    Americas, but after getting caught up in the Salem Witch
    Trials, the Cromwells chose to move forward with creating a
    safe space of their own for beings of magical origin and blood
Dominus Falto *(Dom-en-us Fall-toe)* — Nehemi's former beau and
    a member of King Hermann's circle, killed in the carriage
    accident alongside the king and Queen Lalora
Galdúr *(Gal-durr)* — Heáhwolcen's co-founder, an enslaved
    Black Fairy who became free after the king who imprisoned
    and sold him died. Joined with the Cromwells and provided
    the missing key spell that created Heáhwolcen
Herewosa Donnachaidh *(Hair-eh-whoa-suh Donna-key)* —
    Cailleach wígend and Cath Draíochta practitioner.

Bridgette's feoht trainer

King Hermann *(Her-mahn)* — Former king of Endorsa, killed
when errant magic from Palna overtook his carriage

Lucilla Von Detton *(Loo-silla)* — Witch who acts as the
Samnung's secretary, though her actual employ is to Queen
Nehemi and Princess Cloa

Lymerian Rosu *(Lie-meer-ian Roe-soo)* — Sanguisuge owner of a
crystal and ritual shop

Magister Ephynius *(Mah-jihs-ter Eh-fin-ee-yus)* — The foremost
magical historian at the University in Heáhwolcen

Murthel, Teale, Avengeline *(Muhr-thel, Teal, Ah-vehn-jeh-leen)* —
Members of the Endorsan Modern Kitchen Witch Society,
sisters, and owners of the Coffee Cauldron

Naomi *(Nay-oh-mee)* — Former handmaiden to Queen Lalora,
killed alongside her and King Hermann by errant magic

Pompié *(Pom-pee-aye)* — A lacnestre of mind-health

Queen Lalora *(Lah-lohr-ah)* — Former queen of Endorsa, killed
when errant magic from Palna overtook her carriage

Sheridan Ifans *(Share-ih-den If-ahns)* — Male witch barkeep, friend
to the Fairy ambassadora to the Antaractic

BEINGS OF ECKENBOURNE

Aelys Frost *(Aye-lihs Frost)* — The original founding Elf of
Eckenbourne

Aurelias Parvhin *(Arr-ee-lee-us Pahr-ven)* — Elven fyrdestre, of
Tiefling and Elven heritage

Bennameena *(Ben-ah-mee-nah)* — Elven shopkeeper and the
mother of Bridgette's first violin student in Heáhwolcen

Callithys Eiríkr *(Cuh-lih-thees Air-ih-kur)* — Trystane's mother

Eloise *(Eh-loh-ees)* — Golden-hued Unicorn annwyl of the
Liluthuaé

Eulalia *(You-lah-lee-ah)* — Elven dúnaelfen leader who taught
Trystane to brew and distill his own spirits

Ilori *(Ill-or-ee)* — Njahla's mother, a skilled herbalist and téitheoir

Lessiel *(Less-ee-elle)* — Second-in-command of the Unicorn calvary

Mithrilken *(Mih-thrill-ken)* — Black Unicorn annwyl of the fyrdwisa

Mohreen Conner *(Mor-een)* — Mysterious Elven figure and Bridgette's birth mother

Njahla *(En-jah-lah)* — Trystane's right-hand Elf, without whom he'd be lost

Thorhallsson *(Thor-hall-son)* — Commander of the Unicorn calvary

BEINGS OF FAIREVELLA

Akiko Chidori *(Ah-key-koh Chee-dor-ee)* — Geongre for Fairevella

Apostine *(Uh-post-een)* — Fairy ambestre to the Antarctic, the first Tiefling-blooded being to take such a prestigious position

Djoser Fayek *(D-joe-sir Fah-yek)* — Leader of the Camhnóir Feeric

Emi-Joye Vetur *(Eh-mee – Joy Veh-tuhr)* — Fairy ambassadora to the Antarctic

Etreyn *(Eh-trey-en)* — Geongrestre for Fairevella

Frosset Malvarma *(Froh-set Mahl-vahr-ma)* — Former Fairy ambassador to the Antarctic, now serving as its ambassador emeritus

Garrin Fitzhugh *(Gah-ren)* — Former Fairy ambassador to Palna, deceased and succeeded by Ulerion Mewt

Hafiz *(Hah-feez)* — Fairy guard and warrior

Luthus *(Loo-thuhs)* — A Fairy travel deputy

Oleandra Pappas *(Oh-lee-and-ruh Pah-pahs)* — Aeris of the Fairy Mîleta

Tula & Johannes Vetur *(Too-lah, Yo-hahn-ess Veh-tuhr)* — Emi-Joye's mother and father

Ulerion Mewt *(You-lair-eon Meew-t)* — Current Fairy ambassador to Palna, who disappeared without a trace in August 2017

<u>**BEINGS OF PALNA**</u>

Baize Sammael *(Bay-ze Sam-eye-ehl)* — The late creator of Craft Wizardry and founder of Palna; killed in the Ingefeoht

Caracas *(Cuh-rah-kus)*, Chalamet *(Shall-uh-may)*, and Taurus *(Tar-us)* — Members of the Palnan Royal Guard

Dahvñe *(Dah-v-nyee)* — Ydessa Tinuviel's late mother, the most loyal follower of Baize Sammael

Eryth Tinuviel *(Eh-rehth Tin-oo-vee-ehl)* — Current male witch leading Palna along with partner Ydessa

Fincher *(Finch-er)* — Kobold who works at the butchery as a slátraestre

Glafida *(Glah-fee-duh)* — A leatherwiph known for binding and repairing books, as well as making her own leather goods

Muov *(Mw-ahv)* — Elf who works at the butchery as a slátraestre

Ovidion *(Oh-vih-dee-un)* — Toby's late father, an Elfling who also used to work as a slátraestre at the butchery

Paxson *(Pack-son)* — Baetalüan who works at the butchery as a slátraestre

Queylan, of no surname *(Kweh-lan)* — Sanguisuge jewelry artisan from Düoria

Serrabinx Maudlin *(Sara-binks Maude-lihn)* — Bridgette's hostess and a healer.

Sohli *(Soh-lee)* — Unknown figure whose name appears repeatedly in Ulerion Mewt's ambassador reports about the country

Tobias "Toby" Maudlin *(Toe-by-us Maude-lihn)* — Precocious young Elfling with special abilities. Son of Serrabinx

Ydessa Tinuviel *(Ee-dessah Tin-oo-vee-ehl)* — Current female witch leading Palna along with partner Eryth

Zedolph Maudlin *(Zeh-daulf Maude-lihn)* — Xcthonya's butcher and Serrabinx's brother, considered a host of Bridgette's

Heáhwolcen *(Heh-uh-wall-shen)* —
Literally "continent in the clouds", a magical continent hidden above the cloudline over North America. Includes the countries Endorsa, Eckenbourne, Fairevella, Bondrie, and Palna, as well as the spirit realm Ifrinnevatt. For reference, please see the map at the front of this book.

Beorgdún *(Bay-org-dune)* — Vast rocky mountainous region that stretches from Palna up through Bondrie, Endorsa, and Fairevella. Lower peaks than that of Hlafjordstiepel

Bondrie *(Bon-dree)* — Borderland created between Palna and the rest of Heáhwolcen. Its citizenry largely includes witches and warrior beings descended from indigenous peoples of North America
>	Casa de Piedra *(Cah-suh deh Pee-aye-druh)* — Bondrie's massive, maze-like governmental residence
>	Odalu Digaswodi *(Oh-dah-loo Dee-gah-swoh-dee)* — Majestic river, the Mountain's Tears, that flows from the Beorgdún into Palna

Eckenbourne *(Eck-en-born)* — Elven lands of Heáhwolcen
>	Aelchanon *(Aye-ehl-cannon)* — The capital city and main region of Elven business and government
>	Caisleán *(Case-lee-ahn)* — Elven capital building
>	Estmereamel *(Ehst-meer-ah-mell)* — Elven city of water
>	Faustdúnleshire *(Fao-ust-doon-leh-shur)* — Mountainous region
>	Feormeham *(Fey-ohrm-hum)* — Rural farming region of Eckenbourne, where Collum's apartment is located
>	Hlafjordstiepel *(Lah-fyord-shh-tee-pehl)* — Tallest peak in the mountains of Heáhwolcen
>	Lisweald *(Lihs-wehld)* — Beautiful wooded, natural garden area of Eckenbourne that is primarily

inhabited by Nature itself

Loch Liath *(Lock Lie-ahth)* — A recreational lake in
Estmereamel

Maluridae Wood *(Mah-luhr-ih-day)* — Secret grove in
Faustdúnleshire that can only be accessed by Elves
who know of its existence

Endorsa *(Ehn-door-sah)* — The original country of Heáhwolcen

Coffee Cauldron — Magical coffee shop frequented by
Bridgette

Coven House of Wand and Sword — Similar to
Maluridae Wood, a glamoured shed that serves as the
meeting space for the most prestigious secret society
in Heáhwolcen

Cyneham Breonna *(Chin-hum Bree-oh-nah)* — The
governmental offices and administration building for
Endorsa and the Samnung at large

Deu Medgar *(Due Mehd-gar)* — Residential palace for the
ruling family of Endorsa

Evenshade — Nightclub known for pulsating witchlight
effects, loud music, and a delicious sense of freedom

Galdúr *(Gal-durr)* — Capital city of Endorsa, named for
Heáhwolcen's co-founder

Hologrimoire *(Holo-grim-wahr)* — Salon for fur and hair
owned by Bondrian Sixsi Windwraith

Mimea Botanicci *(Mih-mee-uh Boat-an-ee-chee)* — Magical
botanical garden in the capital city

Minthame *(Mint-haym)* — The training complex of the
Fórsaí Armada

Museo Staire *(Moo-sey-oh Sty-air)* — Historical museum,
considered part of the University

Prifysgol Grantabrych Draíochta *(Riffs-goal Grahn-tah-br-
eye-k Dry-och-tah)* — The full name of what is
colloquially known as the University

Taberna Körtz *(Tah-behr-na Courts)* — an old, original

tavern where Sheridan serves as barkeep

Fairevella *(Fair-eh-vell-ah)* — Home of the Fairies
    Çeofilye *(Seoh-feel-yeh)* — Capital city of Fairevella
    Maremóhr *(Mah-reh-moor)* — Performance and
        ceremonial venue
    Seledreám *(Seh-leh-dree-am)* — The Noble House of Fae
    Seolformúr *(Say-ohl-for-myur)* — Gate at the entrance to
        the Seledreám; the most powerful magical object in
        all of Heáhwolcen

Ifrinnevatt *(Eh-frihn-eh-vat)* — The spirit realm considered part of
    Heáhwolcen

Palna *(Pahl-nuh)* — Baize Sammael's country founded to study
    and teach Craft Wizardry, walled off from the rest of
    Heáhwolcen following the Ingefeoht
    Afon Azúl *(Ah-fahn Ah-sool)* — Winding river named for
        the blue color of its waters. Forms part of the border
        for Terrabruixes
    Afon Verité *(Ah-fahn Ver-ih-tay)* — River that flows from
        Loch Petit Somnis to the border with Bondrie,
        forming part of the border for Terrabruixes
    Ballamúr *(Bah-lah-myur)* — The name of the inner wall
        in Palna
    Bloodwood — Protected lands
    Düoria *(Due-or-ee-ya)* — Palna's capital city
    Forêt Fossile *(For-eh Foh-seel)* — Protected lands of wild
        woods
    Ibaia *(Ee-bye-uh)* — Largest river in Palna
    La Azúlita *(La Ah-sool-ee-tuh)* — Little river that helps
        form the border of Terrabruixes
    Larivuria *(Lah-rih-vur-free-ya)* — An unmapped ocean city
    Loch du Flors *(Lock doo Floors)* — Massive lake that the

Ibaia runs into

Loch Petit Somnis *(Lock Petite Som-knee)* — Small "lake"
in the widest part of the Ibaia, off of which branches
Afon Verité

Tehlalin *(Teh-lah-lynn)* — City north of Düoria, named
for the way it looks while bathed in shadow and
moonlight

Terrabruixes *(Tara-broo-shus)* — The Witchlands, a
sacred space of protected land that only the Tinuviels
go to

Vuoristokylä *(Vyor-is-toe-ky-lah)* — General term for
mountainous villages, where Zedolph claims Bridgette
is from, as to avoid suspicion regarding her origins

Xcthonya *(Ick-thone-ia)* — Sizable city located south of
Düoria

Magical Food and Drink

Blaccattle *(Black cattle)* — Breed of beef cattle descended from the
Kobe cattle on Earth

Brimlad *(Brihm-lahd)* — Dried, seasoned strips of meat, similar to
South African biltong; venison and beef are most common

Caife calabaza *(Cai-fey cah-lah-bah-zah)* — A spiced coffee
beverage developed from pumpkins

Caife mokka *(Cai-fey mocha)* — A milk chocolate-based coffee
beverage

Gingewinde *(Jinj-eh-wihnd)* — Healing, soothing beverage made
from ginger, similar to human ginger ale

Honeycakes — Dessert or breakfast pastry made of lightly
sweetened, fluffy dough, somewhere between a doughnut and
cinnamon bun

The Fórsaí Armada and Associated Terms

Fórsaí Armada *(For-sai Ahrm-ah-dah)* — Heáhwolcen's united

battle forces

Aeris *(Heiress)* — Title for the leader of the Fairy Mîleta

Bondrie Guard *(Bond-ree)* — The armed guard charged with watching over the Palnan border wall

Bródenmael *(Broad-en-mayl)* — Bondrie's most elite on-the-ground warriors

Cailleach *(Callie-ack)* — Endorsa's skilled combat fighters and weapons experts

Caomhnóir Feeric *(Cahm-noor Fee-rick)* — Fairevella's winged fighting force, specifically trained in swordsmanship and knife-fighting

Cath Draíochta *(Cah-th Dry-och-tah)* — The art of spellcasting as part of battle

Comandante *(Cah-man-don-tay)* — Second-in-command of the Unicorn calvary

Fairy Mîleta *(Mih-leh-tuh)* — Heáhwolcen's aerial attack force, primarily skilled in archery and spellcasting from the sky

Feoht *(Fey-oht)* — General term for fighting and battle

Fyrdlytta *(Fyord-light-uh)* — Elven fighting forces, including the Unicorn calvary

Magister Militum *(Mah-gih-ster Mih-lih-tum)* — "Master of soldiers," title for the leader of the Bródenmael

Ingefeoht *(Eeng-fey-oht)* — Heáhwolcen's civil war, which took place approximately around the same time as that of the United States in the late 1850s and early 1860s

Wígend *(Wee-gehnd)* — A singular and plural term referring to trained warriors

Magical Origins and Spiritualities

Biavis Scyllos *(Bee-ah-vihs Sky-lohs)* — Younger of the twin Fyrst Witches

Ceannairí Álfar *(She-an-air-ee Al-far)* — The original magical being

Chrysus *(Cry-suhs)* — The golden god of the Baetalü

Demiurge *(Deh-mee-urge)* — Origin of the world before the worlds existed

Duatha *(Doo-ah-thah)* — Name of the Fyrst Fae

Duathanna *(Doo-ah-thon-ah)* — A distinctive Fairy lineage supposedly created by Ylda, followers of Duatha

Fyrst *(Fy-urst)* — The first group of magical offspring produced following Ceannairí Álfar's procreation rituals

Goddex/Goddexes *(God-ex, God-exes)* — Gender-neutral terms, shortened and inclusive words used instead of the phrase "gods and goddesses"

Ylda *(Eel-dah)* — One of the Fyrst who was charged with designing and creating other magical species and creatures, including the Liluthuaé

Fae Holidays

Imbolc *(Eee-molk)* — A celebration honoring the start of spring

Ostara *(Oh-star-uh)* — The Spring Equinox

Lammas *(Lah-mahs)* — The first harvest, a granary festival

Lunavidad *(Loo-nah-vee-dahd)* — Name used in Palna for the winter solstice holiday celebrations

Lupercalia *(Loo-per-kay-leah)* — Minor holiday, a celebration of fertility

Samhain *(Sow-ihn)* — The time when the spirit world and Earthen planes are no longer separated by a veil of shadows

Wynterwist *(Winter-wist)* — Term for winter solstice feasts in Eckenbourne

Traditional Sayings and Other Words of Note

Aikalé *(I-kah-lay)* — Military response used by the Bondrie Guard

Annwyl *(An-wull)* — A Unicorn chosen to be bonded with an Elf as its steed

Athame *(At-hayme)* — Ceremonial blade used in ritual magic

Cíegan *(Chee-gan)* — A summoning spell for wand magic

Collective — An alleged group of magically talented Palnans who are either captured or recruited by the Tinuviels

Craft Wizardry — The powerful magic of ill-intent hawked by Baize Sammael

Dúnaelfen *(Doon-ayl-fen)* — A group of Elves that follow a selected leader

Diety Dhaoibh *(Dee-ih-tee Doh-b)* — Nondenominational form of "god or goddess bless, honor us"

Elusive Grimoire *(Grih-m-war)* — Baize Sammael's long-missing books of Craft Wizardry lore, spells, and history, hidden for more than a century somewhere in Endorsa for safekeeping

Esoterikos *(Eh-so-teh-rih-kos)* — The version of self that one presents to the world

Etiam pro mundi *(Aye-t-yam pro moon-dee)* — Coded response, "Yes, for the sake of the world"

Fáilte *(Fayl-teh)* — "Welcome"

Gathering of Games — Prestigious annual sporting competition in Palna

Gemaere *(Gehm-air)* — Language of the Fyrst. Appears as a runic language when written

Gimmshoppe *(Gem-shop)* — A store that peddles magical and ritual supplies

Heartsworn — Term for life partner

Hepatizon *(Heh-pat-ih-son)* — Metal alloy that results in a purple shade of bronze

Hexaxis *(Hex-axis)* — Atmospheric research facility in Antarctica, with a miniature replica in Heáhwolcen at Minthame

Hyldájj *(Hihll-dahssh)* — An oath of office for magical leaders

Hringur *(Ringer)* — Palnan resistance

Indictus Magnus Iudicium *(In-dick-tuhs Mag-nuhs Ee-you-dee-cee-um)* — Process of trial, questioning, and judgement of those who used magic with ill intent

Indryhtu Sciccel *(En-dry-too Sih-shell)* — The mark of an office, such as the capes worn by Fairy ambassadors or the embroidered "E" present on Elven leadership's clothing

Ísenwaer *(Eye-sehn-wayr)* — An ability for two people to speak mind-to-mind with one another

Leatherwiph *(Leather-weef)* — Leather artisan

Malouetia *(Mal-oh-ee-cha)* — Plant ingredient that, when the bark is used in certain potions, causes paralysis

Marshwings — Type of footwear common in Palna to keep shoes from sinking in mud during the rainy season

Matla *(Maht-lah)* — The mighty power of the ancient ones

Maylemaegus *(Male-eh-may-guhs)* — An old term for Universal knowledge and power

Mo chridhe *(Moe kree-yuh)* — "My heart"

Neutrinos *(New-tree-nose)* — So-called "ghost particles" that form from great happenings in the cosmos

Nonóir es linne *(Noh-noor es lihn-eh)* — "The honor is ours/mine"

Nunta Alchimica *(Noon-tuh Al-key-mee-kah)* — A magical term for the total solar eclipse, referring to the union of sun and moon

Palnan Artifex Forum *(Art-ih-fects)* — Archivists charged with documenting Palnan history and culture

Palnan sympathist *(Sihm-pah-thist)* — Citizens in greater Heáhwolcen who believe in Baize Sammael's teachings and argue that Palna should be a free country

Rídend *(Ree-dehnd)* — An Elf, Elfling, or other magical being of high rank and friendship to the Elves who is allowed to be bonded with a Unicorn

"Sefnuskrá a Dyfodolden Draiochta Ceáird" *(Sehf-new-skruh uh Die-fold-ehn Dry-och-tah Shay-ihrd)* — The "Manifesto on the Vision of Craft Magic", a three-volume set of books written by Baize Sammael

Seordwiph *(Say-ord-weef)* — Swordsmith, bladesmith

Sierwan / Sierwen *(See-er-wahn / See-er-when)* — The singular and plural terms, respectively, for a gifted Elf who receives knowledge from the Universe and is able to connect dots others cannot

Sóc Láttaew al Hringur *(Soak Lah-tew al Ringer)* — Toby's coded presentation of himself; "I am Guide to the Hringur"

Syndumir *(Sin-doo-meer)* — A spell command, "show me"

Téitheoir *(Teeth-oor)* — Healers

Tráthnóna mistéireach *(Trahth-no-nah mih-stee-ryech)* — Traditional greeting; "A joyous and fair day to you"

Trúwa *(True-wah)* — Divine vow of the Triumvirate

Tunc Triumviratus resurget *(Toon-k Tree-um-veer-ah-tuhs reh-sir-getta)* — Coded call-and-response, "Then the Triumvirate shall rise"

Unt nos liberant *(Oot nas leeb-er-aunt)* — Coded call-and-response, "May they set us free"

Vademecum *(Vah-deh-mee-kuhm)* — Sentient grimoires, guides used by the Triumvirate

Verta verestä *(Vehr-tuh ver-eh-stuh)* — "Blood for blood"

Viltu carleast *(Vill-too car-leest)* — Coded greeting; "Do you desire freedom?"

The Watchword — Palnan newspaper citizens receive three times a week

Wilgiest winedryhtenen *(Wihld-geyst wine-dry-teh-nehn)* — Ceremonial greeting; "Be welcome, friends and comrades"

Witchlight — Spell-cast light, usually appearing acid green, that flickers like flame, but won't blow out except by magic

Wítega *(Wee-teh-guh)* — Birth healer who has certain powers of foreboding

Y gwyr yn erbyn y byd *(Eh gweh-r ehn er-byne eh beh-d)* — "The truth against the world"

~ Acknowledgements ~

Many of the scenes, twists, and turns in "Triumvirate Rising"
lived in my head since my teenage years. It is truly emotional to
see them in print after so long, and I have quite a few people and
places to thank for making this chapter possible.

Mom: Thank you for being an ardent cheerleader for this series,
the first person to buy a copy of "Bright Star", and a test reader!

Daddy: Thank you for helping me bring character visions to life,
for endless encouragement, and your belief that both of us will be
able to retire because of "The Meridian Trilogy". May we never
again have to circle the wagons!

To my test readers — Mom, Annie, Derek, Megan, Barbara,
and Rachel — I am eternally grateful for your patience in
waiting between chapters, for your feedback and edits, and
endless hype. Y'all kept me sane and kept me writing. I hope to
see you back for book three.

For the bookstores and businesses that championed me, an
unknown independent author, in the first two years of
publication: The Bookshelf in Thomasville; Southern Brewing
Company in Athens; Dragon's Lair Bookshop in Jefferson;
Augusta Girls; ConNooga in Chattanooga (Tennessee); Magical
Creature Cabaret in Athens; A Novel Experience in Zebulon;
Silent Book Club – Athens; Neighborhood Books in Athens;
Creature Comforts Brewing in Athens; Sisters of the Moon in
Athens; and Book Tavern in Augusta. A very special thank-you
to Shauna of Dragon's Lair. Your belief in this story and in me
as a storyteller still blows me away. My cup overfloweth because
of our friendship and the audiences you introduced me to.

I'm grateful to those who supported me via Ko-Fi donations and
subscriptions — Liz, Katie, Flavia, Meghan, John, and Justin.

To my cousins, Hadley and Leighton, for helping me create the names of the newest members of the Unicorn population.

Thank you to Dr. Alex Stelzleni and Ryan Crowe of the University of Georgia Meat Science Technology Center, and Chef Kory DePaola. The former two taught me everything I know about butchering, and Chef Kory refreshed my memory. I am grateful to Andrew Wallace and Jen and Justin Barnette for the opportunity to serve in that capacity at the beloved Butcher & Vine in Watkinsville.

For Donovan Fincher, my fellow butcher, the inspiration for Fincher as a character, and my main hype man; and Meghan Britt, my best babe, muse, and eternal hype girl. I love you both.

To author Erik Larson, who has no idea I even exist, and his book "In the Garden of Beasts" — I learned a metric heck-ton from his work, and it inspired much of what happens in Palnan daily life.

For Carolyn Crist and Ed Morales, who took a little college freshman who wanted to write about cows and helped turn her into a full-time storyteller … who still, clearly, writes about cows.

For Ashley Strickland, whose coverage of neutrinos for CNN was heavily influential in Emi-Joye's work and role in this series.

And lastly, to this cute pup named Stitch Evans: When I went to grab a celebratory beer after getting the map laid out, I intended to read a book, eat some fries, and drink an ice-cold IPA or three. Then I locked eyes with this woof, asked the guy holding Stitch's leash if I could pet his dog, and my world shifted.

I have never been so happy to have mistaken a shepherd mix for a black lab.

— The Final Chapter —

Coming November 2025

Chalamet surveyed the utter chaos of the basement room, her eyes struggling to focus on one aspect at a time.

Her king was barely conscious. The room was half-destroyed thanks to the floor mysteriously sprouting tangled roots and reaching branches. Standing water and melting icicles framed where the door had stood, until Chalamet and her force of the Palnan Royal Guard barreled it down. Even the air felt unsettled, as though it waited for something.

And then there was the matter of the corpse.

A foul, reeking stench breached Chalamet's nostrils from where the dead Elf was positioned against the fireplace. It was a wonder the female hadn't fallen backward or been shoved into the flames. Chalamet frowned at the grotesque sight. She edged closer, hiding her nose in the crook of an arm as she examined the body, disgusted but needing to know what led to the death that now presented itself.

Did His Majesty kill her? Chalamet wondered. She removed her helm, allowing her eyes to roam the body. She took in the dark hair and purplish-gray eyes, now dull and void of the Elven flecks of opalescence that would have sparkled in life.

The scene didn't add up. Why would Eryth have killed this strange Elf, but let the Elfling go free?

Chalamet was a commander of the Guard with enough rank that she interacted with her king and queen regularly. They were ruthless. Conniving. A host of negative adjectives Chalamet was careful to not think on too much, especially in the palace, just in case greedy minds were eavesdropping.

She toed the Elf's prostrate hand. Something about the female felt vaguely familiar to Chalamet, though she knew she'd never seen this individual before.

Who were you? she thought, quietly opening herself to what remained of the corpse's aura. Chalamet was a syneath, blessed by Ceannairí Álfar and Ylda with the uncommon gift to perceive energy and intentions by way of color.

As a youngling, it had been overwhelming to constantly sense individuals in such a way. She saw rainbows every time she opened her eyes around living things, including plants and insects. Forcing herself to learn how to turn this ability off was the only way she could have a normal youth. Keeping it in check, so to speak, was also required if she intended to evade recruitment into the Collective. Chalamet may be in the Palnan Royal Guard, but she had no desire for this best-kept secret to turn her into a wielded weapon for Ydessa and Eryth's plans.

Chalamet glanced around to ensure the few guards that remained in the room were otherwise occupied, then pressed two fingers to the bridge of her nose, activating her gift to see beyond. The magic she wasn't supposed to possess, much less use, shifted her eyes to milky white orbs as she inhaled a harsh gasp after the spell. She became blind to all but what she wanted to see.

She did not expect *this*.

The corpse undulated in shades of charcoal gray and brown, like wet soil, with rivers of gold and silver shifting through. This energy was very much still alive, despite its owner's demise. Chalamet ground her boots into the floor to keep herself from stepping backward in shock and alerting fellow guards that something was amiss.

The energy was not only actively flowing, it wafted from the corpse ever so slowly into the floor, seeping between cracks to the earth of Palna itself. A thin tendril reached toward Chalamet. She *knew* this energy, and it came to her why the female seemed familiar. The realization churned in her gut, and she felt her own energy embrace this new touch of power.

Some would describe this as a bond or tether, but it was far more nuanced. Chalamet preferred to regard the connection of the Ealdaelfen as something akin to a mycelial network; an unseen web of power and knowledge that stirred to life when activated by a thrum of command from its thallic body, the almighty Raisarch.

Chalamet, along with most Palnan Elves and some Elflings,

long ago swore fealty to Eryth Tinuviel as the Raisarch. Their Hyldájj was unbreakable. The commander's breath became forced and ragged as she took in what it meant for this energy to peel off the deceased Elf and seep into the ground.

Eryth Tinuviel had never been the Raisarch.

He had been an imposter, a wizard who — like those who gave him their undying loyalty — did not understand that such a role was not one to be *taken* or *assumed*, but one that was handed down by blood. The Ealdaelfen were not bound to this king, this false hope.

By swearing the Hyldájj, they bound themselves to the true Raisarch, who had been this strange Elf Chalamet knew nothing of. And in death, the mycelium of Ealdaelfen was now connected to a new thallic body, one that perhaps had yet to sprout from its dainty web of magic.

She deactivated her color-sight and intentionally slowed her breathing.

Where in the seven hells is this energy flowing to? Chalamet wondered. There were other Elves, other sworn Ealdaelfen, in this group of the Guard. She wondered, too, if they felt the same subconscious recognition as the torch was passed to a new Raisarch.

Recently, Chalamet had gone with three other leaders in the Guard to order provisions for the Gathering of Games. It had been a days-long trip, and most of the interactions with citizens blurred together in her mind. Droll, normal; individuals most pleased to be chosen to proffer goods and services for Their Majesties. But there had been one citizen in the butchery whom Chalamet remembered vividly. Until this moment she had chalked that remembrance up to being because that citizen was the same Elfling she now hunted for.

Chalamet, for reasons she did not understand, had felt compelled to give her name to the female when asked. Her fellow commanders scoffed at her for the decision, but she stood by it, despite not knowing where the compulsion to respond had come from.

My subconscious knew what I did not, she thought now. The new Raisarch was this Elfling, this Bridgette Roberts, Ydessa had called her. The deceased Elf was then either Bridgette's mother, or perhaps an aunt — they didn't much favor one another, so Chalamet was not sure. The new Raisarch also worked for the butchery.

The Elf chewed inside her cheeks. She wondered if the slátrari, the head butcher, knew.

"Oy!" Chalamet jerked her head around to face her guards. "Take His Majesty up to his rooms. Clean this mess up and put *her* somewhere she won't be bothered until the body can be examined."

"Where are you off to?" one of the males accused. "Leaving us to be scullery maids while you go have a tea?"

"Fuck you," Chalamet snapped back. She hated when the males under her leadership attempted to challenge her, as if they could get anywhere close to beating her in combat. "You'll do as you're told, without complaint, or I'm shifting you to Peninsula."

"That a *threat*, Liegefemme?"

She put a hand on the base of her whip, a fierce bitch of a weapon that both knew would slice him senseless if he didn't obey. "Would you like to keep stalling me and find out?"

The guard scowled.

"As I thought," Chalamet said curtly. She pulled her helm on and buckled it under her chin. "Do not leave the palace today. That's an order."

He gaped at her as white whirls filled the spot where she stood.

As suddenly as she disappeared from the basement, Chalamet reappeared in a cluster of stubby trees that struggled to stay standing under the weight of yet another torrential spring rainfall. Chalamet sighed deeply, gathering her wits before stepping out into the hell she knew was about to break loose. She reached for the solar-powered radio at her hip and flipped the volume all the way down. That would be an unwelcome distraction for this undesirable task.

Her helm stayed on as she emerged from the woods and made her way through the muddy fields toward Xcthonya's butchery. Chalamet straightened her posture as she neared the building, wishing to whichever goddess listened that this bloody rain would stop for more than a few hours at a time.

She paused mid-step.

No, the commander thought. *The longer and harder it rains, the easier it will be for the Elfling, the Raisarch, to get out of here.*

Her walk resumed, and it was with a deep sort of resolve that Chalamet pushed open the doors and removed her helm, much to the startled faces of the three slátraestres within. The smallest, a Kobold, was the first to jerk his shoulders back and fist his hand over his heart. His gesture was followed suit by a hulking Baetalüan and a dark-skinned Elf, the latter regarding her with narrowed eyes.

"Well met, Commander," the Kobold murmured.

"Well met, Thighearna. Where is the slátrari?" Chalamet said calmly, though her hammering heart was probably loud enough to be heard across the room.

The Elf gave her a cautious once-over, those eyes remaining narrow and wary. "He is in a meeting."

"I need to speak to him," Chalamet said plainly. "It is a matter of utmost importance."

There was an imploring glance between the three slátraestres. The Baetalüan moved his fingers in some sort of nonverbal communication Chalamet didn't understand. Whatever he said made the Kobold and Elf frown. The Kobold moved his fingers in an apparent reply — or retort, judging from the narrowed brow of the Baetalüan — and looked up at Chalamet.

"What is of such importance that a Palnan Royal Guard commander was sent to see us, after our slátrari has already confirmed your order for the Gathering of Games?" he asked.

"This is unrelated to the Games," Chalamet replied evasively. "There was a death at the palace today."

A collective sharp intake of breath answered her. The Kobold looked like he might be sick, and the Elf blinked, the only sign this news troubled him. Neither moved, but the Baetalüan looked at them apologetically before walking toward a different area of the butchery. Chalamet stood, trying to remain still and stoic, though her heartbeat had yet to return to its normal state.

When the Baetalüan returned, a man and woman walked hand-in-hand behind him. The woman looked as though she'd been crying; her eyes were red and cheeks too puffy. Both gave Chalamet the usual gesture, but the commander did not return it. She wondered if her eyes looked cold and unfeeling, the mask she usually wore.

"You have my son," the woman said. Her eyes, under the redness wrought of grief and fear, were determined. "What do you want for him?"

"I am not here to make bargains I cannot fulfill," Chalamet said carefully, assuming this woman's son was the boy who'd been taken in with the Elfling. "I am searching for the Elfling who escaped." She glanced at the Elf slátraestre. "I am searching for the rightful Raisarch."

The woman blinked, a shrewdness overcoming her sad, hardened stare. "Viltu carleast?" she asked Chalamet.

Chalamet smiled. She knelt to place her helm on the ground at her feet. The shrewd look spread to the woman's entire face, and the butcher's, as the commander folded back one sleeve of her uniform and thrust her tattooed wrist up for all five beings to see. "Etiam pro mundi," Chalamet declared.

Together, the woman, the slátrari, and all three slátraestres revealed their own sigils. "Tunc Triumviratus resurget!" they said, voices raised.

"Ut nos liberant!" Chalamet responded to the call.

She lowered her wrist as the woman walked forward, closing the short distance between them, and took Chalamet's hands in her own.

"The Elfling you seek is more than the Raisarch. Her name is Bridgette Eileen Conner, perhaps more widely known as the Bright Star," the woman revealed. Her mouth twisted into a cruel, pained smile as Chalamet blinked in disbelief. "The Triumvirate has risen, and now, so must we."